WHITE NIGHTS,
RED DAWN

FREDERICK NOLAN

White Nights,
Red Dawn

MACMILLAN PUBLISHING CO., INC.

New York

This is probably not the way it was. Nevertheless, the time
and the place existed. So this, perhaps, is how it might have been.

Macmillan Publishing Co., Inc.
866 Third Avenue, New York, N.Y. 10022
Collier Macmillan Canada, Ltd.

Library of Congress Cataloging in Publication Data
Nolan, Frederick W   1931–
White nights, red dawn.
1. Russia—History—Revolution, 1917–1921—Fiction.
I.   Title.
PZ4.N79Wh   1980   [PR6064.0413]   823'.914   80–16653
ISBN 0-02-589850-7

10 9 8 7 6 5 4 3 2 1

Designed by Jack Meserole

Printed in the United States of America

To Jill and Richard.
With love.

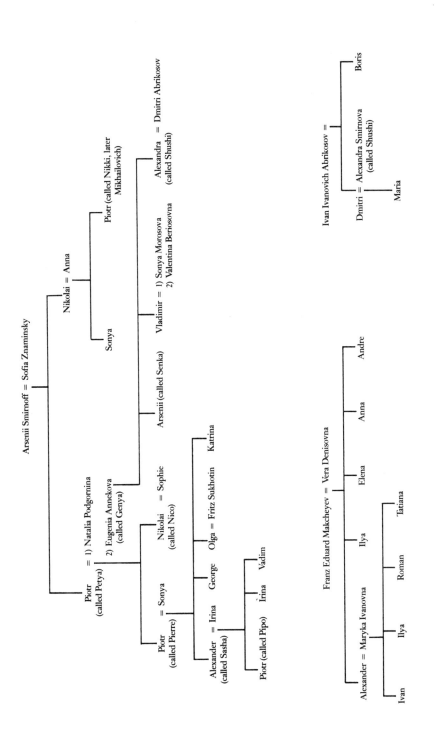

WHITE NIGHTS,
RED DAWN

They came in the gray light before dawn. It was part of the technique of terror they used, bursting into the fetid cell, yelling commands. They knew that was when the prisoners' vitality was at its lowest ebb.

"Smirnoff!" the sergeant shouted. "Vladimir Smirnoff—show yourself!"

"Here!" Vladimir said, scrambling clumsily to his feet. You never kept them waiting if you could help it. They often beat people very badly for keeping them waiting. "I'm here."

"You're what?"

"Present," Vladimir said, correcting himself. They insisted you respond in certain ways. There was a protocol to it. If you ignored it, you were punished.

"Come with me!" the sergeant shouted. Why did they always shout? It was as if they were trying to manufacture an anger they did not feel. The sergeant was a big man with a face like a lump of dough. His teeth were made of steel. He did not look as if he had ever cared about anything in his life.

None of the other prisoners looked up. Nobody looked at Vladimir or the sergeant or the soldiers who had come into the fetid cell behind him with their rifles cocked and ready to fire. It was an understanding all the prisoners had: you were on your own when the soldiers came. No one could help you and nobody was going to try.

"Where are you taking me?" Vladimir said.

The next moment he was on the floor, his head ringing from the blow the sergeant had delivered with his rifle butt. He felt the soft, sweet trickle of fresh blood on his face.

"Who said you could speak?" the sergeant screeched. "Who asked you to speak?"

I

"Sorry, sergeant," Vladimir mumbled. He was conscious of the dirt and blood on his body. His once-fine clothes were in tatters, stiff with sweat. Anger seeped into his veins like acid.

"Move your ass!" the sergeant shouted. "We haven't got all day. There's a lot more to get rid of besides you!"

The soldiers cackled with dutiful mirth at this mirthless jest. They're like animals, Vladimir thought. A picture of men like these butchering his horses at Telegin came to his mind. No, he thought, no, no more of this. Like some baffled bull sensing its inevitable death at the hands of the matador, he shook his head slowly from side to side. Gathering together the remnants of his strength and courage, he surged upward from the straw-littered floor, hands clawing for the sergeant's fleshy throat. He took the man completely by surprise, and for one long, wonderful moment actually clamped his fingers into the thick, giving folds of flesh. The sergeant's eyes bulged with surprise behind which lay real terror. Then he shook his head, as if to clear it, and hit Vladimir in the belly with his fist. Vladimir fell in a heap on the filthy straw, bent double and retching. As if on a signal the two soldiers rushed forward, rifle butts high, eyes dead with the lust to kill.

"Stop!"

The soldiers froze, an obscene tableau. The sergeant's stance changed from predatory to cringing in the blink of an eye. He shrank back as the man who had snapped the command stalked past him into the cell and wheeled to confront him. Dwarfed by the huge Ukrainian, yet dominating him completely, the newcomer was a thin-faced, cold-eyed man with cropped hair and rimless spectacles. He was dressed in an ankle-length leather overcoat, jackboots, and a peaked cap. In his right hand he carried a riding crop.

"Comrade Commissar!" the sergeant blurted. "I didn't mean—"

"Silence," the man said. His voice was almost absentminded, as though nothing that the sergeant might say or do was of any consequence, as though nothing anyone said or did except himself mattered. His contained manner and controlled voice seemed to frighten the sergeant far more than any shouted tirade might have done.

"It was . . . only . . . he . . ."

"Stand back," the Commissar said, quietly. He made an impatient gesture with the riding crop and the sergeant scuttled out of the way, only his burning eyes betraying his hate. He knew this kind only too well. You could never please any of them. If he was in my squad, he thought, I'd have the bastard for breakfast; but there was no chance of anything like that ever happening. Those *Cheka* bastards hadn't the guts for that kind of fighting. They used other weapons, and they killed more men with them than the Army with all its rifles.

The *Cheka* Commissar crossed the filthy room to where Vladimir Smirnoff lay gasping in the matted straw. Wrinkling his nose in disgust, he put a hand under Vladimir's elbow, helping him to his feet.

"Well, Vladimir," he said, almost conversationally. "You're in a mess."

Vladimir said nothing. He turned his head away so that he would not even have to look at the man. No, not a man, he thought. Vermin, something below the reptiles, a creature, not a man.

"It's no use your fighting us, you know," the Commissar said. "No use at all. We've won. Your kind is finished."

Vladimir called him a name, using a word that brought a hiss of disbelief from the prisoners and the soldiers. Many of them had seen men killed on the spot for much less terrible insults than the one that Vladimir Smirnoff had just uttered. The Commissar just smiled, almost dreamily.

"You can't provoke me anymore, Vladimir," he said. "Just go with the soldiers."

"Willingly," Vladimir said. "Willingly, if it means I never have to see your murderer's face again."

"Oh, get him out of here," the Commissar said, wearily. There was utter boredom in his voice. The soldiers jumped forward, grabbing Vladimir's arms. They ran him, his feet dragging, out of the cell and along a stone corridor, heedless of his gasps of pain or the agonies of his battered body. He saw light ahead. It was a gateway which led into an open courtyard. The soldiers pushed him forward and he staggered into the gray daylight, falling face down on the sharp gravel. He lay there for a moment stunned, wracked by pains which immobilized his body. He could hear the heavy breathing of the two soldiers. Then there was the crunch of feet on the gravel beside his head.

"Pick him up," he heard the Commissar say.

Rough hands hauled him to his feet and turned him to face his tormentor. The light was strengthening now. He saw the lines on the thin face, etched deep as though by acid. He studied every feature, as if seeing the man for the first time. What sort of world was it that allowed men like this to become powerful? How could it

3

permit such a man to destroy an entire family, to scatter its wealth and power as heedlessly as a wanton child breaking toys? Vladimir was the last one left alive. He knew that very shortly he, too, would be dead; this courtyard was a place of execution. It stank of death.

"I should have killed you," he said to Boris Abrikosov.

I

THE ST. GEORGE ROOM, the largest in the Kremlin, was a blaze of light on this, the night of the Imperial Ball. Two hundred feet long and nearly half as wide, its ceiling was supported by eighteen pilasters, each decorated with shields bearing lists of Russian victories and the arms of conquered provinces. In the semicircular alcoves between the pilasters, marble tablets bore the gold-inscribed names of officers who had been awarded Russia's highest military honor, the Order of St. George. Among them were the names of Tatiana's father and grandfather. When she was a child, her father had brought her here and showed them to her. They had meant nothing then, although she clearly remembered being awed by the beauty of the room, recalled how her footsteps had echoed no matter how hard she tried to walk quietly. How she would have marveled then, she thought, if her father had told her that one day she would be in this same room, dressed in a beautiful pale blue silken ball gown, ready to be presented to the Tsar and Tsaritsa, longing to dance with the man she loved most in all the world. I wonder where he is? she thought. I wonder if he'll think I'm beautiful? Eyes sparkling as brightly as any of the diamonds glittering around her, Tatiana moved forward through the brilliant throng.

"Isn't it exciting?" she whispered to her aunt. "Isn't it gorgeous?" The Countess Elena Makcheyeva smiled as her niece squeezed her hand. Tatiana was too excited to notice that her shining blonde beauty was turning heads all around them. Just as well, Elena thought. She was a tall, thin woman in her fifties with an imperious expression that was quite misleading, for she was really a generous and sentimental person. Nevertheless, she intended to take her chaperone's duties seriously tonight. Her brother Alex had bidden her to take special care that Tatiana didn't get involved in any

7

romantic nonsense, as he put it, while she was in Moscow visiting the Smirnoffs.

"Far too many young men there with nothing better to do than play cards and make eyes at every pretty girl they see," he rumbled. Well, that was true enough, Elena thought. Too many people these days thought nothing of the old conventions, propriety, standards. Nothing anyone said to them seemed to make the slightest difference; all they thought about was having a good time. The thought made Elena purse her lips and draw her thin shoulders fractionally up; there'd be none of that while she was Tatiana's chaperone. She glanced again at her niece. Tatiana was standing on tiptoe trying to see over the heads of the crowd.

Oh, Sergei, she thought. Where are you? She was thwarted by the sheer size of the crowd slowly ascending the great granite staircase. The black-carpeted stairs were packed with guests. Aunt Elena said that more than three thousand invitations had been sent. Court officials in black uniforms, gold braid gleaming, rubbed shoulders with young Hussars in full dress uniform, their elkskin breeches so tight that it took two servants to pull them on. Elderly women trailed clouds of eau-de-cologne, billowing like galleons in dresses of white satin glittering with jewels. The younger women, fashionably décolleté, displayed the Russian passion for precious stones, their ears, throats, wrists, arms, fingers, breasts and shoulders agleam with diamonds, rubies, sapphires, pearls. They glittered and gleamed and shone and sparkled, smiling and smiling as they ascended the five flights of stairs like pilgrims approaching the gates of Heaven. On every third step stood a trooper of the Garde Chevalier in white full-dress uniform, silver breastplate and helmet bearing the double-headed eagle crest of Tsar Nicholas II. Relays of servants took away cloaks and capes in the marble antechamber dominated by a painting of peasants paying tribute to Alexander III. An enormous Cossack majordomo bent down to listen to the whispered names of the Tsar's guests before bellowing them into the brilliantly lit St. George Room. Tatiana tapped her wrist impatiently with her fan as he called out the names of her party. She saw Nico Smirnoff watching her and thought he looked as if he were suppressing a smile. They had all come together: Pierre and his wife Sonya, Nico and Sophie Smirnoff, and the Abrikosovs. Dmitri Abrikosov was married to Pierre Smirnoff's sister.

"Oh, I do wish they'd hurry," Tatiana said. "I can't wait for the dancing to begin!"

"Tatiana, you're much too impatient," Elena said. "You must

learn the importance of self-control. After all, everyone in Moscow must be here tonight."

"Everyone who is anyone, you mean?" Tatiana said, smiling at Katrina Smirnova. Katrina was Pierre Smirnoff's daughter. Tatiana had seen little of her school friend in the last couple of years, but Katrina remembered their old, shared game of teasing Aunt Elena. In Elena's world proverbs were the guardians of her peace of mind. She had always quoted them, always would. Stitches in time indisputably saved nine, bad pennies never-failingly turned up. The girls always led her on, to see whether they could predict which saying she would quote next.

"Quite so," Elena said, nodding at the girls. "Everyone who is anyone." She thought that Katrina had changed greatly since the last time she had seen her. Hers was as cool a beauty as Tatiana's was warm, Elena thought. Katrina had always been cool, reserved, most watchful, even as a schoolgirl attending the Ekaterina, St. Petersburg's most famous school. It was as if very early in life she had declared herself above trivialities. She had always been religious and had grown into a young woman with the deepest convictions. She took life and people seriously, and her expectations of them were as high as those she had for herself. Elena had once heard one of the young officers tell a friend that Katrina was a cold fish whom everyone called "the Virgin Queen." As if that were reprehensible, Elena thought. She wished sometimes that some of Katrina's reserve would rub off on Tatiana, but she doubted it ever would. Just look at the way the girl's eyes were shining now as she surveyed the glittering throng in the St. George Room. My Heavens, she thought, I've never seen her so radiant!

Sergei, Sergei, Sergei, Tatiana thought, trying to find his handsome face in the sea of faces before her. For once, Aunt Elena's cliché was well chosen. Everyone who was anyone in Moscow was here tonight, for this was the occasion of occasions, an Imperial Ball to mark the Tercentenary of the Romanov dynasty. There was an excited, expectant note in the roaring whisper of the conversation. Silks rustled, jewels flashed, medals clinked, glass chimed. Male voices boomed, punctuated by female laughter. Dozens of uniformed servants wormed their way through the crowd with champagne and more champagne.

"Uncle Pierre is nervous," Katrina observed. "He's probably worrying that his party won't be as successful as this one."

Tatiana followed her friend's glance to where Pierre Smirnoff and his wife stood talking to a group of people not far from the great double doors through which the Tsar and Tsaritsa would come. He was a big, broad-shouldered man with a bushy black beard and heavy eyebrows. He looked much younger than sixty-two, Tatiana thought. Although she and her aunt had been staying with the Smirnoffs for more than a week already, she had hardly yet spoken to Pierre Smirnoff. He was always busy; Katrina said he ate, drank, lived and dreamed nothing but the family business. The Smirnoffs were purveyors to the Imperial Court of vodkas and liqueurs. They made millions of rubles a day, according to Aunt Elena, who made it her business to know such things.

"But money isn't everything, my dear," her aunt told Tatiana. "There are some things that millions cannot buy."

She was referring, of course, to the fact that although Pierre Smirnoff held the title of Count, it was a merely honorary title and not hereditary, as was that of Tatiana's father. In Court circles such a distinction could mean a very great deal indeed, and Tatiana wondered whether Pierre Smirnoff's discomfort stemmed from that fact. It was an uncharitable thought and she chided herself for it, simultaneously aware that it was no less true because of that.

"Tatiana!" The insistent tug of her aunt's hand on her sleeve brought Tatiana out of her reverie and back to the glittering realities of the present. "They're coming!" Elena hissed. "The Tsar and Tsaritsa are coming!"

There was a swell of whispers, quickly rising and as quickly stilled: a tension in the air. A burly man in an ornate uniform marched out into the center of the great room. In his hand he carried a long ebony staff on top of which was mounted the golden double-headed eagle of the Romanovs. He banged the rod loudly on the floor, his face blank with self-importance. A silence, at once immediate and expectant, ensued.

"Their Imperial Majesties!" shouted the man with the eagle-headed staff. Then Tatiana heard a solid, gentle sound like dry leaves blowing in an autumn wind, the sound of hundreds of gowns rustling as the ladies sank in deep curtseys to the Tsar of all the Russias and his wife. Curtsying as low and as gracefully as any woman in the room, Tatiana peeked at the royal couple from beneath lowered lashes. Tsar Nicholas II was not very tall, she saw. He had an open face and a smile that was shy and slightly sad. He had reddish-blond hair and a spade beard, and he was wearing the blue-green uniform of the crack Preobrazhensky Guard with red sash, silver sword belt and tassels. The Tsaritsa Alexandra wore a glittering gown of silvery brocade that shimmered as she walked. She, too, wore a red sash, and long ropes of beautifully matched pearls were looped around her neck. She had red-gold hair piled high on her head, and her eyes were blue-gray. She had a high color, as if a blush were constantly being suppressed. Tatiana thought that the Tsaritsa looked sadly beautiful, boldly shy. She had been told that Alexandra was cold, awkward and remote; they said she was very unpopular. She certainly seemed ill at ease as she came down the packed line of guests waiting to be presented.

By contrast, Nicholas was alert and lively. His bright blue eyes danced with animation as he chatted with everyone. His square face was mobile, his manner warm, and Tatiana could not help but wonder what had attracted him to the proud, regal woman who was his wife. The Tsaritsa said hardly anything to the guests presented to her. A polite "Good evening" or a toneless "How very pleasant to see you again," but no more. Her voice had no inflection at all, and it made the little she did say seem all the more insincere. Her eyes were blank, as though masking panic. Tatiana felt sure that the Tsaritsa was seeing only a blur of faces.

The Tsar and his wife had reached the end of the line now, and as they turned, the same uniformed man who had earlier commanded silence again smote the floor with his staff. The orchestra immediately struck up a stately polonaise, and the Tsar led his wife out onto the floor to begin the dancing. Once again, Tatiana was struck by the feeling that the Tsaritsa was distressed by being in the public eye. It seemed unbelievable that anyone so privileged and protected should be so agonizingly shy, and yet it was obviously so.

Alexandra danced badly. Tatiana could see that the Tsar was leading her very firmly to conceal the fact. Strange, she thought, an Empress who cannot dance. The Tsaritsa's gracelessness clearly shamed her; she danced only because she had to. Poor woman, thought Tatiana with the unforgiving pity of a girl to whom music is second nature and dancing as natural as breathing.

After a few moments the Grand Duke Nikolai Nikolaievich bowed to his wife, and they joined the royal couple on the dance floor. In a few moments more, the ballroom was aswirl with dancing couples, among them Tatiana Makcheyeva and Sergei Tretyakov. If there was a Heaven, Tatiana thought as she swung in Sergei's strong arms to the mazurka, then this surely must be it!

At midnight, supper was served in the St. Alexander Room. Fourteen windows looked out over the ancient walls of the Kremlin across the Moskva River to the twinkling lights of the city's southern suburbs. Opposite the two rows of windows, huge mirrors reflected the guests, the room and the view of the city beyond. It was very warm, and the windows had been opened to let in a welcome breath of air. The tables groaned beneath lobster salad, chicken vols-au-vent, *pirozhki* prepared by the Tsar's own chef, strawberry tarts with fresh cream. Corks popped incessantly. Bewigged servants in frogged uniforms worked their perspiring way around the room with silver trays of champagne in crystal glasses. Faces were flushed, voices raised to carry, eyes met, hands touched, scores were settled, love affairs begun and ended, hatreds magnified, boasts tolerated, bores avoided, rendezvous made, rivalries concluded. All the wealth and beauty of the world were here tonight in this one magnificent palace room, and yet Tatiana Makcheyeva was miserable.

Naturally, she did not let one iota of her misery show. By any standard she had been the success of the evening. Not only had she danced every single dance with the handsomest of the young men and the most distinguished of the older ones, but she had taken wine with the Tsar and Tsaritsa and had been invited to visit them at Tsarskoe Selo. She was the center of attraction, the envy of all the other girls, the cynosure of their mothers' angry looks—all of which would normally have delighted her. Yet still she was miserable.

Her eyes never left Sergei. She watched him dance with Katrina, with Shushi Abrikosova, with Maria, knowing all the time that all he wanted was to be with her. Her heart lifted when he glanced her way. It pounded when he came near her. Yet still he did not speak; still he had not told her that he loved her as much as she loved him. She could not imagine why, and so she was miserable.

In this interval in the dancing, Tatiana was surrounded once more by admirers. On her right Mikhail Subarov, resplendent in the white uniform of Captain in the Garde Chevalier, stood firmly planted. It seemed that nothing his brother officer Paul Dubinsky could think of—and he had tried—would induce Misha to abandon his vantage point. In one hand, Misha held Tatiana's jeweled fan—a gift from Grandmother Ivanovna for her eighteenth birthday—and in the other, his champagne glass. His eyes were so constantly upon Tatiana's face that he utterly failed to see that Olga Narodnova's eyes were flinty with jealousy, or that her mother was glaring at him with the justified anger of a parent who sees the carefully arranged details of her daughter's marriage threatened.

At Tatiana's feet lounged another elegant young officer, Vasilii Kirsanov, scion of the great mill-owning family which supplied most of Moscow's bakeries with their flour. He, too, gazed up at Tatiana with unconcealed adoration, unaware of or indifferent to the smoldering glances being directed at him by Nikolai Vasnetsov, another wealthy young man about town. Nicky was a dark, handsome, slender boy, related to the famous artist whose name he shared. His footstool was strategically placed at Tatiana's side and directly in front of Misha Subarov. Yet another young Guards officer was pushing his way back through the crowd, bringing more champagne for Aunt Elena, who sat nearby, all smiles as she savored Tatiana's success on the one hand and the discomfiture of the Moscow matrons on the other. Elena was a Petersburg girl. *Piter* girls were to Moscow girls as wine was to water.

Still Tatiana was unhappy, and the reason for her misery was easy for anyone with eyes to see. There across the room, apparently oblivious to anyone except each other, sat Sergei and Katrina Smirnoff. Sergei's handsome face was animated, his hands moving constantly to add dimension to whatever he was saying to her. How Tatiana wished she could hear what they were talking about! He had been so gallant and charming when they danced, teasing her until her heart felt as if he had taken it in his hand and squeezed it.

"Well, Tatiana, you're the belle of the ball and no mistake," he had said as they spun around. "What a triumph! Every heart in the palace is at your feet—even the Tsar's."

"Yours, too?" she asked, breathlessly.

"But, of course." Sergei had smiled enthusiastically.

"Oh, Sergei," she said, squeezing his hand. "I don't want any of them. I only want you."

"Me?" he said, his smile slipping a little. "Oh, yes."

He shook his head slightly, and Tatiana was surprised and a little frightened to see what looked like consternation in Sergei's eyes when she had expected . . . something else. Oh, it was so frustrating to be close to him like this and not to be able to talk, not to be able to ask him what was wrong, to tell him that she loved him. Their dance was over before she could say more, and to her

13

chagrin, he had not asked her to dance again. Piqued, angered by what she considered to be his neglect, she filled her card with other names to spite him. Yet all the time she felt the same impotent puzzlement. It was almost as if he was avoiding her, and she did not know why. It was as if she had done something wrong, but she could not envision what it might be. All that she knew was that this was not the way she had planned things.

Why had he acted as though she was just flirting with him, as though what she had told him didn't mean anything? He had been so different in Petersburg, so warm, so understanding, so close to her all through that lovely long weekend at Prince Byelozersky's chateau on Krestoffsky Island, and at the River Yacht Club the following one. She had known then that he cared—known it! Yet now he was acting as if none of it had happened.

She watched him from beneath lowered lashes, careful not to reveal her interest, responding almost automatically to the pleasantries of her youthful companions. She hoped Sergei would notice when Countess Olga Subarovna finally swept across the room to almost drag Misha back to the side of his pouting, tearful fianceé, but Sergei did not even glance her way. Damn the man, she thought, vexed and then instantly penitent. Nice girls didn't swear, and she kept forgetting.

Her face petulant, Tatiana glanced around the room. Her eyes met those of a man watching her, one shoulder against an ornate pillar, every line of his posture cynical and worldly. She realized with a certain delighted chill that he had been watching her for some time, and he smiled as their eyes met. It was a conspiratorial smile, the smile of someone who knows exactly what you are thinking because he has thought the same thing many times. Tatiana was shocked to think that the man could read her so plainly. His corn-blue eyes were as malicious as those of a tomcat, and he regarded Tatiana in a way that made her somehow feel that her décolleté was . . . well, indecent, which it most decidedly was not. He was tall and well built, with the powerful shoulders and thighs of a horseman. He smiled again, his teeth startlingly white in his suntanned face. He was clean-shaven, and his mouth was mobile and sardonic. Tatiana could see good breeding in his face and his assured posture. His clothes were elegant, beautifully cut. She wondered who he could be and how he could dare to look at anyone in such an insulting way.

"Who is that over there?" she whispered behind her fan to Vasya Kirsanov.

"Who?"

"The tall, fair-haired man leaning against the pillar."

"Oh, him," Vasya said. "That's Vladimir Smirnoff. Haven't you met him yet?"

"No," Tatiana said, wondering why.

"Good for you," Vasya said. "Keep away from him altogether. They say he's a womanizer."

"Oh?" Tatiana said, intrigued. "Why is that?"

"He's got a reputation," Nicky chimed in, mock-whispering.

"Not the sort of thing one discusses," Vasya said, "in front of a lady." Pompous ass, Tatiana thought.

"Quite so," Nicky agreed, and Tatiana fought back the impulse to call him a prig.

"But what has he done?" she asked, tapping her satin-shod foot in vexation. Why was it that men seemed to think women were delicate little hothouse blooms, in need of protection from everything? Great Jehovah! She could probably outride and outshoot every single one of them. She used her father's favorite expletive without even realizing it. Tatiana was much more the daughter of Alexander Makcheyev than she knew.

"Well," Vasya said, looking at Nicky. They glanced conspiratorially toward Aunt Elena to make sure she wasn't listening too closely. "If you promise not to say who told you . . . ?"

"Of course I won't," Tatiana said, agog to hear something a little more interesting than the vapid compliments she had been receiving all night, when she wasn't listening to equally boring stories of pranks in the officers' mess.

"Well, he's the black sheep of the family," Nicky said.

"Very black," Vasya said. "He was married to one of the Morosov girls, wasn't he?"

"Years ago," Nicky said. "She divorced him."

"Who's that?" Paul Dubinsky said, coming over to join them. He had been detailed to make sure that Aunt Elena got plenty of champagne, and he had been working with a will. Now the old lady was nodding happily in time with the music, off in a world of her own. The youngsters could have been plotting to blow up the Kremlin with her in it for all the notice she was taking of them.

"Vladimir Smirnoff," Nicky said.

"Who divorced him?" Paul asked. He was a willowy, handsome youngster with brown hair and eyes. His father was director of the Konstantin Observatory in Pavlovsk, about twenty-five versts from Petersburg.

"Oh, God, not again!" Vasya said, with heavy patience. "His first wife. Sonya Morosova."

"Oh, that," Paul said, sniffing. "My parents know the Morosovs quite well. It was one of those family things. They were awfully young, you know. Sixteen, or something. I mean, they weren't in love, or anything. It was all arranged by the families."

"Oh, yes," Vasya said, his voice rich with scorn for anyone who would believe a story like that. "The families arranged everything, eh? Including the other woman, no doubt."

"What?" Paul said.

"That was the real reason," Vasya said, darkly.

"Oh, for Heaven's sake, Vasya, do get on!" Tatiana said. "Getting you to tell a story is like pulling teeth from a chicken."

"Who was this other woman?" Nicky asked.

"Ah," said Vasya.

"Oh, you goose!" Tatiana said. "Who, who?"

"What are you children whispering about over there?" Aunt Elena interposed, returning suddenly if reluctantly to her duties. Her head was quite aspin. Goodness gracious, how many glasses of wine had she drunk?

"Nothing, Aunt," Tatiana said, hastily. "Just gossip."

"How many times have I told you, Tatiana Alexandrovna, that gossip—"

"—needs no carriage. I know, Aunt."

"The Devil makes work for idle hands, child. Idle tongues as well." When she could not think of an appropriate aphorism, Aunt Elena simply took the nearest one to hand and bent it into shape.

"Well, what happened?" Tatiana muttered to Vasya.

"He married this other woman," Nicky said. "An actress." He said the word with considerable disapproval, making Tatiana want to shake him.

"Oh, that's not the half of it," Vasya said, with the air of someone who knows he has the advantage over everyone else. "There was another big scandal before that one."

"Really?" Nicky said, trying to sound as if he really wasn't very interested, but betrayed by the intensely curious glitter of his eyes.

"Really," Vasya said, confidently. "I heard my parents talking about it once. They didn't know I was listening. It was something to do with a gypsy girl who danced at the Yar. Vladimir's supposed to have fallen for her, hook, line and sinker."

Everyone knew the Yar. It was one of three restaurants in

Petrovsky Park outside the city. In the summer, all the young blades of Moscow went to the Yar or to the Mauretania. In the winter, everyone went to the Stryelna. All three restaurants were within easy reach of the Khoduinskoye Field, on the far side of which was the summer camp of the Moscow garrison. Vladimir Smirnoff, Vasya went on, had begun frequenting the Yar when he was eighteen— and already a divorcé.

"Without his father's knowledge, of course," he said.

"Old man Smirnoff was a tyrant, they say," Nicky said.

"He was indeed."

"Tell about the gypsy dancer, Vasya," Tatiana urged. "Oh, come on, tell us."

There was a gypsy chorus at the Yar, Vasya said, and Vladimir had become acquainted with all its members. One of them had taught him how to play the guitar. Later he would get up on the stage and sing the *tzigane* songs with them. Well, one knows what one is like when one is eighteen, Vasya said, with all the infinite wisdom of a man three years older. Young Vladimir fell in love with one of the dancers, a girl named Katja. He ransomed her from the chorus for fifty thousand rubles, giving a note to a Jewish money-lender to raise the money.

"Fifty thousand rubles," Nicky sighed. "Imagine having that kind of money to throw away on a gypsy dancer."

"He must have really loved her," Tatiana said.

"He must have been crazy!" Paul said, shaking his wise old head at such folly. He was the same age as Vasya.

"Crazy is right," Vasya said. "Crazy to think old Petya Smirnoff wouldn't find out about it. He did, of course, and when he did, he let out a roar that would have frightened a bear. He called in that moneylender and paid his son's debt, and while he was at it he told the old Jew that if he ever loaned money to a Smirnoff again, he'd stick him in a room and feed him on nothing but pork for the rest of his life."

"He was a bas— bad old devil," Nicky said, catching himself just in time.

"What happened then?" Tatiana said, ignoring Nicky. If he thought he had to watch his language because of her, he was wrong. Tatiana's father was a soldier, and her three brothers were in the services. She'd heard people called a bastard many times before tonight, and if anything, she preferred the crude accuracy of the word to the euphemisms people used for it.

"Well, the old man paid off the girl and sent her back to her people," Vasya said. "Then he made arrangements to send his son to work in Vladivostok for a year."

"Good Heavens!" Tatiana said, pretending a shock she did not at all feel. What was wrong with falling in love with a gypsy girl? Why had old Petya Smirnoff sent his son into exile on the far side of the world because of it? Old people didn't know anything about love, none of them. Papa and Mama, Aunt Elena, old people like that, didn't know how young people felt these days. It was all so different now than the way it had been when they were young; they simply couldn't comprehend the changes. Her sympathy was all with Vladimir Smirnoff. She looked over toward the pillar where he had stood watching her, but he was no longer there. He must be quite old, too, she mused, thirty-five or so. She looked up as a shadow fell across her face and saw Boris Abrikosov standing before her, his thin face alive with anticipation.

"Well, young lady," he said, with just enough of a bow to show that he had given one. "How are you enjoying Moscow?"

"Wonderfully well, thank you," Tatiana replied.

"I see you are surrounded by admirers as usual," Boris said, his strangely colorless eyes alight with what might have been malice. Tatiana did not reply. She wondered what on earth Maria's sinister uncle could possibly want. She had been vaguely aware of him staring at her earlier while she was dancing, and she was not so young or so naïve that such a stare meant nothing to her.

"I was hoping, Tatiana, that you might have one empty space on your dance card for my humble name," Boris said, taking her card in his hand and opening it before she had a chance to prevent him from doing so. She had never been so pleased in her life that it was full.

"I am desolated," she said without regret, "but I fear my card is already full."

"So I see," he said, smiling like a snake. "What a shame." He made no move to go as the orchestra struck up for the next dance. Paul, Nicky and Vasya exchanged glances.

"My dance, I think," Paul said, stepping forward. As if accidentally, his shoulder caught Boris's, and Boris was jarred aside. "I say," Paul said, "I beg your pardon, old boy." He put undue emphasis on the last two words, and Boris's thin face flushed faintly beneath its habitual pallor.

"You will excuse us," Paul said, rubbing it in, "won't you, old boy?"

"Of course," Boris said, his voice sibilant between tight lips. "There will be another time. Perhaps when you are less . . . well guarded, my dear."

He turned away, pleased with himself. He would never be what the smart set called witty, but Boris knew that his jibe had struck home. Vasya actually took a step forward, but no more. Boris saw the movement, however, and raised one eyebrow, smiling the snake's smile again. His eyes were full of contempt.

"Gentlemen," he said, bowing, making the word an insult. No one spoke. How could one challenge the fellow? Everyone said he was in the *Okhrana*. No matter how obnoxiously he behaved, no one wanted an enemy in the Tsar's secret police. So the young officers watched in silence as Boris Abrikosov turned on his heel and eeled off through the crowd.

"What a rotter!" Nicky said, as Paul and Tatiana swept away to the music of Johann Strauss.

"Oh, come on, now," Vasya said. "He's not bad."

"Not bad?" Nicky said, almost rendered speechless by Vasya's defense of the man. "Not bad?"

"No," Vasya said, grinning. "Revolting. Repulsive. Ugly. But not bad." They both laughed, but there was still an undercurrent of unease in their laughter.

"He gives me the creeps," Nicky said at last.

"He gives everyone the creeps," Vasya said. "They all do."

"My father says they're a necessary evil."

"He's right. The country's swarming with anarchists making bombs, assassins, revolutionaries, lunatics who want to overthrow the Tsar. They want to reduce us all to chaos. They have nothing to offer but chaos. Papa says that they'd do it, too, if it wasn't for the *Okhrana* keeping an eye on them."

"I still wouldn't want him on my heels in a dark alley," Nicky said, with a shudder. "The fellow's a monster."

"Who's a monster?"

The two young officers turned at the sound of the familiar voice. When they saw that one of the two young women clinging to Sergei Tretyakov's arms was Maria Abrikosova, they flushed with embarrassment. How could they reply that the "monster" was none other than Maria's uncle?

"Oh, it's nothing, Sergei," Nicky said, a shade too heartily. He evaded the question by asking one of his own. "Did you get a chance to talk to the Grand Duke?"

"I did," Sergei said.

"And?"

"He said yes," Sergei said, with a smile. Katrina and Maria watched with puzzled expressions as the two younger officers nodded, smiled, shook hands and clapped each other on the back as though they had won an important bet.

"Well, well, will someone tell us what's going on here?"

Tatiana and Paul had finished their waltz, and she had seen Nicky and Vasya slapping each other on the back as Sergei and the two girls looked on. Her eyes were on Sergei and no one else; her question was for him alone.

"It's a surprise, Tatiana," he said, almost defensively.

"A surprise?"

"Yes, my little chickens, a surprise," Vasya said. "It was all my idea."

"No, it wasn't, Vasya," Nicky said. "It was all of us."

"Oh, for Heaven's sake, Sergei," Katrina said. What is this great secret?"

"I've just had confirmation from the Grand Duke Andrei," Sergei said. "You have been invited to see the great parade as his guests. All of you."

"How wonderful!" Maria said. "Oh, you are clever boys!"

As for Tatiana, she could not take it all in. All the music was back in her heart. Now she knew why Sergei had been spending so much time with Katrina Smirnova. It had all been on her account, all part of his making the arrangements for them to witness the Tsar's triumphal entry into Moscow and all the festivities surrounding it. And she had been jealous of them! Overcome with remorse and delight, she threw her arms around Katrina and hugged her.

"Oh, Katrina, I'm so lucky to have such good friends," she said, sniffling slightly. She kissed Katrina's cool cheek. "And you, dear Sergei," she said softly. "I must thank you, too." She stood on tiptoe and kissed him on the cheek. He smelled of bay rum and soap, and Tatiana thought, what a fool to have imagined that he could ever love anyone but me!

"Here!" Nicky said. "Part of it was my idea, you know."

"Me, too!" Vasya said.

"And me!" said Paul.

"Oh, you're all so sweet," she said, and kissed them all, one by one, laughing. Aunt Elena watched them fondly. It was so nice to see the youngsters having a good time, although she would have to speak to Tatiana later about all that kissing.

"But with whom shall I go?" Tatiana asked. "Will you all be there?"

"We shall be there, Tatiana," Nicky smiled. "You'll see us out there on the parade ground in all our finery, while you sit in the Grand Duke's shady pavilion and sip iced champagne."

"Well," Sergei said, "it wouldn't be much of a parade if there were no spectators, would it?" His smile was boyish, mischievous. If it had not been for all the people around them, Tatiana was sure she would have hugged him. He was so dear, so sweet.

"Oh, it will be so marvelous!" Maria said. "Sergei, you're a darling to go to so much trouble. Isn't he, Tatiana?"

"Yes," Tatiana said, looking right into Sergei's eyes. She thought she saw a flicker of that uncomfortable look in them again, but he banished it with a smile. Once again she shook her head, impatient with her imagination, casting such nonsense to the winds. "Oh, my goodness!" she exclaimed, as the thought flashed into her head. "What about Aunt Elena?"

She had completely forgotten her aunt, who was presently deep in conversation with Maria's mother, nodding and smiling at whatever it was that Shushi Abrikosova was saying to her.

"My goodness, indeed!" Maria parroted, laughing. "You'll need no chaperone in the Grand Duke's pavilion, Tatiana. Your aunt can stay at home and knit. Nothing can compromise you while you're sitting with the Grand Dukes and Duchesses of the Imperial Court, for Heaven's sake!"

"Unless Gritschka gets you," Vasya said, putting on a scowl and making his hands into claws with which he pretended to grab at Tatiana. They all laughed, glancing automatically toward the Tsar and Tsaritsa. Everyone was talking about the Tsar's wife and the monk Grigory Rasputin, referred to by everyone as "Gritschka." It was widely assumed that the *starets* had made the Tsaritsa his mistress. Educated people repeated such gossip with distaste and disbelief in their voices, but they repeated it nonetheless. After all, they said, why else would the Tsaritsa keep that smelly libertine constantly close to her, defending him against all attacks, forbidding any punishment for his many and flagrant misdeeds? It was a great scandal and Tatiana longed to hear more of it, but Aunt Elena forbade talk of such things.

"Gossip needs no carriage, Tatiana," she would say, quoting her favorite maxim and wagging a sententious finger. Such stupid strictures, Tatiana thought. Were she the respectably married wife of some dull bourgeois merchant, or even for that matter of a grinning young ensign in the Corps of Pages, she would be able to talk about Gritschka to her heart's content. Because she was young and single, the subject was considered taboo. Could the regal, distant woman she had met earlier in the evening truly be in love with the *starets*, as people said? It seemed unlikely, but it was not impossible. In love, nothing was impossible. She wished she were married to Sergei. They would talk about such things for hours and hours, she sitting at his feet beside a big fire while he explained all the things she did not understand, lifted her mentally and physically into his world. If they were married, they would go to parties together, to the opera, to the theater, all the places Tatiana kept intending to go to and never somehow finding time to do. Everyone would envy her then, married to one of the most handsome, the most dashing officers in all of Russia.

And yet . . . when you were married, people expected you to settle down. You had babies and lost your slender waist and had to wear dull clothes and talk about things like sewing and recipes. You hardly ever went to balls, and even when you did, you could only dance with your husband or perhaps the husband of some very close friend, or an elderly relative who would be as exciting to dance with as a cow. You had to relinquish the center of the stage and watch other girls having all the fun you used to have. You weren't even allowed to flirt. Any of that, and people would shake their heads and tut-tut, and you'd get a reputation for being "fast," like Larisa Gonsarova. Instead you sat with the other married women and gossiped about royal scandals or the youngsters together at the balls, just as the married women around the room tonight were doubtless gossiping about her. Such a short time, the days of wine and waltzes, of teasing, downcast eyes that promised kisses only the most reckless ever allowed to be stolen. Her mind sped back to that day with Sergei on Krestoffsky Island. It would always seem magical to her: precious, unique.

There was a lake below the Prince's chateau, and all the young couples took boats from the landing stage to the two small islands in the middle. There was a pretty wrought-iron bridge across which the guests walked from one island to the other. The servants set out trestle tables laden with cold meats and salads, salmon, sturgeon

eggs, fourteen different kinds of bread, caviar, warm soups and con-
sommés, and huge tubs filled with ice in which had been laid slim
bottles of light Moselle wine.

The islands were tree-shaded and large enough so that couples
could sit apart from each other, far enough away for privacy and
near enough to observe the proprieties. As dusk approached, the
servants built a roaring wood fire to keep away the chill of the
spring evening, and a gypsy orchestra was ferried out to serenade
the guests. When it became too cool to stay longer, the fires were
put out and the servants lit huge torches to lead the guests back to
the landing stage in their boats. As they rowed slowly in, the gypsy
violins lamenting the parting of this lovely day, the shadows flickering on the water and the muted passion of the music, the star-scat-
tered sky above the lake, were the backdrop of a dream. Sergei was
so near, so strong, so warm. Tatiana's hand stole into his and he
turned, as if startled, toward her. His eyes were dark, unreadable
pools. Tatiana knew she should not do what she did next, knew she
must not, and yet, and yet, somehow her lips met his. Soft, warm,
willing wantingness flooded her entire body. His hand tightened
convulsively on hers and his lips responded hotly to her own for
what seemed like an eternity. Then, with a strange, abrupt sigh, he
pulled back.

"Tatiana, Tatiana," he murmured, shaking his head as if baffled,
frustrated. "We mustn't. I—it was unforgivable of me. I must tell
you—"

"Hush," Tatiana said, laying a finger across his lips and nestling
her head against his strong shoulder. "You don't need to say anything. I understand."

"Tatiana," Sergei said, his voice soft and urgent. "I have—no
right to kiss you."

"Love gives you every right," Tatiana said. Her mind was float-
ing on a fluffy pink cloud, soft and warm and lovely. "Do you . . . do
you love me, Sergei?"

"Dear child, you're so sweet and pure and innocent—how could
anyone help but love you?" Sergei said. "But I must—"

"Sergei!" someone shouted. "Hey, Sergei, you're drifting off
course!" There was a slight bump as another boat touched theirs.

"Good Lord, so I am!" Sergei laughed, plying the paddle perhaps
more vigorously than he had to. Their canoe moved back to join the
main party and the moment passed, but Tatiana did not mind. Her
hand trailing in the soft, cool water, she lay back on the seat and

watched Sergei's strong arms as he gently brought the boat alongside the landing stage below the house. He jumped out and held out his hand to help her up. She hugged him around the waist and he stroked her hair. Oh, no evening could ever be more wonderful than this, she thought, immersed in her own delight, in love, in love, in love.

2

SOKOLNIKA was a legend.

It stood on the eastern bank of the River Yauza where the river ran southward through Moscow, beyond the Sokolniki Park with its bandstands and promenades. It was approached by a semicircular driveway that began in the Potveshnaya, where a huge gateman in Cossack uniform swung back the huge wrought-iron gates with their gilded coat of arms. The gateman's name was Vanska. He was seventy-eight years of age, but his back was still as straight as a ramrod. He had opened these gates for a thousand princes, a dozen kings, and three Tsars of Russia.

The drive was lined with fine old oaks which screened the big house until visitors came to the curve on the southern side and saw Sokolnika before them, a long, gracefully proportioned mansion set on a gently rising hill that looked out over all the tumbling low roofs of the city.

Everyone knew the story of the building of Sokolnika. It had been one of the wonders of its time. Old Petya Smirnoff, Pierre's father, had been out hunting in the then-country environs of Moscow when he had taken a fancy to a low hill with a fine view down toward the river and overlooking the far-off spires of the Kremlin. Petya bought the hill and the hundred and twenty acres around it from the bankrupt merchant who owned the land, and work was begun on the house in 1861, the year after Petya's second marriage. First, a piece of the hill was sliced off, like the top of a boiled egg, to make a site for the house. Then a railroad was built by means of which the masses of material needed to build the house could be brought from Moscow. While a horde of builders seethed around the foundations and the rising walls, another thousand workmen slaved to transform the bleak brown farmland into a mellow park, complete with trout lake, formal gardens, and fountains. Every one of the huge oaks lining the drive was transplanted. Twelve teams of sixteen horses were used to drag them from the city to their new location. Petya supervised everything, inside and out, with an artist's eye and an accountant's brain. When he saw what he wanted, he told his builders to buy it. If they could not, he told them to copy it, stone for stone, window for window. He commissioned a Londoner named James Christie to act for him over the years Sokolnika was being built, authorizing Christie to spend enormous sums on the furnishings: Beauvais and Gobelin tapestries, Savonnerie carpets, Sèvres porcelains. The finished house had seventy rooms, and when it was completed in 1866, a formal reception for one thousand guests was held to mark the event, which coincided with the sixteenth birthday of Petya's oldest son, Pierre. James Christie came all the way from England; later that year he established his own auction house in London.

Tonight, Sokolnika shone like a beacon on its hill. The courtyard in front of the house was flooded with light, and the endless procession of carriages showed no sign of growing smaller. This was a night of nights, a reception in honor of the Tsar himself, another glittering event in the long procession of celebrations of the Romanov Tercentenary that had begun in February with a great choral *Te Deum* in the Kazan Cathedral in Petersburg. There had been a scintillating ball given by the nobility of the capital in honor of the Tsar and all the Romanov Grand Dukes and Duchesses. There had been a state performance of Glinka's *A Life for the Tsar* and a hundred other ceremonies. In May, the Imperial family had made a dynastic pilgrimage to trace the route taken by Mikhail Romanov, the first of the Romanov Tsars, from his birthplace to Kostroma, where, in March 1613, this grandnephew of Ivan the Terrible and grandfather of Peter the Great was elected Tsar. Now, in June 1913, his descendant, Nicholas Romanov II, had come to pay homage to the city in which Mikhail and every Tsar succeeding him had been crowned. From the plush-lined carriages stepped ladies dressed in the very height of fashion, glittering with jewels. As they entered the house, Pierre Smirnoff, his brother Nico and their wives were waiting to welcome their guests. Behind them stood their huge majordomo Yuri, a majestic Circassian clothed in flowing *burnous* who directed the activities of the grooms and house servants in a magnificently threatening basso profundo. The cloaks and wraps of the beautiful women, the top hats and shakos of the

26

elegant men were whisked away as if on conveyor belts, as the guests ascended the white marble staircase to the ballroom, their feet soundless on heavy red carpet. The walls were hung with mirror after ornately framed mirror, each framed in turn by potted palms or baskets of sweet, fresh orchids. On every second step stood a servant in red frogged jacket and white breeches, holding in white-gloved hands small trays of sweetmeats on delicate silver skewers. On the landing, with its reclining and arising Cupids, was an artificial lake with a golden fountain at its center. In it swam three swans.

"There must be two thousand people here," Dmitri Abrikosov said to his wife as he helped himself to a tiny piece of smoked sturgeon.

"At the very least," she said, ladling Beluga caviar from the iced dish onto a wafer of toast. She nodded her thanks to the servant, who bowed low to acknowledge the honor of being noticed.

The brilliantly lit ballroom was enormous, taking up all the first story of this not-inconsiderable house. Even so it was packed, and Tatiana could discern the same expectant, excited note in the way people were talking that she had heard in the Kremlin.

Oh, it was so wonderful to be here in Moscow, she thought, almost hugging herself with excitement. It had been a dull winter, the season of old vitiated by the fact that the Tsaritsa did not care for the social whirl, preferring a life of cozy domesticity with her husband and their four children at the summer palace in Tsarskoe Selo, "the Tsar's village," twenty-two versts from the capital. "The heads of the young ladies here are filled with nothing but thoughts of young officers," she had commented, tartly and accurately. Her unconcealed dislike of large functions had made it steadily more difficult for the hostesses of Petersburg to celebrate the old season, which began after Christmas and ended with Lent, in anything like the style or on anything like the scale of former times.

Once, Tatiana's mother told her, it had been an endless round of concerts, ballets, banquets and balls, operas and private parties and midnight suppers. Everyone had gone, everyone. It had all been different in the old days.

"If you were young and unmarried, you went to the Bal Blanc," Maryka Makcheyeva said. "One dressed only in white silk. Nothing else was permitted. One could then see easily who was truly beautiful. Ah, my darling, you would have danced the soles off your slippers at the Bal Blanc!"

"But what if one was married?"

"Oh, there was a ball for young married couples, too. That was called the Bal Rose. There were so many, so many. What a time you would have had."

Even Maryka blamed the dearth of such events in Petersburg upon the Tsaritsa, although she did not go the lengths that some of her friends did and call the Empress *Nemka*, "the German one."

"Can't understand it myself," Tatiana's father would say. "As I recall it, when Nicholas was Tsarevich before his marriage, he was as much of a playboy as any Grand Duke before or since."

"So, it must be her fault," Maryka said, with unbudgeable conviction. For herself, the lack of social whirl mattered not at all. She had never really cared for it, knowing herself to be a plain and simple woman whom no one would ever call beautiful or stunning or dazzling. Her daughter, however, was another matter, for Tatiana was beautiful, and Maryka never ceased to be irritated by the absence of those glittering functions of years gone by when girls were introduced into society, "taken up" by the royals, assured of good marriages. So, when Tatiana's fellow *Institutka* in Petersburg, Katrina Smirnova, had invited her to spend the summer months in Moscow, Maryka had urged her to go and softened up her husband for a week or two before Tatiana asked Alex for his permission and blessing.

"Well, as to all that, I'm not so sure," Alexander Makcheyev said when Tatiana excitedly told him of Katrina's invitation. "Not so sure at all. Moscow's not Petersburg, you know. Altogether a different kettle of fish."

He saw Tatiana's face fall and patted her shoulder gently. He was not entirely unaware of the fact that Maryka had been working on him; he just wanted to enjoy his moment. He had no intention of forbidding Tatiana to go, and he said so.

"But we must decide who's to be your chaperone, *malyutka*," he said. He always called her "little one" or "baby." "A pretty girl like you. Moscow's not Petersburg. It's not so civilized, not so *kulturny*. Full of clerks and factory workers." He smiled at her indulgently, as if she could not possibly comprehend how awful Moscow was, puffing on his blackened old briar pipe. As always, he sat in his studded leather chair beside the big marble fireplace. Whenever she smelled leather and pipe tobacco, Tatiana saw instantly in her mind's eye a picture of her father.

"Now, Alex," Maryka said, softly.

"No culture, Moscow men," Alex said. "Seen plenty of them in my day. No style, any of them."

"Oh, Papa!" Tatiana laughed. "You're just old-fashioned, that's all. Moscow is a beautiful city. If it wasn't, why would people like the Smirnoffs, who have all the money in the world and could live anywhere, make their home there?"

"*Nouveaux riches!*" Alex growled. "Moscow's full of them."

"Now, Alex," Maryka said again, this time a little less softly. "You haven't been to Moscow for ten years. Tatiana is probably right. Things will have changed there, just as they have here in Petersburg."

"Wish I was as sure of that as you seem to be," Alex grumbled. "Never liked the damned place. Never will." He reached for his stick and stood up, broad back to the roaring fire. He always assumed this position when he sensed an argument brewing. He loved to argue, fierce but good-natured, and it was as if, old soldier that he was, he wanted to be sure that his rear was secure.

"Stubborn woman," he grumbled, half beneath his breath.

"Bad-tempered devil," muttered his wife.

"Papa, Mama, stop," Tatiana laughed, clapping her hands to bring their mock argument to an end before it became a serious one. They had those, too, once in a while. "Can't we talk about my going to Moscow? After all, it's not everyone who's invited to visit Sokolnika."

"It's very generous of Katrina to invite you," Alex said.

"Yes, isn't it?" Maryka said, unwilling to back down all the way just yet. "Typical of Moscow, rather than the penny-pinching style of Petersburg."

"We pinch no pennies in my household, woman!" Alex growled. "And no one knows it better than you."

"I know it, my dearest," Maryka said, her voice saccharine. "If only some of your former fellow officers could take a lesson from you, how nice it would be. One gets so tired of the drab evenings we have to spend at their homes."

"Not all of them have a royal pension like me."

"Not all of them earned one like you," she said.

"Don't start that," he said.

There was a silence. Thirty years after losing it, Alexander Makcheyev was still touchy about his leg. He had been one of the honor guard escorting the carriage of Tsar Alexander II back to the

Winter Palace from the Field of Mars when a terrorist group calling itself *Narodnaya Volya*, The Will of the People, had assassinated the Tsar. It had been a clumsy, almost botched affair, not the first attempt on the life of the Tsar and like those which had preceded it, bungled and so very nearly unsuccessful.

They had come down Engineer Street and turned right onto the Catherine Canal. There had been no warning. The first bomb burst under the Tsar's coach, killing two Cossacks and three horses and badly damaging the carriage itself. Shaken but unhurt, the Tsar had stepped out of the carriage and run back to see what could be done for the wounded.

"Thank God, your Majesty is safe!" Alexander Makcheyev said, as he swung down from his curvetting horse and ran to the Tsar's side. In that same moment, another of the terrorists, Grenavitsky, who had been huddled behind a gatepost, burst out into the open, eyes wild.

"Rather too early to thank God!" he shouted, and his arm moved. Glass winked in the spring sunshine, and Alex looked at it and knew what it was in the instant that the bomb exploded in a sheet of flame. It blew the Tsar across the street and against the railings of the canal, his belly ripped open, his right leg torn off, his left shattered, his face a mask of blood. Alexander Makcheyev, standing beside him, was hurled up into the air and smashed against the wrecked coach. When he awoke the next day in the hospital, they told him that the Tsar had died of his injuries. A little later, the doctors came and told Alex that they had amputated his left leg below the knee. Thirty years later, he still sometimes awoke shouting in alarm as the bearded assassin in his dream threw the bomb between the Tsar's legs and all the world turned crimson.

"Well," he said at length, "I want you to know I'm not giving my permission just because you two have bullied me. I'm giving it—"

"Oh, Papa!" Tatiana squealed and threw her arms around his neck and kissed him and kissed him until he disentangled himself from her clinging arms and pushed her away at arm's length, the mock frown on his face no more disguising his pleasure than Maryka's smile concealed hers.

"All right, all right," he said, loudly. "I just hope you're still as pleased with the idea when you're stuck in that pesthole down south." He was unable to resist the one last little jab, but Maryka smiled and said no more. She knew her husband very, very well.

30

They had met in 1885 when, still garlanded with the glory of an Order of St. George from the new Tsar and the title of Count, freed by the death of old Franz Eduard Makcheyev the preceding year, Alexander Makcheyev had presented himself at Vlakerskoye, the estate of Prince Dmitri Ivanov.

Ivanov was himself a descendant of one of the most decorated Russian generals of the Seven Years' War. He was a wealthy but eccentric man with but one daughter of marriageable age, Maryka. She had been given the education thought proper for a young woman of her class: tuition in French and German from governesses, instruction in sewing, needlepoint and crochet, together with piano and recorder lessons. Maryka proved competent at them all without showing great skill at any. She played the piano prettily but without style or feeling. She spoke French reasonably well, as one had to; it was the language of the court. German she rapidly forgot and never felt the lack. She was at heart what she had been born and would always be, a simple country girl, strong, honest and without artifice.

Alexander Makcheyev was honored but without great wealth. Maryka Ivanovna was wealthy but without suitors. His name would have ordinarily been more than enough to recommend Alex to any young heiress in Russia, but there were not so many prepared to marry a one-legged man, whatever his pedigree. He was not bad-looking, Maryka thought at their first meeting, seeing not just the clumsy artificial leg but the wavy brown hair, the upright stance, the frank eyes. Alexander spoke French fluently; his uniform was smart and his manners were acceptable. If perhaps his disability made him awkward, Maryka saw that Alex had acquired the ability to conceal that awkwardness very well.

As for him, he saw a homely girl with dark blonde hair in braids, dressed peasant style. She was young, fresh, and innocent, Junoesque, he thought, but not unattractive. He sighed, and so did she. Next day, negotiations with a view to their marriage were begun. To the surprise of everyone, including the principals, it was a good match. If Maryka was not passionately in love with him, she learned to love and respect Alex. He, in turn, felt affection and esteem for his new wife. They moved to Shuvalovo, where Franz Eduard had established a small estate on the banks of Lake Suzdal, taking with them the four hundred serfs who were part of Maryka's dowry. With a determination that he was surprised to discover that he owned, Alexander set himself the task of earning a degree in jurisprudence at the university. Exactly six years later he was appointed a district judge. He bought an apartment in a big sandstone house on the corner of the Zakharevskaya and the Potemkinskaya. They lived there when court was in session, spending their summers at Shuvalovo, where their nearest neighbors were the Tretyakovs. Stepan, Sergei's father, was related to the family which had donated the famous Moscow art gallery to the city in 1892.

He was so proud of Tatiana, Maryka thought, looking fondly at her husband. He was proud that she was pretty, proud that she was making her own way, glad that she had well-placed friends, confident that she would eventually marry one of the sons of his good friend Stepan Tretyakov. Sergei or Andrei, it didn't matter a damn, he said. His three sons were already embarked upon their respective careers; Alex had taken all that firmly in hand from the start. Ivan was already qualified as a doctor, Ilya was a rising young officer in the artillery, and Roman, the youngest of the boys, had his commission in the Garde Chevalier.

So Tatiana Makcheyeva came to Moscow in the early summer of 1913. Six hundred versts! It was hard to imagine such a distance if you had never traveled more than a hundred on a train before. The journey took them nearly twelve hours, twelve rattling, rocking, noisy hours in the express train that thundered through the rushing night across the black and endless land. Once in a while, Tatiana could see little clusters of light in the darkness, some tiny hamlet lost in the immensity of the land. On the seat opposite her, Aunt Elena nodded wearily, her face slack. How anyone could sleep on such an exciting journey Tatiana could not imagine. She vowed she would stay awake the whole way to Moscow.

For all that, she was half asleep when they reached Tver. She heard them shouting the name of the town, but she found she was too tired to wipe the steamed-up windows with her sleeve to see out. The next thing she heard was the clattering rumble of the train as they crossed the Moskva River on a bridge that roared and shook. People were stirring in the neighboring compartments, stamping their feet, coughing. Tatiana was glad now that Papa had insisted they buy four tickets so that they would have the compartment to themselves. She cleaned the window with her hand and looked out. There, soaring above the early-morning mist on the river, were the graceful golden domes of the city. Forever afterward she remembered that first day in Moscow as one of golden domes and the sound of church bells.

"Tatiana, I have to speak to you." Sergei's voice brought her out of her reverie and back to the glittering ballroom. Her heart opened like a flower. Sergei stood in front of her, gallant and smiling, sternly handsome in his white dress uniform. He offered his arm and inclined his head toward the open French windows leading to the long stone balcony overlooking the lake.

"Not in here," he said. "Let's go outside."

She could not speak. She twined her fingers into his and led and was half-led across the room. She saw Katrina watching her and thought her friend looked sad. Jealous, perhaps, she thought. It was warm outside, dreamy. Sergei was puzzled by her intensity, she by his uncertainty and reticence. Say it, she willed him. Oh, why don't you say it? Sergei looked at her shining eyes. How shall I ever tell her, he thought, agony searing his soul.

"Oh, Sergei, I wish we were really alone," Tatiana whispered. "All alone, the way we were that night on Krestoffsky Island."

"Tatiana," he said, firmly, "there is something I must tell you. I cannot put it off one moment longer."

He took her hands in his. His touch thrilled her. The sky was velvety blue, and it seemed as if the stars were afloat in it. He is going to say it now, she thought, just the way I always knew that he would. Her mind was immobile, cocooned in dreams. She could scarcely breathe as she looked into his serious eyes.

"I am going to marry Katrina," he said, his voice not quite as level as he had wanted it to be. "Katrina," he said, as though speaking her name would strengthen his resolve. At first, Tatiana's mind would not accept what Sergei had said. She shook her head impatiently, as someone will who has been given the wrong answer to a simple question. It was not possible, she had not heard him say it, she would not believe it! And yet, simultaneously, it was, she had, she must. Sergei was going to marry Katrina!

"It's true, Tatiana," Sergei was saying. His voice was full of a sort of self-hatred. "Her father will announce our betrothal tonight. Everything has been arranged. Everything."

"How long?" Tatiana heard herself ask. It seemed as if her voice was coming from someone else's throat, a croak she did not recognize. "How long has all this been arranged?"

33

"For a very long time, Tatiana," he said, untold depths of sadness in his voice. "Our families . . . I thought you knew. I thought everyone knew."

"No," she said, dully. "Nobody told me."

"It's true," he said. "You must understand."

"Understand? I can't understand," Tatiana said, fighting back the tears. I won't cry, she thought. I won't let him see me cry. "You told me . . . you said you loved me. I . . . I thought—"

"No!" he said, a little sharply. "I never said that."

"Do you love her?"

"Tatiana," he said, patiently. "Dearest Tatiana, do you think that's all there is to marriage? Do you think life is some sort of magazine story?"

"Does she love you as I do?"

He shook his head; how could he answer her? "I should have known that you wouldn't understand," he said quietly. "It was unfair of me to expect it."

"Oh, I understand," she said, her breath coming a little faster. All at once she was angry, angry at herself for being so blind, so stupid, so naïve. Angry at Katrina, angry at Maria, angry at everyone for not telling her that she had been making a fool of herself. She thought of Katrina in Sergei's arms and jealousy seared her heart like acid. She struck blindly at his face. The slap was as loud as a pistol shot, and the conversation around them ceased abruptly.

"Liar!" Tatiana said. "Coward! You love me and you know it!"

"Tatiana," Sergei said, glancing around. People were staring at them with undisguised curiosity. Everybody liked a juicy scandal. "Please! Lower your voice, I beg of you."

"Yes," she said, icily calm as suddenly as she had become angry. "Yes, of course. Don't let me embarrass you."

She turned and walked away from him. Sergei's face was as white as the gloved hand he raised to touch his cheek. He stood like a stone and watched her go, shamed and saddened by what had happened. As for Tatiana, her icy calm melted as she crossed the room, to be replaced by a stricken panic. There was a taste in her mouth like ashes. She could not get the picture of Sergei's shocked face, and the red, red mark upon it, out of her mind. She hurried from the pink and gold room, her body trembling, her eyes blurred with tears. Somehow she found the dressing room and collapsed into a chair, staring at the mirrored image of her own face as if it were that of a total stranger.

Aghast at her folly, she contemplated the immediate future. I suppose all Moscow will be talking about me tomorrow, she thought. How could she face them? What could she tell Aunt Elena, who was sure to hear what had happened? And Sergei—he would hate her for so humiliating him in front of everyone. The thought made her want to weep, and she hated herself for what she had done. She could hear the music coming through the curtained doorway as she sat in front of the gilded mirror, mind blank, eyes unseeing. Over her shoulder she saw Maria Abrikosova come bustling into the boudoir, her dark eyes full of concern.

"Tatiana, darling, are you all right?" she said, putting her arms around Tatiana. Tatiana drew herself away.

"Why did you not tell me about Sergei and Katrina?"

Maria was silent. Both Sergei and Katrina had instructed her not to discuss their forthcoming engagement with Tatiana.

"Darling, I'm sorry, truly sorry," Maria said. "I thought you knew about it. I thought everyone did." It was a white lie, but white lies were better than black ones, Maria always thought.

"Everyone but me," Tatiana said. She was silent for a moment, and then looked toward the curtained doorway. "I suppose everyone's talking about me out there," she said, trepidantly.

"No such thing, silly!" Maria laughed. "There are more than two thousand people here. I don't suppose more than twenty or thirty of them are aware that anything happened, and I doubt that any of them has the slightest idea who you are."

"I hadn't thought of that," Tatiana said.

"Won't you come back and join the party now?"

"In a minute," Tatiana said. "You go ahead. I'll come in just a minute."

"You're sure?"

"Yes, yes!" Tatiana said, impatiently. "Go on, goose!"

Relieved, Maria smiled and went back into the great ballroom. The orchestra was playing one of the Strauss waltzes, glorious, lilting music. Tatiana looked at herself in the mirror again and nodded. I'll make him weep for this, she silently vowed. One day, I'll make him weep. Then she walked out into the ballroom, head up, eyes challenging. The dancers swirled by, a changing pattern of brilliant colors.

"Not dancing, mademoiselle?"

It was Vladimir Smirnoff, and he was smiling at her in the same way that he had done when she first saw him at the ball in the

Kremlin. For a moment, she considered cutting him dead, but something stopped her. If they were going to talk about her, she thought, a devil stirring in her breast, then Great Jehovah, she'd give them something to talk about!

"Perhaps I might have the honor?" Vladimir said.

Tatiana smiled and lifted her arms. Vladimir Smirnoff smiled too, a cold, sardonic smile that she had not seen before. He took her in his arms and she discovered, to her surprise, that he was a graceful and accomplished dancer.

"I couldn't help seeing your, ah, contretemps with Sergei Tretyakov," he said, urbanely. "Something serious, I trust?"

Tatiana was taken aback by his effrontery, and it was a moment before she could reply.

"How—how dare you?" she said, her heart sinking as she realized that if Vladimir Smirnoff knew about it, her hosts already did or soon would. Tatiana controlled her temper. I won't let him anger me, she thought, gritting her teeth and smiling, smiling, in case anyone was watching them. She wanted everyone to think she was having the most wonderful time, that she hadn't a care in the world. Frowning crossly at Vladimir Smirnoff wouldn't do it.

"You sound as if you don't like Sergei," she said, coolly. "What has he ever done to you?"

"Nothing at all," Vladmir said.

"Then why—?"

"He's a fraud."

"He is a fine person," Tatiana said, letting a little of her anger boil over. "You have no right to call him names."

"You've misunderstood me, girl," he said. "The reason I don't like him is that he's a play actor; he's never showing you the real person. It's as if he's always afraid to let anyone see what he's really like. That's why I called him a fraud."

"I suppose you think that of all of my friends," Tatiana sniffed.

"Your soldier boys? Oh, they're harmless enough, providing there isn't a war," Vladimir said. "Put them where real shooting is going on, and they'd be as much use as stuffed dummies."

"Oh, not you as well," she said, with a theatrical moue of boredom. "Doesn't anyone ever talk about anything but war?"

"I talk about everything but," Vladmir Smirnoff said, smiling his devil's smile. "Would you like to try me?"

For some reason, his words made Tatiana feel flustered. She covered her uncertainty with words. "No, I most decidedly would

36

not!" she retorted spiritedly. "I would like to return to my friends."

"Oh, shut up," he said lazily, ignoring her request. "You're having a good time, aren't you? And you've got to admit I can dance better than those jackbooted chimpanzees you've been surrounded by all evening."

Great Jehovah! The man's vanity beggared description, she thought, simultaneously realizing that what he said was no less true because of it. He was a wonderful dancer. She could not recall when she had enjoyed a waltz so much, but she would have died before admitting it to him.

"What the devil do you see in that fellow Tretyakov, anyway?" Vladimir asked her. She sensed puzzlement, irritation in the question and smiled to herself. Vladimir Smirnoff needed taking down a peg or two, and he was giving her the means with which to do just that. It was going to be a pleasure.

"My feelings toward Sergei are nothing to do with you," she said, averting her face. "And it betrays your manners that you even ask."

"Oh, you're marvelous!" he said, smiling widely. "Really terrific. Do you think that sort of nonsense works on someone like me?"

"I think you are intolerable," she said.

"You think I'm right, Tatiana," he replied. "And you'll remember it one day. There's something vaguely nasty in your Sergei's life and—"

"I am sure," she interrupted, her voice dripping with venom, "that Sergei would be fascinated to hear that someone as . . . celebrated as you thinks that he has things in his life of which he should be ashamed."

Vladimir looked at her and smiled again, but this time sadly. He shook his head in a gesture not entirely spurious.

"I'm disappointed, little Makcheyeva," he said. "You can do better than that."

"I'm sure I don't know what you mean," Tatiana said, huffily. Then, piqued: "Disappointed?"

"Exactly that. You're playing a silly game, the kind these people play." He jerked his head toward the assembled guests. "They mock-love, and they mock-fight. Nothing they do is real."

"Whereas you, of course . . ." she said, leaving the jibe unfinished.

"Touché," he said. "It doesn't alter the truth of what I said, though. Would you like me to fight a duel with your brave captain?

37

Would that make your little heart flutter, seeing him put a bullet through me for sneering at him?"

"If you want to know the truth," Tatiana said coldly, "it would."

"Alas, for love at first sight." Vladimir grinned. "Well, I knew you had spirit, and I was right. All I ask is that you don't waste it on popinjays like Sergei Tretyakov and his clique."

"I think you are quite insufferable."

"Then you won't dance with me again?"

"I am sorry that I ever consented to do so at all."

"Drat!" he said. "Then I suppose there's no chance at all of your having dinner with me one evening?"

"Dinner?" Tatiana pulled away from him, horrified. "I wouldn't dine with you if you were the last man alive."

"If I were the last man alive, you might have to join a line," he said with a sly grin. "You won't reconsider?"

"Tell me," Tatiana said, trying sarcasm as a weapon, "are you married?" She knew he was. She knew all about that from what Vasya and Nicky had told her, but she wanted to see what he would say.

"Sort of," was the reply.

"Your wife is not with you this evening?"

"No," he said with that devil's grin. "She had some letters she wanted to catch up on."

Tatiana shook her head in vexation at his capriciousness. As if anyone would stay home writing letters when he could be at an Imperial reception! Before she could say more, the music ended. The dancers applauded politely, and Vladimir led Tatiana back to her friends. She slowed visibly as they got nearer. He took her elbow firmly in his hand and squeezed it gently.

"Courage, Makcheyeva," he whispered. She could have killed him for so accurately reading her trepidation.

"Hello, Smirnoff," Vasya Kirsanov was saying. "How are you?"

"Well, thank you," Vladimir said. He made a small bow in Tatiana's direction. "Thank you, mademoiselle," he said. "If you will excuse me?"

"Of course," Tatiana said. "With pleasure." His grin told her that he had not missed the shaft. He bent over her hand. "Enchanté, mademoiselle," he said, and then he was gone, leaving Tatiana irritated, unsettled, puzzled, intrigued.

"I say, Tatiana, it's a bit much, you know," Vasya said. He looks like a pouting baby, Tatiana thought.

"What do you mean, Vasya?"

"Dancing with old Smirnoff," Nicky said. "That's what he means."

"Especially after what happened between you and Sergei."

"Bad form, Tatiana," Paul Dubinsky said, glumly. "There'll be quite enough talk as it is, without your flirting with Vladimir Smirnoff."

"I was not flirting with him," Tatiana said, wondering whether in fact she had been.

"Well, you certainly looked as if you were," Nicky said, a note of aggravation in his voice. Why, they're jealous, Tatiana thought, pleased that they were.

They were all so sweet and so dear, and Vladimir Smirnoff had no right to say such cutting things about them. Caught up in the fun of the moment, her woes momentarily forgotten, she was beautiful again. From across the room, Vladimir Smirnoff watched her with the kind of smile a man might have on his face as he watches a baby learn to walk. After a while he turned away to join his party, not realizing that he had not been the only one watching Tatiana. Behind a pillar near the doorway another pair of eyes was fixed upon her, the smoldering eyes of Boris Abrikosov. There was no smile on his face at all.

"She's a beauty, isn't she?"

Boris Abrikosov turned to face the speaker, quickly masking his anger. He hated anyone to know his innermost feelings, but there was no use showing it. He had obviously been watching the Makcheyeva girl far too openly and far too long if even his stupid brother had noticed it. Next, the fat fool would be prattling to his wife about how Boris couldn't take his eyes off the girl. Dmitri was a dolt, but even dolts can cause trouble.

"They all are, brother," he said, putting enough of a leer into his voice and expression to cause Dmitri to smile conspiratorially. Dmitri was forty-two, overweight and complacent, a direct contrast to his whip-thin, gimlet-eyed younger brother. Boris looked considerably more than his six years his brother's junior, but Boris had always taken pride in being fit, his body hard and in good shape. As heir to the family business and most of the estate, Dmitri had been overindulged and self-indulgent since childhood; he had even married self-indulgently. With the Abrikosov name and money he could have married any one of a dozen beauties, but Dmitri had done his father's bidding—Dmitri had always done his father's bidding—and

39

married Alexandra, the dowdy half-sister of Pierre Smirnoff. Dmitri always took the line of least resistance. He didn't even have the gumption to go out and take a mistress the way any sensible rich man stuck with a frump for a wife would have done. Indeed, the thought of Dmitri taking a mistress was so farfetched as to bring a contemptuous smile to Boris's thin lips. Misreading the smile, Dmitri nodded and smiled in return. He was relieved that his little jest had not offended Boris. Boris was damned touchy, Dmitri thought, his face radiating anxiety to please. One never knew for sure what Boris was thinking.

Dmitri never dared to tell his parents anything about Boris, although there were many times when he knew he should have done so. He knew that in the village, the girls there were terrified of Boris and called him *dyavol*, devil. When Boris went away to school, more than one farmer's daughter breathed a sigh of relief—and more than one farmer's wife, too.

Dmitri hated gymnasium; Boris loved it. Dmitri was hopeless at sports; Boris excelled in all of them. Dmitri was a poor student; Boris a brilliant one. When in his eighth and final year Dmitri faced the so-called test of maturity which preceded graduation, he was ill for a week beforehand. Boris sailed through the series of written and oral tests, indifferent to the atmosphere of awe and tension which the authorities deliberately fostered. It was not uncommon for students of his age—eighteen—to suffer mental or nervous breakdowns during the ordeal. Boris showed, during the examinations as in all his later years, that if he had nerves at all, they were made of steel.

He completed high school graded excellent in every subject except logic. His conduct in class and his interest in studies were judged exemplary. He passed his examinations with distinction and went on to the university as if it had been preordained. None of his teachers admired him. None of his fellow students liked him.

His social standing seemed to bother him as little as anything else. Boris knew he had a superior brain, and he looked upon the antics of his peers with scarcely concealed contempt. He was interested in one thing only—power—and he knew where power lay. He had been recruited by the Tsar's secret police, the *Okhrana*, upon his entry into the university and throughout his years there was an "insider" for the organization. In this activity, as in every other aspect of his life, Boris shared with no one. If he attended the student rallies, if he took girls to the zoological gardens, if he watched the troops drilling in the Ménage with a group of classmates, Boris

40

did so for his own reasons, not theirs. Quiet and watchful, he was always ready to be a confidant, never to confide. His acquaintances —he had no close friends—thought him cold, studious, distant. He went to their meetings in the Alexander Garden and listened to what they said. Students were by tradition radical, and there was always political argument, talk of revolution, change. Most of it was hot air, but the *Okhrana* still wanted to know about it. Without compunction, Boris told them.

He went once a week to an anonymous apartment, where he reported to a granite-faced man named Astrov. Astrov rarely spoke or showed emotion of any kind. Whether the information Boris provided was valuable or worthless, whether any action was ever taken because of it, Boris never discovered.

"What happens to the information I bring you?" he once asked Astrov. The big man looked at him as if he had committed some unspeakable indecency.

"You do not need to know that," he said, stiffly.

"Does it get sent to Headquarters?" *Okhrana* headquarters was in the Ministry of the Interior.

"Everything gets sent to Headquarters."

Boris nodded and mentally filed the information. He did not tell Astrov, or anyone else, that he kept his own files, although he knew that it was dangerous to play a double game with the *Okhrana*. There was something in him which balked at giving without qualification; perhaps, at some future time, the information he passed to Astrov might be valuable. So he kept his files and his dossiers in a meticulous code that a man who had been in the prison of Saints Peter and Paul told him the prisoners—condemned to utter silence during their imprisonment—used. He knew it would never present problems to a real cryptoanalyst, but casually prying eyes would see only coded numbers, meaningless without the key.

"I never cease to be surprised at how much people are prepared to tell you about themselves if you give them half a chance," he would say. His father, Ivan Abrikosov, was a wealthy man with many connections in business and at court; Boris used them. He had dossiers on family friends, their friends, their servants and their servants' friends. His secret knowledge gave Boris a clear vision of the tangled skein of their emotions and relationships. His clear vision increased his contempt for them.

By his thirtieth birthday, Boris had risen to the rank of Examiner in the *Okhrana*, controlling a team of spies—insiders such as he himself had once been—and had access to all confidential memoranda, personal dossiers, and the biweekly *Okhrana Gazette*, which listed all cases under action throughout the country, with lists and descriptions of wanted men. From all these he carefully enlarged his own files on the people he knew and the people they knew. His family paid lip service to the fiction that he was a legal adviser working for the Rossiya Insurance Company—Boris had studied juridical science at the university—and since he saw them all infrequently, the fiction was not too difficult to maintain. His personal life was a closed book to everyone. He had never married.

"Time you found yourself a wife, Boris," Dmitri said, smiling like the fat fool that he was. His tone was heavily jocular so that Boris would not snap his head off. "Isn't that so, my dear?" he said to his wife.

"What's that, my lamb?" she said, turning toward them. Someone had once praised her to Boris, saying that she was that rare thing, a truly modest woman.

"Indeed she is," Boris had agreed. "And she has a great deal to be modest about."

Dmitri's wife—called "Shushi" by her friends and family—was a very plain woman, the kind who always has to do the best she can. Her clothes were expensive, tailored by Madame de Brissac, couturière to the Tsaritsa, yet Shushi Abrikosova managed to look dowdy. Endless hours in the hairdressing salon did not improve her lifeless hair. Her eyes were a watery green—she was shortsighted—and her full mouth was too big for the rest of her face. She was no beauty, Boris thought, and not very bright.

"Oh, hello, Boris," Shushi said. Her voice was flat and uninteresting, and there was no warmth in it at all. What a cow, he thought, smiling.

"There's someone I must talk to," he told her, neither knowing nor caring whether she believed it. Shushi was boring, vacuous and slow. There was nothing to know about her and nothing to learn.

He walked briskly away from his brother and Shushi, but he did not get very far before someone called his name.

"Well, Boris Ivanovich! Not dancing?"

"As you see," Boris said, cursing his luck. Was there no end to the fools he was going to have to suffer before he could talk to the Makcheyeva girl? He saw her being whirled onto the floor by another of her pretty Guardsmen and swore beneath his breath. He had no time for any of the Smirnoffs, and especially Vladimir, who had the most uncanny ability to get under Boris's skin in one sentence. But they were all too rich, too powerful, too well connected to be snubbed.

"Well, man, what's the news?" Vladimir said with mock impatience. "What's happening in the real world?"

"News?"

"No revolutionaries tunneling beneath the Winter Palace? No mad bombers sneaking through the cordon at Tsarskoe Selo?" Smirnoff drawled, raising an elegant eyebrow.

Boris leaned forward slightly. Did he know something? Or was he just drunk?

"Why do you say that?" he asked, regretting the question the next moment, when a wickedly knowing grin touched Vladimir's face.

"Boris, Boris," Vladimir said, shaking his head in mock sorrow. "Always looking for plots. I'm not talking politics, man, just regretting the fact that all this can't go on much longer."

"Nothing is forever," Boris found himself saying. Once more he saw the hateful smile touch Smirnoff's face.

"Well, well," Vladimir said. "A philosopher. An *Okhrana* philosopher."

"You flatter me," Boris said, fighting back.

"Poor Boris," Vladimir said. "So wrong, so often."

Damn you, Boris thought. Vladimir Smirnoff had always been arrogant, yet he sensed somehow that tonight Smirnoff's heart was not in his taunting. It was mere habit, something he always did. There was a faraway look in his eye. Marital problems? Boris wondered. Everyone knew about Valentina Smirnoff.

"Something worrying you, Smirnoff?" he said, offhandedly.

"Everything worries me, Boris," Vladimir said, with a slow smile that indicated he had seen the ploy coming and had no intention of playing Boris's game. "Especially you. Why don't you let the rest of us in on what you know, tell us what's really happening out there? Then maybe we could do something about it. The world's coming to an end, Boris, and you and your ilk stand on your dignity. You're nothing but a herd of damned ostriches. Forgive me, I need another drink."

He pushed himself off his chair and snapped his fingers at one of the servants. Boris took the opportunity to turn and walk away, and Vladimir watched him go without regret. Needling Boris Abrikosov was a poor enough pastime, God knew, but he needed something to take his mind off his own dark thoughts. The champagne wasn't doing a damned thing; alcohol always let you down when you needed it most. He went back to his chair in the gilded alcove, thinking about Valentina again in spite of his own determination not to. It wasn't that he felt betrayed so much as disappointed. Perhaps he always expected too much of people. Perhaps they just couldn't ever give as much as he hoped for.

Or perhaps I'm just a damned fool, he thought, with a wry smile. That's an infinitely likelier proposition.

3

VLADIMIR had watched his wife brushing her hair in front of the mirror just a few hours earlier, before the ball began. Bitch, he thought dispassionately, bitch in heat, making yourself beautiful for someone else. The thought of her with Oleg Baranin made the ugly green thing in the pit of his belly stir, burning, burning. What happens to us all? he wondered, looking at her. I loved her so much once, so very much. Now, finally, I detest her.

Valentina was still a beautiful woman, even if her once-slender waist was thicker now, her hips and thighs fuller, her upper arms heavier. Arms raised to help her maid arrange her coiffure, she was beautiful and she knew it. She saw him watching her and misread the emotion in his eyes. A small smile of triumph touched her well-shaped lips. Beautiful, yes, but also selfish, shallow and vain, he thought, knowing she did not know that at all. Perhaps it was inevitable that an actress be selfish and vain. Life, after all, was always artifice to them, each movement a pose, each pose an attitude. Their very words were counterfeit, the self they showed the world a shell. Perhaps they grew so used to make-believe that they mistook it for reality. Or perhaps they were just stupid.

Seven years, he thought. Somewhere in there something happened. It ended, something else began. Was it all at once, was it a gradual thing? Was the flaw in me, in her, in both of us? Had it always been there, right from the beginning, like cancer, a mole for all those years, and then suddenly death? No, he decided. I know I tried, and I know she did not. So it was stupidity, like his stupidity in thinking, as the infatuated always do, that no one can see their infatuation. He might have forgiven her for taking a lover, had it been someone anonymous. He could not bear it because it had been Oleg.

It was in *Hedda Gabler*, a dark comedy about affectation and pretension, that Vladimir first saw Valentina Beriosovna. The play had originally been presented by the Arts Theatre in 1899, with Stanislavsky himself playing Ejlert Løvborg. Anton Chekhov urged Vladimir to see it. Ibsen was now, he said, his favorite playwright in the whole world, and he had written to Stanislavsky's partner Nemirovich-Danchenko to say so.

"Who is that?" Vladimir said to Blumenthal as they watched the play.

"Who is who?"

"The blonde, you fool," Vladimir hissed, as though everyone on-stage except Valentina had become as invisible to Blumenthal as they suddenly had to him.

"That's Valentina Beriosovna," Blumenthal said. "Surely you've seen her before?"

"No," Vladimir said. "I would have remembered."

"Well, she's been with the ensemble for a year or more, to my knowledge," Blumenthal said, cocking a shrewd eye at his companion. Short, fat, and cunning, Blumenthal produced operettas at the Nikitski Theater near the Nikitskaya Gate. He was planning to ask Vladimir to invest in a new show he was putting together. Vladimir had promised to dine with him after the theater, and Blumenthal was optimistic. Everyone knew that Vladimir was as openhanded as his father was a skinflint. People said that Petya's meanness had turned Vladimir into a spendthrift—he knew that his cavalier attitude to money would further enrage his frugal father. Vladimir was also a bit of a ladies' man. So, since he had presented him with the opportunity, Blumenthal saw no reason why he should not profit from it.

"Would you like to meet her?" he asked.

"You know her?"

"Only slightly," Blumenthal lied. He knew Beriosovna a lot better than slightly, and so did a lot of other producers. But he did not say that.

"She's very aloof," he told Vladimir, "very proud. But if you wish it, I could try."

"Try," Vladimir said. "Ask her to join us for supper."

"Well," Blumenthal said, putting on his face the bravely resigned expression of a man being sent on a suicide mission, "if you wish."

Ten minutes later he came back to the box, smiling and nodding and rubbing his hands like a pushcart peddler. Vladimir looked at him with unconcealed impatience; the fool was acting like a match-maker. Vladimir had a lot of things on his mind but marriage wasn't one of them, especially to an actress. He tried to imagine his father's reaction if he suddenly came home and told the old man he planned to marry an actress. It was like trying to imagine a volcano erupting.

"Well, man," he said, "what did she say?"

"Mademoiselle Beriosovna would be pleased to join us after the performance, but just for a little while," Blumenthal said. "She cannot stay longer. A previous engagement."

"Of course, of course," Vladimir said. He sent one of the red-capped messengers always available at theaters to Echkin's livery stable to order a *troika*, and they settled back to watch the second act.

The *troika* was waiting for them when they emerged into the bitterly cold night, the *yamshtchik* bundled up on his seat, eyes screwed up against the icy air in which shining crystals danced. His beard looked like a great snow-filled sponge. The three horses, blankets steaming, shifted and stamped impatiently as the passengers climbed aboard and wrapped the heavy, slightly damp blankets around themselves and covered them with a bearskin rug. Then, with a lurch and a scattered jingle of bells, silver harnesses gleaming beneath the street lights and powdered snow spraying their faces with feathery fingers, they glided through the Tverskaya Gate and into the Petersburgskoe Chaussée. Alongside Petrovski Park the pines glistened ice-white with frozen snow. The bare birches scattered between them looked like feathered bone. Falling flakes of snow fluttered earthward, a million tiny moths. The driver sang lustily as they sped along, something about a girl he knew in Buda. Through the trees they saw the glass-walled Stryelna, looking for all the world like some huge block of ice lit from within.

A uniformed servant rushed out to help them from the *troika* and brushed the snow from their clothes. Vladimir told the driver to wait for them in the nearby *traktir* and gave the fellow some coins for tea. They went inside, to be immediately assailed by the roar of conversation, the sound of music, a solid wall of heat, the smell of food. Attendants took their coats. The head waiter hurried across, anxious to please.

"Hello, Vanka," Vladimir said. "It looks crowded."

"A private room, perhaps?" the man suggested.

"I think we'd better," Vladimir said, and Vanka nodded, snapping his fingers to bring three waiters running to help him. They went through the Palm Court and into a large pine-walled "kabinet" with a roaring wood fire in an open grate. The waiters bustled about, setting the round table and arranging the chairs. The only other furniture in the room was a sofa and an upright piano covered with a shawl.

"Will you be dining tonight, Excellencies?" Vanka asked.

"No," Vladimir said. "Just some champagne, Vanka. With icicles in it."

He turned to smile at Valentina Beriosovna. She returned his smile politely, without warmth. A cool blonde, he thought; not warm, as some blondes are, but coolly beautiful instead. Eyes emerald green, lips mobile and full, hands and arms slender and expressive. The waiter brought in the ice bucket and lifted out the Veuve Clicquot.

"Champagne," she said, smiling. "What a lovely idea."

Vladimir nodded to the waiter, who poured the wine.

"*Na zdorovye!*" Vladimir said, looking into Valentina Beriosovna's eyes.

"*Na zdorovye!*" she replied automatically, without either warmth or interest. It was not an auspicious start, and things went downhill from there. Vladimir found he could make no headway with the actress at all. She was most certainly beautiful and she seemed intelligent, but nothing that he said seemed to engage her interest. She was friendly, but only in the slightly patronizing way that theater people are with the public, not quite at ease without the footlights between them. Vladimir had not expected to find himself reduced to the status of an autograph hunter, and he listened impatiently as she talked theatrical gossip with Blumenthal about people whom Vladimir did not even know by repute. Whenever he tried to change the subject, she would listen politely to whatever he had to say, remark "How interesting" or "Oh, is that really so?" and return to her theatrical in-talk with the producer.

Piqued by his failure, annoyed by her rudeness, surprised at his own feelings, Vladimir was at a loss. He knew he was usually successful with women. He had been told enough times that he was a good-looking devil to be aware of it. He was no vainer than he had to be. It was just something useful he had, like hands, a brain, good coordination. She knew who he was; Blumenthal would scarcely have failed to mention that. She was still apparently not interested, and that in itself was unusual. Vladimir had discovered that wealth was like power; it affected some women.

Maria Nikolaievna came in, followed by eight gypsies: four men with guitar, violin, accordion, tambourine, and four dark-eyed girls with sinuous bodies and tangled hair.

"No *charochkas* tonight, Maria Nikolaievna," Vladimir smiled, holding up a hand. "Just sing us a song."

"What would Your Excellency like to hear?" the woman said. She was about forty, plump and heavily built. Her large gray eyes were infinitely sad, and her face was lined as if with sorrow.

"How about 'Don't Leave'?" Vladimir said.

Maria Nikolaievna nodded to the musicians and began to sing. As she did, the age disappeared from her face, the sadness from her eyes.

> Don't leave, stay awhile with me
> Tomorrow will come soon enough, you'll see . . .

After a while, Valentina announced that she must leave for the engagement she had told them about: a party at the Haritonenko house. She was adamant about going alone, insisting that they stay and not worry about her. Vladimir was tempted to tell her that he, too, had been invited to the Haritonenko party—as who was not? Something stopped him; he did not want to look as if he was trying too hard. Valentina bade him a cool farewell as she got into the waiting *troika*. She embraced Blumenthal and kissed him on the cheek, and then she was gone in a flurry of snow. The two men hurried back to their warm kabinet, Vladimir shaking his head, Blumenthal following with a small smile concealed.

"Well, Leo," Vladimir said ruefully, "I made a mess of that. She's like an iceberg."

"I did warn you, my dear fellow," Blumenthal said. "She is very, very difficult. But she liked you. I could tell that right away."

"It's hard to believe, Leo."

"You treated her like a lady, my dear fellow. She is a woman who is impressed by such things. So many men think all actresses are tarts. Take my word for it, Vladimir, you made a big impression upon the Ice Princess."

"Is that what they call her?"

"You didn't know?" said Blumenthal, who had just made it up.

"I can see why." Vladimir grinned. He was feeling better; perhaps the evening hadn't been a total waste after all. "I'll send her some flowers tomorrow."

"That's the idea, man." Blumenthal chuckled. "Now, let's have something to eat, for God's sake!"

"All right," Vladimir said. "I think I can manage something, too."

"Good," Blumenthal said. "Good. One or two things I'd like to talk to you about, anyway."

Thinking back on it now, Vladimir could only smile. No one is more readily fooled than he who wants to be fooled, he thought, and Blumenthal did a terrific job. So did she. And nobody told me. No one ever does, until afterward. They all knew I was making a fool of myself. Olga could have told me, Kolya Stanislavsky, any of them. Later, they said they would gladly have done so, but they had been reluctant to interfere. It was a delicate matter, after all; one didn't wish to appear meddlesome. He couldn't really complain, Vladimir thought, looking at his wife's petulant face. He'd been ready to be fooled, and all they had done was to oblige him. Valentina thought she was still fooling him. He smiled slowly; not anymore, he thought.

"What are you smiling at?" Valentina said, half-turning.

"I was just thinking about the night I met you," Vladimir said. "And how you made me suffer."

"Oh, darling, really!" she exclaimed.

"I remember how I couldn't wait to see you again," he said. "All those flowers I sent you."

"You were a darling," she said, absently. "Get my stockings, Serafima," she said to the maid, gesturing toward the flimsy things draped on a nearby chair.

Wasn't I, though? Vladimir thought, forgivingly contemptuous of his own folly. Bouquet after ornate bouquet delivered daily to her dressing room. Luncheons at the Hermitage, suckling pig and horseradish at Testov's, Siberian specialties at Lobachev's, balalaika music at the Sadko. How he had talked and talked, pouring out his ideas to her, his hopes, his ambitions. How she had listened, encouraged, smiled. Was she as bored with me then as I am bored with her now? he wondered. She had taken her time, becoming friendlier slowly, like a glacier melting. She kept him at arm's length; she would not go to bed with him. She smiled as he praised her acting, her beauty, her understanding.

"You are a darling," she would say, patting his cheek with a perfumed hand. He thought that was charming, then. He could not see enough of her; he wrote her passionate letters which he destroyed, cursing his own cowardice. He laid siege to her heart and in doing so surrendered his own, throwing himself madly into love like a suicide off a cliff.

Of course, he married her, sweeping her off her feet with an ease that should have surprised him.

His father's bitter opposition to the match and the guarded cool-ness of his family toward Valentina did not deter him. If anything, they made him more determined. He was twenty-six years old, for God's sake; he knew what he wanted. It took him less than two years to discover how wrong he had been. It was hard to admit it to himself and even harder to go on trying to make it work, knowing that it was so, but he did both. He tried to understand Valentina rather than judge her. He tried to change himself until he realized that to do so was the worse surrender. He told himself that he had been the one in a fever to marry, and that if he was unhappy about it, then perhaps she was too. He tried, doomed to fail because Val-entina did not care and had never cared for him except as a passport to a world of moneyed luxury where she could indulge her passion to buy endless quantities of useless trash.

Valentina was not unintelligent, but she was intellectually lazy. Her responses were slow, her memory for anything except the words in a script bad. She had no wit worth the name. Although she could memorize a part so perfectly that she would never forget a line of it for as long as she lived, the names of Vladimir's friends or business acquaintances seeped out of her head moments after he reminded her of them. Of music, art, history, literature she knew little and cared less, while professing herself enthralled by all of them. Sepa-rately, none of these traits would have made her tiresome; collected in one envious, petty, spiteful personality they made her impossible. He took her to galleries and museums in Petersburg, Paris, London, Rome. Back with her friends she could talk only of the boutiques in the Faubourg St. Honoré, the chic little shops in Bond Street, the place one bought those pretty shoes on the via Condotti. She denied that she ever felt envy, malice or spite, while exhibiting all three. If a conversation was over her head, her face became vacuous and her lack of interest so obvious that it made Vladimir want to strike her. She looked for life's meaning in the occult, attending séances run by charlatans and patronized by fools, sulking like a child when Vladi-mir stormed at her gullibility. She had her fortune told and believed what the *tzigane* said, clinging to the golden future they always promised her. She loved to gamble, but since she had no memory for which cards had been played, she simply threw away the money. That was part of the pose: to be seen throwing it away, because it was chic, not because it excited her.

Still Vladimir persisted, wishing he could give up and not know-ing how to. He did not want to give Petya yet another chance to draw parallels between Vladimir's wasteful life and the misfortunes which had befallen him. Petya was a dominating, impulsive man who brooked no folly in any man, let alone his sons. Teaching his sons that his word was law, he had grown to believe it himself and was baffled by his inability to enforce it once they grew up.

Petya had been married twice, both times extremely happily. His first wife, mother of Pierre and Nico, had died in the eighth year of their marriage. In the same year, Petya buried his father, old Arsenii Smirnoff. When Petya took over the running of the distillery, it was a small enterprise employing nine people in a building at the southern end of the Tchugguny Bridge. Ten years later, the Smirnoff distilleries were among the largest enterprises in Russia. Vladimir couldn't help but wonder what the old man would have said had he been here now, if he had just learned what Vladimir knew about Valentina.

"Always said you'd end up with your foot in your mouth!" he would have roared. "Now let's see you hop!"

Petya had married his second wife, Genya, when he was forty-four and she was eighteen. Despite the difference in their ages, it was a happy if occasionally stormy match. Genya respected Petya's judgment, his energy, his experience. He was delighted and refreshed by her gaiety, her youth. She was the rock to which he was anchored in all the years left to him, and she gave him three fine children: Vladimir, Arsenii, and Alexandra. Petya's two sons by his first marriage were made directors of the company, renamed "Societé Pierre Smirnoff et Fils" in accordance with the preferred language of the Imperial Court, to which Petya was purveyor of vodkas and liqueurs.

Nikolai got into woman trouble and turned to drink. Petya disowned him. Arsenii—Senka—was bookish and intellectual. Petya had no time for him. Alexandra—Shushi—was married off to Dmitri Abrikosov, and Petya was relieved of her. His second son, Piotr—Pierre—was a born businessman, full of energy and enthusiasm, taking on his share of running the family business with a zest and flair that reminded many of his father in earlier years. Petya embraced him.

Which left Vladimir. It took Vladimir a long time to find himself, and while he was doing it, he had no use for the money he received except to spend it. The more Petya counseled frugality, the more his son spent. The more his father advised him to settle down, the more the son ran wild. After Vladimir told him of his decision to marry Valentina, Petya would have no more to do with him.

"Come back when you'd got some sense in your head," he said, angrily. "Although I doubt I'll live long enough to see it happen."

Valentina was not interested in the family business except insofar as it was the source of her husband's money. She knew that the manufacture of vodka paid for the big houses and the trips to the Riviera and the furs and the cars and the rest of it, but that was as far as it went. Well, perhaps all that was my fault, too, Vladimir thought. I let the years pass and did nothing. I knew she preferred her own world and the people in it, and yet I didn't try very hard to get to know it or to like it. Then he shook his head. Yes I did, he corrected himself. The truth of it was that he had found Valentina's theatrical friends as shallow as puddles. They "darlinged" each other to death, vain as peacocks, jealous as Othello, and they all had the morals of alley cats. Another rock for their ship to perish on, he thought. It had been hard to cling to the belief that Valentina remained faithful to him when he knew, at heart, that all the odds were against its being so. Their mutual bargain—conspiracy?—was that they never talked about it. She never told him and he never asked.

As for Telegin, the lovely house he had built outside Moscow, she had never given it a chance, perhaps never had any intention of doing so. She complained that the house was too small, the windows too big, the bedrooms damp, the view dispiriting. She complained about the mud on her shoes and her clothes, nodded without interest as he showed her the stables and the beautiful animals in them, and shrugged disdainfully when he told her how much he was looking forward to their spending weekends together at Telegin.

"I really wish you'd talked it over with me, darling," she said, "before plunging in so deeply. How much has all this cost, in Heaven's name?"

She always wanted to know how much things cost. He was reminded of the famous Oscar Wilde epigram about the cynic, who knew the price of everything and the value of nothing.

"I want to make Telegin one of the best stud farms in Russia," he said. He wanted to tell her about bloodstock, about his plans to breed Arabs, perhaps crossing them with Trakehners, but her first words preempted his intention.

"I'm sorry, darling," she said. "But horses just aren't me, if you see what I mean."

"Perhaps when we come out here regularly, you can learn to ride," he said.

"What on earth for, darling? I can't imagine what possible use riding would be to me. I don't want a great fat backside. I don't even like the countryside all that much. And as for horses—well, you know what Viktor always says: 'Nasty at both ends and uncomfortable in the middle.'"

Viktor was Valentina's leading man these days. Vladimir did not like Viktor. He was sure that the feeling was quite mutual.

"It will be marvelous out here in the summer," he said. "Away from the city."

"Yes, darling," she said absently, toying with her food. She was obviously deep in thought, and Vladimir's face was touched by a small, sad smile of foreknowledge. He knew what she was going to ask next.

"I imagine you'll have to spend a lot of your time out here, darling," Valentina said, offhandedly. "It's not something one can delegate, is it?"

"Oh, I've got a very good man in charge here," he said. "His name is Pavel Ivanovich Ulyanov. He was once assistant trainer at the Imperial Stables under General von Grunwald."

"Really?" she said, looking past him and out the window. "Can he run everything? I mean, without your needing to be here?"

"Not really," Vladimir said. "You're right about that. I'll be out here most weekends." He saw the calculating light in back of her eyes and felt saddened having known it would be there.

"Well, you'll just have to manage without me," Valentina said, sniffing. "I simply don't see myself slopping around a farmyard in rubber boots feeding your precious horses, my darling, and that's that."

"You could try it a few times," he said. "Come out on Sundays in the summer."

"I might," she said, but she never did. I should have known better than to ever expect it, he thought. He wondered whether her reaction to Telegin was where it had all begun to end, where the first line had been drawn across the ledger of their life together. Perhaps. But then, he reflected, Petya hadn't been all that impressed at first, either.

"All that damned money poured into breeding racehorses!" he raged. "And for what, eh? Another damned toy for you to play with! No sign of it producing anything, I suppose? A prize, perhaps, a ribbon or a purse?"

"It takes time, Papa," Vladimir said.

"Hah! You'll tire of it before then!" Petya snapped.

Pierre interceded for Vladimir in this argument, as he nearly always did. He felt that his half-brother's commitment to Telegin was a sign of a growing maturity he wanted to encourage, and he used his court connections to send Vladimir clients. The trickle turned to a flood when Vladimir's horse Pilyugin, "Little Bullet," brought the Telegin stud fame by winning the Tsarevich's Handicap at Yelagin Island. Within months Vladimir had a waiting list of officers who wished to buy mounts from him, a list which lengthened to formidable proportions when it was learned that the Tsar had personally requested permission to have one of his own brood mares covered by Pilyugin. At least the old man lived to see that, Vladimir thought.

He knew—he had always known—that his cavalier attitude toward the family wealth and its source angered his father. Perhaps it was because he knew that he reacted the way he did. Somehow he wanted a success which owed nothing to the fact that his name was Smirnoff. Now that he had it, he realized—perhaps he had always known—that it was not and never had been of paramount importance. He had missed the thing that was, and all at once it was too late. Petya's sudden sickness and the even more unexpected slide toward death were shocking, unbelievable. Vladimir had always thought that his father was made of iron. Now he wept to see the frail creature in the huge four-poster bed at Sokolnika, plucking at the sheets with hands that looked like the feet of a chicken.

We have given each other wounds that will never have a chance now to heal, he thought, as he sat silently by the old man's bedside. And for what? He was thirty. To a stranger, he would seem to have everything anyone could want: a beautiful home, a famous actress for his wife, wealth, success. He took spring vacations in the Crimea, wintered on the Riviera, lost small fortunes on the green baize tables of half a dozen spas, dined at the finest restaurants in the world. People often remarked upon how lucky he was, and he nodded and smiled and agreed. There was absolutely no point in confusing them with the truth.

The truth of it was that, apart from Telegin, his life was empty and his wealth meaningless. Not exciting, not even interesting: pointless. He no longer cared for Valentina, for whom he had turned his back on his family. Now he found himself alone. He wished that wisdom had come sooner.

He looked at the thin old man in the snowy white bed. The doctors said there was nothing they could do. The thing that was eating Petya Smirnoff alive could no more be stopped than could the advent of the morrow. Vladimir had no idea how long he had sat beside his father's bed. He had sent the others away, promising to call them if the old man awoke. Their vigil had been longer than his. Genya had slept only a few hours in the last ten days. Exhausted, with black circles beneath her eyes, she looked many years older than she was. Vladimir's heart opened to her, for he saw in her dark eyes the same fear of being alone that he had discovered in himself. She was not yet sixty. How many more years would she have, to live alone with her memories?

The old man slept and slept. Vladimir sat beside the bed, not knowing why he stayed. He wondered if his father realized he was there, if he realized anyone was there. Or if he cared; what did it matter who was with you when you died? That was something you went through on your own. It was hard to believe that the figure in the bed was really Petya. The face looked like a skull. After a long, long time, Petya's eyes flickered and opened. He seemed to be surprised to find himself where he was, as if he had expected to awaken somewhere else.

"Hello, Papa," Vladimir said, starting to get up.

"No," Petya whispered. "Don't go."

"I'll just call the others," Vladimir said, gently. "They're all here, Papa. Everyone is here."

"Wait," Petya said. He had to work very hard on each word. "Let them . . . wait. Want to . . . tell you . . . something." His eyes closed, as though the effort had exhausted him. His breathing was feathery, fragile.

"Papa?" Vladimir said, thinking the old man had fallen asleep again.

"Just . . . sorry," Petya said. His fingers moved on the coverlet, hardly more than a twitch. Vladimir took the skeletal hand in his own. "Sorry, boy," Petya whispered.

"Sorry? There's no need to be sorry, Papa," Vladimir said.

"Gypsy," Petya said. "The gypsy."

It shocked Vladimir. He hadn't understood. He had thought his father was sorry about dying, but he was apologizing for what had happened all those years ago. He had not thought of the gypsy girl for a long time. Katja, he thought; once I loved her, too. Was he doomed to go through his life falling out of love?

"Cruel," Petya was saying. "Shouldn't have . . . sent you . . . away . . . like that."

"It doesn't matter, Papa," Vladimir said. He could do nothing about his tears. They splashed on his father's hands, but if he felt them, the old man made no sign.

"Cruel, boy," he said. "I hurt you."

"I survived, Papa," Vladimir said, trying for a smile that somehow slid off before he could make it fit his features. "It doesn't matter anymore."

"Mistakes," the old man sighed. "So many mistakes."

There was infinite regret in his voice, as if he had just counted up how many mistakes there had been.

"It was a long time ago, Papa," Vladimir said. "A long time ago."

"Everything was, son," the old man sighed softly. "Everything was."

He died that night and was buried, garlanded with honors. Nobles, bishops, dignitaries, ambassadors, and princes attended his funeral. A thousand people followed the cortège to the family plot below the big house. There was a wreath of lilies from the Tsar and Tsaritsa. Valentina refused to attend the ceremony.

"Oh, darling, what's the point?" she said. "Your family hates me. The old man never liked me nor I him, and that's the truth. There's no point in pretending otherwise, is there?"

No point in pretending, he thought. What ironies we all visit upon each other! She had been pretending for years, pretending an affection she did not feel for a man she did not care about, pretending in their bed and in public a closeness which simply did not exist, pretending their life together was normal when in fact it was empty. Empty, empty, empty! And now this final sham, pretending that she and Oleg were merely friends when for more than twelve months they had been lovers. The word made the green thing in his belly uncoil slowly, like a stirring snake. Why did it have to be Oleg, with whom Vladimir had shared many a bottle, many a hangover, many a good time and one or two bad, Oleg, whose wife Kira was one of the sweetest women Vladimir had ever met? Perhaps, he thought, it was for all those reasons that it had to be Oleg. Bitch, he thought again, feeding the fire of his anger.

"I'm nearly ready," Valentina said.

"I want to talk to you," he said. "Leave us, Serafima."

"Wait!" Valentina snapped, and the maid froze, looking uncertainly from her mistress to Vladimir. "You will leave when I say so."

"Go, Serafima," Vladimir said, and something in his voice made Valentina's face change. She nodded to the girl, who scuttled from the room.

"You have no right—" Valentina began, angrily.

"Be quiet," Vladimir said. "I want to ask you something."

"Ask me on the way to the Cathedral," she said, tossing her head. "We're late enough as it is. The traffic—"

"Sit down!"

Valentina looked at him for a moment; then her lips flattened and her eyes flooded with contempt.

"What have we here?" she sneered. "Are you suddenly becoming the tyrannical husband? God, what a joke!"

"Don't anger me, Valentina," Vladimir said, and again his voice made her face change. "Don't under any circumstance anger me at this moment."

"What—what on earth is the matter with you?"

"I have something to ask you. About Oleg."

This time Valentina's face really changed. It was as if a door had slammed somewhere. Her mouth went ugly.

"I'll answer no questions about Oleg or anything else," she said, getting to her feet and snatching up her wrap. "And if you think you can make me, then you, my darling, are in for one of the most catastrophic disappointments of your pampered life. Now get out of my way!"

She was good, he thought. Many men would have been convinced by it. Not so long ago, it would have convinced him. But not anymore.

"No," he said. He stood in her way, barring the door. He did not see her hand move, but the slap rocked his head, and for a moment he saw stars. Something clicked in his head, all the anger bursting through whatever floodgate had opened, all the hurts, all the disappointments, everything. He found himself towering over her, fist drawn back, ready to kill. His mind registered her terror, his own lust to hurt her. In that same instant, all the rage went out of him like exhaled smoke. His hand fell to his side. He felt exhausted.

"Are you insane?" she whispered, edging away from him. "Have you gone raving mad?"

My God, he thought, I could have killed her! As easily as that, and not regretted a thing. He shook his head.

"Stop," he said, wearily. "Finally, now, Valentina, stop this senseless charade."

She looked at him suspiciously, like an animal which senses a trap.

"You and Oleg," he said. "I know."

"Know?" she hissed. There were two bright red spots on her cheeks. Anger? Fear? He could not tell. "What do you know?"

"You are lovers," he said, dully.

"Oleg and I?" she shrilled, forcing a laugh that did not work. "What a stupid thing to say." But the color was gone from her face, and the defiance and hauteur were as spurious as the laugh.

"You deny it?"

"Of course I deny it, you stupid, stupid man!" she snapped. "Of course I deny it."

Vladimir went across the room and took from its hook above the bed the silver-framed icon of the Virgin. He brought it over and held it out to his wife.

"Place your hand on the icon and swear that it isn't true," he said. Valentina looked at him for a moment, a long moment in which her eyes went opaque, and there was no expression whatsoever on her face. Slowly she extended her hand and laid it on the icon.

"I swear," she said, her voice thick and venomous. "Does that satisfy you?"

Vladimir looked at her. She glared back defiantly. The silence grew until she could bear it no longer. She whirled around and picked up the photograph of her parents that stood on her dressing table.

"See?" she hissed. "I swear on the lives of my parents. I swear on the holy icon. Now will you believe me?"

It was the end and he knew it. He took the bundle of letters from his pocket and threw them on the dressing table. The family lawyer already had affidavited copies. Valentina looked at the letters as if they were a scorpion in her bed. Then she looked at Vladimir. Her eyes were hollow caves, her mouth a wound. He went out of the room and out of the house.

4

PIERRE SMIRNOFF was not just the director of the family concern which bore his name. He was also the friend and confidant of nearly every member of the sprawling dynasty begun by Arsenii Smirnoff, his grandfather. A solidly built, handsome man of sixty-two, Pierre had an authoritative, forceful manner, yet paradoxically he was far easier to approach than rough-tongued old Petya, his father. Petya had been the one who built the foundations of the family business, but Pierre was its anchor, the one to whom they all brought their worries, their fears, their debts, their confessions. Despite the innumerable demands made upon his time and energy by the running of the business, and by his own family which, as he sometimes smilingly remarked, seemed to grow without any help from him at all, he was always available to them: father, financier, Dutch uncle, marriage counselor, confessor.

The business was run from a thickly carpeted and richly ornamented room in the Administration Building of the Moscow distillery. It was known to everyone as "The Office," just as everyone in the family referred to the business as "The House." In it were three beautiful Directoire desks: one, the largest, for Petya, the other two for Pierre and his brother Nico. The walls were paneled in oak and hung with family portraits, the place of honor occupied by an oil of an imperious-looking Arsenii Smirnoff, the founder of the House. Around the walls were various framed memorabilia: the deed for the original plot of land on which the first distillery had stood; the royal decrees signed by Tsar Alexander III making The House purveyor to the Imperial Court, flanked by similar decrees from King Oskar of Sweden and his successor, King Gustav. There was a long velvet case in a glass display unit which housed a double row of gold medals won by Smirnoff products at expositions around the world: Brussels, Bordeaux, Milan, Paris, Barcelona, Stockholm. There was a framed certificate confirming the Tsar's authorization of the change of company name from "Vinakuryennay Zavod Smirnov" to "Societé Pierre Smirnoff et Fils." The centerpiece of the display was the sash and medal of of the Order of St. Anna, awarded to Pierre by Tsar Nicholas II in 1895. It was a room as familiar to the family as any in Sokolnika. It smelled of cigar smoke and beeswax and leather.

"Well, brother," Pierre Smirnoff said. "What are we to do with Vladimir?"

Nico looked across at his brother and raised his eyebrows and shoulders simultaneously. There was more than a streak of Petya's stubbornness in their half-brother, and Nico was not sure that it was a bad thing. Sometimes Pierre steamrollered people without realizing that he was doing it, making them live up to his expectations. He did it with me, Nico thought, but with Vladimir it is less easy.

"He'll have to divorce that woman," Pierre said, with exasperation in his voice.

Valentina's conduct had been the subject of family gossip for more than a year. Everyone in Moscow knew Vladimir's wife was sleeping with Oleg Baranin—everyone, it seemed, except Vladimir. Nico's personal opinion was that Vladimir would be well rid of the woman, but he would have been the last man on earth to say so. Pierre did all that. He deferred to Pierre's judgment in such matters. In all matters, come to that, he thought; they had not differed substantially since "then." Nico always thought of the two years which had ended with his being committed to an institution for alcoholics as "then." Pierre had been the only one who cared. Petya had disowned him, shamed by his son's fall, and forbade Genya to go to him. It had been a bad time, but Pierre had pulled him through, sent him away to the Crimea to convalesce, brought him home, given him a place in the business, trusted him not to slide back into the gutter. He had never looked back since then, and his devotion and loyalty to his brother were complete.

Nico knew, as no one else in the family knew but Genya, of old Petya's deathbed request to Pierre to somehow involve Vladimir— he was thirty, but Petya still called him "the boy"—in the affairs of The House. It was not an easy task. Vladimir had been surrounded since birth by wealth and ease. There were always *nyanyas* and servants, valets, grooms, chauffeurs, maids. Especially maids. Vladimir had a way with them that had caused many a scandalized late-night session at Sokolnika. There were always horses, dogs, guns. There had always been the *dacha* in Yalta, the hunting lodge in

Pyatigorsk, the mansion in Petersburg. There had always been carriages, motor cars, yachts; and most of all, there had always been money. All three of Petya's children by his second marriage had grown up in a world where they were not required to lift a finger if they did not want to. It was really not surprising that none of them showed any real interest in the source of all the luxury surrounding them; it would have been more surprising if they had.

It had not been like that for Pierre and Nico. They knew just how hard the early days had been, when Petya had fought for every kopeck.

"Do you remember the berry season, Nico?" Pierre asked, musing on the past. "Do you remember the confusion, the pandemonium?"

"I remember." Nico grinned. "It always started the same way, with the policeman coming to the house. What was his name?"

"Anatoly Zobrodin," Pierre said. Zobrodin was the chief of gendarmes in the Pyatnitzkaya district, and Pierre could remember Petya's rumbling roars of laughter as he poured drink after drink into the man.

"Your berry pickers are going to bring the traffic in the Pyatnitzkaya to a complete halt again, I suppose, Piotr Arsenievich?" Zobrodin would begin heavily.

"They're not my berry pickers!" old Petya would shout. "They don't belong to me!"

"They'll still stop the traffic, and well you know it," the policeman would grumble. "Well you know it."

"You're right," Petya would say, switching tack abruptly. "No doubt of it at all. Have another?"

Disarmed as usual, Zobrodin would have another. "Just the same, Piotr Arsenievich," he would protest, "it makes things very difficult for me. Very difficult indeed."

"I wouldn't be surprised," Petya would rumble. "Here, what do you think of that ashberry liqueur?"

"Splendid, splendid," Zobrodin would reply. "As good as, if not better than, last year's."

"We've been blessed with good summers," Petya would say. "Same again this year. Harvest should be excellent."

"More wagons," Zobrodin would say morosely. "It causes me endless difficulties, Piotr Arsenievich, and every year it gets worse. Every year I have to take men off other duties to supervise this affair. It all costs a great deal of money, you know. A great deal of money."

"I know, I know," Petya would sympathize. "Here, try some of this rowanberry. It's really rather good."

"Thank you, thank you. I wish I could drink it all the time, but on my salary, and with prices going up all the time, the way they are, it's harder and harder to make ends meet. The wife was saying to me only yesterday—"

"Yes, yes," Petya would interrupt. . . . "Come on, man, drink up! *Do dna!* Bottoms up!"

"*Do dna!*" Zobrodin would say, emptying the glass in one gulp. "You appreciate that I do not like to burden you with such matters, knowing how busy you must be?"

"Of course, of course."

"But I would be derelict in my duty if I did not draw these, ah, difficulties to your attention. You appreciate that?"

"Naturally, naturally."

"You can see that the assembly of so many berry carts in a crowded thoroughfare like Pyatnitzkaya creates problems?"

"Certainly, my dear fellow," Petya would say. "Of course."

It was a ritual which both men observed every season, Zobrodin pretending that he had not come to have his palm greased and Petya pretending that the money he gave the man was a donation for the welfare of the gendarmes of the Pyatnitzkaya district. There were similar rituals everywhere he went, for he wanted things done his way and he brooked no delays.

"Wheels need oil," he would say afterward by way of self-justification.

"It's bribery, Petya," Genya would say, wagging a slim finger at him.

"Ha!" Petya would shout, grabbing her and planting a juicy kiss on her nose. "You think I don't know it?"

How many times had the old man gone through the same formal ritual with Zobrodin, Pierre wondered, twenty times, thirty, more? Yet he had never seemed to lose his roaring enthusiasm, his lust to live. Sometimes, as a young man, Pierre had believed that his father must know every minor official and every farmer in Russia. Those were the days, he thought.

Vladimir hadn't been much more than a sprout then. Genya would bring him to The Office with his brother Senka, sailor-suited, heads shaven for school as a protection against lice, and they would plead to be allowed to come to the factory when the berry harvest was brought in. Petya would take them on his knees and kiss them and promise that they could both come one day, "maybe next year."

Then they would ask if they could bring friends. Everyone wanted to come. The event drew crowds of fashionable Muscovites every year. When all the buying was done, Petya would throw a lavish party in the great cobbled yard where the berries were brought in and open the factory to visitors, with conducted tours and souvenir bottles of vodka for every visitor. In 1894, when the prime minister, Count Witte, announced the government's intention to nationalize the manufacture of vodka, Petya swore that there would never be another Smirnoff party as long as he was alive. There never was.

The berry farmers came in from all the outer suburbs and surrounding countryside, sometimes a hundred versts and more, wagon after cart after dray, so many of them that not even the enormous cobbled courtyards of the Smirnoff distillery could accommodate them. They spilled out into all the side streets for a distance of a verst, then two and then three. Each load was inspected, weighed, sampled, haggled over and paid for by Petya's fruit inspectors, supervised by the old man himself. They all called him *starik*, "old man," but it was a name used with respect, affection. On the streets near the distillery the harassed gendarmes redirected traffic, apologizing to the ladies who had come down to see the show for the juicy cursing of the waiting peasants. Most of them smiled indulgently; they had heard the same or worse on their own estates. Some of the younger women blushed and covered their ears or hid behind their parasols as their coachmen guided their horses past, trading insults with the farmers or winking at their rosy-cheeked daughters. The air was heavy and sweet with the fresh, tangy aroma of raspberries or wild strawberries. At the gate leading into the courtyard Petya always placed a huge samovar, and the waiting farmers would draw tea from it so hot that the moment they drank it, sweat stood out on their foreheads.

Then from one of the wagons someone would produce an accordion, a balalaika, two, four. They would sing some of the old songs, softly, harmonizing with each other as if trained by a choirmaster: "Two Guitars," or "Once Again," "Black Eyes" or "I Cannot Forget." They sang anything, everything, folk songs, hymns, waiting patiently as oxen for their turn on the huge scale in front of the office. From dawn until dusk, day after day, Petya would stand out in the cobblestoned courtyard next to the scales, bargaining with every new arrival as though it was the first and only transaction he had conducted all year.

"Ten kopecks?" he would roar. "Ten kopecks? Do you think that

I'm made of money, Yvgeny Petrovich? *Grabetyel!* Robber! Do you know it takes seven pounds of your berries to make one bottle of my fine liqueur?"

"Aye, I knows it, all right, your Honor," the farmer would say, squinting down from his cart at Petya. "And I also knows you can't make it without 'em!"

There would be good-natured shouts of encouragement and laughter from those nearby. "You tell him, Yvgeny Petrovich!" "Make the old tyrant pay!"

"Tyrant?" Petya would shout, indignantly. "Tyrant? Charitable institution, more likely. I'll tell you what I'll do, out of the kindness of my heart. I'll give you five kopecks, but not a kopeck more."

"Nine!"

"Six!"

"Eight!"

"Seven, and that will bankrupt me!"

"Seven and a half, and I'll be behind you in the bankrupt's court!" the farmer would shout. "Seven and a half and that's final!"

"Get them unloaded, you bandit," Petya would tell him, pretending annoyance at having been bested. The farmer would gig his horses or oxen forward, out of the way, and another would move onto the scale as Petya plunged his hand into one of the baskets of fruit it was carrying, smelling the berries, squashing them between his fingers to see how juicy they were, gently touching his tongue with the juice, his eyes closed, while the farmer watched the ritual in awed silence.

"Well, Georgi Mikhailovich, I suppose you want ten kopecks a basket, too?" he'd say, purple-stained hands on hips, head back, looking as if he had grown out of the ground right on that spot. "Well, you'd better think again!"

So it went on, day after day. The farmers brought in raspberries, strawberries, bilberries, plums, damsons, black currants, mulberries, rowanberries, ashberries, tens of thousands of puds of them to be bargained for as soon as they were picked—to guarantee freshness—and as quickly as possible, to forestall competition. Then the berries were sampled and sorted, washed in distilled water by hundreds and hundreds of women working at long trestle tables. They were prepared for the fermenting vats by further teams of women. In those days, every single process had been done by hand. It was different now, and all in all, Pierre did not regret the passing of the old ways. Modern equipment and mass-production techniques had rendered obsolete the old wooden presses and stone mills. The mules that had once provided power, like the women who had stood seventeen hours a day washing the fruit, were all gone, and in their place were white-coated technical staff and gleaming stainless steel machinery. There was no reason to expect Vladimir to understand, as Pierre and Nico understood, how it had been in the old days and why Petya was as he was because of them. Vladimir had never really seen what it had been like, and no teacher of history yet born has ever truly communicated to a child who has never wanted what famine is like, or made a youngster from a good home appreciate the grinding shame of poverty.

So he watched Vladimir with compassionate trepidation as his half-brother blundered through a turbulent adolescence. Whenever it was possible, Pierre headed off the more predictable collisions, interceding for Vladimir when Petya's impatience turned to a sometimes cruel anger.

"If only you could learn to handle Papa with a little more tact," he told Vladimir, "you'd be much better off."

"I try, Pierre," Vladimir said. "But he doesn't. Why can't he bend a little, too?"

"It's harder for him," Pierre said.

"It isn't easy for me. He's always picking on me."

"That's because he expects so much of you."

"He hasn't any right to!" Vladimir would explode. "It's not his life, it's mine!"

He said it only once to Petya. The old man glowered at him for a moment and then shook his head, angrily impatient.

"You ready to go out in the world and make your own way, boy?" he snapped. "Without any help from me?"

"No, Papa," Vladimir said, sullenly. How could he go out and make his own way? He had no trade, no skill. What could he do?

"Then it's not your life yet," Petya growled. "When you can pay your own bills, you can make your own decisions."

Vladimir glared at his father with eyes full of hate. Sons do not ever understand a father's need for dependency, Pierre thought, any more than fathers understand their sons' need for freedom.

Certainly there was never any chance that Petya would see Vladimir's entanglement with the gypsy girl for what it really was, a desperate expression of the need to love someone who returned that love. Petya saw it as defiance, a foolish attempt to establish an independence for which Vladimir was patently unprepared. He

66

reacted—overreacted, as usual—by sending his son to work for a year in Vladivostok, capital of the Maritime Province, headquarters of the Fourth Siberian Army Corps and precious little else. It was the surest way possible to ensure that Vladimir would grow to hate the family concerns, and it worked.

As if that punishment were not enough, Vladimir returned to Moscow to find that Petya had made arrangements for him to be married to a niece of the great industrialist Sava Morosov. Sonia was a sweet child, but the marriage never had a chance. As soon as the ceremonies were over, Vladimir told his father he had no intention of either sharing a bed with or consummating his marriage to Sonia. He also told Sonia's father, with the result that the Morosovs never spoke to Petya again as long as he lived. Papa and Vladimir had more in common than blood, Pierre thought; they were both immovably stubborn. Papa would never admit that he had made a mistake. Vladimir would never let him forget he had.

Then there were the years of wine, women, fast cars and a dozen scrapes that it had taken a considerable amount of Pierre's time and Smirnoff money to smooth over. Pierre kept telling himself that Vladimir would sow his wild oats and then come home, that one day he would see the difference between good living and a good life. He was wrong; Vladimir married Valentina Beriosovna. He did so in the teeth of howling opposition from Petya, saddened resignation from Genya, and the appalled dismay of the rest of the family. If anything, it made Vladimir more determined.

Pierre heaved a huge sigh and brought himself back to the present.

"It's not like you to daydream, Pierre," Nico said, smiling.

"I was just thinking about Vladimir," Pierre confessed. "I've got an idea."

As the oldest son, he was now the owner of Sokolnika, the director of the affairs of The House. Genya was well provided for. Pierre had bought her a beautifully furnished house on the Nikitski Boulevard, where she had taken her personal servants and staff. Every Friday, Pierre went to see her and discuss business. He had the highest respect for his stepmother's business acumen. Genya had learned a great deal from Petya.

Other than that, there was very little noticeable change at The Office. Things continued as before, except that Petya no longer arrived in his carriage at ten each day, to be saluted and helped from it at the Pyatnitzkaya entrance by Tomchek, the uniformed commissionaire who had once been coachman to old Arsenii Smirnoff himself.

"Are you going to tell me what it is?" Nico asked.

"I thought we might send him to see Darbellay."

Darbellay was a Smirnoff importer in Paris. He was not earning his keep. His business with The House had fallen off thirty percent in the last twelve months, and it was still falling. Pierre suspected that some inadvertent slight, some failure of which Darbellay had not complained, was causing the disaffection.

"You think Vladimir might bring him around?"

"It's worth a try," Pierre said. "Don't you think so?"

He always tried his ideas out on Nico. In all their years together, Nico had never once told him outright that he was mistaken, or that what he was doing was wrong. Yet Nico could always communicate his disagreement, always signal his feeling that Pierre would do well to reconsider. Pierre never said it, but he valued Nico's opinion more than any man's. Nico knew he did, and so it did not need to be said.

"Yes," Nico said. "I think you may be right."

So Pierre asked Vladimir if he would consider doing a favor for him.

"I can't spare anyone just now," he lied. "And it's, well, it's not something I can give to just anyone to do."

"Well," Vladimir said.

"All you have to do is to to see Darbellay," Pierre said. "Wine him, dine him, take him out on the town, do whatever you think is best. He's a very valuable customer and we don't want to lose him. Use some of that fatal charm of yours on him."

"Not too much, though," Nico said in mock alarm. "We'd rather have a little life left in him."

"Well," Vladimir said again, "I suppose I could do it."

"Splendid," Pierre said. "That's splendid." He looked at Nico and winked, and Nico smiled. Sometimes Pierre was as much a big boy as any of them.

So Vladimir went to Paris—and fell in love with the city, as all romantics do. The importer, Maurice Darbellay, was a charming fellow, something of a bon vivant. He was a true Parisian, and he loved the city, too. He showed it to Vladimir with all the pride of a fond parent. They went to Maxim's, of course, and they looked in at the Moulin Rouge, where the whores sat in bright-ribboned rows waiting for a "touch" and the dancers cavorted to pounding music by Offenbach. They sat like lizards in the sun outside Fouquet's, watching the world go by on the Champs Elysées. They went to a restaurant that Darbellay knew on the Ile St. Louis, another in a corner of the Place Contrescarpe. They went to the races at Longchamps and won, and won again.

"You Smirnoffs are a strange lot," he told Vladimir. "Your brother has never even mentioned you to me, yet I find that your stable—what was its name?—"

"Telegin."

"Telegin, *voilà!* It's famous, renowned. And you know horses."

"They're not that hard to understand, Maurice," Vladimir smiled. They celebrated their success at Longchamps by hiring a chauffeur-driven limousine and driving down to Epernay, where they visited the famous *caves* of Madame Clicquot and ate a magnificent meal at a coaching inn called La Briqueterie.

They parted with genuine regret.

"Ah, *mon cher*," Darbellay said sadly. "If only you came to Paris regularly, what good times we could have together! I thought all you Smirnoffs were sticks-in-the-mud."

"Maybe I'll come again sometime," Vladimir said. He returned to Moscow with an empty purse, a huge order for Smirnoff vodkas and liqueurs, and an idea which he put to Pierre as soon as the chance presented itself.

"What are you going to do with your old desk, Pierre?" he said. Pierre had taken over the one which had been Petya's domain (and sometimes barricade).

"I haven't really thought about it," Pierre said. "Why?"

"Well I wouldn't mind doing a trip like that again. Once in a while, anyway. If you wanted me to, I mean. If it would help." He wanted to tell Pierre that he had enjoyed it but he couldn't.

"Trips like that entail a lot of responsibility, Vladimir," Pierre said, frowning furiously so that he would not smile. "You'd have to learn all about the business. We can't send just anyone to visit foreign distributors. You have to know what you're talking about when you're dealing with the royal courts of Sweden, Spain, Holland."

"I could learn," Vladimir said. "It's not all that difficult, is it?"

"It's not all that easy, either," Nico said.

"You really want to?" Pierre said. "This isn't just one of those whims of yours?"

"I really want to," Vladimir said.

69

"Hmm," Pierre said, pretending deep thought. "What do you think, Nico?"

"There's that business with Berglund," Nico offered.

"Berglund?" Vladimir said.

"He's our agent in Stockholm," Nico explained. "Ragnar Berglund. He's a nice enough man. Bit dour, perhaps."

"What's the problem?"

"Deep pockets and short arms," Pierre smiled. "His account is a little too much overdue, and we think a visit would be worthwhile. What do you think, Vladimir?"

Vladimir smiled. "About that desk," he said.

ANOTHER ONE," Guchkov said, sourly.

His assistant nodded. Hardened as he had been by working for more than five years with Viktor Guchkov, five years in which he had seen most of the varieties of butchery of which the human animal was capable, Piotr Bunin still found it hard to look at the body on the marble autopsy slab in the dripping, clammy police morgue on Tverskoi Boulevard. Instead he kept his eyes on Guchkov. To tell the truth, Bunin had been taken aback by the ferocity of the Chief's anger, for Guchkov was a cerebral man, not given to violence of any kind. Yet it was plain from the light in his green eyes, from his very physical demeanor, that had he been able to lay his hands on the perpetrator of the murder they were now investigating, Guchkov would have killed without conscience.

Guchkov rubbed his chin, hearing the stubble rasp. There hadn't been time to shave this morning. As soon as he got the call about the finding of the body, he had hurried to police headquarters. He was surprised to find himself angered, but it was anger that he felt: anger at such senseless butchery. They had a maniac running loose on the streets of Moscow. It was an affront to Guchkov; it angered him.

"Same sort of injuries as before," Bunin said. He had picked up the report of the police surgeon and leafed through it quickly. It was like reading about the procedure in an abattoir. He put it down again, feeling his throat tighten.

"Worse, if anything," Guchkov said.

He sighed and sat down dispiritedly on one of the rough wooden stools, anger slowly seeping away, his shoulders hunched against the chill of the cellar. Anger was no use, he thought. Anger solved nothing at all. He was a small, wiry man, thirty-six years of age, with brown hair parted on the right-hand side, already flecked with gray. There were lines of fatigue around his eyes, which had the saddened wisdom of one who has seen every kind of human folly and found himself able to forgive most of it. He wore neither beard nor moustache, and he looked older than he was.

He had joined the Ministry of Justice fourteen years ago, after studying law at the university. He had been an assistant investigator then, as Bunin was now. Seven years ago he had become Senior Judicial Investigator of the Ministry of Justice, a post independent of either police or gendarmerie. He valued his independence greatly and defended it jealously. He had been approached many times by senior officers of the *Okhrana* seeking to recruit him, but he would have nothing to do with the secret police. He made no effort to conceal his distaste for them and their methods, and it was noted in his *Okhrana* dossier accordingly. His superiors considered Guchkov to be a brilliant but difficult fellow, too prickly to be raised much further up the ladder. Asks too many awkward questions, they agreed. He was respected for his abilities, but he was not the type to seek or care for popularity. As a result, he tended to get the cases no one else wanted or could solve. More often than not, he solved them in his own unspectacular way and quite frequently saw others take the credit—and the promotion—for what Guchkov alone had done. That did not seem to perturb him either. Bunin, after five years, thought the Chief without question the finest investigator in the Ministry and quite probably the best in all Russia. He also admired the man as a man. Guchkov was a realist, but he worked intuitively. Apparently guileless, he was in fact shrewd, analytical and observant. Most importantly of all, by Bunin's reckoning, he was compassionate, which made his anger easier to understand. It stemmed from pity for the poor torn creature on the marble slab.

"You've checked the police files?" Guchkov said, knowing it would have been the first thing Piotr did. He was speaking more to break the silence than for any other reason. Somewhere a tap was dripping, like a slow, liquid metronome.

"Of course," Bunin said. They had gone through all the likely files the first time. Known offenders, child molesters, pimps, musclemen from the dives scattered all over the city, even the more epicene of the brothels. Nothing. Even the ones who had no police blotters but who were "known," the ones who picked up poor girls in the working-class districts and debauched them, all had been checked and interviewed, the transcriptions copied and cross-referenced and filed. And still nothing. They went through the files of men already convicted, knowing it was hopeless. Child killers didn't last long in Siberia. If their fellow convicts didn't kill them, the climate and the hard labor did.

"Nothing, eh?"

"You didn't really expect there would be, did you, Chief?"

"No," Guchkov sighed. "Not really."

He scratched his stubbly chin gloomily, wondering where to begin. They had been through every routine that they knew, explored every criminal file that might give them a lead, twice. There was no common denominator, no telling clue such as there always was in trashy detective stories, nothing except the brutal manner of the victims' deaths. He rubbed his eyes. God, I'm tired, he thought. No wonder, after three months of hunting a ghost, three months since Hova Kaminsky had reported the disappearance of his daughter. He was a lawyer, and he had a few friends in the right places, so action was immediately taken. Statements by her school friends, from her parents, all were neatly laced in the standard blue dossiers and filed in the Office for the Location of Missing Persons. Hova Kaminsky paid for the circulation of privately printed leaflets describing the girl. Copies were sent to every district governor in Russia.

Some days later, children playing among the bushes in the Sparrow Hills, which overlooked the city from the southwest, found what they thought was a bundle of old clothes. Then they saw what it really was and ran screaming for help. The mutilated corpse was identified as being that of Irinia Kaminsky, aged seven. The police surgeon said her body had been torn apart like a paper bag.

The case was passed to the Ministry of Justice, where it landed, perhaps inevitably, on Guchkov's desk. There were no clues, no witnesses, nothing—just a Missing Persons dossier with a photograph and a few statements from people who had known the girl. Guchkov interviewed them all again, anyway. He put together a picture of Irinia Kaminsky's life and concluded, as had everyone else who knew her, that she had been a bright, lively youngster without a worry in the world. The conclusion had to be that she had simply been a random victim. It happened. Kids the same age as Irinia were sold every night in the Khitrovka, the thieves' market. God alone knew what happened to them. Nobody ever asked.

They plodded on. Armed with photographs of the dead girl, Guchkov and Bunin began visiting *traktirs*. Bunin had never realized that there were so many places in Moscow where you could drink tea. The autopsy report said the child had drunk tea not long before she was killed. She had not done so at the home of any of her friends, nor at school. There was just a faint chance the killer might have bought it for her, as a bribe, an inducement to go with him. It was the slimmest of hopes, but Guchkov was willing to try it just the same.

"I think we can assume she wouldn't have gone with just any man," he told Bunin. "She wasn't the type."

"Then how did he get her to go with him?"

"I don't know!" Guchkov said, his voice sharp with exasperation. "I'm damned if I do. But someone must have seen it, someone somewhere. And we've got to find out who. That means we talk to coachmen, cabdrivers, doormen, street peddlers, whores, ice-cream vendors, anyone who might have seen it happen. And the place we'll find all of them is in the tea huts.' "

God, the dives they had been in! Some of the *traktirs*, where coachmen and taxi drivers went to gulp down pots of scalding tea, weren't so bad, like the Egorov or the Golubyatnya, the "Pigeon Loft." The names they thought up for such sleazy backwaters! Gradually, working their way inward toward the center of the city, they homed in on the Khitrovka. Huddled beside the Yauza, here no longer a sweet brook but a stinking sewer, the Khitrovka was a vast market area riddled with doss houses, brothels, drinking dens and God alone knew what other sorts of establishments. Along every narrow street, huddled together like derelicts, rows of shabby stalls dispensed sausages, herrings, soup, cucumbers, bread, fruit, greasy secondhand clothes, boots, anything that might turn a few kopecks' profit. There seemed to be a permanent mist, like a thin fog, over the place, lying just above head height, eddying into doorways and shadowed alleyways. From this murk, phantomlike, lurched scarecrow, toothless hags, beggars in tattered sacking, cripples, drunks, raddled whores. In the Khitrovka, the *traktirs* had no pretensions of gentility. They stank of filth, sweat, urine and *mazhorka*, the cheap tobacco that the peasants smoked.

Down foul, narrow streets that reeked of excrement, past low, huddled houses with façades of peeling plaster, up rotting wooden stairs slimy with damp, jostled by menacing shadows, the two investigators went from tavern to filthier tavern, crossing the smoke-filled dens off their list as they went. There were four principal buildings in the Khitrovka, each named for its putative owner. The Rumyantsev housed two dens, the Peresylny and the Sibir. The Katorga,

"Hard Labor," was in the Yaroshenko. Each had its own type of clientèle. The homeless, the destitute, and the whores too old to earn enough money gathered in the Peresylny. Pickpockets, horse thieves, footpads in the Sibir; escaped convicts, felons, murderers in the Katorga. Then there was the Kulakov, "The Stage," a group of houses which ran from Khitrov Square to the Svininsky Pereulok, into which not even Guchkov and Bunin dared go. Up to a point, the Khitrovka tolerated the police, but only up to a point.

As they pushed through the noisy crowds, child prostitutes of both sexes importuned them. Stinking harpies clutched at their sleeves. Women with faces furrowed with age and pain thrust shivering, scabby babies into their faces, whining for kopecks. They hurried on. Bunin saw that Guchkov's face was like iron.

"You thinking what I'm thinking?" he said.

"There's no use thinking about it," Guchkov growled. "Come on!"

Bunin shivered. The Khitrovka was an appalling place. He wondered whether men like Hova Kaminsky, secure in their solid stone houses, their bellies full, their needs attended to by servants only too well aware of the lack of options available to the workless and homeless, even knew that places like the Khitrovka existed. Here there were men who looked as if they would cheerfully kill you for the price of a drink, women who would do unspeakable things for far less. If Hova Kaminsky were a starving pickpocket and not a wealthy lawyer, there was no question what his seven-year-old daughter would have been in the Khitrovka. He felt moved with pity by the misery and horror that he saw all around him, but he knew better than to give any money to the beggars who constantly approached them. The beggar women hired the screaming, undernourished babies by the day, trailing them through mud and cold to make them the more miserable and thus the more effective a begging tool. Often the babies died of exposure. If they did, the women carried them until dark anyway, so as not to waste the rental.

Guchkov and Bunin spent three nights in the Khitrovka, prowling its filthy streets in search of some, any kind of information, the smallest, most insignificant recollection, thrusting the now-battered photograph beneath the noses of bearded coachmen, drunken *izvostchiki*, the surly concierges of apartment houses. They talked to thieves and escapees from Siberia, pickpockets and whores, icecream peddlers and balloon sellers, for these were the street people. Invisible to the wealthy upon whom they depended for alms, they were everywhere. If anyone had seen what happened to the Kaminsky girl, it would be someone from the Khitrovka. They were asked a hundred times if there was a reward; Guchkov always said no.

"They'll tell us anything we want to hear for a few kopecks, lad," he told Bunin. "Come on, let's keep going."

"Do we have to?"

"Not if you can think of some other way."

So they plodded on. They went to the "Meat Market" where the child prostitutes lined the alley in their pathetic finery, none of them much more than ten or eleven, graduates from street begging begun at five. There were places where you could buy an eleven-year-old for fifty rubles and do with her what you would. The women of the Khitrovka were called *tyetki*, frumps. It took a little more than three months from the time a child went on the street until she became a *tyetok*, with nothing to look forward to from then on but death—in a prison, in a charity hospital, or on the floor of some scabrous *traktir*. There were horrifically deformed beggars everywhere, pus oozing from the sores on their bodies, stumps for arms or legs. They passed derelicts frying up the filthy mess of food they called "dog's happiness" and were jostled by the *kotshki*, the "cats," as the whores called their pimps. The *kotshki* vied with one another to wear the fanciest braided jackets and pants, ready to sell their little charges for a ruble a night. The air was lambent with the stink of horse sweat, manure, onions, burning meat, fish, ordure. Bunin shook his head. How could a place like this exist, not a verst from the brilliant gold and white palaces of the Kremlin, the privileged world of the princes and nobles?

"Can't something be done about this place?" he panted, as Guchkov pushed inexorably on. "Can't anything be done?"

"What would you suggest?" Guchkov asked.

Burn it down, Bunin thought. Raze it, disinfect the ground, cauterize it. People should not have to live in such squalor, no matter what their sins, and as far as he could see, the great majority of the people in the Khitrovka were condemned to it by poverty and nothing else. Penniless and illiterate, what else could they do? Let the students advocating revolution in the gardens below the Kremlin come here to demonstrate, he thought, and they'd find willing enough listeners.

No one knew anything in the Khitrovka, or if they did, they were not saying anything. Both investigators realized without even verbalizing it that the man they were looking for could come here any day of the week and purchase a child for his satanic needs.

"It's the fact that he has killed a decent child that bothers me, Piotr," Guchkov said, lower lip thrust out in thought. "Whatever his sickness is, these filthy little animals here obviously don't satisfy it."

So another week went by, and then another. No information came to them, nothing from their underground informers, the *shpioni*, not a whisper. The murder of Irinia Kaminsky was still unsolved when the second victim was found.

It was a month almost to the day. Two workmen loading a barge near the Yauzki Bridge noticed something sticking up from the mud at the side of the river. One of them went down to investigate and came back almost too sickened to tell his friend to call the police. What he had seen was a hand; the rest of the girl's body had been covered by the filthy sewage that clogged the Yauza. The police arrived and put a cordon around the place. In due course, it was established that the girl's name was Zoya Terzakova. She was identified by her sobbing father, who told Guchkov that his daughter was ten years old. She had left home to walk across town to visit her grandmother five days earlier. As in the case of the Kaminsky girl, her disappearance had been reported to the police, but unlike Hova Kaminsky, Pavel Terzakov knew no one higher up. His report of his daughter's disappearance had been filed and forgotten. Not for the first time, Guchkov found himself cursing the stupidity and venality of the city police force. The civilian population had only contempt for it, and it was no wonder.

He and Bunin went through the same exercise and came up with exactly the same result: nothing. Now, only three weeks after the discovery of Zoya Terzakova's ravaged body, a third mutilated corpse had been found by two railway workers on waste ground just south of the Bryansk Station.

"I suppose we'd better get started," Bunin said without enthusiasm.

"Yes." Guchkov nodded. "The usual, Piotr. Go and see Skolnikov and ask him very nicely if you can see his Missing Person dossiers. You've got the girl's description?"

"Yes, blonde, about ten or eleven. Blue eyes. No scars, no physical defects. Height—"

"All right, all right, check it," Guchkov said. "They've probably got a file on her. At least we'll have a name, something to go on."

"And then?"

"Bryansk Station is a busy place," Guchkov said. "Someone down there may have seen her. Seen something, anyway."

"Maybe," Bunin said without optimism.

"We'll check her friends, relatives, anyone who knew her. It probably won't get us very far, but we'll do it anyway. Then back to the *traktirs*, I suppose."

"Not the Khitrovka again," Bunin groaned.

"If we have to," Guchkov said. "Listen, Piotr, we're not looking for some hothead who's bashed his wife's face in, or a petty thief who's run off with the milk money. This is a sadist, a monster. He isn't going to be easy to find."

"I know that," Bunin said gloomily. "And he's clever, too. He doesn't leave anything behind. Not a thread, nothing."

"An intelligent man," Guchkov said. "Probably well educated."

"Yet he can do—things like that?"

"You're thinking with your heart, Piotr," Guchkov said. "It's because he's intelligent and well educated that he can take these children off the street like a pike taking a duckling. They wouldn't even speak to him otherwise."

"But how does he persuade them to go? How does he do it and remain invisible? A gang? Confederates?"

"I think not," Guchkov said. "This is the work of one man. He's insane, of course, but clever too, wary and careful. How does he persuade them to accompany him? Why don't they struggle or cry out? Why hasn't anyone seen anything?"

"I don't know," Bunin said.

"Neither do I, lad," Guchkov said. "We'll just have to wait."

"Wait? Wait for what?"

"Until he makes a mistake, Piotr," Guchkov said softly. "An error, a misjudgment. Sooner or later he has to make one, and then we'll have him."

"Yes," Bunin said, shaking his head. "But how many kids do you think he will have killed by then?"

They both looked at the poor thing on the autopsy table, their eyes solemn.

"God alone knows," Viktor Guchkov said.

6

ENERAL YAKOV ZHILINSKY was a strange duck, Tatiana thought, with his fishy pallor and his surprised expression. He looked as if he was constantly on the point of death, a gray, bony old man with a stiff back and a voice so dry that it sounded like dead leaves blowing. Nevertheless, he was Governor-General of Warsaw and a firm favorite of the Dowager Empress Maria Fyodrovna, mother of the Tsar.

"Well, m'dear," Zhilinsky said, "lovely day for it, eh, hm? Tsar's sunshine, hm." He ended each sentence with the same strange humming sound. It was surprising how quickly one grew accustomed to it.

The carriages had taken them to the pavilion of the Grand Duke, one of perhaps half a dozen on the huge military review ground which lay on the southern side of the Petersburgskoe Chaussée, opposite the Petrovski Park. Young soldiers helped them alight, saluting as they closed the doors. Officers standing nearby wondered who Tatiana was and grumbled good-naturedly about old fogies like Zhilinsky having all the luck. Tatiana was wearing a wide-brimmed yellow straw hat, her blonde hair shining brightly, her corn-blue eyes matched perfectly by the ribbons around the slender waist of her airy Chantilly lace dress.

It was a splendid day. Stands for spectators had been erected in sloping tiers on both sides of the parade ground. All the way to the Iberian Gate there were crowds lining the streets, flags decking the buildings, children excitedly awaiting their opportunity to cheer the soldiers and to see, perhaps for the only time in their lives, the Tsar of all the Russias. The special stands were already thronged with people. Fat old generals staggering under the weight of sword and medals clanked up the wooden stairways. Gorgeously uniformed officers and noblemen thronged the multicolored pavilion tents, sipping ice-cold champagne. There was a huge, oriental-looking pavilion for the royal party and several smaller ones, like the one in which the Grand Duchess Maria Pavlovna would hold court with her son, the Grand Duke Andrei, cousin of the Tsar. There were carriages and automobiles lined up to the right of the tiered stands. In them, rich merchants and their wives nibbled on game pâté and breast of chicken from the sumptuously stocked picnic hampers their dozens of servants had brought from Moscow. Children in sailor suits or Cossack uniforms, copied from those of the Tsarevich, played happily on the grass verges.

Zhilinsky escorted Tatiana into the pavilion just as the sun emerged from behind a cloud. After the formal introductions, everyone moved to the entrance to see the opening ceremony. As far as the eye could see, there were serried rows of soldiers standing in rigid immobility. Here and there the eye caught the bright golds, blues, reds of the Guards regiments, the flash of a medal, a saber, a spur. Pennants and flags fluttered in the slight breeze. Then someone said, "There's Nicholas!"

It was noon precisely.

To the accompaniment of a thunderous roar of cannons the Tsar, mounted on a white horse, appeared off to the right. As he came into sight, the flags trembled and the band crashed into action, drowning the sound of the cannon in the strains of "God Save the Tsar." At a gentle gallop, the Tsar moved to the review position. He was wearing the white tunic of the Garde Chevalier, and over it the blue ribbon of the Order of St. Andrei. Behind the Tsar came his escort, in uniforms of red and green and white and blue. The Tsaritsa followed in an open carriage drawn by six white horses. With her sat the four Grand Duchesses—Olga, Marie, Tatiana and Anastasia—and the Tsarevich Alexis. Each was in uniform, for each of the Tsar's children was Colonel in Chief of a crack Guards regiment.

Sunlight flashed on cavalry sabers whipping to the salute. The massed ranks of infantry were an immobile force that erupted into noise when the Tsar shouted, "*Zdorovo, rebyata!*"—"Greetings, children!"

"Good health, Your Imperial Majesty!" every man on the field roared back in unison.

The Tsaritsa and the children moved to the central pavilion, accompanied by a group of ministers and other courtiers. The Tsar remained on horseback on the parade ground. His horse tossed its head frequently. A second salvo resounded, and the parade began.

"Infantry first, hm," said General Zhilinsky at Tatiana's shoulder. She nodded, not sure what to look for. She wanted to see the royal family, but she did not want to miss the boys as they passed in review. She could see the Tsaritsa and the Grand Duchesses very clearly, and she studied the girls with more than ordinary interest. If she was to visit the royal palace at Tsarskoe Selo, the more she knew about them, the better.

The Tsarevich Alexis, the Tsar's only son, was a thin-faced, wan-looking little boy of about eight. He was dressed in the fur cap and boots of a Cossack colonel. A bejeweled dagger hung at his belt. He looked sickly, and it had not escaped the attention of anyone that he had been carried from the carriage to his place in the pavilion by a huge Cossack from the Tsar's personal escort. Tatiana asked the general a question.

"Can't say I know what ails him," Zhilinsky said, referring to the Tsarevich. "They say he's got some sort of anemia, hm."

"Poor little man," Tatiana murmured. "He looks so brave in his Cossack uniform."

"Hetman of all the Cossacks, hm," Zhilinsky said. "Purely honorary, of course, tradition and all that, hm."

The boy wasn't a great deal like his sisters, Tatiana decided. Olga, the eldest of the Grand Duchesses, had long, chestnut-colored hair. Her blue eyes sparkled with interest as she leaned forward to hear something one of the courtiers was saying to her mother. She was seventeen and would attend her first ball during the coming winter season. She was not a beauty—none of the Romanov girls were—but she looked lively and intelligent. Tatiana decided that her namesake, the Grand Duchess Tatiana, was the best-looking of the four girls, tall, slender, and gray-eyed. Marie was thirteen, two years younger, with rosy cheeks and big round blue eyes and light brown hair. She was short and a little bit dumpy, like her younger sister, Anastasia, who looked hot and uncomfortable in her military uniform, as if she would have preferred climbing trees to watching this grand parade.

"My God!" the Grand Duke Andrei said behind Tatiana, making her jump. "How long does all this go on for?"

"Quite some time yet, Andrushka," his mother said, as if enjoying her son's ennui. "You know how dear Nicky just loves to play soldiers."

"He thinks he looks dashing," Andrei drawled. The contempt in his voice had a vicious edge on it. "I say, Mama, couldn't we have some champagne to keep the dust down?"

"Good idea, Your Highness!" someone shouted, and there was laughter as the servants hurried to pour wine for everyone. The crystal glasses popped as the champagne foamed in them. The hands of the servants were blue from handling the icy bottles.

Outside, the massed regiments marched and countermarched in the stifling heat. Rising dust filmed the spotless leathers and brasses, dulled the shining glint of sabers, mantled the glossy coats of the prancing horses. Spectators in the stands followed the example of the Tsaritsa, who had covered her nose and mouth with a lacy handkerchief as phalanx after phalanx passed in review, sunlight flashing on golden helmets and cuirasses. If the Tsar noticed the heat and dust, he gave no sign of it, remaining rigidly at attention as his crack regiments went by.

First the infantry: the Preobrazhensky and the Semionovsky regiments, then the Pavlovsky, wearing the gilded miters of the grenadiers of Frederick the Great. Before passing in front of the Tsar, they changed to parade step.

"Notice anything about them, my dear?" Zhilinsky said. "Hm?"

"I wish you'd tell me, General," Tatiana said, smiling. "You seem to know so much more about it all than anyone else."

"Well, hmph, yes," the old man said, his bony features startled into something approaching a smile by her flattery. "Ones in front there: Preobrazhensky. All tall fellows with beards, see, hm?"

"Yes, I see."

"Next, Semionovskys. All fair-haired. Pavlovsky tradition is pug noses. Tradition goes back to Tsar Paul. He had a pug nose, you see, hm?"

Smaller men, he said, went into the Hussars, bearded or not. Thin men went into the Horse Guards, and so on. It was a tradition. Grand Duke Andrei's father, the Grand Duke Vladimir, had sorted all new recruits personally at the old Mikhail Riding School.

"Color and size, he used to say," Zhilinsky told her. "Color and size. Dear old Vladya. He was quite a fellow. Miss him, you know. Yes, hm."

The sun was high in the sky now, but still the troops rolled past. Behind the infantry came the cavalry, a litany of names that even Tatiana, a soldier's daughter, could not recite. Volynsky and Litovsky, Knight's Guards and Horse Guards, Hussars and cavalry, artillery with ponderous cannon and howitzers, rattling munitions

82

wagons making the ground tremble as they thundered past. Cuirassiers and Uhlans armed with long lances tipped with pennants, Cossacks in purple tunics, the Tsar's Hussars in gold, embroidered vermilion tunics, blue breeches and white dolmans with black fur on the shoulders. Bugle calls lanced the golden air with silvery notes. The Tsar's hand moved in a final salute. A huge Cossack ran forward to take the reins of his horse, another to stand by as the Tsar dismounted. An escort of them accompanied him to the royal pavilion. He looked short and stocky beside them. All the ladies in the stands curtsied low as the Tsar approached, the men saluting rigidly until the Tsar was out of sight.

"Is that the end?" Tatiana said.

"Good Lord, no, just the beginning, hm," Zhilinsky said. "We'll take lunch. Then the Tsar will lead the procession into the city. We'll all drive back together, hm." He patted her shoulder clumsily. "Come and sit by me, hm?" he said.

Now that the royal family had retreated to the cooler depths of their pavilion for luncheon, the staggered review stands quickly emptied as the spectators hurried to get out of the sun and the sifting dust. From the cool comfort of their marquee, the guests of the Grand Duchess Maria Fyodrovna laughed at the discomfiture of those less fortunate than themselves and snapped their fingers for more champagne.

"How astonishingly easy it is to bear the misfortunes of one's friends," she heard someone drawl, and the remark made Tatiana angry. When one had as much as this, there was no need to sneer at anyone.

She looked around the pavilion; she had never seen anything like it. All along the back wall, long trestle tables had been placed and covered with spotless cloths of white damask, with cabinets of silver cutlery and battalions of crystal glasses gleaming in the muted sunlight. Food and still more food was beautifully arrayed upon the tables, arranged by the armies of servants brought out here from the Grand Duke's palace in Moscow. The centerpiece of the table display was a peacock, tail spread as proudly as in life. Only on closer inspection did one realize that the bird had been plucked, cooked and sliced, and then reassembled piece by piece and feather by individual feather. Around the bird spiced meats had been artfully arranged, and spreading outward from the centerpiece was an array of foods which defeated the eye. Here a huge Beluga sturgeon, there an equally large salmon lying on a bed of ferns and cucumber.

There a baron of cold beef, sliced razor thin and flanked by silver dishes of fresh-ground horseradish sauce. Four enormous turkeys had been carved and carefully reassembled on plates so that they might be the more easily dismembered. Roquefort cheese and smoked trout, fresh or pressed caviar, herring fillets, cucumber in brine, *balak*, roast suckling pig, a dozen different kinds of pâté, game pies, great silver tureens of consommé and vichysoisse, freshly baked bread and rolls, butter lying in beds of ice, celery, radishes, and a dozen other delicacies with a dozen more beyond them. On a side table rose towers of plates, pillars of saucers. At the far end of each table there were huge wooden tubs filled with ice, into which had been jammed champagne bottles or still white wines from the Loire and Burgundy. Bottles of Smirnoff's *Tsarskoevodka*, fruit liqueurs and cognacs in profusion, stood in gleaming lines. Samovars steamed silently at each end of the marquee.

General Zhilinsky's face was pinker now, and he was perspiring freely. He was drinking vodka at a prodigious rate, and Tatiana excused herself. The conversation between Aunt Elena, Princess Volintisin and Countess Birovna was about the difficulty of finding a decent couturière in Moscow, a subject in which Tatiana had not the faintest interest. More to the point, General Zhilinsky was being a nuisance. His knee had for some time been insistently nudging hers beneath the table.

Her eyes met those of Katrina Smirnova, who was standing at the far end of the pavilion, talking to Zhilinsky's aide, Count Sukhotin, and some other people Tatiana did not know. She half turned away, embarrassed, when Katrina called her name.

"Tatiana, come and talk to us," she said. She linked her arm through Tatiana's and drew her toward the group of people to whom she had been talking. Confused and unsettled, Tatiana acknowledged the introductions without remembering a single name. It was as if Katrina was going out of her way to demonstrate to anyone, to everyone, that she and Tatiana were the closest of friends. Her eyes held an unusual sparkle, as though she was forcing herself to be gay. It was not like Katrina to gush over anyone, Tatiana thought, and after what had happened at the reception between herself and Sergei, it was positively unnerving. She must know what happened, Tatiana thought. Sergei must have told her about it.

"Isn't it a wonderful parade, Tatiana!" Katrina was enthusing. "Isn't the whole thing just splendid?"

"Yes," Tatiana said. "Marvelous."

She did not mean to make it sound blasé, but it came out that way and she saw Sukhotin glance sharply at her. She felt irritated with the man, swiftly followed by pardon; he could not know that her mind was in a whirl. She had expected a confrontation, some kind of scene, ever since that awful moment she had slapped Sergei's face. Instead, both he and Katrina had acted as though nothing whatsoever had happened. The matter had not been mentioned again at the reception, nor had it been raised at Sokolnika afterward. Tatiana had been as nervous as a cat, waiting for Katrina's eyes to flash, for her to say, as Tatiana knew she would herself have fiercely said, that Sergei was hers alone, and that Tatiana must never again so speak to him. Instead, Katrina acted as though Tatiana was dearer, closer to her than ever. She simply could not understand it. It never occurred to her that Katrina was trying as valiantly to cope with her difficult situation as Tatiana.

"I beg your pardon?" she said, realizing that one of the men to whom Katrina had introduced her had asked her a question.

"I asked whether you live here in Moscow," the man said. His French was strangely accented, and she looked at him properly for the first time. She saw a tall, good-looking man in his late twenties or early thirties, with light brown hair and fine green eyes beneath a broad forehead. He had the longest lashes Tatiana had ever seen on a man.

"No, I am staying at Sokolnika," she said. "With Katrina's family. My home is in Petersburg."

"Could I ask you a personal question?"

Tatiana raised her eyebrows.

"Well, it's not all that personal," the man said with a smile. "I was just wondering whether you were in any way related to the General Makcheyev who defended Sevastopol during the Crimean War."

"He was my grandfather," Tatiana said. "I'm sorry, I didn't—"

"Castle," he said. "David Castle. I work for the American Embassy."

"Oh," she said, "an American."

That explained the gaucherie, she thought, and the accented French.

"Is your father also a soldier?" Castle asked.

"No, a judge," she said, absently. She could see the young officers trooping toward the pavilion, and she did not wish to be stuck with some boring American when they arrived. Vasya, Nicky, Paul and the others were such fun, and Sergei—her heart bumped. What would she say to him? How would he look at her?

They all came into the pavilion, noisy and cheerful, shaking hands, dusty and hot, bringing the smell of horses with them, calling for champagne. They unbuttoned the collars of their tunics and stood around in distinctly unmilitary fashion, arms around each other's shoulders. Sergei came in alone. He looked sullen and resentful, as though he had been forced into doing something he did not want to do. Tatiana glanced at Katrina and saw her eyes meet Sergei's. Some message passed between them; a slight frown from Katrina brought an infinitesimal nod from Sergei. He came toward them, smiling uneasily.

"Well, Tatiana," he said. "How nice to see you."

He bent low over her hand, the unease still behind his eyes. Oh, Sergei, please don't be like this, Tatiana thought, trying to put the thought into her eyes so that he could read it. Be angry, be cold, be sarcastic, be anything, but please don't just be polite!

"Now, ladies, you must tell us what you thought of our performance," said Vasya Kirsanov. "Weren't we marvelous?"

"I thought you all looked wonderful," Katrina said. Her eyes were on Sergei, and there was almost a pleading look in them. Look at me, they said, notice me. But Sergei averted his gaze, staring out at the empty parade ground.

"Hello, Tatiana," Nicky said. "You're very thoughtful. Aren't you having a good time?"

"Of course I am," Tatiana said, donning an instant smile. It would not do to let them all sense the tension between herself and Sergei and Katrina. There was gossip enough as it was.

"Didn't we look splendid?" Paul said. "Best regiment in the Army, eh, boys?"

"Hurrah!" the others shouted.

"Here, Kolya, come and pay your respects," Vasya said. "You have not met our goddesses of beauty, Katrina, Tatiana."

Dressed in the uniform of the Garde Chevalier like all the others, Kolya Bakhronshin was a sturdily built young man of perhaps twenty-two. He was tall and very broad-shouldered; his good-looking face was marred by a broken nose.

"At your service, ladies," he said, bending low over their hands and clicking his heels.

"And here's young Andrei," Vasya said. "Do you remember Sergei's little brother? Come along, little brother, don't be bashful."

Andrei Tretyakov was wearing the uniform of a cornet in Sergei's regiment. Tatiana smiled as he bent to kiss her hand. Dear Andrei! She had not seen him for such a long time. They had all grown up together, friends through the golden years of childhood. But Andrei was always the baby, and to her he always would be. He boasted neither beard nor moustache, nor was there yet any character around his mouth. He had that same innocent air she remembered, the same gentle, shy eyes. Although she was only a year his senior, somehow Tatiana felt immeasurably older and wiser than Sergei's brother.

"Well, well, now that we're all together, let's have some more of that champagne," Nicky said. He turned to one of the servants and told him to bring a tray.

"I say," Paul Dubinsky was saying. "The Grand Duchess is in full spate, I see."

Tatiana turned to look. There was a large group of sycophants clustered around the chair of the Grand Duchess Maria Pavlovna, laughing uproariously at whatever it was she was saying. One of them, Tatiana noticed with a faint chill of recognition, was Boris Abrikosov. What was he doing here? She caught a glimpse of the cat-wicked eyes of the Grand Duchess, the expressive mouth, the fluent hands, and pitied whoever it was that she was talking about. Her son, the Grand Duke Andrei, was leaning back in his chair, slapping his thigh and roaring with laughter.

Grand Duchess Maria Pavlovna was the widow of the Tsar's uncle, a handsome woman in her late fifties. Sister-in-law to Tsar Alexander III, she and her husband Vladimir—old General Zhilinsky's friend Vladya—had been the alternative court in Petersburg and took no pains to conceal their contempt for their weak-kneed nephew Tsar Nicholas II and the Darmstadt-born princess who was his wife. The more Nicholas and Alexandra withdrew to their cozy little palace at Tsarskoe Selo, avoiding parties and disdaining society, the more Maria Pavlovna took their place. In the vast drawing room of her Florentine palace facing the Neva, flanked on one side by the Hermitage and the other by the Marble Palace, the world of rank and richesse rubbed shoulders with artists, musicians and writers. Grand Duke Vladimir, military commander of St. Petersburg, had been president of the Academy of Arts and a patron of Diaghilev. His widow had been and still was energetic, poised, intelligent and well read—everything, in fact, that the Tsaritsa was not. The articulate and sharp-tongued Maria Pavlovna, third lady of the Russian Empire, gave her nephew's wife very few chances to forget it, or how closely in the line of royal succession her three sons stood. Neither she nor they made any secret of their belief that any one of them would make a better Tsar than Nicholas. They thought him a fool and his wife a dullard and did not hesitate to say so, publicly and frequently. Tatiana knew all this, as did any Petersburg girl. Unlike those who chose to find such conduct amusing, however, she thought them worthless, and wondered how anyone who lived lives of such indolent uselessness could ever imagine themselves ruling Russia. At least the Tsar was a man dedicated to his work and his duty. Tatiana was far too much her father's daughter to admire people whose principal aim in life was self-gratification. There were far too many of them in Petersburg.

"Your champagne, mademoiselle," a voice said, interrupting her reverie. It was the American again. Great Jehovah, would no one let her have two consecutive thoughts today? Tatiana thought irritably. She took the glass from the man and made herself smile.

"Thank you, Monsieur—?"

"Castle," he reminded her.

"Oh, yes," she said. "The American Embassy. Let me introduce you to my friends."

"An honor to meet you all," Castle said. "Gentlemen, that was a most impressive display out there, today."

"You are a soldier, sir?" Count Sukhotin said. Sukhotin was a tall, thin man who wore a monocle that gave him an air of constant condescending superiority. He was related to the Smirnoffs by marriage and known by the nickname "Fritz" because he was descended from a branch of the Hohenzollerns. There was an edge of hostility in his voice for which Tatiana could detect no cause. The others noticed it, too, and there was a wary silence. All eyes turned to the American expectantly, as if what Sukhotin had said was some sort of test Castle had to pass. Watching him, Tatiana realized that Castle's youthful good looks were deceiving; there was no immaturity whatsoever in the eyes. If anything, there was contemptuous confidence in them, a look that seemed to say, go ahead, try me.

"No, I'm not," Castle said, crisply. "But I'm a student of soldiers, Count. I know a real one when I see one."

Two small red spots of anger stained Fritz Sukhotin's cheeks, and in the long instant that it took them to appear, Tatiana perceived the wicked subtlety of the shaft. She saw her young officer friends stiffen with a mixture of apprehension and delight. Sukhotin was an overbearing and unpopular officer and reputed to be a lone wolf. But even if one disliked the man, it was unwise to incur his enmity. He was said to be one of the best pistol shots in the Army.

"Like all students, you consider yourself an expert," Sukhotin sneered. "Is your knowledge a product of your stay in Berlin?"

Castle refused to be drawn further. "My father was a soldier, Count," he said, deliberately taking the sting out of the confrontation. He did not know the reason for Sukhotin's hostility, but there was no point in exacerbating it. He was a guest of the Grand Duke Andrei. The Ambassador was standing not six feet away. The last thing they needed was for Castle to be challenged to a duel. "And so was my grandfather."

"In America?" Sukhotin asked. Again, the invitation to take offense was implicit in the way he spoke. To be a soldier in the American Army was to be no soldier at all, his voice implied.

"My grandfather was in the same army as you," Castle said.

"Your grandfather was Russian?" Katrina said, coming to the American's rescue. "How interesting, Monsieur Castle. You must tell me all about him."

She was rather beautiful, he thought, cool and Nordic, with a heart-shaped face, wide, vulnerable eyes, and long, straight blonde hair that hung to her shoulders.

"You're Katrina Smirnova, aren't you?" he said.

"That's right," Katrina said. "But how—"

"I know your uncle," he said. "Vladimir. We met at the open day at the Smirnoff distillery. He showed me around. There's a photograph of you on his desk."

"Oh," Katrina said, with a faint blush. "Yes."

Vladimir had told Castle that Katrina had seriously considered taking the veil. It was not hard to imagine her in the long white robes of a nun. Out of the corner of his eye he saw Sukhotin shrug and turn away to talk to someone else. Well, there goes another beautiful friendship, he thought.

"I understand you're to be engaged," he said. "Let me offer my congratulations. Who's the lucky man?"

"You met him a few minutes ago," Katrina said. "Sergei Tretyakov." She smiled fondly toward the other side of the pavilion, where Sergei and the other young officers were returning to the parade ground. She lifted a hand in farewell, but Sergei either did not see or did not respond. Castle thought Katrina's smile looked just a little fragile as she turned back toward him.

"Are you going to be in Moscow long?" she asked.

"A few more days," Castle said. "Perhaps a week."

"Then you must come to our engagement party," Katrina said. "I'm sure Vladimir would want me to invite you. Where can we reach you?"

"The American Consulate on the Archangelski Pereulok," he replied. "In care of the Consul. His name is Snodgrass."

"Oh," Katrina said. "Really?" She had deep dimples when she smiled that invited a smile in return.

"He's not crazy about the name himself," Castle grinned, and both girls laughed out loud. Perhaps I misjudged him after all, Tatiana thought. He's quite handsome when he smiles. Then she remembered the cold knife edge of his voice when he had insulted Fritz Sukhotin and wondered which was the real man, this smiling Embassy official or the other she had glimpsed.

"How do you plan to see the Tsar's entry into the city?" he asked them. "Would you like to ride in the Ambassador's car?"

"Is that the enormous Rolls Royce I saw earlier?" Tatiana said. "That great black and gold machine?"

"That's it," Castle said.

"It's in quite appallingly bad taste," Katrina said. Then the dimples showed again. "But I'd love to ride in it. Tatiana, why don't you come, too?"

"I'm supposed to return with General Zhilinsky—" Tatiana began.

"Let Aunt Elena have him all to herself," Katrina said, taking her hand. "We shall ride with Monsieur Castle. That will give us a chance to have a talk on the way home."

When Katrina said these words, Tatiana's nerve nearly failed her, but she went with them. The ride back to the city was pleasant enough. David Castle kept making Katrina giggle by telling her patently nonsensical stories about the Consul with the strange name, Snodgrass. Tatiana smiled and nodded, but she was not really listening to the American. Her mind was empty of anything except what Katrina was going to say when they were alone. She found herself wishing desperately that she could get out of the car and walk back to Sokolnika, yet paradoxically looking forward to a clearing of the air with Katrina. She had suppressed her true feelings because it was the polite, the correct thing. Well, if Katrina wanted the truth, she could have it.

The Tsar's entry into the Kremlin was a great occasion. He rode alone into the Red Square, sixty yards ahead of his Cossack escort, the massed regiments of his army following in phalanxes. In the center of the great square, the Tsar dismounted and took his place behind a line of chanting priests who led him through the Spasskiya Gate and into the Kremlin. He took his position on the wall as the regiments came through the Red Square one after another. It was nearly dark by the time they had all passed in review. The crowds would stay on the street until well after midnight, or throng to the cafés to listen to the balalaikas and the gypsy singers. Castle got out of the car and bade them both goodbye.

"I've got something to do," he explained. "The chauffeur will take you back to Sokolnika."

Katrina was silent as the car threaded through the crowds and turned north. Tatiana waited, apprehensive and simultaneously eager, but her friend remained silent. Great Jehovah, will she never speak? Tatiana thought vexedly. The silence was worse than any tirade. Finally she could wait no longer.

"Katrina . . ." she ventured. "About . . . the other night. About Sergei . . . and me . . ."

Katrina turned toward her. Her heart-shaped face was shadowed, and her eyes were unreadable. She put a cool hand on Tatiana's arm and shook her head.

"Dear Tatiana," she said, "you don't need to explain. I think I understand what happened."

"I was angry," Tatiana said. "I didn't mean—"

"I know," Katrina said. "You're so full of life, Tatiana, so beautiful, yet there is still so much that you don't understand. Oh, how I wish I had your courage, your confidence!"

"But Katrina, you're—"

"Please," Katrina said, "listen to me, Tatiana. What I am going to tell you now is very hard for me to say, but I have to say it. Maybe then you will understand a little better. I'm not like you, you see. I'm not clever, Tatiana, not bright and witty like other girls, not beautiful like you—no, please don't interrupt me. I don't know how to flirt, and I don't think I could ever learn. I only know how to be honest, and so I will be honest with you. Sergei and I are going to be married. I ask you—beg you—not to come between us."

Expecting a tirade, Tatiana was nonplussed by the confession. She had always thought of Katrina as regal, confident, with all the wealth of the great Smirnoff vodka empire behind her. Yet she revealed herself as the very opposite; the anxiety in her voice and the tears in her eyes were undoubtedly genuine. Disarmed by them, Tatiana could think of nothing to say except the truth.

"But I love him," she protested.

"I know you think you love him," Katrina said, softly. "But I don't think you know him at all."

"Not know him?" Tatiana said. "I've known him since we were children. And he and I—" She was about to blurt out the story of what had happened at Krestoffsky Island that lovely weekend, but something stopped her. Katrina looked at her with eyes that brimmed with tears.

"Please try to understand," she said. "Try to truly understand. This is very hard for me."

Not understanding at all, Tatiana said that she understood. Katrina shook her head again, that slight, sad gesture that was so typical of her.

"In a way, it's funny," she said, her voice almost inaudible. "I asked Papa if we could invite you to Sokolnika. I had it all planned. I was going to tell you that you were never to see Sergei again, never to even think of him . . . like that. Then you came, and somehow I found myself putting it off, not wanting to hurt you or Sergei. Now it . . . it all seems so pointless. How can I tell you not to love someone just because I need him more than you, because I believe in my foolish vanity that he needs someone like me? It's just . . . that I'm no good at lying, Tatiana. I can't pretend; I never learned how. When our parents made the arrangements for the marriage, I went down on my knees and thanked God for giving me . . . for the fact that it was Sergei. When I think of . . . some of the men I might . . . Sergei is kind. I know that he is fond of me. I know that I can make him love me if . . . if nothing happens, if no one interferes."

Tatiana said nothing. He loves me, she thought petulantly, he always has. He had been different from all the others, as a boy and now as a man. She loved him, loved his black angers and the sunny smile that dispersed them in a moment, his unpredictable moods, his introspection. He didn't love Katrina. She had said so herself.

"Tell me you understand, Tatiana," Katrina said, taking her hand and pressing it between her own. "Say you agree."

"You didn't lie to me," Tatiana said, "so I won't lie to you. I love Sergei. I always have. Can you honestly say that he is happy to be marrying you?"

"Yes, yes," Katrina said. "He is. Ask him."

"No," Tatiana said. "If he is happy, then I am happy too. I won't bring him pain, or you either. I'll dance at your wedding—on one condition."

"Name it, dear Tatiana," Katrina said. "Name it."

"That you understand . . . if you and Sergei . . . if it doesn't work out . . . that I will be there waiting. I will become his mistress if I have to. But I will be there, and you will not come between us."

"If he decides that, Tatiana, I won't stand in your way," Katrina said, her voice pitched low. "I would not want to live anyway."

"Katrina!" Tatiana said, shocked. "You must never say such things, never even think them!"

Katrina shook her head again in that pensive, sad way she had.

"Dear Tatiana," she said softly. "How much you love life, yet how little you know of it."

Tatiana frowned and was about to make a piqued reply, but before she could do so, the automobile came to a stop at the great iron gates of Sokolnika. As they glided between the oaks lining the curving drive, Katrina put her arms around Tatiana and drew her close.

"Thank you, darling," she whispered. "Now we can be friends forever."

That wasn't what I wanted, Tatiana thought, petulantly. That isn't the way I wanted it at all.

The Smirnoff family was assembling. Tatiana could hear the busy babble of voices as guests were welcomed at the *porte cochère*, the grinding rattle of carriage wheels on the long drive leading to the house. Four-in-hands, landaus, and automobiles arrived in a never-ending procession, stopping to decant their occupants into the welcoming embrace of Pierre Smirnoff and his brother Nico. Behind the brothers stood the Circassian majordomo Yuri, his granite face wreathed in smiles. Grooms in bright *rubashkas* led away the horses, while a continuous stream of young boys in Cossack dress hurried to and from the kitchens, carrying dishes of food into the dining room, the ballroom, and out onto the verandah, where a continous buffet was being served. Every dish was silver, each beautifully garlanded with fresh flowers. More servants circulated with trays of wine, and on each table stood a silver tray on which, in a silver chiller filled with ice, lay a silver-labeled bottle of Smirnoff's most exclusive product, *Tsarskoevodka*, "the Tsar's vodka." As each gentleman arrived, one of the gardeners would take him to select flowers to present to his lady. There were baskets of flowers all over the house, banks of them along the walls of the ballroom, a sea of color on the verandah, islands of them on each table.

In the little bandstand with its wrought-iron chairs a military band was playing, alternating with a string quartet in the library. At nine, the family assembled for the formal announcement. Elegantly but simply dressed in an ice-blue sheath, her golden hair piled on top of her head and cascading down in ringlets around her ears, her mother's diamond clip on her right shoulder and the diamond earrings that had been Alexander Makcheyev's wedding present to his wife glittering in her ears, Tatiana looked beautiful and she knew it. When Sergei's eyes caught hers across the room, she smiled, trying to make her smile forgiving yet heartbroken, loving but brave. He smiled back uneasily.

Servants brought ice-cold champagne, Pierre made a speech, Katrina blushed, Sergei smiled. Then Sergei replied, and everyone smiled and applauded. After the announcement, everyone assembled on the steps of the house so that a photograph of the occasion could be made by the Court photographer, Vezhenyertzh. After dinner, Sergei Rachmaninoff was to play.

Tatiana decided to go for a walk in the gardens, away from all the Smirnoffs and Tretyakovs and Abrikosovs. It would be ages before she could talk to Sergei, if at all. She had smiled and smiled until she thought her face would grow fixed in the same grimace, and she could smile no longer. She wanted to be alone for a little while. The brass band was playing "Zigeunerbaron." There were people in canoes on the lake, their voices gay in the softening sunlight. Without reason, Tatiana resented their happiness.

"Hi," someone said. It was the American, David Castle.

"Hello," she said, no encouragement in her voice. She didn't want company. Maybe he would take the hint and go.

"Quite a party," he said.

"Yes."

"Mind if I walk with you awhile?"

Tatiana said nothing; she drew in her breath and let it out again.

"Something wrong? You look unhappy."

"No," she said, too brightly. "Nothing is wrong."

"You sure?"

Damn the man, couldn't he take a hint? "I'm sure," she said.

"I'm supposed to be looking for the Ambassador," he said, smiling. "But to tell you the truth, I'd rather talk to you."

94

"Do you work for the Ambassador?" she asked, more to stop him asking her any more questions than anything else.

"Sort of," he replied vaguely.

He wondered what she would have said if he had told her why he was in Russia. Probably wouldn't believe me, he thought. He wasn't sure he believed it himself.

They walked a little further without speaking, turning a corner past some tall bushes. As they did, they met a man with narrow shoulders and a thin face, wearing rimless spectacles, coming the other way. His clothes were ordinary and his hair was cropped short. He looked somewhat out of place among the well-dressed people wandering around the garden.

"My dear Tatiana," the man said. "What a pleasant surprise." His voice was gloating, almost caressing. Now I've got you, it seemed to say. Castle felt his hackles rising. The man looked at him and back at Tatiana.

"This is David Castle of the American Embassy," Tatiana said.

"Castle," the man acknowledged, not bothering to state his own name. "Will you forgive us? There's something I wish to discuss privately with Tatiana."

Before the American could say yes or no, the man took Tatiana's arm and led her off ten yards or so. She looked over her shoulder, her face twisted slightly as if in pain. Should I go over and interrupt? No, Castle thought, it's none of my business.

"What do you want, Boris?" he heard Tatiana say. "What are you doing here, anyway?"

"I came because I knew you would be here," he said. "I want to talk to you." His eyes were intent, fixed on hers.

"To talk to me?" Tatiana said. Her unease was obvious. Who was this fellow Boris, Castle wondered, and why was she so frightened of him? He saw Boris glance at him, the wary look of a predator at a waterhole, alert for enemies. He obviously thought that Castle could not understand anything he was saying.

"I want to see you," he said. "Alone."

He put an emphasis on the final word which was unusual. It seemed to fluster the girl, who did not know how to reply. Then her courage reasserted itself.

"I am afraid that is out of the question," she said, drawing herself up straight. Good girl, Castle thought.

"No, no, Tatiana," Boris said. "That won't do at all." His voice was silky. He laid his hand on her forearm, affecting not to notice her flinch. "You would be wise to be nice to me."

"Please," Tatiana said, "you're hurting my arm."

The man's eyes turned cold, cruel. Dismay twisted Tatiana's face. This has gone far enough, Castle thought, taking a step forward. Before he could take another, the tall, powerful figure of Vladimir Smirnoff appeared as if from nowhere and laid what looked like a friendly hand on the shoulder of Tatiana's tormentor. Friendly it might have looked to any casual observer, but Castle saw the thin-faced man wince.

"Well, well, Boris," Vladimir said. His voice was cheerful, but there was polar ice in every syllable. "Sweeping the ladies off their feet with your usual charm, I see."

"Take your damned hands off me!" Abrikosov said, bucking ineffectually against Vladimir's steely grip. "Let go, I say!"

"Of course, Boris," Vladimir said, his voice still bright and cheery. "As soon as you've apologized."

"Ap—? Damn you, I'll do no such thing!" Abrikosov snarled. "Aaaaagh!" His voice changed, and Castle realized that Smirnoff was applying painful pressure to the delicate nerve endings at the base of Boris's neck, smiling all the while he was doing it. He must have hands like iron, Castle thought.

"Apologize, you animal," Smirnoff said, still smiling as if he were in a drawing room talking of theatricals.

"Ahhh . . . ugghh . . . I—all right, damn you!" Boris groaned. "I apologize."

"Very gracious," Vladimir said. "Try again. Say 'I am truly sorry for being such a disgusting wretch.' "

"Go to—aaagh!"

"Say it!"

"I apologize for being . . . aaggh . . . such a disgusting wretch."

"That's better," Vladimir said, his voice still soft and without rancor. "Now get out of here, Boris. If I ever hear that you've been bothering this young lady again, I'll take a horsewhip to you." He pushed Abrikosov disdainfully away from him, turning his back on the man and taking Tatiana's arm.

"I'll have to have a word with the gardeners," he said urbanely, as though nothing had happened at all. "We don't often get rats in here."

Trembling with a rage he dared not show, Boris Abrikosov stood for a moment glaring at the broad back of the man who had so contemptuously shamed him. Castle watched, hypnotized by the hatred in the man's eyes. If looks alone could have killed, Vladimir

96

Smirnoff would already have been lying dead on the beautifully kept lawn of Sokolnika. Without another word, Boris Abrikosov turned on his heel and shouldered his way roughly past a group of people coming along the path. One of the men turned to remonstrate, but when he saw Boris's face, he remained silent.

"Ah, isn't that our American friend over there?" Castle heard Vladimir say. He turned to see Vladimir waving to him. "Come, join us, David," he said. Castle nodded, smiled, and walked across the garden toward Tatiana and Vladimir, wondering as he did whether the man had any idea what a merciless enemy he had just made, or whether Vladimir simply did not care one way or the other.

7

BORIS ABRIKOSOV never forgot an insult. He not only never forgot, he never forgave, either. A sly and vengeful boy, a cold-eyed youth, a devious and conspiratorial adult, Boris was constant in this one thing all his life. No one could ever alter that implacable resolve, not even his father, who loved him as much as any man could have loved so unloving a son.

"Hatred corrodes the soul, Boris," he would say, gently. "Try not to harbor grudges, my dear, no matter what the provocation."

Doddering old fool, Boris would think.

" 'If thine enemy smite thee, turn thou the other cheek,' " Ivan would say. "That is the mark of the true Christian."

"I'll try, Papa," Boris would reply, acting a contrition that he had no intention of ever experiencing. "I'm sorry."

"There's a good boy," Ivan would say, and potter off, vaguely satisfied, incompletely reassured. He was an ordinary man, without a great deal of ambition or imagination, happily married, a good father. He was proud of that. He loved his sons in an undemanding and unconstructive way. He never really understood why Dmitri was so stolid and dull, never realizing that Dmitri had modeled himself upon those aspects of his parents' characters. He was baffled by Boris's secretive, dark nature, never even suspecting the contempt in which his son held his parents. But then, Ivan was a kindly man by nature, and it pained him that when they grew to manhood, he found that Dmitri bored him and Boris frightened him. He wondered where he had gone wrong and, like many a parent before him, decided that the fault was in the children rather than himself. It was all too late now, anyway; no use fretting. He had done the best that he could with them and for them. So Ivan Stepanovich found a new outlet for his love: his three grandchildren, from whom he received in abundance the affection and esteem he felt he deserved. And was overjoyed that it was given without any criticism.

Boris rejected his entire family with a will. He insulted and offended them and patently did not give a tinker's curse for any of them. Not unnaturally, they responded by treating him with disdain and then contempt, and finally expressed themselves pleased not to have anything at all to do with him. Boris would have nothing whatsoever to do with the family business. Making chocolates was a job for women or for fools. Since Dmitri was patently the latter and more than a little of the former, he sneered, let him be the one who went into the business. Boris never forgot an insult—unless it was one he had given to someone else.

So Dmitri became the director of the family firm, bustling about in the store on the Nevsky, making displays of candied fruits with Boris's contemptuous approval. That he would never make the business any more than it already was, Ivan Abrikosov well knew and did not care. He wanted now only more time with his grandchildren and his watercolors. A man was entitled to take things easier in his sixty-fifth year. As for Boris, Ivan knew what he was up to. He had no special regard for the *Okhrana* or any fear of them, either. They were a necessary evil. Someone had to do it, and, Ivan reluctantly concluded, Boris was well fitted for such work.

Knowledge was power, and Boris thrived on power. There was something about possessing copies of all the documents relevant to a person's life, the secret information people thought only they had access to, the configurations of the skeletons in their cupboards, that gave Boris a heady sense of superiority. It was similar to the feeling that a man might get from owning an old master, a first folio of Shakespeare. The possession in itself was not important. What was important was knowing that no one else in the world except you had it.

So as the summer of the Romanov Tercentenary year turned toward fall, Boris worked upon a new project: a dossier on the Smirnoff family. Like all his other dossiers—and there were many hundreds of those now—he set out to put it together without knowing precisely what he was going to do with it when he had compiled it. The information, he generally found, suggested its own use.

He started with the first of the Smirnoffs, old Arsenii. There wasn't that much to find out, and most of it came from the Registrar of Births, Marriages and Deaths. Arsenii Smirnoff had not been a particularly important person. Born 1796, died 1855, married Sofia Fyodrovna 1825, two sons Piotr and Nikolai. Boris frowned. He knew all about Piotr, or Petya, as he had been called. He had never heard anyone in the Smirnoff family speak of another brother: Nikolai Smirnoff, born 1827, two years after Petya. He sent for a research assistant and gave him the relevant details. Within two hours the assistant was back with a red-tabbed *Okhrana* wallet, and Boris knew he had found real meat and red to boot. A tabbed wallet meant that there were files in the Archives of the Third Section of the Imperial Chancellery. A skeleton in the Smirnoff cupboard, he thought, smiling like a cat at a mousehole, and a nasty one, by the look of things.

"Smirnoff, Nikolai Arsenievich," he read aloud from the printed form in the wallet. "Born November 4, 1827. Family nickname Kolya. Educated at the Petershul and Moscow University. Advocate of Social Revolution. Member of Action Committee in University. Exiled to Novaya Uda 1849. See Report BEL/438-49 of Third Section Investigator K. A. Rozhin."

Boris leaned back in his chair and laid the wallet down on his desk. "Well, well," he said. So one of the Smirnoffs had been exiled, and by the Third Section at that! There was a family secret that had been hushed up, he thought. How the very rich could bury things under their money! The Third Section had been the forerunner of the *Okhrana*. Founded in 1826 by Tsar Nicholas I, it consisted originally of fifty men, officers and civil servants implicitly trusted by the Tsar and headed by a Baltic-German nobleman named General Count Alexander Benckendorff. The files of the Third Section, disbanded long ago, would be in the cellars of the Ministry of the Interior.

It took only a few days for the papers to come through. He opened the thick, wax-sealed envelope with its black legend "State Secrets." A fat little collection indeed, he thought, spreading the contents on his otherwise empty desk.

"Imperial Chancellery, Third Section. Report by K.A. Rozhin," he read, his eyes moving swiftly over the copperplate writing of the special investigator who had compiled the report in 1849.

"Well, I'll be damned!" he muttered to himself as he read. Nikolai Smirnoff, old Petya Smirnoff's brother, had been a member of the famous Petrashevsky group.

Mikhail Petrashevsky, as everyone knew, had been a junior member of the Foreign Ministry, situated in the General Staff building on the Palace Square in *Piter*. He was also the leader of a group of young men who met regularly on Friday evenings to discuss politics, current affairs, literature. They were known to the Third Section, of course. All such groups were known, and within reason tolerated. As long as they stuck to talk. Talk was the national disease. If half of the people who talked about revolution, the overthrow of the autocracy, the urgent necessity for change actually did something about it instead of talking, Boris thought, we'd need an *Okhrana* the size of the Army.

The Petrashevsky group was one such. They debated censorship, they criticized serfdom, they argued in favor of the abolition of property. One of the group, an informer, provided précis of some of the discussions. They were the usual muddled liberalism of the bourgeois class and of little interest to the Third Section until, one evening in Petrashevsky's house, the writer Fyodr Dostoievsky read aloud a letter to the writer Nikolai Gogol from Vissarion Belinsky, a noted dissident. The letter denounced Gogol as "a prophet of the knout, apostle of ignorance, champion of obscurantism and panegyrist of Tatar manners," and had become a manifesto of the radicals before being banned by the authorities. Dostoievsky's reading it aloud was treason. All twenty of the young men at Petrashevsky's house were arrested and thrown into the dungeons of the Peter and Paul fortress under sentence of death.

In that vastly silent place, where no one had a name, where no prisoner was allowed to speak, where the stone cells, set between the outer fortress walls and the inner, dripped moisture all summer and were lined with ice all winter, they remained under sentence of death until they were taken out to be shot, in public, by direct order of the Tsar himself. The whole ghastly ritual was observed in front of a huge crowd on Semionovsky Square. Some of the soldiers even went to the macabre length of dressing the prisoners in shrouds as the priests administered the last rites. Then the firing squad took its position, and the front line knelt as the rear aimed its rifles. Only at this point did the officer in charge stop the whole ghastly farce and read to the huddled men that they had been "graciously reprieved" by His Imperial Majesty, the Tsar. Reprieved from death by firing squad to death by inches. Petrashevsky was sentenced to life imprisonment, the others receiving sentences of a severity linked to the state's view of their guilt. Fyodr Dostoievsky was sentenced to ten years' imprisonment, as was his friend Nikolai Smirnoff. Four of these years were to be spent in the prison at Omsk and the balance as a private soldier in the Fourth Siberian Army. Following that there would be a period of exile as a civilian, but in the case of Nikolai Smirnoff the sentence was academic. He did not survive to serve in the Army. The fortress prisons of Siberia were not rest homes.

"Well, well," Boris said again, pushing the files back and stretching his arms above his head. "Well, well, well."

Further delving into the thick file revealed that Nikolai Smirnoff had married one Anna Mikhailovna in 1846, and that there had been two children. There was no notation by the name of the firstborn, a girl, Sonya, born in 1848. By the side of the name of the son, Piotr, born the following year, there was the cypher Д°, followed by the coding H/B 663-29. Boris knew what that cypher meant: *access restricted*.

He put in a call to Central Registry at the Ministry of the Interior, drumming his fingers impatiently on the desk while he waited for his call to be connected. It always took ages, despite the boasts of the St. Petersburg telephone exchange that its equipment was the finest in Russia and as good as anything in Europe. When he finally got through, Boris told the clerk what he wanted and gave his own security clearance reference.

"It will take awhile to extract the file from the archives, sir," the clerk said. "We will call you as soon as we have it."

"Call me not later than one o'clock this afternoon," Boris said coldly. "This is a matter of the utmost urgency."

"But, sir—" There was a hesitation, but Boris said nothing. The clerk muttered that he would do his best, and Boris smiled his thin smile.

"Be sure you do," he said and hung up.

The clerk was on the phone by midday with the information that Boris had asked for. Boris did not thank him.

"Well?" he snapped.

"This is the dossier on the assassination of Tsar Alexander the Second, sir," the clerk began, reverently. Boris's eyes gleamed; he had struck gold.

"Just go through the index and read me what it says about Piotr Nikolaievich Smirnoff," he said, heart bumping.

"Ah," he heard the clerk say. "Here we are."

"Come on, man, I haven't got all day!" Boris barked.

"Yes, sir, sorry, sir," the clerk stuttered.

"Investigator Bakushin reports that Smirnoff had met Sofia

Perovskaya through his sister, Sonya, who attended the same school. Smirnoff claimed he never knew Perovskaya was a member of *Narodnaya Volya*. Do you wish me to read you the details about the group, sir?"

"No," Boris said. He knew all about *Narodnaya Volya*. They had been the most infamous of all revolutionary groups, dedicated to the assassination of the Tsar. Formed in 1879, they succeeded in killing Alexander II in 1881. What had Nikki Smirnoff had to do with Perovskaya and the organization known as "The Will of the People"?

"Smirnoff stated that since Perovskaya was the daughter of a former Governor-General of St. Petersburg, he never suspected that she was a revolutionary, or that her lover was Andrei Zhelyabov, leader of *Narodnaya Volya*," the clerk droned on. "Investigator Bakushin states that in his opinion, Smirnoff was undoubtedly a member of the cell, along with Mikhailovich, Grenavitsky, Kibalchich, Rysakov and the others. However, none of them would incriminate him, and Investigator Bakushin was unable to find any evidence to support his conviction."

"Does he say what he thought Smirnoff's role was?"

"Just a moment, sir," the clerk said. Boris could hear him mumbling as he read on through the report. Come on, man! he thought, impatiently.

". . . no tangible evidence. Ah, here we are, sir. He says he believed that Smirnoff was funding the assassins, drawing money from the family business. However, no proof of this could be found, and the Smirnoff family would not make any complaint against the man. Investigator Bakushin goes on to say that Petya Smirnoff interceded with the Tsar, whom he had known as a young boy. Piotr Nikolaievich Smirnoff was sentenced to permanent exile from Russia and taken to the border under escort on April 2, 1881. The others, as you know, were all hung."

Boris nodded thoughtfully. How incredible that the Tsar had refused to listen to Tolstoy's pleas for clemency on behalf of the members of "Will of the People" while the vodka maker succeeded in getting his nephew's sentence remitted. Old Petya Smirnoff had been a powerful man in more ways than one.

"Where did Smirnoff go? Does it say?"

"No, sir."

"And that's all we have on him?"

"All that is in this file, sir. If you have any other references, I can—"

"No," Boris said abruptly. "Send me copies of the dossier." He hung up the telephone before the clerk could even acknowledge his order and leaned back in his chair. The sweet smell of revenge to come filled all his senses.

8

COLONEL-GENERAL COUNT HELMUTH VON MOLTKE, Chief of the Imperial General Staff of the German Army, marched imperiously into the *Konferenzsaal* of the red-brick General Staff building on Berlin's Konigplatz, flanked by his deputy, General Count von Waldersee, and their respective aides. Tall, heavy and bald, Moltke was not a very impressive figure. It was said that he lived under the shadow of his illustrious namesake, the uncle who had been, with Bismarck, the architect of the German Empire. That earlier Moltke was the hero of 1870, immortalized by heroic statues all over Germany. One such stood outside the portals of this very building. The younger Moltke was a melancholy, pessimistic man—the Kaiser called him "Gloomy Gus," and so did many others—who "lived above the shop," as they said, maintaining a sumptuous apartment on the top floor of the General Staff building while forever protesting that he preferred the country.

The claim was not without an element of truth. Moltke hated Berlin, with its pretentious, florid, gilded public buildings and its self-satisfied, well-ordered air. The place was too brash for him, too raw. There was no patina of age upon it, even though it was now the third largest city in Europe. Somehow, the mile-long Unter den Linden, with its double avenue of limes ending at the ornate Brandenburg Gate, was just that shade too obviously trying to be the most beautiful avenue in Europe. Somehow, the marble statues of the Hohenzollerns which lined the Sieges Allee were oppressive instead of inspiring. Somehow, the Friedrichstrasse and the Liepzigerstrasse, with their sleek stores and ornate banks jammed with inelegant women and corpulent men, were gross and tasteless. Vice was sold with a world-weary air in the lobbies of Kranzler's and Bauer's and the Hotel Adlon. Such society as there was, was stiff and dull. Unless one was a *von*, one did not mix with the nobility or receive invitations to court. No class mixed with any other. The Junkers, Prussian nobility, dominated the Army and the Civil Service despite the fact that most of them had little money, less taste, and no ability. Looking down the length of the shining conference table at the men assembled around it this July day, Moltke wished yet again that he was on his country estate. God, he thought, I hate Mondays.

"Gentlemen," he snapped, "this meeting is called to order."

Now von Waldersee rose to his feet, clearing his throat self-importantly and glaring at this august gathering of ministers and generals to conceal his nervousness.

"The discussion this morning is to center upon the protocol circulated to you last week. Please signify by raising your right hand if you do not have a copy with you."

One or two hands were raised. Waldersee nodded to one of the two aides, Colonel Gunther von Hummel, who hurried down the room, heels clacking on the parquet floor as he handed out copies of the documents in question. Then he returned to his own seat as noisily as he had left it.

"Gentlemen," von Waldersee said, clearing his throat once more, "I am required to remind you that the contents of the documents in your possession are *strengste geheim*, utterly secret. The contents of these documents or any of the matters reviewed here today are equally secret and may not be spoken of outside this room. The penalty for so doing is death."

The assembled officers and ministers glowered back at von Waldersee, insulted to be reminded of the secrecy of this meeting. Among them von Waldersee recognized the Foreign Minister, Gottlieb von Jagow; his Under-Secretary, Artur Zimmerman; and the Political Secretary, Wilhelm von Stumm. To Stumm's right sat *Reichskanzler* Theobald von Bethmann-Hollweg, and directly across the table from him was the bull-necked figure of General Erich Ludendorff, Chief of the Mobilization Section of the General Staff. General Count von Waldersee sat down, glad that his part in the proceedings was over. You never knew, with people like these, whether they would take as a personal affront the warning one was required to give them as a duty. It was not wise to offend people with the power of a Jagow or a Ludendorff. Gloomy Gus wouldn't back you up if they went after you.

Now Moltke rose slowly to his feet, chair scraping noisily on the floor, saber rattling.

"I have just come from a conference with the Kaiser," he announced. "He has sanctioned the Petersburg Plan."

There was a murmur of interest and approval from the men around the table.

"He agrees, then, that we must declare war?" Jagow said.

"He does," Moltke said. "I have informed him that we of the General Staff consider that war is rapidly becoming inevitable. Imperative! Our plans are drawn up. The Army is ready. The country is ready—eager, even, for war. The Kaiser thinks, and I concur, that the sooner we act, the better."

He paused, as if expecting an interruption. Bethmann-Hollweg opened his mouth to say something and then appeared to think better of it. Moltke nodded, as if pleased with them all.

"You may wish to know the Kaiser's exact words," he said. "I will tell you what he said to me. 'This country' he said, 'has won its position in the world by the sharpness of its swords, not the sweetness of its words. This country's greatness,' he said, 'this country's sole source of greatness is arms—and war!' "

Ludendorff grimaced; he hated breastplate beating of this kind. The Army was riddled with it, almost as if no staff officer could make a decision without exhorting himself to arms on behalf of the Fatherland. He glanced at Gottlieb von Jagow and thought he saw a faint, cynical smile touch the Foreign Minister's lips. Supercilious bastard, he thought. God knew there were fools enough in the Army, but it seemed these days that the career diplomats and the senior civil servants were being recruited exclusively from the ranks of fools, and supercilious fools into the bargain.

"The document which has been circulated," Moltke was saying, "considers the pros and cons of a declaration of general war. It considers also—and hence the importance of the Petersburg Plan—the implications of such an action vis-à-vis Britain, France, and Russia."

"Ah," Bethmann-Hollweg murmured. "Russia. Yes, Russia."

Everyone nodded. Knowing glances were exchanged. Yes, Russia, that was the fly in the ointment, the Russian steamroller. The proposed declaration of war, the march through Belgium to Paris, was based on the old Schlieffen Plan, with modifications by Moltke. It postulated a *blitzkrieg*, a lightning war in which Germany's Army would occupy Paris within forty days of its commencement, before the Great Powers could mobilize properly. The problematic factor was Russia, for Russia was France's ally, and if France were attacked, Russia would immediately mobilize for war. The Russian Army was awesomely large; even in peacetime it numbered one and a half million men. Placed on a wartime footing, four times that many soldiers would be deployed in the field.

"Given that we should contemplate a declaration of hostilities," Bethmann-Hollweg said, choosing his every word with infinite care —"and I am not yet convinced that the moment is opportune—the Reich could in no way countenance the fighting of a war on two fronts at once. Such an error of judgment—" he congratulated himself silently on not using the word "folly" "—would be insupportable."

"We are in agreement on that, Theo," Moltke said gravely.

"There is also another aspect," Bethmann-Hollweg said in his thin, placatory voice. "As aggressors—which is what we would be— we would bring down upon our heads the obloquy of all civilized nations."

"My dear *Reichskanzler*," Moltke said wearily, "we must put aside, the nation must put aside, all platitudes about the responsibility of the aggressor. We are speaking here of Germany's destiny, of historical inevitability. War will come, *Reichskanzler*, be sure of that. What we must do is to ensure that it comes at our behest, at a time chosen by us, at our moment of maximum readiness. What we are talking about is grasping the nettle firmly, bravely—and first!"

"By God, you're right!" Ludendorff growled. "What we need now is action, not talk!"

There were nods and calls of agreement from the men around the long, shining table. Friendless and forbidding Erich Ludendorff might be, but he was hugely respected, tough, granite-hard, a glutton for work. He had risen to Staff rank without the benefit of noble birth, in itself the most enormous feat. All you had to do was look at him, that thick body, the blond moustache and the downturned mouth, the bulge at the back of the neck, the harsh and unforgiving expression. You knew right away that he was a soldier through and through. Not like Moltke, who was thought to be "soft." What else could one think of a man who preferred to play the cello and read philosophy rather than play cards or billiards with his fellow officers? They said he was working on a translation of Maeterlinck. *Maeterlinck!*

"We must!" General von Staab said. "And we can! We're ready!"

His words, too, carried enormous weight. As Chief of the Railway Division, it was he who would carry the burden of mobilizing

108

the Army, of moving two million men and countless hundreds of thousands of tons of artillery, supplies and ammunition through four sectors across the length and breadth of Europe. Merciless with anyone who questioned his judgment, a stickler for detail and possibly a greater glutton for work than even Ludendorff, Staab was one of the most feared men in the German Army. When he talked, people listened.

"You all know the basics of the Schlieffen Plan," Moltke said now. "You will see that for obvious reasons I have added strength to the right wing. Schlieffen's motto was 'Be bold!' Mine is, 'Be bold, but not too bold.' If you will refer to the protocol before you, you will see how it has been revised. The right wing of sixteen corps will attack Belgium, taking Liege and Namur. We do not expect Belgium to resist by force of arms. She will protest, of course, but by that time we shall be in command and on the French frontier. That is vital. If we do not march first through Belgium—and neutrality be damned!—we may be sure the French will, *nicht wahr?*" He allowed himself a slight smile and then proceeded with his exposition. "Now, simultaneously with the right wing pushing through Belgium, our center will invade France via Luxembourg—eleven corps, four hundred thousand men. The left wing of three hundred thousand will entrench itself on the front line in Alsace-Lorraine, south of Metz. The schedule, as you see, is carefully formulated thereafter."

It was indeed; every day's schedule of march was fixed in advance, every contingency considered. The roads through Liege would be open by the twelfth day of mobilization. Brussels was to be taken by M-19, the French frontier crossed on M-22 and Paris occupied on M-39. Victory in forty days.

"It's ambitious enough," the Foreign Minister murmured, urbanely. "The question is whether it's flexible enough. After all, as Klausewitz—"

"We have taken due account of Klausewitz," Moltke said, his voice as urbane as Jagow's but with just a little more edge on it. "I am well aware that military plans which leave no room for the unexpected can lead to disaster. Let me assure you, Gottlieb, that every officer at the *Kriegsschule* and in the field has been trained to supply the correct solution for any given set of circumstances which might arise. Every contingency has been thought of. We are fully prepared: munitioned, armed, poised. We must begin, and soon!"

"Yet still as aggressors," Bethmann-Hollweg said, his voice

faintly aggrieved. He had been ridden over roughshod and he did not like it, and he wanted everyone present to know just how much he did not like it. "Must we go to war without occasion?"

"There will be occasion, *Reichskanzler*," Jagow said, smoothly. "An occasion will present itself. You may rest assured of it."

"May we know what it is to be?" Ludendorff said, his voice as sour as his expression. It was well known that he had little time for the clever-clever boys of the Foreign Ministry. "It does not appear to be in these documents."

Moltke smiled, watching Jagow wriggle. Ludendorff had the most remarkable ability to assimilate information at speed and like a sponge. He had no doubt that, had he been asked, the General could have quoted from any part of the protocol verbatim. An amazing man, Moltke thought, not liking him any better for it. Not for nothing was there a saying in the Army that the best brains produced by the War College went first into the Railway Division. And ended up in the lunatic asylum, Moltke reminded himself, remembering the rest of the saw. He smiled at the thought and Ludendorff scowled, thinking that Moltke was even more than usually condescending this morning.

"I'm afraid not," Jagow said, after noticeable hesitation. "The matter is in the hands of the *Sonderabteilung*. I cannot say more."

There was a silence after he had spoken. Everyone present knew about the special section known as AMSA—*Aussen-ministeriums-sonderabteilung*. It was rumored that it dealt exclusively with international provocation and political assassination, but no one knew very much about it, except that it was controlled by the bland-faced Gottlieb von Jagow. The Foreign Minister's face was impassive, giving no one any clues at all.

"You'll have to give us more than that, Jagow," Bethmann-Hollweg complained, agitation in his voice. "One needs more information than that."

"What one needs does not concern me," Jagow said. "You have asked for an occasion, and I have promised that you will get it. That is all you need to know. In matters of such secrecy, I can do no more. However, I will at least indicate one further aspect: an occasion will arise in the Balkans." He smiled, a sour and worldly smile. "Indeed, an occasion arises in the Balkans every day of the week."

"Very well," Moltke said, bringing the Chancellor's complaints to an end. "Let us now consider the matter of Russia."

"Let us indeed do that," Ludendorff growled. "We have, as our *Aussenminister* has indicated, the guarantee of an occasion to mobilize. Nevertheless, as soon as we do, France will do so too, calling on her allies, Britain and Russia, to support her. At which point we shall be committed to war on two fronts."

"Untenable," Artur Zimmerman said. "Totally untenable."

"With respect, Artur, I am not so sure," Wilhelm von Stumm said. "I think we may be overestimating the abilities of the Russian Army."

"Why so?"

"I spoke at great length with a British military attaché named Hamilton," Stumm said. "He was with the Japanese when they were fighting the Russians. He says that their generals were poor, their intelligence bad, their planning appalling and their security non-existent."

"There are still four million or more of them," Staab growled. "It doesn't make any difference whether they're good, bad or indifferent. Once they are mobilized, they will roll over us like the waves, like the sea! We could not contain such an assault on our rear without reducing our strength on the Western front."

"Which is why we have taken, ah, other measures," Jagow said.

"Other measures?" said Staab, looking up quickly.

"The Petersburg Plan," Jagow said.

"We felt that if we had to fight the Russians," Moltke said, "and it appears inevitable that we may have to, then we should do so on the terms most advantageous to ourselves."

"By knowing their every move before they make it, and their every plan in detail the moment that plan is drawn up," Jagow said.

"A spy?" hazarded Ludendorff.

"A spy," Jagow confirmed.

"He would have to be highly placed indeed," Staab said dubiously, "to have access to that kind of information."

"He is highly placed."

There was a murmur of interest. If Jagow said the man was highly placed, then it was so.

"What do we know about him?" Bethmann-Hollweg said. "Is he reliable? Some of these Russian noblemen would sell their grandmothers for another spin on the roulette wheel, you know."

"Bethmann's right," said Moltke. "You really ought to tell us a little more, Gottlieb."

"I will tell you only this: that the man came to us highly recommended. *Aus* Essen."

Another impressed silence followed his words. If the spy had been vouched for by the Krupps, then the Reich had an espionage coup of the most formidable proportions.

"Are we to be told more?" Ludendorff asked. "The man's name, perhaps, or his background, or how he happened to come to us *aus* Essen? Or is he also to be the personal property of the *Aussenministerium*?"

Jagow smiled his thin, unforgiving smile once again. He knew what lay behind Ludendorff's question. Ludendorff believed that the Foreign Ministry controlled certain matters which would be better and more properly handled by the Army. For his own part, Jagow thought the Army had far too much power already, and he had not the slightest intention of giving them more.

"No names, I'm afraid," he said. "If our man is to be truly effective, he must remain totally anonymous. That is the essence of the Petersburg Plan."

"What a lot of tripe!" Ludendorff barked, but Jagow refused to be drawn. He glanced at Moltke, who nodded. Jagow stood up and surveyed the men around the table with his lordly glance.

"This man is dedicated," he said harshly. "He will work from within Russia to ensure that every move Ivan makes we shall know. Every battle plan that is drawn will be in our hands before the first cannon is fired. We shall make substantial sums of money available to finance the revolutionaries there. Our plan is to destroy Russia from within, and I am confident that we shall do so. A Russia in disarray will be no threat to our Eastern front, and we can concentrate upon the conquest of Britain, France and, if we wish, the rest of Europe too."

He nodded to von Waldersee, who had taken his position by the high double doors at the far end of the conference room. The doors were opened, and orderlies came in bearing trays on which stood glasses of champagne. When everyone had a glass, Moltke proposed a toast.

"Gentlemen," he said, "I give you the Petersburg Plan."

"The Petersburg Plan!" they echoed.

"*Gott strafe Russen!*" Staab shouted.

"*Gott strafe Russen!*" they yelled, emptying their glasses at a gulp and hurling them into the ornate marble fireplace, smashing them to smithereens.

9

CASTLE said goodbye to Moscow with very real regret. He had gotten to know the city and found that in many ways he preferred its atmosphere to the chill sobriety of the capital. But the festivals were done, and he was running out of excuses to stay longer. The rich and fashionable who had graced the glittering balls and banquets were leaving, too, heading for warmer climes: to Tiflis or Sevastopol, to their country *dachas*, to London, to Paris, to the Riviera, to Capri, to take the waters at Pyatigorsk or in Baden, to push small fortunes across green baize tables in casinos in Monte Carlo or Nice. The young officers had returned to their duties, and the royal train had steamed self-importantly out of the Nicholas Station en route to Petersburg. There was already an autumnal lethargy in the Moscow air.

The journey back to Petersburg was as dull as it had been on the way to Moscow. Bare plains, puny trees, long vistas of misted marshland and peaty bog stretching to the limitless horizon. Nearer Tver, the prospect grew steadily more depressing. Networks of drainage channels, peat piled high like rows of coffins, dark woods in which the bare birches looked like bleached bones. Once in a while he saw an onion-domed church, blue and gold, or a huddle of cottages. Otherwise the land was featureless and empty, as devoid of life and personality as the far side of the moon.

At Bologoye, Castle ate a *pirozhk* and drank some tea with a voluble government official named Makarayev, who was sharing his compartment. Like all Russians, Makarayev smelled of tobacco smoke.

"You know Petersburg?" he asked Castle.

"A little," Castle said. "Not at all well."

"Dreary place," Makarayev said, stuffing bread into his mouth with all the delicacy of a baboon. "Hate it myself."

"Why is that?" Castle asked, pushing his plate aside.

"All that rain, fog, damp. All those empty, wide streets. All that red tape, all those uniforms. Hate it. Arrogant place. Don't you want that pie?"

"No," Castle said. "I'm not as hungry as I thought."

"No sense in wasting it," Makarayev said, whipping it away before Castle could comment. "Is there?"

"Are you from Moscow?"

"I am," Makarayev said, pompous as a performing seal. "Proud of it. Wouldn't live in Petersburg to save my life, sir, not to save my life. Every time I have to go there, I say exactly that to the wife. And she agrees with me, sir, she agrees wholeheartedly."

"Look at the place," Makarayev said. "Built on a swamp by a madman. Peter the Great. Indeed. What was so great about killing ten thousand men building his 'Window on the West,' eh? Forty thousand men slaving away day and night in a climate so bad that even the bears avoided it. Only a madman, surely, would begin to build a city where there was no soil and no stone, where every pud of building material had to be dragged there by boat and wagon, where canals had to be dug to drain the water out of the ground, and people had to be ordered to live in the place by Imperial *ukaz*! Who but a madman," Makarayev wanted to know, jabbing a finger into Castle's chest to emphasize every point, "would want to establish his court beneath the strange green skies of Petersburg, where the air was damp and the sting of stagnating water seeped into every building in the city?"

"Sea salt, carbolic acid, smoke and decay," Makarayev said, jabbing away. "That's the smell of Petersburg, sir! Wouldn't live there to save my life. You staying long?"

"I have to," Castle said. "My work, you know."

"Poor fellow," Makarayev said, patting Castle's shoulder in an avuncular fashion. "Still, you're young. That makes a difference. Find yourself a pretty girl—it'll take your mind off the climate. Ha! Ha, ha!" And off he went, still nodding like a Dutch uncle. Castle smiled; perhaps he would take old Makarayev's advice at that, he thought. What had Tatiana Makcheyeva said, the family was "at home" on Thursdays? Friendship with the Makcheyev family would enable him to cultivate the young officers who danced attendance on Tatiana. Like all their breed they were arrogant and thoughtless, and like all their breed they were indiscreet.

The last time he had seen Tatiana had been at the Smirnoff

house. Again, Castle smiled. Calling Sokolnika a house was like describing its owners as generous. One needed a bigger word. Vladimir had invited him to a Sunday luncheon.

"Nothing special," he said. "Just a few people dropping in, sort of goodbye-summer party. Quite informal, so do come if you're free."

"You're going away?"

"Up to *Piter* for the officers' races. Then a business trip to Paris, and on to the Riviera. We've a place down there."

"Lucky old you," Castle said.

"Would you like to go?" Vladimir said. "We've plenty of room."

Castle smiled and shook his head. "I can't get away," he said. "Tell me about these officers' races you mentioned. Where are they held?"

"Every year, before he goes hunting at Spala, the Tsar visits his old regiment at Krasnoe Selo, the Army camp outside *Piter*. There are horse races, and a regimental dinner in the evening."

"And you're going?"

"To the races, yes." Vladimir smiled. "The dinner is very much a royal affair, and I'm afraid I'm not on Nicky's visiting list. Not that I'd want to go, anyway. I haven't much time for the military. I like the races, though."

"You breed horses, don't you?"

"That's right. Half the animals running at Krasnoe will be from Telegin. You must come out next time you're in Moscow. I'm rather proud of it."

"You're very kind," Castle said.

"Sometimes," Vladimir replied, with that self-mocking tone in his voice that Castle had detected several times. It was almost as if Vladimir felt that the character he played in life was a faintly ridiculous one. Yet Castle had seen his confrontation with the thin-faced Boris Abrikosov and knew that beneath the smile and the lazy exterior there was steel; unexpected, perhaps, but no less real.

So he went again to Sokolnika and wandered around the great house as the Smirnoffs greeted their guests, admiring the paintings in the gallery, the splendidly bound books in the library, the fine tapestries and carpets, the ornate ceilings, the intricately patterned parquet floors, the marble staircases. Maidservants curtsied as he passed them, and young men hurrying on errands grinned and bobbed their heads as they went by.

"I thought you said it was a small party," Castle said, when he finally managed to speak to Vladimir. "There must be five hundred people here."

"I don't know," Vladimir said, with a shrug. "One never does at these affairs. Anyway, that's not a big party, is it?"

He means it, Castle thought. Five hundred people was not a big party by Smirnoff standards.

"Big enough," he said with a grin.

"Come along," Vladimir said. "Bring your drink. I'll introduce you to everyone."

He was as good as his word, introducing Castle to so many people that he had all his work cut out to remember their names. Ivan Morosov, director of the huge textile, machine-tool, and manufacturing empire of Vikula Morosov, a thickset, slow-spoken man with dark eyes and fleshy lips; Nikolai Ryabushinsky, a friend and rival of Ivan Morosov's father, Savva; Mikhail Mamontov, son of the railroad baron, tall, thin, elegantly languid, a patron of the arts; Sergei Shchukin and his brothers; the brothers Tretyakov, who had donated an art gallery in their name to the city of Moscow; and, of course, Pierre and Nico Smirnoff. Pierre was huge, bearded, bluff, genial. His brother, although a year younger, looked by far the older of the two, with his pale complexion and beardless face. Nico was as retiring as Pierre was forthright, but Castle did not fail to notice how Pierre turned always to his brother for confirmation of what he said, as if Nico were his constant sounding board.

"We must all be nice to David," Vladimir said when he had introduced them. "Maybe he'll show us how to sell Smirnoffka in America."

"Have you ever tried?" Castle asked, surprised.

"Yes, yes, of course," Pierre told him. "We exhibited at the Centennial Exposition in 1876. But it was impossible to interest anyone in becoming an agent."

"Well," Castle said, "I imagine Jack Daniels would have the same problem here."

"Jack Daniels?" Nico asked. "Who is he?"

"It's the name of an American whiskey," Castle told him.

"Whiskey." Pierre shuddered theatrically. "Isn't that what your Red Indians called 'fire water'?"

"You've never made whiskey here?"

"Never," Pierre said, like a man refusing a blindfold in front of a firing squad.

"How many varieties of liquor do you make?"

116

"More than a hundred," Nico said. "You must realize that there are more than that many vodkas alone, Mr. Castle. Regional types, special blends, local preferences."

"Since nationalization, we have concentrated upon those brands which sell well abroad," Vladimir explained. "All our plain vodka is taken by the government and distributed through the state network along with everyone else's. That is a major aspect of our production here in Moscow. In the Petersburg distillery we concentrate on the luxury lines: the Tsar's vodka, Smirnoffka, and the various liqueurs. Pierre, do you know where Senka is?" asked Vladimir.

"He's around somewhere," Pierre said.

They could not find Vladimir's brother in the house. They went out into the garden, and Vladimir led the way past the lake and beneath a long, sweet-smelling avenue of limes.

"Well, what do you think of all these people?" he said, waving his arm in an all-encompassing movement.

"The ones you introduced me to seemed charming," Castle said, tactfully.

"They're all champagne communists," Vladimir said. "The Morosovs, the Shchukins, Mamontov, Ryabushinsky, all of them. And especially Senka. He's been mixed up with the revolutionaries for as long as I can remember."

"Revolutionaries? Your brother?" Castle echoed. "It sounds like a contradiction in terms."

"I suppose it does," Vladimir said, ruefully. "Yet it's so. Senka was involved in the workers' march, Bloody Sunday, in 1905. He's worked for the Cause ever since."

The way he said the words "the Cause" indicated exactly how he felt about it.

"That's all you'll ever hear from Senka, revolution and the need for it. God knows how many thousand rubles he's given for the Cause. Not to mention the others—Morosov, Mamontov and all the rest of them."

"Why do they do it?"

"An opinion? Well, apart from men like Senka, the ones directly influenced by personal experience, I'd say it's because none of them cares for Nicholas. It's pretty certain that he doesn't care for them. He has no time at all for the 'white city capitalists,' as he calls people like Morosov and we Smirnoffs. The older nobility holds them all in total contempt. They're not welcome in Petersburg circles and they're made to feel it, in spite of the fact that if it wasn't for men like Morosov or my father or old man Mamontov, Russia would still be a backwater of Byzantium."

"And they resent it?"

"I'm sure of it. They're social Darwinists. They believe in free enterprise, in reaching the top because of skill and hard work. They believe in the same democratic freedoms as your American industrialists seem to."

"They believe it, perhaps," Castle said. "But they don't practice it much."

"They can't," Vladimir said. "The Tsar and his clique run this country pretty much the way they want to. The Duma is responsible to the Tsar; we all are. All decisions are ultimately made by Nicholas, and that's why the capitalists can't abide him or his court. That's why they're prepared to finance even the Bolsheviks, if it means getting that vacillating fool kicked off his throne and replaced with a democratic governmental system."

"You sound a little revolutionary yourself," Castle observed.

"Perhaps," Vladimir said, with a shrug of the shoulders. It was plain that he did not wish to answer questions about himself, and Castle wondered why. It was as if he permitted only a limited intimacy.

"You said that Senka lives in Petersburg?"

"Yes, he does," Vladimir said. "He's got a big house on the Fontanka, by the Inzhernerny Bridge."

"That's near the Champ de Mars," Castle observed.

"The Petersburg Sahara," Vladimir smiled. The huge open parade ground, with its sand pockmarked and tossed by the daily drills of the Guards regiments, was known to everyone in the capital as the "Sahara."

"Is he married?" Castle asked.

"Senka?" Vladimir laughed, as though the idea was astonishing. "Hell, no, he's a confirmed mysogynist. He shares the place with Sasha and his family."

"That's Pierre's son."

"You'll get us all sorted out in due course. Yes, Sasha is Pierre's son. His wife's name is Irina."

"Are they here today?"

"Sasha's around somewhere. Irina had a baby a little while ago. Sasha thought it better if she didn't travel just yet. If you want my opinion, I think he was glad to get off on his own for a while."

"She's hard work, then?"

"Irina? Good God, no, she's a delight. But she gives Sasha a hard time. You'll see. I'll take you to meet them when I come to *Piter*." He stopped, as an idea struck him. "But wait, I've got an even better idea. Where did you say you're living?"

"I have a couple of rooms at the Embassy."

"Didn't you say you were trying to find someone to teach you to speak Russian?"

"Yes, I did."

"Then we shall kill two birds with one stone. You must go to Irina for lessons," Vladimir said. "She used to teach history. You two would get along famously."

"But—there are children, aren't there?"

"Oh, Heavens, man, she's got *nyanyas* and maids and all the rest of it. She'll probably be glad of the chance to use her brain. I don't imagine living with Sasha taxes it all that much. And that great big place—come on, let's go and see if we can find Senka."

Half an hour later it was all arranged. Not only would Senka introduce him to Irina Smirnoff when he returned to Petersburg, but Castle would move into the Fontanka house until a suitable apartment could be found for him. It wouldn't be for long, Vladimir promised him; Senka knew everyone. Bemused by their unforced generosity, Castle could find no adequate way to thank them.

"Tush, my dear chap," Senka said. "You may be able to do something for us, one day."

"If I ever can, you won't need to ask," Castle said.

"Good, good," Senka said, smiling absently. He was as unlike Vladimir as one could have imagined. Where the younger man was elegant, Senka was shabby; where his brother was confident and muscular, Senka was hesitant and frail. He had the vague air of an unsuccessful university lecturer and seemed constantly as if he was trying to remember something important that he had forgotten. That such a man supported the cause of the revolutionaries seemed as hard to imagine as the fact that he had marched on the infamous Bloody Sunday of 1905.

"Your brother tells me that you marched with Father Gapon," Castle said. "On Bloody Sunday."

"Yes, that's right, I did," Senka said, patting his pockets one after the other. "Dangerous times, those. Damned nearly got my head shot off, yes, nearly got killed."

Well, almost, he reflected; but no use saying that to this young *istranyetsy*. Foreigners would never understand the Russians, and there was an end of it. Trying to explain to the American why he had marched with the workers that day, and the real truth of what had happened, would be a waste of time. How could he ever comprehend why a man like Senka Smirnoff would become a revolutionary? All that was locked away in Senka's mind and memory; he spoke of it to no one.

It had begun in 1901. He was young then, just another well-to-do young man about Petersburg, with spring just around the corner. He could remember everything about that day, as if it were photographs he was looking at in an album: March 4, 1901, a crisp Monday morning. He decided to go for a walk: along the Fontanka to the Nevsky, and then up the Nevsky to the Winter Palace, back along the Neva embankment to the Troitsky Bridge, across the Sahara and home. He set off early, without a care in the world, a good-looking young man of twenty-two, the son of one of the richest men in Russia, director of the great Smirnoff distillery which stood on an island in the Neva just to the west of the Birzhevoi Bridge. There were not a few ambitious Petersburg mothers who had their eye on Senka as a spouse for their daughters, but none of the vapid beauties he had met at the fêtes and balls of the Petersburg season had so much as quickened his pulse.

Like his brother Vladimir, Senka had grown up rich. The same Petershul education, the same battalions of servants, the same wide range of privilege. He had never questioned his right to any of them. If anyone had asked him, he would have said he had evolved into being a fairly liberal socialist. He did not believe in sweated labor, and went to a great deal of trouble to ensure that the conditions in which people worked at the distillery were decent, insofar as doing so did not interfere with productivity. He was not a fusspot. He left the day-to-day running of the works to his managers and pursued his own interests: the theater, the opera, the ballet, art. He was building a small collection of Impressionist paintings—nothing as grand as that of the Shchukins or Ivan Morosov's, but respectable, as Senka described it, respectable.

March could be a beautiful month in *Piter* if the rains stayed away, as they had done this year. The sparkling air was pearly, opalescent, and the bright cloudless sky a perfect pastel blue. The keen wind from the Baltic stung his nostrils, and he was glad he had worn the overcoat with the beaver collar; there were precious few windbreaks along the hundred-foot-wide Nevsky Prospect. As he stopped to look at the posters outside the Arcade Theater, the smell of fresh coffee from the Café de Paris tempted him. He decided to finish his walk first. There were plenty more cafés.

Up ahead, near the Catherine Canal, there seemed to be some sort of disturbance. He could see crowds and black-uniformed policemen. He noticed a gray-uniformed officer running toward them and shrugged. *My kalutsky*, he thought, it's none of my business. He turned off the Nevsky into the semicircular colonnade leading into Kazan Cathedral. He gave a mock salute, as he always did, to the statue of Marshal Kutuzov, and, as always, Marshal Kutuzov took no notice. Once again, Senka heard shouting, as though a crowd of marchers was approaching. He could see no one. He walked across the front of the cathedral to the western side and realized that the sound was coming from the small garden square beyond it. Frowning, Senka decided to investigate.

It wasn't a square, actually; it was a semicircular patch of ground with trees and benches and an old drinking fountain, the curve of the semicircle bounded by ornate iron railings. It was packed with shouting people, workers, women. The cutting wind made Senka turn up his coat collar as he stepped across the wide Kazanskaya. He saw a familiar face, a foreman at one of the bottle factories.

"*Gospodin* Pavlov!" he shouted. "What's going on here?"

Before the man could answer, a wicked blow across the shoulders knocked Senka sprawling to his knees. As he fell, he heard the clatter of hoofs and scuttled aside instinctively. People nearby were shouting in panic, and now he could hear the hoarse yells of the Cossacks. They rode their horses into the people, whacking at them with sheathed sabers, with thick knotted knouts, batons. Anyone who raised a hand was instantly struck down. A man sprawled moaning at Senka's feet, and a woman—his wife?—fell on her knees beside him, her face streaming with blood. There were flat, loud reports. My God, they're shooting, he thought. He saw two other men pick up a woman, whose body was wet with blood, and run out of the square with her. People were screaming with fear, running like field mice from a thresher. The Cossacks wheeled into a formation and herded the people ahead of them out of the little garden. Some of them were laughing.

Senka could not believe what he had just witnessed. His whole body trembled with outrage. He saw a policeman coming toward him. He stepped forward and stopped the man.

"You!" he snapped. "What's all this about? I demand an explanation!"

The policeman looked at him, and Senka realized that his clothes were soiled and disheveled from the fall he had taken. For no reason that he could identify, he felt the first faint feather touch of fear.

"What's your name?" the policeman snapped back.

"Smirnoff," Senka said, realizing as he said it that the name would carry no weight with the policeman. It was the fourth most common name in Russia. He reached into his pocket to get one of his visiting cards, and as he did, the policeman's face changed suddenly, blind panic obliterating his expression. He flailed wildly at Senka with his baton, catching Senka above the left eye and slamming him back against the railings, blood streaming from a deep cut above his eyebrow.

"Watch out, this one has a gun!" the policeman shouted to one of his fellow officers. Rough hands grabbed Senka and tore his coat open, ripping his cravat and shirt. His pockets were rifled and his wallet was pulled out. Then he was pushed into the milling crowd. His anger flared through his dizziness and he burst forward toward the policeman who was going through his wallet, taking out the money.

"Give me that, you—!"

He got no further. The big policeman simply hit him in the face, and Senka fell unconscious at the feet of the cowed onlookers. When he awoke, he found he was in a cell with a dozen other men. His face was swollen and stiff with blood.

"Well, comrade, you've learned what it's like to be a worker today and no mistake," one of the men said with a sneer. The others all laughed; there was no sympathy in the sound. If there was anything at all, it was satisfaction, Senka thought, a vengeful pleasure that for once, someone of his class had been beaten and kicked, too.

"Where is this place?" he managed to say through swollen lips. "Is there any water?"

"Oh, yes, Your Excellency," one of the men said. "Would you like it in the silver cup or the golden one?"

"Come on, leave him alone," a younger man said. "If he was in the square, he was with us, not against us."

"His kind are always against us," someone said. "He's probably Okhrana." There was a silence. It was well known that the Okhrana put informants and spies into prison cells with other prisoners, hoping to get information that would help hang them.

"My name is Arsenii Petrovich Smirnoff," Senka said. "My father is Petya Smirnoff, owner of the Smirnoff distilleries. You must have heard of him."

"My name is Smirnoff, too," said the dark, thickset man sitting on Senka's right, who had been one of the first to speak. "But that doesn't make me one of the vodka Smirnoffs."

"I had visiting cards in my wallet," Senka said. "I could show them to you. But that policeman took everything."

"Well, brother, at least you're alive," the man said. "Thank whatever God you believe in for that."

"I don't know why I was arrested," Senka said. "I don't even know what the demonstration was about."

He learned that the demonstrators had been protesting the "temporary" rules which had been imposed on the universities by Nicholas Bogolepov, the former Minister of Education. Although Bogolepov was dead—he had been assassinated the preceding month—his "temporary" rules had remained in force. They provided that in some cases students involved in demonstrations could be forcibly inducted into the Army.

"Yet, knowing that was so, you demonstrated anyway?" Senka said, in amazement. Now that his eyes were becoming accustomed to the gloom, he could see that a number of his cellmates were young students.

"What do you expect us to do?" one of them asked. "Sit still, do nothing?"

"We have to do something," another said.

"We can't live under repression forever, being beaten with Cossack sabers and whips every time we protest!"

"We must overthrow the autocrat!"

"Give the land back to the people!"

Hotheads, he thought, idealists. The country was full of them. They all wanted change; none of them knew how to effect it. Some were for murdering the Tsar. Every time it was tried, the repression which followed grew more brutal, the pogroms that decimated the people of the villages more awful. Some were for giving all the land back to the peasants, but the peasants did not know what to do unless they were told. Illiteracy was staggeringly high: seventy percent and more among adults between the ages of sixteen and sixty. Power to the peasants was not the answer either. There were a dozen groups, a hundred propositions, a thousand ideals. They were all useless. Nothing changed; no one wanted change badly enough, and most certainly not the people with the power.

He was, he learned, at the Spassky police station. The woman he had seen being carried from the square had been dead, shot by one of the Cossacks. He learned that there had been others in the demonstration than students: Piotr Struve, Professor Baranovsky from Moscow University, the theatrical director V. E. Meyerhold.

"What did you think we were, rapists, murderers, thieves, derelicts?" His namesake Smirnoff laughed, roughly. "You think all demonstrators are rabble?"

"I have to confess," Senka said, "that I've never given it any thought at all. Except that they were a nuisance. Strikes, marches, slogans. Always the same: more money, more food, more freedom, more this, more that. They never seemed to want to give anything. Just take: whatever they could get."

"Brother," the dark man said, "you've got a lot to learn."

Senka was in the Spassky cells for three days with the other demonstrators. By the time he was released, he was a convert. "My eyes were opened," he was to say afterward. "I could never close them again."

A few days after his release, he visited his lawyer, Anton Maslov. Anton was Senka's age. They had been at school together, and Anton had visited Sokolnika many times. He was a big man now, balding slightly, deep-voiced, broad-chested. He looked as fierce as a brigand, a fervent fighter for the rights of the young radicals and revolutionaries who fell into the hands of the police or the *Okhrana*. He often defended them in court, charging no fee. He had been arrested several times himself.

"I can always justify such cases," Anton would laugh. "I simply charge clients like you more."

"Why do you do it?" Senka would ask him. "Surely you know that if they got their revolution, you would be among its first victims."

"But, of course," Anton said, spreading his hands in a gesture entirely French. "*Naturellement*. You and I, dear Senka, will be the first to go when the revolution comes. They'll have no use for the likes of us, with our country estates and our little palaces on the Fontanka. Oh, they'll shoot us with a great deal of relish."

"Yet you defend them. Support them."

"They are right, Senka," Anton had said, with quiet conviction that stilled all argument. "They are right to want to change this sick society of ours. And if you give it any sort of intelligent thought, you will know it."

They had argued often along such lines, then. After the incident in the little garden square near the Kazan Cathedral, they argued no more. He had enough, Senka had always thought. A decent house, a job to do, decent clothes, a useful life. Now he realized how utterly self-centered he had been, how totally ignorant he was of the conditions in which his fellowmen lived and labored. Even the fairly liberal way in which he treated his own employees was no better than it had to be, although even that was far better than the lot of the average man. There was no welfare for unemployed workers; if you didn't work, you starved. There was no pension for the aged, few hospitals, no free medicine. The system which Senka and men like him condoned by their apathy had no more respect for human life than a hawk has for a sparrow. The poor lived lives of grinding squalor, while the Tsar and his minions vacillated in Byzantine splendor at the apex of a pyramid of privilege unmatched anywhere in the rest of the world. The Minister of the Imperial Court, Baron Fredericksz, had under his command fifteen great officers of state, all with imposingly grandiloquent and meaningless titles: Keeper of the Privy Purse, Master of the Household, Officer of the Almonry, Master of the Ceremonies, Master of the Imperial Music. Altogether, the court could call upon the services of more than one and a half thousand persons of noble blood, all of whom in turn had their personal servants, and on and on, ad infinitum. And for what, Anton would shout, incensed as always by the sheer, senseless waste, for what? To attend to the needs of two adults and five children whose sole contribution to the welfare of their people was to appear infrequently on public occasions and wave to the crowds.

"I agree with you," Senka said. "That whole business is nothing but a pantomime. But how can it be changed? What will we put in its place?"

"A world of social equality, Senka," Anton said. "A world where it isn't a sin to be born poorer than another man. A world where a father needn't sell one of his children so he'll have enough kopecks to feed the others. A world with justice in it for everyone, not just the rich and the powerful."

"It's a pipe dream," Senka said. "It can't be done."

"It can," Anton said, quietly. "And it will."

There was a long silence between them, thinking time, not at all uncomfortable. Each knew the other's mind well by now. Anton slowly filled his pipe, lit it and puffed away, savoring the bite of the tobacco. He waited until Senka spoke.

"I know nothing about making revolutions, Anton."

"Don't worry," Anton said, with that gentle smile. "There are more than enough teachers."

Senka was eager to learn and plunged into this new world with all his energy. If some of the comrades he encountered seemed to regard his efforts with ill-concealed contempt, he did not let that upset him. Each man, he believed, could do something that another could not. He was not a violent man, and did not believe that violence ever justified itself, but he did not argue against those who did. They were just as likely to be right as he was. He preferred, however, to try more peaceful means, and labored assiduously to build up the circulation and distribution network of the revolutionaries' newspaper, *Iskra*, "The Spark." It was produced in Paris by Vladimir Ulyanov—Lenin, as he preferred to call himself. Many of the revolutionaries used nicknames, or *klichkas*. His life became a strange mixture of what it had been before and something new. He still lived the life of a well-to-do young man about town, still saw to his duties at the distillery, still attended the round of teas and dances and balls, concerts, operas, ballet and theater and art gallery as he had always done. At the same time, often only minutes after some formal reception or grand function, Senka and Anton and other young people like them put themselves at the disposal of the growing revolutionary underground. They were part of a chain stretching from Paris to Petersburg, via Berlin, Warsaw, Moscow, Riga, and the Finnish border. They helped nameless men with hooded eyes to cross the frontier in or out of Russia. They manhandled crates of arms and ammunition and explosives, stenciled with Turkish hieroglyphics or peremptory German. They circulated forbidden newspapers and pamphlets, feeling rather brave and fine about it, and pretending not to notice the contempt of men like Azev and Sazonov and the dead-eyed Boris Savinkov, the Socialist Revolutionaries who had vowed to rid Russia of its cancers with fire and the sword.

For four years Senka worked hard, a committed man, but he was too intelligent not to see that he and his friends were merely being used by the harder elements of the revolutionary underground. Lenin, Trotsky and the rest of them did not care who they used or how; the end justified any means. Even that would have been acceptable had there been any end in sight, but there was not. The Tsar was still the Tsar, giving thanks to God for the birth of a baby son who would perpetuate his dynasty. Nothing changed.

Senka went, on the night of January 8, 1905, to a meeting of the

Society of Factory and Plant Workers at the old Tashkent Cafe on the Peterhof Chaussée. He had heard that Father Gapon was to appear, and he was anxious to meet the priest. They said he was from the Poltava region and had studied at Petersburg University before becoming Chaplain at the Kresty prison. He had a strong following among older, conservative workers.

He arrived late, a good-looking, black-haired man with dark eyes and a thin face.

His voice was hoarse and he looked distraught, as though he had many urgent decisions awaiting him. He told everyone in the crowded, smoky room that he had informed the Minister of the Interior, Mirsky, that on the morrow the workers would come to see the Tsar at the Winter Palace and submit a petition of their demands to him.

"And what do we ask for, comrades? An eight-hour day, a decent working day for every man. Is that so much? A rule of law, freedom of speech, of press, the right to assemble. Is that so much? The right to strike. Is that so much, comrades?"

There were cheers from the crowd, applause from the workers, several hundred of them, roughly dressed men with lined faces and gnarled hands, their caps clutched tight in their fists. No revolutionaries these, Senka thought. He recognized one or two from his own factory in the crowd; they avoided his eyes.

"We will go the Tsar!" Gapon shouted. "We will tell him how we suffer. We will ask him—Father, forgive us. Understand us. Help us, we are your children. We know that you love us and work for us, but they don't tell you how they beat us and starve us! They don't tell you they treat us like animals, that we don't know how to read or write. Help us, *Batyushka*, we will say. We are your children!"

They were children indeed, Senka thought, moved in spite of himself. He heard someone ask what they would do if the Tsar would not receive them.

"He will receive us," Father Gapon said.

"But if he does not?" the worker persisted. "What shall we do then?"

"We will do nothing violent," the priest said. "Understand me, children—nothing violent. If the Tsar will not receive us all, perhaps he will receive a small delegation, chosen from among us."

"And what if he won't do that, either?" someone said.

"Then this is not our Tsar," the priest said, very sadly. "This is not the Tsar."

"Then he is not the Tsar," the workers muttered like a litany.

"Then there will be no more Tsar." They said the word "Tsar" as others would say "God."

Father Gapon held up both his hands in a gesture of benediction. "If we need to die, we shall die together," he said, his voice soft as gossamer. "We will swear to stand, all for one and one for all. Go now, and may God go with you."

The people began to rise from their seats slowly, as if reluctant to face the bitter January cold outside. Some of the men went to the front of the hall and shook the priest's hand. Mothers held out their babies to be blessed.

Strangely moved and somehow uneasy, Senka made his way to the home of Anton Maslov. Anton opened the door himself, his face concerned.

"My God, man, come in," he hissed. "I was sure you'd been arrested."

"What on earth for?" Senka said.

"There's trouble," Anton said. "Have you got a gun?"

"Of course I haven't got a gun," Senka said, smiling foolishly. Perhaps this was Anton's idea of a prank, he thought. "What would I want with a gun?"

"Haven't you got eyes, man?" Anton said. "Are you deaf as well as blind? They're moving troops all over the city. They're setting up guard posts on the bridges, on the boulevards. They say regiments have been brought in from as far away as Revel and Pskov."

"My God!" Senka said. "I'd better try and warn Gapon."

"Take this," Anton said, thrusting something into his hand. Senka felt the cold metallic bulk of the pistol, and a chill touched his heart.

"No," he said. "I can't. I won't."

"Take it!" Anton hissed.

Shaking his head, Senka turned away and hurried down the street, not looking back. A raw wind whipped tendrils of snow through the gloom. There were halos of frost around the street lamps. As he walked toward the Admiralty, he could see Red Cross posts and field kitchens had been set up at intersections, but nobody stopped him as he hurried across the frozen Neva toward Georgi Gapon's little house in the worker's quarter. When he arrived, breathless and perspiring despite the bitter cold, the priest was not there. No one would tell him where Gapon was. It was already growing light.

At about eight thirty, the sun rose. Workers were already gathering in the street, smoking cigarettes, huddled in small groups. Someone was assuring his comrades that even if the troops were on the streets, they would not open fire on the marchers.

"We'll take them by the hand and say, 'Brothers, you wouldn't fire upon your own, would you?' "

"Course not!" someone shouted. "Stands to reason!"

The stewards decided to organize the march with women, children, and the more elderly workers in the front, so that the Tsar— and the troops—could see that everyone was in this, not just the militants. A people's manifestation, they kept saying; they'll see that it's a people's manifestation. At the head of the column was to be a very big portrait of the Tsar, flanked by two smaller ones of the Tsar and Tsaritsa. Someone had made a large white banner, on which were painted the words "Soldiers! Do not fire upon the people!" Many of the men and women were carrying icons and crosses and religious banners.

At eleven, when the sun was high and bright and it was growing steadily warmer, the procession set off. Father Gapon and his bodyguard of workers led the way. They began to sing "Save Us, O Lord, Thy People," and policemen lining the route took off their caps as the portraits of the Tsar were borne past. Senka could not get near the priest. Every time he tried, one of the bodyguards pushed him away.

"Keep back!" they yelled, pushing him away. "Stay in formation!"

Five columns of marchers, all moving at the same snail speed, began converging on the great square before the Winter Palace. From Kolpino they came, twenty-four versts outside the city. From the workers' quarters on Vasilyevsky Island. From the teeming slums of the city, thousands and thousands of shuffling men, women and children, bearing icons, singing hymns, exalted in their hope. Senka's heart was beating wildly. Something awful was in the air; he knew it. The very wind smelled strange.

Ahead of them lay the Narva triumphal arch, commemorating the victories of the Russian Guard during the Napoleonic war. Sunlight glinted on Klodt's Victory, her chariot drawn by six horses. The procession moved into the square and suddenly, like magic, a squadron of cavalry burst into view, breastplates gleaming in the bright morning sunlight. They rode straight into the crowd, scattering people like ninepins. There were hoarse shouts of fear, screams, as the marchers streamed to the safety of doorways, away from the center of the street and the flailing hoofs of the horses.

"Re-form!" Senka heard someone shouting. "Have faith! Don't be afraid, join hands!" It sounded like Gapon's hoarse voice, but he could not be sure. He joined hands with a young worker marching on his right and a boy of perhaps sixteen on his left. The procession moved forward again, singing solemnly, confused but still confident. It was all a mistake; it would be all right now. Senka heard the clatter of hoofs as the cavalry turned behind them. In the same moment, or so it always seemed to him when he tried to recall the exact sequence of events in later years, there was a noise like a string of firecrackers being set off. There were screams up ahead. For a moment, no one realized what was happening. Then Senka saw the elderly men carrying the portrait of the Tsar fold to the ground like dropped washing. Hidden troops were firing on them from the shelter of the bridge. People were rushing in all directions, mindless with panic. Here and there they lay on the ground, blood staining the hard-packed snow. The boy holding Senka's hand was catapulted backward, his head a pulped mass of splintered bone and jellied brains. Men, women and children slipped to the ground as though someone had cut strings in their legs. There were shouts of fear, disbelief. Some of the marchers were still, incredibly, moving forward into the hail of bullets, chanting hymns. Confused, astonished, Senka started forward as though to stop them. Then he saw Georgi Gapon fall to the ground. His heart bounded into his breast, and terror coursed through him as he realized his own peril. Oh, Jesus, they're going to kill us all, he thought, and turned and ran without volition to the shelter of a low wall nearby. He scrambled over it, heard the shouts of the soldiers, the popping rattle of the rifles. It did not seem possible that such a sound could connote danger, yet the rain of fire on the street had felled dozens. Senka lay face down on the cold ground, body heaving in panic.

After a while, he crawled down the slope below the wall to the safety of the Yekaterinhof Park. He was trembling, harrowed with guilt and grief. He had run like an animal to save his life. There had been absolutely nothing else that he could have done, and yet the knowledge that he had done so seared his soul. Who had seen him? What would they think? What would they say?

The bloodshed and killing went on all day. In the Shlisselburg Tract and near the Academy of Arts on Vasilyevsky Island, the marching workers were ruthlessly decimated. The angry mob broke into gun shops for weapons, tore down telegraph poles to make barricades. At the Troitsky Bridge more were killed: forty-eight dead and more than a hundred wounded. Even so, the surging march was irresistible. The workers went forward into the Palace Square. Imperial troops were already in formation there. The crowd milled forward against them like sea against rock. Two thousand soldiers were arrayed around the Winter Palace; cannon had been aligned, facing the mob. A little after two in the afternoon a short, red-faced officer marched about, shaking his fist at the people who were waiting for the Tsar to appear.

"Get out of here!" he kept yelling, his fat jowls shaking. His face glistened with perspiration, his anger covering an obvious fear. He waved his saber at the Kolpino marchers again and again. "Get out of here! Get out of the square! You've been warned!" he shouted. "Disperse or we'll fire!"

"We're here to see the Tsar!" a woman in dark clothes shouted. She had a red kerchief tied around her hair. "We're here to find the truth. Will you shoot us for that?"

A bugle sounded. Heads turned in the crowd. A detachment of the crack Preobrazhensky Guard marched out into the square and formed two lines opposite the Alexander Garden.

"What are they doing?" people said. "Is it a parade? Is the Tsar coming?"

The front rank dropped to one knee. The bugle sounded again, and both ranks leveled their rifles at the crowd. There was a stillness, a silence. The people could see what was going to happen, but they could not believe what they were seeing.

"You wouldn't fire on us, lads, would you?" someone shouted to the iron-faced soldiers. As an answer, the rifles blazed. Again and again and again and again. The bullets scythed people down like ripe corn. Broken bodies lay sprawled and torn, like smashed dolls, bleeding, dying. In the gardens, in the square, there was panic. People clawed at each other as they tried to escape the relentless, random death coming at them. The rifles roared in a regular rhythm, like a woman beating a carpet. Bugles sounded again above the shouts of terror. The guardsmen wheeled about-face, the front row dropping again to one knee. People knew what that meant now. They scattered like birds as the soldiers volleyed first at those on the Palace Bridge and then at the crowd near the Admiralty.

Another bugle call, another formation, and the Preobrazhensky unleashed the fury of their fire on the defenseless spectators near the arch of the General Staff building. At the same time, Cossacks on the Isaakievskaya began to shoot indiscriminately into the crowds, some of whom were innocent Sunday afternoon strollers. Troops fanned out from the Admiralty, driving panicked civilians before them like stampeding cattle, shooting them in the back as they ran. The slaughter went on until the merciful coming of darkness, swirling snow, bitter winds.

Senka slowly made his way back to the center of the city. His terror had vanished. In its place was an icy vacuum. He slouched along, head down, shoulders hunched against the snow and the wind, drowning in shame, torn between feeling that he should have stood his ground and the knowledge that had he done so, they would have killed him. Cossacks came down the street, sabers drawn, dark eyes alert. Senka slipped into side streets to avoid them, passing stores whose windows had been smashed in by looters.

Snow fell and more, snow on snow, silently blanketing the city. In the vast Dvortzovaya, dark figures were moving slowly around the square, huddled, iron-faced, from body to crumpled body, finding their dead. Carts bearing coffins creaked across the bridges and down the Nevsky, followed by silent men and sobbing women. Senka bared his head in tribute as they passed in the whirling snow. Nobody even looked at him; they were locked in the prison of their own grief.

Much later, or so it seemed, he found himself beneath the vast granite monument to Alexander I in the center of the Palace Square. He looked up at the lighted windows of the green and white Winter Palace, a tiny figure alone in the white emptiness. The soldiers were gone now, back to their barracks. All the people were gone. The merciful snow covered all. Bloody Sunday was over.

"*Ubetsa!*" Senka shouted at the top of his voice. "Assassin!" He did not know that the Tsar was not even in Petersburg, that the whole march and all the killings had happened to no purpose, to no avail. It would not have mattered then if he had known. The word was torn from him, an eruption of his own shame and grief. The sound was lost in the soft, swirling vastness of the snowy square. After a while, Senka turned away. The wind was like a razor, but he did not feel it.

Bloody Sunday was his turning point. Until that day he had been prepared to listen to both sides of the argument, but not anymore. He espoused the cause of the Bolsheviks, unfashionable though that was, and made generous donations to Party funds, even persuading his own friends and his father's friends to do the same. He argued revolution on every occasion that he could and lived his life "on the edge of the very edge," as they said in those days.

They were all confident that Bloody Sunday was but the beginning of a total revolution. It never came. The years went by, four, six, eight years, and still it did not come. No one could make it happen, not even Lenin. Revolution was out of fashion.

"What difference would it make, my dear Senka?" the titled fops would ask him in the white-painted drawing room of Margarita Morosova's mansion on the corner of the Smolensky Boulevard. "What earthly difference would it make?" And they would leave to attend their séances, their teas, their mistresses. The country was detached from reality. Day by day and week by week the terrorists killed the Tsar's minions. In reprisal the Tsar's other minions murdered the peasants and nothing changed, nothing changed.

In 1912, when the first legal Bolshevik newspaper appeared, Senka was its financier. Its editor was a little fellow from Georgia with dark brown hair, beard and moustache. His face was long and narrow, pockmarked and swarthy. Lenin wrote that he had been his chief lieutenant in the Caucasus. His name was Josif Djugashvily. From other sources, Senka learned that Josif had also been the brains behind a holdup in Tiflis which had netted the Bolsheviks an enormous influx of funds in 1907. Expecting a bandit, he found an idealist. Josif was well read, softly spoken. They talked of Thackeray and Balzac and Darwin and Victor Hugo as they worked on plans for a new newspaper. It was to be a direct competitor to the Menshevik journal, *Ray*.

" 'Heaven'!" Josif said, contemptuously. "What sort of name is that for a workers' newspaper? Ours will be better. Like the one I edited in Tiflis."

"What was it called?"

"*Brdzola*, 'The Struggle.' "

"That's good. We could use that."

"No," Josif said. "We were in hiding then, underground. Now we don't need to hide. I want to call this paper something more . . . victorious. *The Workers' Truth*, how about that?"

"Bombastic," Senka said.

"Oh?" Josif said, his dark face twisting. He did not like to be contradicted, and even the mildest and most gentle mockery was taken personally. There was something of the brigand in him after all, Senka decided. Perhaps it was because he was so short that he reacted so violently to everything. Well, it took all sorts to make a revolution as Lenin said. One did not do it wearing white gloves.

"Truth is a word which stands alone, Josif," he said. "It belongs to no one."

"That's good!" Josif said. He had an attractive smile. "I like it. *Pravda*, 'The Truth'! That's what we'll call it."

"Good idea," Senka said, concealing his own smile.

"Now, we'll need lots of money," Josif said. "Lots of that Smirnoff money."

Senka nodded, just a trifle wearily. There had been so many false starts, so many thousands of rubles poured down the drain for pamphlets full of inflammatory nonsense. Well, perhaps this shoemaker's son from Gori would be different.

"Stalin," he said, absentmindedly.

"I beg your pardon?" Castle said.

"Oh, excuse me," Senka replied, coming back to the present with a jolt. "It's the name of someone I know. Not his real name, his Party name: Stalin."

"The man of steel," Castle said. "Sounds ominous."

"Josif?" Senka smiled. "No, he's a talker, a dreamer."

"There seems to be a great deal of talk about revolution," Castle observed.

"You're right, yes, absolutely right," Senka said. "They all talk and talk and talk, but that's all. Ask anyone here, any of them, they'll all say the same thing, they hate the Tsar, he's got to go. Just ask them and they'll tell you, yes? Down with Bloody Nicholas! Then they go home to their soft beds and their fat wives and they forget it."

"What about this man Rasputin?" Castle asked. "Do people feel the same way about him?"

"Yes, definitely so," Senka said. "All Petersburg is in a furor over the man. They say he has a hold over the royal family. None of the people who sponsored him into society will have anything to do with him anymore, none of them, no. They all say the same thing; you'll hear it all when you come to *Piter*. It's all part of the same sick society we live in. You see, that's it exactly. Just a symptom of the disease."

"In what way?"

"Look around you; tell me what you see. In the theaters, in government offices, everywhere, what do you see? Indolence, that's what! Bewilderment! What's it all about? People don't know. They're bewildered, and they ask someone to tell them what to do. Only nobody knows, you see. Nobody cares. What does it all matter, they say. See how they all want the latest thing, the newest fad, a motor car, a new dress, anything. Then, when they get it, they find they never wanted it, and they're confused, yes? Bewildered. They have run out of wholesome things to want, yes? So now, they want séances, yes? Tarot, palmistry, fortune telling, other men's wives, crystal gazing, astrology. None of them is worth the gunpowder it would take to blow them up!"

"You feel strongly about it," Castle said, trying to just keep Senka talking. He was surprised by his sudden eloquence.

"No example to follow for anyone," Senka said. "Empty pantomime from our rulers. How can one expect anything else from their clique? Precious scoundrels, every one of them, yes? Not a trace of integrity, not a trace. Idle, jealous, and dull they are. Very, very dull, divorcing and remarrying for no other reason than that it is something to do, that's all. No artistic sense whatsoever, no talent. Yet somehow, they control our destiny. All Russia is at the mercy of a religious fanatic and a disreputable *starets*, and nothing changes, nothing! Well, you know, I've enjoyed our little discussion, yes? We must talk again. You seem to have the right idea."

Off he went, patting his pockets like a pipe smoker who has mislaid his tobacco. Bemused by the waterfall of words which had fallen upon him, Castle watched the man walk away and permitted himself a wry grin. There was something about Senka Smirnoff that he couldn't quite pin down. It was almost as if the man had assumed a role, like an actor who has after many attempts finally mastered a part and will never alter his performance.

He decided to take a walk beside the lake, watching Pierre Smirnoff's guests enjoying themselves. They must know where all this comes from, he thought. They must be aware of the great mass of peasantry and workers who make all this possible. Is that why they talk so much of change, of revolution, yet do so little? Is that why the rich use their wealth to encourage revolutionary organizations? Guilt, a sense of not deserving to own what they possess? Did that account for Vladimir's diffidence, Senka's anger?

Right now, while beautifully dressed women trailed delicate hands in the warm water of the little lake, the workers in the Smirnoff bottling plants would be halfway through their fifteen-hour day. Smirnoff was an enlightened employer and paid above-average wages, with many benefits for his people. There were plenty of other factories where a man would work the same fifteen-hour day for six days a week and be paid less than five rubles for it, two and a half dollars. Twenty rubles a month for a man, ten for a woman, seven or less for a child; children worked alongside their parents. A family of five working in a factory might make fifty rubles a month, out of which their employer would deduct money for rent, fines for lateness, and so on. Twenty-five dollars a month gross, and they lived in a dormitory provided by the factory, nothing more than a warehouse for labor divided into tiny rooms called *kamorki* in which as many as four families might be housed. The bare plank beds were crowded together, touching each other. There was no privacy, unless flimsy cloth partitions or plaited matting could be said to provide it. One table and one chair served ten people. Toilets were communal. Castle had seen the *kamorki*. They were worse than prisons. He could not understand how people could be made to live in them, knowing that others lived in palaces. His thoughts angered him. By God, they'll make a revolutionary out of me if I'm not careful, he told himself. He almost laughed aloud at the thought.

The train was pulling into the Nicholas Station now and the *provodnik* came in to get the luggage, letting in the Petersburg smell of sea and salt. Castle walked toward the waiting line of *izvostchiki*. The trip to Moscow had been well worth the taking; he had added a dozen more names to the list he was compiling. Some of them were part of the clique surrounding the *starets*, Rasputin, the puppetmasters to those tune it was said the holy man danced. There were others, however, and although he did not yet know whom, one of them was the man David Castle had been sent to Petersburg to find. And to kill.

10

BY THE TIME Tatiana came home to Petersburg, her broken heart was beginning to mend. She knew that she would always cherish Sergei in a special place in her heart. His marriage to Katrina Smirnova was, after all, not by choice but by the arrangement of the two families. Katrina was not Sergei's type; she was altogether too serious a person, altogether too deeply committed to God. Tatiana had never seen her so much as angry. Sergei could never love someone like that. He liked to dance, to laugh, to have fun. He loved her and always would. She quite enjoyed the thought of its being a little tragic.

In the middle of September, a royal page delivered to the Makcheyev house on the Zakharevskaya a personal invitation from the Tsaritsa, bidding Tatiana to come to Tsarskoe Selo for the winter months as maid in waiting to her namesake, the Grand Duchess Tatiana. On the same Thursday afternoon, there was an inundation of visitors: Nicky Vasnetsov, on his way back to join his regiment, with Vasya Kirsanov, jaunty as ever, and dear Paul Dubinsky. They drank wine and told Alex jokes and all the military gossip. He wanted to know all about the royal summer: the pilgrimage made by the Tsar to retrace the route of his ancestor, Mikhail Romanov, to the throne of Russia.

"It was fantastic," Nicky said. "Awesome, I'd say. We went to Vladimir, to Suzdal, to Bologyubovo, Nizhni Novgorod, and Yaroslavl, Rostov, Kostroma. What a procession! You can't imagine it, Alexander Frankovich. All the way down the Volga, miles and miles and miles, you could see peasants lining the banks, on both sides, thousands of them!"

"Some of them dashed into the water," Vasya said. "To get a better look at the royal steamer. And in the towns, I saw people fall to their knees and kiss the Tsar's shadow as he passed. Everywhere we went, the people cheered and cheered, women, children, everyone! We were deafened by the noise."

"It was incredible," Paul added. "So was the parade in Moscow. You saw it, didn't you, Tatiana?"

"Of course," Tatiana said. "You were all very handsome, very smart."

"What a day it was," Paul said. "What a day!"

A brilliant blue-sky day in June, Nicky told Alex. Alone, sixty feet ahead of his Cossack escort, the Tsar rode through the Iversky Gate and into the Red Square. Tatiana could see it all again, the crowds everywhere shouting and cheering, the clatter of the horses' hoofs on the cobblestones of the great open space, the sun striking flashes off the golden clock in the Spasskiya belfry, St. Basil's Cathedral down the hill looking like a huddled group of Turkish sultans.

"Bit risky that, letting the Tsar ride unescorted," Alex huffed. "Wouldn't have been allowed in my day."

"Well, sir, things are a little different now," Nicky said, tactfully. "There aren't any assassins waiting to kill the Tsar. The people love him; that was plain to see everywhere we went."

They sat for an hour or more, talking about the sights of that day and other days. They had gone to Berlin as escort to the Tsar and Tsaritsa, for the wedding of the Princess Victoria-Louise to the Duke of Braunschweig-Luneburg.

"Sergei knows Berlin well," Paul said. "He knew all the best places to go."

Oh, Sergei, Tatiana thought, if only I could have been in Berlin with you! She let her mind wander, only half-listening to the boys telling Papa about the royal family's traditional week at Krasnoe Selo, the camp of the Imperial Guard. The Tsar and his wife stayed in a little wooden chalet built in the Swiss style by another Alexandra, the wife of the first Nicholas.

While they all chattered, Maryka busied herself with her sewing. She liked to have something to occupy her hands; she wasn't a woman who could just sit. It was strange, the sewing helped her to concentrate: an aid to deep thinking, she called it. She was doing some deep thinking now as she convertly watched her daughter. Tatiana had been withdrawn and quiet ever since her return from Moscow. She had not said why, but Maryka knew anyway. She had heard it all from Elena, who couldn't wait to get her alone to tell her all about Tatiana's quarrel with Sergei Tretyakov, and of the announcement of his engagement to Katrina Smirnova. She had known, of course, that Tatiana was fond of Sergei; they all were. The two families had been friendly for many years, and Stepan Tretyakov often rode across to join them for dinner when they were at Shuvalovo. Maryka had simply not realized that there was anything between Sergei and Tatiana. It had not occurred to her that there could be, because they were so obviously totally unsuited. Sergei was a good-looking boy, Maryka thought, but shallow, even vain, the last person in the world she would have imagined Tatiana finding attractive. It always came as a surprise, she thought. You were never ready for your children to be grown up, suffering exactly the same hurts you suffered years before. You could do little to alleviate them and nothing to prevent them. She had hoped that Alex . . . but that was not to be, either, she feared. She knew that one day they would have to do something about marriage. The girl couldn't stay single forever, and it was clear that she felt no strong attachment to any of these young officers who came so constantly to call. Which was just as well, she supposed. Alex made no effort to conceal his conviction that none of them was halfway good enough for his only daughter. He hated the thought of "bargaining" her away, as he put it, and avoided the topic like the plague. She looked at her daughter's face, shining at the center of the laughing group, and sighed. Yes, they would have to face it one day, but perhaps not yet awhile.

To be invited to Tsarskoe Selo was a great honor, although there were more than a hundred ladies in waiting and as many maids in waiting attending them. Tatiana had been told that she might really consider herself to be a royal guest, for her "duties" would be nominal. The Tsar and Tsaritsa felt it their duty each year to introduce to court some of the sons and daughters of the nobility who had not previously been there. So it came about that in the early part of October, a cold, blustery day with a wind like a knife coming in off the Neva, a royal carriage arrived at the doorway to take Tatiana to Tsarskoe Selo.

"Goodbye, Mama, goodbye, Papa, goodbye, Ivan Pavlovich. I'll see you soon, goodbye, goodbye!" It was all like a dream, hugs and kisses and the sound of the horses snorting and the grooms in their scarlet livery taking her bags and stowing them away. Then off through the busy streets, past the Nicholas Station and down the Zabalkanski Prospect with its mean houses leaning together as if to support each other, and the workers on the street outside the cattle yards and the slaughterhouse, through the great Moscow Triumphal Arch, twenty-five versts to the Tsar's village.

Tsarskoe Selo!

Tatiana fell in love with it, a world within a world of beauty. In the lovely English park stood two palaces, the Catherine and the Alexander. The former was an ornate greenish-blue and white splendor of two hundred rooms built by Catherine the Great from the designs of Rastrelli in 1747. Fifty years later, Catherine commissioned the Italian architect Quarenghi to draw up plans for a new palace, the Alexander. Simpler and smaller—it contained only a hundred rooms—this had become the home of the present Tsar and his wife soon after their marriage in 1894.

It was a beautiful, beautiful place. Its windows were wide and high, and from them every prospect pleased: terraces and wide lawns, grottos and pavilions, gardens and statues. In the formal gardens below the palace stood a Chinese village complete with its own theater. Inside the Alexander Palace were long polished halls and tall shaded rooms. The furniture was rich and ornate: mahogany, gold, crystal, marble, velvet. Huge chandeliers brilliantly illuminated each room. The finest Oriental and Persian carpets lay everywhere. Footmen walked from room to room carrying censers of sweet-smelling incense, its perfume mingling with the sharper tang of the wood burning in the huge porcelain stoves which heated the palace to give it its own special aroma. Throughout the year, blooms glowed in every room on tables and pedestals: roses, violets, chrysanthemums, lilies in tall Chinese vases, hyacinths, daffodils in hundreds, all selected by the Tsaritsa herself. When the greenhouses were exhausted, special trains brought fresh flowers from the Crimea.

The palace itself was a simple two-story building in the classical style, made up of a center and two wings. In the center building were the state apartments and formal rooms. The ministers of court and the ladies and gentlemen in waiting had apartments in one wing. The Tsar and his family occupied the other, which, under the direction of the Tsaritsa, had been decorated throughout in the style of the home of a wealthy English country gentleman. The entrance to these quarters was through a pair of heavy doors guarded by a quartet of Ethiopians. They wore scarlet trousers, gold-embroidered jackets, white turbans and strange shoes with turned-up toes. They were not soldiers, and had no function except to open and close doors or to signal, by their sudden silent appearance, the imminent arrival of one of the royal family. Tatiana was awed by them at first.

Later, she learned that one of them was an American. His name was James Hercules, and he had originally been a servant of Tsar Alexander III. James always smiled at her and called her *ditya*, child.

The complicated hierarchy of the court was explained to her. State officials of the second class—the Grand Marshal, the Grand Chamberlain, the Grand Master of the Court, the Cup Bearer and Esquire Trenchant, the Master of the Horse and the Master of the Imperial Hunt—were to be addressed as "Your High Excellency." Officials of the next class, such as the Marshal of the Court, the Grand Master of Ceremonies, the Equerry, Huntsman, and so on were to be addressed as "Your Excellency." The court of the Tsaritsa consisted of a Grand Mistress, several ladies of honor, and a number of maids of honor. Each of the Grand Duchesses had a similar, if somewhat smaller, retinue.

The royal family themselves lived a life of almost cozy domesticity amid all this splendor. The Grand Duchess Olga was like her father, a modest and indecisive man who liked very much to be alone. Marie was a cheerful, lazy girl. Anastasia was a practical joker. Tatiana, to whose "court" Tatiana Makcheyeva found herself attached, was by far the most self-assured of the Tsar's daughters, devoted to her mother and known to all the others as "the governess." As for the Tsar himself, Tatiana rarely saw him. He spent most of his day in his study or receiving ministers. Occasionally she met the Tsaritsa walking in the gardens, sometimes accompanied by the Tsarevich, a frail-looking boy. She thought the Tsaritsa regal, beautiful, dignified and utterly unpretentious, not at all the distant, self-centered snob which gossip said she was. In spite of the grandeur of the palace, the host of ever-present servants, the rituals of changing guards, the fierce Cossacks who constantly patrolled the grounds, the Alexander Palace was a homely and comfortable place, more like a country estate than the home of the Tsar of all the Russias. For Tatiana, it was a magical time; the weeks flew by. She could have lived like that forever, with the world shut out.

One evening, she was sitting in the antechamber awaiting the summons of the Grand Duchess when she became aware of a presence close behind her and of a smell—not the faint body odor that one often detects when someone comes close but a barnyard smell, positive and powerful and totally alien in such regal surroundings. She turned around, and her heart leaped to her throat. It was the *starets*, Rasputin.

She had seen him once before, visiting the Tsar and Tsaritsa.

They seemed to treat him with the utmost humility and respect, but whatever passed between them did so behind closed doors. The *starets* smiled at her, his hands clasped in front of the heavy gold crucifix he always wore, a gift to him from the Tsaritsa. His smile was almost beautific, his bright eyes gentle.

"What are you doing here, daughter?" he asked. His voice was soft, yet resonant, reassuring. Tatiana told him she was waiting to be summoned to the Grand Duchess Tatiana. She felt uneasy, and she did not know why. Nothing could happen to her here in the corridors of the great palace—could it? She said a silent prayer that the summons would come quickly.

"You are happy here in Tsarskoe Selo?"

"Very happy," Tatiana replied.

"Praise God, daughter, for your good fortune. All that is good and wonderful in life comes from Him."

"Yes, holy father, I know that."

"Are you married, daughter?"

"No, I am not."

"Have you a lover?"

Shocked by the directness of the question and the fact that it was being asked by a *starets*, Tatiana flushed and shook her head vehemently. Rasputin nodded and smiled, reaching to one side without taking his eyes from hers, pulling a chair toward him. He sat down on it, very close to her, his knee touching hers.

"Be still, daughter," he said, deepening Tatiana's unease. She sensed, without quite knowing how, that beneath the outward appearance of quiet repose, something mysterious and corrupt burned in this man. Yet his eyes were so gentle, so compassionate.

Almost as if he had read her thoughts, Rasputin edged closer to her, putting a gentle hand on her shoulder. Now it seemed to her that all at once his eyes changed color, the gentle blue darkening and deepening. His gaze took hold of hers and held it and held it and held it. She began to feel suspended, emptied, as if even to inhale would be the most enormous effort. A shadow touched her mind, and her eyelids drooped as if she was weary. She saw his face coming nearer, his eyes still holding hers, nearer, nearer. His hand touched her breast and still she did not move, could not move, did not want to move. She was terrified of what he might do, and yet she could not repel him. She was conscious of him saying something, whispering into her ear, but the words meant nothing. Her body overpowered her mind. She wanted him to do whatever he wanted

142

to do with her. Her thoughts were in a closed box. Her skin was flushed, and she could hear the steady pounding of her own heart.

No, the something said, and the closed box opened slightly.

His hands moved on her body and her eyelids drooped again. The muscles at the back of her neck felt soft, pliable.

No, the something said again.

Rasputin seemed at once to be aware of her increasing resistance. He pulled away from her, and his burning eyes became hooded. His hands left her body. Aware of his touches now, what he had done, her face went scarlet with shame, but Rasputin was not even looking at her. His eyes were raised toward the heavens, as if he was praying. He bent over her, took her face in his rough peasant's hands, and pressed a paternal kiss on the top of her head. If he felt her shudder he took no notice, and if there had been desire on his face it was gone now, washed away. He was as he had been before.

"God's blessings upon you, daughter," he said, his voice soothing and gentle. "You will have much happiness in this house. I will pray for you tonight."

Tatiana said nothing, hoping that the trembling of her hands and legs was not visible. How could he act as if nothing had happened? In an almost dreamlike state, she watched as Rasputin turned and walked silently out of the antechamber, soundless on the soft kid soles of his handmade boots. Tatiana did not move for a long time. When her duties were over that night, she rushed to the bath and scrubbed herself cruelly, almost as if punishing her body. Even so, she felt unclean for a long time afterward. She never looked at Rasputin again without seeing in the hypnotic eyes the other man who lived behind them, the sensual animal who had touched her.

Every day when it was fine she walked in the great park, wandering through its arbors and beneath its arches, crossing bridges over ponds frozen solid by the bleak November nights. One of the bridges had a balustrade on which sat four Chinamen with parasols. Around the ornate fences, guarding the imposing iron gates of the Imperial Park, rode Cossacks in heavy greatcoats, shining sabers on their shoulders day and night, night and day. In the mornings the eight hundred acres of lawn were like white carpets of frost. As the pale November sun appeared, water dripped from the fine old trees. Sometimes the yellow marble column, erected to her lover Orlov by Catherine the Great, was swathed in swirling mist that rose from the great lake, hiding the pink Moorish baths and the Admiralty with its little fleet of rowing boats and the gilded barges which had once belonged to Catherine. On cold mornings, the shouts of the soldiers being marched along the Kadetskaya sounded like shots. Late at night, with her little lamp burning on the bedside table, Tatiana would think of her parents and her friends, so close to her and yet as far away as if she—or they—were in Egypt. She thought of Sergei often, no longer sure of how she felt about his marrying Katrina. She hated the idea of it, and yet strangely she felt no sadness at the thought. It was almost as if the future was unreal, something destined never to happen. Perhaps, she daydreamed, some nameless tragedy will intervene. She pictured Sergei coming to her, weeping, with the news that Katrina was dead—some painless disease, a fall from a horse, something that would leave them without guilt. She saw herself, noble and kind, listening to his confession that he had always loved her, begging her to understand. Forgivingly, she would kiss him, and after that . . . after that her thoughts rarely proceeded further. She would suddenly realize, with a chill of superstitious terror, that she was wishing for the death of another human being, and turn conscience-stricken to the icon of the Virgin over her bed, praying for forgiveness, vowing never to think such thoughts again.

She remained in the small court of the Grand Duchess Tatiana until Christmas, after which the royal family would move to the Winter Palace in St. Petersburg. The season was to open with a coming-out ball for the Grand Duchess Olga, who was eighteen this year. It was to be an occasion of the utmost splendor with three thousand guests. Knowing that this awaited her made Tatiana's homecoming party the most wonderful experience.

Alex and Maryka had invited every one of Tatiana's friends, a houseful of people who brought with them all the news and gossip from Moscow and the salons of Petersburg. Nicky Vasnetsov, dark and slender and handsome as ever; Paul Dubinsky, who listened respectfully while Alex meandered through his ragbag of recollections of life in the Garde Chevalier.

"It's all different now," he complained. "They'll take anyone, no discipline, nothing. Sloppy, some of them. Seen them. Outside the Winter Palace. Great Jehovah, they'd've been shot if they'd turned out for parade like that in my day!"

"Yes, sir," Paul said, rolling his eyes heavenward and wondering if he would ever get a chance to talk to Tatiana alone. He did, of course, and when he did he talked of everything but what he wanted to talk about. She was so beautiful in her woolen dress with the gold chain belt, he thought. Some girls just had a way of dressing. It didn't make any difference what they were actually wearing; they made every other girl in the room look, well, ordinary. Tatiana was one of those. He looked across the room at Olga Narodnova, clinging like a leech to the arm of her fiancé, Mikhail Subarov. Stupid creature, he thought, he's welcome to her.

Olga's smugness had nettled Tatiana, too. Frankly, she had always thought Misha a little on the dull side, slow on the uptake. He never got a joke. When it was finally explained to him, a slow smile would dawn on his face, and he would nod eagerly and say, "I get it now, I get it now!"

"He gets it now," all the others would chorus mockingly, and laugh. Misha never seemed to mind. He would just shrug and smile that oxlike smile. So Olga Narodnova hadn't got all that much to be smirking about. Yet one by one, all her friends were announcing their engagements. Even dowdy little Maria Abrikosova was becoming engaged, to Sergei's baby brother, Andrei. From what Tatiana heard at her party, it seemed as if everyone she knew would be married by the end of the year.

Vasya Kirsanov was full of questions about life in court, especially about the *starets*, Rasputin.

"Is it true the Tsaritsa's in love with him?" he asked, grinning like a devil incarnate. "Everyone says so, although it's hard to imagine that woman loving anyone."

"Oh, Vasya, you misjudge her," Tatiana protested. "She's warm and gentle and very kind to all of us."

"Maybe," Vasya said. "You'd have a hard job convincing most people of that, though."

"He's right, you know," Alex said. "She gives the impression—true or not—of being aloof. Remote. Indifferent. And people think it's directed at them, and so at Russia, too."

"If only you could meet her," Tatiana said. "You wouldn't say that."

"What about this Rasputin fellow, then?"

"He must be terrible." Nicky laughed. "Just look at the way Tatiana shivers when you mention his name."

"He's a strange man," Tatiana said, knowing that she would never say more, never even hint more. "The Tsaritsa reveres Rasputin because he makes the Tsarevich well. No one else can do it.

All the doctors, all the specialists, they come away shaking their heads when the little one is sick. Then Rasputin comes, and soon the boy is well again."

"What's wrong with him, anyway?" Alex asked his daughter. "Is he anemic?"

"No one seems to know for sure," Tatiana said. "We're not allowed to discuss it at the palace."

"But you do!" Vasya grinned.

"Of course we do," Tatiana said, spiritedly. "We'd hardly be human if we didn't feel sorry for the poor little chap "

"And what do they say at the palace?"

"Everyone seems to think it's some sort of circulation trouble," Tatiana said, wrinkling her brow. Her knowledge of medical matters was practically nil. "The blood circulating too near the surface of the skin, or something."

"I heard he was an epileptic," Vasya said, darkly.

"No," Tatiana said. "We would know if it was that."

"There have been rumors about the Tsarevich for as long as I, for one, can remember," Maryka said. "He always seems to be ill. They say it is a sprained ankle, a sort throat, a chill. No one believes these things. How can one feel sympathy for the child when they lie about him? Do they think we haven't eyes to see with?"

"I think perhaps the Tsaritsa is . . . overprotective of him, Mama," Tatiana said. "He seems a perfectly normal little chap to me. He teases the girls dreadfully."

"Well, perhaps we should leave all that to the Tsar," Alex said heavily. "He must know what he's doing. As for me, I want something to drink. Now, where the devil is that lazy valet of mine?"

"Zubov!" the boys all shouted. "Ivan Pavlovich Zubov!" It became a chant, a continuation of an old game that Alex's three sons had played since they were very small. Ivan Pavlovich appeared, his face set in a fierce frown.

"What's all this yelling about?" he said. "Can't a man have any peace in this house?" He had been Alex's servant in the Army and had stayed on as his valet. The two men were more like brothers than master and servant.

"Where's the damned vodka?" Alex roared. "We're all dying for want of a drink!"

"Take more than the lack of a drink to kill off this useless lot!" retorted Ivan Pavlovich. "Hydrochloric acid might do it, but I doubt even that."

"Don't stand there arguing with me!" Alex shouted. "Get us something to drink."

"By all means, Your High Excellency," Ivan said with mock humility. "Right away, Your Mightiness." He went out, and they all laughed. Ivan Pavlovich's sarcasms were no more dangerous than Alexander Makcheyev's anger.

How fine and manly they all looked in their uniforms, Maryka thought. Her heart swelled with pride. She was proud of Tatiana, proud of her three sons, proud of all their friends. Tears brimmed momentarily in her eyes; she was very lucky. She thought of the poor German woman with her sickly son and praised God that her own boys were healthy and strong, grown to manhood, deep-voiced strangers inhabiting the bodies of the little boys who had sometimes come creeping into her bed on bitterly cold Petersburg nights to snuggle warmly up to her.

Darling Vanya, always the clever one. They had expected more of him because he was the eldest, and he had exceeded all their expectations. If Alex had been disappointed when his son chose the Marine Army instead of the regular, Vanya had swept away that disappointment by qualifying, first as a doctor, and then accepting a commission. Just a few months ago, he had married his childhood sweetheart, Nikitina Neledinsky. She sat beside Ivan now, her eyes rarely leaving his face.

Ilya was the second-born, as different from Vanya as chalk is from cheese. Dark where Vanya was fair, secretive where his brother was sunnily frank, Ilya's moods were as unpredictable as Petersburg weather. Smiling one moment, scowling the next, he seemed as a child to have no special talents. Then when he was about fourteen, he had suddenly become the one to whom all his friends brought things to be repaired. Anything mechanical, easy or complex, Ilya would take to pieces, frowning furiously at the thing for hours until the problem revealed itself. And look at him now in his artillery uniform, sitting next to Natasha Narodnova!

"Not too much vodka for Misha, now," Ilya was laughing, as Ivan Pavlovich poured the drinks. "Otherwise he'll start singing."

Olga Narodnova pouted visibly. She didn't like the way all the boys teased Misha, and she wished he would buck up and give them back some of their own medicine. Instead, he just sat there grinning like a fool. Sometimes she wished she wasn't engaged to him. She envied her sister Natasha. Who could have foreseen that sulky little Ilya Makcheyev would become so good-looking? She remembered him as she had always known him, with broken nails and oil-stained hands, always wearing the same greasy coverall. They had all called him *myekanik* then, the mechanic.

"Here, are we going to have any music at this party?" Roman Makcheyev said. "I don't want to sit here gossiping like an old maid all night. I've got to be back in barracks on Monday."

Tatiana put her arms around her brother and kissed him on both cheeks. Roman had always been her special brother, the youngest next to herself, and her ally against the older boys. It seemed no more than two yesterdays that they had snuggled together in bed while Mama read them the old stories of Alyonushka and Ivanushka, about the evil witch Baba Yaga, or the story of the golden fish: *"Head in air and tail in sea, fish, fish, listen to me . . ."* Now he was grown to manhood, tall, almost too good-looking for a man.

"Me, too," Andrei Tretyakov said. "Come on, Roman, put some records on." As he spoke, Tatiana saw in his face and posture the boy that Sergei had been, and she felt a pang of love for him. He wasn't really like Sergei at all, she decided, with his tousled hair and calflike eyes. Just a sweet boy. She wondered what on earth he saw in Maria Abrikosova.

"Come, Ivan Pavlovich!" Vasya shouted. "More vodka over here!"

"We don't get this stuff free, you know," Ivan Pavlovich scowled as he refilled their glasses. "We don't get a regular supply direct from Smirnoff."

"Maybe you should ask Tatiana to have a word with Vladimir Smirnoff, then," Kolya Bakhrushnin said. "She saw a lot of him last summer. Maybe he'll give you a discount."

"Kolya, you're a bad boy, telling tales like that," Maria said. "You make it sound as if Tatiana was flirting with him or something."

"Is that what I was doing?" Kolya said with hugely mock surprise.

"Oh, take no notice of him, Maria," Tatiana said, smiling. "He's only jealous because he hasn't got half the money the Smirnoffs have."

"Nobody's got half the money the Smirnoffs have," Vasya laughed. "Not even the Kirsanovs."

"*Na zdorovye!*" they all shouted. Ivan Pavlovich brought some light wine for the ladies, and they joined in the toasts.

"Oh, this is lovely," Tatiana said. "Isn't it, Mama?"

"Delicious," Maryka said, sipping as if the wine was poison. "Now don't you drink too much, Tatiana."

"*Na zdorovye!*" the men shouted again, clinking glasses.

"I'll tell you what," Andrei said. "This is a lot better than being on maneuvers."

"Maneuvers?" Alex said. "You were on maneuvers? Where were you quartered?"

"Same place as always, sir," Andrei said. "The beautiful Polish Spa of Kalisz."

"Hellhole, you mean," Alex growled. "I know the place. Near Lodz, on the German border, isn't it?"

"Yes, sir," the boys said.

"Been there many a time," Alex grunted. "Pigs in the streets, filth. I remember it well."

"A toast to Kalisz!" Vasya said. "May none of us go there again."

"To Kalisz!" they all said, clinking glasses. "*Do dna!*"

It was a boisterous, happy, noisy homecoming. They all ate and drank far more than they should have done, and even Maryka drank a third glass of wine that made her face flush and her eyes sparkle. As for Alex, he was having the time of his life, telling the boys tall stories about his soldiering days. They encouraged him, making sure that his glass was never empty.

"Give you 'nother toast," Andrei said. "To Sergei's promotion!"

"Sergei has been promoted?"

"Attached to the Tsar's staff, sir," Andrei said. "On the personal recommendation of General Zhilinsky."

That dirty old man, Tatiana thought, remembering his clumsy hands and stertorous breathing that day in the pavilion in Moscow. She had never dreamed that the day would dawn when she would bless his name, but it had come and her heart sang. Sergei was coming to Petersburg!

"When will he come?" she heard herself asking, hoping her voice sounded as casual as she was trying to make it.

"May, June, I'm not sure," Andrei said. "*Na zdorovye!*"

"To Sergei!" the boys all said.

"Is he coming alone, then?" Tatiana heard herself ask artlessly. "Or will Katrina be coming with him?"

"With him, I should think," Andrei said, offhandedly. "They'll be married in April."

"See here, you fellows, what about that music?" Roman shouted. "Do you want to dance or not?"

"Wait, wait, if there's going to be music, I'll be off out of it," Alex said. "I can't stand all that racket you kids seem to think so marvelous. Here, Ivan Pavlovich, where's my stick?"

"Right where it always is, Your Excellency," the valet said.

"What are you gawping at, man, didn't you hear me say I was going to take a nap?"

"No, Your Incredibility, I did not."

"Well, I did, and I am, so give me a hand instead of standing there giving me lip." Alex turned toward Maryka, who was standing within reach, and gave her a hefty whack on the bottom. "How about you, madam? Must I sleep alone?"

"Alex!" Maryka protested. "Really! At your age, you should know better!" He grinned unrepentantly and put his arm around her shoulder.

"Many a good tune been played on an old fiddle," he said, with a huge wink. Maryka smiled at him fondly. He would be asleep the minute his head hit the pillow, after all the vodka he had drunk. It was somehow as if men never wanted to grow up at all, and soldiers even less than most.

She looked at all the bright young faces and sighed. Where does it all go, so soon, so soon? she thought. Telling her daughter not to be too late, she bade them all good night and followed her husband up the stairs. It's their turn now, she thought, and somehow the thought made her sad. Come along now, my girl, she said to herself, you've had your share of good times. Count your blessings the way you always do. Tonight it did not work. She went into the bedroom, burdened with regrets.

The coming-out ball for the Grand Duchess Olga was the most glittering, brilliant occasion Petersburg had seen for many years. There were quadrilles, Egyptian dances, Hungarian dances, Cossack dances, followed by waltzes and more waltzes. After the sumptuous supper, announced in the traditional fashion by the playing of the Wedding March from *Lohengrin*, there was a cotillion, surely one of the most stunning events of this or any season. Wicker carts of flowers—roses, carnations, violets and mimosa—were reverently trundled into the great Nicholas Salon by the servants, filling it with the sweet perfume of Maytime, while outside, the Baltic wind sweeping across the frozen Neva drove the temperature down to thirty degrees below zero Centigrade. The dancing went on until five in the morning, although the Tsaritsa left at midnight.

It seemed, indeed, as if all Petersburg was conspiring to make this season the most glamorous of all. There was an unending succession of balls and parties. Among the most notable was the party given by Mathilde Kschessinka, mistress of the Tsar before his marriage and now the consort of Grand Duke Andrei. It was for Kschessinka's son Vova, a lavish Russian Christmas party at which the clown Durov entertained, and whose finale was the appearance, on a huge bed, of a real elephant trained to use an enormous chamber pot—much to the delight of the children. The Countess Kleinmikhel gave a brilliant costume ball at which she presented the daughters of her sister-in-law to Petersburg society. To have been invited to the Kleinmikhel party was almost as great a social coup as to have been at the Imperial Ball, perhaps even greater.

Everywhere along the Neva and the frozen canals lacing through the snowbound city, the tall windows of the fine houses and the great palaces blazed with light. There were crowds in the opulent Fabergé establishment, where elegant women sat on blue and gold chairs spending small fortunes on the shining trifles clerks brought to them on red velvet trays. In the salons and the parlors of the rich, in the hairdressing establishments, fashionable women gossiped about Nijinsky's expulsion from the Royal Ballet, occasioned by his having worn in *Giselle* a costume so unusually brief and so extraordinarily revealing that the Dowager Empress, who had been in the royal box, had risen majestically to her feet, fixed Nijinsky with a basilisk stare, and stalked out of the Maryinsky. The dancer was dismissed the next morning.

There were plenty of other things to gossip about. The women pouted about how terrible it was with all these strikes; one couldn't get anything done these days. There were more than a million workers on strike, they said, the idle devils. There was even talk that the peasants were becoming militant; could you imagine that? The revolutionaries were the cause of it all, fomenting discontent in the factories and in the fields, even in the State Duma. It was a scandal, of course, but it was too much to expect, one supposed, that anything would be done about it. Instead of sending out the Cossacks to whip these troublemakers into line, Nicholas fiddled about with governmental appointments, no doubt at the bidding of *Nemka*, the German one. And everyone knew who told *her* what to do! Dear, sweet Count Kokovstov, successor to the martyred Piotr Stolypin, was dismissed in February, and everyone knew it was the work of that Siberian *moujik*. Rasputin didn't like Kokovstov and wanted his own lackey in the Premier's office. No one was taken in for a second by the Tsar's announcement that he had dismissed Kokovstov because he had opposed abolition of the tax on vodka. And look who had taken Kokovstov's place: that old fool Goremykin, who would paint himself with black and yellow stripes if Nicholas told him to, and then pass a law that required everyone else to do so as well! The whole thing was a disgrace, but no one would do anything about it; no one ever did. The country was going to the dogs, no doubt of that at all. The best thing to do was to put one's money into jewelry or gold or gilt-edged stocks or property. One heard that the banks in Switzerland were quite good, or the ones in Monte Carlo. One had to do something. The way things were going, nothing one owned would be worth more than ten kopecks in a couple of years' time.

Through this glittering winter, Tatiana sailed with her head held proudly high. She danced with all the young officers in their blazing crimson Guards uniforms, rode with them in *troikas* through the snow-piled streets, silver harness bells jingling, laughter bouncing off the dark façades of the huge buildings, the frozen Neva a wasteland of ice. Champagne fizzing in her head, she kissed them good night—Nicky Vasnetsov tonight, Vasya Kirsanov tomorrow, Kolya and Paul and Andrei and someone else and someone else in all the nights that followed. The golden palaces in which she danced meant nothing, any more than the kisses which she gave to her suitors. She took them as much for granted as her own safe, secure life, just as everyone she knew took them for granted. So they danced and danced and drank their champagne and gossiped and flirted. They whirled home in the bone-freezing cold, past the haloed gas lamps in the Champs de Mars, tumbling up the stairs to be undressed by sleepy-eyed servants who tucked them into warmed beds, while in the Narvskaya and the Vuiborgskaya, and the barracklike dormitories huddled against the bleak factory walls of the industrial districts, the workers struggled from beneath their thin quilts to face another day of drudgery. Pulling on their rough clothes and their felt boots, gulping down a glass of hot tea and a hunk of black bread, they went out into the piercing cold, breath freezing as it met the air, hurrying to be in their places before the six o'clock whistle sounded, for they would be fined half a day's pay and more if they were late. Heads down, eyes down, huddled against the murderous wind, they did not look at the little red sleighs jingling by with their occupants snug and satisfied beneath piles of woolen blankets and bearskin rugs. Things were as they were. If the knots of faceless, shuffling people the sleighs sped past envied them or resented them or hated them, no one in the speeding *troikas* knew, no one in the glittering palaces cared.

One after another, the events of the year proceeded. Felix and Irina Yussupov were married in panoplied splendor, their union bringing together more wealth than existed in any other family anywhere on the face of the earth. Everyone knew it was a *mariage de covenance*, for Felix had made no secret of his predilections for many years. *Maslenitsa*, Shrovetide, came and went; Lent followed. At Tsarskoe Selo the royal family began to prepare for their annual vacation in Livadia. The end of the social season, marked by Lent, was also the beginning of the official one, an endless round of functions, receptions, parades and reviews. In June, the King of Saxony would make a State visit, and in July, the President of France, Monsieur Poincaré, would arrive. There was to be an official visit by the British Navy under the command of the dashing young Admiral Beatty. It would be an exhausting time for the Tsar and even more so for the Tsaritsa, who so hated to appear in public at any time. Some of the more precious gossips of the Petersburg set sneered and said that Nicky and the German woman were always on vacation: the Crimea, or Poland, or on the *Standart* or in Peterhof. Tatiana did not begrudge them any of the few days they snatched for themselves, the days when they tried to act like any ordinary Russian family. She had seen them many times when they came back from watching maneuvers at Krasnoe Selo or some State banquet in one of the palaces. The Tsaritsa would be wan with fatigue, the girls drooping with weariness. When they were called upon to watch parades or military exercises, they came back coated with a film of dust, their clothes gritty with dirt. The girls would sink into their hot baths with such grateful sighs that Tatiana knew what they did was work, not pleasure, duty, not fun. The remarkable thing to her was that they did it, and so much of it, without duress and in such high spirits. Only the Tsaritsa flagged, and anyone could see that she was a woman living entirely on her nerves.

She said goodbye to them all and wished them a pleasant trip to the Crimea in the royal train. She shook a finger at Alexis and told him not to play too many practical jokes upon his sisters, and to take care of his spaniel, Joy. She kissed shy, kind, innocent Olga, hugged her self-confident namesake Tatiana, and petted the younger two, Stana and Marie. She curtsied before the Tsar and Tsaritsa, and Nicholas smiled at her, his blue eyes twinkling.

"Well, Tatiana, don't go and get married on us, or anything silly like that, now, will you?"

"Nicky, dear," the Tsaritsa said gently, "you'll make her blush with such remarks."

"Nonsense!" said the Tsar. "She has plenty of young men paying her court. I've seen them with my own eyes—never seen one girl with so many beaux!"

"Your Majesty may be sure I won't get married," Tatiana said with a smile. "My father will see to that."

"I expect he will," Nicholas said. "How is your father? Well, I trust?"

"He is well, Sire," Tatiana said.

"Good, good, well, mustn't keep you," the Tsar said. "Have a lovely summer, my dear. Perhaps you will come and visit us again next winter?"

"Oh, yes, Papa, please!" Grand Duchess Tatiana said.

"We shall see, dear," the Tsaritsa said to her daughter. "Next winter is a long way away."

"Thank you, Your Majesties," Tatiana said, curtsying again and withdrawing. An hour later, she was on the train back to Petersburg. The royal carriage took her to her door.

It had been an unusually quiet homecoming.

It seemed to Tatiana that her parents had not heard a single thing she told them about the parties, the balls, the events at Tsarskoe Selo. Even Papa's appetite seemed strange, she thought. He picked at his food in a manner most atypical, looking anxiously at Maryka from time to time, as if silently seeking her guidance. Even dear Ivan Pavlovich had been gloomy and uncommunicative. There was none of the usual banter between him and his master. He brought in the wine, supervised the serving of the food and as silently departed. Finally, Tatiana could stand it all no longer.

"Papa, Mama," she said, exasperatedly, "I've been talking and talking for hours and *hours*—and I don't believe that either of you has heard one single word I've said."

"Tatiana . . . darling—" Maryka began. Alex gave his wife a dark look, and she lapsed into an uncomfortable silence.

"What's wrong?" Tatiana said. "What is it?"

Alex did not answer, fumbling instead for his pipe, taking a long time to find it in his pocket. He's grown old, Tatiana thought, he's grown so old all at once. Her father's hands trembled constantly, as if with ague. She watched him frowning furiously over the simple task of filling and lighting the old pipe, as though what he was doing required his full concentration, as though he had learned to do it only a little while ago, when in fact he had been doing it for thirty years and more without even looking. Something that felt like a frozen feather touched the furthest edge of Tatiana's perception.

"Something's wrong," she said. Her father's agonized look and her mother's guilty jump confirmed her suspicions as nothing else could have done. "What is it? What's happened?"

Alex stared at his beautiful daughter with his soul trapped in purgatory. Something happened, he thought, something happened all right, my little one, and how will I tell you what it was?

The caller had been a complete stranger. Ivan Pavlovich showed him in, a thin-faced man with colorless eyes behind rimless spectacles. His hair was cropped short, his clothes ordinary.

"Abrikosov?" Alex said, perhaps a shade too heartily. "Are you related to my daughter's friend, Maria?"

"Her father is my brother," Boris Abrikosov said.

"Of course, of course," Alex said, wondering what it was about the man that made him nervous. The eyes? There was no friendship there. "It is an honor to meet you, sir. A privilege. May I offer you something? Some tea, a drink?—"

"This is not a social call," Boris said coldly.

"I see," said Alex, although he did not. "Would you like to sit down?"

"Standing suits me," Boris said. He took out his *Okhrana* credentials and showed them to Alex, who nodded, his normally ruddy face paling slightly. What could the Tsar's secret police want in his house?

"What exactly is the nature of your business, sir?" he asked.

"You have a son, Roman."

"Roman? Is something wrong with?—"

"Nothing like that," Boris said, waving a hand. "Your son is an officer?"

"He is, sir," Alex replied proudly. "In the Garde Chevalier."

"You have other sons, I believe?"

"Two others. One is a doctor in the navy, the other an officer in the artillery. Why do you ask?"

"You are a military family," Boris said. "With a military tradition."

"Yes, yes," Alex said, testily. "Will you now tell me what all this is about, sir?"

"I will tell you, Count Makcheyev, in my own good time. Please be good enough to be quiet and listen."

"Damn me, sir, I don't think I care for your manner!" Alex growled. "I'm not accustomed—"

"Then get accustomed!" Boris snapped. "You're going to have to put up with my manner, as you call it, until this distasteful matter has been resolved to my satisfaction."

"Distasteful—what are you talking about?"

"I am talking, sir—" Boris's lip curled as he used the title— "about your son Roman Makcheyev's homosexuality."

Alex looked at Boris, horror and disbelief on his face. The colorless eyes of the man facing him held no expression. No warmth, no pity, no sorrow, nothing.

"You dare to . . . suggest . . . ?"

"It is not a suggestion, Count," Boris said. "It is certainly not a suggestion."

"You—you damned—!" Alex started to get up out of his chair, his face suffused with anger. As he did, Boris Abrikosov shook his head impatiently and stiff-armed him back. There was no anger on his face.

"Sit still, old man," he snapped, "and listen to me."

"You damned scoundrel!" Alex growled. "If you don't get out of this house immediately, I'll get a pistol and shoot you!"

"While I stand still and let you," Boris sneered. "You're a fool, Makcheyev. You'd better listen to me, and listen well. Do you think I would come here and say what I have just said if I couldn't prove it?"

"I've been told you people are capable of anything," Alex said. "And now I believe it. I refuse to listen to another word."

Boris smiled his snake's smile. The old man's anger was empty; he could hear the fear behind it. The very way Alex's voice had changed told Boris that he had won. He felt no elation. The issue had never really been in doubt.

"I can prove what I say, Count," he said. "Every nasty little rendezvous, every sleazy little detail. Would you like me to read you some of my agents' reports?"

"No," Alex said weakly, holding up a hand. "No, don't."

"You're very wise," Boris said. "So, let us get to our business."

"Business, sir? What business?"

"You accept that I can prove what I say about your son?"

"Yes."

"You know what would happen if these facts were published?"

"It—there is no crime," Alex said hoarsely. "My son is not a criminal."

"Nor is he accused of being one," Boris said, urbanely. The old man had taken a long time to go for the bait, but he had it now. Boris waited.

"Then . . . why is the *Okhrana* involved?" Alex said. "What is your interest in my son's private affairs?"

"Personal," Boris said.

"I don't understand."

"Such information comes my way all the time. Most of it I discard as useless. But not in this case."

"Why not in this case?"

"I have brought the dossier with me," Boris said, ignoring the wary question. "I propose to give it to you, on certain conditions."

"Ah," Alex said. "Conditions."

"You didn't think it would be free, did you?"

"I didn't think anything. If it's money—"

"Not money!" Boris snapped. "I have no interest in money."

"What then?"

"I want your daughter."

"*What?*"

"You heard me, old man."

"Never!" Alex shouted. "Never!"

"Never is a very long time, Count," Boris said, not raising his voice. "You would do well to reconsider. Unless the name of Makcheyev means nothing to you?"

Alex glared at his tormentor. Boris smiled his hateful smile.

"Don't worry," he said. "I'll marry her if it eases your bourgeois conscience."

"You dare to speak to me of conscience, you blackguard?" Alex growled. "You wouldn't know the meaning of the word!"

"Make the arrangements, Count," Boris said. "I mean to have Tatiana, do you understand? I mean to have her."

"But . . . why? There are other girls, plenty—"

"Because . . . it would please me," Boris said.

"I cannot permit you to speak about Tatiana as if she were an animal—"

"You are in no position to issue edicts, Count," Boris said. "Unless you wish—" He waved the dossier.

"No," Alex said. "No." He stared at Boris, who said nothing.

"I need . . . time," he managed. "Time. To think."

"I have no time to give you," Boris said without sympathy.

"I . . . have to tell . . . my wife. It . . . will be a shock, you see. I . . . a little time. It would help." He dreaded the thought of telling Maryka. He could not even bring himself to think of what it would be like to tell Tatiana. In one short half hour, this empty-eyed man had destroyed the future completely.

"All right," Boris said. "You see that I'm a generous man. I give you forty-eight hours' grace. Many others would not do so."

Great Jehovah, Alex thought, the man actually expects praise, a poisoner seeking compliments because his victims had felt no pain.

"You will advise me of your agreement in two days, Count Makcheyev. Otherwise, I shall act without further consultation. Do you understand me?"

"Yes," Alex groaned. "I understand."

"Then there is no more to say," Boris said. "Don't bother to call your man. I'll let myself out."

He went out of the room. Alex heard his footsteps on the marble floor in the vestibule and then the sound of the door slamming. A silence like the silence at the end of the earth came over the house. He stared sightlessly at the wall, trapped and helpless. The face of his youngest son came into his mind, and then a series of images of Roman and other men, faceless, nameless, dark figures in perverted poses, laughing, ugly. He grabbed the bell pull and yanked on it, again and again. He kept on pulling it until Ivan Pavlovich came running into the room, his brow knotted with anxiety. The old man had not pulled the bell like that for years. Relief flooded the valet's face when he saw that Alex had not suffered another seizure. The relief vanished when he saw that Alex's face was dark with stifled rage.

"Get me a bottle of vodka!" Alex shouted. "Vodka, damn you, and quick!"

"You know what the doctor—"

"God damn your soul, Zubin!" Alex roared. "Do what I tell you!"

Ivan Pavlovich skittered out of the room in panic, aghast at the way Alex had spoken to him. What had happened? Was it connected with the visit of the thin-faced man in the leather coat? Abrikosov? What had the Abrikosovs to do with Alexander Makcheyev? He brought the bottle upstairs and took it in nervously to Alex on a silver tray. The old man opened the bottle in the peasant way, grasping the neck firmly and smacking the bottle sharply with the palm of his hand. The cork popped out. Pushing the tray and the glass aside, Alex tilted the bottle to his mouth, drinking the vodka like so much water.

"Sir," Ivan Pavlovich said, distress and fear in his voice, "please, don't—"

"Get out of here!" Alex roared. "I want to be alone. Get out, get out, get out!"

Awed, astonished, afraid, Ivan Pavlovich backed out of the room and quietly closed the door. There was nothing he could do, nothing anyone could do. He went downstairs and told the maid what was happening. She said she would go across to the Nevsky and see if she could find Madame, who had gone to the shops in Gostinny Dvor. In the meantime, Alexander Makcheyev got roaring drunk. It was the only way he could face Maryka. When she came home, he blurted out his version of what had happened. Then he fell unconscious into his bed.

Two days later, they told Boris Abrikosov that they accepted his proposal. There was absolutely nothing else that they could do. The idea of his daughter being married to the man was almost more than Alex could bear. Yet the family name, the family honor, they meant something too. They had been hard won; he could not easily toss them all onto the dunghill to be gossiped over by Petersburg fishwives.

"You . . . your mother and I . . . we've been thinking about your future," he said. "You're growing up, a woman."

"Time you thought of settling down," Maryka said. "A home of your own, children . . ."

"Children?" Tatiana said, so astonished that she laughed out loud. "I don't intend to have any children for years and years and years."

"That's all very well," Maryka said. "For you. Your papa and I have to consider the future now. After all, you're our only dau—"
She choked with emotion, her eyes suddenly flooded with tears. Startled, Tatiana rose and came around the table, putting her arms around her mother.

"What is it, Mama?" she said, looking over her mother's head at her father. "Papa, what is it?"

"In a moment, little one," he said, his voice gentle. "Come, Maryushka, no weeping. No more weeping."

"Yes," Maryka said, wiping her eyes with her apron and sniffing. "Yes, I know. I know, Alex. It's just—"

"There, there," he said, patting her clumsily. "Don't cry anymore. You'll only make it harder for us all."

"You're right," Maryka said, sniffing again. She sat up and looked at Tatiana, who was watching them with a deep frown on her face. She had never seen her parents like this before.

"Go ahead, Alex," her mother said now. "I'm sorry."

"I'm sorry, too," Alex said. "But we must talk about it. We must discuss Tatiana's marriage."

A terrible cold hand clamped itself suddenly on Tatiana's heart, and she thought for a moment that she would never be able again to draw another breath. It was as if someone had blindly struck a chord on the ends of her nerves. They had arranged a marriage for her! She could not believe it.

"I don't want to . . . get married," she said, plaintively. "Not yet, Papa. Papa?" Her father did not answer for a long time; then he looked at her and sighed. He took her shoulders in his big paws and turned her around so that she faced him.

"Your mother and I have discussed the matter, Tatiana," he said, heavily. "We have decided that—"

"*You* have decided?" Tatiana looked at her parents aghast. "You have decided without even asking me?"

"Tatiana, you don't understand," Maryka said. "Listen to what your father says, child. Please, listen."

"No!" Tatiana shouted, jumping to her feet. "No, no! I won't be forced into marriage. I can't believe you'd ask me to marry someone I don't love. I can't believe it. Mama, tell him not to make me do it. Tell me it isn't true!"

"Listen to me, *malytuka*—" Alex began.

"Don't 'baby' me, Papa!" Tatiana said. "You can't do this to me and call me 'baby'!"

"Tatiana, darling," Maryka said, reaching for her daughter's hand. "Please give us a chance to explain—"

"No!" Tatiana said. "I won't listen to it. I won't listen to any of it!"

"Unfortunately, you must," Alex said, and there was something different in his voice that made her look at him as if for the first time. She saw an old man with deep pain in his eyes, and all at once the knowledge that her father was dying swept over Tatiana like a tide. With a heartbroken sob, she threw herself into his arms, laying her head on his shoulder as she had done when she was a child, so many years ago.

"Papa, Papa, why?" she sobbed. "Why?"

"Because there is no choice," Alex said. His voice was without hope; his eyes burned with self-hatred as he spoke. "You will marry Boris Abrikosov in August. Now be quiet, and I will tell you why."

When he had finished speaking, the awful things he had said hung in the air like vultures above a dead animal. This must be how they feel when the hangman takes them up onto the scaffold, Tatiana thought: sick and angry and afraid, cold and alone and soiled. She could not believe what she had heard him tell her about Romasha. It was too vile, too loathsome. Yet she knew he could not lie to her, not about something like this. She felt sick.

"You see how it is, darling," her mother was saying. "How we have no choice in this."

"I see," Tatiana said, dully.

"Well," Alex said, with a long, long sigh. "That's settled, then?" He could not hide his relief, and Tatiana hated him for it. Silently she vowed that she would never marry the hateful Boris Abrikosov, never, never, never. She would kill herself first.

"You're sure you understand?" Maryka said. Tatiana's silent acceptance of the shocking things her father had told her was unnerving. "You'll go through with it?"

"Yes," Tatiana lied.

"Well," Maryka said, her voice still uncertain. She knew her daughter and feared so ready a capitulation. "Perhaps it won't be so bad," she said, without conviction. "After all, the Abrikosovs are a wealthy family, and . . ."

Quite coldly, Tatiana shut the sound of her mother's voice out of her mind. Let them believe she was going to marry that evil old man if it made them happy. She would marry the Devil first. For no reason, the thought conjured up the sardonic smile of Vladimir Smirnoff.

Putting on a tired mask, Tatiana went to her room, filled with a rare sense of purpose and determination. Alex and Maryka watched her so anxiously, but Tatiana said no more. She knew exactly what she was going to do. When Annushka came to undress her, she sent the girl for some paper, ink and a pen, swearing her to the utmost secrecy. Then, in the dark safety of her pretty bedroom, beneath the fringed shade of a little oil lamp, she wrote a long, long letter to Pierre Smirnoff.

II

ANATOLI IVANOVICH KURASOV, senior assistant to the First Secretary of the Ministry of Justice, was a prim, methodical, unimaginative man. He saw himself, first and foremost, as the amanuensis of the First Secretary and, through him, of His Majesty the Tsar. Small, drab and cunning, Kurasov's life was spent avoiding situations which could lead to criticism of his performance. His every action was weighed. His standing in the Table of Ranks was of more importance to him than anything else in his life. He never took chances of any kind.

Which made it difficult for Viktor Guchkov. Guchkov had no time for *tchinovniki*, especially when they were infinitely more interested in their own advancement than they were in the work by means of which they were supposed to earn it. He knew, to his cost, that the First Secretary did not consider criminal investigation an art to be held in high respect; it was hardly to be expected, then, that Kurasov would be any more sympathetic. Nevertheless, it was to Senior Assistant Kurasov that Guchkov reported and from Kurasov that he received his instructions. As he was doing now, with as much good grace as he could muster. He did not like Kurasov. The man was a cipher, an excrescence, toadying, fawning, self-serving. He was also, thanks to Peter the Great, Tsar of all the Russias, 1672–1725, a nobleman by virtue of his office and the Table of Ranks.

In 1722, dissatisfied with the quality of his civil service, Peter the Great instituted a major change in the nature of the nobility. He insisted that merit, and not heredity, should determine a man's role in government or the services, and that service to the State should be as glamorous—and rewarding—as the bearing of arms. Thus the Table of Ranks, the *Tchin*, came into being. There were fourteen ranks; the upper eight automatically conferred hereditary nobility, and the lower six nonhereditary. Thus, top civil servants held a rank equal to that of successful soldiers, could call themselves "General" and wear the appropriate uniforms, like that fat old fool Sukhomlinov, Minister for War. The eighth grade, for example, gave the holder of a doctoral degree and an Army major equal status, conferring hereditary nobility upon both. Promotion was, of course, eagerly sought, and the pronouncements of the *Tchin* were to the *tchinovniki* what market prices were to stockbrokers on the Bourse. And no more ardent *tchinovnik* lived than Anatoli Kurasov. His rank and position were matters to him of the gravest concern, and he never failed to draw them to the attention of people he considered his social inferiors.

"Disgraceful!" he said to Guchkov. "The whole matter is quite outrageous, Guchkov, and I will simply not accept it!"

Guchkov said nothing. There was nothing to say, and anyway, he knew Kurasov wasn't finished yet.

"You have the nerve to come to me with this—this farrago of, of nothing, that's what it is, nothing, and expect me to put it before the First Secretary? Well, do you, man?"

"I'm afraid it's all we have," Guchkov said.

"Disgraceful!" Kurasov said again. "Here we have at least half a dozen brutal murders, and you tell me that neither you nor the police have the slightest idea who has committed them, or why."

"We don't know who," Guchkov said. "But we can make a fairly educated guess as to why he does it."

"Go on."

"We feel sure that the man we are dealing with is a sexual sadist, someone who derives sexual gratification from the degradation of children."

"Now you are a psychologist."

"No, I'm not," Guchkov said, concealing his irritation. "But I have discussed the matter at length with Professor Doctor Lobano-vich at the university. He was kind enough to prepare a psychological portrait of the murderer which I think we will find an enormous help. You see—" He stopped speaking as Kurasov held up an imperious hand.

"Spare me the jargon, please," said Kurasov. "No high-flown theories or psychological portraits. Just give me the bare essentials for my report to the First Secretary. He is very anxious to hear what you have to say."

"Perhaps if I were to speak to him—" Guchkov began, but the look on Kurasov's face froze the words on his lips. Fat chance of that, he thought. With the slightest of shrugs, he took out the dossier and laid it open on Kurasov's desk.

"The first murder was that of Irinia Kaminsky. She was abducted somewhere between her school and her home. Her body was extensively mutilated. You may refer to the autopsy report for details."

"Good God, man," Kurasov shuddered, "d'you think I'm some sort of ghoul? Wait, though. Kaminsky, you said? Is that the daughter of Hova Kaminsky, the lawyer?"

"That's right."

"But he's the one who's been making all the commotion! Came in and demanded to see the First Secretary—can you believe it, *demanded*! And when he was told that he would have to make an appointment, he stormed out, making all sorts of threats. Dreadful fellow."

"Did anything happen?"

"Yes, something happened. Do you know, Guchkov, I received a reprimand from the Minister? A reprimand, because I insisted that the fellow make an appointment? Thirty years in the Ministry, without a mark on my record, and then I get a ministerial reprimand because of some damned ambulance chaser!"

Guchkov shook his head, which Kurasov took for sympathy. It was not; Guchkov felt nothing but contempt. He sighed; it was useless, hating the Kurasovs of this world. They were everywhere: vain, petty, pompous little men, often wearing some sort of uniform, futile, self-centered failures worth nothing, using their rank to bolster their own inadequacy. It took no imagination to visualize Kaminsky's angry reaction to Kurasov's supercilious dismissal, nor did he feel any surprise at Kurasov's wounded reaction to Kaminsky's revenge. Men like Kurasov always felt aggrieved when one of their victims bit back.

"Shall I proceed?" he said wearily.

"Proceed, proceed," Kurasov said, waving a magniloquent hand in a way that made Guchkov want to slap him.

"Second victim, Zoya Terzakova, late August," he said doggedly. "*Modus operandi* apparently the same. The third victim, Lara Lazareva, was found seventeen days later, on waste ground near the Bryansk Station. The police surgeon stated that the injuries inflicted on her were more severe than those inflicted on the previous victims. She had been—"

"Guchkov!" Kurasov hissed. "You know that I do not wish to hear the ghastly medical details. I will not listen to them and I will not read them."

"But how can you understand what kind of man we're up against if you don't examine the manner in which he commits his crimes?" Guchkov said.

"I do not have to explain my decisions to you, Guchkov," Kurasov snapped. "Please be kind enough to remember your position."

"Sorry," Guchkov said again. He was well aware that Kurasov's stomach turned queasy when confronted with autopsy evidence. By God, I'd love to get the bastard down in the morgue on the Tverskoi when the police surgeon made that first long, deep incision from the sternum to the groin, he thought.

"Now, what about the Starovna girl?"

"He picked her up in the Petrovsky Park, took her off somewhere they couldn't be seen, and killed her almost immediately. That tells us quite a lot about our man."

"What, for instance?" Kurasov said. He had no idea what Guchkov was talking about.

"He is driven, impelled to do what he does, by some deep, twisted need. In the case of the Starovna girl, he was in a hurry. He killed her in a frenzy. There were forty-two—"

"Guchkov!"

"Sorry, I forgot," Guchkov muttered, knowing that he had not. "If our murderer was in a hurry, terrified lest someone come while he was at his bloody work, then there is a chance that he was less careful than usual, that someone may have seen him. He may have lost something near the body. I've got teams combing the area around where it was found. The girl's clothes are being examined microscopically. Fingernails, too. There's just the chance that she scratched the man."

"Anything yet?"

"No."

"It's taking a long time, isn't it?"

"It always does," Guchkov said. "Do you want me to go on?"

"How many more?"

"Another two."

"Anything specially significant about them?"

"No. He sticks to a type: blonde, pretty. There is one other thing."

"And that is?"

"I'm sorry," Guchkov said, "I have to be specific. The scale of the injuries being inflicted on the victims is increasing with each murder. It almost seems as if the man is going further with each, like some insane explorer. The most recent victim, Tereshkova, was most terribly mutilated. The father had to be taken to the hospital after he identified her. He's still under sedation."

"This is dreadful, dreadful," Kurasov said with a theatrical shudder. "I suppose all this is in your report?"

"Naturally."

Kurasov looked at the file as if it might leap off the desk and attack him. He shuddered again. "And your conclusions?"

"There aren't that many," Guchkov said, rubbing his eyes. God, he was tired. He felt as if he had been on his feet for a month, and it was not all that far from being true. "There seems to be nothing to get hold of. No common denominator. He has killed by night and in daylight. No pattern. I think that very fact indicates that this is no ordinary murderer."

"A lunatic, you mean?"

"Not in the conventional sense of the word," Guchkov said, choosing his words with care. "He's not a wild-eyed monster, foaming at the mouth and brandishing a carving knife. This is an apparently normal man, living an ordinary life. Quite possibly he is well educated, certainly well dressed. He is shrewd, intelligent, and cautious. Only once has he taken a chance, the time he killed Anna Starovna. Despite that, he has given us nothing to work with, not a scrap. Our man is cunning, and he is no fool. But that's all we know about him. We still don't know what he looks like or where to look for him."

"You're not very encouraging, Guchkov," Kurasov said petulantly. "I can't very well go to the First Secretary and tell him we simply haven't any idea what to do."

"I didn't say I haven't any idea what to do," Guchkov said, emphasizing the personal pronoun to alleviate his asperity. "I didn't say that at all."

"You had better tell me what you mean," Kurasov said. "And I hope that it's going to be good."

That was his way of letting Guchkov know he had caught the tone of his voice. Sometimes he felt the man simply hadn't the correct attitude to his superiors at all. He waved a patrician hand to indicate that the investigator might proceed.

"Vanity," Guchkov said.

"I beg your pardon?"

"I told you that Professor Doctor Lobanovich had prepared a psychological portrait of the kind of man our killer might be. It's in the file. I'd like to read it to you before I explain what I mean."

"Is it long?"

"Not very."

"Proceed, then," Kurasov said, leaning world-wearily back in his chair. Guchkov took the headed sheet of paper out of the file and began to read it.

From the information provided by Senior Judicial Investigator V. I. Guchkov, and from the autopsy evidence which I have examined, I venture to conclude that the perpetrator of these crimes may be found to be that far from uncommon creature, a sadistically impelled psychotic. Such a man commits these acts to relieve his own sexual tensions, which he can do no other way. Let me endeavor to put it in lay terminology.

The sadistic tendency lies, generally speaking, in the fact that the perpetrator compels the victim, by either psychological or physical force, to submit to indecent treatment. Satisfaction is gained from the supremacy of the perpetrator over the delicate and powerless victim. The knowledge that he is influencing the child's mind by force may perhaps play a decisive role in the excitement of his sexual impulse. The overcoming of a shy, weeping, struggling girl also satisfies the sadistic sexual urge. If the child is also pretty, this further enhances the sadist's enjoyment.

Such acts are usually planned cold-bloodedly and carefully, for the pervert is well aware of what he is doing and of society's view of his aberrations. This man has given more than sufficient indication that he is both cautious and intelligent, therefore no ordinary brute. In sexual pathology, it is not unusual to find the kind of escalation being encountered in these murders. One might go so far as to predict that they will continue to escalate in violence. All the evidence tends to indicate that the killer sees himself as a kind of *ubermensch*, above the law and contemptuous of it. I would like to comment upon this factor.

Quite often such aberrants try to draw attention to themselves. As an arsonist leaves clues by which he may be identified, such a murderer will frequently try to contact the authorities or the newspapers to claim credit for his ghoulish success. It is the more unusual that this man has made no attempt to do so, for a factor in the makeup of a sexual murderer is on the one hand his knowledge that identification will mean punishment, conflicting violently with his need to "show off," to tell people how clever he is to kill and get away with it, how he deludes his victims, makes fools of the police, shocks everyone. As I hope I have indicated, this murderer shows classic symptoms of typical degeneration. The absence of any evidence of superego is therefore most unsettling.

> I respectfully submit my observations for your perusal.
>
> P.A. Lobanovich, P.D.

"That's what I meant about vanity," Guchkov said, laying the report to one side.

"I'm sorry, Guchkov," Kurasov said. He looked slightly green around the gills, Guchkov was gratified to notice. "I don't follow you at all."

"Professor Doctor Lobanovich has mentioned a departure from the classic type—the absence of the super-vanity. So far, as Lobanovich points out, our man hasn't advertised himself at all. No letters telling us what fools we are, no samples through the mail."

"Samples?" Kurasov said, faintly.

"Sex murderers often send a body fragment to the police to prove that they are indeed the killer," Guchkov said. "A strip of flesh, or—"

"Guchkov, will you please refrain from offending me in this manner!" Kurasov said, shrilly. "Do you hear me?"

"I want to see if we can encourage our murderer to come out into the open," Guchkov said, avoiding apology. "He's too damned modest by half. I'd like to see if we can get him to tell us something about himself."

"How do you propose to do that?"

"I want you to get the First Secretary's permission for me to go to one of the newspapers; it doesn't matter which. Once we get the ball rolling, they'll all join in anyway."

"Ball? Rolling?"

"I want to give the murders to the papers."

"The First Secretary has forbidden the censors to permit anything to appear in the papers about these killings!" Kurasov bleated. "He says, and I agree, that there would be panic in the streets if it was known that this maniac is on the loose."

"You may be right," Guchkov said, "although I doubt it. Tell me this: do you think the First Secretary would prefer our killer to go on killing without let or hindrance? He isn't going to stop, you know. Not until we stop him."

"Well," Kurasov said, dubiously.

"Let me talk to the First Secretary—" Guchkov said, eagerly.

"Just a moment, just one moment!" Kurasov said, his voice waspish. "We'll see about that in due course. First, tell me what you have in mind."

"I want to give the newspapers a series of articles written by me. Us," he added, seeing Kurasov's expression change. "My idea is to write the articles with certain inaccuracies in them, things no one would know about except the murderer. If Professor Doctor Lobanovich is right, he won't be able to resist showing the writer up as a fool. If we can get him to put pen to paper, we might have a chance. We might even get fingerprints."

"Oh," Kurasov sniffed. "Fingerprints."

Guchkov sighed. He knew how his superiors felt about his fingerprint files: the same way Kurasov had felt about every innovation he ever made or suggested: nervous, hostile, and threatened. Although the science was still in its infancy, Guchkov was convinced of its eventual effectiveness and he had fought hard to get it adopted in the Ministry of Justice. Unlike most of his confreres, Guchkov was widely read in criminology. His shelves bulged with works by the experts: Faulds, Anderson, Irving, Lombroso, and the American, Geyer.

Guchkov had won his fight, but it had been a long haul. The system now in use in the Justice Ministry was based on the well-established principles laid down by the Englishman, Sir Edward Henry, a disciple of the true pioneer of the science, Sir Francis Galton. Galton, a nephew of Charles Darwin, had been one of that breed of Victorian all-rounders who dabbled in science and anthropology, searched for the source of the Nile, tilled the virgin soil of statistical research. He published, in 1892, a book on fingerprinting which remained the definitive work until Henry, at that time Inspector-General of Police in Bengal, devised the cataloging system which had since become standard throughout the world. Henry had discerned five basic patterns in all fingerprints and assigned codes to each of them. He then broke down the five main patterns into many hundreds of subdivisions, giving each of them a secondary code number. In 1900, his report to a London committee so greatly impressed it that fingerprinting was made the official criminal investigation system in Britain, and he was appointed head of the new Criminal Investigation Division based on the Thames Embankment in Scotland Yard. His book, *The Classification and Uses of Fingerprinting*, was one of Guchkov's bibles. The fact that many of his colleagues did not share his enthusiasm for the technique bothered Viktor Guchkov not at all. He knew what he knew; that they did not know it or care to learn it was their loss, not his.

"It's worth a try," he said to Kurasov. "Damn it, we haven't got anything else!"

"There could be repercussions," Kurasov said, dubiously.

"There'll be repercussions if we leave this maniac running around Moscow," Guchkov said. "You can be sure of that."

"I hadn't thought of it that way," Kurasov said. "I'll speak to the First Secretary tomorrow."

"Why not do it right away?" Guchkov said, hoping that he wasn't pushing too obviously. "The sooner the better, I'd say."

Kurasov frowned. "You may be right, at that," he admitted. "I'll go up and see if he's free."

Smiling, Guchkov watched him go.

12

VLADIMIR looked out across the harbor at the old castle on its hill. It was warm in the Ane Rouge, and the bright sunshine outside gave the sullen Mediterranean the false glitter of a rhinestoned whore. The tall palms along the Promenade des Anglais clacked their fronds in the wind. Inside the glass-fronted restaurants on the sea front, waiters unstacked chairs with the desultory, lackadaisical air of men who know no one is coming. Vladimir sighed. A man ought to be happy, he thought, sitting in a cozy restaurant on the Riviera when the rest of the world was still shivering beneath the onslaught of winter. Somehow the thought did not cheer him. Dark, depressed imaginings threaded their way through his mind; the future seemed bleak and uninviting.

It would be *shirokaya maslenitsa* soon, the Saturday of Shrovetide, the great Russian winter holiday: carnival time, the time of feasting on *bliny* filled with herrings or caviar, drowned in butter or *smetana*, with toasts in vodka drunk *do dna*, to the bottom. In every park and public place there would be snow slides, and girls with apple-red cheeks would shriek with mock fear as their laughing escorts took them careering down the hills in furious flurries of snow and laughter. Along all the sidewalks street vendors would sell spiced bread, nuts, hot pancakes, sweetmeats, fishcakes, *pirozhki*. Peddlers' huts would sprout on the Devitchy Field, and the street musicians would play their hurdy-gurdy tunes while the *sharmanka*, the tame monkey with his red tarboosh, would clank a kopeck in this tin cup, vying for attention with the balalaika players, accordion players, tumblers, storytellers. There would be fairgrounds with carousels and dancing bears, acrobats and shooting galleries. The restaurants would all be full, and so would the theaters and the circuses. Crowds would jam the liquor stores to buy vodka. The girls in the brothels would be doing a roaring trade; even the *tyetki* in the

Khitrovka would be doing better than usual. Merchants would parade on the Taganka side in their carriages, the horses and harness decorated with ribbons and colored paper flowers, their owners dressed in their finest clothes. Others would walk the broad sidewalks, their wives and daughters wearing their finest jewelry, solemnly greeting their neighbors as they passed by.

Vladimir had left the villa early and walked along the promenade, watching the gulls being blown about like scraps of paper above the roaring surf. He always enjoyed walking through the market among the housewives buying their vegetables, savoring the peachy tang of the fruit and the flowers. He came the same way almost every day, partly to get away from the villa, which was beginning to oppress him, and partly to clear his head of the smoke and drink of the preceding evening at the casino. God, what a thieves' den that was! Half the Russian nobility was on the Riviera at this time of year, and some evenings it seemed as if every single one of them was crammed into the outrageously ornate palace on the promenade, gambling sums that raised the eyebrows of even the blasé casino croupiers.

He smiled at his own misanthropy. He gambled a bit himself, but it was not a compulsion. Some of the people he had watched last night had been betting as cheerlessly as if the markers were worth no more than the wood of which they were made. One had no right, he supposed, to criticize the way others spent their money; but it did seem such a sad waste. He shrugged, knowing the cause of his reaction. He was tired of Nice, tired of the neat gardens which looked as if someone had manicured them, tired of *cuisine gastronomique*, tired of traveling, tired of newspapers with blaring headlines about war and assassination in Montenegro and Serbia and Rumania, tired of Monsieur Proust, whose new book he had tried (and failed) to read, and tired of Lilian Donaldson, the Englishwoman he had picked up at the Folletts' cocktail party in Grasse. God, yes, he thought, very tired of her. The French had the right word for it: *anomie*. It described how he felt much better than *boredom* or *weltschmerz* or the Russian word, *skuka*.

It had started in Paris.

The French were very partial to Russians this year, and they all seemed to be in Montparnasse. He stopped at the Rotonde with Maurice Darbellay and was astonished at how many of them there were: artists, painters, actors, dancers, beggars, whores, gypsies, poets, thieves, poseurs arguing and drinking and drinking and arguing. There was no tomorrow for any of them. They believed that they could change the world at will without suffering any consequences. How could anyone be as sure of anything, as were Martov, say, or Ehrenburg? How could anyone be as openly fraudulent as Diaghilev and get away with it? He didn't like the man and never had. In fact, he didn't like any of the theater crowd he had come to know so well, thanks to dear, sweet Valentina. What he especially did not like was men wearing makeup, and Diaghilev was always surrounded by those. He was full of plans for his new ballet. It was to have a score by Igor Stravinsky.

"It will be a sensation, dear boy," he told Vladimir. "A veritable astonishment!"

"Sergei, you're a fraud," Vladimir said.

"I know, my dear boy," Diaghilev said. "But a brilliant one, non?

He was a great charmer and utterly unscrupulous. Despite the fact that he had no talent of his own, he attracted the talented as if he possessed some strange magnetic force: Juan Gris, Chaliapin, Fokine, Nijinsky, Braque, Picasso, Debussy, Erik Satie all clamored to work with him.

"You seem unhappy, my friend," Darbellay said to him as they walked down the Boulevard St. Michel. "Is there something wrong?"

"It will pass, old friend," Vladimir told the Frenchman, knowing it would not. He had been feeling low ever since he had talked to Nikki. If there had ever been any possibility of his having a good time in Paris, Nikki had seen to it that he did not.

Of course, he didn't call himself that anymore. To the seedy gang of would-be revolutionaries with whom he mixed, Nikki was Mikhail Mikhailovich, a klichka, which honored the assassin of Alexander II. They met in a dismal café on the Avenue d'Orleans. Traffic clattered incessantly outside. Around the huddled tables the surly exiles played endless games of cards and chess, forever talking of the revolution to come in Russia. Vladimir felt conspicuous in his good clothes; perhaps he was supposed to, he thought. He felt very aware of the gulf between himself and these men, even between himself and Nikki—Mikhail, he corrected himself. By either name, he was still a Smirnoff, a cousin. The gaunt, gray-haired man sitting opposite him looked considerably older than sixty-four and nothing like any cousin Vladimir had ever imagined having.

"You'll let me have the money, then?"

173

"Of course," Vladimir said.

"You can afford it." There was contempt in the old man's voice. No gratitude. One never expected gratitude from them. Senka had told him that many times.

"I expect so," Vladimir said. "How much this time?"

"Ten thousand francs."

"Another ten thousand? I gave you ten thousand in October."

"Revolutions don't come cheap," Mikhail snapped. Damned right, Vladimir thought, recalling being told that Lenin paid nearly a thousand francs a year for his elegant apartment on the rue Beaunier.

"It's still a lot less than it would cost you if I came back to Moscow and claimed what's due me," Mikhail said.

"If you came back, it would cost you your life," Vladimir told him. "And well you know it."

"No," the old man said, "they've forgotten all that. Nobody knows who I am anymore. Not even this lot." He jerked his head at the men playing chess under the guttering oil lamps. There was scant respect in his voice.

"They're a poor bunch," Vladimir observed quietly.

"Hard times," Mikhail said unfeelingly. "How are things in Moscow?"

"Very quiet," Vladimir said. "No revolutions lately."

"It's not funny!" the old man snapped. "Don't make fun of us, Vladimir."

"You're quite right," Vladimir said. "I'm sorry."

"We're going to win in the end, you know. Maybe not this year or next. But we shall win."

"Nikki—"

"Don't call me that!" the old man hissed, eyes widening with anger. "I gave that name away a long time ago—when your illustrious father traded my birthright for my life."

"You'd have preferred to hang?"

"Nobody asked me!" hissed Mikhail. "Nobody asked *me!*" He banged his fist on the checkered tablecloth, and the cruet jumped and jangled. The men at the other tables looked up to see what the disturbance was. A huge fellow dressed in what looked like the remnants of a sailor's uniform came across to them. He leaned over the table, brow knotted with manufactured anger.

"Something wrong here?" he growled, looking at Vladimir. "You causing trouble, or something?"

"It's all right, Yuri Danielovich," Mikhail said, laying a liver-spotted hand on the sailor's bunched fist. "He's a friend."

"Strange friends you have, Mikhail Mikhailovich," the man growled. "We don't want his kind here."

"It's all right, Yuri," the old man said again. The sailor glowered for a few moments longer and then deliberately spat at Vladimir's feet.

"We'll bury your kind in millions," he said, "one day." Then he lurched back to his companions and sprawled in his chair, a satisfied look on his brutish face. Vladimir looked at him and then at the gob of spittle on his shoe. Anger swept over him, but he did not allow it to show. The sullen brute was just waiting for someone upon whom he could vent his frustration and purposelessness. Somehow, it seemed sad that a man should be ready to fight, even die, for a cause which no one cared about.

"About the money," Mikhail said.

"Ah, yes," Vladimir said. They still wanted the money, of course. They might call you a capitalist pig and spit on you, but they still wanted the money. "What are you going to use it for?" He just managed to avoid adding the words "this time."

"To keep our newspaper going."

"Your newspaper?"

"Yes, our newspaper. Our revolutionary newspaper. The only one which tells the workers of the world the truth."

"Spare me the polemic," Vladimir said. "I've heard it all before."

"One day you will be glad to be given the chance to hear it," Mikhail said. "The truth will set the workers free. That is our by-word, the name of our newspaper: truth."

"*Pravda?*" Vladimir said, suddenly dismayed. "Isn't that the one that Senka—?"

"The same," Mikhail said.

"You're going to publish it here in Paris?"

"Not in Paris," Mikhail said, his old face wreathed in a savage grin. "We shall publish where we have always published—in Petersburg."

"You plan to send the money to Petersburg? I could have taken it there for you."

"No need," Mikhail said. "I'll take it myself."

"You?"

"Yes," the old man said, pleased with his bombshell. "Me."

"You'll get us all hung!" Vladimir said.

"Do you think I give a damn about that?" Mikhail snarled, venomously. "Do you honestly think I give a damn about any of you?"

There was no possible answer. The old man's hatred went back to a time before Vladimir had been born, yet it was directed at him as though he, personally, had been responsible for what happened to Nikolai Smirnoff in 1849. This rheumy old man had spent sixty years or more dreaming only of revenge. He was not going to be persuaded now that it was useless. It had become a sort of insanity.

"Stay away from us. Stay away from Russia, cousin."

"I won't promise that," the old man growled.

"Yes, you will," Vladimir said. His eyes met without fear the glare which the old man directed at him. If Nikki came back to Petersburg, he would be *Okhrana* meat. No matter how welcome the Smirnoffs might be at the court of Nicholas II, not even that indecisive bumbler would countenance the reappearance in the capital of one of the plotters who had murdered his grandfather.

"No money without your solemn oath," he said.

"Damn you!" the old man replied. Vladimir saw Yuri look up sharply at the sound. Stay put, Yuri, Vladimir thought, relieved when the big man turned back to talk to his comrades.

"Your oath, cousin," he insisted.

"All right," the old man muttered, pretending sulky acceptance. He had no intention of ever keeping his word. If there was a God, which Mikhail seriously doubted, he would understand and forgive the necessity. The cause needed the money; the end justified the means. If what Lenin's informants in the *Okhrana* said was true, Josif Djugashvily was to be arrested and exiled to Siberia. There would be no one to run the newspaper who was *au fait* with the attitudes of the leaders of the movement in Paris. It had been decided, at his own request, that Mikhail Mikhailovich be permitted to take on the task.

"There are plenty of skeletons in Petersburg cupboards, not a few of which have been there since Mikhailovich's time," Lenin said, smiling that strangely self-satisfied smile of his. "Perhaps it is time to fling open the doors. And Mikhail Mikhailovich is the man who can do it."

"You give me your solemn oath?" Vladimir said.

"Yes, yes," Mikhail said, impatiently. "Now, when will you bring me the money?"

"Tomorrow," Vladimir said. The old man was lying, but there

176

was nothing he could do about it. He felt soiled and used, like a whore paid in counterfeit. His own attitude toward the Bolsheviks and the other revolutionaries was mixed. On the one hand, he saw them, as did most liberal thinkers, as the only way by means of which the lot of the workers and peasants could be changed. The change must come from below since it would never come from above. And yet, when he was confronted by the dingy reality of the revolutionary cause, he saw clearly that it was in the hands of small-minded men with venal ambitions, men intent on personal gain, men pursuing small revenges who cared as little for the downtrodden poor as any bloated plutocrat. Depressed and saddened, he walked down the avenue toward Montparnasse. A soft rain was beginning to fall and he was glad that in a few days' time he would be on the Riviera, away from this gray, disconsolate city.

If Paris was a disappointment, Nice was a disaster. Sergei and Katrina had come down, and he invited them to dinner at his favorite restaurant. It stood on a corner just a few hundred meters from the Promenade des Anglais, a bistro run by an elderly couple to whom Vladimir had loaned the money to buy the place some years earlier. They had long since repaid him, and paid him in more than money. He was their patron, their always-honored guest. Marcel Charpentier and his wife served plain, simple food, good fish and a decent Hyères. Vladimir never ate better anywhere else in France.

He had not seen either Sergei or Katrina for a while. It seemed to him that she was pensive and sad, but Katrina was always pensive, and perhaps he was imagining the sadness. As for Tretyakov, he had no time for the man or any of his precious, pomaded friends. They were part of the system that was ruining Russia, but men like Sergei would never realize it. Even if it was thrust under their noses, they would be far too indolent to try to change. He remembered his short, sharp, furious argument with Pierre, when Pierre had first announced that Katrina was to marry Sergei.

"You oppose the match?" Pierre had said, as if astonished that anyone should challenge him.

"Of course I do," Vladimir said. "The man makes my flesh crawl."

"He is the son of Stepan Tretyakov, one of the most respected men in Russia," Pierre said. "Not to say one of the richest."

"Genya approves the match, too, Vladimir," Nico murmured.

"Does she, by God?" Vladimir said. His mother, stepmother to Pierre and Nico, was still a power behind the scenes in the Smirnoff family. For all her frailty—she was past her seventieth birthday—few of the affairs of The House or the family escaped her attention. Pierre discussed everything with her. She still treated Vladimir as if he was a boy, shaking her head at follies he no longer committed, convinced he was still guilty of them.

"Vladimir," Pierre said gently, "believe me, I have given it the most serious thought. Surely, you don't think I would allow my daughter to make such a match if I was not certain—*certain*—that it was what she wanted, too?"

"You've asked her?"

"Of course, I've asked her," Pierre said testily.

"Then I'll not be the one to oppose it," Vladimir said. "But I'm damned if I'll say I like it."

Looking at them both now in the restaurant, Vladimir realized that there was something seriously amiss. Sergei was ill at ease and avoided Vladimir's eyes. He had the air of a man who is afraid he won't be able to get away before someone asks him the one question he doesn't want to answer. As for Katrina, she replied to all Vladimir's remarks in monosyllables, head down, toying with the honest food the Charpentiers had served them. After the main course, Sergei excused himself.

"An appointment," he mumbled. "Couldn't break it."

Vladimir watched him go without allowing his annoyance to show. There was something about the man, something he could not put a finger on. He did not mind the evasiveness, the uneasy feeling that much of what Sergei said was merely words, used to avoid direct response to anything you said to him. It was something deeper than that. Instinct told him there was a factor missing in Sergei's personality, an inability to respond to other humans in the same way that everyone else did, an inability he concealed with an apparently gregarious nature and a somehow spurious generosity. He turned to face Katrina and was distressed to see that her eyes were brimming with tears she was fighting to avoid shedding.

"What is it, Katrina?" he said.

"Don't be angry with him, Vladimir," she said. "I asked him to go."

"Why?"

"I wanted . . . I need to talk to you."

The huge tears trembled on the brink of her eyelids and then overflowed, trickling down her face like mountain rivulets. And yet she was not crying.

178

"Tell me what's wrong," Vladimir said.

"He hates you," she said. "He hates us all. All the family."

"Including you?"

She fumbled in her purse, avoiding the necessity to answer by coming up with a tiny lace handkerchief and dabbing ineffectually at her eyes. She drew in a faltering breath and let it out slowly and then looked at him.

"I . . . don't know, Vladimir. That's what's so awful. I don't know. I have no standards to measure him by, so I don't know."

He said nothing, just let the silence stretch. Questions did not always bring replies, but silence nearly always did. It was as if people wanted to fill silences with speech. But Katrina said no more. They sat in the lengthening silence, uncomfortably aware of the surreptitious stares of the other diners. They think I'm her lover and she is the betrayed plaything I am discarding, Vladimir thought. At any other time he might have smiled at the irony of it, but Katrina's distress was too real for him to care about what anyone else thought. She had been his darling ever since he could remember. The idea of being an uncle, a real uncle at fourteen was so heady that he had gone to the bank and opened a savings account in her name, putting money in it every birthday and at Christmastime. She was a sweet child, bright and intelligent and full of love. That same sweet innocence had stayed with her into adulthood, but as it had been a shield in childhood, so it had rendered her vulnerable as she grew up. She was a serious schoolgirl. Year by year she grew more interested in the Church. At the ornate Ekaterina Institute, with its smoking candles and chanting priests, she seemed to find a contentment, a reward that nothing else in life provided. She even talked for a while of taking holy orders, but Sonya gently steered her away from that, and when Katrina came home from school, she went to work instead in the little school provided for the children of their workers by the Smirnoff family. As she got older, she went into the *kamorki*, to look after women in labor, to wash their babies, to read the children stories from the Bible. At first they were wary of her, as the grindingly poor are always wary of the motives of the rich. Her goodness and inner radiance shone from her and won them over. They called her *Dabryachka*, the kind lady.

"Would you like a cigarette?" Vladimir said, after a while.

"No."

"Come on, let's go for a walk. We'll have coffee somewhere else."

He signaled to Marcel, who looked at their plates and raised his eyebrows.

"I am desolated that you do not like your meal, monsieur," he said. "And mademoiselle has eaten hardly anything."

"It's nothing to do with your fine cooking, Marcel," Vladimir said, patting the old man's arm. "Please give your wife my apologies and tell her I'll try to do better next time."

He took Katrina's arm, and they walked down the street to the promenade. A bus went by, and the people in it stared at them incuriously. There was a café open a little way along. The waiter was standing by the zinc with that disengaged look they have in mid-evening. When Vladimir asked for two coffees, the man nodded as if his worst fears had just been realized.

"Did you like the bistro?" Vladimir said, lighting a cigarette. It was more for something to say than for any other reason. He was trying to find a way to put her at her ease.

"It was very nice," she said, absently.

"Do you know how bistros got their name?" he said, not waiting for a reply. "When Paris was occupied by Russian troops in 1814, and they found a restaurant closed, they would hammer on the doors and yell at the owner to cook them some food quickly. After a while, the restaurant owners realized that the only way to stop the soldiers banging on their doors and yelling 'Quickly! Quickly!' was to always have something ready. So the Russian word for 'quickly'—bistro—became the French word for a little restaurant."

Katrina did not answer. He wasn't even sure that she had been listening, and by and large it didn't matter if she had not.

"Would you like something? A cognac?"

"No," she said. "I don't like the stuff."

"A real Smirnoff." He smiled. It was a funny thing, but none of the family had ever been a serious drinker, except Nico, and even he was now teetotal. Old Petya had been strict about it, because it was always so easy for them to get. He quoted Arsenii's maxim: first the man takes a drink; then the drink takes a drink; and then the drink takes the man.

He noticed that Katrina had looked away and thought he saw the gleam of tears again. Damn, he thought, realizing how clumsy he had been. Before he could speak, however, the waiter brought their coffee, pushing it under their noses with the air of a man performing a most unpleasant duty.

"Does Sergei's drinking worry you?" he said, stirring his coffee and not looking at Katrina.

"He . . . it's not just . . . oh, Vladimir, yes, yes, I'm so terribly worried."

"It's bad, then?"

"Not like that. He doesn't get stupid drunk or fall down or get angry. He just . . . seems to drink to dull his senses. To be morose. I don't know why."

"Have you told him that it distresses you?"

"No . . . I thought . . . perhaps later. When we're married."

Vladimir said nothing. You didn't have to be a drinker to know how hard it was to convince a real one that he was killing himself, killing the love of the people around him. Nobody ever believed he could slip from just having a social drink to serious drinking, and from there to drinking to survive, the living death of alcoholism. He wondered why Sergei had turned into a drinker. There always was a reason. He made a mental note to ask some questions when he got home.

"Try to get him to talk about it," he said softly. "Tell him it makes you unhappy."

"That's not the important thing, Vladimir," she said.

"It is to me," he said. She shook her head in that sad way she had, and laid a soft hand on top of his.

"Dear Vladimir," she said. "I've always brought you my problems and you've always helped. But this time . . ."

"You want me to speak to him?"

"No!" she said, sharply. Then more softly, "No, don't."

He remembered the time he had brought her a pretty woven basket to collect mushrooms. She had whispered in his ear that she wanted one more than anything else in the world, and when he brought it, he called it an "unbirthday" present and told her he would bring her 363 more for all her other unbirthdays.

"Vladimir, you're spoiling her," Sonya would protest, smiling. "You're always bringing her presents."

"She'll be grown up soon enough, Sonya." He smiled. "Let me spoil her while I can."

Well, she was grown up in earnest now, he thought, and it made him want to strike Heaven in the face for what was happening to her. Whatever Sergei Tretyakov's fear was, or guilt was, he had handed it to her like a bouquet of flowers, and she was accepting it like a gift.

"I'm sorry," she whispered. "It's not fair of me to burden you with my problems."

"I would be angry if you didn't," he said. "I just wish there was something constructive I could say or do right now."

"Just . . . talking helps."

He let the silence lengthen once again. The waiter and the man behind the bar were watching them with unconcealed interest. Strange how people love other people's tragedies, he thought. As if they're secretly glad someone other than themselves is being hurt, feeling pain.

"Do you love him, Katrina?" he asked.

"He needs me."

"Is that enough? Enough for the rest of your life?"

"I don't know," she said. "Perhaps I'm not meant to know. Perhaps God in His infinite wisdom saw Sergei's need and put me here to fulfill it. Perhaps that is my task in life."

"That's a lot of perhapses," Vladimir said.

"I know."

"But you're still going to go through with it."

"Yes," she said. "Yes, I am."

"It's a mistake, Katrina," he said. She was committing herself to a kind of prison, a life sentence in which the punishments were loneliness, contempt, jealousy and fear. Sergei Tretyakov would break her heart and never even know he had done it. For a moment, Vladimir felt the rage surge up. God damn it, why did the weak always have to fasten onto the strong like some awful cancer, eating them away, using their strength to survive on—and why did the truly strong ones always let them do it?

"Come on," he said. "I'll take you home."

"You go ahead," she said.

"Where are you going?"

"To church," she said. "I'm going to church."

"Say one for me," Vladimir said.

She smiled. They had talked about religion, about faith and God, many, many times. Katrina believed; her faith was as unshakable as a mountain. Vladimir doubted; that there might have been a man like Christ he could not argue, but that there was a God of the kind the priests talked to, he seriously doubted. It always seemed to him that their God was too small-minded, too vengeful. If there was a God, He was everywhere and not just in some perfumed *lavra* where only priests could address Him. Vladimir would not accept a God from whom a man had to *beg* forgiveness. Katrina was different. Her God was a shining reality, the center of all existence, inaccessible,

182

mysterious, awesome, all-powerful. Her faith was sweetly certain. It shone from her and people saw it, and were humbled by it. She would talk to her God and somehow find the peace she needed in doing it.

"I'll see you later," he said, and kissed her. Her cheek was cool and slightly damp from the sea air. After she had gone he stood for a long time outside the café, not thinking, not seeing anything, not moving. The surf slid up on the shingle and roared back again. He realized that there was a cold edge on the wind and began to walk back toward the villa, wrapped in a cloak of foreboding.

Max, the butler, took his coat and told him that Mrs. Donaldson was waiting for him in the drawing room. He went in; her face looked as if it had been chiseled from a glacier.

"Lilian," he said, going over to her and taking her hand. "How long have you been here?"

"An hour," she said frostily, withdrawing her hand. Her voice was as cold as her expression. "Did you forget our arrangement?"

"Our arrange—?" He clapped a hand to his forehead. "Oh, *mon Dieu! Chèrie*, how can I explain? It was—"

"Don't trouble yourself," she said.

"Lilian, please," he said. "It was unavoidable. A family matter. I had no—"

"No choice?" she echoed. "Nor had I, my dear Vladimir. I stood in the foyer of the casino for the better part of an hour, listening to cloakroom girls sniggering at me. And wondering why I was such a damned fool as to wait at all."

"I am sorry, Lilian," Vladimir said. "Truly sorry. It won't ever happen again."

"In that, at least, you are right," she said, icily.

"I beg your pardon?"

"I waited for you so that I could tell you to your face. It's finished, Vladimir. I never want to see you again."

"Please, Lilian," he said. "Don't do this."

"It's overdue anyway," she said. "Tonight was just a confirmation of it. Will you ask your man to bring my wrap, please?"

"Lilian, I beg of you—stay. Let's talk it over."

"There's nothing to talk about," she said. "Are you going to ring that bell, or must I do it myself?"

"I'll do it," he said, pressing the bell. It really was the strangest thing. She was telling him what he had been trying to find a way of saying, and he was pleading with her not to say it.

"Let me call you tomorrow," he said. "We can talk—"

"My coat, please," she said to Max. "No, Vladimir. Don't call me or come to the house again. Do you understand?"

"I hear," he said. "But I don't understand."

Liar, the voice in his head said. You are flooded with relief, you are glad to see her walk out of your life.

"I am going now," she said, as Max helped her into the silken wrap. Her voice was as sweetly precise as a Swiss watch. "But there is one thing I wanted to tell you before I leave."

"Yes?"

"I know women who fuck better than you do," Lilian Donaldson said, and pushed past him out of the room. A few moments later, he heard the door slam. A car started up; headlights flashed against the walls, and she roared away. Vladimir shook his head, bemused, a little shaken by her not altogether atypical Parthian shot. Lilian had been like that. He had once read about an African animal called a honey badger. They said when it was cornered by a man, it went straight for the groin. That was Lilian's way of fighting. She always liked to be in control; she had right from the start. God, how he had wanted her when he first met her at the cocktail party in Grasse! She had been wearing a pale green sleeveless dress of crepe-de-chine. It clung to her and revealed every contour of the elegant body beneath it, a fact of which Lilian Donaldson was completely aware. He saw her look at him when he arrived. The Folletts greeted him with hugs and kisses and pointed him at the bar. He looked around and discovered that he didn't know a soul. Ken was a writer, and Vladimir didn't know any of his literary friends. He got himself a glass of champagne and turned around to find himself facing the sexy woman in the green dress. She had a drink in one hand and a cigarette in the other.

"Hello," she said. "I'm Lilian Donaldson. Who are you?"

He told her his name, and she smiled.

"Russian?" she said, putting a lot into the word, as if being Russian was the very distillation of everything male, attractive. "You must tell me something about your country. I'm quite fascinated by Russia. *La charme Slav* is very big this year, isn't it?"

She was looking right into his eyes as she said it. He hadn't seen her put down her glass, but she had done so. Her right hand, hidden from all the other guests by Vladimir's body, slid into his crotch and grasped his genitals firmly.

"Mmm," she said, softly. "I thought so."

He could hardly believe it was happening to him. He was standing in the middle of a crowd of perhaps fifty or sixty people and this elegant, horsey Englishwoman was stroking his penis as if they were alone and naked in a bed. He reacted immediately to her touch, and a smile parted her beautifully painted lips.

"Well," she said approvingly, "you'd better come and dance with me, darling."

There was a four-piece orchestra playing on the patio beside the swimming pool and she slid into his arms, molding her body against his, one slender arm draped around his shoulder, the slim fingers caressing his ear and the short hairs at the nape of his neck. He was enormously aroused. His throat felt so thick that it was all he could do to make the polite conversation that convention seemed to demand. She told him that she was a widow, that her husband had been very old, very fat, and very tiresome.

"Thank God, darling, he was also very rich," she murmured with a wicked little laugh. "So I can indulge myself now." She moved her hips slightly, looking into his eyes with her own eyes parted widely. When his arms tightened around her lithe body, she smiled her panther's smile again. "Steady, darling," she said, lifting her chin and responding with her body. "All in good time."

They danced for what seemed a very long time. The warmth of the sun, the sound of the music, the chatter of the guests seemed to be muted, as though he was half deaf. He was conscious of her every movement, every nuance of the strong, slender frame in his arms. They went across to the buffet and poured Veuve Clicquot from the magnums into fresh glasses. They sipped the wine slowly, looking at each other over the rims of the glasses. They could have been totally, utterly alone, for all the notice they took of the other people around them.

"Well, darling, I'll go up first, shall I?" Lilian said, as if she was discussing taking a walk. "It's the third door on the left at the top of the stairs. Give me five minutes." She kissed her fingers and laid them on his lips, and then she was gone. She had a strong, almost mannish walk, he thought. He felt conspicuous now, as if everyone was watching him and waiting for him to follow her, but when he glanced at the other guests, no one seemed to be remotely interested in him. After five minutes that seemed like an eternity, he walked across the lawn and went into the house. It was cool and dark inside, and he had to wait for a moment until his eyes grew accustomed to the shaded interior. The staircase was ornate and curving, with a wrought-iron balustrade. He went up the stairs two at a time and through the gold-inlaid doorway into her room. She was lying naked on the bed, smoking a cigarette. There was a bottle of champagne in an ice bucket by the side of the bed.

"Who's a clever girl, then?" she said, lifting her chin. He stood there looking at her. Her breasts were not large. Her thighs were long and smooth. He could not take his eyes off the provocative tuft of pubic hair at her groin.

"Yes, darling, I'm a natural blonde," she drawled. "Now take off those boring clothes and come here."

In bed, Lilian Donaldson was agile and shameless. Her hands, her mouth, her tongue explored him as urgently as he explored her body. He took her roughly, hastily, explosively, and she shouted with pleasure as he climaxed inside her. Unlike many women he had known, she held him firmly to her afterward as if savoring the racing thunder of his heart and his raggedly uneven breathing. After a while, she loosened her grip.

"Well," she said, "is that the best you have to offer?"

It sounded like teasing then, that first time. It wasn't until much later that he realized that Lilian said things like that to make men feel inadequate, to dominate the situation. The first time, her words were just sweet, spoken in warm intimacy.

"Just for the moment," he said. "See for yourself."

She sat upright and looked down at him. Vladimir grinned up at her, and she grinned back.

"Well, darling," she said in her impeccable Home Counties drawl, "if that's the only problem . . ."

Her mouth enveloped him, drowning him in sensation. He felt himself stirring and she murmured something without words, her left thigh sliding across his face. He was swamped by the salt and musky tang of her as she squirmed and pushed against his seeking tongue. He was ready for her within moments, and she no less ready than he. Just as he was about to reach a climax she slid forward, easing her body around and under his, her legs wrapped around his back, her head thrown back upon the disordered bed.

"Now, now, now, now, now!" she hissed, her sinuous body moving as if impelled by some volition other than its own. "Now, now, *now!*" Then it was done and they were two again, not one, all slipping away from them, lying joined and yet apart once more, their bodies damp with perspiration.

Lilian Donaldson sat up, her eyes glowing with an almost feline

186

satisfaction. She reached across Vladimir's naked body, flattening her breasts against his belly as she reached for the champagne and the glasses on the bedside table. She put the icy base of the bottle on him, and he gasped with shock.

"Stay awake, darling," she said, and there was warning in her voice. "I don't want you dozing off, or anything."

"Don't worry," Vladimir said. "I want some of that champagne."

"Three glasses," Lilian Donaldson said. "No more."

"Why?"

"I may need you again," she said, with that same feline smile.

That had been the beginning and, taken for what it was, it was a fairly pleasant relationship. He clothed her and fed her, wined and dined her, took her to the theater or the casino, and paid her bills. She, in turn, graced his arm at dinners where he would otherwise have been that perennial thorn in the hostess' side, the unaccompanied male, and provided a mutually satisfying sexual partnership with no strings attached to it. It didn't matter a damn to Vladimir that everyone who knew her said that Lilian was playing him for all he was worth, and that when she got bored she would drop him and find another lover. In fact, it suited him; it was a straightforward business arrangement. Love didn't come into it. He was finished with love. Love was a bundle of clinically descriptive letters you found in a drawer. Love was a promise nobody ever kept. He could manage without it.

So they shared no intellectual pursuits or argued over the merits of book or play. They had nothing to say to each other except in bed, where they were eloquent for as long as it took for it to become repetitive. Then it became petty and boring, and he found himself trying to think of excuses not to see her, and angry when she expected more of his time than she had the right to expect. They would have parted anyway; tonight he had inadvertently—was it inadvertent? —given her the opportunity to do it in her own way. She probably needed to be able to say that she had walked out on him. He smiled a wry smile. She would probably tell everyone exactly what she had said when she did, too.

Well, that was all over without regret, he thought, as he sat the following day in the Ane Rouge and watched the fishing boats pottering in and out of the tiny harbor. Katrina and Sergei would be married at Easter. The thought did not make him feel any more cheerful. He laid down the copy of *Le Matin* he had been reading and called goodbye to Jules, the *patron*. Time to go home, Vladimir thought, without pleasure.

Sergei and Katrina preceded him to Moscow; Katrina was anxious to be home for the ceremony of anathema in the Cathedral of the Assumption in the Kremlin. She observed these rituals with meticulous care. On the Day of the Forty Martyrs, March 9, she would serve the little loaves shaped like birds with folded wings, with eyes made of raisins, which celebrated the arrival of the larks. In the sixth week of the Great Lent, she would decorate all the icons with willow branches to mark the beginning of Holy Week, see to it that the palms had been blessed, take some of the workers' children to the Red Square to buy their balloons and carry in their catkins. Katrina would see to the organizing of the Easter feast, the preparing of the dough for the *kulich*, the sugared white cheese for the *pashka*, and the dyes for the eggs. Meanwhile the days grew longer. The ice broke on the Moskva, and crowds went to see the tumbling blocks swirling turgidly beneath the great bridges. Freed from the icy grip of winter, people opened up their windows to catch the hints of spring breeze. In the big houses there was a frenzy of activity. Glaziers came to remove the double frames from the windows; the sleighs were greased and put away, and the carriages once more emerged from the carriage houses. Servants were everywhere, polishing, dusting, sweeping. The doorknobs shone, the chandeliers glittered, the floors mirrored the image of anyone who walked across them. There was a smell of beeswax and wet earth. The first buds were swelling the black branches, and in the woods, the only snow left was banked on the northern edges of the close-set stands of trees. Once in a while there was a fresh flurry, but spring was just around the corner. The wide streets became alive with the shouts of street vendors, *morozhonoye*, selling ice cream and itinerant cooks with trays of *pirozhki*. Peddlers of old clothes, flower sellers shouting "*Tzvyeti, tzvyetotchki!*"; fish merchants, fruit vendors, Tartars selling linen and long ornate dressing gowns, old women with baskets full of mushrooms, gypsies telling fortunes thronged the street. Carriages rattled by, splashing through puddles, wheels coated with yellow mud. The sidewalks were crowded with people: soldiers, policemen, students, nurses, schoolboys, sailors, businessmen who nodded greetings to the old *dvorniki* sitting outside the doors of the houses in their charge, snug in their short fur coats. Inside the big houses, women tried on their new dresses, their new hats.

At Sokolnika, the activity had been doubly intense, for the approach of Katrina's wedding day had involved a whole protocol of planning. Now it was here. Radiant in a gown of white lace, Katrina drove to the Church of the Redeemer with her father at her side, her two maids of honor sitting opposite her in the carriage.

A crowd of people, hundreds of them, stood outside the church. In honor of his daughter's wedding day, Pierre had given the workers at his factory a day off with full pay. Many of them were among the crowd which pushed and argued and jostled outside the beautifully decorated church. After all, it wasn't every day one got the chance to see a Petersburg nobleman marry one of the daughters of the Tsar of Vodka, old Pierre Smirnoff himself. Dozens of carriages had already been arranged around the square outside the church by the perspiring policemen, yet more and more kept on arriving. Women, their hair decorated with bright spring flowers, got out delicately from the coaches, stepping onto the red carpet laid across the muddy sidewalk, escorted by men dressed in cutaway coats and white ties, or the bright uniforms of the Garde Chevalier. They took their position on the right-hand side of the church, brilliantly lit by a thousand candles, doffing their top hats and helmets as they entered, greeting one another in informally hushed whispers, smiling, bowing, a chiaroscuro of colored silks and braids and satins and velvets, glinting sword tassels and epaulets, shining boots. On the left-hand side of the church, people who had crowded in off the street hours before watched in awed expectancy, their faces shining in the light of the candles in the lusters and around the icons on the scarlet eastern wall. The golden frames of the paintings gleamed, the soft silver lusters and candlesticks glowed warmly. Coughs, shuffling feet, the throaty whispering of the guests made a solid sound that echoed from the marbled pillars.

The bride arrived and entered the church on the arm of her husband-to-be. The priest walked ahead of them to the lectern set in the center of the church, and the crowd of friends and relations, with a surge of whispers and a sigh of silks, followed them. Maria Abrikosova stooped down to rearrange Katrina's train. The bride smiled at her and her other maid of honor, Tatiana Makcheyeva. There was a silence in which the sound of the wind in the trees outside the church could be clearly heard. Now the priest lit two candles wreathed with flowers, and holding them at an angle so that the wax dripped off them, turned to face the bride and groom. His eyes were large, shining as if with some special inner laughter. He held up his hand in blessing and gave the candles to Katrina and Sergei.

"Bless us, O Lord," intoned the head deacon.

"Blessed be our God now and hereafter, for ever and ever," chanted the old priest, his eyes still brimming as if with laughter. Then the sound of the choir, invisible in their stall high above the heads of the congregation, filled the whole church with sweet sound, music that swelled and hung and slowly faded.

The deacon read the litany and then the priest turned to the young couple, prayer book in hand.

"Eternal God who unitest those who were separate, and hast ordained their indissoluble bond of love; Thou who blessed Isaac and Rebecca and hath shown Thy mercy to their descendants according to Thy holy word, bless now Thy servants Sergius and Ekaterina, inclining their hearts to good. For Thou, God, art merciful and forgiving. Glory be to the Father and to the Son and to the Holy Ghost, now and forever more."

The choir's "amen" sounded like the voices of the angels as the priest picked up the wedding rings and, drawing Sergei's hand forward, placed one ring upon the tip of his finger.

"The servant of God, Sergius, plights his troth to the servant of God, Ekaterina."

He then placed the larger of the two rings on Katrina's hand and repeated the words. They exchanged rings; their faces were expressionless as they did so.

"From the beginning created Thou them, male and female," the priest read. His voice droned on, and Vladimir found his attention wandering. There were a lot of things on his mind, among them the young woman standing to Katrina's right before the lectern. Pierre had acted with typical forthrightness when her letter arrived. He told Alex and Maryka to close their apartment in Petersburg and come at once to Sokolnika, bringing Tatiana with them.

"That damned Abrikosov!" he raged. "I'll go to the Minister personally. I'll have the man kicked out on his ear. He'll be lucky to get a job directing traffic on the Kuznetsky Most!"

"You will do no such thing," Genya said. Although she no longer lived at Sokolnika, she still took a very lively interest in the family business. She was still a good-looking woman. Her eyes were clear, her back straight, her mind as sharp as that of a woman half her age. She attended the ballet and the opera regularly and made a point of reading at least one new book every week. None of these pastimes, however, held half as much interest for her as the affairs of the family. She had been involved with those for more than half a century, ever since the day she had married old Petya Smirnoff, when he was forty and she was eighteen and as innocent as a kitten.

"You'd rather let him go unpunished for his blackmail?" Pierre said.

"I think it might be better if you let me handle it, Pierre. I shall speak to Zubin Gorbichev about it."

Zubin Gorbichev was Deputy Minister of the Interior and the day-to-day head of the *Okhrana*. Vladimir looked at his mother in surprise. "I didn't know you knew him," he said.

"I know him," Genya said. She smiled at some memory. "Dear Zubin. He was very much in love with me. He wanted me to leave Petya and go with him to Paris."

"Why didn't you go?" Vladimir said, smiling.

"Oh," Genya said, and behind the old face, just for a second, Vladimir caught a glimpse of the pretty girl who Zubin Gorbichev had tried to steal from Petya Smirnoff. "He was—just—resistible."

"What will you do?" Pierre asked.

"I shall tell him that the Makcheyev family are our guests at Sokolnika, and that we consider them to be under our protection. I shall tell him that I will have no hesitation in bringing the matter to the attention of His Majesty should they be persecuted by any member of the *Okhrana* while they are our guests."

"Do you think he will listen?"

Genya smiled again. "I propose to make sure that he does."

"How?" Nico asked.

"By telling him about Vladimir's friend, Mikhail Mikhailovich. Cousin Nikki. I shall tell Gorbichev that he plans to return to *Piter*, and that we feel it our duty to advise him accordingly."

"You agree with this, Pierre?" Vladimir said.

"Well," Pierre said, dubiously.

"We have no choice anyway, Pierre," Genya said, sternly.

"They'll put him into prison and throw away the key," Nico said. "We can't—"

"We can and we must," Genya said. "Pierre, you know what I say is true. Any other way, and he will cause irreparable harm to the family and to the business."

"I suppose you're right, Genya," Pierre sighed. "I regret the necessity of it no less for that."

He and Nico left soon afterward. Vladimir decided to accept his mother's invitation to stay for tea. He did not spend enough time with her, and it was a lack of which he was specially conscious. He liked her very much indeed, and admired her mind. She had always treated him like a son, never like a child. There were very few like her.

"Pierre's distress is understandable, I suppose," he said. "It does seem . . . treacherous."

"I don't care what it seems like, Dimi," she said, using the nickname she had given him as a baby and never stopped using. "I will not allow that . . . that brigand to harm this family in any way. Pierre is soft-hearted, that's all. And he's going through a bad time."

"In what way?"

"Katrina and Sergei, for a start. He's having second thoughts about that. Then Nikki threatening to return to Moscow and make trouble. And Senka mixing with these Bolsheviks. All these years, everyone has done exactly what Pierre told them to do. Now all at once, no one will listen to him. To top it all, we hear that Irina is having an affair."

"What?" Vladimir said. "I didn't know about that."

"My dear boy," Genya smiled, "you don't know a quarter of what goes on in this family; you never have. You've always hidden away from the responsibility, played with your horses and your women, while someone else did the worrying."

"That's not fair, Genya," Vladimir said.

"Perhaps not, my dear Dimi," she replied. "But it's true."

At four o'clock precisely, the maid brought in tea. Not the samovar, but tea served in the English manner on Genya's pretty porcelain china. It tasted bitter and weak to Vladimir, who was accustomed to the more robust flavor of Russian tea.

"What's all this about Irina?" he said.

"Ah," Genya said, pouring herself another cup of tea.

"Don't be coy, Genya." Vladimir grinned. "What's it all about?"

"It's your fault, really," she said.

"My fault? How?"

"You were the one who introduced Senka to this American."

"The American? You mean Irina is having an affair with David Castle?"

"That's what Olga says," Genya replied.

"How would she know?" Vladimir said, not troubling to hide his scorn. Olga was Pierre's oldest daughter. She was married to Fritz Sukhotin, aide-de-camp to old General Zhilinsky, and she was as empty-headed as a china doll. Vladimir had no time for her or any of her social-climbing friends. "Olga knows as much about love as—"

"You, perhaps?"

"My, we've got our claws on today," Vladimir said. "You know it's true, Genya. Olga's only telling you to make trouble."

"She is telling me for the best," Genya said.

"She's feather-brained," Vladimir said. "You can't rely on a word she says."

"We shall see," Genya said. That was the only concession she would make. "It's a little more complicated than you think."

She poured him more tea and bade him tell her about his conversation in Paris with Nikki Smirnoff.

"You'll have to remember to refer to him as Mikhail Mikhailovich, Genya," he said, repeating the gist of what they had talked about. He left out Yuri and the sleazy café that smelled of rainwater and cats and the hopeless look on the faces of the exiles.

"You think he was serious about coming back, then?"

"Absolutely."

"Did he say when?"

"He didn't need to," Vladimir said. "He's sure to contact one of us as soon as he arrives. Pierre, probably, or Senka anyway."

"It will be too late then," Genya said. "So give me a kiss and run along. I have some telephoning to do."

"Your old flame Gorbichev?"

"Get along with you, now," she said, and he would have sworn, were she any other woman, that Genya Smirnoff was blushing.

The Makcheyev family arrived three days later. They looked for all the world like people who have had a death in the family, and, he supposed, that was not too far from the truth. He tried to imagine what his own reactions might be if someone told him what Boris Abrikosov had told Alex. You would try to understand, but could you? You would say that you forgave, but would you? As an abstraction, the thing was bearable. Close up, it was repellent. Alex looked old and tired, his wife pale and drawn. Tatiana was subdued and silent, but that had passed as they were all caught up in the excited preparations for the wedding. It was as if the very knowledge that Boris Abrikosov's baleful attentions had been removed from their life—Genya said Gorbichev had assigned him to the Ukraine and that he would leave within the week—was medicine itself. Old Alex became his gruff, crusty self, Maryka smiled once

193

more, and Tatiana—Tatiana had flowered, Vladimir thought. He looked at her now across the crowded church, her bright golden hair shining in the candlelight. She was beautiful, no doubt of it. But not too bright, he reminded himself. After all, the girl had been enamored of Sergei Tretyakov, and Sergei was as poor a fish as ever swam in the marital sea.

"Wife, obey thy husband," Vladimir heard the priest intone. The first part of the ceremony was over. The choir above sang a psalm as the priest spread a length of rose-colored silk in front of the lectern, and, turning around, motioned Katrina and Sergei onto it. Katrina's expression was one of near-exaltation. She was lovely in her white silk dress with its long veil, her bouquet of white flowers. Her hair was dressed in a chignon above the scalloped lace collar, and her cornflower-blue eyes were as misty and faraway as if she was dreaming. Neither she nor Sergei appeared to hear the arguments among the spectators about which of them had stepped first upon the rose-colored carpet. There was an old saying that whichever of the couple stepped on it first would be the head of the household.

Now the priest asked them for the first time whether they wished to be married, and whether either of them was pledged to anyone else. Heads bowed, they listened to the prayers that their union be fruitful, that God would bless them as He had blessed Isaac and Rebecca, Joseph, Moses. Now the orange-blossom crowns were held high above their heads.

"Put it on!" the people said. "Put it right on!"

Katrina nodded and Sergei, with trembling hands, gently placed the crown of orange blossoms on the golden head. The epistle was read; the deacon thundered out the last verse so that the crowds outside would know that the ceremony was nearing its end. Bride and groom drank the warm, watered red wine from the proffered cup, and the priest took their hands in his, leading them around the lectern while from the choir above, a voice rang out: "Rejoice, O Isaiah!"

Now the best man and the maids of honor joined the circle that moved and stopped and circled and stopped until the priest lifted the blossom crowns from the couple's heads. It was time for the last prayer.

God, help them, Vladimir found himself thinking. God, help us all. It surprised him; it was a long time since he had prayed.

"Sergius, kiss your wife," he heard the priest say. "And you, woman, kiss your husband," he took the candles from their hands. Katrina and Sergei were married.

Now everyone rushed to congratulate them, hug them, kiss them, tell them how beautiful the service had been. It was hot in the church, the heat of close-packed people amid many candles and tension. Vladimir caught a glimpse of Pierre among the press of people, his face held stiffly in a grimace of pleasure. He saw Tatiana Makcheyeva standing to one side. Her face was sad; he wondered why.

"Well, Vladimir, that was quite an experience."

Vladimir recognized the accent immediately and turned to see David Castle smiling at him. The American didn't seem to have changed the slightest bit since the last time he had seen him, and it somehow surprised Vladimir. He smiled a little at his own fancy. Did he expect the man to have grown horns and a tail?

He said, "What are you doing here in Moscow?"

"Just a flying trip," David Castle said.

"How is life in Petersburg?"

"Splendid, thanks to your brother," Castle said. "I'm almost embarrassed by the number of invitations that I receive."

"*Piter* is like that," Vladimir observed. "If they like you, you're invited everywhere. If they don't, you could be the Tsarevich and never go out. You're obviously popular."

"A curiosity, I suspect," Castle said. "An American who speaks Russian."

"You've mastered the language well."

"Most of the credit for that belongs to Irina."

"How often do you have lessons?"

"Three afternoons a week."

"At the house?"

"Mostly. Sometimes we go for a walk down the Nevsky or in the Alexander Garden. So I can practice."

"How long will you be in Moscow?"

"Just a few days. When Irina said they were coming for the wedding, I decided to take a few days off. The house was going to be empty anyway, and there were some things I had to do here."

"Oh?"

"There's a man I have to talk to," Castle said. "You probably know him. His name is Marius. Gustave Marius."

"The banker? Yes, I know him. He's a German, isn't he?"

"I believe so," Castle said.

"Who's German?"

It was Senka, patting away at his pockets as usual. He looked strange in the formal clothes and very uncomfortable, like a man forced to do something silly in public.

"We were talking about Gustave Marius," Vladimir said.

"He's got a place on the Tverskoi, hasn't he?"

"That's right," Senka said. "Have you business with him, David? You didn't say anything before we left *Piter*."

"It's not important," Castle said, offhandedly. "Just an errand for the Ambassador."

"Well," Vladimir said, "I imagine the bride and groom are back at Sokolnika by now. Why don't you ride out with us, David?"

"Thank you," the American said. "I've already arranged to come with Sasha and Irina."

They walked out to where the carriages were being brought to the gate of the church, waiting among the crowd of guests for their private landau.

"You know, I don't know any of these people," Senka complained, not so *sotto voce*. "Not a single one."

"Neither do I," confessed Vladimir. "They're all friends of Pierre's or the Tretyakovs."

"Noisy lot," Senka said as they got into the carriage. "Like a flock of starlings." The word seemed to remind him of something. He fell silent and remained so as the coach rattled over the yellow road toward Sokolnika.

"You know about Nikki?" Vladimir said, after a while. "You know what Genya is going to do?"

"Yes, I heard it all from Pierre," Senka said. "And about the Makcheyevs, too. Probably all for the best, yes? Although I can't say I think it'll do the trick."

"Why don't you think so?"

"Let me ask you a question. What sort of man do you think Boris Abrikosov is, eh?"

"I think he's an unmitigated shit."

"Yes, of course." Senka smiled. "Would you say he was vengeful?"

"Certainly."

"Then what do you think will happen when he finds out what the family has done?"

"What can he do?"

"I haven't any idea, Vladimir," Senka said. "But I can't see him doing nothing."

"Don't worry so much," Vladimir said. "Pierre knows what he's doing."

"I hope you're right," Senka said.

The wedding feast was a vast and noisy affair for more than five hundred guests. Tables were set out in the great dining room of Sokolnika, each place setting marked by an individual arrangement of flowers in which nestled a miniature bottle of the special vodka made by The House for the Tsar. Around the neck of each bottle was tied a little label on which was printed the name and title of the guest. Buckets of ice stood on each table; in each lay a bottle of Smirnoffka and a bottle of vintage champagne. Servants were already bringing in trolleys laden with food, bustling busily up and down the aisles between the tables to serve the wedding guests. Children in party dresses and neat sailor suits scampered about, their faces flushed with excitement. There were many toasts to the happy couple, to the parents of the bride and the parents of the groom, and to the maids of honor. Telegrams of congratulation were read out by the best man, Andrei Tretyakov, and bouquets of flowers arrived by special messenger at what seemed to be almost planned intervals. Greetings came from all over Russia, including one from Count Fredericksz in the name of the Tsar. Everyone seemed to know everyone else. Family groups wandered from table to table, hugging and kissing each other, exchanging family gossip, sitting together for a while to drink some wine before moving to the next table, the next group of friends.

"Hatchings, matchings, and dispatchings," Alex Makcheyev said. "Always the same at weddings."

"Wasn't it a wonderful service?" Maryka said. "I thought Katrina looked so lovely. Was that her mother's wedding dress she wore, Vladimir?"

"It was indeed," Vladimir said.

"Your brother certainly does things on the grand scale," Alex said. "I shudder to think what this lot is costing."

"Don't worry about it," Vladimir smiled. "Just enjoy it."

"He will," Maryka said. "That's what's worrying me. Alex, you've already had quite enough to drink."

"Oh, Mama, it's a wedding," Tatiana said.

"Wedding or no, you know red wine always gives you a headache," Maryka said. "Yet you drink it anyway."

"Being married to you gives me a headache too," Alex grinned. "But I stay married, don't I, eh?"

"Anyway, save a little space for my party on Sunday," Vladimir said. "I hope you'll all be coming to Telegin. I'd like you to see my stables."

"Kind of you," Alex said. "But I'm not sure I'm up to a jaunt across country. Old bones creak a bit these days, y'know."

"I'll see to it there are a lot of cushions in the carriage, sir," Vladimir grinned. "Do try."

"We'll see, we'll see," Alex said. "Eh, missus?"

"Well, perhaps Tatiana would like to come? Do you know how to ride, bridesmaid?" Vladimir grinned at Tatiana, a grin that widened as he saw her chin come up.

"I can ride anything you can saddle," she said.

"True enough!" Alex echoed. "She can do just that."

"Splendid," Vladimir said. "You'll come, then?"

"I'll think about it," Tatiana said, coolly. Before Vladimir could say more, there was a sudden chorus of shouts and cheers from the center of the room, and they realized that the bride and groom were about to leave. Everyone clustered around them to wish them good luck and a happy journey, and it took the couple nearly fifteen minutes to cross the room. The carriage was waiting outside; first, they ran the gauntlet of a hail of orange blossoms, rice, and confetti, surrounded by cheering, laughing friends. Katrina caught sight of Vladimir's face in the crowd and blew him a kiss as she ducked into the carriage. He watched the vehicle depart with the strangest feeling of sadness and turned to find Tatiana standing next to him.

"Well," he said, "that's that."

Tatiana said nothing. The sound of the horses and the wheels of the carriage faded and was gone.

"How do you feel about it now?" Vladimir said, jerking his chin in the direction in which the carriage had gone.

"I don't know," she said. "Numb, I think."

"It passes," he said, and Tatiana turned and looked him full in the eyes. He had not realized how much hurt showed in his voice. Without even thinking about it, she took his hand and laid her cheek on it. They stood like that as the noisy crowd ebbed back into the house, looking into each others' eyes, not moving. Then the silent night shrouded them, and she moved into the circle of his arms. The kiss was long and soft and tender, a promise, an affirmation of all that lay unspoken between them.

"I must go," Tatiana whispered.

"Stay," he whispered back.

"Tomorrow," she said. "At Telegin."

"Tomorrow," Vladimir said. "At Telegin."

He did not follow her into the house. He walked down the steps and into the garden, a silent figure moving soundlessly between the sturdy lime trees. I thought you said you didn't need any more love, a little mocking voice repeated in his head. And he had no reply.

It had been a glorious morning.

The grooms had readied horses for those who wished to ride and chilled two dozen magnums of champagne for those who did not. There was a splendid buffet luncheon in the big old oak-beamed dining room, followed by a conducted tour of the house and stables. Pavel Ulyanov detailed grooms to take small parties of five or six people at a time around the paddocks, stables, and stalls, and out to the little race track where the trotters were put through their paces. The sun was bright, the animals were sleek and handsome, and everyone was having a good time, which gave Vladimir pleasure. He enjoyed showing people around Telegin; he was proud of his house, enthusiastic about his horses. He had a couple of good paintings, decent furniture, a fine cellar. His cook had been a disciple of Cubat, chef to the Tsar. He stinted in nothing—for his guests. His own requirements were considerably less ostentatious. It was the place he loved, not the gewgaws money could add to it.

He had bought Telegin six years earlier, in 1908. Friends who had been at a party there told him casually that the house was for sale and he rushed to see the agent, only to learn that it had already been sold to a Polish officer. Without really knowing why he did so, Vladimir told the agent he wanted to talk to the owner. The agent was very reluctant to upset the applecart, but Vladimir insisted.

"This Kovacs," Vladimir asked the owner of the farm. "What will he do with the place?"

"I don't know," the owner, whose name was Vinin, said. "Summer house, I suppose."

"You don't care what happens to the place?"

"I'm not in a position to care," Vinin said. "I need the money."

"What's he paying you?"

"Seventy thousand."

"I'll give you a hundred."

"A hundred?" Vinin's eyes lit with a small fire of greed. "It would cost me money to break the contract."

"I'll pay your expenses, too."

"That might be another ten thousand."

"My lawyers will handle it," Vladimir said, impatient with the man for cheating. It was one of the greatest advantages of being wealthy, not caring about money, not having to cheat and lie for it. He always felt a little sorry for someone who had to, but he understood why Vinin was doing it. What he knew he would never be able to explain to the man was that the money meant absolutely nothing to him anyway.

When the sale was completed, Vladimir went to see the architect Ivan Gorobinsky and told him what he wanted to do. Intrigued, Gorobinsky agreed to accompany him to Telegin. They sat on the hillside overlooking the farm and talked for most of one long afternoon.

"I don't want one of those Gothic funeral parlors they all seem to love in Moscow, Ivan," Vladimir said. "I want something light and airy and comfortable."

"I understand," said Gorobinsky, with a sly smile. "Not like Sokolnika, eh?"

"Not like Sokolnika," Vladimir agreed gravely. "Definitely not like Sokolnika at all."

"You remember what M'dvani said when he first saw Telegin?"

"I remember," Vladimir said. Prince M'dvani was the Tsar's aide-de-camp. He had been with the Tsar when His Majesty had first visited Sokolnika. "What a marvelous folly," M'dvani had drawled languorously. "One can scarcely imagine anything more perfectly planned to ensure discomfort."

"I take it you will not entertain as, ah, lavishly as your brother Pierre does?" Gorobinsky said.

"Nobody entertains as lavishly as my brother Pierre does," Vladimir grinned. "No, Ivan, I plan to live quietly out here. I want to breed horses, fine horses, champions. I want you to build me a home for them."

"I accept," Gorobinsky said. "I will build you a home kings would envy."

He had been as good as his word, and done work of pure genius. He re-created, in the lovely river valley from which the farm took its name, a country mansion in early Georgian style, with twelve bedrooms and four splendid reception rooms. Some distance from the main house, screened by fir and birch trees, were four servants' cottages. The terraced gardens sloped gently down to the river from a stone patio, shaded by a loggia on which vines grew busily. Vladimir had specified, on Pavel Ulyanov's advice, seventy loose boxes, four stallion boxes, and eight foaling boxes, as well as a sitting-up room. There was a covering yard, a trotting track, and a big old Dutch barn to house fodder.

Within the first year of its existence, Vladimir's horse Pilyugin, "Little Bullet," brought the Telegin stud fame by winning the annual handicap held in Petersburg to mark the birthday of the Tsarevich, for a purse of two hundred thousand rubles. Since then, Telegin horses had won at all the great racecourses of the world: Chantilly, Ascot, even Saratoga Springs. Pilyugin's portrait hung in a place of honor above the great stone fireplace in the main house.

Everyone wanted to see him, of course, and Pavel Ulyanov made sure everyone got a chance to pet the old boy. The horse was outrageously spoiled and pampered now. Vladimir always said that he had the perfect life: the most comfortable quarters, all the love and attention that could be bestowed upon him. He didn't even have to leave home; his mates were brought to him, ready and eager for his regal favors.

Toward evening, with most of his guests gone or ready to leave, Vladimir excused himself and went down to the stables to see Pilyugin, as he usually did.

"I'll be back in ten minutes," he said to Tatiana. "Then we'll ride over to Sokolnika together."

"That will be lovely," she said. She had enjoyed her day at Telegin, and seeing it had added a dimension to her understanding of Vladimir Smirnoff which surprised her. She had thought him something of a playboy, out only for a good time. Yet here at the stud farm he was so unpretentious, so boyishly proud that his wealthy friends admired what he had achieved, that she could no longer maintain that image of him.

The more you get to know people, the more interesting they become, Vladimir thought as he opened the door and went into Pilyugin's stall. Seeing Tatiana handling the horses with the confidence of someone who has grown up with them and knows their idiosyncrasies had been a revelation to him. So many of these Petersburg pretties winced at the thought of getting a fleck of mud on their satin slippers and reacted to the sight of the horse as if it were a winged dragon, that to see someone who obviously liked the animals was a distinct pleasure. Pilyugin nudged him, butting at his pockets for the sugar he knew was always there. Vladimir slapped the arched, glossy neck.

"Fat old carthorse!" he scoffed. "You couldn't beat a fairground donkey around Yelagin now."

He stayed with the stallion for a little while longer, petting him while a boy cleaned out his stall. Strange that a girl as seemingly levelheaded as Tatiana should get mixed up with two such utter shits as Sergei Tretyakov and Boris Abrikosov. He had asked Katrina if she could think why.

"She's just a baby, Vladimir," Katrina said. "She thinks that just because she grew up in a house full of boys, she knows all there is to know about men, and of course, she hasn't anything like the guile to cope with someone like Boris."

"But if she's such an innocent," he said, "why are they interested in her at all?"

Katrina looked at him with a sad, gentle smile. "My dearest Vladimir," she said, "that is precisely the reason."

He remembered Katrina's words as he handed the bridle to Pavel Ulyanov and excused himself, walking back toward the house without haste. There was no one in sight. He saw one or two of his guests in the terraced gardens as he passed the gap in the box hedge, but that was all. Nearly everyone had gone by now; evening was drawing in. Vladimir's footsteps crunched on the gravel; he had insisted on gravel paths because there was less danger to the horses during the winter. Just as he rounded the corner of the paddock, he stopped short. He shook his head; it had sounded like a scream, and that could not be. Or could it? He looked up and saw one of the servants running toward him, shouting something. His blood went cold. He ran toward the man.

"Come quickly, Your Excellency!" the man panted. "For God's sake, come quickly!"

"What is it?" Vladimir said "What the devil is it?"

There was a carriage standing by the front entrance of the house, the reins looped around the curved iron rail beside the driver's seat. There was no one in it. Vladimir started to run toward the house, and as he did, he heard the woman scream again, twice, three times.

He ran into the house. In the hallway stood Boris Abrikosov, trying to drag Tatiana toward the waiting carriage. He saw Vladimir, and his face went dark with rage. He released the girl, who fell backward in a half-faint. Boris's colorless eyes were swimming with hate as he confronted Vladimir.

"Get out of my way, Smirnoff!" he hissed. "Get out of my way!"

"Boris," Vladimir said evenly, "I am going to break your filthy neck." He saw it all now. Boris knew he had no chance at all of

202

getting past Vanska into Sokolnika, but no doubt he had bribed someone to tell him if Tatiana left the house at all and, if so, where she was going. Then he had come over here and waited for his moment. Vladimir stepped forward, intending to grab the man, but as he did, Boris produced a revolver.

The muzzle of the gun looked like the entrance to a cave. Vladimir stared into it for a moment, then made himself look away.

Boris made a gesture of command with the pistol. "The girl was promised to me. I'm taking her," he said.

"Over my dead body," Vladimir said.

Boris smiled his snake's smile cocking the pistol. Vladimir flinched instinctively, and Boris stepped forward. "Get out of the way," he said.

Vladimir moved aside, and as he did, his hand fell against the elephant's-foot stand in which he kept walking sticks and riding crops. Boris half-stopped, reaching behind and to his side to grab Tatiana's arm, still keeping the pistol pointed at Vladimir. Then, as his eyes shifted toward Tatiana, Vladimir snatched up a riding crop. Even as Boris caught the movement and whirled around, the steel-cored crop whistled through the air in a murderous arc. It took a strip of skin an inch wide and four inches long off the back of Boris's hand, spraying flesh and blood everywhere. Boris screamed with pain, reflexively firing the pistol, which made a noise like a cannon. A huge chunk of plaster was blown out of one of the pilasters in the hall. His face twisted with agony, Boris tried to turn the gun on Vladimir again but Vladimir gave him no chance, no chance at all. Once again the riding crop whistled through the air, its arc ending again with that awful cracking *whop* on Boris's forearm. This time the gun fell with a solid thud to the floor. Boris scrabbled after it, but Vladimir kicked it to one side and laid the crop across the man's back. Boris's body arched upward, and he yelled in pain. Before the sound had died, Vladimir hit him again, and then again and then again, putting every ounce of his strength into the blows. Screeching in agony, Boris fell. He lurched, he crawled, he writhed, he wormed, he wriggled down the long hall and out of the house, pursued by the iron-faced Vladimir, who stalked behind the weeping, shouting thing on the floor like some awful automaton. Out of the house Vladimir drove the sobbing, cursing, bloody thing, past an open-mouthed group of guests who had come running up to the house when they heard the shouts and screams of pain, out to the drive where the carriage stood. The horse shifted its feet nervously, eyes rolling in fright at the sound of the cracking crop and Boris's hoarse shouts of pain. With a gesture of the utmost contempt, Vladimir shoveled the reeling, bloody figure into the carriage. Boris lay slumped on the floor, his body shivering with pain and humiliation.

"Bastard!" he hissed. "You bastard! One day I'll make you wish you'd killed me!"

"You're not worth killing," Vladimir said, and lashed the skittish horse across the rump with the crop. The animal leaped into movement, careering off down the drive and on toward the road in a flurry of flying gravel.

Now Vladimir turned and went back into the house. Tatiana was standing in the hallway, distractedly running her hands through her hair, while a servant tried to pull the torn pieces of her dress together. She looked at Vladimir as he came through the door with the bloody riding crop in his hands, his eyes like the eyes of Satan. Without hesitation she ran to him, and suddenly they were in each others' arms.

C**ASTLE** stared at the sheets of Embassy paper on the desk in front of him. They stared back, blank and accusing, but he did not pick up the pen. The report for Landis could wait. There wasn't all that much to say anyway. Castle was angry, angry at himself. His involvement with Irina Smirnoff was not only unprofessional, it was downright stupid. Their affair might very easily imperil everything he had succeeded in doing since he came to Russia. He could not take the chance of that happening. He wondered what Landis would do if he found out about it.

Landis was the Counselor of the State Department in Washington and he was also Castle's immediate, only superior. He had the reputation of being a flint-hearted, mean-mouthed, tight-fisted son of a bitch, and by and large it was an underestimate. Castle was Landis's troubleshooter, his very special agent. He had been ever since the Department sent him into Nicaragua six years ago. It had been a dirty job, but the assassination of Zelaya had seemed unavoidable to Castle. If he hadn't shot the man, someone else undoubtedly would have. The way he worked, the methods he employed, came to Landis's attention. Landis was looking for someone just like Castle. There had been other assignments since, all of them covert, none of them much concerned with the kind of diplomatic activities that the man in the street fondly imagined the State Department indulged in.

"America is coming of age, Castle," Landis growled. "That fool Bryan doesn't know it, and even if he did, the silly bastard wouldn't do anything about it. Make a speech, maybe. So we have to do it for him."

And for yourself, Castle thought. Landis had his eye on higher office than the one he held. After all, what was the competition? Taft? William Jennings Bryan, the man who had sent an invitation to the admiral of the Swiss Navy on the occasion of the opening of the Panama Canal? The new incumbent in the White House, Teddy Roosevelt? Landis thought himself a smarter animal than all of those. He was as ruthless as a mongoose, so when Castle was summoned to his office, he didn't expect good news. It was a cool, high-ceilinged room looking out onto Pennsylvania Avenue. Landis was a short man with cropped hair and a pockmarked face. His voice was as abrasive as pumice stone.

"Castle," he said, "sit down. This is Sir Myles Hetherington."

Hetherington was a tall, thin man with lank hair and prominent cheekbones above which dark eyes looked out of cavernous sockets. He looked as if he had never had a good time in his life.

"You're going to Russia," Landis barked.

You grew to expect the unexpected in Castle's line of work. Just the same, Landis's announcement surprised him.

"Been telling Sir Myles about your work in Nicaragua," Landis said. "And elsewhere."

There was nothing to say to that, either.

"Sir Myles is from the British Foreign Office," Landis said. "Political Information Division."

Castle knew what that meant. Hetherington was a British intelligence chief, one of those Whitehall mandarins he'd heard about but never met. Hetherington nodded, but he did not speak.

"How's your Russian?" Landis asked.

"Pretty poor, sir," Castle said.

"French?"

"Better."

"You can brush up on your Russian," Landis said. It wasn't a request. "Tell Sir Myles about yourself, Castle."

Fraud, Castle thought. Every man in the Department had a dossier. His was kept in Landis's office, and he had not the slightest doubt that the Englishman would have already gone through it with a fine-toothed comb. Mexico City, Madrid, Luzon, Managua, all of it. I hope you know what you're doing, Landis, he thought. Hetherington's silence and his brooding stare were a little unnerving. Castle wondered what all this was about, but he did not make the mistake of asking.

"I wonder," the Englishman said, leaning forward, "if we might hear about your grandfather, Castle? I understand he was Russian?" His voice was as sepulchral as his appearance. Landis nodded as if to say, answer him.

"I only know the family stories, sir," he said. "How much is fact I can't say."

Hetherington nodded expectantly, so Castle told him the story of Yuri Zamokin, born in Odessa in 1804, third son in a family of four. In 1825, serving as a captain in the Russian Army, he had become involved in a revolutionary society led by his superior officer, Colonel Pestel. On the eve of the planned revolt, Pestel was betrayed by informers and arrested. Yuri Zamokin fled and managed to secure passage on a boat bound for Piraeus. He arrived in America in 1826.

"He settled in Liberty, Missouri," Castle said. "Changed his name to Castle—*zamok* is the Russian word for a castle—and married a local girl. They had one son, my father."

He had never really known old Yuri—*Dedyushka*, they called him, Grandfather. Such childhood memories of the old man as he had brought to mind only a stern face, great bushy white eyebrows, a deep voice, and his own sense of awe in his presence. He had been told that he was a great bear of a man, jovial and full of life, but all he ever did was to scare Castle. The only question Castle could ever recall his asking him was whether he was a good boy. He had answered yes, of course. He would not have dared to say anything else.

"My father studied law at the university until the war. Then he joined the army. The wrong one," he added, with a wry grin. His father had always said he only made two mistakes in his whole life. The first one was joining the Confederate Army and the second one was admitting it afterward. George Castle came back from fighting with the Third Missouri Light Battery to find that there was a Federal statute prohibiting anyone who had borne arms against the Union from practicing law. Like many another of his kind he went West, to the New Mexico territory. He knew a few lawyers out there, one of whom was now a Senator, Stephen Elkins. He was admitted to the bar and hung out his shingle in Santa Fe.

"You were an only child?" Hetherington asked.

"No, sir," Castle said, wondering what he wanted to know for. "I had a brother, George, who died when I was about six. My sister died in infancy. Diphtheria, I think." He had no memory of either of them other than what his mother had told him about them. He often wondered why.

Landis took a humidor of cigars out of the cupboard behind his desk and offered one to the Englishman, who shook his head without attempting to conceal his distaste. Landis, who was about as sensitive as a cannonball, proceeded to make a performance out of cutting and lighting the cigar. Castle had seen the ritual before; he knew that Landis used it for thinking time. He wondered whether men who smoked cigars and pipes didn't get more enjoyment out of getting the damned things ready to smoke than they ever did after they'd put a match to them. Landis lit the cigar and squinted at Castle through the smoke.

"The British Embassy in Petersburg put someone onto checking the background of Yuri Zamokin," he said. He pushed a folder across the desk. It had the red "secret" tab fixed to the top right-hand corner. "You'll find it all in there. Read it later. The gist of it is that the Zamokin family was a noble one. Your great-grandmother was a countess with estates near Yelisavetgrad in the Ukraine. Her name was Lara Svobodina. Yuri was her third son. The fourth child was a daughter, Kira. Her grandson is Michael Tereschenko, senior assistant to the President of the State Duma in Petersburg, Rodzianko. So, to coin a phrase, you have a friend at court. A cousin."

He gave a small smile, as though he rationed them very severely.

"How old is he?" Castle asked.

"Fifty something," Landis said.

"Is he one of your people?" Castle asked Hetherington. The Englishman smiled for the first time. His teeth were stained and brown.

"Good heavens, no!" Hetherington said. "He's Russian through and through. But you'll find him a great help in making the right contacts."

"Sure," Castle said.

There was a little silence. Landis puffed away on his cigar and waited. The Englishman cleared his throat.

"What I am about to tell you now is a matter of the utmost secrecy, Castle," he said. "You understand?"

"Yes," Castle said.

"The British Government is becoming increasingly concerned that Germany is actually fomenting war in Europe," Hetherington began. "You're familiar with the situation in the Balkans?"

Castle concealed a smile. Nobody was familiar with the situation in the Balkans. The riotous complications of Balkan politics were the stuff of comic opera. Andrew Ettinger, the tall, slow-spoken Californian who had the Balkan desk, was known as "Octagonal Andy" because he had to present so many different faces in so many different directions at the same time.

"In general," Castle replied.

"The gist of it is simple enough," Hetherington said. "Old Franz Josef of Austria-Hungary is rattling his saber, looking for an excuse to invade Serbia. Up to now, he hasn't been able to find one. Our intelligence is that the Germans plan to manufacture an incident—probably in Serbia—which will give Franz Josef the excuse he needs."

"Do you know what the incident will be?" Castle asked.

"No, we don't. As you can imagine, we're not getting a lot of information out of Berlin just now. Rather tricky situation altogether."

"What we do know," Landis said, "is what will happen if Franz Josef gets an excuse to attack Serbia."

"Russia, as Serbia's protector and ally, will immediately mobilize for war," Hetherington said. "Germany, as Austria's ally, will do the same. Whereupon Russia will call on *her* allies—"

"Britain and France," Landis intoned.

"—to do likewise. The result will inevitably be war." He said it with the gloomy certainty of an old man talking about death.

"The German General Staff has already decided upon the means by which it will conquer France," Hetherington went on. "The idea is to put France out of the running before the shooting really gets started. They call it the Schlieffen Plan. You'll find it outlined in these papers."

He handed Castle another folder, twin of the first down to the little red "secret" tab.

"And Russia?" Castle said.

"Ah," Hetherington said. "Yes, Russia. What do you know about Russia, Castle?"

"The usual statistics, I suppose," Castle said. "Not much more."

"We can get statistics from an almanac," Landis growled. "What we need is information, and I don't mean the kind we get once a month in the Ambassador's letter."

"Our intelligence people have discovered that the Germans have a plan for Russia," Hetherington said. "It is called the Petersburg Plan. Its intent is simple: to vitiate the Russian High Command and to finance and foment industrial and political unrest. We also know that there is a group of Germans—or German sympathizers—working in St. Petersburg and Moscow to achieve those ends."

"Already?" Castle said.

"The Germans are very careful planners," Hetherington said. "Here's the theory our political intelligence people have postulated:

Germany conquers France and the Low Countries as per the Schlieffen Plan. Shorn of her allies—France gone, Britain powerless across the Channel—Russia collapses from within because of revolution. Britain must now either invade Europe or stand by and watch Germany march eastward—perhaps even to India. The British Government does not consider that to be desirable," he added, almost apologetically.

"Where do I come into all this?" Castle asked.

"Somewhere in Russia," Hetherington said, "is the man controlling the Petersburg Plan. We want to know who he is, who else is in it with him. Our people on the spot are handicapped by the very fact that they are British. Being American, you can ask anyone anything."

"This man at the top," Castle said. "What do you know about him?"

"Nothing, I'm afraid," Hetherington said. "Except his code name: *Verschwender.*"

"That doesn't give me much to go on."

"I realize that. Nevertheless, I'm afraid it's all we have."

"What about this Rasputin?" Landis said. "Tell Castle about him."

"Ah," Hetherington said. "Yes, Rasputin. He's some kind of holy man."

"Strange name," Castle said. "The Russian word *rasputnay* means dissolute. 'Rasputin' would be 'a dissolute fellow.'"

"We don't know much about him," Hetherington said. "He seems to have arrived in St. Petersburg around 1906. The point is that Rasputin is very close to the throne of Russia. In fact, unhealthily close. There are stories of the Tsar's wife being his mistress."

"Does that concern us?"

"It does if he is working for the Germans, and there is some ground for believing that he is," Hetherington said. "His associates are all pro-German."

"What have we got on him?"

Another folder was pushed across the desk. This one was the usual buff, nonsecurity type. Castle leafed it open. It contained three sheets of paper: a memorandum from the American vice-consul in St. Petersburg dated July 19, 1912, and a two-page biographical sketch, presumably also by Vesey. There was a photograph clipped to the memo. It showed a bearded, shifty-eyed man with long hair plastered close to his skull. One tendril of hair had fallen, artfully or otherwise, into an S above the right eye. It was not an attractive face: cunning, perhaps even a little crazy. He did not look as if he could be the lover of the Empress of all the Russias, and Castle said so.

"Nevertheless, that's what everyone in Petersburg says," Hetherington assured him. "You'll find out soon enough."

"I suppose so," Castle said. "One last question."

"Fire away," Hetherington said.

"When I find this man—what did you call him?"

"*Verschwender.*"

"When I find him, what happens then?"

"Ah," Hetherington said. "Yes. I think we'd quite like you to kill the bugger, if you wouldn't mind."

A long time ago, Castle thought, staring out of the Embassy window at the people walking along the path bisecting the grass-covered island that divided the Furshtatskaya. He had put on a *persona* for Russia—the expected, clean-cut, naïve American, full of wide-eyed wonder and an endless fund of questions. He did not feel the slightest bit guilty about using people to make his job easier; he had not been sent to Russia for pleasure. His desk had become a heaped repository for files of every kind, on every topic, most of which were totally devoid of interest or information. He read them anyway. You made no judgments. You were just looking for information, and you had no idea where the vital piece you were looking for would come from. There were reports on the building of rolling stock written by American entrepreneurs hired by the Imperial Engineering Works, on the construction of boats or dams or canals and the grading and improvement of roads by engineers from the States. There were letters and memoranda from Americans working for Kodak in Moscow, at the Nevsky Cotton Mills in Petersburg, or the Giraud silk works, the Smirnoff distilleries, the Baku oil fields, the Siberian gold mines. They were all thorough, detailed, analytical and useless. So he had pulled strings, using Michael Tereschenko to give him introductions to the society people, the merchants and industrialists, the military. He pumped them all, the Mamontovs and Morosovs and Haritonenkos, the Grand Dukes and the Generals. Through Senka Smirnoff he heard the revolutionary talk and attitudes of the day, learned names that were unknown to many even inside Russia, let alone outside. He sent Landis and Hetherington reports on Vladimir Ulyanov, the leader of the revolutionary Bolshevik party, who called himself Lenin; on terrorists like Savinkov and Azev; on politicians and ministers and court officials. Throughout his first year, he diligently checked and double-checked name after name after name of German sympathizers. He sometimes felt that either Sir Myles Hetherington and the British Secret Service were crazy or the German High Command was crazy. Or that all involved in this maniac business were crazy. That any of the men whom he investigated was an *agent provocateur* of the kind Hetherington had described was as likely as seeing the Tsar do a clog dance in the Palace Square.

He went over the names in his mind. Vladimir Sukhomlinov, Minister of War and *ex officio* General of the Army, a small man with a cat's face hidden behind white whiskers. Vain as a peacock, sly as a snake, Sukhomlinov was greedy and selfish and as emptily charming as a high-priced whore. Fat, bald as an egg, he considered himself a dashing Lothario. His private life was a disaster, his wife an empty-headed spendthrift whose follies Sukhomlinov supported by cheating the government and accepting bribes from everyone. He was known, not affectionately, as General Fly-off. That he was in the pocket of the Austrians was as certain as the fact that he was a liar. But the controlling genius behind a baroque plot to overthrow the autocracy? Never, Castle concluded. Sukhomlinov was doing far too well out of the autocracy to want to see it end.

Aron Simanovich, then, Rasputin's political mentor? He heard all about him around the samovar at the Smirnoff house.

"You don't know him at all?" Sasha Smirnoff asked, when Castle asked about the man, making it as casual as he could. "Slimy toad. He's got gambling dens and sleazy cabarets and other places."

Yescho kudato, they said in Russia, "somewhere else," meaning brothels.

"How did he come to be involved with Rasputin?"

"They say he cured Simanovich's son of St. Vitus' Dance," Sasha said. "In Kiev. Simanovich comes from Kiev."

"I hear he is Rasputin's political adviser," Castle said.

"Ha!" Sasha snorted. "Can you imagine anything more bizarre? Like saying one is teaching an ape to play the harpsichord!"

"Yet he is welcomed at Tsarskoe Selo."

"He sells the Tsaritsa cut-price jewelry. Everyone knows she's a penny pincher. She and her fat friend Vyrubova, they're like two suburban housewives, watching every kopeck."

"Tell me about Madame Vyrubova," Castle said.

"She is a dull-witted, superstitious gossip and a middle-class prig. She gets on well with the German woman because Alexandra, too, is dull-witted, superstitious and all the rest of it. It is thanks to Vyrubova that Rasputin has gained access to the court, and that's why, if you want anything from that worthless crowd at Tsarskoe Selo, you go through Simanovich. Simanovich controls Rasputin. Rasputin controls the Tsaritsa. And she controls the Tsar."

Sasha Smirnoff was three years older than the American, bustling and self-important. He liked everything to be in its appointed place at the proper time, including himself. Punctilious almost to the point of mania about appointments, the time of his arrival at the distillery, the timekeeping of employees, the feeding times of the babies, train departures, dinner engagements and luncheon dates, he was the very opposite of his wife. Irina was a small girl, a year Castle's junior, with lively brown eyes, high cheekbones, a mobile mouth and a vivacious manner. She seemed congenitally incapable of taking the remotest interest in what time of day it was, a characteristic which occasionally drove Sasha into paroxysms of petulance. Irina never ceased poking fun at Sasha's pomposities, which he chose to find endearing. Castle, however, soon sensed the impatience underlying Irina's teasing. It was almost as if she wished her husband would get his mind working faster to keep up with her own. By and large, he thought, she kept her keen intelligence well concealed, always letting Sasha believe that the decisions at which he had arrived were his own and only his. Her children were delightful. Pipo was five, the girl a year younger. Both were in the charge of their governess, Madame Blon, and both were already conversing fluently in "the language of Voltaire." The new baby, Vadim, was cared for by the old *nyanya*, Annika. Annika was a peasant woman from Simbirsk, well over sixty, illiterate, superstitious, talkative, and as untiringly devoted to Irina's children as she had a quarter of a century earlier been to Irina herself.

The Smirnoff household was a wealthy one. There were a host of servants, their duties carefully supervised by Sasha. There was a chef, two valets, two chambermaids, a laundress, a sewing maid, a coachman, a groom and an odd-job man. There was a tiler who came twice a year to inspect the roof, a German clockmaker who came weekly to wind and adjust all the clocks, a stove setter who cleaned out all the porcelain stoves which heated the house, a polisher who each week brought two laborers to clean and wax the parquet floors.

Irina had a personal maid, Ulyana, and Senka Smirnoff had a personal valet and coachman. He lived in his own apartment on the western side of the house.

In the stable behind the big house, entered through the gate opening onto the Fontanka, were eight horses, all from Vladimir Smirnoff's Telegin stables, including a pair of trotters said to be worth at least ten thousand rubles. There were landaus, sleighs, calashes and hunting brakes in the carriage house, as well as a Mercedes-Simplex automobile with side doors, which belonged to Sasha. It was his pride and joy. He polished it personally every Sunday morning, unable or unwilling to allow anyone else to touch it.

They often took breakfast together. Sasha always rose first, and he and Senka would read the papers until Castle joined them. Irina would appear last, if at all, wearing a pale white wrapper buttoned to the neck and decorated at the wrists with lace. She had a fine, slender figure, unmarred by having babies, with high breasts and a narrow waist. It took Castle a long time to get used to the sight of Sasha sitting at the table wearing his cashmere dressing gown and a strip of gauze across his upper lip to protect his newly trimmed moustache, and even longer not to smile indulgently as Sasha left, in a flurry of instructions to Irina, who would kiss him and say "yes, dear" and wave goodbye from the window. As befitted the senior director, Senka would leave a little while later. He soon became Castle's most important source of information on what was happening in Petersburg. Senka seemed to be *au fait* with everything, for all his vague manner. He had the most formidable range of connections, from the cheapest thugs of the revolutionary movement all the way up to the holders of the highest offices in the land. He was rarely at home in the early evening but usually came in late to join everyone around the samovar in Irina's sitting room. Looking out across the Fontanka at the strings of lights reflected in the still waters of the canal, sipping the scalding hot tea, Castle listened as they talked and talked and talked, avalanches of conversation, usually about the need for change, the inevitability of revolution, the shortcomings of the Tsar, and the scandals surrounding the Rasputin *camarilla*. It was all talk, nothing more. None of the dozens of people Castle listened to seemed to do anything else but talk. After all, they said, with that Russian shrug, what could one do? One's hands were tied. The lunatics were running the asylum.

"Tell me about this Manuilov," Castle said, one evening. "Someone told me he was a spy."

"A spy? Manuilov a spy?" Senka said, his head coming up abruptly, as if he had been startled by the use of the word. "That's a good one! He might be a musical-comedy villain, David, but a spy? No, never! He's beneath contempt, beneath it. A homosexual. A police informer. A rat, most of all. He betrayed Witte to Plehve and Plehve to Witte. He had his grubby fingers in the death of Georgi Gapon, yes, even that. He posed as a revolutionary and sold the names of his friends to the police. Ach, the mention of his name makes me angry!"

"Yet he has power," Castle said. "Thanks to Rasputin."

"Rasputin is a credulous peasant," Senka said. "Men like Simanovich and Manuilov can manipulate him, use him any way they like. It is they who dispense the favors in that so-called salon at Sixty-four, Gorokhovoy, not that sex-crazed *starets*. No."

Once, he told Castle, the "salon" had been something special in Petersburg life: the famous "Wednesdays" at the home of Vyacheslav Ivanov on the Tavrichevskaya, at the Merezhovskys or the Bloks or at Margarita Morosova's house in Moscow, where the judgment of the host or hostess could make or mar a reputation, yet attract the very best of all the talents notwithstanding.

"Now, what do we have, tell me, what?" Senka said angrily. "We have intrigue, gossip, scandal, yes. We have that degenerate Andronikov and his lover, the Tsar's Groom of Chamber, daring to call their gathering of other degenerates a salon! We have other salons—they call them salons, they dare to do that!—at the houses of adventuresses and thieves. Count Burdukov or the Baroness Rosen, yes, that's what we have! But you asked about Manuilov, so I will tell you, yes, gladly. If you are looking for a swindler, try Manuilov. A blackmailer? Manuilov again! A thief, a Judas, a liar, a charlatan, a Jew who is a rabid anti-Semite? For all of these, the man you want is Manuilov. Yes, undoubtedly. For myself, I'd rather consort with the lowest scum in the Haymarket slums."

He glared at Castle, anger in his eyes. Castle smiled.

"Ah, my young friend, I am sorry," Senka said, seeing the smile. "I am too passionate. Yes, we Russians feel everything passionately. We cannot be moderate—I cannot, at any rate—when adventuresses and thieves are tearing our world apart like buzzards, yes, buzzards! They flourish, as Rasputin flourishes, because there is no one strong enough to put an end to them. No, no one!"

"Surely, one day, the Tsar will—"

"No, no, no!" Senka said. "God knows, the Romanovs have been responsible for many of this county's woes, yes, certainly, but at least in the past they were strong, decisive. This Nicholas—" his lip curled with contempt—"this Nicholas is a weak-kneed mama's boy, a henpecked, vacillating coward. Yes! He is the first Tsar in the history of Russia who is neither respected, feared nor hated. Nobody gives a damn about him, nobody! He isn't even worth assassinating."

"There's talk of war," Castle said. "What will happen if it comes?"

"It will be the end of this charade, yes, I'm sure of it," Senka said. It was strange the way the anger fell away, and he reverted to the absentminded professor mannerisms, almost as if aware that he had stepped out of character to be angry, concerned, involved. The longer Castle knew the man, the more frequently Senka surprised him.

So the seasons had turned. The royal family moved from palace to palace, from the Crimea to Finland, from Tsarskoe Selo to Moscow, everything as preordained as the movement of the stars in their courses. If anyone in the Russian court was aware of the far-off rumblings of war resounding around the rest of Europe, Castle could discern no sign of it. He had long since concluded that if Sir Myles Hetherington's German agent existed at all, he could operate within this Russia with complete impunity, surrounded by people more than willing to listen to and support the proposition that Tsar Nicholas II should be disposed of, done away with, rendered harmless. As for Rasputin, the notion that he was in German pay was so naïve as to be laughable.

He met the ugly, disreputable *starets* for the first time at the Yulitsky house. He went there as escort to Sasha's sister Olga, a young woman who had no earthly excuse to be as dull and silly as she was. She spent all her time visiting women as empty-headed as herself, dabbling in clairvoyancy, séances, the reading of tea leaves in cups, and other such nonsensical pursuits. Olga was by no means unique. There were hundreds, thousands like her in the capital, women with plenty of time and money, and nothing better to do than pursue the latest fad or *frisson*. Among such women, the height of social éclat was to have Rasputin visit their home.

By the time he encountered Rasputin in the flesh, Castle almost felt he knew the man. He was one of the most common topics of conversation in Petersburg sitting rooms. The city was constantly scandalized about the man and his hold on the royal family. He was a lecher and an exhibitionist, no longer welcome in the homes of the Grand Duchesses Militsa and Anastasia of Montenegro, his original sponsors. What did he care for that? they said. He had the patronage of the Tsaritsa herself, and she would hear no ill of the man. Let any policeman, politician, or priest question Rasputin's evil ways and he would be out of work faster than you could say *da svidanya*.

Castle had been told by Michael Tereschenko that Piotr Stolypin, when Premier, had ordered a full investigation of the *starets* in 1911. The Tsaritsa had simply refused to read the damning dossier.

"Of course, you know what everyone said then," Tereschenko said. "That the Tsaritsa and her friend Vyrubova share the devil's bed, fighting for his favors."

"That's pretty scurrilous," Castle said.

"You'll hear worse," Tereschenko predicted, and he was right. Petersburg gossip was virulent and specific. It wasn't just the German woman and her fat friend who were sharing Rasputin. He had raped all the Grand Duchesses, too, and turned Tsarskoe Selo into his private harem, where the four girls fought for their turn to sleep with him. As for the Tsar, one story went that he had to take off Gritschka's boots and wash his feet, before being turned out of his own bedroom so that Rasputin could rut with his wife.

"Nonsense," Castle said, when people told him the story. He asked Tatiana Makcheyeva as delicately as he could about Rasputin and the Tsaritsa. He felt strongly that she did not wish to talk about it at all, but he pressed her. There was no question, she said, but that the Tsar and Tsaritsa were devoted to each other. The idea of Her Majesty submitting to the caresses of the *starets* was ridiculous, unbelievable. Castle wondered why she shuddered when she said it. He got the feeling that she was trying to convince herself as much as him that it could not be true, while all the time believing it might be possible. It was not, he felt sure. It could not be. He said so frequently, never ceasing to be amazed at the way educated, intelligent people still shook their heads, unwilling to surrender their preconceptions.

Of course, they would admit, one takes such stories with a pinch of salt, but, untrue or not, one had to consider them. There was no question of Rasputin's power, was there? No argument that he dominated the royal family completely, that his friends were favored and their enemies persecuted by royal command? And what about those letters that had been circulating? Everyone had heard about them: love letters to the *starets*, written in her own hand by the Tsaritsa. Didn't that prove she was his mistress?

No, Castle maintained, it did not. He had seen the letters. They were certainly florid and more than indiscreet, but if one took into account the hothouse fervor of the Tsaritsa's religious beliefs and the fact that both she and her husband were convinced that Rasputin had been sent to them by God to restore the health of their puny, ailing son, then the letters were understandable. Passionate, to be sure, he said, but not inspired by passion.

"Oh, yes," people said in reply, tapping their noses and winking. "Of course. Trouble is, you don't know the fellow. Wait till you meet him, then you'll see. He hypnotizes them. Everyone knows that."

"Hypnotizes them?" Castle echoed. "What for?"

"To make them do things that they would not otherwise do," they said, darkly. "Everyone knows he was a disciple of the Khlysty."

"The what?"

"Ah, see how our fair-minded young American defends the good name of the German woman, yet does not know what the Khlysty is!" they scoffed, as if to say, you don't know the half of it.

The Khlysty, he discovered, was a religious order. As a young man, Rasputin had made the pilgrimage to the monastery of Verkhoturye, where the sect—who believed in reaching God through the transports of sexual delight—lived. He had stayed there for four months.

"Four months!" they said. "What do you think he was learning, then? Greek, maybe?" They all laughed at that. Everyone knew what Rasputin had been learning at Verkhoturye. They did not want to separate truth and lie; they preferred the slanders. Why, they said, he had even tried to seduce a nun, and when that failed, to rape her. And what had the German woman done about it? Nothing. You see? If that wasn't proof, what was?

If that was proof, Castle said, he hoped to God he never had to appear in a Russian court.

Igor Yulitsky was an importer of oriental carpets. Olga said he had made a fortune selling to the *noblesse*. He owned a big house on the Moika, not far from the Yusupov palace, and his dinner parties were lavish affairs. Olga was excited and giggly all the way, like a child on her way to a party. She was as unlike her sister as two girls could be, plump and flushed, badly overdressed in colors which did not suit her. She was not alone in her breathless excitement. All the women at the Yulitsky house had that same air of heightened anticipation, so that it seemed as if the men sipping their champagne in the ornate morning room, with its tasteless Empire furniture and cane bric-a-brac, were mere decoration, backdrop against which the star, Rasputin, would shine.

Everything Castle had heard about the man was beggared by the actuality. He simply could not believe that this drunken illiterate could have inspired so much speculation, or so much fear. It did not seem possible that he could be even admitted to a royal palace, much less welcomed there. To begin with, Rasputin was ugly. Silk blouse, black velvet trousers and soft kid boots did nothing to lessen the repellent effect of the pockmarked face, the matted beard and unkempt hair, the crafty eyes, the goaty smell. The men looked at him with faces on which fear fought with disgust. The women's eyes were alight with something altogether different.

"Well and well and well, my dears!" Rasputin said, striding into the room and taking possession of its center as if he owned it. "I am here, it has begun!" With his hand on his hip, his head thrown back, he struck a pose that in any other man would have been ridiculous. But no one laughed at Rasputin.

"You will all excuse my late arrival?" he said. "Many wish my help. And as you know, my dears, I give and give. Those I can help, I help with all my heart and with all my soul. With everything in my body." He leered as he said this, his eyes rolling like a Tartar carpet seller.

"You are welcome, holy father," said Madame Yulitsky. She was an imposing woman, with a vast bosom which swelled beneath her double chins like some huge loaf sprinkled with diamonds. "Our house is honored by your visit."

"We will eat soon, perhaps?" Rasputin said. "I hunger. I thirst. The work of God is arduous. I give much love, much love." Once again the crafty eyes rolled from side to side, lingering openly on the décolleté of the women near him.

Castle looked at the women. Their faces were rapt, their eyes intent upon the *starets'* every gesture. Olga's hands were clasped tightly together against her bosom, which was rising and falling quickly. Castle watched Rasputin slide closer to a young woman standing beside him; her name was Larisa something or other. He put his hand on the girl's bare shoulder. Her back arched slightly, as if she were in heat.

"Ah, my little one," Rasputin said sibilantly, as if he and the girl were alone in the room. "You arouse me. My cock stirs at the sight of your lovely breasts."

There was an indrawn gasp of breath from one or two of the ladies, but it was not a sound of horror or dismay—more a *frisson* of anticipation. Castle looked at the men. They were all wearing the same expression of strained horror, as if one of them, and not Rasputin, had made the remark.

"Ah, perhaps we should all go into dinner?" Yulitsky said, his voice perhaps half a note higher than normal, and with something approaching apology in it. I know, he seemed to be saying, but don't worry, he's always like this.

"Yes, yes, we must to the table!" Rasputin said. He held the upper arm of the young woman firmly in his own far from clean paw. "You shall sit next to me, my lovely little mare, and we shall talk of the delights of the body, the raptures of the soul."

Bird hypnotized by snake, the young woman went into the dining room with Rasputin. The rest of the guests followed. If they noticed Rasputin's hands openly caressing the woman's breasts, they affected not to. During dinner, the *starets* dominated the conversation. Whenever he spoke, everyone stopped to listen, although practically every word he uttered was banal, his perorations littered with clichés and the moral values of a wayward child. They asked him questions about the Tsaritsa, the Grand Duchesses, life at Tsarskoe Selo, coyly vulgar questions to which Rasputin shook his head.

"No, no, no, my dears, I will not speak of those whom I love," he said. "What they are to me, and what I am to them, I speak of to no one, except God."

Good answer, Castle thought. Maybe Rasputin wasn't so peasant-stupid as he acted. He watched, saying little, all through the meal, and everything he heard confirmed the feeling. The *starets* ate without either manners or style, cramming food into his mouth. He ate no meat. Wine spilled on the expensive silk shirt, but he took no notice or did not care. When he wiped his hands on the napkin, he left streaks of greasy dirt on the brilliantly white linen.

"Ah, such fine foods, my dears!" he exclaimed, wiping his mouth with the back of his hand and taking another swig of the madeira he had asked for. "They are not good for us, not good at all. They take us further from grace, not nearer to it. They are sent to us by the Devil, who tempts simple peasants such as I with the sweet pleasures of the flesh. We should all renounce this life, for it is slothful and sinful."

"Renounce it for what, holy father?" one of the women asked.

"We could all go to Siberia together," Rasputin said, waving his arms. "You would be happy with me there, away from this pampered life. Ah, the freedom there! We could work together in the fields in the summer, and go down to the river to catch fish. In the evenings, we would sing and tell stories. There, you would be closer to Almighty God and come to understand Him. You will never do that here in the sinful city."

"Do you go often to Siberia, holy father?" Castle asked.

"Ah, who is this?" Rasputin said, sitting up suddenly in his chair, the crafty eyes narrowing. "This is no Russian who speaks."

"No," Castle said. "I'm an American."

"American?" Rasputin said. He pronounced it "Amyerikin." "And what has America to do with Holy Russia?"

"My grandfather was Russian," Castle said. "His name was Zamokin."

"Zamokin?" Rasputin said, sloshing more wine into his glass. "And now his grandson wishes to know whether I go often to Siberia?"

"I believe you come from Pokrovskoye?"

"You are not my friend," Rasputin said. His non sequitur put a cold chill on Castle's spine for a moment; everyone around the table seemed to stop moving, freezing into a strange tableau. The *starets'* piggy eyes opened wide. Castle felt the lambent power behind them.

"You are not my friend," Rasputin said again. "I feel it."

The bright blue eyes held Castle's unwaveringly. He felt the noises of the room recede slightly, as if a layer of gauze had settled on his mind. A note of disbelief sounded in his brain, and he almost laughed out loud. Good God, he thought, the lunatic is trying to hypnotize me across the dinner table!

"I can't claim to be your friend, since we have never met before," he said. "But I'm not your enemy, either."

"No, no, no," Rasputin said, moving his head from side to side jerkily, a movement almost spastic. "Some things are. Some things are not. I can feel this: you do not think well of Grigory."

"I believe many things are said about you that are not true," Castle said. "But why should I not think well of you?"

"The great and all-powerful God who knows all our hearts has given His servant special powers," Rasputin said, somberly. "I see what I see. I know what I know." He took a deep breath and let it out in a gusty sigh. "It is of no importance," he said abruptly. With an imperious gesture, he turned away, excluding Castle from his consciousness. His entire demeanor changed as he addressed the young woman he had brought into dinner.

"Thou art troubled, my child," he said to her.

"N—no," she whispered. "No, holy father."

"Thine appearance is troubled," he insisted. "Tell me."

"Well . . ." she said. She looked at Madame Yulitsky, who nodded eagerly, as much as to say, go on, go on. "Well . . . it, actually, I am upset about something," the girl said.

"Tell me!" Rasputin said commandingly. "We are in the presence of the Almighty, child. There are no secrets in His presence."

If he hadn't seen it, Castle would never have believed the story from the lips of someone else. He watched astonished as, with little nods and winks and gentle touches on the arm, smiling and smiling, the *starets* persuaded Larisa to tell him her story. Haltingly at first, and then with ever-increasing confidence, she recounted the story of her unhappy love affair with a Guards officer. Her husband, she said, was serving in the Crimea and had not been given leave for almost a year. She was torn between passion and duty, she said, and did not know what to do.

"Come to see me," Rasputin said, his grimy fingers lingering on her upper arm, stroking infinitesimally. "Come to my house. We cannot talk properly here. There is better. There I may see your soul."

Larisa stared at him with awed eyes, as if he had just bestowed some great honor upon her. Madame Yulitsky arched her eyebrows and inclined her head slightly to the right as if to say, isn't that nice? Larisa smiled shyly and nodded. Castle realized that he had just witnessed Rasputin invite the woman to come to his house and sleep with him, Larisa's acceptance, and their hostess making noises of approval, as if she had performed some notable social feat.

Shortly after dinner, pleading further engagements, Rasputin left the Yulitsky house. The ladies retired to the drawing room, atwitter with envy of Larisa, while servants brought in brandy and cigars for the gentlemen. Igor Yulitsky noticed David Castle's expression and nodded.

"Well, young man," he said. "And what do you think of Rasputin now?" He spoke with the satisfied confidence of a teacher asking his favorite pupil how he has done in an examination.

"He is amazing," Castle said, using his words carefully.

"He's not your usual holy man, I'll say that," Yulitsky said, to guffaws from the others around the table. "But he's damned useful, eh, Koltsov?"

Koltsov was an immensely fat man with a shaven head. He gave off an effluvium of bay rum powerful enough to knock down a horse.

"Damned right " Koltsov said.

"In what way?" Castle asked.

"Gets things done, know what I mean?" Yulitsky said. "Specially if you're in the business of selling to the government or the court."

"How?" Castle asked, deliberately obtuse.

"Knows everyone who's anyone, doesn't he?" Yulitsky said, puffing on his cigar and then stirring his brandy with the wet end. "Word from Rasputin, everything's fixed. Scratch his back and he'll scratch yours, know what I mean?"

"A word in the right ear," another man said. "Worth a good deal, isn't it?"

"Wouldn't tolerate the blighter otherwise," Yulitsky said. "Man's an absolute beast. However, doesn't do to upset the apple cart, know what I mean?"

"Yes, sir," Castle said. "I know exactly what you mean."

"Know his friend Simanovich, do you?" Koltsov asked.

"I've met him."

"And Manuilov?"

"Him, too."

"Know what I mean, then," Yulitsky said. "Don't you? Do yourself a bit of good, boy. Keep well in with them. What do you say to that, Grigor?"

"Damned right, and that's the end of it!" Koltsov said.

Olga had drunk a lot of wine and was in a giggly mood on the way home. She snuggled against Castle in the coach and looked up at him from beneath lowered eyelashes, in what she no doubt fondly imagined was a seductive way. Castle sought refuge in questions about Rasputin.

"Yes " Olga said, pouting slightly. "He's married. Some peasant woman from his own village. She doesn't care what he does, they say."

"Are there any children?"

"Two daughters," she said. "And a son who is an epileptic."

"How long have you know him, Olga?"

"Oh, ages," she said impatiently. "You're not very romantic. Why don't you kiss me?"

"Dear Olga," he said. "You're very beautiful and it would be nice to kiss you, but I'm in love with someone else. She fills my whole heart; I can only kiss you like a brother."

He kissed her forehead lightly, thinking she would never swallow such twaddle. To his surprise, she sighed, and looked up at him with teary eyes.

"That's so sweet," she said. "Oh, you're such a nice man."

Her voice was sleepy; she snuggled up beside him, soft and warm as a little bird. He felt sad for her, sad for all the dumpy little Olgas in the world who felt unloved and unspecial, who filled their empty heads with romantic notions, who thought an animal like Rasputin was exciting.

"Tell me, Olga," he said. "Do you find him attractive?"

"Whosat?" she murmured sleepily.

"Rasputin."

"Mmmmm," she said, snuggling tighter against his side. "He's lovely, lovely . . . those eyes. So strong, so sure."

It was dark inside the lightly swaying coach, warm. There were haloes of light around the lamps on the Nevsky Prospect. Olga giggled as they crossed the Anitchkov Bridge and turned toward her house.

"What's so funny?" he asked softly.

"You," she said. "Why don't you ask me what you really want to know?"

"Ask you what?"

"Whether I've slept with him. That's what you want to know, isn't it?"

Castle was silent for a moment; then he shrugged.

"All right," he said. "Have you?"

"Of course," Olga said.

"I'm . . . surprised," he said.

"Oh, David," she scoffed. "You disapprove, don't you?"

I guess I do at that, Castle thought as the coach clattered along the canal. It bothered him enough to keep him awake for a long time that night. When he finally fell asleep, he dreamed strange distorted dreams of pursuit and fear.

And then Irina.

Sasha and Irina and their children lived a hectic, noisy life, and they swept Castle up in it as unthinkingly as if he were one of their own children. On weekends they would rush off to Peterhof, where

Sasha had a country house, or at the last possible moment decide on a picnic on the shores of Lake Ladoga. Everyone would scurry about, and there would be shouts of laughter from the children as they dashed to catch the steamer. A reticent man, Castle found their disarray charming and not a little seductive. It was as if they knew a secret of living that had eluded everyone else, cramming more into one week than many families did in a year. They joined the glittering crowds at the Maryinsky to see Pavlova with as much enjoyment as they bought ice cream from the *morozhonoye* on the Nevsky. They went to the restaurant at the Zoological Gardens, had tea at Oranienbaum, went to Ciniselli's circus, to parties, to cotillions to the opera. When Vladimir Smirnoff came to Petersburg for the races, Sasha reserved a box at the track in Novaya Derevnaya. There was a seemingly endless supply of champagne, and servants in gay peasant costumes served piquant *okhroshka* and black, salty caviar with onions and eggs. At sunset they all went to the Stryelka, the point at the western end of Yelagin Island, and watched the sun sinking into the darkening blue of the Baltic, then turned about-face and waited for it to reappear, almost at once, in the fresh bright glow of morning. White nights, they called them.

In these activities, in everything they did, Irina was the one who made the decision; Irina was the instigator. Sasha was the willingly docile follower, happy to be the support man, logistician, quartermaster.

"Wouldn't do any of these things on my own, you know," he would pant to Castle as they hurried off on some new quest impulsively announced not an hour earlier by Irina. "All her, all of it."

Irina.

Her name brought a series of images into Castle's mind, one after another. At a birthday party for little Rina, in a sleeveless shift that would have looked shapeless on another woman, yet which accentuated the soft symmetry of Irina's body as no close-fitting dress could ever have done. Poised at the edge of a swimming pool, on tiptoe, slim arms outstretched above her head, bare back glittering with drops of water, lovely as a heron, then gone into the water in a flash of movement. Sprawled on her stomach in front of the fire, face cradled in hands, frowning furiously at the newspaper. Sitting in a boat with her eyes closed, trailing her hand in the water, her mobile face in a repose that made her look strangely sad. Dancing across a sunlit lawn like a dervish with a child on each hand, singing a nonsense song. They were the no more than ordinary things that a thousand other women do just as regularly and with no less grace, but they impressed themselves upon his consciousness like photographs on film. And as it would theoretically be possible to make strong hawser from cobwebs, if enough cobwebs were used, so these thousand remembered images fused into an entirety which enchanted him.

It was stupid to have fallen in love with her, he told himself. An affair, a quick bout of sexual aggression for mutual pleasure, ending without regrets, that would have been forgivable, even sensible. But loving her was stupid, and stupidity always angered him.

At first, it was simply an hour in the afternoon, three times a week: Russian lessons, a refresher course in the language learned effortlessly as a child and forgotten before he was sixteen. Some things had stuck in his head. He could still count to ten, *odin*, *dva*, *tri*, and still recite the names of the countries of the Russian Empire: Byelorussia, Moldavia, Lithuania, Latvia, Estonia, Georgia, Armenia, Kazan and so on—doubtless learned by rote. He was a quick learner, and she was a good teacher. Their relationship was pleasant, warm, comfortable. They enthused over similar things and laughed at the same kind of joke. It was no more than that, at first.

Then one day he looked at her and truly saw her, saw the way she moved and the intelligence in her eyes, the whole fine-tuned machine of mind and body. He did not plan it, or even think about it. He simply bent down and kissed her. She did not pretend outrage, innocence, anger, shock. Her lips were firm and cool, her eyes unreadable.

"Why, David?" she said.

"I don't know." He shook his head. "I want you."

"It isn't love. It can't be."

"It'll do," he said, and took her in his arms.

So then the Russian lessons became a routine observed only so that they could be together, a formality for the sake of convention. They talked in Russian, but the teaching was ended. Now both of them were learning. He told her about himself, some of it. They explored each other's lives and minds as eagerly as children. He was charmed by the unexpectedness of her insights, she pleasured by his ability to evoke in words the places he had been and the things he had done. She learned to recognize his moods and he hers, and there were secrets between them that no one knew.

They began to meet away from the house, at the Hermitage or

the Stroganov art gallery. They stood before Tintoretto's painting of an old general with a white beard, their shoulders touching, the back of his hand against the back of hers. His body ached to possess her; he knew she wanted him, too. They had never spoken of it. It was implicit; when they could, they would. But there was never anywhere they could go, no way they could be together, and so in the end he reserved a suite at the Astoria, and she came to him there.

Their lovemaking was a disaster. He had no sense of her urgencies, nor she of his. It was clumsy and unsatisfactory, and it was over for him before it had begun for her. They lay silent afterward in the impersonal hotel bed. The traffic on the Morskaya sounded very loud.

"I have to go soon," she said.

"I know."

"Does it bother you—what happened?"

"What do you think?"

A clock ticked somewhere; in the hall, she thought.

"I'm sorry," he said. He turned toward her. Her body was golden in the sunlight coming through the drawn shades. He fought against feeling angry; that was no good at all.

"God damn it!" he said.

"Oh, darling," Irina said. "Don't. Don't, please. It doesn't matter that much."

"But it does."

"It shouldn't."

"It was my fault. It was no good for you, was it?"

"Not very," she said, in a small voice that told him she was fighting back tears. "I was—I don't know what I'd expected. Something special, I suppose. This was . . . just . . ." Her voice trailed off, and silence flooded the room again. She got up off the bed and started picking up her underwear. He lay on the bed and watched her, feeling as if she was a stranger he had never seen before, a woman behind a window in a room across a street.

"Will you walk down with me?" she said, and something happened to him. He felt as if someone had taken hold of his heart in his hand and crushed it. In that moment and for the first time, he fell truly in love.

"Irina," he said, unable to say more. She looked at him and saw the tears.

"David?" she said. Her voice was hardly more than a whisper, as if she feared that speaking would shatter this fragile moment. She came to him soundlessly, the cool lips soft on his, and he drew her down on the bed. For the smallest moment she hesitated, and then, as if making some sort of decision, she sighed and slid into his arms.

He kissed her face and her chin, his mouth against her throat, her breasts. She held his head in her hands and then her arms went around him, rocking him against her body. He could feel the steady pulse of her heart through the silky skin. He ran his hands down the long valley of her back and over the soft swell of hip and thigh, finding the warmer center of her. Interwined, they explored each other without haste, eyes half-closed, like cats in a sunlit garden. She was not as schooled as some women he had known. Her responses were natural and unforced, and when she was ready, she turned to him and smiled.

"Second time lucky," she said, closing her eyes as he entered her. Then the long joined movements became less slow, the languor evaporating and changing as they went together faster into nothingness, quicker into darkness that deepened and throbbed and then swelled and then thundered and then burst over them like a wave over a groyne, huge, engulfing, on and on and on and then over, then eddying, swirling, dying, falling, eddying, swirling, gone.

"I love you, Irina," he said, afterward.

She did not answer at first.

"I mean it," he said.

"I know," Irina replied. "I'm glad."

"Are you? Are you glad?"

"Yes. And sad, too."

He did not ask why because he knew she was thinking of Sasha. She was saddened by the knowledge that she had betrayed him, just as Castle was saddened to think that he was stealing from him. They were silent. Do I really want this, he wondered? Is this what I want? He did not know the answer; not then, and not now.

14

THE LETTER was written, as all of them had been written, on cheap paper, pages torn from a cheap exercise book of the kind you could buy in any one of two hundred shops in Moscow. The handwriting was crude and obviously disguised. The envelope was as common and, like all the others, the letter had been mailed from one of the central post offices, in this case the one in the Upper Rows. Guchkov had gone through the pointless routine of testing the paper for fingerprints, but it had been useless. The writer was far too clever and much too careful to make so elementary a mistake.

"*My dear Investigator Guchkov,*" it began. Very friendly; well, they were old friends now. This wasn't the first letter. The killer had begun writing quite a while back. "*So you thought you were rid of me, did you? Well, I've left you a little surprise in the garden of the Alexeyevski Monastery—I took my usual cut, ha, ha! What fools you policemen are. I am going to give you two for the price of one next time—not that it'll help you. All that newspaper stuff didn't fool me, by the way. I was going to write to you anyway. I like the name they've given me, though: Gospodin Palatch.*"

Viktor Guchkov pushed the letter aside with an exasperated grunt, running a hand through his thatch of gray-flecked hair and giving a cavernous yawn. It was nearly two in the morning. He and Bunin had been working eighteen hours a day for the past few days, ever since they had been called out to the gardens behind the Alexeyevski Monastery, where the mutilated body of Maya Levasova had been discovered by a workman taking a shortcut from his home to the Krasnoprudnaya. There was not the slightest doubt whose handiwork it was: the mass murderer whom the newspapers had dubbed *Gospodin Palatch*, Citizen Butcher. There was no mistaking his fiendish work. The mutilations that were his trademark were the same, and then, as if to remove even the faintest possibility of doubt, the man had written to Guchkov to boast about his filthy achievements.

Bastard, Guchkov thought, brazen bastard!

It was the sheer frustration of it that maddened him. The killer's brazen, taunting letters had turned out to be no help to them at all, and there were many times when Guchkov bitterly regretted having been the one to suggest opening this particular Pandora's box. He consoled himself with the thought that the killer would in all likelihood have written his taunting missives anyway, but that got them no nearer to the man. The handwriting—if you could call such ill-formed capitals handwriting—told them nothing about the personality of the man. The experts analyzed it, of course. They told Guchkov that it had probably been written with his left hand by a man who normally wrote with his right, rendering worthless any assessment of the calligraphy, leaving only the maddening taunt that he planned to kill again, soon, and that there was not a damned thing Guchkov or the entire Moscow police force could do about it.

The newspaper campaign had worked perfectly. Once the First Secretary gave his consent, Guchkov approached the editors of the two leading Moscow newspapers and set out the salient facts about the murders for them. He went over the final copy with the feature writers before it was published to make sure that in each article and in all succeeding ones, there was a common factual error. The articles created a furor and drew massive correspondence from the public, divided about fifty-fifty between demands that Citizen Butcher be caught immediately and suggestions as to how it might be done. Crackpot letters rolled in by the hundreds. Many of them were published, generating more in their turn. Others were not published, including the short note in straggling capitals which, the moment he saw it, Guchkov knew had been written by the murderer.

"*To The Editor*, Moskovsky Listok, *Sir—Your article about the murders in Moscow is almost laughably inaccurate. Most notably it states that the girl Starovna's face was not mutilated. You know better than that, Sir, and so do I. I sliced her up nicely. One who knows.*"

Guchkov had seen to it that the papers all said the same thing: that Starovna's injuries were all confined to the body. Apart from himself, Bunin, the police surgeon and one or two other officials who had read his reports, no one except the murderer knew any differently. Ergo, the letter writer was the murderer.

A further series of articles was published, each of which drew a reply, sometimes several, from the murderer. Gradually, the whole thing assumed a life of its own, for the newspapers—hitherto prevented by the censors from reporting the murders—had a field day when in February 1914, the body of eight-year-old Natasha Albedinski was found on waste ground behind a factory in the Serpukhovskaya district. High-minded citizens condemned police inaction, and pressure was put on Guchkov from above to enlist a fifty-man Murder Squad to mount an intensive hunt for the man whom the newspapers had now dubbed Citizen Butcher.

"The man we are after," Guchkov gently explained to Secretary Kurasov, "is far too intelligent to be flushed from his den like some rabid fox frightened by yapping dogs. We will only capture him by using the same kind of guile he uses himself."

"If you insist, Guchkov," Kurasov said, sourly. "But be warned: if we don't see some results soon, heads will roll. Mark what I say, Guchkov: heads will roll."

Guchkov nodded and left. Heads rolled at the top first, he knew. There was no point in firing the policeman doing the investigating, because his replacement would take too long to become familiar with the nuances of the case. Anyway, the public never heard much about the investigators, wasn't interested in them. If someone was to be the scapegoat for the Ministry's lack of success in catching *Gospodin Palatch*, Guchkov felt pretty confident that it would be Anatoli Kurasov. It was not a prospect which filled him with sympathy or horror.

"Got any ideas, Chief?" Bunin said.

"Not really," Guchkov replied. "The only chance, if it is a chance, is that he seems to have killed the child where he found her. He's only done that once before."

"You think he's making it harder for himself? Or is he challenging us?"

"Could be either," Guchkov said. "Making it harder for himself, certainly. That would add excitement, you see. And making it, as it were, easier for us heightens it even more."

He got up and went across the room to the big blackboard which they had asked for. On it were written the names of the victims and the dates of their deaths, together with any other relevant information. The brutal facts mocked his helplessness. Kaminsky, seven years old. Killed July. Terzakova, ten, a month later. Three weeks after that, Lazareva. Then Starovna, and little Valentina Tereshkovna. He remembered Tereshkovna, the poor mutilated little thing they had looked at in the police morgue. There had been something almost demonic in the way that the soft, girlish body had been defaced. Anger coursed again through him, the slow, pulsing anger he always felt when he thought of that monster walking the streets free. He looked again at the letter from the killer about the girl in the Alexeyevski Monastery garden. He wondered how Kurasov was enjoying the newspaper headlines which the latest slaying had generated. WORST MASS MURDERER IN LIVING MEMORY KILLS AGAIN! one screamed. GOSPODIN PALATCH STRIKES DOWN ANOTHER VICTIM! shouted another. The stories were all pretty much the same, recapitulating the bare facts of the first murders, a summary of bloodshed ending with the few facts which had been released about the murder of Maya Levasova.

"Maya Levasova left the home of her grandparents, where she had gone to show them a new watch bought for her by her parents, at 9:40 P.M., after declining an invitation to stay because she had not brought any nightclothes. Twenty minutes' walk from the home of her grandparents, the girl met her murderer. She was most brutally killed less than five minutes' walk from the doorway of her own house, and within sight of other houses. The killer is thought to have been stalking his victim and surveying the area for some time, and the police wish to interview anyone who was in the area of the Alexeyevski Monastery between 8:30 P.M. and midnight. At the head of the inquiry is Senior Judicial Investigator V. I. Guchkov.

"At the back of our minds is the knowledge that between July last year and the present, this man has killed seven times. There is every reason to expect that he will kill again. No one is safe. We adjure all parents to tell their children to avoid open ground, lonely places, empty streets. Ensure that they have an escort, the company of friends. Instruct them on no account to speak to any stranger, no matter what the pretext. This man strikes without warning, and it is obvious from what has happened that he appears to be quite normal when he approaches his victims.

"The suspicion increases that someone is sheltering *Gospodin Palatch*. Investigator Guchkov says, 'This fiend returns from his crimes bespattered with the blood of his victims. Either he lives alone, so that no one can see him when he returns from his atrocities, or someone other than he knows who he is and what he is. I appeal, I beg of that someone, if he or she exists, to come forward before another innocent child loses its life.'

"The murderer knows that random murders are the hardest of all to solve, and taunts the investigators by sending them letters, and even, in one case, going back to the scene of one of his murders to put the body in a place that made it easier to find.

"Meanwhile the lights in the Ministry of Justice burn all night. The race that the investigators have lost so many times is on again."

Somewhere in this city, Guchkov thought, a man is sitting in a room beneath a light, reading these same words. What is he thinking? Does his heart pound with excitement to see how infamous he has become? Does he laugh contemptuously at the journalese descriptions of his exploits, the ham-handed efforts of the police to apprehend him, the inability of one living soul to describe him? Is he tall, short, dark, fair, young, old? What color are his eyes? Is he a sailor? Is that why the intervals between his killings are so irregular? Is he a soldier, a foreigner, or perhaps just some meek-looking little clerk in an anonymous office doing an anonymous job? Guchkov sighed, wondering if he would be able to come up with any answers at all before Citizen Butcher fulfilled his ghastly promise to kill twice on the same night.

15

JUNE is a beautiful month in Siberia. The weather in Irkutsk was fine and the skies were a cerulean blue, but Boris Abrikosov derived no comfort from them. The wide, empty steppes mocked his isolation and his powerlessness.

They had given him no options. There was no nonsense about *habeas corpus*, representation by a lawyer, or any of the other amenities of legal procedure. He had used *Okhrana* power for his own ends, which would have been bad enough. He had been publicly humiliated into the bargain. The *Okhrana* did not care to see its officers humiliated and itself without a defense. The Smirnoff family had laid charges against Boris, bringing the matter directly to the attention of the Minister of the Interior; there was no question of closing ranks. It was decided to make an example of Boris Abrikosov *pour encourager les autres*.

The section doctor, a pompous old fool who ought to have been retired years ago, had concluded that Senior Examiner Abrikosov had suffered from a fit of temporary insanity brought on by monomania. The diagnosis was not offered as a defense; it merely provided a means by which the Department could wash its hands of involvement. The hearing, conducted by the Head of the Department of Security Affairs and his aide, was held in a private office at the Ministry of the Interior. It was brief and clinical. No witnesses were called, no testimony was taken, no defense was permitted.

"You know why you are here, Abrikosov?" Gorbichev, the Head of the Department, said. He was a big man with peasant's hands and heavy eyebrows that grew together over the bridge of his nose. His eyes were unfriendly.

"I am sure you will inform me, Your Excellency," Boris said smoothly.

"Insolence will not help you, Abrikosov!" Gorbichev snapped. "You would be wise to be circumspect."

Boris would have smiled, but he knew better than to do so. Gorbichev was quite capable of doubling whatever punishment he had in mind if he felt he had been insulted. Vain as a peacock, Boris thought. They said Gorbichev was a bit of a ladies' man. He couldn't see it himself. "I beg your pardon," he made himself say.

"Have you anything to say here which would be relevant to our decision?" Gorbichev's aide Kalnikov asked.

"Nothing," Boris said. He wasn't telling them anything. Let them smack his wrist and be done with it.

"Very well," Gorbichev said. He picked up a sheet of paper from his desk and looked at Boris. There was neither rancor nor interest in his expression. He looked like what he was, a man doing a job.

"You will be exiled for two years—"

"What?" Boris shouted. "*What?*"

"Be silent!" Gorbichev shouted back, starting to his feet.

The guards on either side of Boris grabbed his arms. "Be silent, prisoner!"

As he glared at Gorbichev, the word sank into Boris's mind. For the first time he realized what he was now: a number, a nothing.

"You will be exiled for two years," Gorbichev repeated, "without choice. You will subsequently serve for one year in an Army unit with the rank of private, such unit to be designated by the appropriate authority at the appropriate time. You have been consigned to spend your exile in the city of Irkutsk. Have you anything to say, prisoner?"

Boris clamped his mouth shut and said no more.

"You will be given forty-eight hours to arrange your affairs," Gorbichev said. "Then you will report for deportation. Have you any questions?"

"No." He was damned if he'd call the man by his title, and he was gratified when he saw Gorbichev's lips compress with anger.

"Take him away!" Gorbichev snapped.

The police escort stayed with Boris throughout the forty-eight hours he had been given to settle his affairs. He made arrangements for his secret dossiers to be lodged in a vault at the Imperial State Bank on the Sadovaya. The two *gorodovoi* even helped Boris to carry the boxes down to the waiting carriage, an irony of which Boris was not unappreciative. He wrote two pages of instructions for Dmitri on foolscap paper and had them delivered by messenger.

He wanted no one from the family coming to see him off for Siberia, as if he were going on vacation. He wanted nothing from them at all except money. Money smoothed all paths, even in faraway Irkutsk.

Two days later he was taken with fifteen other deportees to the Nicholas Station in Petersburg. Two ordinary trains left there daily, bound for Tchelyabinsk. There were special carriages for the prisoners, guarded by soldiers. Traveling via Vyatka, they covered the two thousand-odd versts from Petersburg to Tchelyabinsk in three days. At Tchelyabinsk they were transferred, in the same coaches, to the Trans-Siberian Express, at the rear end of which they traveled another three thousand versts to Irkutsk. The windows were painted black; they saw nothing except each other the whole way. At no time did Boris speak to any of his fellow prisoners. He had already closed his mind to everything except survival.

It would have been easy to hate Gorbichev and Kalnikov and the rest of them, too easy. They were only lackeys, doing the bidding of the people with the real power, people like the Smirnoffs, with their money and their connections. He had never had more than the scantest respect for the Head of the Department and his aide; now he considered them beneath even contempt.

Boris could not concede any failure except their failure to support him. Nor would his pride allow him to consider that he had fallen. It was a world full of crass idiots. He knew his worth, knew it was only a matter of time until it was recognized. His time would come, he was sure. Meanwhile, he would wait it out.

So he simply shut himself down, like a boiler which is allowed to go out and will not function again until the fire is relit. He maintained no illusions, expected nothing, gave nothing. He did not mix with the other exiles. He felt nothing but contempt for their pathetic attempts to act as if Irkutsk was some kind of home away from home, going out with local girls, renting little houses and setting up literary circles and discussion groups.

It could have been worse. He could have been sent to prison, and that would have been hell on earth. There was a huge compound at Alexandrovskoye, about seventy versts northwest of Irkutsk. He had been up there and seen the shuffling convicts with their leg irons and their shaven heads and their "dressing gowns" with the diamond-shaped prisoner's mark on them. He had seen them being herded down to the sheds on the riverbank to work in the furnace-hot brick kilns or the lung-choking dust of the alabaster bakeries. He had seen their watery cabbage soup—they didn't even bother to scoop the dead black beetles out of it—and their lice and their cockroaches, and he had seen their eyes, with death in them. Most of them were illiterate serfs, but he knew that some of them were "politicals," educated men, from good homes and soft lives. He did not know how they could endure such privation and misery, but he did not care. The only person Boris cared about in the world was himself.

Irkutsk, he discovered, was not so bad. The air was fresh and mountain-steppe dry, pleasant after the sea-level dampness of Petersburg. The River Angara was swift and clear, six hundred yards wide at the point where it passed the town, and there were plenty of fish in it. In the summer there was a pontoon bridge across the river below the point at which it was joined by the Irkut. There was a theater on the Bolshaya, and a little farther along on the opposite side was the museum of the Imperial Geographical Society. Most days Boris would call in and pass the time of day with Nikolai Nikolaievich Bogorodsky, the librarian, and on Saturdays, like everyone else in town, he went to the baths at Kurbatov's on the Savinsky Pereulok. He read a great deal, getting his books from the Makushin Library. From time to time he would see one of the other exiles in there, a striking-looking man with penetrating dark eyes and a spade-shaped beard. He learned that the man was Felix Dzerzhinski, a Polish aristocrat turned Social Democrat, then Bolshevik. After a while, they began to greet each other, and then to exchange a few words. Dzerzhinski was a close friend of Lenin, the leader of the Bolsheviks, so Boris listened attentively to what Dzerzhinski had to say. He soon learned that Felix was interested in the same thing that he was: power. Their talks became longer as the acquaintanceship ripened, and Boris allowed Dzerzhinski to believe he had converted him to Bolshevism. It might be useful later, he thought. If it was not, he would discard it and Dzerzhinski without so much as a second thought.

Meanwhile, he ate, he walked, he slept. He lived poorly but not badly, roughly but without privation. He was indifferent to his circumstances. There was only one thought in his mind: the passage of time. I can do it, he told himself. Day after day, like a litany, he repeated it: I can do this. I can live through this. I can wait.

16

GOSPODIN PALATCH was as good as his word. On the night of June 20, 1914, he disemboweled a young girl named Sofia Naryshkina in an alley behind a workingmen's club in the Pryesnenskaya district. The body was found at about one in the morning by a steward from the club called Stepan Svobodin, who had left by the rear entrance to go home. Blood was still pouring from the body when the police surgeon arrived, and he estimated that she had been killed only minutes before Svobodin stumbled over her. When he realized that he had probably interrupted the murderer in the middle of his butchery, Svobodin hurried back into the club and locked himself in, swigging at a bottle of vodka he'd saved for a rainy day.

Less than an hour later, *Gospodin Palatch* struck again. The name of the girl he killed was Vera Pilova, an attractive, lively youngster of fourteen. Unlike all his other victims, however, Pilova was a prostitute, probably the only kind the murderer could find on the streets at that hour, Guchkov told Bunin.

Pilova had made the mistake of taking the man who picked her up back to the room she rented in a house near the Pryesnenskaya Ponds. Her body was found the next morning when her landlady waddled across the courtyard to see if her tenant wanted any milk. The door swung back beneath the weight of the landlady's fist and they saw Vera lying on the bed. Or rather, what was left of her.

The murderer, according to the police surgeon, had taken at least two hours over his fiendish work. This time he had not torn the body apart in his usual satanic haste but had carefully, almost methodically, sliced Vera Pilova apart, like a butcher preparing a display. The throat had been cut from ear to ear, the face obliterated, kidneys and heart removed, breasts cut off the body and laid neatly to one side. There was blood everywhere. Parts of the body had been hung on nails and from the picture rails. It was the most ghastly sight Guchkov had ever seen.

"Don't go in, Piotr," he said to Bunin. "You don't have to."

Bunin shook his head and went in. He emerged after just a few moments, white and horror-stricken.

"God," he choked. "Oh, God!"

"Piotr?" Guchkov said.

"All . . . right, Chief. I'll be all right," Bunin said. "In a moment."

"Listen, Piotr," Guchkov said, "pull yourself together. I need you."

"All right. All *right*, dammit!"

"You know what we have here, Piotr?"

"Hell!" Bunin said. His eyes were full of tears. "The bloody pits of hell!"

"I know how you feel," Guchkov said gently. "But we have to act, Piotr. Swiftly, now. I want a photographer out here. I want pictures of the room, the body, everything. Exactly as it is now, do you understand? Nothing is to be moved, nothing. Cordon the place off. Let no one in here, not the Chief of Police or the Governor-General—not even the Minister himself!"

"I don't think he'd be too keen," Bunin said, with a weak attempt at a grin. He wished he had Guchkov's iron will. "Where are you going?"

"Back to the office," Guchkov said. "I need some things. Now, don't let me down, Piotr. No one in there, except the photographer. And make sure he doesn't move anything."

Bunin shuddered. He didn't imagine for a second that the photographer would want to stay in that blood-spattered abbatoir any longer than he had to, or touch anything he didn't need to touch, and he was right. The photographer was as green as grass when he came out, even though he was a twenty-year man.

Guchkov was back within the hour. "Right, lad," he said. "Let's get started."

"Chief," Bunin began, but Guchkov cut off his words with an impatient gesture.

"Don't talk, lad, listen!" he said. "Door to door, now. Every house that has a view of this courtyard, every house on the street, every house that overlooks the intersections at each end. I want to know if anyone saw Pilova at all, any time between—what shall we say? Three yesterday afternoon and eight this morning. And most especially, Piotr, I want to know whether anyone—"

"—saw a man with her?"

239

"Right, lad," Guchkov said. "Get to work!"

"What will you be doing, Chief?"

Guchkov inclined his head toward the doorway of the apartment. He did not relish the prospect, but he was going to go over it with a fine-toothed comb. This was probably the nearest they had ever come to their quarry, and the hair on Guchkov's neck bristled at the thought.

The room still stank of death, the strange metallic-sweet odor of dried blood and meat, the smell of the charnel house. The walls and the few cheap sticks of furniture were still sticky with the blood of the murdered girl, and flies buzzed abominably everywhere. Guchkov cursed at them, swiping blindly to drive them away. He bound a handkerchief around the lower part of his face, pulled his hat low over his eyes, and pulled on the thin cotton gloves he had brought in the murder kit. Then, trying to ignore the awful thing on the blood-soaked bed, he set about doing what he had come to do.

There were ashes in the fireplace: some remnants of cloth, by the look of them. With infinite care he brushed them into one of the envelopes he had brought. There were other fragments on the floor; these went into another envelope. From each of the spattered gobs of blood around the room he took a scraping, placing it on a glass slide which he covered with another before numbering them, ready for use in microscopic analysis. He searched every place in which a weapon might have been concealed, finding nothing. There were a few clothes in the cupboards, cheap, shoddy stuff. He went through them all, dress by dress, jacket by jacket, pocket by pocket, seam by seam, carefully enveloping and annotating everything he found. There were shoes, some with mud on them; in each case he took a scraping. He took specimens of the hair on the brushes that he found in the bedroom and others from the rim of the girl's chamber pot. When he had finished his minute examination of the apartment, he began at the doorway again. This time he dusted every smooth surface he could find, anywhere which might have taken a finger-print. He grunted; there were a great many. Hardly surprising when you considered Pilova's profession.

Two days later, they made a list of what they had.

They had three fingerprints which did not belong either to Pilova or to her "cat," Shunikov the pimp. That they could very well be and probably were the fingerprints of any of a hundred "clients" Guchkov was only too painfully aware. He filed them, anyway. You never knew.

They had a report on Shunikov. The pimp was known to the police, and more pleased with his sudden celebrity than he was upset by the death of the girl. They turned him loose. There was no way Shunikov could be the killer; he could neither read nor write.

They had a forensic report on the ashes which Guchkov had raked out of Pilova's fireplace. It said that they were remnants of merino wool, dark blue or black in color. A second forensic report said that all the blood samples from the room were of the same type: that of Pilova. The various scrapings Guchkov had taken from her shoes were street mud, unidentifiable except as such. They gave no indication of where she might have been, or when.

Disappointing, to say the least of it. They would have been no nearer to *Gospodin Palatch* than ever had it not been for Piotr Bunin's house-to-house search of the neighborhood in which Pilova had lived. Out of that had come two eyewitness descriptions of a man with whom Pilova had been seen on the night of her murder: a tall, dark-haired man wearing a blue jacket, according to the first witness. The second was even more specific: thirty years old, give or take a few years, five feet nine or ten, with a small moustache, dressed in something like a blue blazer, with light-colored trousers. Definitely not a workingman, the witness said. Someone slumming, more likely. They got a lot of them down here.

They had one more thing: another crudely lettered note from the maniac himself.

Goodbye, Guchkov!
The last one squealed a bit, but it was good fun in the end! Stop hunting for me—I'm leaving Moscow tomorrow and won't be back for ages. Better luck next time
Gospodin Palatch

As abruptly as they had begun, the murders ceased. The reign of terror was over.

17

T HAT MAN, Tatiana decided exasperatedly, was more interested
in Papa than he was in her. Torn between feeling that Vladimir
ought to take more notice of her and the fear that he would do
just that, it seemed to her that Vladimir was almost deliberately keeping her at arm's length.

Somehow the very knowledge that Boris had been arrested eased
the strain that had existed at Sokolnika. Alex and Maryka sent word
to Ivan Pavlovich that they would soon be returning to Petersburg
and bade him prepare the house. Tatiana looked forward to returning home with mixed feelings. She had grown to know Sokolnika
and loved its leisured pace, her equally leisured days. As for Alex, he
was always delighted to have one of the Smirnoffs to talk to. Nico
would often stop to chat, and before long he would be explaining
this process or that to Alex. Alex, in turn, would recite what he had
learned over the dinner table, proud of his newly acquired knowledge and sometimes awed by it.

"D'you know how many bottles they use, any idea?" he would
say. "Fifty million a year! Fifty million! They subcontract the work
to seven bottle factories, each one of which works exclusively for
Smirnoff. What do you think of that, eh?" Or, another day, "Pierre
was explaining the filtering process to me; fascinating business. Introduced by his grandfather, old Arsenii, you know. He was just a
young fellow, then, twenty or so. Just got out of the Army, fought
against Napoleon, imagine that! Bought a few *desyatina* of land by
the Moskvoretzky Bridge and got a license to make vodka. There
was a scientist in Petersburg, Theodr Löwitz, who'd just discovered
a technique for using charcoal as a filter in the process of distilling
alcohol. Old Arsenii decided to use Löwitz's process and then ex-
perimented with it until he had his own method. Produced the
best vodka in Moscow, then Russia. Fascinating! Know how much

charcoal they use now, just the Moscow distillery? Two hundred and forty thousand tons a year! What do you think of that, eh?"

Thus, willy-nilly, Maryka and Tatiana got an education in vodka making and a small idea of the size and wealth of the Smirnoff family business. The cost of corks alone, Alex told them, was more than one hundred and twenty thousand rubles. So how much, he asked rhetorically, for the hundred million labels and tags produced by the four lithographic printers exclusively employed by Ste. Pierre Smirnoff et Fils? How much more to pay the two hundred drivers whose wagons were loaded daily in the cobbled courtyard of the factory, the hundreds of others in Petersburg and Odessa and Lvov? How much more for the casualty ward, the pharmacy, the doctor and nurse at each factory, and how much more on top of that for the schools provided to give the workers' children some sort of education and the automatic pension granted to any worker who had been with the company for twenty-five years?

"Staggering!" Alex would say. "That's the only word for it, staggering!"

One could not begin to imagine the enormous quantities of berries needed by the distillery to produce, besides vodka and the purified wines, the fruit liqueurs, among them the famous ashberry liqueur "Katyushka" which was a Smirnoff specialty, invented by Petya Smirnoff. Well, as Nico said when he brought Alex a bottle to try, sort of. They had been talking about old Arsenii.

"You said he had two sons," Maryka pointed out. "What happened to the other one? Wasn't he involved in the business at all?"

"No," Nico said, abruptly. There was an awkward silence for a moment, as if Maryka had touched a tender spot. Alex asked another question.

"Competitors?" Nico smiled, his frown disappearing as quickly as it had formed. "By the hundred! In Central Russia alone there were more than seven hundred distilleries making vodka. A further four and a half thousand in the rest of Russia and Siberia!"

"I had no idea," Alex said. "No idea."

"How could you know?" Nico said. "My grandfather, who began the business, did not know. Perhaps if he had known, he would never have started."

Nevertheless, he went on, Arsenii had succeeded well enough to make a comfortable living for himself and his wife and sons. The little building with its primitive distilling equipment grew, becoming a large building on what was now the Pyatnitzkaya, employing twenty-five people. Arsenii had a steady stream of satisfied regular customers.

"But you asked me how 'Katyushka' came into being, and I will tell you," Nico said. "My father, Petya, was not quite twenty-one when his father died. He took over the management of the company and soon decided that vodka alone would not be enough to make it grow. One day, he was visiting the home of one of the landowners from whom he bought his berries and he was persuaded to try a homemade liqueur from ashberries, which grew in profusion in the area. From the first sip, Petya—the family always called him Petya and my brother Pierre, to avoid confusion—knew he had stumbled onto something. He couldn't wait to get back to the city."

The following morning Petya sent every worker in the factory out to the huge fruit and vegetable market in the nearby Bolotnaya Square, with instructions to purchase every single punnet of ashberries they could find. Smirnoff's workers cleaned out the entire stock of the astonished fruit merchants in a single twenty-minute period. The following New Year's day, P.A. Smirnoff's "Katyushka" Ashberry Liqueur, named for the wife of the friend whose recipe had given him the idea, was launched with huge success.

Petya—a publicist to his fingertips—took full-page advertisements in the big newspapers and magazines, featuring well-known actors, actresses and other public personalities who endorsed his liqueurs in return for free space to promote their own activities. Demand grew. Petya put on extra workers to cope with the flood of orders coming in from wine merchants throughout the country. He made it a condition of their purchasing "Katyushka" that they purchase an equal amount of other Smirnoff products.

"And that's how 'Katyushka' was born," Nico said.

"We'll have a glass," Alex said. "You'll join me?"

"Thank you," Nico said. "I don't drink."

Never anymore, not since "then." He could remember exactly where it had started, that night he had gone out to "drown his sorrows," joking about it. God, he had been in love with her, though! Just thinking about her had made his bones ache, every fiber longing to be with her. Vera, Verushka, where are you now, he wondered? Still married to that fool of a stockbroker, still living in your house-proud world of dreams? He had drunk too much that night and wakened the next day with the most terrible hangover. There were at least ten thousand "cures" for a hangover, but he took the one nearest, the hair of the dog which had bitten him. He found himself feeling good, braced, ready to face what had looked like another dreary Petersburg winter day. So it began. Around and around and around it goes, and where it ends up nobody knows. Why does someone commit suicide when all his senses and reason insist he live? He did not need drink. He did not like what it did to his coordination, which became erratic, or his memory, which grew poor, or his walk, which turned into a shamble, or his speech, which was slurred. The more the thing took hold of him the more he hated it, and it seemed as if the more he hated it the more he did it. There were times when he literally felt he would have to force the revolting stuff down his throat, disgusted by its taste and smell, just so he could function. He made a hundred determined vows to do without the first drink of the day until ten, eleven, midday, and failed as many times. He hated himself when he was half-sober, and he was swamped with self-pity when he was not. He was haunted by remorse, soiled and sordid, mired in chaos. He knew that everyone knew, even if no one spoke of his condition. He was consumed by guilt, while knowing he did not care for anything except the next drink and the next. He woke every morning with a throat that felt as if it were full of ashes, belly twisting with the first movement, nausea and the need to defecate coming simultaneously. He learned not to drink any water, no matter how bad the thirst. If he did, he was again immediately intoxicated. Often, it made him vomit.

Then he had to sweat it out, the charade of routine, getting ready to go to "work." Servants know everything. He knew that now, but then he had pretended they did not, and they had supported his pretense with one of their own. Skin crawling, sweat cold on the body, nerves screaming, he would pick at the breakfast they placed before him, surviving the minutes until he could leave the house and get what he wanted. Every day was a patchwork quilt of lies and deceit, forgotten meetings, encounters with strangers, arguments with other drunks in other dives, noise, smoke, smell, sweat, rain, cold, heat, light.

They found him one December night lying in a gutter on a side street behind the Kuznetsky Most, half-frozen, wasted. He had no recollection, when they revived him, of who he was or where he had been for the past three days and nights. He had severe frostbite and pneumonia, and he was aswarm with lice. His name meant nothing to the doctors in the charity ward. No one looking at the derelict in bed number twenty-two would have dreamed of connecting him with the wealthy family of which he was a member.

It was Pierre who had found him, Pierre who arranged for him to be transferred to a private "clinic" in Pyatigorsk as soon as he was able to be moved. It was ruthless, yet it was the only decision which Pierre could have taken. If Nico was not treated for his illness, he would die of it. The Ryashensky Clinic in Pyatigorsk was renowned for its success with alcoholics. It was Nico's only chance.

He still remembered, as if it were yesterday instead of thirty years ago, the sudden, safe sensation he felt as he was taken into the great sprawling country house. It was like coming home to a warm house and loved ones. He never took a drink again; that was the miracle they wrought for him. The way you did it was simple. You got through each half hour without taking a drink. Then you got through the next one without taking a drink. Then the next, and then the next. There would never be any time when you would not want to have one, they said. You just had to decide whether you wanted to be alive or dead. If you wanted to live, you gave it up. If you didn't give it up, you would die. It was a very simple formula, and he clung to it as a shipwrecked sailor clings to a spar. Two years after he was "cured" he met Sophie Tamarova, fell in love with her warmth and beauty, and married her as soon as she would have him. Supported by Sophie, encouraged by Pierre, he returned to the family business. Old Petya accepted, grudgingly, that Nico was cured.

"I'd written you off, Nikolai," he said. He always called Nico by his full name. "I made myself do it. Otherwise you'd have dragged us all down." He put his arm around Nico's shoulder and hugged him in that offhand, almost embarrassed way that he had.

Liquor was just a series of names now on the invoices Nico perused, the advertisements he sanctioned, the labels he authorized: Smirnoffka and Spotikatch, Zubrovka, Pertsovka, Ryabenovka, Katyushka, Vishnyovayanalevka, all the rest of them, kummel, crème de cacao, cassis.

"I'm more of a wine drinker, myself," Alex said. "Next time you're in Petersburg, I'll show you my cellar. Rather proud of it. See no sense in paying inflated prices for French wines when we've perfectly good ones of our own. Better, if you ask me."

"You know our wines?" Nico asked him.

"Yes, they're not at all bad," Alex said. "Not top class, you understand, not as good as an Alushta, say."

"Ah, Tokmakov and Molotkov." Nico smiled. "But their vines are of German origin, Alex."

"If they grow in the black earth of Russia, they are Russian enough for me, young fellow!" Alex retorted.

Nico was still smiling as he left, having promised Alex that he would arrange for him to be taken around the factory before they returned to Petersburg. Alex watched him go almost regretfully. He was becoming quite interested in the history of the Smirnoff family.

"Wonder why he didn't want to talk about Petya's brother?" he said. "Black sheep of the family, eh? Skeleton in the cupboard?"

He was nearer to the mark than he knew, but as there seemed no polite way to return to the topic, he let it lapse. They saw little of Pierre, for which Tatiana, at least, was grateful. Papa seemed these days to talk of nothing but vodka, and when it wasn't vodka, it was war, war, war. Even Vladimir Smirnoff's talk of horses was a change, if not for the better. Why wouldn't he *look* at her? she asked herself as Alex and Vladimir talked about Telegin and the various faults of this breed and merits of that until she was sure that she would scream. Once in a while she caught her mother watching her with a strange sort of half-smile on her face. It was as if Maryka knew exactly what Tatiana was thinking. Somehow the thought made Tatiana more rather than less uneasy.

They decided to celebrate Alex's seventieth birthday on June 29 with the Smirnoffs. The boys were all away, anyway, Maryka said. Alex could cut his birthday cake as well in Moscow as in *Piter*. They ordered it from Siou in the Dzhamgarov Arcade, a magnificent thing of chocolate and icing and piped lettering, with six large candles and three small ones. Sixty-three, Maryka thought as she took the cake from its box, how could he be sixty-three? It seemed like only yesterday that he had arrived at Vlakerskoye, a tall young man with brown hair and gentle eyes.

Everyone called: Pierre and Sonya came, Nico and Sophie. Vladimir stayed after all the others were gone, and Tatiana thought it must surely be to speak to her. She was wrong; it was to her father he again addressed himself.

"I took the liberty of bringing you a present, Alex," he said.

"More presents?" Alex gruffed. "That's . . . well, seems to me you've all given me more than I've any right to expect already, you Smirnoffs. Now, a present, too! You shouldn't have bought . . ." He tore away the wrapping paper, and his eyes widened. He looked at Vladimir with eyes glistening, as close to tears as Tatiana had ever seen him. It was a beautifully bound book, the leather tooled, the titling and the top edges of the pages gilded. "Look," he said. "My father's book," Alex said. "*The Defense of Sevastopol.*"

"I saw the name, Franz Eduard Makcheyev," Vladimir said. "I knew it had to be your father."

"I don't . . . I don't know how to thank you," Alex said. "I've tried many times to find a copy. Never could. Told me it was unobtainable."

"I was just lucky," Vladimir said, neglecting to add that he had commissioned an antiquarian book dealer to find the memoirs of the old soldier for him.

"See, Maryka, look at this," Alex said. "Isn't it splendid?"

Maryka picked up the book, and her face softened. She looked at Vladimir with a strange, baffled expression that seemed to ask: why are you doing all this for us?

"He must have been an interesting man," Vladimir said. "I'd like to hear about him sometime."

"More than welcome, I can tell you, young fellow," Alex said. "Anything you like. Mind you, watch out! Nothing more boring than one old soldier talking about another, you know."

"Amen to that!" Maryka muttered, and Vladimir smiled. These two might needle each other constantly, but their whole relationship gave off an aura of solid security, which added a further facet to his understanding of Tatiana. He had thought her awe of the parades and the glittering levees of Moscow where he had first met her to be a sham, a sophisticated pretense of a delight she did not truly feel. He realized now that her enjoyment had been real, her wonder genuine. He watched her now as she arranged the flowers in the dining room. She was so fair. Her hair was like a golden nimbus, backlit by the sunshine coming through the tall windows, the soft contours of her face bathed in pale light that made her blue eyes transparent.

He stayed talking comfortably with Alex for a very long time. They talked at first of horses. As if, Tatiana sulked, anyone cared whether the profile of an authentic Arab should be concave or whether it might also be straight! What nonsense, the way men had to dress up their little games with jargon! Would anyone normally refer to a horse's head as "very dry and harmonious," as Vladimir Smirnoff did? Would they insist that a good horse's tail should be high set, its crop comparatively horizontal, as Papa was doing? Now he had Papa started on *Dedyushka*! Good Heavens, they'd be at it for hours!

She had never known Franz Eduard Makcheyev. He had died ten years before she was born, but she had heard so many stories about him that he was as alive to her as if he were in the next room, a great, bearded man with button eyes and a big belly. He had been the third child of an Austrian diplomat and a Russian soldier's daughter who met and married—against the wishes of their respective families—in Vienna, in 1814. They had settled in Kiev, where they had two sons and two daughters. The oldest son, Johann, Ivan in Russian, became one of the most able executives in the huge Bobrinski firm, which dominated the sugar industry. Franz Eduard, named for the Austrian grandfather he had never seen, graduated as an engineer and joined the Ninth Army Corps, whose headquarters was in Kiev. By the time he had reached his mid-thirties, he had something of a reputation as an original military strategist and had attained the rank of Lieutenant-Colonel, one of the youngest men in the Army ever to have done so.

On March 26, 1854, France declared war on Russia. The following day her ally, Britain, followed suit. Quite how it had come about nobody seemed altogether sure, but it was an indisputable fact that a vast enemy army had landed on the shores of Mother Russia. It was now that General Prince Gotschakov remembered Makcheyev and sent for him. He was told to inspect the defenses of Sevastopol and report on their condition to the commandant, Prince Mentschikov. His report was terse and unflattering. Mentschikov ordered him to leave Sevastopol forthwith, telling Makcheyev that he was lucky he wasn't being charged with treasonable utterance. Fortunately for the Prince and for Sevastopol, Makcheyev could not leave immediately.

"And of course," Alex went on, "the French and British attacked a few days later, leaving Prince Mentschikov looking decidedly foolish. Had to reinstate my father. Put him in charge of making the city impregnable and gave him three days to do it."

"Three days?" Vladimir said. "To fortify a city?"

"Should have been three months," Alex nodded. "Even that wouldn't have been enough."

"But he did it."

"He did it. Worked night and day, never off the back of that black horse of his, all along the line of fortifications. Great Jehovah, he was a man!"

"He was wounded during the attack, wasn't he?"

"Yes, he was. Very badly, too. On the Grand Redan, right in the thick of it as always, shouting to encourage his men."

"We used to think he could see right inside our heads," Maryka said, smiling. "He had such sharp, sharp eyes. And a huge, bushy black beard. The children said it had birds nesting in it!"

"Is your mother alive, Alex?"

"No, she died three years after my father," Alex said.

He had married Vera Denisova, the daughter of a brother officer, in 1852, and their first child, Ilya, was born while he was fighting in the Crimea. There were four more children, the last of whom was Alex. His father called him *Myedvedka*, "little bear," because he was so soft and cuddly. As for himself, he was back in the thick of it, with his own brigade, during the war with Turkey in 1877 and the following year. By his sixtieth birthday he was Deputy Commander of the Army, and in the process, according to the laws of Russia, had acquired the title of Count.

Tatiana made a moue of displeasure which neither man saw. Would they never stop talking about horses? She watched Vladimir when her mother was not looking; no use giving Mama any more ideas than she already had. Since that terrible day at Telegin when she had run so instinctively into the safe shelter of his strong arms, Tatiana's emotions had been in turmoil. No man had ever spoken to her as he had done that evening. She was fiercely attracted to him and at the same time more than a little frightened of him, and it was too much for her to handle.

"Well, Tatiana," he said. His voice was soft, and his eyes danced with the light from the huge fire in the great marble fireplace. "As you see, I have taken off my armor."

He was wearing a velvet jacket, a ruffled shirt, corduroy breeches. He poured her some of the Sancerre the servant had brought in.

"I . . . I don't know how to thank you," Tatiana whispered.

"Yes, you do," he said. He came across the room and put his hand beneath her chin, tilting her head so that she looked into his eyes. He nodded, and took her into his arms. His kiss was heady, passionate, and Tatiana felt herself surrendering to him in spite of the tiny voice that whispered in her ear, Wait, wait! Take care, take care!

"I want you, Tatiana," she heard him murmur. "I want you naked in my arms now. And you want to be there, don't you?"

Everything in her ached to say yes. She said the opposite.

"You're lying," Vladimir said, frowning. "Why?"

"Vladimir," she said, heart pounding, "you're right. I do want you. But I want more than just this. More than a glass of wine, a casual fling."

"Love, you mean?" he said, a small and slightly bitter smile touching his mobile mouth. "Ah, that! I'm afraid I'm not in the market for love right now. No orange blossoms and violins and wedding marches. I am *hors de combat*, my dear, a casualty in the battle of the sexes."

"You're making fun of me," she protested.

"Not really, Tatiana," he said. "I am telling you the truth. I want you, but not on your terms. You want me, perhaps, but not on mine. Such irony! Well, you're not the first girl to find that a man wanted only her fair white body while she wanted a wedding ring." It seemed to Tatiana that he was sneering at her. She reacted accordingly. "I think I would like to go back to Sokolnika now," Tatiana said. "And if you think I had any idea of marrying you, you're sadly mistaken."

"What a pity," Vladimir said, smiling that sardonic smile she now knew so well. "Very well, I'll take you back."

"I'd rather ride with Pavel," Tatiana said, haughtily. She was taken aback when Vladimir pulled the rope to summon his servant.

"Just as you wish," he said, pouring himself another glass of wine. "Sleep with your pride, my dear, and see how warm it keeps you."

"That is a detestable thing to say!"

"Isn't that the truth," he said, unaffected by her anger. She had not seen him since. She watched him talking to her father and examined her own emotions. He was a good-looking man, she had to admit that, the sort that a lot of women seemed to find attractive. There was strength, unexpected strength in him. He was a man who had learned to recognize what he wanted, and who would never apologize for being what he was or saying what he thought. Attractive, but a little frightening. She found herself resisting his attraction as some people will resist alcohol or tobacco, somehow sensing that they will become addicted. If he had spoken to her, she would have challenged what he said automatically. She had been ready to fight with him from the moment he came into the house and was completely nonplussed when he all but ignored her.

He rose to go, and she stifled her exclamation of protest. Damn the man! she thought. If he doesn't want to talk to me, that's his loss, not mine.

"By the way," he said, as the servant brought his coat, "they sent Boris Abrikosov to Irkutsk."

"Pity they didn't shoot the scoundrel!" Alex said. "Great Jehovah, I'll do it myself if he ever shows his face again!"

A picture of Vladimir standing over Boris Abrikosov's writhing body with a face like iron and the bloody riding crop in his hands flashed through her memory, a picture totally at odds with that of the civilized country gentleman she saw before her now.

"Tatiana," Maryka said gently, "see our guest out, please." Tatiana glanced sharply at her mother, but Maryka's face was bland and expressionless. She walked out into the garden with Vladimir. The groom brought his horse and departed. The scent of roses hung heavy in the evening air.

"You . . . make it difficult," she said at last.

"Difficult?"

"I never really thanked you. For . . . about Boris."

"Forget it," he said. "Pretend that I was being the gentleman you wish I were."

"You are no gentleman for putting it this way!"

"Is that what you want, Tatiana?" he said. "A gentleman?"

"If by that you mean someone totally unlike you," Tatiana flared, "that's exactly what I do mean!"

"Is it?" he said, and now she saw in his eyes the anger that he had thus far kept damped down. "Is it, by God! Then tell me if any of your damned gentlemen ever kisses you like this!"

Once again, he took her into his arms before she could move. She had no chance to give more than the merest wriggle of resistance before his lips were on hers, crushing, burning, demanding. Without volition she surrendered, her head spinning. She could feel his heart pounding against her own, and it seemed like a million years before the realization of where she was and what she was doing flooded into Tatiana's mind, and outrage took the place of surrender.

"How dare you!" she panted. "How dare you?"

He laughed out loud. "Well!" He grinned. "What an accolade! Didn't you enjoy it, Makcheyeva?"

Tatiana gave him a withering look. What unbearable vanity!

"Do you really think," she asked icily, "that I enjoy being mauled by an old man?" She realized what she had done the moment the words left her mouth, but it was already too late for regret.

"Ah," he said softly. "I didn't think you'd fight dirty. Don't worry, Tatiana, I won't ever bother you again."

Next morning she learned that he had left on an extended business trip: Berlin, Stockholm, Paris. By the time he got back, she would be home again in Petersburg. Her dismay did not last long. Larger events overshadowed those at Sokolnika. Vladimir had been away only a week when they heard the news that Archduke Franz Ferdinand had been assassinated in the little Serbian town of Sarajevo.

The talk at the dinner tables of Moscow and Petersburg was of nothing else.

"Strange, you know," Pierre Smirnoff said, one evening. "Franz Ferdinand was a superstitious fellow. He told me once that a gypsy had said he was destined to be the cause of a world war."

"And he took it seriously?" Nico said.

"I don't think he did," Pierre said. "He said it pretty much as a joke. But as it turns out . . . they say everyone begged him to stay in Vienna and not go to Bosnia, you know."

"But he went anyway."

"He would have avoided it if he could, I think. I'm told he talked very morbidly before he left. Said he expected bombs to be thrown at him. Well, it wasn't bombs."

"The poor man!" Maryka said. "Why did he go, feeling as he did?"

"You want my opinion?" Alex chimed in. "I think he wanted the world to acknowledge his wife as his consort. Wanted the world to see what the court of Austria-Hungary would not recognize, that Sophie would one day be its Empress."

"She was a commoner, wasn't she, Pierre?" Sonya Smirnoff asked. She was an elegant, dark-haired woman who looked hardly old enough to have been married to Pierre for thirty-three years.

"More or less." Pierre shrugged. "A mere countess—if you'll forgive me, Maryka? Hardly good enough for the heir to the throne. No one at court would have a thing to do with her. She was dreadfully humiliated, especially by that old goat Franz Josef. He was like a rock about it, no matter how much Franz Ferdinand roared and raved. The old boy would not recognize the woman, and that was the end of it."

"Sad," Maryka said.

"Stupid," Alex corrected her.

"That poor old man," Sophie Smirnoff said. "He has had the most terrible things happen to his family. I can't help but feel sorry for him."

It was true; Emperor Franz Josef's entire reign had been marked by tragedy. His brother, Maximilian, had become Emperor of Mexico, only to be executed by the rabble. His son, the Crown Prince

Rudolf, had died in a mysterious suicide pact beside his mistress in the royal hunting lodge at Mayerling. His wife, the Empress Elizabeth, had been stabbed to death by an Italian anarchist in Switzerland. Yet still he alienated his heir, Franz Ferdinand, and his wife.

"More wine, Alex?" Pierre said.

"Thank you, no."

"He doesn't like Smirnoff wine." Nico grinned. "He prefers that rubbish from Tokmakov and Molotkov."

"No, no, nothing like that!" Alex protested.

"He gets a stomachache if he drinks too much these days," Maryka said, with the relentless benevolence of all wives.

The story of the events at Sarajevo was one of blunder and anarchy, perhaps both. The Archduke and his wife had traveled separately to Ildize, a few miles south of Sarajevo, arriving on June 25. The Army maneuvers they had come to see were to begin at Mostar the following day. During the maneuvers, the Archduke expressed his intention of visiting the capital. To expand this gesture of a friendship he could have been far from feeling, he announced that his wife would accompany him.

"That's the official version, anyway," Pierre said. "What has been left out we can only guess at."

"He must have known it was dangerous," Alex observed. "That they might be attacked."

"You'd think so, wouldn't you? Yet the fact of the matter is that he—or someone on his staff—told the authorities to dispense with the usual security arrangements, lining his route with troops and so on."

"Of course," Nico said, slowly. "He is not available to be asked whether he said it or not."

"Precisely so," Pierre said.

The Archduke's six-car procession was moving quite quickly along the Appel-quai. There were a lot of people out, not all of them cheering; it was not a triumphal passage. Nevertheless the crowd on the sidewalks was six deep, waving or shouting. One or two even had Serbian flags. The police learned afterward that there had been six assassins at various points along the route. The first one missed his chance to throw his bomb because there was a policeman standing right by him. The second one couldn't bring himself to murder the mother of three small children. The third, Cabrinovich, threw his grenade at the Archduke's car, but the Czech chauffeur saw it coming and banged his foot down on the gas pedal. The car surged out of the way and the bomb, which would otherwise have landed in the Archduke's lap, bounced off the tonneau of the limousine and exploded beneath the following car, wounding two officers. Cabrinovich had meanwhile swallowed poison and jumped into the River Miljacka. Security police hauled him out as the speeding car bore the Archduke and his wife safely past the other assassins and on to the Town Hall.

Police now descended on the Appel-quai in droves, beating the confused spectators back into the side streets. No one was altogether sure what had happened. There had been an explosion; someone was hurt. Who? Why? What? Meanwhile, at the Town Hall, the Archduke berated the unfortunate *Burgermeister* for this outrage. Pale, shaken, and furious, the lanky Archduke banged on the table with the flat of his hand and roared out his insistence that a military escort be provided for the remainder of his tour.

"Does Your Excellency think that Sarajevo is filled with nothing but assassins?" General Potiorek asked with cutting sarcasm.

"One could certainly be forgiven for thinking so, sir," the Archduke angrily replied. "Do you contend that there is no further danger, then?"

"I guarantee it," Potiorek said. "The danger is over."

"You may be right," Franz Ferdinand said. "But I doubt it. There'll be more bullets later, if I'm any judge of it. By God, sir, this is not the way I expected to spend my wedding anniversary!"

"I regret—"

"Enough!" Franz Ferdinand said. "Harrach, what was our next engagement to have been?"

His aide snapped to attention. "A visit to the museum, Your Excellency," he said, referring to a meticulously drawn schedule. "Followed by a—"

"Never mind that," the Archduke said. "We will go to the hospital to see the two officers who were wounded. We wish to be sure that they are being well cared for."

"They should be safe enough," Potiorek said, and if he noticed the flush of anger that stained the cheeks of his distinguished visitor, he affected not to. "The Appel-quai has been completely cleared. We can drive straight to the military hospital."

"So," said Franz Ferdinand, putting on his cockade hat with the ostrich-feather plumes and striding grotesquely out, lifting his legs high as if he were a marionette marching the goose step. The municipal officers lining the staircase got not so much as a glance from the Archduke and his ample, pinch-faced wife as they descended the stairs; Franz Ferdinand was showing them that he was not afraid. As they started the engines of the cars, Count Harrach jumped onto the running board, his sword drawn.

"Don't be a fool, Harrach!" Franz Ferdinand snapped. Harrach skipped off and saluted as the car speeded up and moved away from the Town Hall. Whether by design or stupidity, the leading car, carrying the Deputy Mayor and a member of the Bosnian *Diet*, came to the bridge and turned right, following the original route to the museum. The Archduke's Czech driver automatically followed around the corner, only to have General Potiorek clout him on the shoulder and bawl into his ear: "Not this way, you fool! Down the Quay."

The chauffeur shrugged, braked, put the car into reverse and began to move back to the Quay. The Archduke, resplendent in the green uniform of an Austrian Field Marshal, his white-plumed hat set at a jaunty angle, leaned over and patted his wife's hand. She grimaced sympathetically; was there to be no end to the stupidity of these graceless people? The sidewalks were crowded, a blur of faces from among which, suddenly, materialized that of the assassin.

"So the whole thing happened by chance?" Alex said. "By accident?"

"It would seem so," Pierre said. "How could any assassin have known that the car would take the wrong turning? Who could have been sure, even if they knew it would, that this schoolboy would go through with it?"

"Schoolboy?" Nico said.

"Twenty," Pierre said.

Gavrilo Princip, puny son of peasant serfs, his twentieth birthday still two weeks away, stood on the corner of Franz Josefstrasse as the Archduke's limousine made its wrong turn and stopped. He could not believe his eyes. There was the hated Austrian, not five feet away. Princip hesitated for a moment because of Sophie Chotek. Then he pulled the pistol from his pocket and ran across to the car, aiming at the Archduke. A policeman saw him and started forward to intervene, but he was tripped by an out-of-work actor named Pusara. Gavrilo Princip put a bullet into Franz Ferdinand's throat and then turned the pistol on Potiorek. Someone struck down his arm at precisely the same second that Sophie Chotek rose in terror from her seat. The second shot hit her in the stomach, driving her back across her husband's body. His green uniform was splattered with their blood.

"Get us out of here! Get going, get going!" Potiorek screeched, as the police and the Archduke's entourage fell on Princip. They swarmed all over him, beating him with the flat of their sabers, kicking him on the ground in pointless retribution.

"Sophie was dead before they got the car started," Pierre said. "Franz Ferdinand died a quarter of an hour later. Do you know what his last words were?"

"What?"

"*Es ist nichts*," Pierre said. "It's nothing."

There was a silence. No one wanted to be the one to say what all were thinking.

"Well," Alex said, clearing his throat, "I think we all know what will happen now."

"I'm afraid so," Pierre said heavily.

"It can mean only one thing," Alex said.

"War, Alex?" Maryka said. Ilya, she thought, Vanya, Romasha. My babies.

"Yes," Alex said. "War."

18

O N the very same day that Gavrilo Princip gunned down the Archduke Franz Ferdinand on the streets of Sarajevo, there was an attempt on the life of Rasputin. All Petersburg was in a furor when the news was telegraphed from Pokrovskoye. Reluctant to even consider the implications of coincident assassination, Castle went to see his "friend in court," Michael Tereschenko.

Tereschenko was an enormous man who weighed over two hundred pounds. He had all the lusty appetites of a man half his age. He boasted that he laughed louder, ate bigger, fought dirtier and fucked better than anyone in Russia, and it wasn't all bombast. Senior Assistant to Mikhail Rodzianko, President of the Duma, Tereschenko was a former cavalry officer, born an aristocrat in this city of aristocrats. He was a man of stern and unbending honesty who, like his superior, hated Rasputin and everyone connected with the man. Unlike many of those in high-ranking government office, however, both of them were uncompromisingly hostile toward the *starets* and made no effort to conceal it.

"You've heard about Rasputin?" Castle said.

"I've heard," Tereschenko said. "Frankly, it makes me very sad."

"Sad?"

"Apparently he's going to live."

Rasputin had gone, as he often did in summer, to his home in Pokrovskoye. The royal family was going cruising in the fjords of Finland aboard the royal yacht *Standart*, and without their protection, Rasputin feared for his safety in Petersburg. With his daughter Maria, he set off on the long journey, five days on the train to Yakutsk, then two more by steamer. What he did not know was that he had been followed (or preceded; no one seemed to be sure) by a demented woman named Kinia Guseva, a disciple of Rasputin's bitterest rival, the *starets* Ilyodr. At about two-fifteen in the afternoon, the postman brought Rasputin a telegram. The *starets* came out of the house to ask the postman to take a reply, and as he did, the woman Guseva rushed up to him and buried a knife in his belly.

"I've killed him!" she screeched. "I've killed the anti-Christ!"

She then tried to stab herself to death, but villagers grabbed her and wrestled the knife from her hands. She was taken into protective custody; the crowd was ready to lynch her. Meanwhile, Rasputin was put on a special train and taken to the hospital at Tyumen, his entrails protruding from the great gash in his belly. By special order of the Tsar, an Imperial physician was sent to care for him. The gossips said the Tsaritsa had insisted upon it; she was beside herself with anxiety for her lover.

"You want a drink?" Tereschenko said. "Something to eat?"

"No, thanks," Castle said. "I'm fine."

If he lived in Russia a thousand years, he thought, he would never get used to them drinking vodka at ten o'clock in the morning. All the same, he liked Michael Tereschenko.

"You need tutoring to be a Russian," Tereschenko told him soon after they first met. "And I'm the fellow to teach you."

Their pact was simple. If Castle would occasionally keep Tereschenko informed of things only he could hear at the Embassy, Tereschenko would do the same for David. One of the first things he had done was to show Castle Rodzianko's exhaustive report on Rasputin. He made no bones of his dismay that the Tsar had not acted upon it.

"What do you make of it?" Castle asked him now.

"Seems straightforward enough," Tereschenko said.

"No nagging doubts at all?"

"Well," Tereschenko said, "I'd like to know more about this journalist. The one who gave his name as Davidsohn."

"Me, too," Castle said.

Who was the "journalist" who had ingratiated himself with Maria Rasputin on the long journey to Pokrovskoye? Why had he gone all the way to remote Siberia? Not to be with Rasputin's sixteen-year-old daughter, surely.

"And what was this Davidsohn doing on the porch of Rasputin's house at the exact moment that Guseva tried to kill him?" he asked Tereschenko. "And where is he now?"

"Good questions, my friend," Tereschenko said. "I wish I could give you the answers."

It was like a handful of fine sand. You could make nothing with it. If you tried, it sifted between your fingers and left you with air.

"I brought you our file on Princip," he said, changing the subject. "It just came in from Vienna."

"I'll read it later," Tereschenko said. "What does it tell you?"

"Another mystery man," Castle said. "This time, someone called Ilitch. Princip lived in his house. There's talk that he was behind the assassination."

"I smell our German friends," Tereschenko said, darkly. "I smell their beery breath everywhere."

"You think the Germans—?"

"I think nothing," Michael said. "However, I will remark that the Governor-General of Bosnia-Herzegovina, our friend General Potiorek, could not have done much more to make it easy for the assassins."

"You think he deliberately omitted the necessary security precautions?" Castle said. "That doesn't seem credible, unless he had been guaranteed that there'd be no investigation afterward."

"Agreed," said Tereschenko grimly, as though he had rather liked the idea of Potiorek's involvement. "Anyway, I suppose he wouldn't have ridden with Franz Ferdinand if he'd known that someone was going to shoot him."

"What about someone in Franz Ferdinand's entourage?"

"Possible, boy, possible. Was the confusion deliberately engineered to make the *attentat* feasible?" He shook his head. "No, one couldn't guarantee anything with a Serb. They're as brave as bulls and they shoot well, but as terrorists they're a disaster. It's not that they lose their courage—they lose their heads. No, that won't do either."

Coincidence, then?

They could not bring themselves to believe that no connection existed between the two events, yet nothing in the evidence indicated that one did.

"The proposition would be that if murdering Franz Ferdinand makes war possible, then killing Rasputin makes it probable," Tereschenko said.

"How so?"

"Rasputin is against war. He tells the Tsar—through the Tsaritsa or Vyrubova—that war will mean the end of Russia and bring about the fall of the Romanovs. So with him out of the way—"

"Nicholas might go more readily to war?"

"He would almost certainly mobilize. All the Ministers are agitating for him to order mobilization, and if we mobilize then there'll be war."

"But Rasputin isn't dead, and they say he won't die," Castle said. "He'll still exhort Nicholas not to declare war."

"I suppose so," Tereschenko said, with an elephantine sigh. "We're not having any luck with our conspiracy plan, are we? Both these affairs were badly bungled, David. I can't believe that if our German friends were behind them, they would have been so clumsy."

Castle had taken Tereschenko into his partial confidence from the beginning. He told him of the intelligence reports about the Petersburg Plan, financed by Germany and designed to undermine authority in Russia. He was glad that he had, because Tereschenko told him that he already knew about it. Russia, too, had her spies, he said. So they concluded that *Aussenministeriumssonderabteilung* would never be so clumsy as to attempt to achieve its ends by means of halfwitted anarchists and religion-crazed women. Castle was not the first intelligent man to make the assumption that his opposite number would not do anything obvious or crass. He might have thought considerably differently had he been, later that day, a fly on the wall of the home of the Petersburg banker Frederick Streicher.

The man the German High Command knew only as *Verschwender*, the man Gottlieb von Jagow had placed in control of all German espionage in Russia, sat in the beautifully porportioned library of Frederick Streicher's elegant town house on the Moika, a few doors along from the Club of the Noblesse. Opposite him, filling the big leather armchair, sat the banker, huge, jowled, gross. His belly rose to where his double chins ended. There was a fine sheen of sweat on his upper lip. His eyes were tiny, hidden in the folds of flesh above and below them. What was left of his hair was slicked across his shining scalp. He was dressed in a black coat, striped trousers, patent leather shoes, and a pearl-gray Ascot tie. His breathing was the loudest sound in the room.

Subverting him had been easy. Not only was the man greedy, he had been slighted a dozen times by the Romanov court. No matter how assiduously the fat man had curried favor with the powdered princes and their self-satisfied wives, no matter how many times he rushed to the aid of the indolent Grand Dukes who held the keys to all court appointments, Streicher was rebuffed. What made it worse was that he was rejected so casually. They did not even seem to find it worth the effort of disliking him. So Frederick Streicher passed from admiration through disappointment to hate. He hated the Romanov court and everyone in it, and there was nothing to which he would not now stoop if it brought about the humiliation of those people who had so contemptuously humiliated him. Patriotism, as was so often the case, had nothing to do with it.

"I have had word from Moltke," he said to Streicher. "He has given me full authority to proceed. The budget for our first year of operation will be twenty million rubles."

"Twenty million!" Streicher said. "That's a very great deal of money."

"And you may be sure they will expect a very great deal for it, my dear Streicher."

"But of course," Streicher said. "I see that. Tell me, how are we to proceed?"

We? the man thought. The fat fool thinks he is my partner?

"I shall instruct you," he said, coldly.

"Yes, yes," Streicher said, hastily. "Yes, of course."

"I shall delegate through you. You will have a great deal of power."

"Thank you, thank you," Streicher said, thinking, yes, and I'll be the one taking all the risks.

"Don't worry, Streicher," his visitor said, his thin smile chilling Streicher's blood. Did the damned man know what he was thinking? "You'll be very well paid."

"How much?"

"Ten percent."

"Two million rubles? For that kind of money, I'd strangle my own grandmother."

I have no doubt of it, the man thought, but he said nothing.

"What am I to do, then?" Streicher asked.

"You will function as my paymaster," the man said. "I will send people to you. They will not be your usual clientele, Streicher. They will be wild-eyed revolutionaries, assassins, murderers, thieves. They may be Bolsheviks or Mensheviks or Social Democrats or Octobrists. Men like Savinkov or Trotsky or Lenin—men who have only one thing in common: the desire to see the autocracy trampled into the dust."

"Is that all?"

"Not quite, Streicher. While those rats are gnawing at the foundations, I want to start the rot at the other end. Aron Simanovich badly needs money. Give him what he wants. We shall need him when Rasputin returns to Petersburg."

"I heard Rasputin was stabbed."

"He was indeed," the man said, urbanely. "I think you will find that when he returns he will be . . . different. Easier to deal with."

"You think so? I find it hard to believe."

"He will do as we wish," the man said. "Take my word for it." His eyes were cold and empty, and the fat man suppressed a shudder. He asked no more questions; he did not wish to know the answers.

"Find me fools, Streicher. Dolts with political ambition, nonentities who wish to lead brigades, wasters whose accession to rank will bring about chaos."

"But who will put these men into office?" Streicher said. "Such appointments are within the gift of the Tsar alone."

"Not the Tsar, my corpulent friend. It is Alexandra who makes the decisions. Nicholas merely ratifies them. And we all know who 'advises' Alexandra."

"Rasputin."

"None other."

The man got up, as though to leave, but Streicher did not follow suit. He looked up uncomfortably, a man with a question he does not know how to ask.

"This American," he said.

"Castle? What about him?"

"He has been to see many of . . . our friends. Marius in Moscow. Simanovich. Sturmer. Sukhomlinov. They all say the same thing: he knows something."

"He knows nothing."

"You are sure?"

"I'm certain."

"He wants to come here. To see me," Streicher said.

"See him. You have nothing to hide."

"But—"

"Find out what he wants. Use your own judgment. If you think he is dangerous, I will take care of it."

"You mean—?"

"You worry too much, Streicher," the man said.

War seemed to come all at once. No one wanted it, and yet no one seemed able to prevent it.

"Damn, damn, damn, damn!" Michael Tereschenko said, banging on his desk with a fist the size of a small ham. He looked drawn and distraught. His suit was rumpled and his shirt soiled, as if he had slept in his clothes. There were piles of folders on his desk and a sheaf of telegrams clipped together with a clothes peg. "That stupid old goat Pourtales!"

"What about him?" Castle asked.

"Why didn't he warn the Kaiser that war was inevitable?" he said aggrievedly, rooting among the piled papers. The Tsar had formally declared war on Germany three days ago. Castle knew Tereschenko had been to see the Tsar the night preceding the declaration. He wanted to hear exactly how it had happened.

"Pourtales didn't think war *was* inevitable," he said. The American Ambassador had told him that Count Pourtales, the venerable German Ambassador in Petersburg, had confided in him that he was sure that Russia could not and would not go to war with Germany. Weren't there a million and a half workers on strike? Had he not seen with his own eyes the riots in the streets of Petersburg? How could a country torn by such dissensions go to war? "Russia is like a sick cat," he had told Marye. "And I have so informed my Emperor."

"Well, it wouldn't have made any difference," Michael said. "The whole damned thing seems to have a will of its own."

It was true. There had been a dreamlike inevitability about the series of events which had triggered the war, as if the whole thing was too big, too complex, for any one man or one nation to call a halt to it. Austria delivered what everyone agreed was a totally unacceptable ultimatum to Serbia. The Tsar remarked that it was outrageous, and then went to the races. Next day, his Ministers exhorted him to make some show of action. Austria's intention was to humiliate Serbia and Russia was, after all, the protector of the Slav states in the Balkans. Nicholas ordered partial mobilization, the recall of all volunteers, the canceling of leave. Everyone had forgotten Schlieffen's uncompromising dictum: mobilization means war. Then, with just enough reservations to save face, Serbia accepted the Austrian ultimatum.

"Thank God," said the Tsar. "Now all cause for war has been removed."

He had no sooner spoken the words than an equerry handed him a telegram. Notwithstanding the Serbian capitulation, Austria had declared war. Nicholas sent a telegram to the Kaiser, imploring him to intercede with the Austrians.

"He forgot to mention to Willy that the entire Russian General

Staff was screaming for full mobilization," Tereschenko growled. "But they were, boy, they were."

In any case, he said, the Tsar's telegram made no impression on Kaiser Wilhelm, who had been intractable ever since he had heard of Russia's partial mobilization.

"Sazonov went out to Tsarskoe Selo," Michael said. "He told Nicholas that war was unavoidable. Can you credit that? All Nicholas had to do was to cancel the order for general mobilization, nothing more than that. Yet we go to war—to protect the Serbs, who would cut all our throats if they had half the chance!"

"It's all pointless, Michael," Castle said. "Can't they see that? Russia has nothing to win and everything to lose."

"Tell me something I don't know," Tereschenko said, darkly. "We're not fighting for ourselves, boy. We're going to war for the French and the Belgians and the fucking Serbs!"

The Tsar acceded to Sazonov's request for general mobilization on June 30. At midnight, Count Pourtales delivered a German ultimatum to the Premier: halt mobilization within twelve hours. It did not say "or else"; it didn't need to. No move was made to halt the Russian mobilization, as if anything could have been done in so short a time to halt something so vast. At noon on the first day of August 1914, Kaiser Wilhelm of Germany ordered general mobilization of his army. At five in the afternoon of that same day, Count Pourtales was ordered to declare war on Russia.

"Sazonov told me the old boy looked like death warmed up," Michael said. "His hands were shaking. He looked as if he was going to break down. He asked several times that the order to mobilize be rescinded. Sazonov said that only the Tsar could do that. So Pourtales said he had no option; he handed over the Kaiser's declaration of war. Then he leaned against a window and cried like a baby."

"You saw the Tsar that night?" Castle asked. "How did he react to the news?"

"He was very shaken by it, my friend. Very shaken indeed. The whole family was. The Tsaritsa had been weeping, not the slightest doubt of it."

"Who was there?"

"Rodzianko, Sazonov, Goryemkin, myself, all of us. The French and British Ambassadors. Quite a gathering."

The Tsar had received his ministers in the audience room. His face was serious. He was still in uniform.

"General, gentlemen, these are grave times," he said.

"They are indeed, Your Majesty," Sazonov said. "Has there been any further word from the Kaiser?"

"I should say there has," the Tsar said. "It has made me most angry, gentlemen. Most angry. I asked Willy—the Kaiser—to agree, as I had already promised upon my sacred word of honor, that mobilization need not lead automatically to war, that we should continue to negotiate. Listen to what he replies, listen! 'I must ask you most earnestly that you without delay order your troops under no circumstances to commit the slightest violation of our frontiers.' There, gentlemen! What do you say to that?"

"Perfidy, Sire," Goryemkin said. "Perfidy!"

"Just so," Nicholas said, prim as a schoolgirl. "The Kaiser is hopelessly entangled in his own treachery and lies. He pretends that it depends on me whether war is arrested or not. He instructs me not to allow my troops to violate his frontiers. Have I gone mad, gentlemen? Did I, or did I not receive, less than three hours ago, the Kaiser's declaration of war on Russia?"

"It's madness, Your Majesty," Sukhomlinov huffed. "The Germans are mad with the lust for war."

"Perhaps the German telegram was delayed, Your Majesty," Rodzianko suggested, nearer to the truth than he dreamed.

"Perhaps, perhaps!" Nicholas said, petulantly. "I don't want to hear any more perhapses! This farcical message is my cousin's way of trying to shake my resolution, that's all, to disconcert me. Well, he'll find out it's had exactly the opposite effect, hm, yes. All is over between Wilhelm and me. My responsibility is now to God and my people. I know what I must do. Gentlemen, you will oblige me by helping to draft a formal proclamation of hostilities. I shall issue it at the Winter Palace tomorrow."

"Does he really talk like that?" Castle asked.

"Those very words," Michael said.

"About being responsible to God—?"

"—and his people, yes."

"But he's going to war with Germany, with Austria! Doesn't he realize what that means? Doesn't anyone?"

"I do, my friend," Michael said, shaking his head. "And we'll need more than Nicholas and God to help us now."

Every man, woman and child in Petersburg seemed to be on the streets the following day when the Tsar and the royal family stepped onto the quay beside the Dzvorzovy Bridge. Wave upon wave of cheers bombarded them, washed over them, engulfed them. The Neva was teeming with boats: yachts, canoes, pirogues, sailboats, anything that would float, all festooned with bunting and loaded to the gunwales with cheering spectators. Thousands more clogged the quays and the bridges, cheering, cheering, singing, weeping. Old men fell to the ground and kissed the place where the Tsar's shadow had fallen. The sky was brilliantly ablaze—Tsar's sunshine again—and in the great square before the Winter Palace a huge crowd waited, carrying banners, flags, icons and posters, their cheering a solid wall of sound.

"*Batyushka, Batyushka!*" they shouted. "*Pobyeda, pobyeda!*"

They stood in the sweltering heat before the baroque palace with its glittering windows, hundreds of thousands of them, in the same square where the Preobrazhensky Guard had massacred their brothers, shouting for their Little Father and for victory as the Tsar's procession moved across the quay and entered the palace by the Jordan Gate. The Tsar was wearing the plain uniform of the Fourth Imperial Family Rifles. His wife was dressed in pure white, the wide brim of her hat turned back so that the people could see her face. Slowly they made their way through the immense crush of people on the ornate staircase of Carrara marble, faces grave. Men and women sank to their knees as the Tsar passed, many of them trying to catch hold of his hand and kiss it. The Tsar looked proud and determined, the Tsaritsa pale and exalted.

"She looked . . . well, the only way I can describe it is to tell you that she looked fulfilled," Michael said. "As if this was a moment she had been waiting for all her life."

"I don't think I've ever seen that many people in the Dvortzovaya," Castle said. "Or in the palace, come to that."

"Where were you? I didn't see you."

"I'm not surprised," Castle said. "There must have been five thousand people in the Nicholas Room. I was with Mr. Marye and Sir George Buchanan."

"God, it was hot in there, though, wasn't it?" Michael grinned. "Rodzianko swears he lost five puds."

An altar had been placed in the center of the white marble hall, and the priests had set upon it the legendary Vladimir, Mother of God, icon. It was reputed to have turned back Tamburlaine. Kutuzov had prayed before it prior to going to Smolensk. The fine chandeliers gleamed in the bright sunlight coming through the tall windows. Outside, the cheers of the crowd surged like surf on some nearby beach. The chanting priests in their bejeweled finery performed their timeless rituals as the Tsar asked for the blessing of the icon. Then, raising his right hand, Nicholas turned to face his assembled nobles, calmly reciting the oath sworn by Alexander I in 1812.

"I solemnly swear that I shall never make peace as long as a single enemy remains on Russian soil," he said, his voice clear and precise. The Tsaritsa looked proudly at her husband, her face that of a fond mother. Then, together, Tsar and Tsaritsa walked out onto the balcony overlooking the great square. They were greeted by an explosion of sound, a roar of cheers almost tangible in its intensity. Slowly the sound died. As if on signal, in an extraordinary act of homage, the hushed mass below knelt. The Tsar began to read the proclamation he had helped to draft the preceding night, but his voice would not carry above the sound. Renewed cheering had begun among the crowd pushing through the General Staff Arch from the Nevsky and on the bridge by the Admiralty. The sound grew and grew and grew, and the Tsar bowed his head, overwhelmed. Then, in growing volume, the people below began to sing the national anthem. It was astonishing, uncanny, intensely moving. Many stretched their hands upward, weeping.

> God save the Tsar!
> Mighty and powerful
> May he reign for our glory
> And the confusion of our enemies!
> The orthodox Tsar!
> God save the Tsar!

Hand in hand on the red-draped balcony, Nicholas and Alexandra wept.

The change which came about in Petersburg was startling. Only a month earlier, it would have been difficult to find anyone with a good word to say about Tsar Nicholas II. Now peasant and well-born alike gathered voluntarily around the advertising pillars to read the portentous propaganda displayed upon them by order of that same, formerly despicable individual. Workingmen, who only weeks before had been rioting in the streets, students who only a few days ago had advocated revolution as the only possible salvation for Russia, stood reverently reading aloud the endless titles of the autocrat whose overthrow they had been trying to achieve.

By order of His Imperial Majesty Nicholas the Second, Emperor and Autocrat of all the Russias, Tsar of Moscow, Kiev, Vladimir, Novgorod, Kazan, Astrakhan, of Poland, of Siberia, of Tauric Chersonese, of Georgia, Lord of Pskov, Grand Duke of Smolensk, of Lithuania, Volhynia, Podolia, and Finland, Prince of Estonia, Livonia, Courland and Semigalia, Samagotia, Byalistok, Karelia, Tver, Yougouria, Perm, Vyatka, Bulgaria, etcetera, etcetera; Lord and Grand Duke of Lower Novgorod, of Tchernigov, Riazan, Polotsk, Rostov, Yaroslavl, Belodoero, Oudouria, Condia, Vitebsk, Mistislav and all the region of the North; Lord and Sovereign of the countries of Iveria, Cartalinia, Kabardinia, and the provinces of Armenia, Sovereign of the Circassian Princes, and the Mountain Princes, Lord of Turkestan, Heir of Norway, Duke of Schleswig-Holstein, of Storman, of the Ditmars, and of Oldenbourg . . .

And so on, seemingly ad infinitum, until the message began:

At the call to arms, Russia has risen . . . with iron in her hands and the Cross upon her heart . . . we have taken up arms not from martial ambition or for earthly glory but in a just cause—to defend the integrity and safety of our own Holy Empire. . . .

The entire population seemed to believe this flatulent nonsense. War had become crusade. All Russia was caught up in the fervor, and the proof of that fervor was there in the streets to see.

Day after day, infantry regiments marched down the Izmaily Prospect toward the Warsaw Station, rank after dusty green rank, smiling, singing. Coming into the city from Tereschenko's house in the country, Castle was awed by the sheer mass of military movement to the west. Infantry, cavalry, artillery slouched along— Russian soldiers rarely marched in close order except on ceremonial occasions—spilling over into the fields on either side of the highway, sloppy, apparently undisciplined, like some modern incarnation of the hordes of Ghenghis Khan. In their dusty wake, baggage carts lumbered, field guns clattered, ammunition trucks lurched. Remount horses ambled along in herds, tended by lackadaisical Cossacks. Ambulances bounced ahead of jangling field kitchens steered by bearded, pipe-smoking veterans. Behind them all hung a climbing pall of dust fifteen feet high, marking their passage like a thundercloud. Some of the soldiers had women with them, and some of the women carried children.

At the Warsaw Station, dust motes spun like miniature galaxies in the sunlight slanting through the glass-domed roof. The departing soldiers, their green uniforms swamped by the press of civilians packing the platforms, shouted and waved. Fathers, sons, mothers, wives, children, sweethearts smiled bravely as their loved ones packed themselves into the open-slatted cattle trucks. More phalanxes of green came marching into the station all the time, their officers shouting commands that mingled with the cries of the spectators. Brave smiles, kisses, tears. Some had brought flowers, chocolate, fruit for the departing heroes, "Uncle Kostya" cigarettes. Priests pushed through the throng chanting blessings. Somewhere someone was playing "Kalinka" on an accordion.

Then there were more shouted commands, a crescendo of them, culminating in the shrill blast of a whistle, which galvanized the crowd into a panicked flurry of hugging, kissing, blessing. The driver let off steam, a huge *whoomphf* of sound. Wives embraced their husbands for the last time, mothers their sons, sweethearts their own true loves.

"Take care of yourself," they said to each other.

"Write as soon as you get there."

"We'll miss you."

"Not as much as I'll miss you."

"Goodbye, my darling."

"God keep you safe, my love."

"We'll be thinking of you every moment."

"Wish me luck."

"Say a prayer for me."

"Don't forget me."

"Give my love to Mama."

"Goodbye, be brave, don't cry, we'll be back before you know it, don't cry, it's not for long, *Da svedanya*! Goodbye!"

Then the goodbyes and the cries of the children and the sobs of the wives and mothers were drowned by the second shrill blast of the whistle, signaling departure. The officers shouted at the crowd to move back from the train, but nobody took any notice. They clung to each other's hands, they embraced, they kissed hungrily as the engine gave a heavy continuous roar, like a giant awakening in Hell, and the train jerked into movement. The clutching hands were torn apart, the seeking lips separated. The women were all crying, and the younger men watching the train go out of the station looked ill at ease, as if they felt guilty because they were not on it. The older ones gently consoled their wives and their daughters and their grandchildren. Be brave, Daddy has gone to the war but he'll be home soon, be brave, don't cry, see how proud everyone is. The train went *shun-shunshunshunnashunnashun* and then it was moving fast, trundling out of the station. As it moved into the summer twilight, the people on the platforms could hear the soldiers singing.

> Uncle Willy's gone quite barmy, wants to have a boxing match
> So who leads the German Army? Willy Whiskers, stupid cat!
> Ho, there, so there, ho, there, so there,
> Willy Whiskers, stupid cat!

The silent, bareheaded crowds stayed until the last sound of the train and the singing faded, drowned by the louder sound of marching feet as fresh arrivals were shouted into place by perspiring officers. The ones whose men had left were pushed aside by others as anxious as they had been to see their husbands and sons and lovers off to the war. Castle watched them as they came out of the station afterward. Their faces were as blank as paper.

19

WELL, all I can say is, thank God we have this chance to be together before you all leave for the front," Alexander Makcheyev said. He smiled proudly as he surveyed the crowded dining table, and only his wife saw the faint flicker of pain behind his eyes as they fell upon their youngest son, Roman. The party was Alex's idea. He had decided to have it as impulsively as he did everything, riding roughshod over her disinclinations. To Maryka, saying goodbye to the boys opened the door to the thought that they might not be coming back. Even to contemplate that made her throat tighten with fear.

"Nonsense!" Alex had said. "Great Jehovah, woman, you want to see them again, don't you?"

"Of course I do," she said. "It's just that ... Romasha ..."

"He's still our son, Maryka," Alex said, softly. "Just tell yourself that ... it never happened."

"Oh, Alex, I can't forget it," she said. "I can't!"

"Put it out of your mind," he told her. "You can do that. For one evening."

"I ... I suppose so," Maryka said.

Now that the house was full of people, hot, noisy, and festive, she was glad that Alex had insisted, glad to see him cheerful. He had been depressed for the last few weeks, dispirited, unwell. She smiled as he clapped young Vasya Kirsanov on the shoulder.

"Just the same, I'm glad no more of you came," he said. "Otherwise I'd have had to rent a bigger place."

"Better do that now, sir," Vasya said. "You'll need a lot more room when we're celebrating victory."

They all laughed. How fine and manly they looked in their uniforms, Alex thought. Was it possible that he had only been their age when Grenavitsky had thrown his bomb? They all look so very, very young, Maryka had whispered to him earlier.

"Not too young to do their duty," he had said, knowing it sounded jingoistic and not caring. "Not too young to serve their Tsar."

"I suppose so," Maryka said. She knew that Alex did not approve of her anxiety for their safety. A man had to go out into the world and take his chances, no matter whether it was peacetime or wartime. Mothers worried too much anyway, he said. She knew how he felt; how else would an old soldier feel? He did not see their sons as she did, grown all at once to manhood, not quite strangers but set apart from her, with their own secrets, their own intimacies, their own private worlds where she would never be able to go.

Yet, children still. Vanya, in his naval officer's uniform, his hand resting lightly on his wife's shoulder, was a tall, good-looking man with level green eyes and wide shoulders. Just the same, there was still that summer sprinkling of freckles that he had always had, right from the start, and when he spoke, she could not forget the little boy who had once startled them by suddenly asking where babies came from and falling asleep while they were trying to answer him. He had only been three then, bright, intelligent, handsome Vanya. And look at Ilya, glamorous in the black leather flying jacket of the Observation Corps. He seemed to change his girl friends as often as his shirts, but they all adored him. He used to tell us jokes, she remembered, and always get them wrong. Vanya would hoot at him derisively, and Ilya would scowl and then smile, his sunny nature triumphing every time.

"Those Germans aren't going to know what's hit them when we get up to the front," Paul Dubinsky was saying.

"We'll put Misha in the lead!" Nicky Vasnetsov shouted. "One look at his ugly mug and the Germans will run like rabbits!"

Everyone laughed again, except Misha's wife Olga. Maryka concealed a smile. Olga had always hated them teasing dear Misha, who was so slow on the uptake. Olga herself looked around the room, her dark face petulant. Misha was such a dull stick, she thought. Even the American was laughing. He was tall and fair and rather good-looking, she thought. He was sitting next to Irina Smirnoff, their shoulders just touching. When they looked at each other, they seemed to be exchanging secret messages. Olga Subarova glanced at Irina's husband, Sasha. He was having a good time, one of the boys. Very interesting, Olga thought.

"You gentlemen don't seem to think too highly of the German Army," the American observed. In fact, their air of superior invincibility surprised him, the more since not one of them had ever heard a shot fired in anger.

"Germans!" Nicky said. "The only thing Germans are any good for is making sausages."

"And eating them," Paul added.

"Our colonel says that all we'll have to do to annihilate them is to throw our caps at them," Vasya said. "Now, Alex, we need your advice. Do you think we ought to take our dress uniforms with us?"

"To the front?" Alex said. "What the devil for?"

"For the victory parade, of course," Vasya said. "In Berlin!"

"That's right, Papa," Roman Makcheyev said, grinning. "We can't march down the Unter den Linden in field uniform, now, can we?"

Oh, Romasha, Maryka thought. She had been only half-listening to the boys' boastful chatter until her son spoke. He knew nothing of what had happened, about Boris Abrikosov, none of it. Alex had insisted that it be so, and for all the ache in her heart, Maryka was glad that he had. She could not have borne to see guilt on Roman's boyish face.

"Well, now, Nikitina," Ilya said to his brother's wife. "I'm surprised you traveled all the way up here to *Piter*. What's the matter, can't you bear to let Vanya out of your sight for one moment?"

"I came to say farewell to these brave soldier boys," Nikitina said, with a shy smile. "If I'd known you were going to be here, too, Ilya, I might have thought twice. You have plenty of girls of your own to wish you luck."

"Aha!" Nicky said. "That's not good enough, Nikitina. I've got the feeling that there's something going on we don't know about."

"No," Nikitina said, blushing. "Nothing is going on."

"Is that so, Vanya?" Misha asked, naïvely. "Have you got a guilty secret or something?"

"Oh, the devil take you all!" Vanya said, flustered by the unexpected turn of the conversation. "Can't a fellow have any private life?"

"Yes, come on, Nicky, leave them alone," Andrei Tretyakov said, smiling. "Let's just be glad that Nikitina is here to make our farewell so much more pleasant." It was a gallant little speech, and Nikitina looked at Andrei gratefully. Maryka smiled again to herself. Men!

she thought. One could see just by looking at the girl that she was going to have a baby. Nothing more astonishing than that. Why on earth Vanya hadn't admitted his "secret" she did not know. Probably keeping it until just before he leaves, she thought, making a mental note to be surprised when he did. It wasn't like a man to keep a thing like that secret. They usually wanted to proclaim their manhood like cocks on a dunghill.

"All right, all right, let's hear from Ilya," Vanya said, successfully turning the spotlight away from himself. "I want to know more about his marvelous flying machines."

"Flying machines?" Nicky said. "They haven't got airplanes in the Observation Corps. They send them up in balloons."

"Oh, shut up, Nicky," Ilya said, good-naturedly. "Of course we have planes. Not many, but a few."

"What type are they?" Castle asked.

"Anatras, mostly," Ilya said.

"Biplanes?"

"Yes, but quite fast."

"What do they do?"

"About ninety miles an hour."

"That's nearly as fast as Sasha's car," Irina put in slyly, to hoots of laughter and derision.

"Have they got any guns?" Vanya asked his brother.

"Have they—? Of course they have guns, you idiot," Roman said. "A machine gun for the pilot and a Lewis gun for the observer. Isn't that so, Ilya?"

"That's right."

"You wouldn't get me up in one of those things for a bet!" Misha said, with a theatrical shudder. "My father says airplanes are death traps."

"He would," Olga muttered, so quietly that only Maryka, sitting next to her, heard the words.

"I'd much rather be up in a plane than stuck down in some muddy hole in the ground," Ilya said, stoutly. "Which is where your lot will all be."

"Not us, old boy," Vasya said. "We are officers and gentlemen. We don't fight in mud. If it rains, we go home."

"And we are cavalry," Roman added, "we don't fight on foot, even when the weather is good."

"In fact, we don't fight at all if we can help it," Nicky said, and they all laughed again.

"My bet is that there'll be precious little fighting of any kind," Andrei said. "The Germans can't match us for firepower."

"Or *esprit de corps*," Misha said.

"We'll have half a million men under arms before the end of the month."

"France, Britain and Russia. How could the Germans hope to win against such an alliance?"

"Let's have a toast to that," Nicky said. "A toast to the Triple Alliance!"

"Britain!"

"*Britanya!*"

"France!"

"*Frantzya!*"

"To the Fatherland!"

"*Atyechestvo!*"

Amid their cheers, Maryka pushed back her chair and smiled toward her husband.

"Come, ladies," she said. "We shall leave these men with their boring war talk and find something more interesting to discuss. Now, Tatiana, don't you sulk. You must tell the girls all about the Tsaritsa's hospital at Tsarskoe Selo. They can't wait to hear what Her Majesty's plans are. Besides, the boys want to let their hair down."

Everyone stood as their hostess left the room, followed by the Narodnova sisters, Nikitina, Irina Smirnova, Maria Abrikosova and Tatiana. When they were gone and Ivan Pavlovich had closed the door, Vanya grinned at his father.

"Tatiana was very quiet tonight, Papa," he observed.

"Well," old Alex said, inventing excuses, "probably thinking about that hospital business. You know the Tsaritsa's turning the Catherine Palace into a hospital, don't you?"

"When will Tatiana go to Tsarskoe Selo?" Andrei asked.

"Almost immediately," Alex said. "Some of the buildings are already being converted."

"What's the mood of the court, sir, do you know?" Nicky Vasnetsov asked.

"There's a mood of great optimism, Tatiana says. The Tsar and his Ministers are convinced the war will not last long, and that we shall be victorious."

"I hope it isn't too short," Andrei protested. "Otherwise I'll not see any action."

He was still awaiting confirmation of his promotion to Lieutenant. His brother Sergei, he told them, had been appointed to serve as Adjutant to the Grand Duke Nicholas Leuchtenberg, on the personal staff of the Tsar. He had left Moscow at the end of June to join the Grand Duke at Krasnoe Selo and was now at the *Stavka*.

"And you, Roman, where have you been posted?" asked Andrei.

"To the front, in East Prussia. What's the name of that town, Nicky?"

"Ostrolenko," Nicky said.

"That's not the *Stavka*, is it?"

"No, sir," Nicky said to Alex. "Ostrolenko is just the headquarters of the Second Army. *Stavka* is at Baronovichi."

"Will the Tsar go there?"

"Why on earth should he do that?" Alex said.

"As Supreme Commander of the Army," Misha replied.

"Oh, that's just his official title," Nicky said. "The actual Commander-in-chief is Nikolasha, the Tsar's uncle."

"Grand Duke Nikolai Nikolaievich," Alex said. "A damned fine man."

"Damned fine soldier, too, sir," Nicky added.

"Best in the business," said Ilya.

"Amen to that!" chorused Vasya and Andrei. "Here, Alex, you're pretty mean with your brandy."

"Don't tell me we need another bottle?" Alex roared. "Where is that lazy scut of a servant of mine? Ivan Pavlovich! Ivan Pavlovich Zubin!'"

Ivan Pavlovich came without haste into the dining room, his eyebrows slightly raised, as if to say, what's all the fuss about?

"Bring us another bottle of cognac, man!" Alex said. "These young fellows are off to the war, dammit!"

"They won't fight any better with hangovers," Ivan Pavlovich observed sourly. "But I'll get another bottle if you insist."

"Good, good," Alex said, absently. He was in much too good a humor to rise to Ivan's little jibes tonight.

"In the meantime, sir," Vasya said, mischief in his eyes, "we'd value your opinion of our officers." He grinned at Castle as he said it, and Castle grinned back. He was quite interested in hearing what Alex had to say about the Russian commanders, too, but for reasons different from Vasya Kirsanov's.

"All right, all right," Alex growled. "Let's hear it, then. Who are they?" As he spoke, Ivan Pavlovich appeared at his elbow with the brandy bottle.

"Well, don't just stand there, man!" Alex shouted. "Pour it out, pour it out!"

"Yes, Your Honor," Ivan Pavlovich said sardonically. "If it will stretch far enough."

"Get another if it doesn't," Alex said.

"I hope you still feel as generous next month, when you can't buy any more," Ivan Pavlovich muttered. It was rumored that the Tsar was going to ban the sale of alcohol for the duration. Nobody believed it; the government made too much money out of the tax on alcohol.

"I want to hear who you boys will report to," Alex said.

"General Zhilinsky, sir," Nicky Vasnetsov said.

Castle remembered Zhilinsky in the Grand Duke Andrei's pavilion at the Moscow Tercentenary parade, a gray-faced, skeletal old man. He wondered why the Russians put these ancients in charge of their armies. War was a young man's profession.

"Zhilinsky, eh?" Alex said. "You know what we used to call him?"

"No, sir," Vasya said, his face angelic. "What was that?"

" 'The Living Corpse'!" Alex said. "Man always looked as if he'd been dead a week."

"Is he a good general, sir?" Misha asked. His eyelids were beginning to droop, and he was having trouble staying awake. Misha always got sleepy if he drank, but he felt a fellow had to keep up with the others. Olga often scolded him and said he should not, but Misha didn't listen. It made him feel one of them, as if he belonged. It also eased the knot of apprehension coiled in the pit of his stomach. Misha was afraid that when the time came for action, he would funk it. He knew that if he should do so, he would kill himself.

"Wouldn't say that," Alex said, referring to Zhilinsky. "Man's a damned fool. Wasn't it he who promised the French we'd have half a million men in the field fifteen days after mobilization?"

"It was Zhilinsky," Castle said. "And it was eight hundred thousand."

"No difference," Alex growled. "It's what caused this panic. That's why you boys are being rushed up to the front. Need every man they can get out there."

"Hardly that, sir," Andrei protested. "They say the Army is pushing forward so fast that there aren't enough men to garrison the towns which have been occupied."

"That's what they're saying, is it?" Alex said. More likely they

278

haven't got enough cannon fodder, he thought, but he bit the words back. To have spoken them in this room, with his sons present, would have been to invoke black misfortune. "What do the younger officers think of Zhilinsky? Tell me that?" he said.

"Well," Paul Dubinsky began, "they say he's a sly old devil, sir. They say he's pretty clever."

"Clever, is he?" Alex pounced. "Then if he's so clever, tell me why he gave Rennenkampf the First Army and Samsonov the Second. Doesn't he know those two hate each other, eh?"

"I didn't know they did, sir," Nicky said.

"Have done, ever since the Japanese war," Alex said, triumphantly. "Samsonov accused Rennenkampf of failing to support his Cossacks at the battle of Mukden. Nearly fought a duel over it. Terrible scandal! Poor old Samsonov."

"Why do you say that, sir?"

"Look at his record, boy," Alex said. "Man hasn't had an active command for years."

"Well," Misha said sleepily, "hope we don't get posted to him, then."

"Doesn't matter whose command you're posted to," Alex said. "Jealousy's part of the day-to-day routine in the Army. Everyone knows that. Tell me about the Corps Commanders instead. Who have they got out there?"

"First Corps, General Arlomontov," Nicky recited. "Sixth Corps, General Blagoveshensky. Thirteenth Corps, General Klyuev. Fifteenth Corps, General Martos, and Twenty-third Corps, General Kondratovich."

"Mmm," Alex said, thoughtfully. He put a smile on his face. "Well," he said, more cheerfully than he felt, "Nikolasha will lick them all into shape, don't you worry."

"Of course he will!" they shouted. "Here, pass that brandy bottle along. If the Tsar's going to stop the sale of liquor, we'd better make the most of it!"

Castle smiled at their optimism and enthusiasm. He had never been in a war, but he knew from the stories that his father had been told by *Dedyushka* Zamokin about the American Civil War that whatever else it was, war was not fun. He also knew, as apparently his young acquaintances here did not, or did not want to know, that the entire Russian Army was riddled with mistrust, venery and favoritism. He and Tereschenko had discussed it only the preceding day.

"Look at the picture, boy," Michael had said, storming about his office, waving his arms excitedly. "Our Minister of War, Sukhomlinov, hates the Commander-in-chief, because he wanted to be—and believes he deserved to be—Commander-in-chief himself. Can you imagine it?"

"It's hard to believe," Castle said.

"The unsavory bastard!" Michael said. "He stinks to high Heaven of graft and corruption. He's a fool, an idiot, a moron!"

"But powerful."

"And dangerous," Tereschenko agreed. "They all are, all that Rasputin *camarilla*. He'll undercut Nikolasha, you'll see, the bastard. He'll use Zhilinsky for that. Zhilinsky is Sukhomlinov's man. He owes his command to him. In fact, if it hadn't been for Sukhomlinov, General Samsonov would be Commander of the Army Group in Prussia, not Zhilinsky."

"How come?"

Tereschenko smiled, a tired but genuine smile.

"You say you'll never get used to us drinking vodka in the morning," he said. "Well, my friend, I'll never get used to what you Americans do to the language. 'How come,' indeed! I'll tell you 'how come,' boy. Zhilinsky can do Sukhomlinov some good in court, which Samsonov could not. *Ergo* . . ."

"Zhilinsky got the job. And Samsonov?"

"He got the First Army. Under Zhilinsky."

"So there'll be no love lost there," Castle said.

"A masterpiece of understatement," Michael said. "The whole thing is damnable, the more so since we in the Duma are powerless to interfere. Sukhomlinov has the ear of the Tsar and may do as he wishes. Zhilinsky is his creature, as Rennenkampf, who commands the Second Army, is Zhilinsky's."

"Which leaves Samsonov—"

"—up to his eyes in ordure," Tereschenko said angrily. "There'll be disaster in East Prussia, David. I feel it in my bones."

"Because of the politics, you mean?"

"Because of these childish rivalries, boy! Our soldiers are brave, strong, honest. They'll fight with their bare hands if they have to. What I'm afraid of is that it may come to just that."

"You can't be serious."

"You've heard that the Tsar plans to ban the sale of alcohol?"

"Yes, Senka Smirnoff told me."

"It's true. He apparently wants to convince the French that our soldiers will be arriving at the front spick, span, and most importantly of all, sober. The only way to be sure of that is to introduce prohibition, says our brainless Emperor."

"Michael, you've got to admit liquor is a problem," Castle said. He'd seen plenty of drunken soldiers on the streets, in the railway stations. A lot of the kids they were sending east had never had money in their hands before. All they knew to spend it on was vodka or whores, and there were no whores in barracks.

"Simplistic!" Michael shouted, banging his desk. "Like all Nicholas's ideas. We've gone to war with one of the biggest military machines on earth in front of us. We need guns, shells, bullets, rifles, bombs, planes, munitions! How are we to buy them if the first thing we do is to cut off the Exchequer's largest single source of income? For God's sake, man, alcohol produces nearly one-third of the total taxes levied in all of Russia!"

"But surely, there'll still be enough—"

"We haven't enough *now*! Our boys are going out to the front without rifles, without machine guns, without ammunition, without shells for the artillery they are taking. The only way they will be able to get rifles will be to advance empty-handed and take them off the dead bodies of their comrades or the Germans."

"Empty-handed?" Castle said. "Surely the generals, the Commander-in-Chief wouldn't countenance—"

"They don't know! That fat fool Sukhomlinov has blocked every attempt that Rodzianko or myself has made to get word to them. He prevents us from even putting the arsenals on a wartime footing. Can you believe it? The workers are performing prodigies, but there are simply not enough of them. I swear to God, he couldn't be helping the Germans more if they were paying him direct."

"I'm looking into that," Castle said. "I think maybe they are."

"Bring me proof, for God's sake!" Tereschenko said. "And I'll hang the fat bastard myself."

Castle recalled Tereschenko's gloomy prognosis as he listened to the noisy celebrations of the young officers in the Makcheyev house. He wondered whether he ought to have said something to Michael about Frederick Streicher. It was to Streicher that Sukhomlinov was deeply indebted. Indeed, the German was an extremely liberal source of loans to a number of highly placed government officials and military commanders. Castle reluctantly decided to say nothing. All he had was hearsay, not an ounce of proof. He put one of the Embassy staff onto the task of making a list of all who attended Streicher's weekly luncheons, the Wednesday *stammtische*, as he called them. Streicher's generosity was unstinting. No expense was spared, and pretty girls encouraged the guests to relax in an intimate atmosphere.

"Tell us about General Samsonov, sir," Nicky Vasnetsov was saying. Castle tuned back to the conversation. He wanted to hear this, too.

"Senior to me at the Academy, as I recall," Alex said. "Didn't really know him all that well. Tubby chap, with asthma. Thorough, I'd say, the sort who would stick to his guns right to the end. Not a fighting soldier, though he did have some experience in the Japanese war. Don't think he's had an operational post since. Who's his Chief of Staff?"

"Major-General Postovsky, sir."

"A book soldier!" said Alex, with a snort.

"And Major-General Filiminov, sir?"

"What's he?"

"Quartermaster-General, sir."

"Pompous ass," Alex said. "Remember him well."

"How about General Rennenkampf, sir?" Nicky asked now. "What is he like?"

"You watch your step with Rennenkampf," Alex bade him, sternly. "He and Zhilinsky are like that." He crossed his forefinger with the one next to it and held them up for all to see. "Like that! And worse, not only is Rennenkampf's brother-in-law head of the Tsar's Field Chancellery, but his Chief of Staff is also close to the Tsar."

"Isn't Zhilinsky a great friend of the Grand Duke Andrei?" Castle said, turning up the flame a little.

"Damned right," Alex said. "Means he has the ear of the Dowager Empress, and woe betide any young officer who falls foul of *that* old battleaxe." He reached for matches to light his pipe.

"Anyone else?" he said, puffing fiercely. He was having the time of his life, Castle thought, an old firehorse hearing firebells.

"First Corps, General Arlomontov," Nicky began to recite again, "Sixth Corps, General Blagovesh—"

"All right, all right," Alex said testily. "I remember, no need to go through it all again. Now, let me see. Leonid Arlomontov I hardly know. I think he was two years junior to me at the Academy. Blagoveshensky is stupid, a fact as well known in the Army as is the fact that the bullet comes out of the muzzle of the rifle. Klyuev, you said? Rear-echelon general, been in the Army forty years and never seen action once. One of His Majesty's pretty-boy soldiers, that's Klyuev."

"How about General Martos?"

"Know him only slightly," Alex said. "Stickler for detail. Sort of fellow who worries about how many paperclips are being used in Headquarters rather than how many men are dying on the line."

"Well, at least he's been stationed in the general area of the fighting," Vasya said. "Otherwise you'd be making me feel that our best plan would be to desert, sir."

"Oh, you mustn't listen to him," Vanya said. "Papa always looks on the gloomy side of things."

"He most certainly does," said a woman's voice, interrupting them. They looked up as Tatiana came back into the room. "And it's time he stopped." They would go on all night, drinking, smoking, talking about Ilya's airplanes or Vanya's battleship or their silly generals. There was only one way to stop them.

"Papa," she said, "couldn't we have a little music?"

"What a splendid idea," Vasya said, scrambling to his feet. "I claim the first dance, Tatiana."

"And I second!" shouted Nicky.

Tatiana smiled at them all, pleased with her ploy. Maryka and Nikitina came in, and the two Narodnova girls, followed by Irina Smirnoff. Alex glowered at his daughter, but it was mock anger. He had been having such a damned good time that it seemed a shame to stop for silly dancing and chatter. Well, it was their war, not his.

"One last toast!" he shouted. "A toast to the brave Kozma Kryuchkov!"

Kozma Kryuchkov was a Don Cossack who had sighted twenty-two enemy horsemen approaching his position in Prussia. He had attacked them fearlessly, singlehanded, cutting his way through their formation with the pent-up fury of a wounded tiger. By the time his comrades came galloping to his assistance, Cossack Kryuchkov had killed thirteen Germans. He was awarded the first St. George's Cross of the war by the Tsar. His exploit had been headline news. Now the gypsies sang songs in the taverns about the brave Kozma.

"To Kozma Kryuchkov!" they all shouted.

"*Do dna!*"

They gulped their brandy down in one—to the bottom, as the toast required—and then began to move the furniture against the walls, rolling back Maryka's beautiful Persian carpet. Andrei shuffled through the records and put one on the green baize turntable, winding the phonograph furiously. He tested the needle with a forefinger, gently opened the double doors at the front of the cabinet, and pushed the lever to start the turntable. Tongue between teeth, he lowered the needle onto the record. After a moment or two, the sound of the music filled the room. It was all the rage in Paris, Ilya said. It was known as *les temps du chiffon*.

> Un, deux, trois!
> On lance le ventre en avant
> En tenant les bras ballants
> Comme un orang outang . . .

Well, I'll be damned, Castle thought.

"That's called 'ragtime' in my country," he said.

"You must not talk English," Tatiana admonished him as she swept past in Vasya Kirsanov's arms.

"There's no word for it in Russian. The French isn't quite right. *Synkopeska musika*. It's American."

"No," Ilya corrected him. "It is from France."

"Before that," Castle said. He was watching Irina dance with Sasha. Sasha danced awkwardly, but she was graceful and lightfooted. He felt the same old tug again. If only . . . He put the thought out of his mind. She would never leave Sasha; she had told him that, and he believed her. Her reasons for staying with her husband were not romantic, but realistic. He could even understand them; that was what irritated him. He wanted her all for himself, like a child wants to monopolize whoever he is talking to.

"Wherever it's from, it's splendid," Nicky called out. He was doing a highly exaggerated cakewalk with Natasha. "Do they play it a great deal in America?"

"Quite a lot," Castle said. "Especially black people."

"Aha!" Ilya said. He was dancing with Misha's wife Olga. He was holding her very tightly, Castle thought, but Olga didn't seem to mind. Neither, it appeared, did Misha, who had fallen quietly asleep in the corner, his head slumped on his chest.

"Do you know how to play this ragtime on the piano, David?"

"A little," Castle said.

"Good, very good!" Andrei shouted. "Then we can dance all night."

They didn't, of course, but they did their best. It was well after three in the morning when they all finally tumbled out into the street and clambered into taxis to be taken back to their barracks. They were all singing-drunk, their voices echoing in the empty streets. Castle could hear their bawdy soldier songs long after they had disappeared from sight. Somehow or other, his feeling of well-being evaporated all at once. Irina and Sasha had gone home hours ago. Castle looked at Alexander Makcheyev. The old man looked tired, unbearably sad. Castle left them. They had their own good-byes to say. A line from a poem kept repeating itself inside his brain:

Wait for me and I'll return, just to spite all death . . .

He shivered in the cool night air. God help them all, he thought, and went down the street to see if he could find somewhere to buy a drink.

On August 27, General Pavel Rennenkampf's entire Second Army began its advance. Along a vast line drawn north and south through Prussia, it drove the German frontier troops before it. Rennenkampf's tactics were classical. He had used them in the Japanese war, where he had learned them from generals who had used them in the war against Napoleon. As Rennenkampf's army advanced, the German artillery laid down a withering fire from its entrenched positions. Rennenkampf brought up the cavalry and ordered them to take the guns. They were a fine, a glorious sight. Their breastplates and helmets glinted as they moved up, from the walk to the trot, from the trot to the canter. Then, yelling and screaming to unnerve the Germans in front of them, they thundered into the gallop, hurling themselves upon their enemy, sabers flashing.

In the very first charge, more than three hundred young Guards officers, among them the very flower of Russia's aristocracy, were scythed from their saddles. The field was a hell of screaming men, thrashing horses, whistling death. Undeterred, Rennenkampf sent in a second wave, and after it a third, to die on the bloody bodies of those who had gone before. It was the first day of what was to become the battle of Tannenberg. It raged for six awful days of carnage without mercy. When it ended, two and a half Russian army corps had been annihilated. Ninety-two thousand Russian soldiers had been taken prisoner, and another thirty thousand were dead. Among them were Nicky Vasnetsov, Vasya Kirsanov, Misha Subarov, Paul Dubinsky, Roman Makcheyev and Andrei Tretyakov.

The bad times had begun.

20

War brought many changes to Moscow, too.

As in Petrograd, soldiers gray with dust were packed into cattle cars and left singing for the front, while the silent, bare-headed crowds on the station platforms stood motionless until the last faint echoes of the marching songs faded. Here, too, the wives of the rich bourgeoisie competed with each other in the setting up of hospitals. There were gala performances at the Bolshoi, thousands cramming night after night into the white and gold theater, filling the five balconies to overflowing. Their patriotic fervor was almost religious in its intensity. Every night, at the opera and ballet, orchestras played the national anthems of England, France, and Russia. When Lemberg was taken, there was a gala performance of Rostand's *L'Aiglon*. At the end of the first act, a young girl in a white dress walked onto the stage and read aloud a telegram from Marshal Joffre announcing victory all along the Western front. In a storm of cheers the orchestra struck up the "Marseillaise." Men hugged and kissed each other. Paris was saved! Women smiled and wept in the emotion of the moment, and all at once, the most stirring thing of all happened. There were several hundred French reservists in the gallery; in glorious unison they sang their anthem:

> Aux armes, citoyens! Formez vos battaillons!
> Marchons, marchons! Qu'un sang impur
> Abreuve nos sillons!

It was memorable, it was epic, but it was not to last. In the summer of 1915 the war turned against Russia. As the Germans advanced and advanced, as the refugees poured into Moscow, the mood of the people changed. Sacrifices which at the beginning everyone had gladly made were now made grudgingly, if at all. It was not thought shameful to purchase exemption from the Army. It was not thought remiss to "negotiate" for a permit with which to replenish one's private stock of wine, even if the proletariat could no longer buy alcohol.

The Smirnoffs remained major contributors to the Russian cause. Although the distilleries were producing only nominal amounts of liquor, The House still paid the wages of every employee, even those who were serving at the front. After all, Pierre said, their families still had to eat. He had turned all but one wing of Sokolnika over to the Red Cross for use as a hospital; both his wife and Nico's were working in it as nurses. Vladimir immediately tried to get a commission. He was turned down because he was color-blind, an act of bureaucratic stupidity which so enraged him that he almost struck the examiner. When it became clear that nothing could change the decision, he made one of his own. He had good contacts at *Stavka*, Sergei Tretyakov and Olga's husband Fritz Sukhotin among them. Suvanov, editor of the newspaper *Russkiye Vedomosti*, jumped at the chance to have Vladimir as a war correspondent, especially since he wanted no salary. Then Vladimir went back to Telegin, gave the best of his horses to the Army, and handed the keys to Katrina.

"Turn it into a hospital," he said. "Spare nothing."

He could not believe what he saw at the front.

By the beginning of 1915, after only five months of war, more than a million Russian soldiers—a quarter of the entire Army—had been killed, wounded, or taken prisoner. In spite of this, morale was extraordinarily high among the common soldiers. It was amid their officers that Vladimir found the schisms. There was a new breed among them now, for as the scions of noble families were decimated in the early months of the war, they were replaced by men who came to the front direct from law offices and engineering works or even from universities. They did not subscribe to the hidebound social and regimental traditions of yesteryear, which required soldiers to respond to praise by answering, like automatons, "Eager to serve, High Well-born." They besieged him with requests for news from home, from *Piter* or Moscow. Was it true that the Tsaritsa openly favored the Germans, as rumor had it? Was it true that a radio station communicating directly with Berlin had been discovered in the royal palace? Was it true that when she visited hospitals, the Tsaritsa would stop and talk to the German wounded but pass Russian soldiers without a glance? Was it all true about her and Rasputin, as people said? Was it true that the Tsar was going mad, was it true that he was Rasputin's puppet, was it true that he had begun drinking heavily?

He told them what he knew. He told them that *Piter* and Moscow were under partial blackout for fear of Zeppelins, and that by night the streets were dangerous because of footpads. He told them that it was hard to get wood and coal, that prices were soaring, that there were lines for bread and milk. Despite the shortages, he told them, the private receptions in the great houses were as brilliant as ever.

"Naturally," they said, contemptuously. "Of course."

Just the same, he told them, the gossip about the Tsar and Tsaritsa was just that, gossip. He tried to reassure them, knowing he was not succeeding. They believed that Rasputin and the German woman were the source of all their woes, and that nobody gave a damn about the troops or the war.

"Do you know that in the Ninth Army they are forming companies of axemen to protect the artillery?"

"We need three, four, six times as many guns as we are getting. How can we send our boys forward bare-handed, against machine guns?"

"Why doesn't someone shoot that old pig Sukhomlinov?"

"Why doesn't the Tsar do something?"

"Why doesn't anyone do anything?"

Vladimir went to the *Stavka* at Baronovichi. *Stavka* was an old Russian word; it meant the camp of a chieftain. Surrounded by three concentric rings of sentries, the field headquarters of the Russian Army was an enclave of a dozen interconnecting railroad trains, drawn up in a fan-shaped formation beneath the branches of a forest of birch and pine. Roofs had been built over the cars to shield them from heat and snow and wooden catwalks laid from train to train. The Grand Duke Nikolai had his quarters in a six-car train: offices in one car, bedroom in another, dining salon in a third, and so on. His bedroom wall was completely covered with religious icons, more than two hundred of them in golden frames, the icon lamps kept constantly burning. Over the doorway of each room a piece of paper was stuck, to remind the six-foot-six Nikolasha to duck his head as he entered.

At the *Stavka*, as everywhere, the talk was of the lack of weapons.

"The system is appalling," they told him. "In fact, it's no damned system at all. Look, we have six arsenals. The larger three are in

Petrograd, in Perm, and in Obukhovo. The others are in Tula, Izhevsk and Sestrovesk. Only the Petrograd arsenal is capable of producing new guns, and even then it must rely on outside foundries. Perm is inefficient, Obukhovo produces only naval ordnance, and the others have no capacity to manufacture artillery or small arms at all, unless you count the fact that they make a few machine guns at Tula. How can a system like that cope with our needs?"

"What are your needs?" he asked.

"Our needs?" They laughed at the naïveté of the question. "Do you know what they're sending us? Twelve percent of our needs. We need two thousand machine guns a month on this front alone. God knows how many more in the Carpathians. We need five, six thousand field guns! A million rifles! Do you know that there are regiments where the men are forbidden on pain of death to fire their rifles more than three times a day? Three rounds each day! How can we fight if there is an offensive?"

"Are there signs of an offensive?"

"There are always signs of an offensive, *reportyor*," they said. "What we need are signs that anybody gives a damn."

Vladimir sent it all back in his dispatches. Alexei Suvanov, the editor of the newspaper, cut them savagely, taking out anything Vladimir had written which might, to use Suvanov's words "cast fear and despondency into the hearts of our readers."

"Don't they want to know?" Vladimir shouted at him. "Don't you want to tell them?"

"Of course I do," Suvanov said.

"Then why don't you do it?"

"If I don't take this stuff out, the censors will."

"It's the truth, damn you!"

"They don't want to hear it, my dear fellow!" Suvanov said, and there was more than a little evidence to support his words. On the home front, plenty of people were making pots of money out of the war. For those in the know, there were lots of ways to make a fast ruble, and there were more than enough people in the know: bankers, industrialists, prelates, courtiers, heads of commissariats, mandarins and the mistresses of Grand Dukes and Generals. Everybody splashed in it, everyone who could.

The poor suffered. There were always food shortages, and they were intensified by the thousands of refugees flooding in from the war zones. The bureaucracy was floundering, unable to cope. Voluntary organizations sprang into being, spontaneously taking control of the purchase of commodities for the civilian population and the Army. It was not at all accidental that they made their headquarters in Moscow. They soon became an almost parallel government, but with one vast difference to the one in *Piter*: they were, by their very definition, socialists to a man.

Vladimir went back to the *Stavka* from Galicia, where he had watched the devastating advance of the Russian armies. Early in April the Tsar himself entered the conquered province, clambering over the ruined buildings of Przemysl, sleeping in the bed formerly reserved for the sole use of the Emperor Franz Josef in Lemberg.

"To watch our soldiers advance," Vladimir wrote, "is to watch heroism beyond any power of mine to describe. We have very little artillery and ammunition, and our gallant soldiers attack heavily fortified positions, manned by crack Austrian troops, without the benefit of an artillery barrage. Each hill, each ridge, each bloody foot of these craggy, forested peaks must be stormed by bayonet. Line after green-clad line advances, wilting beneath the withering fire of the enemy machine guns, only to be replaced at once by another line, and another, and then another. Inch by inch they advance, up hillsides soaked with the blood of their comrades, magnificent, awesome, contemptuous of death. They take the hill, and the next and the next. We are winning the Carpathian passes, but the cost is beyond all reason."

He sent it to Suvanov, knowing that it would not be used. Somehow it made him feel better to have written it down. He arrived back at the *Stavka* on May 1, and dined that night with the officers. Their talk was still the same: no rifles, no ammunition, no confidence in the men running the war.

The next day, one and a half thousand German guns opened fire on a single sector of the Russian line. For a distance of five miles along the enemy front there was an uninterrupted eruption of artillery fire, a whooshing, whistling, thundering, obliterating maelstrom of death that continued for more than four hours. In that four hours, three quarters of a million German shells fell upon the Russian trenches, wiping them off the face of the earth. Casualties in the division stationed at the center of the Russian line where this happened were fifteen thousand, five hundred men—ninety-seven percent. The line disintegrated. Panicked commanders pulled their men away from the useless, senseless slaughter. New lines were quickly formed, reinforcements rushed forward. The Third Caucasian Corps advanced upon the Germans, forty thousand strong. By the end of the first day, it had been reduced to six thousand. That gallant, incredibly brave six thousand then made a bayonet charge, at dead of night, returning from the German lines with two prisoners for every Russian that came back. Not even such gallantry could alter the fact that the Third Army had been cut to pieces. Nothing could stop the advancing German horde.

There was an air of feverish activity at the *Stavka* as the news started to come in, a fever which turned to stunned disbelief when the scale of the disaster became apparent. No longer did the bugles blare. The runners who had sped between the command posts like startled rabbits were no more to be seen. It was as if, for a long summer afternoon, the High Command was paralyzed. Vladimir hurried to the command post to find Sergei Tretyakov coming out of it. He had not seen his niece's husband for a long time, and he was struck by the changes in the man. Sergei's face was drawn and there were dark, dark shadows beneath his eyes. He did not recognize Vladimir at first and plainly did not wish to talk to him. Vladimir planted himself firmly on the duckboard walkway, impelled by a strange anger to make the man confess what Vladimir already suspected: that there was no plan, no policy, no strategy. The High Command, like a chicken with its head cut off, was still running but dead on its feet.

"Sergei," he said, "I want to talk to you."

"I can't stop," Sergei said, trying to get past. "There's no time now."

"Make some," Vladimir said. "This is important."

Sergei looked at him properly for the first time, and Vladimir saw the dislike in the man's eyes. And something else: contempt?

"Important to whom?" Sergei said, chin lifting. "You? Or me?"

"To all of us," Vladimir said, controlling his temper. "Can you tell me what's going on?"

"I would have thought that was apparent," Sergei said, "even to the most limited intellect."

"It's a rout, then?" Vladimir said, controlling his temper. He would get nowhere with Sergei by antagonizing him. He could see the fire in the other man's eyes. He was looking for a fight.

"I'd get back to Moscow, where it's safe, if I were you," Sergei said, not concealing the sneer. "There'll be real bullets flying around here before long."

"Would you be able to tell?" Vladimir said sweetly.

"Always the clever remark, Smirnoff," Sergei said. His voice was breathy, slightly slurred. "Always know it all, don't you?"

"Sergei, let's not quarrel," Vladimir said. "I need some information. Is there to be a counterattack?"

"We have lost too many men."

"Then you'll stand here?"

"The ground is too flat here for a successful stand."

"So it's retreat?"

"I have heard nothing about any plan to retreat."

Vladimir shook his head, baffled. It was as if he was talking in one room and Sergei in another. The words were not connecting properly with each other. He tried one more time.

"Sergei, if it's neither advance, stand, nor retreat, what is the plan?"

"It is in the lap of the gods," Sergei muttered. "It's all in the lap of the gods."

"Look, I want to see the Grand Duke," Sergei persisted. "Who do I have to talk to?"

Now sentience came into Sergei's eyes, and as it did, dislike flooded them. There was something else there, too, Vladimir thought. That same contempt he had seen earlier.

"You have to talk to me," Sergei said, not troubling to conceal his satisfaction. "Don't waste your time by beginning."

"Suppose I report you?"

"I'll get you kicked out of *Stavka*," Sergei said. "If you don't get out of my way, I will anyway."

"You haven't got the authority to do that."

"Try me!" Sergei snapped. "I have the complete confidence of the Grand Duke." The slur was there again, slight but noticeable. Bombast, aggression, scornful superiority—the man was drunk, Vladimir realized. He decided to change his tack just once more.

"Why won't you help me, Sergei?" he said.

"Because I don't like you and I never have," Sergei said. The moment he had said it, a faint look of surprise touched his face, as though the words had been uttered by someone else.

"All right," Vladimir said. "You don't like me and I don't much like you, but we've both got a job to do. Let me talk to the Grand Duke."

He saw the smile that touched the thin mouth for a moment and realized that Sergei was enjoying himself. The damned man had no intention of helping him; he just wanted to see Vladimir beg.

"You won't help?"

"You didn't really think I would, did you?" Sergei said. "You damned Smirnoffs are all the same. You think all you have to do is snap your fingers and the whole world comes to heel. Well, now you're learning differently. Perhaps it will teach you to keep your nose out of what doesn't concern you."

"You mean, like Katrina?"

"Especially that!" Sergei hissed. "Stay out of my private life, Vladimir, or you'll regret it."

"Is that a threat?"

"Take it any damned way you please," Sergei said, pushing past Vladimir and striding away, his back rigid with contained anger. Well, well, Vladimir thought. There were fires in Sergei Tretyakov's belly after all. Not quite the morose skulker I imagined. It was like hearing one of those stories about the henpecked husband who finally kicks his wife down the stairs; you knew it happened, but it was always a surprise. He wondered what pressure Sergei Tretyakov was under that made him so aggressive, so angry.

He stayed as long as he could, learned as much as it was possible to learn about the military situation. He asked the other officers about Sergei but found out nothing he did not already know: that he went frequently to nearby towns, where he drank a lot and alone, that he had no friends and few admirers. He wondered what had happened to the man, but it was all washed out of his mind by his disgust at the incompetence he saw at the front. The High Command was totally divided, riddled with rivalries and intrigues. At the front the officers fought like lions; their men died without complaint in attacks which were little short of suicide. They told Vladimir it was as if the Germans always knew from which sector the next sortie would come and were ready for them. Every day thousands were dying, and nobody at the *Stavka* seemed to have the slightest idea what to do about it.

"Too many Germans back there," the young officers would tell him, their faces smeared with powder smoke, their uniforms gray with dust and often stained with the blood of brave soldiers who had died in their arms. "Too many damned Germans." They were not gesturing at the enemy lines. It was toward *Stavka* that they jerked their thumbs.

Vladimir told it all to Pierre, and Pierre acted in his usual forthright fashion. He called a meeting of all the major factory owners in Moscow. Dubbing themselves the War Industry Committee, they demanded of the government that it permit industry to organize the production of arms and ammunition. They met with the predictable opposition of Sukhomlinov and responded to it by telling the War Minister to go straight to hell. Pierre systematically reorganized the flow of food to Moscow and the shipment of arms and ammunition to the front. In short order there was a *Voinsky Industryetskamityat* in every city in Russia, and Pierre found himself traveling far and wide, helping different *gubernaya* to set up their own self-help organizations.

When Vladimir went to see his editor, Suvanov flatly refused to commission any more dispatches from the front.

"You simply don't know the trouble your stuff has been getting us into, Smirnoff," he complained. "I've had all sorts of people around here asking about you. The censor's department first, then the security police. Your articles could not be permitted to appear as you had written them. They said they were going to refer your case to the *Okhrana*."

"What the devil for?" said Vladimir, astonished.

"They said you were fomenting treason and desertion in the Army."

"How could I do that if they censored it? There's no logic in what you're saying."

"Since when did the *Okhrana* need to be logical?"

"I can't believe it," Vladimir said. "Alexei, doesn't anyone in Russia want to hear the truth? Doesn't anyone care about the way our boys are dying out there?"

"You had better believe what I say," Suvanov said, fiddling with his pen. He was clearly uncomfortable, as if afraid that someone would come in and find Vladimir with him.

"You want me out of here, don't you?"

"Yes, I do," Suvanov said, anger in his voice. Vladimir regarded the man sadly. Suvanov needed to justify himself and could only do so by getting angry. "Yes, I wish you'd go and not come back."

"Poor Alexei," Vladimir said, picking up his hat and gloves. "They'll bury you with your head still in the sand."

As Vladimir turned and went out closing the door behind him, Suvanov let out his breath in a long, relieved whistle. People like the Smirnoffs never learned the rules because they had always made their own. That was fine when you were making vodka, he supposed, but in the newspaper business one needed to trim one's sails to the prevailing wind, slip the right people a few rubles, and most of all, keep on the right side of the law. He still shuddered when he remembered the cold-eyed bastard from the *Okhrana* who had come in asking questions about Vladimir Smirnoff. He didn't want anything to do with that one, or any of them. Alexei Suvanov was looking out for Alexei Suvanov first, last and always. If he didn't, nobody else would.

In the autumn, Warsaw fell. There were violent changes at the top, and the Tsar himself assumed command of all the Russian armies. In the hospitals the lines of wounded and dying grew and grew. They were all brave lads, and they died as they had fought, without complaining. *Nitchyevo, syestruchka*, they would say, it's nothing, little sister. The endless procession did not slacken until November, when winter closed down the front. The line was stabilized, but now all of Russian Poland lay in German hands. There were no great parties that winter, no galas in the silent, snow-covered cities. The young men who had once danced in the great ballrooms, so heedless of the morrow, lay moldering in East Prussia or the foothills of Galicia. There were no flags, no bands on the station platforms, no cheering crowds. Huddled groups, shoulders hunched against the biting wind, stood reading the casualty lists in the shop windows on the Nevsky and the Kuznetsky Most. Hatred of all things German reached almost pathological heights. Bach, Brahms and Beethoven were banned from the concert halls. French-speaking people traveling in Moscow streetcars—anti-German feeling was much stronger in Moscow than in Petrograd—were hissed at and spat upon by Russians who knew no language but their own, and who reviled all "foreigners" with the filthiest insult they knew: *Nemtsy*, German.

Vladimir spent his time helping with the administration of the hospital at Telegin. There was always more work to be done than could be handled. The numbers of wounded streaming back from the front had become so great that even the stables had been converted into quarters for them. Vladimir was no doctor, but he did what he could, and tried to see to it that Katrina got at least a few hours' sleep every night. She was greatly changed. It was as if all of her life and all of her soul had been poured into a new mold. There was an exalted, almost religious fervor in her dedication to the wounded and dying. She would often sit for hours holding the hand of some shattered, mumbling boy, showing herself no mercy until he slipped away. In the operating theater she held ether cones, sterilized instruments, assisting in even the most difficult operations.

She took amputated hands and legs from the bloody hands of the surgeons, changed filthy, lice-ridden dressings, and daily endured all the sights and the smells and the agonies which passed through the hospital.

"I don't mind it," she told Vladimir, when he begged her to rest. "It is as if I am somehow repaying Our Lord for keeping Sergei safe."

She wore a headdress and uniform that looked like a nun's habit. The soldiers called her *Byelaya*, the White One. As she moved down the aisles between the beds, they would reach out their hands to touch her; they wept when she knelt by their beds to pray for them. When it was time for them to go to theater, they would call for her: "Stand near me, *Byelaya*," they would say. "Hold my hand and give me courage."

Katrina never saw envy or hatred, but there was some there, and Vladimir knew it. It was understandable, of course, but no less saddening for that. They brought these peasant boys in from the battlefields and put them into spotless beds in the great houses, kids who had never had anything better to sleep on in their lives than bundles of rags. What else could that stir in some but hatred and envy? Inequality in luxury was harder to take than inequality in misery and poverty.

One day, walking through the gardens, he overheard two convalescent soldiers talking. They took no notice of him. Vladimir was wearing stained old army fatigues and carrying a ladder on his shoulder: just another worker.

"By God!" the taller of the two said to his mate. "The way these people live! Those stables they so kindly let us sleep in used to be full of thoroughbreds, you know, every one of them worth a fortune. Houses for the servants. Why, the pigsties are better than the house my family lived in. And all the property of one man, brother! One man had all this while we slaved twelve hours a day in the factory just to get enough bread to feed our kids. By God, there's no justice in the world, is there?"

"There will be one day, brother," his friend growled. "You'll see. When this bloody war is over, we'll kick them all out. There'll be no more rich living in places like this."

"By God, there won't!" said the first man, glaring at the walls of Telegin as if his very anger could bring them tumbling down. "By God, there won't!"

And we thought nothing was too good for them, Vladimir

thought with a shrug. He hoisted the ladder on his shoulder and went on his way. Perhaps it had been too much to expect gratitude, he thought, but he had not expected hatred. It had been a long time since he heard that kind of revolutionary talk. There was some unrest among the workers here and there, disaffection among the troops, but no organized agitation. All the revolutionaries had been arrested and exiled in February 1915. The ones in foreign exile, in Switzerland and Paris, could communicate neither with them nor with each other. Revolution was in abeyance for the duration, the cynics said.

When his brother came to Moscow, Vladimir asked him what had happened to Mikhail Mikhailovich, their "cousin from Paris."

"He was picked up by the *Okhrana*," Senka said. "Whether it was because of Genya telling Gorbichev or because they had a line on him anyway, I don't know. It makes precious little difference, either way. He's been sent off to exile with the rest of them, yes. Good riddance, says I."

"Where was he sent, do you know?"

"Irkutsk, I think. They send them to all sorts of places. My young friend Josif was shipped off to Kureika."

"Have you heard from him?"

"Only that he is there, and that he does a lot of hunting and fishing," Senka said. "Yes, he says he does a lot of that."

"Haven't heard from our friend Mikhail, though." Vladimir grinned. "Funny they should send him to the same place as Boris Abrikosov." He asked Senka another question.

"I haven't really seen them," Senka replied, "although I heard old Alex was ill. Meant to call and see him, but you know how time goes. Quite poorly, they say, yes. Tatiana is working as a nurse at Tsarskoe Selo, in the Catherine Palace. Yes, Castle told me that."

"I wanted to ask you about him. And Irina."

"Castle? Moved out last summer, yes. Just as well, I'd say. Getting decidedly uncomfortable with them both under the same roof, I can tell you. Couldn't make up my mind what to do, you know. That was the dilemma. Tell Sasha, or not?"

"They're still seeing each other?"

"More now, with Sasha away in the Army, yes? Nothing to stop them, really, nothing."

"I suppose not," Vladimir said. "Do you think Genya?—"

"Let it be," Senka said, patting his pockets one by one in that familiar, maddening way. "Sleeping dogs lie and all that. That's my feeling. He'll probably go back to America before long."

"What makes you say that?"

"Can't say I remember what, no, but something he said. Yes, along the lines of his having wasted time, wasted too much time in Russia, something like that. Yes, that was it."

"Well, let's hope you're right," Vladimir said. "I shudder to think of what might happen if Sasha were to find out."

21

THE HOUSE of the banker Frederick Streicher was imposing, exuding an air of solidity and wealth. Castle was passed from *dvornik* to doorman to maid, guided up a wide marble staircase whose walls were crowded with oil paintings. They looked old and valuable, although Castle was no connoisseur. He was conducted through ceiling-high doors into an airy, warm drawing room whose windows looked out across the ice-covered Moika and the frozen streets as if denying their existence.

The heavily gilded double doors at the far side of the room were opened by a silent butler, and Streicher waddled through. He was a fat man, ugly. The butler closed the doors as silently as he had opened them.

"Mr. Castle, I presume?" Streicher said. His voice was throaty, the gutturals hardly noticeable. Castle took the soft, warm hand and made himself smile.

"I've been looking forward to meeting you," he said.

"Come into the library," Streicher said, taking Castle's elbow and piloting him through the double doors. "You're somewhat younger than I expected, yes indeed, quite a bit younger."

The library was as beautifully furnished as was the drawing room, its walls lined from floor to ceiling with mahogany book-shelves filled with books by British, Russian, French and German authors, all in rich bindings. The floor was carpeted. In the center of the room stood a long mahogany Regency dining table, on which were scattered dozens of newspapers and magazines. At the far end of the table, a set of decanters sparkled in the pale sunshine. On the left-hand side of the room there was a huge fireplace, with a log fire crackling heartily in it. Before the fire, a leather Chesterfield and two chairs were arrayed around a small oak table. At the side of one of the chairs stood an ice bucket holding an already-opened bottle of Veuve Clicquot. A silver tray with crystal glasses stood on the table.

"You will take a glass of wine, Mr. Castle?"

"With pleasure."

The champagne was ice-cold, almost tasteless. Russians always drank it nearly frozen, no matter how many times one protested that to overchill champagne killed its delicate flavor.

"Well, sir," Streicher said, lowering his great bulk into the armchair farthest from the door and motioning Castle to a seat. "How can I help you? Here, let me fill your glass."

He smiled as he poured the wine into Castle's glass and then leaned back, as confident as a king on a throne. Shock tactics, then, Castle decided. He reached into his inside pocket and produced a piece of paper, which he laid on the table. Streicher frowned and turned it around with a porcine finger so that he could read it.

"What is this?" he said, frowning and pursing his lips.

"A list of names," Castle said.

"I can see that," Streicher said, irritably. "What is their significance?"

"They all have one thing in common," Castle said. "Aron Simanovich, Boris Sturmer, Alexander Protopopov, Manuilov, all of them have one thing in common."

"And what is that?"

"You," said Castle.

The fat man moistened his lips with his tongue; his eyes were like the eyes of rodents beneath rocks. The fleshy lips became a bloodless line, and his huge belly rose and fell rapidly.

"I am not sure that I understand you, sir," Streicher said.

"The names on that list are all your clients," Castle said.

"I am a banker, sir. I have a great many clients."

"I know that, too."

"Come, sir, come!" Streicher said. "I think I have the right to know what your interest is in these people."

"I'll tell you," Castle said. "I'd like to know about the large sums of money Protopopov brings back from Stockholm. And I'd like to know about the banker who gives it to him. And what it is for."

Streicher said nothing. His eyes did not leave Castle's face, but his whole demeanor had become tense and waiting.

"What about Manuilov, then?" Castle continued. His manner was breezy, almost insouciant. Streicher stared at him as if he expected Castle to turn into Satan before his very eyes. "Have you any idea who financed his arrangements with Rasputin? Or Simanovich, there's another one. Perhaps you can tell me who set him up in that new gambling club of his along the canal. What about Sukhomlinov? Who paid all his gambling debts after he was kicked out of office? Or Boris Sturmer. Do you know who provided him with enough money to buy that country estate he now owns?"

He stopped talking and let the silence work for him. It took a while. When the banker spoke, his voice was quite different. Gone were the false bonhomie, the expansive style. The gross body was as still as that of a coiled snake.

"Young man," he whispered, "I owe you an apology."

"For what?"

"Because I underestimated you," Streicher said sibilantly. "You have style. Imagination, even. They are qualities one so rarely encounters these days that one is inclined to forget they still exist. Petrograd is the city of the bludgeon, not the rapier. I mistook your apparent youth for inexperience. I apologize."

"Don't bother," Castle said harshly.

"You're right," Streicher said. "Apologies are a waste of time. All right, young man. Two hundred thousand rubles."

"What?"

"Two hundred and fifty thousand, then. Don't try my patience, please. You are asking questions that I do not want asked. I will pay you to stop asking them. What could be more simple than that?"

Castle smiled.

"Now it's my turn to apologize," he said. Streicher nodded, misreading the American's expression and tone. It was always the same, he thought. Money bought anything one wanted. It was only a question of how much to use.

"No apology necessary," he said graciously. "As long as we understand each other." In this moment of self-congratulation, he idly speculated whether he might have bought the fellow for less. Not that it mattered; it wasn't his money.

"We do," Castle said, and something in the way he said it brought Streicher's head sharply up, the piggy eyes glaring suspiciously. One look at Castle's face confirmed what Streicher had suspected.

"You . . . refuse?" he whispered.

"You didn't really think I'd accept, did you?"

"I did not think you would be so stupid as to do otherwise."

"You can't buy me off, Streicher."

"Then you are a fool!" Streicher hissed. "And I have nothing more to say to you. Good day, sir."

He must have pushed a bell somewhere because the tall double doors opened soundlessly. Castle saw that the butler who had earlier shown Streicher into the drawing room was standing there, Castle's coat over his arm.

"Show him out, Ivan," Streicher said. The butler looked at Castle, as expressionless as a lizard. For the first time, Castle saw that Ivan was a very big man, wide-shouldered and powerfully muscled.

"Call off your thug, Streicher," he said. "I'm going."

"Don't make the mistake of coming back," Streicher said, his eyes hooded.

"One final question," Castle said, half-turning as if to leave. "Who is Helphand?"

Streicher's face changed abruptly. Half-rising from his seat, he looked at Castle with stricken eyes. Then caution flooded them, and the suety face became a wary mask.

"Wait outside," he told the butler.

The big man by the door frowned and then went out. Once, Castle had seen a black bear fishing by the side of the Yellowstone River. It had caught a trout with a swipe of its paw, but just as it was about to sink its teeth into the fish, the trout wriggled free and was gone in a flash of silver movement. Ivan's expression had been much the same as that bear's, cheated of its prey.

Now Frederick Streicher put both hands on the arms of his chair and heaved his huge body upright. He waddled across the room until he was face to face with Castle. His face was ashine with sweat, and he thrust it forward, lips curled in anger.

"You damned fool!" Streicher hissed. "Do you realize what danger you are in?"

"Tell me about it," Castle said. "Tell me about Helphand. And while you're about it, tell me about the Petersburg Plan."

"Ah," Streicher sighed. He shook his head slowly. "I had hoped you were bluffing."

"I'm not bluffing."

"Neither am I, Mr. Castle. So listen to what I say. Do not on any account pursue this matter further. Ask no more questions of me or anyone else. Go while the going is good."

"And if I don't?"

"You will find that you have made a fatal error of judgment," Streicher said, turning his back.

Castle was dismissed. The fat man stood immobile in the middle of the room, his back a wall. The door silently opened, and Ivan came back in. With a small shrug, Castle went with him down the stairs. Ivan held the door open and smiled as Castle went out into the street. His very politeness was more menacing than any hostility could have been. It put a chill into Castle's body which had nothing to do with the icy wind coming up the Nevsky.

22

IN LATER YEARS, Tatiana could never remember the proper sequence of the events of the war. Time blurred. So very much seemed to happen that it was as if some demon were piling event upon event, too fast for anyone to do anything but live through. She grew up all at once. The change was not altogether of her own making. Confronted by the wreckage of war, the maimed, shattered men sent back to the Tsaritsa's hospital at Tsarskoe Selo, it was impossible to do otherwise. You saw too many die who had never really lived; too many with ruined lives before them who had never really had half, a quarter of the opportunities someone like herself had known. You saw too many who had lost their loved ones not to realize that convention meant nothing, that life was all, that there were no guarantees, no promises, no certainties other than those you held in your hand this day. For the first time she regretted kisses she had not surrendered, kindnesses she had not offered, sorrows she had been too self-centered to share. She thought very often of Vladimir and wondered where he was. Senka came to see her, and said he had been a war correspondent on the western front and in Galicia. He was changed, more absentminded, older-looking; Tatiana knew it was true of them all. It was impossible not to realize, however slowly, however reluctantly, that her life and the life of everyone she knew would never be the same again.

Almost as if trying to make amends for what she now began to see as wasted years, Tatiana threw herself into her work, thinking of nothing else until she collapsed into exhausted sleep on her narrow cot. She had grieved for her lost friends and for her dead brothers, and she would never cease to miss them, but she could not let grief stand in the way of what needed to be done. Life was for the living and for the survivors; the dead had no rights to anything, except their place in your memory. Russia was dying, bleeding to death.

The evidence of it was there in the immaculate wards, winter, spring, summer, autumn and winter again. She worked like an automaton, her only reward the praise of her patroness, the Tsaritsa Alexandra.

The Tsaritsa had forgotten her own illness in caring for others. She took her nursing seriously, unlike many of the titled ladies who also endowed hospitals in their names but took very great care not to become involved in the bloody work of repairing the broken bodies which filled them.

Everyone was busy all the time. The Tsaritsa, who had formerly stayed abed till noon nursing her ailments, now rose at seven for Mass, breakfasted at eight, and wearing the long gray-white habit of the Sisters of Mercy, arrived at the hospital at nine for her nursing course. Her two older daughters and her friend Anna Vyrubova also attended. The two younger girls were allowed to become patronesses of hospitals for other ranks, mainly from the Guards regiments, whose officers were sent to Tsarskoe Selo. After lunch the Tsaritsa would usually visit other hospitals in Petrograd. Throughout the day, she continued her endless correspondence with her husband. The Tsar was frequently at the front now, and she wrote him daily, page after page after page in a bold, impulsive hand.

Tatiana heard—how could she not hear?—the slighting remarks some of the other girls made about Alexandra, but she ignored them. The Tsaritsa was little short of saintly in her devotion to the wounded. She did not keep her aloof distance from the suffering, as someone of her rank had every right to do. She worked in the blood-spattered operating theater, held dying men in her arms, sat by their beds and talked to them, wrote letters to their loved ones.

"Acting a part," her enemies sneered.

"Then she does it superbly," her friends would reply.

Tatiana was among the latter. She felt sure that the Tsaritsa's devotion was not a pose, that she really did care for the torn, battered men in the long, silent wards.

"Oh, use your head instead of your heart, Tatiana," the other nurses would say to her. "Don't you see that it's only the privileged ones who are sent to Tsarskoe Selo? Don't you know they're specially chosen at the front? Where are the Ivans, eh? Where are the Fyodrs and Mishas and Kostyas who are being shot to pieces in Carpathia and Masuria? Not here, Tatiana."

"How could they all be here?" she would retort. "What does it matter which soldier is looked after by the Tsaritsa and which not? They are all as badly wounded."

"Simpleton!" they would call her. "Open your eyes."

"Gossipmongers!" she would shout back at them. "Shut your mouths."

It seemed they were determined to condemn the Tsaritsa, although she had committed no crime that anyone could name. They called her *Nemka* openly and sniggered about her friendship with Vyrubova and Rasputin. They referred to the Tsar as "little Mr. Henpecked." No matter what she did, the Tsaritsa would never earn approval from such people, and Tatiana detested them for their pettiness. Even the man she admired most, her friend Dr. Marutinsky, was cynical about the Tsaritsa's endeavors.

"You think you are seeing a representative selection of our wounded, Tatiana?" he asked her one evening after rounds. He was a tall, thin man with deep-set eyes which looked to Tatiana as though they had seen every form of human suffering that existed. "Don't they tell you girls anything here at the palace?"

"We read the papers," Tatiana said. "And the soldiers tell us a great deal, too."

"The papers!" he said, with a laugh like a cough. "The soldiers! What do those poor fools know? Tatiana, we have already lost four million men, and this war is not yet one year old."

You could not imagine four million dead. It was beyond belief, twice the entire population of Petersburg. Petrograd, she corrected herself automatically. Yet the evidence was there. Every day the Red Cross trains brought wounded and dying men back from the front. No more than a few received anything except the most cursory treatment in the front-line dressing stations, because bandages and medical supplies were in as short supply as ammunition and weapons. Dirty, bloody, groaning with pain, feverish after the two days in the cattle trucks that had carried them seven hundred miles from the front, they were brought to the hospitals, lousy with vermin. Many of their wounds had turned gangrenous. Tatiana soon learned what every doctor learns: that there is never any end to the sick, the wounded, and the suffering. It is true in time of peace. During a war, no matter how fine the surgeons, no matter how devoted the nurses, no matter how committed the organizations set up to deal with them, the endless tide of maimed and dying stifles, deadens, dulls the reflexes, until you feel you can no longer care. There are always men dying before your eyes, screaming in agony, moaning in postoperative shock. There are always operating theaters slippery with blood, buckets and tanks filled with the gory detritus of surgery. There is always infection, blood poisoning, dysentery, enteritis. There is always gangrene and the metallic stink of death. And when you have lived through it all once, twice, a hundred, a thousand times, there is more, and then more and then more again. In war there is never any end to it.

There was a German offensive on the Baltic front. They heard about it from a young officer who had been brought in by the last ten soldiers left alive in his battalion. The German bombardment, he said, had begun at five in the morning. At the same time, gas was released, blowing in deadly tendrils across the Russian trenches. After each hour, the bombardment was lifted for five minutes.

"They wanted to see if we were still alive," the young officer said, with a bitter laugh. "Just about, eh? My boys would give them a cheer, or fire a few rounds to show we were still there. We only had a few bullets each, so that was all we could do. Just about still there, eh?"

The bombardment was resumed five times in all, he told them. He began to weep as he spoke, tears trickling down his face.

"After five hours, my battalion of five hundred was reduced to ninety-one men." He sniffled. "All my boys are gone. It was like a butcher's shop out there when the Germans came. They could not advance very quickly because there were so many dead bodies. Like a barricade."

When the Germans got close enough, the Russian troops fixed bayonets and charged them; they had no ammunition. Bayonets against machine guns, bare hands against Mauser bullets.

"Could you not have fallen back?" Tatiana whispered as she bathed the young man's face, which was shining with perspiration. "Couldn't you have retreated?"

"Retreated?" he said. "Do you think my boys would have let me retreat? Do you think I could have done it, left all my boys to be butchered by the *Nemtsy*? Oh, God, oh, God, oh, my poor brave boys!" He was sobbing now, not much older than the boys he mourned, and he was still sobbing when they put him on the trolley and wheeled him down to the theater, where the surgeons did the best they could with the wound which had shattered his groin.

Sometimes, in spite of herself, Tatiana grew attached to one of the never-ending procession of broken, ruined men. There was a boy named Feofan. He was shy, diffident, awed as so many of them were awed by the chasm of education, wealth, and position which separated them from those who now nursed them with such devotion. There were some, of course, who learned other things from being brought to the Catherine, the ones in whom resentment born years ago simmered to boiling point if they felt some noble lady visiting the wards was patronizing them. Their hatreds were especially noticeable after the Tsaritsa's daily call, and they would glower with hopeless anger for hours after she had gone.

Feofan was not one of those. He begged Tatiana to stay with him "just a little longer, just a moment more," to talk, to soothe his fever, to hold his hand and listen to him talk about his mother, his sisters, his life on the little farm in Klin. He was a brave boy with a shining smile, and Tatiana knew she spent more time with him than she should, but it was as if she somehow drew strength from him just as he drew strength from her. He became a symbol. In spite of the awful wound in his belly, she willed him to live. She wanted him to live, to show that some things could be saved, that some of it was worthwhile, that it wasn't all waste and horror and death. Sometimes in the evenings he would grow delirious and ramble, talking about his Army life: the Caucasian campaign, the other boys in his battalion, Misha, Oleg, Mitya.

"Don't grow too attached to that boy, Tatiana," Dr. Marutinsky told her. He had seen such attachments before, and knew the desperation which caused and intensified them. "That's a very severe wound he has."

"He won't die," Tatiana said, confidently. "He's getting better all the time." She dressed his wound. She knew that what she said was not so, and yet still she believed it because she wanted to believe it. They talked each morning and sometimes for an hour in the afternoon, if she was able.

"I must go now," she said to him, one breezy March day. "I've got a lot to do. Do you like your flowers?" Schoolchildren had gathered wild spring flowers and brought them into the wards. They gave the hospital a festive air which dispelled thoughts of war and death, however momentarily.

"They're beautiful," he said, with that shining smile. "And so are you, Tatiana."

"My, my," she said. "I think you're getting better."

"No," he said. "Not just yet."

An hour later they told her that he had died. She ran to her little cubicle in the nurses' quarters and cried until she could cry no more, not just for dear, sad, brave Feofan but for the thousands like him, for every one of the poor, smashed, humiliated creatures who had passed through this hospital and all the other hospitals and who would never stop coming, never, never, never stop.

They sent her home for a week: strain, overwork, emotional debility, Dr. Marutinsky said. Home was a sad place, too. Her father looked so gray and old, her mother so worn and tired. It was as though Death had put a mark on them: *to be collected soon.* She crossed herself to banish the black thought. Alex had never really recovered from the death of Roman at Tannenberg.

The following March, they received word that Ilya's plane had been shot down over the rubbled ruins of Przemysl, and their cup of bitterness flooded over. Nothing could cheer them, not even the visit of dear Kolya Bakhronshin. It was almost as if his call brought back the ghosts of happier days, sunnier times.

There were no sunny times anywhere anymore, Kolya told Tatiana as they walked together in the autumn sunshine along the embankment of the Neva. There had been riots in the bread lines, where starving citizens cursed the profiteering landlords, who hoarded bounteous crops of grain while bread mounted to three times its prewar price. There was hardly any beef or mutton to be had, and when there was, it cost four times what it had formerly cost. Butter was the same, cheese, milk. Men and women joined any line they saw. Whatever was being sold, they would buy, if any was left when they got to the counter. Only the wealthy, who did not care what anything cost and never had, could afford to eat well. For everyone else it was thin soup, or black bread and *kvass.*

"I wish you would think about getting away from Petrograd," Kolya told her. "It's going to be dangerous here."

"Dangerous?" she said, incredulously. "In the Tsar's own palace?"

"Especially there," he said. "Listen to me, Tatiana. I have been with the soldiers. I know their mood. They feel they have been betrayed by the aristocracy, and who can say that they have not? When they come back, when the war ends, they will want to change the system, and they will not do it by talk, as we used to. We have taught them how to fight together, and we have shown them how to use guns. One day they will use them on us."

"Kolya Bakhronshin!" she said. "I can't believe my ears! Is this the same boy who used to live only for fun and laughter, talking now of revolution and death? What happened to you?"

"I will tell you what happened to me, Tatiana," he said, taking her shoulders in his hands and looking straight into her eyes. "What happened to me was a battle. It took place last August in a forest. The name of the forest was the Kammerwald. I was with the Dorogobuzh Regiment. Have you ever heard of them?"

"No," Tatiana whispered, hypnotized by the intensity of his voice. "Never."

"You never will," he said, sepulchrally, "for neither any longer exists. We were drawn into a rearguard battle as we pulled back from Allenstein, what was left of our three battalions. General Klyuev gave our commanding officer no plan for withdrawal save the order to do so. 'Do your duty!' General Klyuev said. 'Do your duty!' He did not tell us what our duty was, but we knew: we knew we were doomed to die. No other course was open to us, for we were outnumbered ten to one by the advancing Germans. All we could decide for ourselves was how to sell our lives most dearly. And that was what we did. We drew our line with a lake on one flank and the forest behind us. There was a chain of smaller lakes on our other flank. There were perhaps twelve hundred of us, exhausted, battered, wounded, dirty. We had no food, water, or tobacco, and hardly any ammunition. Yet there we drew our line, there in the bright sunshine on Assumption Day."

"Kolya, don't," Tatiana pleaded. "Don't torture yourself."

"Let me tell you!" he panted, his eyes haunted, all of himself back there in the hot August sunshine, with the glittering ranks of the German troops clearly visible down the hill on which they had dug in. He lived through it again as he told her about it: how the Dorogobuzh Regiment stood its ground all that afternoon and into the evening, decimated by withering machine-gun fire they could not return, firing sporadically until they had exhausted their ammunition and then—and then—counterattacking three times with bare bayonets.

"Three times, Tatiana!" Kolya whispered. "And they were just kids, most of them, reservists! They hadn't been in the Army a month. They didn't even know what they were dying for! They walked into fire behind their silent bayonets, dropping soundlessly, like marionettes in a dream. A third of them hadn't even got rifles. They marched forward empty-handed behind their comrades until one of those in front fell dead and they could pick up his weapon. They were slaughtered, Tatiana, cut to pieces like hogs in an abattoir—and nobody gives a damn! Nobody gave a damn while we were out there dying, and nobody gives a damn now! High-ranking officers who ought to be at the front sit in the bars of the big hotels, drinking champagne, while their friends congratulate them on their good sense. 'No point in going out to the front and getting killed, is there?' they say. 'Leave that to the Ivans and the Mishas, eh? There are more of them than there are of us.' Don't you people in *Piter* see what's happening?" His voice was full of anger. "Don't you know?"

They walked all the way to the St. Alexander Nevsky monastery at the eastern end of the three-mile-long Nevsky Prospect. Over the low wall on their left, Tatiana could see the scattered old tombstones in the cemetery. Dostoievsky was buried in there, and Tchaikowsky. Somehow the sight of the graves made her shiver, and he saw it.

"I'm sorry, dear Tatiana," he said. "You see enough and do more than most people in this lousy city. I'm sorry to weigh you down with my woes."

"What will you do, Kolya?" she asked. She could not banish the specter of death that had suddenly appeared in her mind.

"Oh, I'll go back," he said. "I'm too stupid to desert. I'll go back for the big push they say is coming. Probably get my fool head shot off."

"Don't say that," Tatiana said. "Don't say such things."

"Oh, don't you fear for me," Kolya said, with forced joviality. "I'll be safe. We have a new strategy at the front, did you know? Shall I tell you what the soldiers say?"

"What?"

"We are going to retreat to the Urals," he told her. "When we get there, there will only be one German and one Austrian soldier left pursuing us. According to custom, the Austrian will give himself up. Then we'll kill the German and win the war." It was a bitter jest; she did not laugh.

"Will you have time to go to Moscow before you go back?"

"I hope so," he said. "My father is very ill. They don't think he will live until Christmas."

"Oh, Kolya, I'm sorry!" Tatiana exclaimed. "I didn't know. Working at the hospital day in and day out, I don't have time to write to anyone. I haven't had any news from Moscow for ages. After Nicky and Vasya and the others were killed, I . . ."

"I know," he said. "So many of the old crowd are gone." He made a distinct effort to brighten up. "However, I can give you a little news. You know the Smirnoffs turned Sokolnika into a hospital?"

"No," she said. She tried to imagine the beautiful old house on its hill jammed with the broken bodies of dying men and walking wounded, like the Catherine Palace. She never ceased to be struck by the bizarre contrast between the elegantly carved doors and ceilings, the frescoes and murals by great artists, and the rows and rows of beds filled with terribly hurt men, the intricately carved marquetry floors stained with blood from countless discarded dressings. "Is Katrina a nurse there?"

"She's a nurse, but not at Sokolnika," he said. "She's turned Vladimir Smirnoff's house into a hospital. They don't accept officers, only enlisted men."

Telegin! The name brought back that awful day that Boris Abrikosov had tried to abduct her. She could still feel the steel grip of his hands on her body, see the lust in his eyes. Yet she had not thought of the man himself in all that time, almost a year. As for Vladimir . . . yes, she admitted to herself, she had thought of him.

"Where is Vladimir?" she asked. "Is he in the Army?"

"No, he couldn't get in for some reason or other, so he went as a war correspondent."

"It would be nice to see them all again," she said wistfully. "Papa isn't well . . ."

"You should all go to Moscow," he said. "I wasn't joking, you know. Petrograd will be a dangerous city when all those soldiers come back. A big change is coming in this country. The ruling class will never make it, but one day the soldiers will, the soldiers and the workers."

"You think there will be a revolution?"

"I am sure of it," Kolya said. "That's why I think you ought to come to Moscow."

Kolya left the next day, promising to write from Moscow.

"I'll send you all the gossip," he said gruffly, and kissed her clumsily on both cheeks. "Remember what I said about coming there, Tatiana. Think about it."

"I will," she promised, but she did no such thing. There was always the endless task of looking after the wounded and the dying brought to the hospital, always more to do than any of them could cope with. She did not go home again until Easter.

Alex insisted on going to the midnight mass at the Kazan Cathedral. He was stubborn about it, brooking no argument from either Maryka or Ivan Pavlovich. And so they all went together to the great cathedral on the Nevsky. The huge bronze doors, copied from those of the Baptistry in Florence, were thrown wide, and the church was already very crowded. Thousands of candles yellowed the huge silver balustrade before the iconostas. The banners and eagles of Napoleon on the pillars and walls above them shone faintly gold, like stars on a cloudy night. They sang the psalms and, at the appropriate hour, the priest approached the sepulcher. Symbolically he lifted the shroud; the body of the Savior was not there. Then the priest went out into the square and walked around the churchyard, seeking the vanished Christ.

"*Khristos voskrese!*" he announced as he reentered the cathedral. "Christ is risen!"

"Truly he is risen!" the congregation replied joyously. Friends, relatives, even strangers then exchanged the triple Easter kiss; it was unthinkable to refuse anyone this sign of brotherly affection. Now all the bells of the city pealed out. In every home there would be colored Easter eggs, and *pashka* and *kulich* decorated with the symbol XB—*Khristos voskrese.*

Tatiana stood beside one of the great Corinthian pillars, inhaling the sweet perfume of the incense mixed with the softer smell of the burning tapers held by everyone in the congregation.

"*Khristos voskrese!*" someone said to her, and she was enveloped in a bear hug by a big man wearing a heavy coat with a fine marten collar.

"*Vo istinue voskrese!*" she replied automatically, and then her heart jumped and she felt suddenly breathless. The man kissing her three times in the traditional Easter manner was Vladimir Smirnoff. He looked older somehow, as if he had suffered or seen much suffering.

"It's a long time since we did this, Makcheyeva," he muttered, and Tatiana felt the blood rush to her cheeks. Damn the man! He could still get under her skin with the first few words he spoke. She pulled away from him, ignoring the devil's grin on his face, and saw that all the Smirnoffs were there: Senka, in a great heavy cape, Sasha Smirnoff in his Army uniform, a young woman she took to be Sasha's wife and their two small children, Olga Sukhotin and her husband Fritz, also in uniform. They hugged and kissed and embraced each other, smiling, excited. Alex beamed like a boy, so pleased was he to see them all again. Maryka's heart lifted to see him smile; it was a long time since he had done so.

Now, beside the altar, the priest was beginning the ceremony of dismissal. Candlelight gleamed on his golden miter, the shining chasuble. One by one, the congregation went forward to kiss the crucifix and his outstretched hand. Then they came out into the sparkling chill of the night, past the nuns and the beggars beneath the statue of Kutuzov, into the crowded Nevsky. Dozens of sleighs

316

waited by the high curb. The horses snorted and pawed at the chipped ice on the streets as their owners climbed aboard.

Tatiana found Vladimir at her side. He took her arm, as if wishing to ensure that she did not slip on the icy sidewalk.

"I've missed you, Makcheyeva," he whispered. "Where have you been?"

"I've been working at the Catherine Hospital. In Tsarskoe Selo."

"Not married yet?" he said, lightly. "Or anything?"

There he went again, Tatiana thought angrily. It was as if he deliberately tried to get her angry by the very tone of his voice.

"No," she said, as coldly as she could manage. To her intense annoyance, he grinned that insouciant grin once more. "Good," he said. "Then there's still hope."

"Are you suggesting that I might marry you?" Tatiana asked, frostily.

"Why?" Vladimir said. His expression was strange: eager yet reticent, serious and flippant, all at the same time. "Aren't I good enough for you? Too old, perhaps?"

She remembered that day her wicked jibe, and his reaction. And the cutting retort she had been about to make died unborn. There was enough cruelty in the world; there was no need to add more.

"I have no thoughts of marriage, Vladimir," she said, softly. "To you or anyone else."

"You know, you've surprised me yet again," he said, and this time his voice was as soft as her own. "You never cease to surprise me. I always knew you had spirit, but now I discover you have compassion as well. I think maybe I'd better marry you, before someone else does."

"Oh, do stop teasing all the time, Vladimir," she said. "Can't you be serious for a moment?"

"I can," he said. "I will. I want you to come to Telegin. All of you. I can look after you better there."

"Why should you want to look after us?" Tatiana said. "We are perfectly capable of looking after ourselves."

"Even so," Vladimir said, "I wish you'd reconsider. We need you at Telegin, Makcheyeva. I need you."

"What?" Tatiana said, scoffing. "Vladimir Smirnoff? I thought you were the one who didn't need anybody or anything."

"Times change," he said. "So do people. At least promise me you'll think about it."

"I promise," she said, thinking no more about it than that. She could not go to Moscow; she was needed at the Catherine. Anyway, Papa was not well enough to travel, and it would be impossible to convince Mama to leave him. So Telegin was out of the question, even if she had wanted to go.

They parted on the corner.

"If you need me," he said, "you know where I am. I'll always come if you need me."

"Thank you, Vladimir," she said. For the very first time, there was no hostility between them, and she felt the warm glow of his affection. Below the carefree exterior she sensed a gentleness that he kept hidden, as if afraid someone might take advantage of him because of it. "Don't worry about me."

He smiled. "Let me worry if I want to," he said. "It gives me that feeling of being needed so lacking in my life."

Tatiana walked back to the Kazan Cathedral. Her parents were just saying good night to the Smirnoff party, and Maryka looked at her daughter curiously.

"Where did you go, Tatiana?" she asked.

"I walked a few blocks with Vladimir," Tatiana said.

"Vladimir Smirnoff? I thought you two didn't get on?"

"Oh," Tatiana said, as she got into the carriage, "I wouldn't say that, exactly."

She smiled to herself as Ivan Pavlovich gigged the horse into motion and they set off down the Nevsky toward home.

23

CASTLE looked at his watch, then got up and put the catch on the door in the open position. He lay down on the bed again, thinking about what he was going to do with the rest of his life.

He had moved into the apartment in the spring. Senka had tried to talk him out of "all that damned nonsense," as he referred to the little apartment on the Morskaya which Castle had found, but it taxed him unmercifully to live in such close proximity to Irina. He had found himself too often reaching out to touch her as she passed him. Nobody had seemed to either notice or care, but that was pure chance, and it was unwise to rely on too much of it. They were often alone in the big house, yet somehow they could never bring themselves to take advantage of the fact, as if some form of disloyalty were involved. How foolish lovers were! They honored such minor conventions while rationalizing the greater ones of deception and lying.

So Castle moved out, and he was glad that he had. The move to the Morskaya gave him psychological distance, a breathing space. Cursing himself for giving a damn about bourgeois morality, he knew he could not ignore it. No one could, not forever. Rules, he thought; they take no account of love.

When they were together, it never occurred to Castle and Irina that they might be seen. It was as if they believed their love conferred a special invisibility on them. Petrograd was, after all, a big city, swarming with people. Who would notice two more or less? It was the confidence of folly, no doubt, but they were no less carefree for that. Being together put out of their minds the things which would always keep them apart.

She would be here soon, he thought. This time he had promised himself that he was going to end it. It had gone on too long, it was too inconclusive, and he did not like the guilt. More than anything else, he hated that. He lived in a world where deception was the norm, and perhaps because of it, he valued his own honesty with himself. Being in love with Irina was altering him, and he did not know if he wanted to be altered. He loved her; he knew that. If she were free he would marry her, but there was never going to be any chance of that. She would never leave Sasha. She had said it many times, and always the same way: you understand that this is a condition of our love? Circles, he thought, we're both going around in circles, and we can't go on like that. He shook his head impatiently; it was always the same. The minute she walked back into his life, he forgot all the resolutions he had made, abandoned all the decisions he had arrived at. He heard her footsteps on the stairs and got up to meet her, wishing he had the kind of mind that did not seek solutions. He had no one to go home to, and Irina had. It was, all in all, as simple as that.

"Sasha, my dear fellow," Fritz Sukhotin said. "Do come in. Let me get you something to drink."

"Thanks," Sasha said. "I don't think I will just now."

The Sukhotins lived in a house on the Catherine Canal just by the Demidov Bridge. They did not see a lot of each other, primarily because Fritz, as a staff officer, was constantly on the move between *Piter* and the front. Sasha wasn't all that keen on Olga's husband, but Olga was Irina's sister, and so Sasha tried, as best he could, to discover in both of them something that he could like. Fritz was a tall, thin man who affected a monocle that made him look like a Prussian. Perhaps it was not entirely accidental, Sasha thought. Fritz's grandmother had been German, related vaguely to the Hohenzollerns. It was a part of his life which Fritz took great pains to play down, just as he made a joke of his name, saying it was merely a childhood *klichka*, and that his real name was honest and Russian: Ivan. He was very friendly with Felix Yusupov, the Grand Duke Dmitry, and their hangers-on, an unsavory bunch for whom Sasha had no time at all. He had heard—as who had not?—about their precious little parties on Yusupov's estate at Archangelskoe and elsewhere. Fritz didn't look the type, but one never knew. There had to be some reason why Olga played around the way she did.

Sasha had heard stories that she was part of that filthy Rasputin's coterie.

For Irina's sake, however, he kept his peace. He found that Olga would always respond to being flirted with, so when he saw her he always pretended to be mildly smitten by her. She ate up his gaucheries like a child. As for Fritz, he moved in more rarefied circles than Sasha, but they still had things military in common, and mutual friends both at Staff HQ and at the *Stavka*. They talked of them now, while Sasha wondered yet again what had prompted Fritz to invite him to call.

"Tell me, Sasha," Fritz drawled, "do you know an American named Castle?"

"Why do you ask?"

"I'll tell you in a moment. Is he a friend of yours? I seem to recall seeing him at the house."

"He lived with us for a while," Sasha said, puzzled. "Irina taught him Russian."

"Ah," Fritz said. "I see."

Sasha frowned. "What do you see?"

"Nothing," Friz said. "It's nothing."

"Why do you want to know about Castle?"

"Sasha," Friz said, reproachfully.

"Damn you, Fritz! Are you suggesting—? Why, I'll break your damned neck if—"

"Sasha, listen to me," Fritz said, and the drawl was gone from his voice now. "It's true. Believe me."

"Irina? And David Castle?"

"He has an apartment on the Morskaya, number twenty-four. They meet there regularly."

Sasha shook his head like a taunted bull.

"I don't believe it," he said. "She wouldn't do it."

"This is very unpleasant," Fritz said. "You understand, I take no pleasure in being the one to tell you."

"The hell you don't!" Sasha gritted.

"My dear fellow—" Fritz said, spreading his arms wide. "I assure you, I thought I was acting from the highest principles." He shrugged. "Now I am not so sure."

"What proof do you have?" Sasha said. His voice was harsh. "How do you know about all this?"

"My dear fellow," Fritz said. "Everyone knows."

"Everyone but me."

"That's right."

Sasha sat down on a padded stool near the door. His face was slack and his eyes empty. I ought to cry or something, he thought. There was no reaction in him; he just felt numb.

"Irina," he said, softly.

"I'm sorry, Sasha," Fritz said.

"Oh, yes," Sasha said.

"What will you do?"

"Nothing," Sasha said, tonelessly.

"Would you like a drink? Let me get you something. You look as if you could use it."

"Don't bother," Sasha said.

"I'm sorry about this, Sasha," Fritz said. "But someone had to tell you."

"Why?" Sasha said, looking up. "Why did you have to tell me, Fritz?"

"I thought you deserved—you ought to know."

"Of course," Sasha said. He stood up. He wanted to get out of this house and go home. Then he realized that the word no longer meant the same thing.

"Where are you going?" Fritz said.

"I don't know," Sasha said. "I thought . . . I might go and talk to him. To Castle."

"You think that is wise?"

"Why not?"

"Why not, indeed," Fritz said. "Look, I'll walk with you."

"All right," Sasha said.

How long does this go on for? Irina wondered in the warm after-glow of their lovemaking. How much more of this can I stand? Today was a "good" day. She had her life in balance today, and David was her love, the most precious secret in her unsecretive life. On days like this all was well, and she was able to tell herself that she was hurting no one but herself by loving him, that it didn't alter the way she loved Sasha or the children, and she was able to believe it. But she knew that tomorrow or the next day, when she could not see him, would be one of the "bad" days, when all the emotion would swell frighteningly inside her without the slightest warning, feelings so strong that she could hardly bear them. She would become obsessed with thoughts of him, and everything in life would become prefaced with the words "if only." She did not even feel the certainty of his love, as she did now, on the bad days. All that mattered then was the need to see him, touch him, talk to him, know he was there. Yet she knew she could never leave Sasha and the children. They were too much a part of her, the consequences of leaving them too frightening to consider longer than a moment. Sasha was as much a part of her as breathing, but so was David. She wanted to shout aloud at the uncomprehending world that it was possible, that she loved them both, for different reasons and in different ways.

She loved both of them and she did not know what to do about it, so she did nothing, hoping that somehow time would provide her with a solution. Time: she looked at the clock.

"I have to go," she said.

"Stay a little longer," Castle said.

"It's late."

"I love you."

She rolled toward him, and he locked her body into the circle of his arms. Her skin was damp and warm. He brushed the hair out of her fine brown eyes and kissed the end of her nose.

"Fool," she said.

"When will I see you again?"

"Tomorrow, perhaps, I don't know."

" 'Tomorrow, do thy worst, for I have lived today,' " he quoted.

"Who said that?"

"Dryden."

When they had first known each other, they had talked all the time. There were a thousand questions to ask and answer, and then a thousand more, leaving another thousand unanswered still. They had argued and agreed, exchanged their likes and dislikes until now, knowing each other with total confidence, they needed fewer words, speaking their loves with their bodies.

"I'm happy," Irina said, snuggling her head against Castle's shoulder. She felt a lovely sense of peace. These stolen hours were not so very much to ask from the demanding world, were they? It was wrong, but not black sin. No one was being hurt but the two of them.

"Me, too," Castle said.

What a damned mess, he thought. He would never win. If he took Irina he destroyed Sasha, and if he did not, he destroyed himself. If only . . .

Sasha Smirnoff shot the lock off the door and kicked it open. Castle's reflexes were very good, but he was only half out of the bed when Sasha leveled the pistol and fired it. The pistol made a shocking sound in the confined space. Castle was smashed sideways out of the bed and hurled against the wall as if by some invisible giant. He held up a hand, trying to say something, as Sasha leveled the pistol again. Blood came out of his mouth instead. The last thing he saw was Sasha's empty eyes and expressionless face as he pulled the trigger a second time, and the world disappeared into a blackening red hole. He did not even hear the sound of the shot, nor the two which followed it.

When the neighbors came running up the stairs from below, they found Castle where he had fallen, blood trickling from his slack mouth. Irina Smirnoff lay dead on the bloodstained bed. There was a hole in her breast just above the sternum; the bullet had killed her instantly. Behind the half-open door lay a ghastly thing with the top of its head missing. It took them some time to establish that it was Sasha Smirnoff. It looked as if he had put the pistol into the roof of his mouth and pulled the trigger.

Doctors will tell you that there is a place to which the mind retreats when the body is hurt badly, a place no doctor knows how to reach. They will tell you that most of those who go there never come back, for it is a place better than life itself. The smashed, the broken, the tortured go there. So, sometimes, do those tired of life for different reasons, past the unmarked point of no return. It is a strange and dreamy and wonderfully comforting place, not quite as far from life as death itself, but a long way past oblivion. The body remains minimally alive, the heart pulses, the nerves respond to stimuli. The mind, however, floats unrestricted by time or memory, across inconceivable boundaries of imagination.

Castle was there.

He felt safe and warm and cherished, caressed by sensual dreams, lit by the love in unknown eyes. Very, very rarely, true memory spilled into his brain like scalding water, and he remembered the blazing eye of the gun and the roaring in his ears and Sasha and something else important, and then he would retreat to the warmer safety of nothingness and the darkness beyond it. There was a girl in a boat on a river dappled with sunlight through willows, and her hair was as golden as buttercups. When he kissed her, he could taste honey and smell hay. He put her arms around her and her eyes looked up into his . . . brown eyes full of pain, liquid with agony, poor dog, poor old Pedro, who died by the side of the road, too old to dodge the clattering truck. The driver took him to the police station, and he carried the dog in his arms. He left the dead animal there in the yard behind the station, covered with a dustbin lid. He didn't cry, there was no point; it was his own grief, not theirs. It didn't matter if the policeman didn't understand. You can always get another one, son, the policeman said, answering the telephone that was ringing . . . bells ringing and ringing, a beautiful sound that remained in your memory long after you forgot the flowers on the Singel and the litter in the market at the Waterlooplein. He remembered the rainbow colors of the Vondelpark, and the baroque barrel organs playing Strauss waltzes, while the men chinked the money in the collection boxes in three-quarter time. The mist rose like smoke over the narrow canals where the houseboats lay and windmills stood tall and lonely in the fields, and there was an old man walking along the bank—the faceless man in Castle's dreams, the man in the uniform which had no insignia. He pursued the man across empty landscapes without trees or grass, mountains like the surface of the moon, swamps that turned to glutinous mud that gripped his body. Always the man in the dream moved relentlessly forward, and although Castle could not see his face, he knew that the man was smiling. He wanted to shout the man's name, and yet he was afraid because he knew that if the man turned and saw him, he would recognize Castle and kill him. So he hid behind a tree, one lone tree in the middle of the empty world, and waited until the tall, dark figure came level and went by. When he went past, Castle knew he had to do it now, now or never.

"*Verschwender!*" he shouted. "Who are you?"

The man turned, and his face was a rotting skull. Castle felt utter dread burst through every cell in his body, and he screamed silently in dreamed terror as he fell upward toward the light.

When he opened his eyes, a man in white was bending over him, making notes on a pad. The sunlight was harsh and bright through the unshaded windows, and he could hear the babble of Russian voices. Hospital? he thought. Why am I in a hospital?

"Well," the man in the white coat said in Russian. "How do you feel?"

"Sensational," Castle whispered, trying for a grin that wouldn't stick to his face. There was a nurse on the other side of the ward. She was a bit like . . . "Irina?" he said.

"Plenty of time for that," the doctor said, soothingly.

Castle tried to sit up, and agony swam like quicksilver through his belly. The blackness closed in again, but it was not the blackness of before. The door of the place beyond memory was closed. He slept.

When he opened his eyes again, the doctor was gone, and Cliff Parker was sitting on the chair at the side of his bed. He looked very uncomfortable, like a man bearing bad news.

"Parker?" Castle said. Cliff was a senior civil attaché at the Embassy, on the new Ambassador's staff.

"You're awake," Parker said.

"What day is this?"

"Tuesday. May fifteenth."

"My God, have I been out that long?"

"You were lucky," Parker said, although his voice said exactly the opposite. Castle knew the answer to the next question before he asked it, but he asked it anyway, awash with dread.

"She's dead," Parker said. "The man too."

"Suicide?"

"Seems that way."

"Oh, God," Castle said. "Why didn't they let me die?"

"We were hoping they would," Parker said grimly. "You're a considerable embarrassment to us, Castle."

"What?"

"You must realize how compromised you are by all this . . . business. Marye is asking for you to be repatriated as soon as you're well."

"Get out of here, you fucking jackal!" Castle said.

How could she be dead? His mind refused to accept that the sentience, the intelligence, the bright light of love in those deep brown eyes was extinguished forever. It simply could not be. Only a moment ago she was in my arms, only a moment ago, he thought. Just by closing his eyes, he could see her breasts lift beneath the thin cotton of a white blouse. He could see the long, sweet line of her throat, golden-brown from the sun. He could remember the softness of her rounded shoulder against his lips. And somewhere in an echoing empty room in his mind, he could hear someone saying the words "never again." That was what death was. Never again to touch her, never to hear her sigh, never to hold her tightly and feel the inner ache of loving her. Never again. He wished that he could cry, but they had trained all that out of him years ago. He was sentenced to life, remembering her.

George Marye, the Ambassador, came to see him. Marye was a San Franciscan, one of those work-ethic-oriented types whose motto was something along the lines of "what's good for business is good for America," and vice versa. Castle had been told that when Marye was presented to the Tsar, he had tried to "sell" that bewildered individual on the merits of American know-how. It had been, according to one eyewitness, like watching someone trying to explain electricity to a kangaroo. Marye sat by the bed with a face like a prune. Coldly and disapprovingly, he told Castle how disappointed he was. Disappointed, for Christ's sake, Castle thought.

"Things like this reflect upon us all," Marye said reprovingly, as if what had happened was infectious. "Damned bad for our image out here. I've got to go back in December, you know. I'd have had a clean sheet here if it hadn't been for this business. Damned shabby of you, Castle."

You've been dining with too many Englishmen, Castle thought. You're beginning to sound like one. He said nothing, waiting for Marye to finish.

"I want you to know I've put in a stiff protest to your people in State. Landis says you're to make a complete report as soon as you're on your feet."

"He'll get it," Castle said.

"Do you have any idea when you'll be out of here?"

"I didn't fall off a bicycle, you know."

"Well," Marye said, "Landis wants a full report. See that I get a copy, will you?"

He was a fussy, interfering fool with an inordinately high opinion of his own worth. Castle had always distrusted the American method of choosing an Ambassador from the ranks of those who could pay to be one. The British system was much better. Diplomacy was something to be carefully learned, not picked up while you were totaling your annual dividends.

"Sure," he said.

"I must be going," Marye said. "There's so much to do. I never seem to have any time. All these changes."

"Changes?"

"People don't realize how difficult it is. Do you realize that in my two years here, there have been three Prime Ministers—"

"Three?" Castle said.

"Haven't you heard? Boris Sturmer is to replace old Goremykin."

"No," Castle said. Another German, he thought, another of Streicher's protégés.

"Three Premiers," Marye went on, "five Ministers of the Interior, three War Ministers. The whole thing is crazy, crazy!"

Everyone was talking revolution, he said; he was glad he was getting out. Nobody had a clear picture of what was happening at the front, although they said the Germans had overrun Rumania. There were strikes everywhere, seventeen factories closed, and the troops did absolutely nothing to suppress them.

"Maybe Kitchener will liven things up," Marye said. "When he gets here."

"What?" Castle said, wincing as he tried to sit up too quickly. "What did you say?"

"It's very confidential," Marye said. "We just heard. The British are sending Kitchener out here to aid the Russian war effort. Assess what they need in the way of artillery, munitions, and so forth. Just the man for the job, I'd say."

Field Marshal Earl Kitchener of Khartoum was the British Secretary of State for War. Probably more than any other man, he personified the British will to victory, as Joffre did in France and Hindenburg in Germany. He had raised a million men by simply putting his face on a poster which starkly stated, "Your country needs you!" Of all the British strategists, Germany feared Kitchener most.

"When does he leave England?" Castle said. The urgency of his tone startled Marye.

"I—I don't know," Marye said. "I don't think anybody does. Here, what the devil do you think you're doing, man?"

"I'm getting up," Castle said, swinging his legs out of the bed. "I'm getting out of here." He stood up, and as he did he felt something slide slickly somewhere inside him. The room tilted, and he fell across the bed.

"Doctor!" Marye shouted. "Nurse! Come at once!"

In the swimming blackness that was trying to swallow him, Castle heard the clatter of their feet. He fought weakly as they lifted him back into the bed.

"Let me go, damn you! Marye, tell them to let me go! Listen to me!" He saw the hypodermic in the doctor's hand. "Don't let them put me under, Marye! Kitchener's in danger. You've got to listen to me!"

Marye nodded.

"Yes, yes," he said soothingly His eyes were on the doctor. Castle saw the doctor shake his head. "Just take it easy and you'll be fine."

"Listen to me!" Castle shouted. He tried to struggle against the restraining hands of the nurses. He had no strength at all.

"What is it?" Marye was asking the doctor. "Is he delirious?"

"*Nyet!*" the doctor said. "*Byezummay*. Crazy. Wiz grieve."

"Damn your thick Russian skull!" Castle shouted. "I'm not crazy with anything! Listen to me, Marye, you've got to get word to the British Embassy. Tell them—tell them Kitchener has got to change his plans." He felt the needle slide into his arm. "Listen to me, Marye, for God's sake!"

They were unfastening the dressings around his middle. The doctor gestured Marye away. I must have opened up the wound, Castle thought.

"Tell Kitchener," he gasped. There was a fuzzy edge on his sight. He had to tell Marye something, but his mind was blank. He could not remember what it was. Something about Kitchener. "Tell him to alter his route," he said. He did not know that his words were slurred, unrecognizable.

"Castle?" Marye said. He looked at the doctor. "What was he talking about?" The doctor shrugged, waving Marye back again.

"Petersburg Plan!" Castle shouted. He could hear their voices. They sounded as if they were in a box full of cotton wool. He tried to speak the name of the banker, Frederick Streicher, but the drug had already done its work. He fell away into soft darkness, dreaming.

He was lying on a bed; Irina was there. She was warm, and her skin was soft and faintly damp. They had made love. He yearned to touch her, and tried to turn on his side to do so. As he did there was a huge explosion, and he saw Sasha with a gun in his hand. There was a flicker of movement behind him—a shadow? He could not see clearly. He tried to tell Sasha, but then the flame grew out of the barrel of the pistol like a sudden yellow flower, and he was on the floor with his mouth full of blood. He looked up, and Sasha fired again. He looked up, and Sasha fired again. He looked up, and Sasha fired again. Castle awoke bathed in perspiration, breathing as if he had run a hundred yards.

Irina, he thought, my sweet Irina. The formless dreams came back, drifting through his mind like smoke. Could there have been a movement behind Sasha, that shadow that only his subconscious had seen? If there had, what was it, who? Ask no more questions of me or anyone else. And if I do? You will find you have made a fatal error of judgment. Streicher? Or the sinister German *Sonderabteilung*? Why? Why would they go to such lengths, why kill two innocent parties? To make it look the way people like Marye saw it: a shameful and sordid adultery and its inevitable outcome? Discrediting me into the bargain, Castle thought; Landis may still recall me. Yes, that would all fit. There must have been some kind of police inquiry, but it would probably have been no more than a formality. The facts were not in dispute. Mad with jealous rage, Smirnoff had tried to kill his wife's lover. He had either deliberately or accidentally killed his wife, and then, in a fit of remorse, turned the pistol upon himself. Case closed.

It was too pat, Castle decided, too easy.

"A telephone," he told the doctors. "I have to talk to the American Embassy."

They told him that Ambassador Marye had left strict orders that Castle was not to talk to anyone. No press, no photographers, no telephone calls, nothing. He was to be incommunicado until further notice. Castle raged at them for a while, and then he stopped. Anger directed against a Russian bureaucrat who has been given a direct order is as much use as throwing pebbles into the sea. You see the splash, but the sea does not change. He tried to tell them that it was a matter of maximum security. He might as well have been saying that it was Wednesday

"*Tyelefon, nyet!*" was all they would say. No letters, no telegrams, no messengers, nothing.

Some days later, on May 30, Parker came in. His face was grave. He told Castle that on the preceding Tuesday, the British cruiser *Hampshire* had been sunk in unknown circumstances off the Orkney Islands. No one knew what had happened. The official release stated that the ship had stuck a mine, but Admiralty intelligence indicated that German submarine activity in the area had been particularly heavy at the time the *Hampshire* sailed. On board the ship, en route to Russia, his departure from England cloaked in the most elaborate veil of security, had been Field Marshal Earl Kitchener of Khartoum. His body was never found.

It was a waste of time blaming anybody. He had been stupid and there was no room for that in his line of business, no room for sloppiness or delay. Most of all, there was no room for love. Love made you vulnerable, and vulnerability was what your enemies were seeking. Parker listened now. He took word to Michael Tereschenko, and Tereschenko saw to it that the ballistic tests Castle wanted done were carried out. As Castle had suspected, the bullets taken from his body did not match the ones taken from the bodies of Irina and Sasha. They had been killed by a gun or guns other than the one with which Sasha had shot the American.

In a way, it was ironic, Castle thought. If he had done what he now planned to do, Irina and Sasha would still be alive. But he had procrastinated because he wanted her, so she and Sasha had died. It was only by the grace of God that he wasn't dead himself. Well, he thought, I won't make the same mistake again.

There was no one he cared about in Russia anymore. Because of what had happened to Irina, he was freed of such considerations as guilt and innocence, the necessity of proof. He had nothing to think about but doing what he had to do. So he made his plans while his body mended. He ate all the food they brought him, did all the exercises that were prescribed for him and more. He was a model patient, and the doctors smiled at him as doctors always smile at patients who do what they are told. Castle smiled back, enjoying their self-deception. He wanted to be strong and fit when he got out of the hospital. Parker brought him the lists of the men who regularly attended Streicher's Wednesday *Stammtische*, and he studied them like Scripture. There was only one way to smash the Petersburg Plan and the men behind it: there had only ever been one way. He lay there and took his medicines and listened to the news about the war and waited. June passed, and then July. In the middle of September, they told him he could leave the hospital, and he smiled and thanked them for all they had done.

Three weeks later, he killed the first of the Germans.

Spring passed, summer came, and still Tatiana was swamped with work at the hospital. They were desperately short-staffed. It was no longer fashionable to nurse the wounded, although there were more now than ever. The fashionable thing was to pretend that the war simply did not exist, to dress for cocktails at the Astoria, to go on to all-night champagne parties with dashing young officers in no hurry at all to return to the carnage, or with "white-ticket" men who had bought or obtained exemption from military service. There were more than enough of those to go around.

The talk about the changes being made by the Tsaritsa now that the Tsar was spending all his time at Mogilyev, the new *Stavka* —at the instigation of the beastly *starets*, of course—meant little to Tatiana. She heard that faithful old Goremykin had been replaced as Prime Minister by Boris Sturmer, one of Rasputin's hangers-on, whose principal claim to fame seemed to be that one of his Austrian forebears had been a member of the guard on Napoleon at St. Helena. Another German, they said. The Alexander Palace is full of them; they're in direct touch with Berlin by short-wave radio, you know. Then Polivanov, the War Minister, was sacked. He had done wonders in the year he had held office after replacing the venal Sukhomlinov, but Rasputin didn't like him, so out he went. The Tsaritsa gave the post to General Shuvayev, an old fool whom they said would jump out of the first window Nicholas pointed to, so devoted was he to the Tsar.

Tatiana took little interest in all this. Her politics had been firmly shaped by her father, who had a soldier's attitude toward men who sought political office.

"The only thing you can ever rely on a politician to do," he used to say, "is lie. Not to change the world. Not to make people richer, better, happier. They are there to get reelected. They're venal and worthless to a man, and my opinion of them is this: the higher the office, the bigger the liar holding it."

Certainly the politicians controlling Russia's destiny this summer of 1916 seemed to be everything her father said, but Tatiana felt no sense of involvement with the events in Petrograd. She was still working a sixteen-hour day alongside Dr. Marutinsky, looking after the wounded men who still came, trainload after trainload of them, as if there were some obscene conveyor belt somewhere, spilling them out endlessly. All the young officers said the same thing: the war was going badly and it was getting worse. The Tsar was no general, and none of the generals were any better. The Tsar took his advice from *Nemka*, who was told what to do by Rasputin. Bad enough to fight the Germans in the trenches, they said, without having to fight them in the royal palace as well.

As for the Tsaritsa herself, she no longer came to the hospitals she had so lovingly established. Instead, she spent more and more of her time cloistered in the Alexander Palace with Vyrubova and the hated *starets*. The gossip about them had always been contemptuous; now it was positively virulent.

"You see, she was only playing at being the gracious sister of mercy. Now that the going is getting hard, she has gone back to her lover and left the dirty work to us."

"*Nemka* cares more for that smelly goat than she does for the men who are dying in order that she may remain on her throne."

"They should get rid of her, shut her up in a convent, where she can't do as she pleases."

"Away with the German woman!" they said, echoing the crowds who had demonstrated in the Red Square in Moscow, demanding that the Tsar be deposed, Rasputin hanged, and the Grand Duke Nikolai crowned as the new Tsar.

Nobody cared about anything anymore, they said. Life was the same as it had always been for the rich, for those who did not choose to care about the war. Society went to the Maryinsky to see Karsavina dance *Sylvia* and *The Water Lily*. Fyodr Chaliapin sang *Boris Godunov* and *Don Quixote* at the Narodny Dom. There were parties as glittering, perhaps even more glittering, than the ones held before the war, while ordinary people could not get enough bread or salt or sugar or meat. It required four thousand railroad cars of supplies a day to feed the people of Petrograd; fewer than three were being delivered. Meat was three and a half times its prewar price, butter and flour two and a half times more. Inflation had halved the value of earnings; rents had gone up as much as three hundred percent. Couldn't the rich understand how poor people must feel, how their folly must look to battle-wrecked soldiers?

"Why do they do it? she asked Dr. Marutinsky one day. "Why does the Tsaritsa permit it?"

"I can't answer you, child," Marutinsky said. "I can only ask you a question in return. If she cares so much for Russia, why does she tolerate the presence of that drunken pig Rasputin? Everyone says he is seen with German spies, even those prepared to believe that he is not a spy himself. Yet the Tsaritsa will hear no ill of him, and anyone who criticizes him is removed from Petrograd. You tell me why."

"I don't know," she said.

"Do you know what people are saying?" Marutinsky said, darkly. "They are saying that all the generals are traitors, otherwise Russian soldiers would have been in Berlin already. They are saying they will sit quietly until the war is over. And then, they are saying, accounts will be settled."

Tatiana shivered. She could think of no answer. If someone with such infinite compassion and humanity as Dr. Marutinsky felt as he did about the Tsaritsa, what did her enemies—and they were many now—think? She was still in this mood when Kolya Bakhronshin's letter found her, and she seized upon the invitation it contained with an almost feverish enthusiasm.

My father died in August, and I was given leave to arrange things at home. As a result, I have much more news of Moscow than might otherwise have been the case. Hatred of the Tsar and his entire regime is very high here. I have heard officers talking openly of assassinating him. They will bomb his car or crash a plane on him, anything to be rid of his awful misdirection of the war effort. They say, not humorously, that since he assumed command, things have gone from worse to impossible. My mother, who is friendly with the Tsar's sister, the Grand Duchess Elizabeth, says that Elizabeth went to Petrograd from Moscow to talk to the Tsaritsa about Rasputin. She told my mother that the Tsaritsa would not listen to her, that everything she said about Rasputin was lies, and that when she persisted, the Tsaritsa simply refused to talk to her anymore and had Elizabeth taken back to the station in her carriage. Her own sister-in-law! Surely, the woman is beyond redemption!

There have been many changes here. Sergei Tretyakov is back home. He was wounded during the Brusilov offensive and invalided out. He and Katrina are living at Sokolnika. The hospital at Telegin was closed down because they couldn't get enough nurses, and the few that were left went to Sokolnika with Katrina. You can imagine what things are like, Tatiana. Nurses are impossible to find, especially nurses with any kind of training at all. Instead of wasting all your time at Tsarskoe Selo looking after those pampered babies, why don't you come to Moscow and do some real war work, where it would be a hundred times more useful and infinitely more rewarding? It would do you good to get away from that hothouse. I am still convinced that if there is an explosion, it will happen in Petrograd.

Katrina sends you her love and adds her entreaties to mine that you come, and come at once. So, too, does Maria. I hope you will be happy to know that I have asked Maria to marry me and she has accepted. We will wait until the war is over before we actually "tie the knot." I am due to leave soon for the Eastern front, and I have been making all my good-bye calls. The Smirnoffs have taken some hard blows this year. As you probably know, Pierre's son Sasha and his wife died very tragically in the spring. They don't talk about it, but one gets the impression that whatever happened, it was unpleasant. To crown it all, the old lady, Genya, died a month later—of a broken heart, according to Maria. Still, life goes on. Pierre is always madly busy with his war committee work, hardly ever at home. Nico runs the business. Now that the ban on selling vodka has been lifted, they are producing what they can. Of course, it's almost impossible to get skilled workers. As fast as they train new ones, they are called up for military service. I went over to see Vladimir at Telegin. He still has twenty or so horses that were kept on a farm while the place was being used as a hospital. He says he's going to go back to breeding horses and drinking whisky, that nobody else gives a damn about the war, so why should he? He's just disillusioned, like all of us.

Now, think carefully about what I have said, dearest Tatiana. In Petrograd you are useful. In Moscow, you would be invaluable. Please give my warmest good wishes to your parents, and ask your mother to remember me to Vanya when she writes. And of course, I send you my fondest love, as does everyone here.

"I don't want to—"

"—seem disloyal, I know," Dr. Marutinsky said, when she told him. "Do you think that either I or Dr. Derevenko would think you disloyal if you decide to nurse soldiers in Moscow rather than in Petrograd? Do you think that even Her Majesty would deny you?"

He did not add what he suspected, which was that the Tsaritsa would not give a damn one way or the other. Now that the Tsar was spending all his time at Mogilyev, the Tsaritsa and the filthy *starets* were running the country. He had heard there had been attempts on Rasputin's life, but that they had failed. He wished they'd send the bastard down here. It would be an honor to cut out his black heart.

"I think Dr. Marutinsky is right," Maryka said to her daughter. "I think you should go." She did not tell her why: she would know that, soon enough. "I'm sure Papa agrees with me, don't you, Alex?"

"What's that?" Alex said, irritably. "What are you on about now?"

"Tatiana is going to Moscow, Alex," Maryka said. "To work in a hospital with Katrina Smirnova."

"Smirnoffs, eh?" Alex said. "That what you want to do, daughter?" It seemed to Tatiana that there was more to his question than the words which framed it. His eyes were soft and sad, and Maryka had to look away. They had seen all the doctors, and the doctors had all said the same thing. It was just a question of time.

"Like that, is it?" Alex had said. "Always thought I'd die on a battlefield, somehow. Funny, really."

It wasn't funny, but his bravery made her weep. She could already see the first hints of the frailty to come. He slept only a little at nights, and his appetite was like a sparrow's. He spent most of the day reading, or sitting by the window looking out at the Tavrichevski Gardens, where there was a little carousel and slides for the

335

children. He liked Maryka to read from the newspapers and magazines to which they still subscribed, and she made a point of marking those passages which she knew would be of interest to him. Strangely, Maryka felt closer to Alex now than she had done for years, and their lonely life did not make her feel at all lonely. They ate together every day, their frugal meals prepared by the ever-loyal Ivan Pavlovich. Alex could no longer afford to pay his salary, and told Ivan he must feel free to find himself another place if he could. Ivan Pavlovich told them there was nowhere on earth he would rather be than with them. All the other servants were gone. With plenty of time on her hands, Maryka found herself corresponding regularly with her daughter-in-law Nikitina, who sent her all the news of Vanya and the children. They were in Kronstadt now. Vanya was an officer aboard the cruiser *Aurora*, commanded by Captain Mikhail Nikolsky. She knitted socks and scarves which she gave to the Red Cross to be sent to soldiers at the front. She often wondered whether they ever gave a thought to who had sent them.

"I . . . I'd like to go, Papa," Tatiana said. "But I don't want to leave you and Mama."

"Tush, child," he said. "We managed for a number of years without you. Manage a few more, shouldn't be surprised, eh, mother?"

"Yes, Alex," Maryka said.

"There, then," Alex said. "That's settled." He leaned back in his chair like a man who has made a difficult decision, and in a few moments he was dozing.

"Well," Maryka said, "you don't have to go right away, do you?"

"No, of course not. I'd like to stay awhile. It's nice to be home. Like the old days."

The old days, Maryka thought. There would never be any days like the old days ever again.

"Yes," she said brightly. "Come, let's make supper."

24

I DON'T BELIEVE IT," Viktor Guchkov said.

Kurasov just smirked at him. For some reason he was enjoying this, and it took Guchkov a few minutes to realize why. It was proof to Kurasov that the great Viktor Guchkov had failed. *Gospodin Palatch* was not dead, as they had surmised a year earlier. He must have been away somewhere, Guchkov thought, and in the same moment made a mental note to send out a tracer to all the *gubernaya* asking for details of any murder case which might have been in the style of the Moscow killer.

"When did it happen?" he asked now.

"Last night, by all accounts. The girl was found in a ditch by the road to Yaroslavl, about ten versts outside the city. The police surgeon says she had been carried there. Murdered somewhere else."

"You've read the report?"

"Good Heavens, no," Kurasov said.

He looked older and more tired than he had the last time Guchkov had seen him. Times were difficult. There had been so many changes of ministerial posts that the senior civil servants were rapidly losing control of their own ministries. Every time a system was put into operation, there would be a change at the top and the orders would be countermanded, new ones substituted. Everyone was weeks behind with his paperwork, and the police department was becoming more and more mired down by the number of arrests they were making on the 'streets—deserters, strikers, looters, thieves. The incidence of murder was very high. More than twice as many people had died violently in Moscow during 1916 as in the preceding year, and here it was only September.

"Guchkov, we can't have a repeat performance of this man's madnesses," Kurasov said. "He must be found, and quickly."

337

"Can I have some help?"

"There is no one I can spare."

Guchkov thought of young Piotr Bunin. He had been killed during the Galician compaign, one more of the millions of Russian boys who had laid down their lives in that futile, bloody series of defeats.

"All right," Guchkov said. "I'll do what I can."

He got the police report and sat down with it. The details were stark and awful. The girl's name was Petra Malevska. She had left her home at about half past five on the afternoon of July 23, on her way to see her grandmother, who lived on the northern edge of the Khapilovski Pond. She left there at seven-fifty, cycling back toward her parents' home in the Lefortovskaya. Her route took her past the old German cemetery where, somewhere around eight that night, passersby had heard screams. All of them had assumed it was just kids playing and had taken no notice. At eleven o'clock, Petra's worried parents sent her brother to fetch her home. His grandmother told him that his sister had left shortly after seven-thirty, and he hurried back home. On the way, he saw some children playing with a bicycle. He recognized it as his sister's, and they told him they had found it in an alleyway. The front wheel was badly buckled. The police were informed, and the next day one of Petra's shoes was found in the cemetery. Nothing more had been heard of her until her body was discovered in the ditch beside the Yaroslavl road. She was lying face down, naked. The policeman who turned her over fainted on the spot.

"Same type of wounds, same everything," Guchkov muttered. He wished he had Piotr to talk to. He sent for all the files, the thick, all-too-familiar files on the deaths of Irinia Kaminsky, Zoya Terzakova, Lara Lazareva, Anna Starovna, Valentina Tereshkova, Natasha Albedinski, Maya Levasova and the two that Gospodin Palatch had killed within an hour of each other that June night a year ago. He read again the notes he and Bunin had made, the reports of the police surgeons and the pathologists, the vast, inconclusive entirety of it.

They had never closed the case. Murder cases always remained open until the perpetrator had been found and dealt with. In the case of this killer, the murders had simply stopped. Bunin had suggested the possibility that the man had killed himself; it was well within the psychological pattern of such murderers to do so. Guchkov somehow felt that the man's final farewell letter had been the truth, and that Citizen Butcher was indeed leaving Moscow.

338

Well, he was back with a bloody vengeance, Guchkov thought. Where had he been? The man might have gone into the services—but there were fifteen million men under arms in the Russian Army, a number impossible to check out.

I played your game before, killer, he thought. Not this time. He asked for and received permission to prevent any mention of the murder appearing in the newspapers. A blanket of security was placed over the entire case. No one was allowed to investigate any aspect of it without first seeing Guchkov.

"I want that bastard to sweat," Guchkov said. "I want him to think he has been wasting his time, and that we haven't found the girl's body. Put a five-man rotating guard where the body was found. Anyone who even comes near the place is to be held for questioning by me."

Three days went by, four, five, and nothing happened, Then on the sixth day, one of the uniformed desk sergeants came up from the offices below with a letter which had been handed in at the inquiries desk. Guchkov took one look at it and was out of the door like a sprinter, taking the stairs three at a time as he hurtled down to the ground floor. He rushed across to the desk, waving the letter in his hand.

"The man who gave you this letter!" he shouted. "Where is he?"

"The—which—oh, he left, sir. About ten minutes ago."

"God damn him!" Guchkov shouted, rushing to the door. The street outside was crowded with people. There was no point in pursuit. Guchkov came slowly back into the building and stopped to talk to the sergeant who had taken delivery of the letter.

"Did you see the man who brought this letter in?" he asked.

"Yes, sir," the sergeant said. "A gentleman, sir."

"Could you describe him?"

"Well," the policeman said, pursing his lips, "I didn't really take all that much notice, sir."

"Do your best."

"Tall, I'd say," the sergeant said, squinting up at the ceiling. "A good-looking fellow, well dressed. Dark suit."

"Not a uniform?" Guchkov said, sharply.

"No, sir, a suit."

"Anything else?"

"I don't think so, sir."

"Age?"

"About thirty, maybe thirty-five."

"Beard, moustache?"

"Moustache, sir. No beard."

"About five nine, five ten?"

"That's right, sir. I take it you know the gentleman?"

"Yes," Guchkov said, slowly. "I believe I do."

He went back upstairs and opened the letter with its familiar capitalized scrawl. It was from Gospodin Palatch.

Well, Guchkov, you tried to fool me. However, the policemen you had on guard aren't as smart as you. They'll all talk for a couple of rubles. The girl was no use—too young. I'll need another before long. To show you how stupid your people are, I am going to deliver this by hand. Glad to know you're still around. I hear that Bunin's dead. Till next time, then.

Guchkov stifled a curse. Petra Malevska had been just a few months over fifteen years of age, and for this sadistic lunatic to make a joke of it was almost more than he could bear. He controlled his temper. It might well be that his quarry had outsmarted himself this time. The note he had delivered so neatly sealed in its envelope had not, like all the others in the files, been handled by a dozen others before it got to Guchkov. He hurried to the laboratory and prepared the various chemicals he was going to need. An hour later, he emerged with a smile on his face. Across the top left-hand side of the letter was a clear set of three prints: a thumb, and the first two fingers of a man's left hand.

"Well, you bastard," he said, "you're one step nearer the grave."

He picked up the phone and spoke to the dispatch clerk in the main building, asking whether there had been any replies to the tracers he had sent out.

"Nothing yet, sir," the clerk said. "Of course, you realize that with things the way they are, it may take weeks for some of this stuff to get through to us."

It better hadn't, Guchkov thought. Gospodin Palatch wasn't going to wait that long.

340

25

By MID-AFTERNOON the blizzard had eased a little, and for a short while it stopped snowing. Even so, the wind had an edge like an open razor as Frederick Streicher got into the *troika*. Damned snow, he thought, nothing but one blizzard after another all month. He pulled the fur rugs over himself and told the driver to hurry. He had no desire to keep the cold-eyed man who controlled his destiny waiting. There were long lines of shivering women outside the bakeries and food stores, their faces without hope. The sky was the color of lead, as if the end of the world was coming. A mood of profound gloom seemed to permeate the entire city. Streicher shivered beneath the thick bearskin rugs and his warm Crombie overcoat.

He was admitted to the house on the Catherine Canal by an expressionless footman and shown into the library. There was a huge fire blazing in the fireplace; the house was almost oppressively warm after the sharp cold outside. Streicher permitted himself a knowing smile. Electricity might be rationed, wood and coal almost unobtainable, but there were always supplies available if you had enough money.

"Sit down, Streicher," his host said, abruptly. "I haven't much time." Damn the man, Streicher thought, as he sat down. At least he could get up and shake my hand. He allowed his anger to show on his face, but the man opposite him took not the slightest notice of it.

"Well, what's so urgent?" he said.

"Ivan is dead."

"Your man?"

"That's right," Streicher said. "He was found on the railway lines outside the Nicholas Station. The police are treating it as suicide."

There was no immediate reply from the man in the leather chair opposite him. Streicher needed none. He knew what the man was thinking. Since October, five of their organization had died; each of the deaths had apparently been an accident or random violence. There was no coincidence about it, both men were sure.

"The American again?"

"It must be," Streicher said. "Who else could it be?"

"He can't know. He can't possibly know!"

"He has guessed, he knows, he doesn't know—what difference does it make?" Streicher said, hoping his fear was not too obvious. "He's killing our people one by one, and you're not doing anything about it!"

"First we must catch our rabbit, Streicher," the banker's host reminded him. "A task at which you have proven singularly unsuccessful."

"Nobody knows where he is. The Embassy people don't even know. He's just disappeared."

"It is not possible to disappear in Russia, Streicher."

"It's not possible to murder people and get away with it, either, but this devil is doing it."

There was another silence. Streicher could stand it no longer.

"Well?" he said. "What are you going to do?"

"Nothing. Not a damned thing. Castle is your responsibility. He doesn't even know that I exist."

"You're going to just sit there and let that—that *assassin* pick us off, one by one?"

"It doesn't matter anymore, Streicher," the man said. "Nothing matters except the task I set out to accomplish. And I am too near victory to be frightened off. Petrograd is a powderkeg waiting for a match, Streicher."

He was right, Streicher thought; it was ready to blow up. People talked of the coming revolution as matter-of-factly as if discussing when it would snow again. There had been riots in October. Police trying to disperse a crowd of strikers had been fired upon by the very soldiers supposed to protect them. There had been riots in Moscow too, it was said, although there was nothing about it in the newspapers. Nothing about the hundred and fifty soldiers executed after the October incident, either; the censors saw to that. Not even the censors could stop people talking, though, or stop the soldiers telling them what was going on. There were thousands and thousands of them in the city, wandering aimlessly about, waiting to be shipped to the front. There weren't enough trains to carry them; the railway systems were in chaos. That was why there was no bread, no food, no kerosene, no salt. Everything came to Petrograd by train, and there were no trains. Just as well, the soldiers said. We haven't got any rifles anyway, and even if we had rifles, we have no bullets to shoot from them. And even if there were enough bullets, who wants to be shipped to the front, to freeze in the trenches to keep Bloody Nicholas on his throne? The Tsar has lost control, they told people. He sits in his train all day at Mogilyev playing dominoes, while *Nemka* and Rasputin fornicate in the Alexander Palace. Everyone was reading *samizdat* copies of a speech made by Pavel Milyukov, leveling charge after charge against the inept government, asking after each, "What is this: stupidity or treason?" Treason, said the people. The workers on strike who mingled with the thousands of deserters from the front told one another that if something wasn't done soon, they would have to take things into their own hands. It was no longer resentment which was leveled at the aristocrats; it was undisguised hatred.

"We are ready now," the man told Streicher. "We have Sturmer in our hands, not to mention that syphilitic old fool Protopopov. The Army is in disarray, the Tsar is powerless. The whole thing is like a house of cards, and tonight I propose to begin its collapse."

"Tonight?" Streicher said. "What happens tonight?"

"I'm going to kill Rasputin."

Streicher allowed himself the luxury of a doubting smile. "You sound sure of yourself. But then, you did last time."

"I made the mistake of leaving the matter to others," the man opposite him snapped. He was touchy about criticism. Streicher had noticed that before.

"Let me put your mind at rest, Streicher. Rasputin is to be killed tonight. It's all over town. Purishkevich has teamed up with Grand Duke Dmitry and Felix Yusupov."

Streicher laughed out loud. "That little *Teilsauger*? You expect him and that precious Dmitry to kill Rasputin?"

"Not really," came the urbane reply. "That doesn't matter. What matters is that they go ahead. I shall see to the rest."

"But why? What's the point of killing Rasputin?"

"Without Rasputin, the Tsaritsa is finished. Without Alexandra, Nicholas is useless. The monarchy will collapse in days, weeks. The exiled revolutionary leaders will then be sent back to Petrograd, with special immunity to cross Germany. They have made an agreement with the *Sonderabteilung* through Fritz Platten in Zurich. In return for this help, and the sum of five million marks, they will sue for a separate peace with Germany as soon as they gain power. The Petersburg Plan will be complete."

"You mean Lenin, Zinoviev, that crowd?"

"All of them."

"You trust them?"

"Why not?"

"They may well turn out to be more treacherous than Nicholas."

"It will not matter a damn to me, Streicher. I'll be out of Russia long before then."

"You're leaving?"

"As soon as I hear that train is on its way."

"What about your wife?"

He was favored with a basilisk stare that, as always, unnerved him. He'd heard the talk, of course. They said that was why the wife had turned to the grimy clutches of Rasputin.

"Where will you go?" he asked.

"Somewhere where it never snows," was the reply. Streicher waited, but there was to be no further information.

"What happens to us?" he asked. "We who helped you?"

"You've all been well paid for your various treacheries," the man said. "What you do now is entirely up to you."

"What happens if things don't go as you plan?"

"You may be assured that they will," was the confident reply. He allowed not the slightest expression on his face. He did not want Streicher to start thinking too deeply about his reasons for wanting Rasputin dead. It might just occur to the fat man that he and the *starets* were the only two men in Petrograd who could link him to the *Sonderabteilung*. He got up from his chair and smiled at the banker. Streicher had been useful, but his usefulness was at an end. He would have to be killed, he and the American. Well, all that would be taken care of before he left.

"So, Frederick," he said, putting a friendliness into his voice that he was far from feeling. "It's time for us to say goodbye to each other. We will not meet again."

Streicher got up heavily. For reasons he could not adequately identify, he felt uneasy, as if ghostly fingers had touched the nape of his neck. He was being abandoned to the American, the lunatic who was killing, one by one, every man who had helped this cold and ruthless man. Well, he thought, I'll have to do it myself. There were ways. In Russia there were always ways.

"I suppose I ought to wish you luck," he said. "For tonight."

"Why not?"

"*Ach*," Frederick Streicher said. "It's a dirty business."

"It always was," said Fritz Sukhotin, and closed the door.

Rasputin sat silently. His eyes were hooded, glazed. He had drunk a great deal of madeira before coming to the Yusupov palace. He drank more of the drugged wine they had prepared. Yusupov put his hand on the *starets'* thigh, stroking upward.

"No, no," Rasputin mumbled. His voice was slurred. "Play me something, *malchik*."

Yusupov picked up his guitar and began to play softly. His face was flushed as he sang the love song to Rasputin. His eyes were soulful, moist with passion. His whole body trembled with the idea of being in the rough embrace of this great, bearded *mouzhik*. Dmitry would be green.

He had gone to a great deal of trouble to arrange the rendezvous, even to completely redecorating the room in which they planned to kill Rasputin. It had originally been a wine cellar, but he had turned it into something not far short of a harem. The room was divided by a low arch, one section of which was quite large, the other smaller and more intimate. The smaller room had a doorway beyond which was a spiral staircase leading to the courtyard. The drapes were red damask, the furniture heavy: carved antique chairs and many small tables draped with brightly colored shawls on which stood *objets d'art* from Italy, Turkey, the Far East. There were several tiny black cupboards, each an intricate maze of drawers, specially purchased for the Yusupovs in China. On top of one of these was a crucifix of rock crystal and silver from Florence. A huge red granite fireplace dominated the room. There were Persian carpets on the floor, and cushions and harem pillows scattered everywhere. In front of the fire lay a huge polar bear skin. It was on this pelt that Felix Yusupov now lolled, singing his gypsy songs, while Rasputin nodded dully in appreciation.

After a while Yusupov stopped playing and moved closer to Rasputin, stroking his hands, his face.

"Don't you want me, Grigory?" he whispered. "Other men desire me. Other men love my soft body."

"I am not as other men," Rasputin mumbled.

"You are," Yusupov breathed, touching him. He was huge. "You see? You are!" His laugh was girlish, triumphant.

"No," Rasputin groaned, but he did not push away the hand. Yusupov bent over him, soft mouth wet, pushing Rasputin back onto the cushions.

The first thing Rasputin said afterward was, "God forgive me." Then he looked at Yusupov.

"I am finished. The Light has been taken away from me."

"Then perhaps you'd better say a prayer," Yusupov said, gesturing toward the crucifix on top of the little cupboard. Rasputin looked at it blearily and got up, fastening his clothes. He lurched across the room. How does he drink so much and stay upright? Yusupov wondered, reaching under the embroidered pillow for the pistol he had hidden there. He watched Rasputin fall on his knees before the crucifix, and he thought, *you ghastly, dirty, filthy animal,* and he shot the *starets* in the center of the back. Rasputin roared in agony and fell across one of the small tables, shattering it. The shot was the signal for the others. They came in, naked, all of them. Dmitry put the lights out as they did. Only the flickering flame of the huge fire illuminated the room, like some scene from Dante. They ripped off the velvet trousers and descended on the body, shouting obscenely, faces like demons. They were all drunk, drunk with fear, passion, alcohol, desire. Someone had a knife, a fine-honed butcher knife from the Yusupov kitchen. They carved away at the supine body and then tossed what they had cut off across the room, laughing insanely.

Rasputin was not dead. Perhaps the terrible shock of the butchery of his body brought him back to consciousness, perhaps that incredible vitality for which he was renowned. His eyes opened. He gave a formless shout and grabbed at Yusupov.

"Felix!" he shouted. "Felix! Felix!"

Yusupov's eyes started from his head in sheer terror, and he screamed like a woman. He pulled free of Rasputin's clutching hands and, grabbing the first thing he could reach, battered away at the *starets'* face and head. It was the Florentine crucifix. He beat it against Rasputin's skull again and again and again. It made a soft, dull, wet sound. He was sobbing like a baby when the others pulled him away, aghast at what he had done. Rasputin's face was smashed in at the temple and the left cheek was a pulped mask of flesh in which one dangling eyeball hung obscenely, held by a slender thread of flesh. Blood matted his hair and beard.

"Jesus Christ Almighty!" Vladimir Purishkevich said, his voice awed by what they had done. "Dmitry, give me a hand. Help me get Felix upstairs. We've got to get this blood off us. Lazavert, come on, now! Come on, all of you!"

They left the bloody body where it lay and hurried up to Yusupov's study on the floor above. There in the bathroom they washed away the blood on their bodies and put on the clothes they had left there.

"Get him out of here!" Felix was sobbing. "Get that thing out of here!"

Their plan was simple. They would bundle up the corpse and tie weights to it, then drop it off the Petrovski Bridge, just above where the Malaya Nevka joined the Gulf of Finland. Once below the ice, it would be swept out to sea. They were going over the details again when Purishkevich heard something.

"What was that?" he said. He was a bald, bearded little man. His pince-nez glinted as he cocked his head to listen.

"It's your nerves, Vladimir," Stanislas Lazavert said, smiling. He was a doctor. It was he who had supplied the drugs with which Yusupov had stupefied Rasputin. A door opened. They all heard it. Vladimir Purishkevich jerked open the door of Yusupov's study.

"Sweet scented Jesus!" he shouted. "He's still alive!"

Somehow, incredibly, Rasputin had crawled up the stairs from the cellar to ground level and managed to open the door leading into the snow-covered courtyard. Fifteen yards ahead of him was the open gate leading to the street. He was dead on his feet, but he was moving.

"Get out of the way!" Sukhotin shouted to Purishkevich, who was standing in front of him. He pulled out a pistol. It was a big Savage revolver. He fired at Rasputin, but the *starets* kept going. They could hear him muttering one word, "Felix," over and over and over. Sukhotin fired again, and this time they saw Rasputin's body jerk as the heavy slug tore into him. Again the revolver boomed, and they saw blood and skin flayed from the bent back. Rasputin went down in the drifted snow, and Sukhotin thrust the pistol into Purishkevich's hand.

"Get down there and finish him off!" he snapped. They watched as Purishkevich ran down the stone steps. He fired into the *starets'* body from a range of about six feet. Now they could hear shouts, the sound of running feet out in the street. Far off, a police whistle wailed.

"Get out there!" Dmitry shouted in panic to Purishkevich. "Don't let anyone in here!" The last thing they wanted now was police in the bloodstained courtyard. Purishkevich was well known; they'd take orders from him. After a few minutes, the politician came back into the yard. He had two soldiers with him.

"I told them we've killed Rasputin!" he panted.

"You damned imbecile!" the Grand Duke Dmitry shouted. "Are you insane?"

"Your Excellency, we're Russian soldiers," one of the two men said. From the shadows into which he had retreated, Sukhotin saw that they were artillerymen. "Have no fear of us."

"Give us a hand, then," Purishkevich said. "We've got to get the body inside before the police come around asking questions. And someone turn that snow over; cover the blood."

"I'll do that," Sukhotin said, hurrying past the soldiers with his head averted. Neither of them so much as looked at him. They carried Rasputin's body back into the entrance hall. Purishkevich went to find Yusupov. He was in the lavatory, vomiting violently.

"Don't worry anymore," Purishkevich said. "He's really dead this time."

"Felix," Yusupov muttered. "Felix, Felix, *Felix!*"

He fell on the bloody body, battering at it with his fists, sobbing. They pulled him away, and Purishkevich told Lazavert to give him something to make him sleep. The doctor led Felix away; he went like a lamb.

"All right," Purishkevich said when Felix was gone. "We'll have to change the plan slightly. Dmitry, take Rasputin's hat and coat; put them on. Get Fritz to drive you back to Gorokhovaya so we can say that he went home. Then take my car to my house. Get a taxi to your house; come back here in your car. Understood?"

"Yes," Dmitry said. He was a good-looking boy, Purishkevich thought. Perhaps they could have dinner one evening, after all this was over.

They were back an hour later. They rolled Rasputin's body into a tarpaulin, together with his coat and hat and boots. Dmitry drove, with Purishkevich sitting next to him up front. Sukhotin sat in the back, his feet on Rasputin's body. He was smiling slightly. Dmitry accelerated down the straight Petrovski Prospect and took the right turn into the Topolnaya on two wheels. Ahead of them was the Petrovski Bridge. The area was silent, empty, white, bitterly cold. Purishkevich and Dmitry carried the body to the edge and dropped it where there was a gap in the ice. Sukhotin threw the clothes and the boots over after it.

"Come on, come on," Dmitry said, as Purishkevich came hurrying back to the car through the snow, breathing heavily. "Let's get out of here."

Neither of them noticed that one of Rasputin's boots lay on the solid, unmoving ice.

26

THEY SAID all Petrograd was in a ferment over the murder of Rasputin. The Tsar had ordered General Grigoryev, Chief of Petrograd Police, to put every man he could spare on the case, and to personally oversee the investigation. Investigation, Guchkov thought, with a snort. What investigation they needed to make he could not for the life of him imagine, when Yusupov and the Grand Duke Dmitry were openly admitting their part in the homicide, and Purishkevich was boasting all over the city of having administered the coup de grace.

The body of the *starets* was brought up from the Nevka by divers soon after a patrolling policeman noticed a bloodstained boot lying on the ice below the Petrovski Bridge. Maria Rasputin identified the body of her father. The police report said that even after all the injuries inflicted upon him, Rasputin had still been alive when the conspirators threw him into the river. There were raw, deep marks on his wrists which indicated that he had struggled to free himself from the ropes with which they had bound him. His right hand lay across his breast, middle finger bent in the sign of the cross, as if giving blessing.

I'm glad I didn't get involved in that one, anyway, Guchkov thought. He had no taste for politically sensitive affairs like the Rasputin murder. Too many tender toes, too many fingers in the pie. He wished they would give him half as many men as they'd told Grigoryev to use, just the same. With that kind of manpower, he would have solved the Gospodin Palatch case long before this. He sighed and looked out at the bleak January sky, then turned to the pile of dossiers in front of him. The tracers he had sent out to the fifty-nine *gubernaya* had yielded only four replies. He hadn't even bothered to do more than flick through the three from Tambov, Samara, and Orel. The Chief of Police in Vitebsk had sent him a report on his investigation of five murders, all young girls, which had occurred in the district town of Orsha, a pretty little town straggling along both sides of the Dnieper, with a mainly Jewish population of some twenty-one thousand souls. It was unquestionably the work of Gospodin Palatch. Guchkov only had to read the first autopsy report to be sure it was so. The dates fitted together nicely as well. The murders had all occurred between June 1915 and September 1916, the period in which the killer had disappeared from Moscow. What interested Guchkov particularly was not the murders themselves, although, God knew, they were as awful as the ones that had happened in Moscow, or even the fact that Grimbikov, like himself, had been unable to find the killer. What interested Guchkov about the Orsha murders was the very fact that they had taken place in that small provincial town. For Orsha lay in a triangle at whose three corners lay Vitebsk, Smolensk and Mogilyev. And Mogilyev, as any fool knew, was where the Headquarters of the Army had been and still was. Ergo, the murderer was a soldier, probably an officer, who had been stationed at *Stavka* between June 1915 and September 1916, or possibly a month or two earlier, since the last murder in Orsha had taken place in June.

Between September 1916 and Christmas, Gospodin Palatch struck twice more. Almost impatiently, Guchkov delegated the investigation to his new assistant, Fyodr Malev. Malev was a dour, unsmiling man, a plodder. Guchkov expected no flashes of insight from the man, nor did he receive any. Malev did what he was told, to the letter, no more and no less. He was short, inclined to overweight, with heavy black eyebrows over brown eyes that could swim with wounded self-pity when Guchkov turned on him angrily, as he perhaps too often did, for not thinking as fast on his feet as Piotr Bunin had in the old days. Ah, the old days, Guchkov thought. The way things were going, there wouldn't be any old days for those alive today to remember. He saw the dwindling power of the police and the growing hatred of all forms of law enforcement by the increasing number of strikers and deserters on the streets. One of these days there is going to be an explosion, he thought. They will expect the police to contain it, as they always have, by calling upon the troops to help. That was all right in the old days, but the crack regiments of yore were not manned now by the scions of noble families, the rigidly educated and totally disciplined graduates of the Corps of Pages. The Preobrazhensky and the Volkonsky and the Litovsky regiments consisted now of peasant boys from the *izbas* of

Siberia, and the only tradition they understood was the tradition of staying alive. Well, he thought, with another sigh, that's thankfully also not my problem.

His problem was simply a long, arduous and uninteresting plod through the records of the Adjutant-General's records of officer postings to and from the *Stavka*. There were hundreds and hundreds of names, of course, and each of them had to be checked. Where had they come from, and where had they gone? One by one by one, he religiously checked them out, crossing off name after unconnected name. He looked at the calendar on the wall. January twenty-first, he thought. Give it another month, and I'll be able to begin interviewing. Maybe the weather will have improved a little by then, he thought. Some of the men on the list lived a long way outside the city. He looked at the sheaf of paper in front of him. Seventeen names. Seventeen men who had been in Moscow between July 1913, when Irinia Kaminsky was murdered, and June 1914, when Gospodin Palatch conducted the bloody saturnalia in the apartment of the woman Pilova. Those same seventeen men had been at *Stavka* at the appropriate time and had returned to Moscow before the second outbreak of murders. Seventeen men, any one of who might be the man for whom Viktor Guchkov had been hunting the better part of four years. He smiled, and thought, it won't be long now. Then he dipped his pen into the inkwell and prepared a memorandum containing the seventeen names, their present addresses, rank, field record, family background. He liked to have it all down in black and white. One never knew what might happen.

27

THE twenty-first of February was a cold day, windy and snowy. Outside every bakery and food store there were lines of people, many of whom had been there all night, waiting for bread which never came. The temperature overnight was −40° Centigrade. Everyone was talking about the strike at the Putilov steel works which had begun four days earlier.

Putilov was the largest and most important industrial complex in Russia, employing more than a quarter of a million people. On February 17 there was an argument in the gun-carriage shop over the dismissal of several workers. By the evening of the 21st, it had escalated into a full-scale lockout. When Putilov closed its gates, one Petrograd family in three lost its income. The men roamed the streets, surly and discontented. Older ones remembered that the revolution in 1905 had begun in exactly the same way and said so.

"It's just a strike," others said. "There are always strikes."

On the 23rd, International Women's Day, the strikers marched through the streets, their ranks swelled by women workers from the Anchar plant and the Obukhov factory. They were not demonstrating for more pay or better conditions. There were no petitions to the Tsar.

"Bread, bread, we want bread!" they chanted.

There was no disorder at all. It was a bright, warm day. The snow was beginning to melt from the balconies and windows on the sunny side of the Nevsky. Senka Smirnoff pushed through the crowds of workers gathered at the Kazan Cathedral shouting hurrahs. Speeches were being made in the little garden on the eastern side of the building. He remembered the cutting March wind, the coarse yells of the Cossacks, the woman's body wet with blood, wondering how the years could pass so swiftly. It was different today; like a holiday, he thought. Everyone was laughing and smiling, even the police.

The next day, Friday, was sunny and warm again. There were more than three hundred thousand workers on strike now. The streetcars gradually stopped running as strikers boarded them and appropriated the power levers. All day long there were crowds on the Nevsky and Liteiny, shouting for bread. Here and there, Senka saw banners that said "Down with the war!" and heard slogans shouted: "An end to the Tsarist monarchy!" "Down with Bloody Nicholas!" But only a few. The police, faced with such crowds, could do nothing and did nothing. The Cossacks would not. They patrolled the quays and streets on their little ponies, armed with carbine and lance, but they treated the people gently. There were no knouts, no whips. The people cheered them, the crowds opening up to let them through.

"Remember we're starving, boys!" they shouted.

Still no one admitted the possibility that revolution was in the air, although it was happening. The Tsar, returned to his *Stavka*, spent his time fretting about his children, who had measles, and the fact that blizzards had prevented food trains getting through to the front lines. He was still concerned about the war; no one else was even interested in it. The Duma debated endlessly. The speeches of Rodichev, Chkeidze and Alexander Kerensky were excised from the morning papers by the State Censor.

Maryka Makcheyeva stood in the long line of women waiting outside the bakery on the Liteiny Prospect. She had been standing in the bleak street, as all of the women had, all night, shuddering in the bone-freezing cold, hoping that today, Saturday, there might be bread for the weekend. Ivan Pavlovich was in another line in the Nevsky, and Tatiana in still another. Day after day, this was the pattern of their life: waiting in endless lines for food that was never forthcoming. Every day, before daylight, the shopkeepers started putting up their signs: *khleba nyet, myaso nyet*. No bread, no meat, no salt, no candles, no kerosene, no wood, no coal, no sugar, no flour. The women shook their fists at the merchants, their eyes filled with helpless rage. They stood in angry groups on the sidewalks and talked about the shortages. Who could pay a ruble and twenty kopecks for a little bag of potatoes that had not cost fifteen kopecks before the war? Who could afford fifty rubles for a pair of decent shoes? Everything cost more than people had, and they were resentful, bitter. Why doesn't somebody do something? they said.

Just after daybreak, old Alexeyev came to the door of the shop and let up the blind. He gave an elaborate, apologetic shrug. His face was lined and tired. *Khleba nyet*, he mouthed through the square of glass. No bread.

"You filthy old liar!" one of the women shouted.

"I'll bet he's got enough for himself, the old goat!" another yelled. "He just won't sell any to us!" A stone smacked against the door. Old Alexeyev reeled back from the door in alarm as the glass panel starred. They heard the locks being hurriedly turned, bolts sliding into place. Alexeyev's face disappeared from view.

Maryka sighed and turned disconsolately away, walking toward the Nevsky. She might as well try, although she did not know why she was bothering. She cared about nothing. If it weren't for Tatiana and old Ivan Pavlovich, she simply would not have bothered. Nothing had seemed important to her since that gray November day when she had awakened to find Alex still and silent beside her in the big bed. Somehow the fact that she had not even known, that she had slept soundly as he left her, wounded her more deeply than anything else could have done. She went through the ritual of her husband's funeral feeling nothing, seeing nothing. The officers of Alex's old regiment had all been very kind, very thoughtful, but none of it meant a thing to her. The mahogany coffin, the black-plumed horses, the iron ground into which they put Alex's body were scenery in a play that did not interest her. She did not even remember who had been at the funeral. Some of the Smirnoffs, she remembered that. They had had their own tragedy: the death of Pierre Smirnoff's daughter and her husband. They had told her all about it. Frowning now, as she walked down the Nevsky, Maryka realized that she could not recall the details. It didn't matter; Tatiana knew. Tatiana was the rock to which she clung now, blessing her daughter's strength. Vanya had come home for the funeral, but it was necessary for him to go back to his ship in Kronstadt. Sometimes it seemed to Maryka that her house was full of the ghosts of small boys playing on the floor, the ghost of her husband, hale, hearty, full of life. In such a mood, what did she care for the sensational events of December, when those powdered princes had murdered the *starets* Rasputin? They had not even been punished, merely banished to the comfortable exile of their own estates. What would Alex have said about the fact that not only had the principal assassin been a member of the Duma, but that he had positively flaunted that fact all over Petrograd? As if it were something of which to be proud, putting four bullets into the back of an unarmed man! Maryka simply did not care to hear the news these days. It was always bad, she told Tatiana, so why listen to it?

There were many, many people on the Nevsky. No trams were running, no trains, no taxis; the entire city was at a standstill. Not one factory in Petrograd was in operation, only the vital services: gas, electricity, water. She stopped to read a proclamation pasted on one of the news pillars by the commander of the Petrograd garrison, General Khabalov. It said that if all the strikers did not return to work by Tuesday, all those deferred already and those with deferments for the next two years would be inducted immediately into the Army. They can't do that, Maryka thought, feeling an irritation with men so stupid. There wouldn't be a worker left in the capital. She pushed through the seething mob. There would be no stores open on the Nevsky today, she thought, wondering where Tatiana would be. She decided to turn back and go home. There was still some cabbage left; she would make some soup. They could put a lot of pepper in it; that would make them warm. Cossacks rode through the crowd, touching their fur caps and smiling as the people shouted hurrahs.

She reached home shortly after eleven and did not go out again. It was just as well. By afternoon the crowd began to become militant. Nobody knew why. Carriages were stopped on the Nevsky and told to divert down the Fontanka. One officer drew his sword. The crowd took it off him and threw it, bent double, into the canal. There was a continuous meeting on the Znamenskaya Square; even the Cossacks were listening to the speeches. Some of the speakers were workingmen. Some of them were students. Some spoke in support of the Duma, others of the war. All kinds of speeches were being made, and Ivan Pavlovich Zubov stopped to listen to them on his way back to the Zakharevskaya. He had been fortunate enough to find a man selling horsemeat from a stall behind the Nicholas Station. There had been a big crowd around him, and Ivan had managed to purchase only a small piece, but it was better than nothing. The thought of seeing Madame smile would be reward enough for the long walk and the long wait.

He was pushing through the crowd on his way to the Znamenskaya, when a detachment of mounted police came out of the street beside the Nicholas Station at a trot, led by a burly officer in gray. The bugle sounded; everyone knew what it meant. There were screams, shouts. People started running blindly, scrambling, colliding, panicking to get away from the charge which would begin momentarily. Suddenly, shockingly, a shot rang out and one of the policemen cartwheeled backward off his horse, falling flat dead to the ground. There was a second of silence which seemed to last an eternity, and then hell broke loose. The policemen charged into the crowd, knocking people aside like ninepins, lashing at them with batons and the flat of their sabers. The packed mass of people scattered into the side streets, cowering into doorways as the clattering police went by, hurrying up the Nevsky to mingle with the bigger crowds there and spread the news. By nightfall everyone in Petrograd knew that the shot which killed policeman Krylov had been fired by a Cossack. The soldiers had turned against the police.

Word was sent to the Tsar, suggesting his return to the capital immediately. "Out of the question!" snapped Nicholas. He dictated a telegram to Khabalov.

I COMMAND YOU TOMORROW TO END THE DISTURBANCES IN THE CAPITAL WHICH ARE NOT PERMISSIBLE IN A TIME OF DIFFICULT WAR WITH GERMANY AND AUSTRIA

The telegram reached Khabalov at about nine that evening. Shortly after ten, he issued instructions that if the crowds resisted tomorrow, the troops should give them three warnings and then shoot. At roughly the same time that evening, a woman named Yelena Sverdlova, who lived in the workers' quarter of Moskovskaya, served her family a slice of good horsemeat each. She told them she had found it clutched in the hand of a man lying in the gutter on the corner of the Znamenskaya after the riot there earlier in the day. If he hadn't been dead, Yelena told her husband, she was willing to bet he would be by now.

Sunday, February 26, was another beautiful day. The sky was a soft, opalescent blue, the air balmy with the promise of spring. The morning was quiet, the streets crowded with marchers again. Shortly after two, soldiers were deployed across the Nevsky at the Sadovaya and laid down a continuous volley of rifle fire. There was blind mass panic. Men, women and children ran screaming with terror for shelter, any kind of shelter, huddling into doorways, throwing themselves flat on the suddenly murderous sidewalks, hiding behind the slender shelter of lampposts. Bullets whipped and whined, ricocheting off stone in blinding fragments. Dozens were

357

killed, more wounded. Their bodies lay in strange lumpy shapes on the empty street. Civilians who worked in the barracks rushed back and told the troops there what had happened. The men of the Pavlovsky Regiment broke open their armory and grabbed rifles, pouring out onto the Catherine Canal, running toward the Nevsky. On the way, they were confronted by a detachment of mounted police, and shots were exchanged. Men fell screaming on the street a hundred yards from where, not a generation ago, Alexander II had been blown in bloody tatters against the canal railings by Grenavitsky's bomb. Eventually the conflict ebbed; the soldiers were persuaded back into their barracks. Nineteen of them were placed under arrest and taken to the Peter and Paul Prison. By nightfall, everyone in Petrograd knew that the soldiers had mutinied.

Maryka and Tatiana waited up all Saturday night and all day Sunday hoping that Ivan Pavlovich would return. They heard the rattle of small arms fire. The woman in the apartment below said that forty people had been killed in the Znamenskaya Square. It didn't seem possible, but they decided it would be safer to stay inside and not venture out onto the street in search of Ivan Pavlovich: protest was becoming insurrection. At nine-twenty that night, the Tsar sent a telegram to his wife to say he would return to the capital on Tuesday. Then he read for a while and played dominoes.

At six in the morning of Monday, February 27, the men of the Volkonsky Regiment mutinied, killing one of their officers and his aide. Within half an hour, the Preobrazhensky and Litovsky regiments had joined them. They rushed into the streets to join the growing crowds on the Nevsky, marching behind their own bands, singing the "Marseillaise." When they reached the Arsenal on the Liteiny Prospect they sacked it, taking more than forty thousand rifles and thirty thousand revolvers, which were quickly distributed among the marchers. The crowd poured through the streets, dangerous as wild beasts. One group attacked the barracks of the gendarmerie on Kirpochny. Another broke into the Engineer Cadets' School. They burst into the Kresty Prison, unstoppable, irresistible, a mass of blond-haired peasant boys, students, soldiers in muddy boots and travel-stained greatcoats, workers, housewives, children, loud-mouthed youths, singing girls, the *narod*, the people. They freed the prisoners in the Litovsky Castle and the House of Detention on Shpalernaya. They set fire to the District Court Building in the Liteiny Prospect and then fought away the fire brigade which came to try to quell the blaze. They danced with joy, passing bottles of vodka from hand to greedy hand, watching the wooden Romanov eagles burning in the fiery inferno. They seethed into police stations, battering the policemen with rifle butts, pistol barrels, clubs. They wrecked *Okhrana* headquarters and the Central Police Building and killed anyone who tried to stop them. They put the telegraph office out of commission and took over the Finland Station. The civil authority was powerless. Events were out of control, and by four o'clock Petrograd was in the hands of the revolutionaries. In Room 13 of the Tauride Palace, the Provisional Executive Committee of the Petrograd Soviet was already in session.

Maryka and Tatiana heard them coming, the great gray mass, the unstoppable tide of people. They filled the streets outside all day, ebbing and flowing in the Potemkinskaya, the Zakharevskaya and the Furshtatskaya, thousands and thousands of them milling outside the headquarters of the Duma, the Tauride Palace. Into the courtyard, into the very building itself they went, dirt-caked men, red-faced with the cold, hollow-eyed from hunger and lack of sleep, victors who did not know that they had won. Someone estimated that there were more than fifty thousand people there.

Tatiana picked up the telephone. To her surprise, it was still working. Such was the disorder that the revolutionaries had not thought to occupy the telephone exchange. She dialed the number of Senka Smirnoff, and her heart bumped with relief when she heard his familiar, diffident voice.

"Tatiana!" he exclaimed. "What's the matter?"

Tatiana explained, telling him about the disappearance of Ivan Pavlovich, the turbulence in the streets around the Duma, outside their apartment, everywhere.

"We're so frightened, Senka. We don't know what to do for the best."

"I understand," he said. "Yes, I do, quite. Same all over the place. I've been on the streets. It's incredible! My advice to you is to stay right where you are. Don't go out on the street, no. Mood of the people's very uncertain just now, yes, very. Wait for things to quiet down a bit. Tomorrow, perhaps, or Wednesday even better. Have you got anything to eat?"

"A little," Tatiana said. "Not much."

"I'll send someone over with something," Senka said. "Keep body and soul together, anyway, yes? Then I'd suggest you both come over here to my house. Yes, that's it. Dress in your oldest clothes, you understand? No jewelry. Nothing. If you have jewels, sew them

359

into the linings. Don't carry them, no. There are all sorts of scum on the streets, yes, all kinds. I'll see what I can arrange. Perhaps you ought to go down to Sokolnika, get out of Petrograd."

"Are you going to Moscow?"

"I? My dear child, of course not," Senka said. She could almost see him smiling. "I've been waiting for this day for more than ten years. I wouldn't miss this for anything, not for all the world! But you'll be better out of it. No place for ladies, I'm sure of that. Come over here. We'll see what can be done. Things will improve in a day or so, you'll see."

"Is it revolution, Senka?"

"Oh, yes," he said cheerfully. "No doubt of that at all."

The fire spread. At Kronstadt the sailors ran riot, and ship after ship joined in the mutiny. Perhaps of all the services, discipline was most mindless and life most brutal in the Imperial Navy. Thus the revenge the mutineers wrought was the more swift and terrible. The first officer to be killed was the commander of the cruiser *Aurora*, Capt. Mikhail Nikolsky. Within hours the telegraph lines had been cut and the entire Naval Quarter was in the hands of the revolutionaries. They occupied the Admiralty, the naval hospital, the School of Naval Engineers. They streamed into the Nikolayevski Prospect shouting slogans, firing rifles taken from the dungeons where they had liberated men who had lain there rotting since the revolution of 1905. They killed Admiral Viren, the commander of the base, and arrested all officers, throwing them into the dungeons so recently emptied. Red flags appeared at the mastheads of the ships *Aurora*, *Krechet*, *Diana*. The naval bases at Helsingfors and Revel caught the fever. Scores more officers were arrested. Those who resisted were shot, beaten, thrown over the sides of their own ships. The men showed no mercy to anyone. They held meetings with the dockyard workers, vowing solidarity and no retreat. They killed Senior Lieutenant Piotr von Vitt on his minelayer. They killed Admiral Nepenin, Captain Rybkin on the *Diana*, Lieutenant General Protopopov and Baron Rudolf Shtakelberg. Anyone in an officer's uniform might find himself suddenly a target for no other reason than that he was an officer. One of these was Lieutenant Doctor Ivan Alexandrovich Makcheyev. Protesting at the way some of the seamen were mistreating a wounded officer, he pushed through the crowd to see what he could do about the wound in the officer's belly. One of the sailors tried to stop him, and Vanya short-armed the man aside impatiently.

"Can't you see this man is dying?" he shouted angrily.

"Can't you see you are?" jeered the sailor and shot Vanya in the back at close range with his Moisin-Nagant rifle, killing him instantly. They threw his body overboard, cheering.

Frederick Streicher watched from the tall windows of his beautiful library as the armed marchers moved down the Nevsky, thousands of them, thousands more behind, armed young people threading their way between motor cars in which drunken soldiers waved machine guns, shouting slogans to the men in the trucks laden with supplies of food, ammunition. More troops edged their way through the crowd. I should have got out earlier, he thought, I should have gone sooner. There was nowhere he could safely go, nowhere safer than right here in the big house on the Moika, behind locked doors.

"Hello, Streicher," Castle said.

Frederick Streicher's eyes bulged with terror as he turned to face the American. The man had made no sound entering the room. How the devil—? He started to speak and found he could not make his mouth utter the words. The doors had been bolted, barred, the house secure. How had the American got inside?

"Alone at last," Castle said.

It had been easy. When the servant opened the judas window in the door, Castle had stuck a pistol into his face and told him to open up. Then he told the man that in five minutes he was going to bring the people in off the street. He looked like a man who could do just that. He was wearing ordinary working clothes, a cap, old shoes. He was bearded now, and his blond hair was long and straggly. There were dark shadows of deprivation beneath his eyes, which burned with a special light as he explained all this to the fat man.

"What?" Streicher managed, somehow swallowing the great ball of fear which was blocking his throat. "What do you want?"

Castle smiled. "Don't be stupid, Streicher," he said. "You know why I'm here."

"Don't," Streicher whimpered. "Oh, no, please, don't."

"Give me one good reason."

Streicher looked at Castle, keeping his face blank. His brain was spinning in turmoil. *Think*, he told himself, *use your brain*. There was a Browning automatic in the desk drawer to his right, fully loaded. He had put it there ready to take with him, kept it there when he saw the violence on the streets. You never knew with the mob. They had broken into some of the big houses and helped themselves to everything in them, vandalizing the rooms, emptying the cellars.

"I can pay you," he said. "A great deal of money."

"We've had this conversation before," Castle said, smiling that cold and cynical smile. He took the pistol out of his pocket and laid it on the table. Streicher looked at it as he might have looked at a cobra.

"Wait!" he babbled. "Please! Wait!"

It wasn't fair. The damned people and their damned demonstration. If it hadn't been for that, he would already be in Switzerland. He had everything organized, everything. A passport in an assumed name, purchased long before the necessity to use it had ever arisen. A suitcase containing English pounds sterling, Swiss francs, Swedish krόner, and plenty more in the bank account in Geneva. He would travel to Stockholm as Bjørn Ellerman, nationality Swedish, destination Switzerland. The down payment on the villa in Vevey was already made, everything arranged. Then this. This damned, damned, damned American!

"Suppose I tell you the name of the man you really want," he said, moving casually toward the desk in the corner of the room. "The man who tried to assassinate you. The man who killed the Smirnoff woman. *Verschwender*."

Castle's eyes narrowed slightly. "What sort of trick is this, Streicher?" he said, hunching his shoulders and thrusting his fists into his coat pockets.

"It's not a trick," Streicher said in his most reassuring voice. He had always been good at that, he thought. There had been countless times when he'd used exactly the same voice and manner with clients, and countless times it had worked. He had the desk behind his thick thighs now, and began to ease it open.

"The whole thing was set up. He followed Smirnoff to your apartment. When Smirnoff shot you, he was right behind him, his own gun ready. He shot the woman, then Smirnoff so that it would look like suicide."

He used short sentences so that he would not babble. All the time he was talking, he was easing the drawer open. He had his hand on the automatic now; his finger slid into the trigger guard.

"His name?" Castle said, harshly.

Streicher whipped the automatic around his body, triumph surging through him. There was no way Castle could reach the gun on the table in time. Castle was still smiling his cold smile. He shot Streicher with the gun he had been holding in his coat pocket. The .38 caliber bullet smashed Streicher back against the wall, and the shot with which he had intended to kill Castle buried itself in one of the beautifully bound books on his fine mahogany shelves. Streicher's eyes bulged. There was no sensation in his legs. He slid to the floor slowly, like some huge beast, and rolled over on his back. His breathing was uneven, stertorous. He could not see anything clearly anymore. Not fair, he thought petulantly. It was all arranged. He reached for a last revenge.

"Castle?" he said. He saw the dark shape of the American loom above him and smiled vengefully.

"Now you'll never—" he said, and died before he could finish the sentence.

Castle looked down at the dead man without regret. He had let Streicher die thinking him outwitted; it was little enough to die with. He already knew the name of the man the Germans called *Verschwender*: Ivan, "Fritz" Sukhotin, husband of little, fat, giggly Olga Sukhotina, who had once asked Castle to kiss her in the back of a dark, warm coach. Sukhotin had gone to ground. Olga did not know where he was, but Castle knew he must still be in Petrograd. He knew how to find him: through Senka Smirnoff. Senka had contacts on every level, from revolutionary thug to wealthy nobleman. He would know where to look for Sukhotin, and when Castle told him why he was looking for the man, Senka would move heaven and earth to help him. He smiled his cold wolf's smile again. Petrograd was in chaos. There was nowhere for Sukhotin to run. Castle went out of the house of the banker Frederick Streicher, leaving the doors wide open. The revolutionaries were welcome to it.

Tsar Nicholas II spent Tuesday, February 28, in his sumptuously appointed train en route from Mogilyev to the capital. At Smolensk, he was greeted, as usual, by the local chief of gendarmes and the local governor. There was no news from Petrograd, but all was quiet in Moscow, they said. At Rzhev, the Tsar got out of the train for a while and went for a walk while coal and water were taken on. He was fond of walking. At Likhoslavl, he was given word of the formation in Petrograd of the Provisional Government. His advisers proposed altering the train's destination to the northern front headquarters of General Ruzky, but no decision was made. The train proceeded to Malaya Vishera where they discovered that the special train which always preceded that of the Tsar had been halted. The next station toward Petrograd, Lyuban, was in the hands of armed insurrectionists. The Tsar did not seem particularly perturbed by the news that revolutionaries were in control of the main railway line into Petrograd.

"Where is the nearest terminal of the Hughes telegraph?" he asked his aide, General Voyeikov. The Hughes apparatus was an American system of keyboard telegraph transmission used as the principal means of communication by the military.

"At Pskov, Your Imperial Majesty," Voyeikov said.

"Then we shall go there," the Tsar said. So it came about that it was at Pskov, at three o'clock in the afternoon of Sunday, March 2, that he signed the instrument of his own abdication.

This morning Ruzsky came and read his long conversation by telegraph with Rodzianko, he wrote that night in his diary. In his words the situation in Petrograd is such that now the Ministers of the Duma would be helpless to do anything, since against them struggles the Social Democratic party and the members of the Workers committee. My abdication is necessary. Ruzsky sent this conversation to headquarters and Alexeyev and all the chief commanders. At 2:30 came the answer from them all. The judgment is that in the name of saving Russia and supporting the Army at the front in calmness, it is necessary to decide on this step. I agreed. From the headquarters was sent the project of a manifesto. This evening Guchkov and Shulgin arrived from Petrograd, with whom I conversed and gave them the signed and completed manifesto. At 1 A.M. I leave Pskov with a heavy heart. I am surrounded by treason, cowardice, and deceit.

Order returned to the beleaguered city on Good Friday. The windows of the Preobrazhensky barracks were lit up. All the church bells rang, peal after silvery peal. There were salvos from the cannon on the perimeter of the Fortress of Saints Peter and Paul. The events of the weeks past seemed like a bad dream. The crowds in the cathedrals were as great as in former times, although in the working-class districts they said the churches were empty. Tatiana took her mother to the midnight mass at Kazan Cathedral, accompanied by Senka and Vladimir. The cathedral was as full as Tatiana had ever seen it, unchanging in a totally changed world. The myriad candles still yellowed the silver balustrade before the iconastas, still picked golden gleams from the trophies of the Napoleonic wars. The psalms were the same, the ceremony, everything.

If I closed my eyes for a moment and opened them again, Tatiana thought, it could easily be last Easter—last Easter, when we all went home together, and there was dear Ivan Pavlovich waiting, and there were hugs and kisses, and colored eggs and *pashka*.

Death, she thought, there has been so much death in this bitter, cruel winter. It had begun in November, with the death of Alexander Makcheyev. Her husband's death seemed to rob Maryka of any will, and if it had not been for Ivan Pavlovich, Tatiana knew that she, too, would have broken beneath the strain of those days. She would carry in her mind for as long as she lived the sound of the half-frozen earth falling on the top of her father's coffin. Then came news of the other deaths: of Rasputin, of Sasha and Irina. Funerals, funerals. In February, Ivan Pavlovich had died, needlessly, pointlessly. Tatiana remembered the awful days that had followed, days in which she trudged from hospital to city hospital until finally she learned where Ivan's body had been taken and seen to it that he was buried, as he had always wished, alongside his friend and master. Death always takes its toll of the living, even the young, the strong. Tatiana glanced at her mother. Maryka was almost frail, her strength sucked out of her by the relentless attrition of death: first Alex, then Ivan, and finally Vanya. They had not even found her son's body, and that had seemed to Maryka the cruelest thing of all.

"*Khristos voskrese!*" Tatiana heard the priest chanting.

"*Vo instinue voskrese!*" the congregation replied. The sound was heartfelt rather than joyous. It was as though people were giving thanks for being alive themselves rather than for the resurrection of Christ. She turned toward her mother. Maryka was crying, her face twisted with memory. They exchanged the triple Easter kiss. Tatiana held her mother tightly, tightly. How thin she has become, she thought. Then she kissed Senka, dear, sweet Senka. He was so absentminded these days, so vague, almost a caricature of his former self. Death had robbed him, too. Vladimir said his brother was only a shadow of himself since the murder of Irina and Sasha. Nothing was the same anymore, she thought. There was no Tsar. "Citizen Romanov" and his wife were under close arrest, and the palaces of Tsarskoe Selo were guarded by revolutionary soldiers.

"The lunatics have taken over the asylum," people said. "Anything that can happen, will happen." Perhaps that was why so many people were crowded into the cathedral, Tatiana thought. They are looking for guidance, reassurance, hope; we all are. She turned toward Vladimir and he held her close, his arms strong around her as they exchanged the traditional Easter kisses.

"You should have listened to me, Tatiana," he said as he embraced her. "You should have come to Telegin."

"Yes," she said softly, sadly.

"You'll come now, though. You and your mother. Don't argue anymore."

"No," Tatiana said.

It would be so wonderful to be away from the cold gray streets of Petrograd, away from the fear and the hunger and the ever-present reminders of death. It would be nice to just let go, let someone else make the decisions, take care of everything, nice not to worry about rents and food and lines. She had been doing it for what seemed a very long time. She was tired, tired of fighting, tired of war. She longed to lay her burden down.

"Yes, Vladimir, yes," she said. "Take me home. Take me home to Telegin."

"We'll leave on Tuesday," Vladimir said. "As soon as the Easter holiday is over. Will you come with us to Moscow, Senka?"

"No," Senka said, smiling. "I am staying here. This is where I want to be, yes. At the heart of it, Vladimir. The heart of it."

They had gone for a walk, then come back to the big house on the Fontanka. There were soldiers everywhere, slovenly and undisciplined, leaning against the railings, smoking. One or two of them were drinking from bottles. It was good to be indoors. Somehow, although they had neither said nor done anything menacing, the soldiers had frightened Tatiana. Senka lived alone now in the old house, only his manservant for company. He still had difficulty in convincing himself that the silence was permanent, that Irina and Sasha and the children were not suddenly going to come shouting and laughing into the house as they had always done. The children were staying with Sasha's brother, George, and his wife Elena. Hardly a day passed that Senka did not miss them.

"How is Pierre?" he asked Vladimir.

"He works too hard," Vladimir said. "Never stops, never. Seventeen hours a day, seven days a week. Nobody thanks him."

"It's the willing horse who gets to plow the field," Senka said.

"Yes, exactly. And the business?"

"At a standstill," Vladimir said. "Nobody wants to work. They're too busy having a revolution. Where did you get all this food, Senka?"

He gestured at the cold meat, the roasted chicken, the traditional *pashka*. By Petrograd standards, it was a banquet.

"Black market, I'm afraid," Senka said. "Yes. It's bad of me, I know, but I thought—just this once, once won't matter, no."

"You said the distillery was sacked?"

"Gutted," Senka said. "Absolutely gutted, yes. They broke in and stole everything—raw alcohol, fruit essence, anything that they could carry, anything, yes. Then they got drunk, wild, crazy drunk. They smashed the place up, axes, hammers, smashing everything, everything, just for the sake of breaking it. Yes. Stupid, stupid." He shook his head, thoughts elsewhere.

"And these are your revolutionaries," Vladimir said bitterly. "These are the people for whom you wished to overthrow the Tsar?"

"The autocracy had to go, Vladimir," Senka said. "Everyone knew that, yes, even you. Democracy, constitutional government, that's what this country needs, yes, absolutely that."

"It's not what we've got."

"Not yet," Senka said. "Give it time, man! Kerensky and Lvov and the rest of them, they won't last, no, not long. They'll step aside in due course. There'll be reform, you'll see."

"I doubt it," Vladimir said.

"You always were a pessimist, Vladimir." Senka smiled. He looked at Tatiana and Maryka. "He always was, you know. Yes."

"Pessimist or not, I think I ought to take Tatiana and Maryka back to Sokolnika, Senka. Petrograd is not going to be a safe place for a long time."

"Well, you may be right," Senka said reluctantly, as if to admit the truth of what his brother had said would somehow reflect discredit upon the entire revolution. "You may be right."

"What do you think is going to happen, Senka?" Tatiana said. "What will they do now?"

"Hard to tell just yet," Senka said, frowning. "I've heard that all the revolutionaries are slowly drifting back into the city. Bolsheviks who have been in exile, yes, and others of even more violent persuasions. Savinkov, Azef, that sort. They say Lenin is on his way back, yes, although I don't know how much truth there is in it."

"He's the Bolshevik leader?"

"That's right, yes. Good man, but a little dour."

"The Bolsheviks took over Kschessinska's house, didn't they?"

"I believe they did, yes. She got out, they say."

Many had not, Vladimir thought. The mob had killed and burned and pillaged without let or hindrance. Someone had told him that more than two hundred thousand rifles had been distributed to the revolutionaries. He remembered the boys at the front telling him that they had no rifles, no ammunition, the stories of soldiers advancing on German machine-gun emplacements unarmed. Yet there were two hundred thousand rifles lying rotting in one Petrograd armory. It was beyond belief.

"What shall we do? About the distillery?" Senka asked.

"I don't imagine there's much we can do," Vladimir said. "The Provisional Government will certainly refuse to entertain claims for civil damages caused during the revolution, and I imagine the insurance companies will do the same. Wars, lockouts and acts of God. Maybe we can sue Him.

"Talk to Pierre about it," Senka said, patting his pockets, a sure sign that he was restless. "When you get back to Moscow."

"All right," Vladimir said as his brother got up from the table, still patting away.

"You'll excuse me, ladies?" Senka said. "The only place to find out what is going on is at the Duma, yes, that's where the news is. I shall go down there, I think. Mitya, bring some more wine for Vladimir. Might as well drink it, no good keeping the stuff! Well, I'll see you all later."

Mitya brought him his fur-collared overcoat, and he turned up the collar as he went out into the bitter cold. There was snow in the air, flying almost horizontally in the strong north wind. He bent his head to keep it out of his eyes. A man fell in step alongside him, bearded, fair, shabbily dressed.

"Good evening, comrade," Senka said. "A cold night, eh?"

"Senka?" It was David Castle. The man was changed out of all recognition, Senka thought. He looked like a vagrant.

"What do you want?" he said, roughly.

"I need your help."

"My help, is it?" Senka said. "I wouldn't throw you a matchstick if you were drowning, Castle, no, not a matchstick."

"You blame me for what happened to Sasha and Irina."

"That's one of the things I blame you for, yes," Senka said, trying to push past the American. "Now, get out of my way."

"They were murdered, Senka," Castle said. Senka looked at him in astonishment.

"Are you mad?" he said. "Do you realize what you're saying?"

"I'm not mad," Castle said. Senka nodded, gesturing toward the Liteiny Prospect.

"I was planning to walk as far as the Duma," he said. "If you can convince me between here and there, I'll help you. Yes. Willingly."

"Don't worry," Castle said. "I'll convince you."

They did not get as far as the Tauride Palace. Instead they went to a café on the Shpalernaya, not far from the French Embassy. It was packed—soldiers with red armbands, young men in working clothes, women with rifles. The air was blue with smoke, and it seemed as if everyone in the place was talking at the top of his voice. There was only vodka or tea, the girl said; take your pick. They ordered both.

"You swear all this is true?" Senka said.

"All of it," Castle said. "The Petersburg Plan, the murder of Sasha and Irina, all of it. That's why I went underground, Senka. I couldn't do what needed to be done any other way."

"All right," Senka said. "What do you want me to do?"

At ten past eleven on the night of Monday, April 3, the "sealed" train from Zurich hissed to a halt in Petrograd's Finland Station, and from the fifth carriage Vladimir Ilyich Ulyanov, Lenin, stepped back onto Russian soil, his dumpy, dark-haired wife Krupskaya behind him. An honor guard of Red sailors from Kronstadt lined both sides of the platform, and a brass band played the "Marseillaise." Outside the waiting room, once reserved for the exclusive use of the Tsar, an armored car was drawn up. There were huge crowds outside, shouting, singing. Inside, the two hundred-strong delegation of the Bolshevik party crowded into the red-draped waiting room to meet their returning comrade. There were red roses, cheers, speeches. The crowd outside roared as Lenin appeared. A band played martial music, and some of the people were singing the "Varskavyanka." Lenin climbed on top of a car and made a speech, shouting over the noise. No one could hear what he was saying: "worldwide Socialist revolution . . . imperialist slaughter . . . European capitalism . . . lies and frauds." When the speech was finished, Lenin climbed on top of the armored car and was driven across the Samsonievsky Bridge and along the walls of the Peter and Paul Fortress, then over the Troitsky Bridge to the Kschessinska mansion on the Moika, his entire way lit by the huge searchlights on the Fortress walls. The cheering crowds followed the cars, the armed detachments, the band. The procession moved slowly, but fifteen minutes after it had left the square in front of the Finland Station, the area was deserted again, lonely and dark. Now the figures of two men appeared beneath the flaring lights, disappearing into the darkness, reappearing beneath the next. They walked close together, breath visible in the chill night air. Across on the Petrograd side they could hear the cheers of the crowd; the lights along the Neva glittered brightly.

The two men came to a halt beneath a street lamp and shook hands. "Goodbye, then, Fritz," Senka Smirnoff said.

"You're not going over to the Kschessinska place?"

"I don't think so, no," Senka said. "They can manage quite well without me tonight."

He turned on his heel and Sukhotin watched him go, a frown creasing his forehead. There was something strange about this, he thought. Something he couldn't put his finger on. He frowned again; he could no longer hear the sound of Smirnoff's footsteps. Imagination, he decided and started to walk across the square toward the Alexandrovski Bridge. Then he saw the American. Castle was dressed in old clothes, bearded, his hair long and untrimmed, but it was him, all right. He just stood there, ten yards ahead, his face shadowed. Sukhotin looked left and right; there was no sign of Smirnoff. He cursed beneath his breath. Set up like a damned amateur, he thought bitterly.

"Castle!" he shouted. "Castle, listen to me!"

"No!" Castle shouted back. "Your turn to talk, Fritz!"

"No!" Sukhotin shouted. "For God's sake, listen! It wasn't me, Castle! He fooled you! He's fooled all of us! It was Smirnoff! Smirnoff is *Verschwender!*"

It was preposterous, and yet it was enough to make Castle hesitate, to glance sideways at where he thought Senka might be. That momentary hesitation gave Sukhotin the chance he needed, and the gun glinted in his hand as Castle whirled around, a second too late all the way.

"Fritz!" he heard Senka shout, and he saw the bulk of the man moving out of the shadows in front of him, shielding him from Sukhotin's bullets. Sukhotin, committed to action, fired anyway, and Castle saw Senka Smirnoff stagger. Then he straightened and started walking toward Sukhotin. Sukhotin looked at him as if he had turned into a demon.

"You killed them," Senka said, inexorably. "You killed Irina and Sasha."

Sukhotin shot him again, and this time Senka was so close that the flash of the gun burned his overcoat. Castle saw the cloth ignite and then smoulder, smoke rising. By now Senka had Sukhotin by the throat.

"You," he said. His hands were around Sukhotin's neck and Sukhotin's eyes were bulging, as much with panic as because Senka was strangling him. "You! You! You! You!" Senka said, over and over. Castle heard the gun go off again, and then again. Now Senka Smirnoff's grip loosened, and his eyes rolled up. He slid down to the ground, and as he did, Castle shot Fritz Sukhotin between the eyes. He went backward into the shrubs behind him as if he had been suddenly blown, like a leaf, by some gigantic wind, dead before he even stopped twitching. Castle rushed to where Senka Smirnoff was lying. The front of his body was wet with blood, and Castle could smell the charred cloth of his coat.

"It was a lie, David," Senka whispered, as the American bent over him. "It wasn't true. I wanted—I wanted—"

"What did you want, Senka?"

"Am I dying?"

"I think so."

"Revolution," Senka said. "I wanted revolution. But not like that. You know."

"I know, Senka," Castle said, softly.

"Is he—?"

"Yes," Castle said. "He's dead."

"Good," Senka said. "I wanted—wanted to—"

"Lie still," Castle said.

"Dying?" Senka said. There was a look of surprise and wonder in his eyes. Castle pressed his pistol into Senka's hand and felt the dying man's fingers tighten on the butt.

"You understand?" Castle said.

Senka smiled and nodded, and said something that Castle could not properly hear. He bent closer. There were voices on the far side of the square near the station. Two soldiers with red armbands had come out. They were carrying rifles and looking around to see where the shots had come from.

"Irina," Senka whispered. "You. Love her?"

"Yes, Senka," Castle said. "I loved her."

"So did I," Senka said, and died.

Castle waved, and the two soldiers saw him. They came running across the grass, boots clattering when they hit the cobblestones. They pointed their rifles at him and told him to get up. They saw he had tears in his eyes, but they did not ask him why. He told them the story he had invented, and later he told it to their officer. There were no police anymore. All police, city, state, political and secret, had been arrested by decree of the Provisional Government on March 1. The officers were unfriendly until he told them he was an American diplomat. America was Russia's ally now; the United

371

States had declared war on Germany just a week ago. In addition, this American was a diplomat, and the soldiers knew better than to get involved with anything to do with matters diplomatic. They told Castle he could go.

"*Amerikyanski, dabro!*" they said, slapping him on the back. "*Amerikyanski, tovarich!*" Castle shrugged; if they wanted to think he was a fine fellow and their comrade, it was all right with him. He drank the vodka they gave him and asked them about collecting Senka's body. Then he went back to the American Embassy in the Furshtatskaya, because he had nowhere else in the world to go.

28

REVOLUTION spread like a stain over Russia. News always traveled slowly, especially in winter, when the relentless snow held the land in its icy grip. Gradually the news of the Tsar's abdication reached the *izbas*. The peasants spoke of it in whispers, afraid to even repeat it. But then, after a while, people came from the cities and told them what had happened. Their sons, who had deserted from the army, came back to the villages and said it was so.

Bolshevik agitators came to each *izba*, telling the elders about the new Russia where every man would be equal, where all land belonged to the people. What was theirs by right they should take, they said.

"All power to the soviets!" was the cry in the cities.

"All land to the peasants!" was the slogan in the fields.

The peasants had always believed that the land was theirs. Now there was no more Tsar; then there should be no more landlords, no more of the old ways. The peasants were far more revolutionary than the workers in the cities, their methods more brutal, their vengeance unrestrained. They simply took the land by force and killed anyone who protested.

In Berezovka, the peasants unearthed the body of State Counselor Luzhenovsky, assassinated in 1906 by the revolutionary Mariya Spiridonova. They placed it on a pile of pine logs and drenched it with kerosene and then set fire to it. They broke into the state liquor store and stole all the vodka. There was some arson, and two men were killed. Near Kishinev, the capital of the government of Bessarabia, the workers drove the overseers off the tobacco plantations, and at Mtzensk, a district town on the Zusha not far from Astapovo, where Count Leo Tolstoy died, they pillaged the cellars of the great Sheremetyev house, causing damage estimated at seven and a half million rubles. In Krasnoyarsk, the peasants set fire to the houses of the landlords. There were bandits in the forests. More than a million soldiers were deserters, and many of them had turned to robbery in order to live. They attacked monasteries and killed the monks, ransacking the churches and setting them on fire as they left.

In Tver, the workers marched upon the barracks, calling on the soldiers to join them. They marched together down the Millionaya and into the Catherine Square singing the "Marseillaise." Nobody yet knew the "Internationale;" that would come later. In Nizhni Novgorod, the same thing happened. The workers marched through the streets, clamoring at the gates of the Duma. The Mayor made a speech, and then the mob marched on to the jail, waving red banners, smashing down all the doors, freeing the prisoners. By evening, eighteen of the twenty-one divisions in the barracks on the Nizhnevolzhkaya had gone over to the Revolution.

"There'll be no fair there this year," Nico said.

"There'll be no fairs anywhere anymore," Pierre replied. He sat in his accustomed place at the head of the table, and not for the first time since their return from Petrograd, Vladimir thought how much Pierre had changed. It was almost as if the revolutionary workers who had sacked the distilleries had taken from Pierre that vitality, that driving force which had always characterized him. Last year, at sixty-five, he had looked fifty. This year, he looked a decade older, almost as if he was constantly crying inside. Perhaps he is, Vladimir thought. Losing Senka had been a terrible blow to them all, but most of all to Pierre. He talked to Nico and they agreed to try to make him talk about Petya, the good, young years. It would keep his mind off revolution.

Things had not been so bad in Moscow, but the changes were just as sweeping. Strikes first, then people in the streets shouting and cheering, "Long live the Revolution! Hurrah!" Workers from the Siou factory marched beneath red banners to the artillery barracks, hugging the soldiers, kissing them, weeping. Crowds surrounded the Duma, a sea of faces tossing boats of red flags, chanting and singing. A soviet of deputies was formed. It was addressed by a man called Felix Dzherzhinsky, recently returned from exile in Siberia. There were one or two bloody incidents, some sniping, but no armed confrontation such as had happened in Petrograd, where they counted over fourteen hundred dead and wounded, eight hundred and nine of them soldiers, sixty officers.

"Do you remember Papa at Nizhni, Pierre?" Nico prompted.

374

Pierre lifted his head, frowning, as though he had not heard properly. Then slowly he smiled, something he rarely did anymore.

"Pass me some of that wine, Maryka," he said. "And I'll tell you about Papa and the dancing bear."

"A dancing bear?" Tatiana said.

"Yes," Pierre said. "Her name was Smirnoffka."

The Great Fair was held each year at Nizhni from the middle of July to the middle of September. There were more than eight thousand exhibitors, more than a quarter of a million visitors from all over Russia. The goods on show were valued at over one hundred and fifty million rubles: gold, silver, ironmongery, raisins, porcelain, rice, dried fruits, Persian carpets, shoes, cushions, chinoiserie, Simbirsk shawls, Turkish sweetmeats, tanned hides, droshkies, felt slippers, soap, accordions, icons, Chinese silks, gems from Yekaterinburg, millinery, ornaments, furs, cottons, scrap iron, salted fish—there was no end to it.

Petya knew that the greatest concentration of visitors came to the Fair between July 25 and August 18, and so for that period he reserved a pavilion on the Kizlyarskaya, the area of the Fair in which the wine trade was traditionally located. Decorated in the Byzantine style, its center was a raised circular dais; low tables faced outward in every direction. Then he hired Anatoly Karpov and his famous dancing bear, Angelina, stars of the Truzzi Circus. For the duration of the exhibition, Angelina was rechristened Smirnoffka, and Petya instructed Karpov to make her dance on the raised dais where everyone could see her. While Smirnoffka did her tricks, Petya's salesmen, dressed in bearskin suits, handed out samples of Smirnoff vodka and liqueurs. "P.A. Smirnoff's Vodka Circus" was such a success that the other exhibitors complained to the police that the crowd around Smirnoff's pavilion was blocking the aisles and no one could get through to them. The police would come along and dutifully move the packed—and well-oiled—crowd along, only to discover that within minutes of their having done so, there were as many people watching Smirnoffka as there had been before. After two days the *gorodovoi* washed their hands of the whole affair and left Petya to it. From then on, there was a solid mass of spectators around the pavilion from opening time until the Fair closed. It was the talking point of the whole exhibition.

By the time Tsar Alexander III visited Nizhni, Karpov had taught the bear a new trick. Smirnoffka ambled forward with a tray balanced on her head. On the tray was a bottle of Smirnoffka and a glass. The bear stopped in front of the Tsar, who laughed and took the glass, sipped the vodka politely, and was about to put it back on the tray when he hesitated.

"Is something wrong, Your Imperial Majesty?" one of the aides hastily asked.

"Not at all, not at all!" boomed the Tsar. He was a big man, with big appetites. "This is very good. Very good indeed!"

"Perhaps His Imperial Majesty would allow me to offer some to his suite?" Petya inquired, boldly.

"You are the maker of this vodka?" the Tsar asked. "What is it called?

"Smirnoffka, Your Imperial Majesty," Petya said.

"Never tasted better!" the Tsar said. "Gentlemen?"

Petya nodded, and his bearskin-suited salesmen hastily poured glasses for the Imperial escort. The Tsar turned toward the packed stands, where spectators were allowed to watch the royal progress from a respectable distance. As they watched in awe, he raised his glass.

"*Na zdorovye!*" he shouted.

"*Na zdorovye, Batyushka!*" they thundered back. The Tsar and his officers tossed down the vodka and then hurled the glasses at the stone dais. The crowd cheered and cheered. Beaming and smiling, the Tsar shook Petya's hand. He said something to one of the aides before moving on down the aisle toward the next exhibits. Petya could only half-hear what the Imperial aide was saying.

"I beg your pardon, Your High Excellency," he said. "It's not every day one receives a visit from His Majesty."

"Quite, quite," the aide said, impatiently. "Now, you understand what is required of you, Smirnoff?"

"I am to send a supply of my vodka to the Imperial Palace," Petya said. "As soon as possible."

"*All* your products," the aide said. "His Majesty will instruct the Court Chamberlain to award you the State Emblem. This, in turn, renders you eligible for consideration as purveyor to the Imperial Court and the Imperial Household, subject of course to the usual conditions, and providing . . ."

He droned on and on, but Petya was no longer listening. He could find all that out later. He knew the requirements, anyway. If he could maintain the quality of the products he supplied to the Imperial Court, he would be awarded the State Emblem, which indicated that he was one of the Court purveyors. That, in turn, meant acceptance by the nobility, the civil service, everyone. In one day he had changed from being a smallish undertaking into a major name in the liquor business.

"I can still remember what he said when he came home," Pierre told them. "He said he watched the Tsar walking away down the aisle and thought, I'd better buy that damned bear."

It was a warm night. They had their coffee and brandy on the terrace. Far away, they could see the lights of the city, the floodlit domes of the Kremlin. It was hard to believe that Moscow was seething, boiling with revolutionary mobs, and Sokolnika was an island, surrounded by hatred. They all knew it, but no one spoke of it.

Sokolnika was no longer a hospital. In the new dawn, the workers and the soldiers wanted no capitalist largesse, however well-intentioned. Katrina and Sergei returned to their house in Dmitrovsk, a country estate given to his son by Stepan Tretyakov at the time of Sergei's marriage. Katrina had exchanged her nurses's uniform for the robes of a Sister of Mercy; she spoke ever more frequently of taking holy orders. At Dmitrovsk, her "patients" were refugees and deserters threading their way east, away from the German advance. No one who came to Katrina's door was turned away hungry or cold. She was known there, as she had been known to all the soldiers in Sokolnika, as *Byelaya*, the lady in white.

Tatiana saw Sergei only once before he left with Katrina for Dmitrovsk. She was walking in the gardens and came upon him, splitting logs with a hand axe. He was not boyish anymore. There were deep lines on his face. His blond hair was thinning and lifeless, his moustache sprinkled with gray-white. His wide shoulders slumped, as if he perpetually carried some heavy burden.

"Hello, Sergei," Tatiana said. She felt shy, strange, uneasy, bold. She could not forget the years binding them together, the years of their thoughtless childhood, when it had been implicit in everything they said and did together that one day they would marry. Not just one sad secret, but all the thousand secrets that they had shared, from schooldays to the magical evening on Krestoffsky Island.

"Well, Tatiana," Sergei said, straightening up and putting his hands on his hips, "you've grown up."

"I think I have," she said. "It was time."

"It's . . . difficult to face you," he said. "There is so much standing between us, now."

"Dear Sergei," Tatiana said, understanding and forgiving all in one moment. "It's all in the past."

"I wish I could believe that," he said, and there was more in the words than she was able to understand. She looked at him as if for the first time. Sergei was thirty-four, but he already looked forty. When he frowned, and he did so often, the once handsome face became a sullen mask, the face of a man whom life has cheated.

"You look tired," she said, unthinkingly.

He gave a short, ironic laugh. "Yes," he said. "Yes, indeed." He raised the axe and slammed it into the stump of the tree he had been using as a base on which to chop the logs.

"What is it, Sergei?" Tatiana asked, laying a gentle hand on his muscular forearm. She was not prepared for the way he snatched it away, as if her touch repelled him.

"What's wrong?" she said, dismayed.

"What's wrong, Tatiana?" He smiled. "What's wrong, indeed? I never cease to wonder why you women ask 'what's wrong' in that manner, as if there is some nice simple answer to the question and some nice simple solution to the problem. What's wrong, my dear Tatiana, is the cessation of expectation, the loss of hope. What's wrong is the realization of eternity. I am in a long, dark tunnel. I see the light, but I am afraid to emerge into it. I know I will, I must, but I fear it no less for that."

"Sergei, you're strong and brave," Tatiana said. "You and Katrina, you expect too much of yourselves."

"Ah, yes," he said. "Katrina's faith is a rock to which we all cling." She had never heard him speak so cynically before, and it surprised her.

"I always thought there was nothing you feared."

"If only that were true," he said. "If only I believed, as Katrina believes. But, of course, I do not. I am cursed by the ability to see myself clearly for what I am."

"You don't believe in God?"

"I don't believe in anything anymore. I used to, Tatiana, once upon a time. Honor, duty, love. I believed them all until I learned the true extent of my own evil."

"Sergei, you frighten me when you talk like this," Tatiana said. "You were always the one who looked ahead."

"Ah," he said. "That was because I didn't know what awaited me, Tatiana."

"My poor Sergei," she said. "Are you so unhappy?"

"I am not unhappy," he said, dully. "I live among the damned, where happiness and unhappiness do not exist."

"Why, Sergei, why?"

He shook his head, the sullen, cheated look back on his face, and although she waited, he did not speak again. After a while she left him, walking back to the house blinded by tears. She could hear the regular *chock*! of the axe behind her and saw again the haunted, lost look in Sergei's eyes. She could not imagine what had cast him into so deep a pit of despair. He left with Katrina for Dmitrovsk before she had the chance to talk to him again, and for several days Tatiana brooded over the things he had told her.

She wondered whether to mention it to Vladimir and decided not to. She felt much closer to him now, much more relaxed in his presence. It was almost as if that challenge he had always seemed to offer her when she first knew him was no longer important, to him or to her. In retrospect, she realized that she had been a little afraid of him, and now she understood why. Vladimir wasn't like any of the other men she had ever known. He was tough, but it was a learned toughness, and it covered a heart as gentle and loving as a child's. Indeed, to see him with children was to see the true man, patient and understanding and able, as so very few adults are, to enter into their enchanted lands. Yet he was not childish himself. No matter how much he clowned, or deliberately made a fool of himself to see the children smile, he was a man and she was never able to forget it. She had known plenty of men, but men who were always controllable, pliant, easy to twist around your finger. The boys, Vasya, Kolya, Nicky Vasnetsov, had been sweet and she had loved them, but somehow, deep down, she had always known they were not of the same mettle as herself. She was beginning to feel that she understood Vladimir a little, but it was no more than that. There was still a contained anger in him, and she walked warily around it, as one might skirt the perimeter of a volcano. Just the same, there were things about him which occasionally puzzled her. Sometimes, turning quickly, she would catch him looking at her with the strangest look in his eyes, as if he was waiting, waiting to see her . . . do something? Say something?

In the middle of May, he told her that they were closing down Sokolnika and going to the Crimea. Pierre needed a holiday, he said,

379

and the way things were at the distillery, he might just as well be in Yalta as anywhere. Conditions were uncertain, but it was possible to travel safely now.

"You've done nothing but your duty since the war began," Vladimir said. "It's time you had some fun. Your mother, too."

"I haven't—of course, I have had fun," Tatiana said, somehow resenting the inference that she'd never had any fun in her life.

"Let me show you how wrong you are," Vladimir said. "Take off that metaphorical nurse's uniform you're still wearing, and let me show you."

"All right," Tatiana said, smiling.

"You can be my best girl," he said, smiling back. "I'll tell everyone I know that you and I are lovers."

"Tell them what you like," Tatiana spiritedly replied. "But it won't be any nearer the truth because you say it."

"You don't see yourself in the part?"

"No," Tatiana said, scornfully, perhaps to conceal her own confusion at the directness of the question. "You're not my type at all."

She had never been in the south, and she fell in love with it, the balmy air, the leisured pace of the days. They did not talk of revolution and war here. Isolated from those grim realities by the thick walls of privilege and wealth, the rich and titled who had fled the embattled streets of Petrograd and Moscow flocked to the shores of the Black Sea in their thousands. Things were terrible now—these dreadful Bolsheviks, these awful little men Kerensky and Savinkov and the rest of them—but it would all pass. Things would return to normal before long. There was much talk of a restoration and a great deal of criticism of the Grand Duke Mikhail, who had refused to become Tsar.

"Mikhail would have made a worse ruler than Nicholas." Vladimir laughed. "The only thing he knows anything about at all is horses. Besides, can you see Natalia Sheremetyeva as Tsaritsa?"

The Tsar's brother, Grand Duke Mikhail, had married the twice-divorced daughter of the famous Moscow lawyer in 1912. They had been living together for years; she had borne Mikhail a son, George, in 1910. Natalia had married one of the Mamontov boys when she was only sixteen. Three years later she divorced him to marry an officer in the Blue Cuirassier Guard, and within three months Natalia had become the mistress of that regiment's Colonel-in-Chief, His Imperial Highness the Grand Duke Mikhail Alexandrovich. It had been a juicy scandal to tattle around the salons of the capital, and Nicholas had never forgiven his brother. Forced by their marriage to give Mikhail's wife the title of Countess Brassova, neither the Tsar nor his wife ever so much as uttered one word to the alluring Natalia.

The journey to Sevastopol took twenty hours, with a stop at Eupatoria.

They all had adjoining staterooms: Pierre and Sonya in one, Nico and Sophie another, Maryka and Tatiana the third. Vladimir had the one next to Tatiana and her mother.

"In the circumstances," he said, with that devil's grin she now knew so well, "I thought it better to be adjacent, but not adjoining." She laughed, too. Once she might have pretended to be shocked, but Vladimir hated such pretense. To her surprise, Tatiana found she did not mind at all. He appealed to the earthy side of her nature, and once she set it free, she found she could as easily dispense with such nonsense as could he.

Vladimir knew everyone in Yalta, or so it seemed to Tatiana. Strangely, though, his most special friends seemed to be not quite gentlemen. They always knew the best restaurants, the head waiters, the finest wines. They always tipped handsomely, dressed elegantly, lived recklessly. Yet Tatiana sensed that in the presence of true nobility, these same self-assured people lost a fraction of their poise, and their mood became uncertain.

"Riff-raff," her mother called them, immediately and accurately.

"They're Vladimir's friends, Mama," Tatiana would protest.

"Well they may be," Maryka said. "They're none the less riff-raff for that. Black sheep, divorcés, third sons of rich families who've never had to work."

"I like them," Tatiana said, her lips firming. Maryka saw the storm signals and smiled gently.

"Of course you do, *malyutka*," she said, "and why not? Just don't let any of them sweet-talk you—"

Tatiana laughed. "No chance of that, Mama. There isn't a man in Yalta that I'd want to marry."

Maryka nodded and smiled and said nothing. Next day, Tatiana told Vladimir about the conversation, omitting the last few sentences.

"I had the feeling that they'd please you," he said.

"Why shouldn't they?" she said, piqued yet again by that familiar smile.

"Because they're exactly what your mother says they are, Tatiana," Vladimir said. "Remittance men, gamblers, paid-off sons of the mercantile nobility from whom all that is expected is anonymity. Don't rock the boat, don't disgrace the family. In a way, I pity them."

"Pity them? Why?"

"The world that supported them is coming to an end, Tatiana. There'll be no place for people like Vesevya and Georgi in the brave new world planned by the comrades. Or for you and me, if it comes to that."

"I don't understand you sometimes, Vladimir," Tatiana said, impatiently. "Why, only the other evening, I sat next to you at a dinner with all those Counts and Princes and their wives, and you talked of nothing but how and when the Tsar would return to the throne at the head of a constitutional monarchy."

"Ah," Vladimir said. "Would you have preferred me to tell them the truth?" He shook his head and smiled at her. "That's why I choose the company of Maryev and Nazarov and Makunin. They never preach honor and sacrifice and duty. They are motivated in ways I can see and touch and hear. I know them for what they are. It does not delight me to know that I am one of them, but I know I am. Time is running out for me, too. However," he smiled, getting up from the chair and going to the door, "nobody said I can't enjoy myself in the meantime. I'll call for you at seven."

"Where are we going?"

"What's the difference?" he said, with that grin.

They went to Alushta, to Syudak, to Feodosia. They drank wine, wine, wine, and more wine, champagnes and liqueurs whose names Tatiana had never heard, bottle after bottle. And the food! Crab and shrimp and oysters, sweetbreads cooked in cream sauce, veal in Marsala, fish baked *en papillotte*, pastries, fresh strawberries, gateaux, chocolate cakes, thick, strong Turkish coffee, endless delights. She ate heartily, like a man, and Vladimir smiled.

Everything she did seemed to please and amuse him, as if she, too, were a child and he some loving big brother watching her learn to walk. It was such fun to be with people who were not gloomy, away from the grim grayness of Petrograd and Moscow.

"How long shall we stay here?" she asked him.

"As long as you like," he said. "We'll stay forever, if it pleases you so much."

"It's a lovely thought." Tatiana smiled.

"Why not?" he said, with that quizzical look in his eyes, as if he was hoping to see something in hers besides pleasure and laughter and friendliness.

"Vladimir, you're being—are you serious?"

"Of course I'm serious," he said. The strange light was still there in his eyes. It made Tatiana uneasy. "Let's have fun. Let's have each other, while there's still time."

"There you go again, with that doom talk. You know I don't like it."

"Very well," he said, and the devil's grin was back on his face. "I see I'm doing it all wrong." He went down on one knee before her in the classic position of the lovesick swain, hand on heart, eyes wide, head thrown back.

"My dear Tatiana," he said, pompously, "it cannot have escaped your attention that I harbor toward you the warmest, nay, may I even dare to say it, the most tender and ardent feelings. You ask me what emboldens me to speak this way, and I shall tell you. It is love, my dear young lady, it is love that prompts my heart! Say, say you will deign to consider my humble proposal. Ah, Tatiana, my dear, my heart—"

She hit him with a cushion, laughing and laughing and laughing at his imitation of a suitor.

"Oh, Vladimir," she giggled. "You looked so funny."

He got up and gave a wry grin. "I suppose I did," he said. "It's not something I've had a lot of practice at."

"You are sweet," she said, and reached up and took his face between her hands and kissed him. It was not intended to mean anything and yet—and yet, somehow, in that second, everything stopped, everything in the whole universe. It was silly, she thought, that the only thing which described the moment was a cliché: her heart stood still.

"Say yes, Tatiana," he whispered. "Say yes."

She started to say no, and his lips were on hers and she could not say anything. It was a gentle kiss, not long, not hard and demanding the way his first kiss had been, that time in the garden at Sokolnika. She laid her head on his shoulder, surprised at how natural it felt to do so. They did not speak for a long time. Then he moved away from her, looking at her with unreadable eyes.

"Did you mean it?" he whispered.

"I don't know," she whispered back, wondering why they were whispering. "I—"

"Words, words, words," he said. He put his hand beneath her chin and lifted her face so that she had to look into his eyes. "Was what your lips said just then the truth?"

This is too sudden, Tatiana thought, too soon. She needed time to think and did not want to think at all. She needed room to maneuver and did not wish to move. She wanted Vladimir to take her in his arms, and yet she did not want to surrender.

"All my life," Vladimir said, softly, "I have been wandering through the world, vaguely knowing that a part of me was missing, something which would complement everything I am. I've been used, and I'm scarred, and my life isn't anything to write a book about, but in spite of all that, or perhaps because of it, I know now that what I was looking for all these years was you, Tatiana. I cannot and will not take any more chances because I'll never get any more. Do you understand me?"

The dusk had crept up from the darkening sea without them even noticing it. There was a soft silence everywhere, a heaviness in the air as there sometimes is before thunderstorms. Tatiana moved into Vladimir's arms as naturally as if she had been doing it all her life, her eyes half-closed, her lips parted. Yes, her heart sang, yes, I'm ready, yes, this is the moment!

"I didn't know," she whispered, thrilling to the strength of his arms. He smiled, and this time there was passion in his kiss.

Love was their cloak of invisibility. All they had to do was put it on and the grim world which surrounded them disappeared. They lived inside a charmed circle. They dined in lovely homes, in fashionable restaurants, bathed in bright sun or soft moonlight. They climbed together up the long path that led to the great waterfall at Utchan-Su, with Yalta laid out below them like a model. They visited the estate of Prince Golitzuin and toured the Roman ruins at Kertch with Mikhail Megalov, the British Vice-Consul. They lay together in the sunshine, listening to the warm wind rustling the grass, watching the clouds.

"Summer afternoons," Tatiana said. "That's all you need to say. "Summer afternoons. Like poetry."

" 'I can only love you,' " Vladimir said. " 'To tell you how much you were beloved, eternity alone will know.' "

"Oh, how beautiful!"

"It's by Vasilii Zhukovsky."

"Say it all."

"All right," he said.

Where is there a name for you,
No mortal art exists to express the wonder of you.
There is no rhyme for you!
A song, What could song do but report too late of you!
If the heart could only be heard,
Its every emotion would be a paean of praise for you!
All the charm of you
The image so pure and so holy is secretly locked in my heart.
I can only love you
To tell you how much you were beloved, eternity alone will know!"

He rolled onto one elbow and kissed her lightly on the end of the nose. "There," he said. "I couldn't have put it better myself."

"You're a strange man," she said, dreamily. "You act so hard, so cynical, yet beneath it all, you're warm, kind, so patient."

"I'm not really," he said. "It's all an act. I'm on my best behavior, so you'll be impressed."

"Nonsense," she said. "You're just afraid to let it show."

"There isn't too much room in the world for softness and kindness these days, Tatiana," he said. "We're making believe there is because we know it isn't going to last very long."

"You mean you and I?"

"No, fool!" he smiled, tolerantly. "I mean our world."

"Oh, let's not talk about that," Tatiana said. "Let's talk about us."

"More?" he said, with a grin. "I thought I'd told you everything about myself by now."

"I want to know more," she said, burrowing into the strong circle of his arms. "I want to know what kind of little boy you were, what you were afraid of, what you wanted to be when you grew up. I want to know about your friends, and the first time you fell in love, and all the places that you've been to."

"That, my dear, would take a lifetime," he said, teasingly.

"I know that," she said, looking up at him. Her eyes were serious, and there was no trace of banter in her voice.

"No, Tatiana," he said. "We're better like this. Marriage is— marriage is something for times more settled than these."

"Marriage is also for people who love each other," she said.

Vladimir thought about Valentina Beriosovna, whom he had loved once and married. You married, never thinking that you would change or she would change or love would change, and all of them did. You married, sure that nothing in the world could ever be as good as what you had, and ended wondering how you could ever have been so naive.

"People who love each other don't have to be married," he said. "It's not one of nature's immutable laws."

"I know. It's just . . ."

"Believe me, my instinct is to say every romantic cliché that was ever invented to you. But I've said them all before, and I'm wary of saying them anymore. How can I take them seriously, how can you? I'm an also-ran in the forever stakes, Tatiana. Here, now, I know I love you. Isn't that enough?"

"Of course it is," she said. "I would not be here otherwise."

Vladimir smiled and shook his head. "How you have changed!" he said. "I remember looking at you the first time I saw you and thinking how beautiful you were, how spirited, not just another of those spoiled Petersburg darlings, all flutter and fans. But I never thought that we would ever be together like this."

"Neither did I," Tatiana said, and it was the truth. "I used to think of the future as something stretching endlessly ahead, and know that at some point I would marry and have children and be happy. Then the war came and I saw all those boys die in the Catherine Hospital, hundreds of them. They were like me. They had the same hopes, the same fears. They loved as much and laughed and cried, but they were killed anyway. They had no say in it. They were just wiped out, like chalk from a blackboard. That was when I realized that there were no second chances."

"You still think that?"

"Most of the time," Tatiana said. "Sometimes I hope that I'm wrong, that perhaps your friends are right and things will return to being as they once were."

"No," he said flatly. "There's no chance of that, Tatiana, and they're fools for hoping."

They were all hiding from the grim reality which encircled them. There was no escaping the finality of what was happening: a naval revolt at Sevastopol in June, more riots in the streets of Petrograd, landlord after landlord driven penniless from his estates, many murdered.

Kerensky, the new Premier, ordered a major offensive on the Western front in June. It fell to pieces in a matter of days. The soldiers no longer saw any sense in being slaughtered in a war they knew they could not win, and their officers were powerless to command them. Early in July, there was armed insurrection in Petrograd, and for a while it seemed that the Provisional Government might be overthrown. This time, however, the soviet brought in loyal troops from outside the city, and the Bolshevik "July Days" came to an abrupt end. Warrants were issued for Lenin, Trotsky and the rest of them. They fled; one or two were arrested. The Revolution went underground, but it did not stop. It could not, would not be stopped.

In the fetid *kamorki* and the smoky *izbas*, in cloth factories and foundries, tanneries and sawmills, in the giant steelworks and armament factories, the revolutionaries moved among the workers.

Throw off the yoke of your bourgeois oppressors!

Down with the tyranny of the upper-class autocracy!

They whispered and plotted and preached and persuaded, many of them young men, some of them old, spreading the seeds of discontent throughout the deadly summer.

All over the country, manor houses were put to the torch, the owners murdered, their livestock slaughtered. The peasants took the land without let, hindrance, permission or decree. If they had the land, no one could take it back. Troops at the front commandeered trains at gunpoint and forced the engineers to take them home. If they got home, no one could make them fight the capitalists' war again. The railroad services deteriorated, then disintegrated, and again the shortages began: *Khleba nyet, Kerosina nyet, Sol nyet.* In the cities the great factories once more fell idle; the workers thronged the streets. Cabs and carriages began to disappear as the horses were killed for food. Vagrants, drunks and robbers proliferated, unchecked. There were no police to stop them.

Yet somehow life in the cities went on, as petty and conventional as ever. Young women still came up from the provinces to learn French and cultivate their voices. Handsome young officers, in elaborate uniforms which still bore the insignia of the Tsar, disported themselves in the bars and lounges of the great hotels. Elegant women took afternoon tea together, each carrying her own elegantly jeweled gold or silver sugar box, perhaps bringing half a loaf of bread as a present to her hostess. Titled ladies complained about the shortage of servants and wished the Tsar was back. They said Kerensky had sent the Royal family to stay in Tobolsk "for their own safety." That upstart! One had heard that he spoke as if he had himself become Tsar. "I and my Government," indeed!

"Is this what we bled for?" the firebrands shouted at the street meetings. "Is this what our comrades died for—so that Kerensky may sleep in the Tsar's bed?"

"*Nyet!*" roared the listeners. "*Nyet!*"

The old gentlemen in uniform going home from the ministries or the government offices would hear the crowds, see the agitators waving their arms beneath the blood-red banners, and detour around them, clutching firmly at the portfolios they were taking home, still intent upon advancement in the Table of Ranks, *Tchinovniki* to their bones.

Gambling clubs blazed with light from dusk until dawn; huge wagers were considered *de rigueur*, champagne the only wine. On the brightly lit sidewalks, bejeweled whores paraded openly. Bolshevik or bishop, it was all the same to them. The cafés were crowded, the shops were open, the trams ran, the cinemas put out "House Full" signs. Great red streamers hung down the fronts of the government buildings and the two-headed eagles of the Romanovs had been torn down, yet all the generals were still Tsarist generals, all the senators and councilors. The books in the schools were the same books children had always studied, and *nyanyas* still told stories of Ivan Veliki and the boyhood of Peter the Great. Everything could still be had for money; there were wild parties everywhere. Eat, drink, and be merry!

There were mass meetings at all the factories, in Nizhni, in Tver, in Moscow, in Petrograd.

Down with the capitalist conspiracy! the agitators shouted.

All power to the workers!

End the tyranny of the bourgeois oppression!

Take what you want, comrades! Don't wait for anyone to give you permission, take! You're as good as the next man now, take! Why should the rich man have it all? Haven't they always had it their way?

All land to the people!

Take!

At Lapotkovo in Tula province, the elderly Princess Urusova was dragged from her sickbed and left shivering with cold and fear in the courtyard while peasants pillaged and burned her house. They dug up the body of her son, who had been killed at the beginning of the war, to see if it had any jewelry or medals on it, and left it stinking where it lay, still recognizable. The old lady was taken, sobbing and half crazy with terror, to the railroad station by some Austrian prisoners of war, and put on a train to Petrograd.

Peace, land, and bread!

The Bolsheviks were resurgent. Government by the workers and soldiers! they shouted. All power to the soviets!

There was a huge assembly of Smirnoff workers in the Pyatnitz-kaya, close to the lowering bulk of the great distillery. They listened spellbound to the gaunt, gray-haired old man on the makeshift dais above their heads. He had a way of talking that belied his years, and there was a zeal close to madness in the crafty old eyes.

"Ah, comrades, I can see what you're thinking," he said. "What's this *starik* doing here? Why isn't he at home with his grandchildren instead of making speeches? I'll tell you why, comrades, I'll tell you why! I've been working for this Revolution since before most of you were born. You don't believe me, eh? I can see that. It's true, just the same. How many of you here have heard of Zhelyabov, eh? How many of you know about *Narodnaya Volya*? One, three, five, ten? You talk of revolution and you don't know these things? Well, I do! We were the ones who killed Alexander. We were the ones who were buried alive in the Fortress of Peter and Paul, or hung like foxes on a tree before the cheering mobs in Semionovsky Square. We were the ones, comrades! We began the march that brings us here today! You have the fruits of our labors! So listen to what I tell you!"

There was cheering, wave after wave of it. The other men on the platform behind the old man smiled at each other.

"I know these capitalist dogs!" the old man shouted. "I know them because I used to be one of them. I know how they think, these imperialist swine! They skulk around the edges of the blaze of our Revolution, hoping that the flames won't touch them. 'Wait till it all dies down,' they tell each other. 'Then everything will be the way it was.' Yes, comrades, that's what they want, everything the way it was. Eleven-, twelve-hour days, fourteen if the factory inspec-tor's palm's been greased. But we're not going to let them do it, are we?"

"No!" the incensed crowd roared. "No! No!"

"We'll stop them!"

"We won't let them!"

"How will you stop them?" the old man shouted. "They're safe behind the walls of their houses, behind barred gates, behind iron fences. You can't get at the Smirnoffs and their like."

"We ought to go and drag them into the streets!" someone yelled. "Drag them out!"

"Yes, comrade, yes! That's the answer!" the old man shouted. "They have to be stopped before they can take control again. They must be cleared away, like the debris of a burned truck. The Smirnoffs have lived on your sweat and blood for three generations, parasites, every one of them! Are you going to let them go on doing it?"

"No!" the mob shouted. "No!"

"Then who will go with me to Sokolnika?"

They roared and cheered and raised fists clenched in the workers' salute, and then they began to march. All through the workers' districts they marched, shouting slogans and waving the red banners, through the Myaznitzkaya and the Yauzskaya. They picked up thieves and footpads in the dank purlieus of the Khitrovka, deserters and looters hanging around the three railroad stations in the Kalantchevskaya. By the time they reached the gate in the Potveshnaya, they were more than four hundred strong. They massed against the wrought iron gates, chanting slogans, shouting, waving sticks and rifles. The old man clambered up on the stone footings of the gold-tipped iron railings.

"See how they hide, the bourgeois scum!" he screeched. "See how their lackeys protect them!"

"Break down the gates!" someone shouted. There was a roar of approval from the crowd. Bottles were being passed from hand to hand. "You at the front, break them down!"

"Follow me!" the old man shouted. As he approached the gates, the old Cossack, Vanska, appeared from his gatehouse. He was wearing the medal given to him by Tsar Alexander III and carrying the rifle that had been a present from Arsenii Smirnoff in the year before his death.

"Stand away from my gates!" he shouted hoarsely. He was very frightened, but a lifetime of pride sustained him in the face of the screaming mob. No one had ever passed through these gates uninvited. He fired the rifle into the air. The men at the front of the crowd shrank back, pressing against those behind them.

"Don't be afraid of one old man!" those in the rear shouted.

"Stand back!" Vanska shouted. "The next shot won't be into the sky!"

"Kill the old fucker!" someone shouted, and there was a pistol shot from somewhere in the crowd. Vanska looked down at his chest, surprised by the sudden pain, unable to believe that this was the moment of his death. He folded to the ground and the cheering, shouting men began to clamber over the railings and the gates. They tore the keys from the dead Cossack's belt and swung the gates open wide. The mob surged through into the park like a pack of dogs.

They trampled heedlessly through the gardens, crushing everything underfoot. They smashed the greenhouses and the outbuildings and set fire to anything that would burn. A group of them went down to the lake and demolished the rowboats with the butts of their rifles. Others tossed burning brands and bunches of straw into the stables. When the flames caught and the buildings began to burn, the horses went wild, shrieking with panic and fear. One or two of them managed to kick down the doors of their stalls, but as they careered out into the cobbled yard, eyes rolling and ears flattened with terror, the waiting men shot them. The others burned alive, their screams going on for more than half an hour.

The old man did not go near the stables. His whole attention was focused on the house, and he was the first one to enter the building. He stood in the entrance hall, awed by its proportions. The hate welled up in him. They had all this while he starved in Paris on their handouts. His blood sang with the power of the men behind him. Glass shattered; doors splintered as the mob smashed their way into the house, picking up the fine antique furniture and hurling it at mirrors, crashing it against the finely gilded walls, ripping down the paintings, throwing vases onto the parquet floor in smithereens.

A hundred men and more were pushing up the fine, ornate staircase when the huge black Circassian majordomo, Yuri, fell upon the leaders, roaring with rage, a curved sword in his hand. Men hung onto his arms, his legs, like dogs on the back of some huge black bull. There were already a dozen small wounds on his body where one man after another had lunged at him with a bayonet. No one could shoot in such a crowd. The black man was covered in blood and the floor was slick with it. Still his great strength kept him upright. He thrust the sword through one man, who screamed like a gull and fell backward over the banister, landing with a sickening sound on the tiled floor. Now Yuri grabbed a rifle off one of his assailants and swung it like a club, smashing yet another man to the floor. The rest backed away from him, away from his mad eyes and inhuman strength.

"Shoot him, shoot him, shoot him!" someone shouted, and four or five pistols spoke almost simultaneously. The great black figure was smashed back against the white wall, leaving a great smear across it. Then he went down and stayed down. The shouting mob surged upon the supine form, stabbing at it repeatedly with their bayonets.

Suddenly another shot rang out, and then another and then another. Three of the men who had been thrusting their bayonets into

Yuri's corpse fell in contorted heaps across the body of their victim. Everyone in the great hall froze. For one long, silent moment it was like some tableau from Hell: the bayed revolutionaries, the dead bodies, the blood-smeared wall, the tall, bearded man at the head of the staircase with the smoking pistol in his hand.

"Get out of this house!" Pierre Smirnoff bellowed at the rabble below him on the stairs. "Get out before I kill you all!"

"We don't take your orders anymore, Smirnoff!" someone at the back of the mob shouted.

"You're finished, Smirnoff!" yelled another.

"Rush him!"

"He's only got three shots left!"

"I warn you!" Pierre thundered, with eyes that dared anyone to make a hostile move. "I'll kill the first man that moves!"

"Kill him!" Mikhail Mikhailovich shouted, forty years of waiting in the words. There was an answering shout in the crowd and then another, and then all the shouts became a roar and the roar became the sound of some unearthly animal, as the men rushed up the staircase and fell upon Pierre Smirnoff. He emptied the gun at them as they came, and heard the bullets striking flesh. Two men faltered, their eyes stricken, and fell as a dozen bayonets were thrust into Pierre Smirnoff's body, his legs, his arms, throat, thighs, belly. He was skewered against the great oaken banister which had known the touch of kings, and the snarling rioters pulled the triggers of their rifles as they wrenched the bayonets free. Pierre Smirnoff was dead long before his body was pitchforked over their heads, from bayonet to bayonet, like some awful bale of blood-soaked meat.

At the foot of the great staircase, Mikhail Mikhailovich stared with baleful eyes at the broken body of his cousin. Then he spat upon the corpse and went out of the house. Upstairs, he could hear the men kicking down the doors of the bedrooms, looking for the women.

29

THE People's Office for the Investigation of Agitations and Disturbances was located in the former offices of the City Governor of Moscow on the Tverskoi Boulevard, and the man installed by Felix Dzerzhinsky to run it was Boris Abrikosov. Dzerzhinsky had two trusted lieutenants, and only two: Martyn Latsis and Boris. To them he had confided his plan to create a new kind of police force, one which would not concern itself with rights and wrongs or such abstractions as justice.

"I want something that will consolidate our power and enforce our will," the spade-bearded, dark-eyed Dzerzhinsky said. "Vladimir Ilyich is namby-pamby about it, but I've told him a dozen times: we don't want another damned investigating commission or tribunal. We want an executive with which to strike down our enemies."

They had talked about it many times in the echoing public library in Irkutsk, many times since their return from exile.

"We should not be interested in individuals," Dzerzhinsky said. "We should devote ourselves to the class struggle, to the extermination of the bourgeoisie in its entirety. We will need an organ which does not seek evidence or witnesses to deeds or words directed against the soviet power. Let us instead ask, to what class does this man belong? What are his origins? What is his upbringing? Where was he educated, what is his profession? The answers to these questions will define the fate of the individual, not evidence, nor words."

There was no question in Boris Abrikosov's mind about which way the Russian wind was blowing. He became a Bolshevik long before he returned to the city of his birth. Here was the new order. In that new order where everyone was equal, some would inevitably be more equal than others. Dzerzhinsky admired his organizational abilities, and so he offered them, with the semblance of humility, knowing that Dzerzhinsky could not refuse them. Martyn Latsis was a firebrand, a leader in the Bolshevik Military Committee. Someone, Boris told Felix, would be needed to keep the dossiers, to set up the organization upon whose back the force which Dzerzhinsky visualized could eventually be grafted.

"Set out your requirements," Dzerzhinsky said, "and I'll see you get what you need."

Within weeks Boris had a staff of ten, and rank within the officialdom of the Moscow Duma which effectively concealed his connections with the Bolsheviks. During the summer of 1917, when Dzerzhinsky and Latsis were forced to go underground like Lenin and the others, Boris remained in his office on Tverskoi, gainfully employed by the city government. They did not know he was a Bolshevik, of course. All they knew was that once a month, Boris provided them with reports of the disturbances and agitations which his office had been set up to enumerate and, where possible, investigate.

The work was not onerous, although it was dull. His administrative assistant was a former policeman named Malev who had somehow survived the March purge of the police force and was now more than happy to work as a menial in the same offices where he had once given orders. Boris showed the fellow little charity and no hope; Malev's kind were there to be shit upon. It was to Malev that he gave the task of opening all new files on disturbances wherever they had occurred: Tambov, Taganrog, Kishinyev, Odessa, Zhitomir, Voronezh, Chernigov, Penza, Nishni Novgorod. In agitations against the wheat monopoly, two food administrators killed. In pillaging private property in Kharkov, four killed. In Simferopol, two, Astrakan, eight, Saratov, four, Ekaterinburg, Tiflis, Tashkent, Dmitrovsk. At Rostov-on-Don, a member of the town council thrown down the stairs of the Duma. Boris read them all, usually giving them only the most cursory attention. Malev was a dull plodder, but he was methodical.

In the middle of August, Malev came to him with a puzzled look on his pudgy face. Boris looked up impatiently, as if he were very busy.

"Well?" he snapped.

"If you have a moment, comrade," Malev managed, "there is something I would like to show you."

"Well, well, show me," Boris said.

"I beg your pardon, comrade, but what I wish you to see is in the cellars. Perhaps, if you could come—?"

Boris frowned. "Is it a secret, Malev?" he shouted. "Am I to trek all the way down to your cellars before you condescend to inform me why?"

"N-no, no, comrade, of course not," Malev said hastily. "There are files, old files. Ministry of Justice files."

Boris frowned again, but this time in concentration. It was most unusual for files to be lodged anywhere but in the archives of the Ministry itself.

"Show me," he said, and followed Malev down the stairs to the dusty basement. It was full of broken desks, battered chairs, split filing cabinets with scorch marks on them. Relics of the February uprisings, he thought, when the people stormed the police stations. Malev led the way to some wooden shelving, slatted and unpainted. On it there was a pile of thick dossiers. Each bore a label on which was written in a copperplate script the name of a woman: Irinia Kaminsky, Zoya Terzakova, Lara Lazareva.

"Well?" he said.

"When I worked here," Malev said, "er—before, there was a man here, Viktor Guchkov. He was the Senior Judicial Investigator of the Department of Justice. I was—he worked here. I knew him. Very briefly, of course."

"What was he working on?"

"That's just it, comrade," Malev said, showing the nearest thing to excitement Boris had ever seen him demonstrate "He was in charge of the hunt for that mass murderer, Citizen Butcher."

Gospodin Palatch! Boris had forgotten all about him; he imagined everyone else had by now. He had killed God knew how many women and then vanished.

Have all this stuff brought up to my office," he said. "And do it now."

"Yes, comrade, of course," Malev said. "Do you—do you think I—?"

"Do you want to drool, Malev?" Boris sneered. "Is that it? Do you want to look at all the photographs, eh? You nasty little snail! Get those files up to my office and then get to hell out of my sight!"

"Yes, of course, sorry, sorry, right away, sorry comrade!" Malev babbled as Boris stalked past him and out of the cellar. As soon as Boris's back was turned, Malev mouthed the words he longed to say but did not dare to utter. One day, you bastard, he thought, one day.

"Mikoyan!" he shouted at one of the clerks. "Quickly, damn you! Comrade Abrikosov wants these files in his office. Well, man, don't just stand there. You know he doesn't like to be kept waiting."

Everyone in the NKOVT hated Boris Abrikosov, but their hatred for him was infinitesimal compared with the way that they felt about Fyodr Malev. Any one of them would happily have strung the sad-eyed little swine from a telegraph pole and paid for a chance to pull on the rope.

"Yes, comrade, right away, comrade!" Mikoyan shouted with mock servility. Malev glared at him and Mikoyan stifled his smile. Kiss mine, he thought, and ran up the stairs with the files.

Boris spent the rest of the afternoon going through the dossiers. Most of them contained very little except gruesome medical reports outlining the mutilations performed by the murderer. It was growing late by the time Boris came to the thin folder which contained Viktor Guchkov's final assessment of the case. Neatly clipped to the inside cover of the folder was a memorandum in neat, sloping handwriting, and Boris read it with quickening interest.

Within a matter of two weeks I expect to be able to name and apprehend the sex murderer who calls himself Gospodin Palatch. My inquiries into this case are almost complete. It would seem that the murders in Orsha (see attached report from V.K. Grimbikov) were quite certainly the work of the same man, establishing that he was in all probability a soldier. Since we know that he is reasonably well educated, well dressed, and not a workingman, we might also safely conclude that he is an officer. I have therefore checked the records of postings to and from Field Headquarters at Mogilyev and from these extracted the names of seventeen men whose movements to and from *Stavka* fit the dates and who are of the appropriate age. Interviews will quickly establish whether their physical descriptions match those of the murderer. With your permission, I propose to begin interviewing as soon as we have located the present whereabouts of the men I now list for your information.

> BUZUNOV, Georgi Nikiforovich
> DZHIRKVEKOV, Yuri Alexandrovich
> GORYUNOV, Georgi Vasilevich
> GRUSHKO, Viktor Fyodorovich
> KOCHEGAROV, Anatoli Nikitovich
> KUSNETOV, Nikolai Ivanovich
> LAPTEV, Yuri Ivanovich
> LEONOV, Vladimir Alexeivich
> MASLOVSKI, Paul Mikhailovich
> NOVIKOV, Lev Aleksandrovich
> PAVLOV, Aleksandr
> RUDICHEV, Gennadi Petrovich
> TRETYAKOV, Sergei Stepanovich
> UDALOV, Ivan Ivanovich

Vasilyev, Nikolai Trofimovich
Yukalov, Semen Ivanovich
Zabivkin, Nikolai Vasilevich

Boris laid down the dossier as though it were made of the most delicate porcelain. The checking the man must have done! he thought admiringly. He knew a thing or two about compiling dossiers. The ones he had so carefully placed in the vaults of the Imperial State Bank in Petrograd before he went to Irkutsk, the ones now as carefully hidden beneath the floorboards of his apartment, were proof of that. He had not even told Dzerzhinsky about them. They were Boris's safety net, his security, his pension.

"Malev!" he shouted. "Malev, get in here!"

His assistant came scurrying, panting, anxious-eyed.

"Yes, comrade?"

"Do you know what happened to Viktor Guchkov?"

Malev's eyes flickered away from Boris's, and that hunted look Boris now knew so well flooded them.

"He was, er, they killed him. In the riots. The February riots," Malev said. "There was an attack on the building. Here, this one. They all came in. They had clubs, rifles, grenades. He tried to talk to them. They wanted to burn the place down, and he tried to talk them out of it. They just—they beat him to death, no warning, nothing. There was nothing anyone could do."

"Were you here?"

"No," Malev lied.

"Very well," Boris said. It was a pity about Guchkov. He would have liked to talk to the man. "Send Mikhailovich in here."

That crazy old monster, Malev thought. He wondered what the devil Boris Abrikosov kept him around for, maundering about the place, muttering about "the old days," as though to have been alive in the days of Alexander II was some sort of miracle.

"Yes, comrade," he said. "Right away."

The news in Nico's telegram was stunning, deadening, and yet there it was in incontrovertible capitals on the buff telegram form.

SOKOLNIKA SACKED BURNED PIERRE SONYA SOPHIE KILLED TELEGIN ALSO BURNED STAPOVNY ULYANOV MURDERED COME IMMEDIATELY DESPERATE NICO

"I'll go at once to Moscow," Vladimir said.

"We'll come, too," Tatiana said.

"No!" Vladimir said. His tone was adamant. "I'll take you and your mother to Dmitrovsk. You can stay with Katrina and Sergei until I send for you."

"I don't want to st—"

"No, Tatiana!" Vladimir said. She wanted to hold him close and tell him not to punish himself, as she knew he was doing, for having been dancing, and drinking champagne, and making love while the mindless mob had killed his family and looted his home. But there was a wall around him, and she could not penetrate it. There was no room in his mind for anything except what had happened in Moscow. The anger seethed in him like molten lava in the crater of a volcano, and she was afraid, afraid of what he might do.

"Please be careful, my darling," she begged him as they stood on the platform of the station in Orel. She could see the river glinting in the sunshine. "Please come back safely to me."

"Of course I will," he said. His smile was mechanical. He was already far away from her, and Tatiana's heart felt like a stone. He left without a backward glance; she cried all the way back to Dmitrovsk. She felt soiled, used, cast off. She had wanted him to take her in his arms and tell her that he loved her, but she could not bring herself to ask him to. He had wanted to explain to her that he hated kisses and tears and promises at railroad stations, but he could not say it.

Nico was drunk.

Not happy drunk; not even sad drunk, Nico was maudlin, filthy, ugly drunk. The servants said he had been like that ever since.

"Ever since?"

They told Vladimir what they knew while he waited for the doctor to arrive. Rioters, sir, all kinds of riff-raff, people from the Khitrovka, that sort. They said it apologetically, as if somehow they could have prevented it. They were all genuinely sad. Every one of them had served the family at Sokolnika, and every one of them loved the old house almost as much as Vladimir himself. There had been eight dead: Pierre, Sonya, Sophie, two maids, Vanska, Yuri and a groom. The rioters stayed at Sokolnika for the rest of that day and all night. They broke open the cellars and by midnight they were all wild, drunk, crazy. People heard the noise, but no one dared to investigate. Next morning, still crazy with liquor, the mob marched across to Telegin. Oh, sir, the servants said, it must have been dreadful. The poor animals, the horses. Everything had been slaughtered, chickens, cats, everything. Piotr Stapovny, Vladimir's estate manager, and Pavel Ulyanov had both been killed.

Doctor Ransel was brusque, efficient, perhaps a little disapproving. He took Nico's pulse, lifted his eyelids, pursed his own lips and shook his head. "How long has he been like this?"

"Three days, the servants say."

"Hm," Doctor Ransel said. "All right, young man, get out of here. This isn't going to be pleasant."

Vladimir went outside and waited. It was more than an hour before the doctor came out, buttoning his coat and wiping his forehead with a none-too-clean handkerchief.

"He'll sleep for twelve hours at least," he said. "Give him something to eat when he wakes up. Eggs or milk pudding, anything easy to digest. He's going to be shaky for a while. I'll give you something to make him sleep. And one more thing."

"Yes?"

"Keep him away from drink."

"I'll do my best."

"Do better than that, young man. Your brother is teetering on the edge of a very severe breakdown. Something has happened to push him as far as any man can be pushed safely. Do you know what it is?"

"His wife," Vladimir said. "His wife was killed. In a riot."

"Ah," Doctor Ransel said. "Well, I must be on my way. Keep him warm, keep him quiet, and most of all—"

"I know," Vladimir said. "No liquor."

He didn't ask the doctor to tell him how you keep an alcoholic away from liquor. No doctor knew the answer to that one. He wondered whether Nico would be able to face reality without the solace of the drunken veil he had drawn across his memory.

He arranged for a nurse to spend the night at Nico's bedside, with instructions to call him immediately if Nico woke. Then he began to make telephone calls. There were a lot of decisions to make, and he was the only one now who could make them. The Moscow distillery, the one at Odessa, must be closed down immediately, all production stopped. He spoke to the directors of each establishment, explaining his decision, warning them that to stay at the plants was to risk being murdered by the revolutionaries.

"The vodka distilleries will be the first places they sack," he told them. "Look after yourselves, look after your families. Leave the factories to the looters. There is nothing you can do to save them."

Some of the older employees argued that the danger was not as great as Vladimir described it. He told them what had happened: that the Bolsheviks now had a majority in the Moscow and Petrograd soviets, effectively giving them political control. They had repeated this success in the Moscow district Duma elections, wiping out the Mensheviks and the Social Revolutionaries. The troops were voting ninety and in some cases ninety-five percent for Bolshevism. And the single simple reason was the war. Russia was sick of it, the troops were sick of it, the peasants were sick of it, the workers, everyone. The Bolsheviks stood uncompromisingly for peace—peace, land, and bread. And so, people voted for them.

The nurse woke him at seven to say Nico was awake, and he went in to see his half-brother. Nico looked sick, tired, and old. His skin was almost transparent, and there were dark, dark shadows under his eyes.

"Oh, Vladimir," he said, starting to cry. "Oh, Jesus, Vladimir, did they tell you what happened?"

"I heard some of it," Vladimir said.

"Oh, Jesus, it was awful!" He looked around, his hands opening and closing spasmodically.

He tried to get up from the bed, but Vladimir pushed him back against the pillows. Nico was as weak as a baby.

"Tell me about it," he said softly. "I have to know."

"Yes," Nico said, with a deep, deep sigh. "I suppose so."

He told him about the workers marching on Sokolnika, about the fires and the dead horses and the ruined house. He faltered when it came to talking about the women, Sonya, Sophie, the two maids. It was hard to talk about. They had all been raped repeatedly, beaten, raped again, killed. The looters had used them mercilessly all through the endless night and then killed them as dispassionately as a man with a newspaper swats a fly.

"They were all drunk, crazy, every one of them," Nico said. He was no longer crying, but tears still trickled down his face as if of their own volition. "The next morning, they marched on Telegin."

Telegin had become as famous, in its own way, as Sokolnika. The visitor's book contained the names of the wealthy, titled and famous of five continents, a dozen Grand Dukes, and even one or two Kings. All of them had come to Telegin for the same reason: because it was, without question, one of the finest stud farms in the world. For this fact Vladimir took no credit at all except the credit for financing it. The work of selecting and breeding the Telegin strain he had placed confidently in the hands of Pavel Ulyanov, and that faith had been rewarded tenfold. The farm boasted two great lines: one from the pure Orlov champion Zenit, the other from Vladimir's own horse, Pilyugin. Telegin was the only stud farm in Russia which boasted two such fine strains. Even Prince Leonid Vyazensky of Lotarevo could not claim to have two Russian Derby winners among his sires. Over the years, Vladimir's estate manager, Piotr Stapovny, a graduate of the juridical faculty of St. Petersburg university who had specialized in agriculture, had stocked the farm with Swiss cattle, chicken, ducks and geese. Most of the peasants in the nearby villages worked on Telegin land. In the nearest, Shkolkovo, the Smirnoff family had built a church and a hospital named for Petya's first wife, Natalia.

That September morning, Piotr Stapovny rode, as he usually rode, across the fields to the big house, to see Pavel Ulyanov before making his customary circuit of the estate. The harvest was in, and it had been a good one. There would be plenty of food for the animals this winter. He planned to spend the afternoon at the mill. The wheat was almost ready to be ground, and haymaking could begin soon.

He saw the mob coming; he knew immediately what their intent was. He was well aware of the mood of the peasants. At the outbreak of war, he had become the chairman of their Mobilization Committee. He had known many of them ever since he had come to Telegin. He could see faces that he knew from Shkolkovo among the advancing men, but there were others in the tattered remnants of uniforms, filthy overalls, working clothes. Many of them were drinking from bottles as they marched. Piotr touched the spurs to his horse's flanks and thundered up to the main house, scattering gravel. Chickens fled in squawking panic as he ran to the door and pounded on it, shouting Pavel Ulyanov's name.

"Get out, Pavel!" he yelled. "Get out of here while you can! They'll be here in five minutes!"

"It's too late!" Pavel shouted, throwing the bolts back to let Piotr in. "We'll have to hold out here!"

The mob was in sight now. They were led by a gaunt old man with gray hair. He wore worker's overalls and a red armband. He was shouting to the men behind him, but they did not seem to be taking much notice.

"Hey, you in there, you'd better come out!" someone shouted from the mob. "Or we'll burn the place down around your ears!"

Piotr Stapovny came to the doorway of the house, a pistol in his hand. He was tall and good-looking, and concealed his fear very well.

"What do you want here?" he said. "What do you men want?"

"We've come to claim what's ours!" someone shouted. Piotr Stapovny recognized the voice and fixed the speaker with a stare.

"Is that you, Yakov Yurievich?" he said. "You own nothing in Telegin. You don't even work the land here."

"Don't argue with him!" another man shouted.

"Stepan Petrovich?" Stapovny said. "Tell me, why are you here?"

"We're here for Lenin!" the man he had spoken to shouted back. "And we retreat for no one!"

There was a huge cheer and the mob began to move forward. Stapovny held up an imperious hand and they stopped, waiting like wolves.

"You cannot come into this house," he said. "This house belongs to Vladimir Smirnoff."

"It belongs to the workers!" the old man with the gray hair shouted. "Everything belongs to the workers!"

"Stand aside!" they shouted.

"Down with the capitalist lackeys!"

"All land to the peasants!"

"Get out of the way, Piotr Grigorievich, we don't want to hurt you."

"No!" Stapovny said. "I'll die before I let you pass me."

He raised the gun and managed to fire it three times before they were on him. Little Pavel Ulyanov had no chance at all. He had never fired a gun in his life, and he was still trying to understand why his pistol would not fire when they swarmed into the house, shouting, cursing, killing mad. It was only after they had killed him that they noticed that the safety catch on the Browning was still on the "on" position. That was a good laugh, they said.

They demolished the poultry houses, killing the chickens, geese and ducks as indiscriminately as foxes. Then they slaughtered the pigs and the sheep, and wrecked the pens and barns before moving on to the cowsheds and the milking pens. When all of those were well alight and smoking, they went into the stables. They brought the proud, sleek racehorses out into the cobbled courtyard, but they did not kill them. Instead they slashed the hamstrings of each animal and watched them thrashing about, screaming in agony, on their now-useless hoofs. That was much better than killing them. They would live a long time like that, if the wolves didn't get them first.

After the horses had been whipped, screaming, into the fields, they set fire to the stables and barns. Then they moved back into the house and systematically destroyed it, room by lovely room. They smashed the blue-tiled stoves with the delicate Delft designs; they threw the gilt-framed mirrors out of the windows to shatter on the paving stones below. They defaced the walls and smeared ordure on the painting of Pilyugin. They defiled what they could not break and stole anything of the slightest value. Once again, they ended their orgy of destruction in the cellars. Vintage champagnes, the finest wines swilled down their gullets, spilled heedlessly on their clothes, poured wantonly on the spotless cellar floors. Howling, reeling, blind drunk all night and well into the next day, they set Telegin alight at two in the afternoon and left singing the "Marseillaise."

"I had to go out there, Vladimir," Nico said. "I had to go to Sokolnika, to Telegin. I had to—look at them. Oh, Jesus Christ, Sophie, Sophie!" He sobbed without tears, great, dry racking sobs that made the muscles on the side of his throat stand out like ropes.

"That was brave of you Nico," Vladimir said, softly. "Were they very badly—?"

"I don't know, I didn't look. I'm sorry, I couldn't bear to look at them," Nico said. His voice was rising steadily, his breathing faster. "I buried them, Vladimir. I buried them right away at Sokolnika. I couldn't bear the thought of having the—of their being in the house. I just couldn't do it, I couldn't, couldn't!"

"You did the right thing," Vladimir said. "It's all right, Nico, it's all over now."

"No." Nico said. "No, it's not, that's not all. I could have taken that, I think, even that. But then—"

"Something else?"

"There's a place," Nico said, sniffling. "On the Tverskoi. The old City Governor's residence. You have to go there to report—disturbances. It's called NKOVT. The People's Office for the Investigation of Agitations and Disturbances."

God, Vladimir thought, the names they choose! "You went there?" he asked.

"You have to. You have to report what happened. Everything, every detail. They write it all down. I couldn't stand it, watching them write it down, word for word. I tried to tell them, but when I saw them writing it down—"

"Take it slowly, Nico. Take it bit by bit."

"That was bad enough, them writing it down. But then him. He came out of the office. I couldn't believe my eyes when I saw him. He's the director of it."

"Who?"

"Boris Abrikosov! That damned Boris Abrikosov!"

"This office, what did you call it?"

"NKOVT."

"Is it something to do with the militia?"

"I don't know, Vladimir. I don't think so, but I was too scared to ask. I just wanted to get out of there. I'd been all right up till then. I was managing. It was awful, but I was managing. And then him. He came over. He was smiling, as if he was glad to see me. 'Well, well,' he said. 'Has something terrible happened here?' The clerk told him and he smiled again, the same smile. He was glad, Vladimir. He was pleased to hear what had happened. I could tell, he wasn't going to do anything, not a damned thing."

He subsided hopelessly, staring at the wall.

"I went out. I went down the street. There was a café. I ordered vodka. Then another and another. I was—it was—oh, God, oh, Jesus, Vladimir, why did they have to tear her to pieces like that?"

He could not cry, but he moaned, whined, wrapping his arms around himself and rocking, forward and back, forward and back, eyes unseeing, spittle drooling from the corner of his mouth.

"Nico," Vladimir said. "Nico, listen, there was nothing you could have done. Nico, it's all right, listen to me!"

Forward and back, forward and back, forward and back. No sentience in the eyes, no expression on the face, forward and back, forward and back. Vladimir got up quickly and shouted for the nurse. The tone of his voice brought her running. When she saw Nico, she went quickly and efficiently to work. The syringe glinted; she waved Vladimir out of the room.

"There's nothing you can do," she said. "This will put him to sleep."

Vladimir nodded and closed the door silently behind him. So Boris Abrikosov was back—and in Moscow! He wondered how Boris had managed to get a post in government. The way things were, nobody was checking credentials too carefully, he supposed. He imagined Abrikosov going over the grim details of the events at Sokolnika, gloating. If the only way to press a claim against the Provisional Government was through the offices of Boris Abrikosov, then the best thing to do was forget it.

I wish Genya were still here, he thought. There were so many decisions to make. He thought of Tatiana, far away in Dmitrovsk. He wondered if, by thinking of her as he was doing now, she could pick up the faintest tremor of his need, all those many versts away. They said sometimes lovers were telepathic. He looked at the clock. Five thirty. He made a mental note to ask her what she had been doing, and whether she had thought of him at that moment. He was still thinking about her when he went to sleep that night. He dreamed he was walking through a ruined world. There were corpses on the sidewalks, and buried in the rubble. Dying horses floundered past on bloody stumps, white bones striking the cobblestones with an awful sound. There was smoke and fire everywhere. No one could tell him what it was he was looking for, or who it was that he had lost.

There is something unreal about an empty factory. It is like an unoccupied house or an empty stage, meaningless without the people who fill it with life and color. Vladimir's footsteps echoed hollowly as he crossed the cobbled courtyard and opened the door of the office building.

The distilleries and adjacent buildings of the Smirnoff vodka manufactory covered eight blocks in all. They stood on the south bank of the Moskva River, where the cast-iron Tchugguni Bridge spanned the Vodoovotni Canal. Four blocks southward on the Pyatnitzkaya they marched, huge, dark, full of crouching power. The tall chimneys of the distilling plant soared high above the streets. They said that from the top you could see 150 versts in any direction.

From the big paneled room they had always called The Office, he could see down into the factory, the maze of piping and machinery. He remembered his father telling them how women had fainted with astonishment the first time the electric lights were turned on in the bottling sheds. That had been in the exciting time, when Petya had been revolutionizing the whole concept of vodka making. In old Arsenii's day, it had needed only comparatively simple equipment to distill the alcohol. The scale of operations envisioned by Petya had required a dynamic new approach, and he had made it. He went to Germany and bought the finest high-efficiency rectifiers available. Even in those days they had cost half a million *Thalers*. They were nearly a hundred feet high. The police had to be called daily to disperse the crowds of goggling spectators wanting to watch them being erected. Then Petya bought dynamos and evaporators, coolers and continuous-flow heaters, stills, flasks, retorts. The only thing which remained constant throughout was the formula for the charcoal used in the distillation. That was a Smirnoff secret.

The plant was silent, and he could see that many of the machines had been badly damaged. The Office had been smashed to bits, the fine Directoire desks reduced to kindling, the paneled walls splintered. Vladimir walked across the room to where his father's portrait had been flung in a crumpled heap on the floor. Someone had slashed at it with a knife. It was hard to imagine people doing things like this just for the sake of seeing it torn, or broken, or smashed. The Bolsheviks were unleashing fury on the land; he doubted that they had the remotest idea how to contain it. He picked up the battered portrait and hung it back where it had always hung. The mien was still haughty, the eyes confident, the stance aggressive. I'm glad you're not here to see all this, Vladimir thought.

They had not found the secret safe set into the concrete floor. Only he, Pierre and Nico knew of its existence. He ripped back the carpet and opened the safe, taking out the steel deed box which contained the secret distilling formula. They're not getting that, he thought. They can have all the rest, but they're not getting that. He relocked the safe and then left the offices without a backward glance. As he crossed the Moskvoretzky Bridge, he noticed that a red flag was flying over the Kremlin. His eyes were cold and his mouth was bitter. You could neither fight the Bolsheviks or join their swelling ranks. Well, he would never join them. Even if they would have me, he thought, grimacing at the red banner; the Bolsheviks had little time for turncoats. A series of pictures flickered through his mind's eye: screaming horses, Pierre's bloody body on the bayonets, sweet, kind Sophie torn and battered by cruel hands, Senka gone, Irina gone, Sasha gone. What had they all done to deserve such deaths? he asked himself, knowing there was no answer and there never would be.

30

OR THREE MONTHS, Castle lived like an automaton. Each night he went back to his apartment from the Embassy, drank half a bottle of vodka, and fell into a dream-haunted sleep from which he would awaken to return to the Embassy. Every day he anxiously scanned the signals, certain that Landis would recall him. No signal came, and he could not understand why. After Sukhotin's death, the Petersburg Plan had been broken. Castle gave everything he had to Tereschenko, who turned the information over to the Ministry of Justice. Perverzev, the Minister of Justice, couldn't keep the lid on it. Despite a governmental edict forbidding publication in any newspaper of the basic facts, there was a pamphlet on the streets in days that told the people Lenin was a German spy, supplied with money through a German espionage *apparat* based in Stockholm. For the moment, at least, revolution—which had been imminent—was staved off. The "July Days" demonstrations fizzled out, and the Provisional Government took firmer control than it had had since its establishment.

Through all these times of turmoil Castle waited, cursing Landis for making him sweat. It was not until August that he learned why he had not been recalled. The man who brought him the news was Raymond Robins, deputy head of the newly arrived American Red Cross Mission.

He was a tall, black-haired man with the striking profile of a Sioux warrior. As a young man, he had given up a thriving law practice in San Francisco to join the Klondike gold rush, where he struck it rich. He always said that the most important thing he had found in the Yukon was not gold, but God. A devout Christian, his eyes held the bright shine of a man on a crusade.

"Robert Landis told me that you are a good man, Castle," Robins said. "We need good men. We need you, your experience, your contacts. As of now, you're seconded to the Red Cross. Landis has okayed it."

He nodded, wondering what Landis had told Robins about him. Not the truth, that was for sure. He could not imagine the Red Cross having any need of his special talents. The fact that Landis was keeping him out in the cold meant that he was not yet convinced that the German *Sonderabteilung* had shot its bolt in Russia. Under the cover of the Red Cross, he would have Castle available should the need arise. What was that old hillbilly saying? Castle thought. It applied to Landis: his ma didn't raise no fools.

"What can I do?" he said to Robins.

"We have a hell of a big job to do here, Castle," the tall man said. "People are dying of hunger, babies starving, old people freezing to death. Our job, as I see it, is to get food to the hungry, clothing to those who don't have any, medical supplies where they'll do the most good. We've got the money and we've got the manpower and we've got the goods. What we need now is coordination, and that's where you come in. You know people. I want liaison set up between the Provisional Government, the Army sanitation people, the Union of Zemstvos, the Russian Red Cross, and the voluntary organizations. And I want it yesterday. When can you start?"

"Yesterday?" Castle grinned. Robins grinned too, and stuck out his hand. He had a strong grip.

"Fly at it," he said. "See Bill Thompson if you need money."

From that day on, Castle worked eighteen and sometimes twenty hours a day, seven days a week. The logistics of moving food, clothing, and medical supplies became his sole concerns. Buried in work, he had little time to reflect on the past and no time at all to grieve. He found he could walk down the Morskaya now, and look at the apartment building in which Irina had died, without it breaking him up inside. It was not forgetting; it was learning to live with remembering.

The streets were dirty and dangerous. There were roving bands of drunken soldiers everywhere, and in the railroad stations hundreds waited day and night for trains that rarely came.

Tereschenko was still working in his old office, although now he shared it with four other deputies, who looked at Castle with surly dislike every time he showed his face there. If their presence inhibited Tereschenko, he did not show it.

"I'm just another deputy now, boy," he said to Castle. "No power at all. But I can take you to meet Kerensky, if he's not off at the front somewhere giving the troops a morale booster."He told Castle that Kerensky was still trying to establish some kind of stable power base from which to resist the Bolsheviks.

"The man's weak, boy, that's the trouble," Tereschenko said. "He'd shake hands with the Devil if it was expedient. Right now he's plotting with Boris Savinkov and that old fool Kornilov to set up some sort of triumviral leadership."

"I don't think I know Kornilov," Castle said.

"Kerensky made him Commander-in-chief in July," Tereschenko said. "He's the worst judge of men I ever met. Kornilov is a dolt, the heart of a lion and the brains of a sheep. But what can you expect in times when the man who plotted the death of Plehve and the Grand Duke Serge is appointed Deputy Minister of Defense?"

"I hear he has sent the Tsar and the royal family to Siberia."

"Yes, for their own protection, he calls it. Others say it's to clear the path for his own coronation."

Castle found Kerensky to be a sallow, exhausted-looking individual, his face always twisted as if in pain. He was a good talker, though, and his enthusiasms were infectious.

"We're only trying to do here what the British, the French and you Americans did centuries ago, you know," Kerensky said. "Only without a Napoleon, without a Cromwell, without a—"

"Benedict Arnold?" Castle grinned. Kerensky smiled, too, that quick, nervous-sparrow smile of his that Castle would come to know so well.

"You know about all that, then," he said.

"I know what Tereschenko told me," Castle said.

Tereschenko said that Kerensky feared Savinkov would kill him, and that even if Savinkov didn't kill him, the former terrorist was plotting to make Kornilov dictator. That was exactly the scenario that was played out in late August. The oxlike Cossack general ordered his troops to occupy Petrograd. With one would-be dictator in Mogilyev—Kornilov—and the other in Petrograd—Kerensky—both being manipulated by Savinkov, chaos ensued. Kerensky issued orders that Kornilov was to be replaced by his aide. Kornilov refused to be dismissed and his aide, General Lukomsky, refused to replace him. Kerensky then named another general to the command, and he, in turn, said no. Finally, on September 1, old General Alexeyev, the Tsar's last Commander-in-chief, was persuaded to accept the post.

"It's like a bloody comic opera!" Tereschenko roared. "Kerensky has handed Russia to the Bolsheviks on a platter! They've been sitting like cats at a mousehole, boy, biding their time. And now they're ready to move. Trotsky's out of the Kresty on bail. Lenin's lurking in Finland waiting his moment. We've got perhaps a month, boy, maybe two. Then all hell is going to break loose."

Tereschenko's prediction was uncannily accurate. By midday on October 26, Petrograd was plastered with posters proclaiming the downfall of the Provisional Government. It was not, in fact, true, but it was true in effect. Although the Ministers were in constant and noisy session in the fairy-tale Malachite Room of the Winter Palace, they had no power to enforce any edict they issued. The Bolsheviks already had control of the telephone exchange, the post office and telegraph station, the railroad stations and most of the public buildings. Yet a strange, inert quiet pervaded the streets. Shops stayed open, streetcars grated by, people lined up as usual outside the bakeries and the butcher shops.

Kerensky was gone. He left Petrograd soon after ten on the morning of October 25 in a Pierce-Arrow belonging to the American Embassy, flying the flag of the United States on its tonneau. Kerensky told Castle on the telephone that it was imperative that he get transport to take him to Tosno so he could meet the troops en route to Petrograd. Not one of the thirty automobiles lined up outside the Winter Palace would start. He was frantic, and Castle sensed that his urgency concealed panic. He watched as Kerensky and his aides piled into the machine and roared out of the great Palace Square. A vast quiet descended as the sound of the motor faded. The calm before the storm, Castle thought. It was strange how people thought in clichés at times of great uncertainty, as though the clichés were themselves reassuring. He had heard that one phrase a dozen times in the last couple of days.

He tried, unsuccessfully, to get into the Winter Palace to ask Tereschenko what was going on, but the soldiers barred his way. Not even the letter Michael had given him worked. They were really frightened, Castle realized.

Late in the afternoon, Lenin made a speech at the Smolny Institute, headquarters of the Petrograd soviet. The Military Revolutionary Committee sent an ultimatum to the Winter Palace: surrender or fight. If it was refused, a red lantern would be hoisted on the tower of the Fortress of Peter and Paul, the cruiser *Aurora* would fire a blank from one of her six-inchers, and the storming of the Winter Palace would commence.

The Ministers in the Winter Palace had received a promise of troops from Mogilyev if they could hold out for forty-eight hours, but even as they read it, Bolshevik infiltrators were entering the vast palace, which had several hundred doors of one kind and another. At about 10:30 P.M. the red lantern winked on the tower of the Fortress, and its guns opened fire as the cruiser fired her blank shot. Nothing happened. No return fire was noted, and after a while the bombardment ceased. A cold, wet wind swept the streets clean of people, apart from the groups of armed soldiers guarding the bridges.

Castle was at the Smolny all evening. The former girl's school, three long blocks of gray buildings dominated by a blue and gold cupola, stood at the farthest eastern end of the Shpalernaya. It was a maelstrom of activity. Soldiers tramped through corridors filthy with mud and detritus, despite signs that exhorted the comrades to preserve cleanliness for the sake of their health. Women carrying dossiers, girls with bundles of leaflets, officers standing in groups, watchful-eyed men in working clothes filled the place with enormous noise. A dining room was set up in the basement, selling cabbage soup, pieces of tough meat, black bread for two rubles, or a cup of tea in a tin mug for five kopecks.

A little after 2:15 on the morning of October 27 a telegram came over the wires. AT 2:04 THE WINTER PALACE WAS TAKEN. SIX MEN OF THE PAVLOVSKY KILLED. The Provisional Government was under arrest; the Revolution had succeeded. Everyone in the Smolny was cheering, hugging each other, kissing one another. Castle ran out and managed to scramble on board a truck that was going to the Nevsky. At every corner the men in the back hurled out leaflets which spread the word that the Winter Palace had been successfully stormed. He piled out of the truck at the top of the Nevsky. The Winter Palace was ablaze with light. There was cheering and shouting, and a huge mob of people was moving across the Square. He ran into the palace. The place was full of packing cases, all full of glass, porcelain, paintings. The crowds were attacking the boxes, smashing them in with rifle butts and crowbars. He saw a small man in working clothes carrying an ornate golden clock, another with an armful of jewel boxes. An officer came into the room and shouted at the people to get back, away from the boxes of treasure.

"No looting, comrades!" he shouted. "Do not touch anything! This is the property of the people!"

Nobody took any notice of him. A woman ran past Castle carrying a wide-brimmed hat with a huge ostrich feather on it. He saw two men going down a corridor with a carpet on their shoulders. Others had vases, clocks, statuettes, icons, small paintings. There were knots of people everywhere, soldiers arguing, dejected-looking civilians shuffling down the vast, echoing corridors with their gritty stone floors. He saw a doorway marked "29" and went through it, up stone stairs with an iron railing, and came out into the Dark Corridor, with its multiple portraits of the Knights of the Order of St. Andrew. He went past another gallery filled with portraits of generals of the Napoleonic wars. The place was breathtaking; no other word would do. Vast rooms, salons, ballrooms, reception halls, dining rooms with pillars of marble, gilded fluting, golden doors, carved ornamental frescos and pillars, awesome, beautiful. He passed from chamber to exquisite chamber. There were Gobelin tapestries on the walls of the private dining room; intricately ornate golden carvings surrounding the screens, the walls, the mirrors of baroque boudoirs; deep reds and golds in the throne room; dazzling gold walls, doors, even ceilings in the Gilt Drawing Room. The mind could not encompass the sumptuous, elegant wastefulness of it. He eventually found his way to the Malachite Room, where the Provisional Government had been arrested. The malachite walls were decorated with angels, the doors painted with gold leaf. His footsteps echoed. There was a green baize table with sheets of paper on it. Someone had been doodling on them.

"Stand still, you!" a voice shouted. Heavy boots pounded on the polished parquet, and Castle turned around to see three Red Guards coming toward him with rifles ready.

"*Amyerikanski!*" he shouted. They looked nervous enough to shoot first and ask questions afterward. This had been a trigger-happy night. "I'm looking for Michael Tereschenko. Do you know where he has been taken?"

"You get out of here!" one of the soldiers shouted. "We don't want any provocateurs in here."

"I'm an American," Castle said. "I'm not a—"

"Out!" the soldier said, gesturing with the rifle. Castle shrugged and let them hustle him through the corridors and down the stairs. At the doorway there were more guards. Piles of pictures, rugs, bedspreads, vases, jewel boxes, rings, mirrors were piled to one side. Everyone who left was being searched. Castle did not protest as rough hands checked through his pockets. When they were finished, he asked the officer if he knew where the Ministers had been taken.

"They have gone to the Fortress," the man said. "They took them to the Fortress."

It was no use going over there, Castle thought. He looked at his watch. Nearly four. Soldiers were grouped around their bonfires in the square and by the Palace Bridge; he could smell tea. The lights were on again in the Nevsky, pale in the growing grayness of dawn. The streets were silent; there were no people about.

On November 9 all bourgeois newspapers were suppressed. All offices of the Kadet party were closed. On the 18th, the Kadet club in Petrograd was wrecked, and on November 28, all party members were declared to be "enemies of the people." The Table of Ranks had already been abolished, and on the 22nd, every citizen with more than one fur coat was ordered to hand over the others to the Army, giving Red Guards a pretext for searching any home they chose. On December 11, control of education was taken from the hands of the Church, and on December 14 banking became a State monopoly. Workers' control of industry was established, and commercial secrecy was abolished. On December 16, all Army ranks were officially suppressed, except for the rank of Commander. On December 17, the sale or purchase of houses was forbidden. On December 18, civil marriage and divorce were instituted. On December 21, the "revolutionary courts" were given a new code which virtually rendered the legal profession superfluous. On December 24, all industry became the property of the State. On December 29, payment of interest and dividends was stopped. Private bank accounts were frozen, and no depositor was allowed to withdraw more than 125 rubles in any one week. There were new elections everywhere for the administration of housing, trade, industry, municipal services. To each were appointed, in due course, cold-eyed men with wills of steel who enforced their edicts with pistols and brutality, men to whom the petty bourgeoisie were no better than contemptible small-time thieves. Leather-coated, jackbooted, relentless, they reorganized everything; factories, apartment blocks, shops, newspapers, mills, restaurants, streetcar operations were inexorably Bolshevized.

Not all the new laws could be enforced immediately. The Bolsehviks simply did not have sufficient hold upon the economy or the country to do so yet. Nevertheless, the blows fell thicker and faster. A decree confiscating private houses was promulgated, confining their former owners to a few rooms in each. Luxury taxes were levied on servants, on bathrooms, even on pianos. All nonworkers under fifty were required by law to join the Personal Labor Corps. It was not uncommon to see former Generals, priests, and Countesses clearing the snow from the Fontanka or the Nevsky. Now another decree required anyone owning jewelry or gold objects weighing more than seventy grams, together with any foreign currency, to surrender it to the State. One or two rich people bribed bank clerks to get their safety deposit boxes out before the banks were searched. This traffic stopped when a number of bank clerks were summarily executed.

One further, far-reaching decision was made by Lenin on December 7 and promulgated immediately by his fanatical disciple Felix Dzerzhinsky: the creation of the All-Russian Extraordinary Commission for Struggle Against Counterrevolution and Sabotage. The Russian initials for "Extraordinary Commission" were "Ch" and "K," and it was by this name that the new Soviet secret police force was to become notorious: *Cheka.*

Felix Dzerzhinsky sent Latsis to Moscow with a message for Boris Abrikosov. Its text was simple, its meaning plain.

You are appointed immediately to the rank of Commissar, Moscow, of the All Russian Extraordinary Commission for Struggle Against Counter-revolution and Sabotage. You will commence duties forthwith. The good of the Revolution now demands a relentless attack upon the bastions of capitalism, saboteurs, and organizers of military insurrection. The enemies of socialism no longer have inviolability of the person or universal suffrage under the law. The matter is arch-important. The Party is responsible. Act with courage and dispatch. Comradely greetings.

Dzerzhinsky, Chairman, ChK.

Boris had talked with Dzerzhinsky enough times to know exactly what his new master wanted. He imagined that fiery-eyed, spade-bearded face, thin and saturnine, totally uncompromising. He remembered how Felix would bang his fist on the table, insisting that only terror and attrition would break the stranglehold of the ruling classes. Well, Boris thought, now he has *carte blanche*, and so do I. He issued his first edict to the men he had enrolled from the Moscow Party Committee.

"Your watchword will be 'no quarter,' " he told them. "The government means to take strong measures against landowners, insurrectionists, and mercenaries in the interests of the workers and peasants."

They cheered, as he had known that they would. Boris smiled cynically. Many of them were smarting for revenges of their own, and he was giving them the power to exact those revenges without retribution. He turned them loose upon the city with a callous disregard for what they might do. If they were to become his creatures, he had first to feed them. It was as simple as that.

Give them until the end of January, he thought, or the middle of February. Meanwhile, he could prepare for his own, long-deferred revenge. It was, after all, no less pleasurable because he had been forced to wait. Now he had unlimited power, and he was going to use it to destroy what was left of the Smirnoff family. First, the weakling brother whom he had seen sniveling in his outer office a few weeks ago. Then Sergei Tretyakov and his wife, the nunlike Katrina. He smiled his snake's smile at the thought of the test to which he was going to put her faith. Yes, he thought. First, Nico Smirnoff. Then the Tretyakovs. And then you, Vladimir Smirnoff. Then you.

"Mikhailovich!" he shouted. "Get in here!"

The streets were full of soldiers, workers, Red Guards. Snow was piled high everywhere; there was no one to clear it. Scaffolding had been erected on the towers of St. Basil's Cathedral in Red Square; Bolshevik cannon had damaged the façade. Bread was in short supply, meat too expensive to buy. The only people who were eating well were criminals, who stole what they wanted. There were riots in the Kuznetsky Most, street disturbances everywhere. The prohibition of the sale of alcohol had still not been rescinded, but the street toughs knew where to get it. There was plenty in the cellars of the rich, and night after night, these were broken into. A traffic grew in the sale of addresses of the rich. The brutal Red Guards would pay anyone a few rubles for such information, but they were not to be trusted. Sometimes they took the address and then shot the person providing it.

The Reds came to 24 Nikitski Boulevard on January 4. It was a bitter, snowy night; their feet were soundless in the fresh snow. They battered on the door with their rifles until the terrified nurse opened it, holding her nightclothes tightly against her body.

"This is the home of the vodka maker Nikolai Smirnoff!" the leader of the mob shouted. It was not a question. "We are told that anti-Bolshevik plots are being hatched here!"

"That's—that's impossible," the nurse stuttered. "There is no one here, only myself and Monsieur Smirnoff."

"Stand aside," the man said, pushing her out of the way. "We'll question him ourselves."

"You can't—he's sick, you mustn't disturb—" the nurse jabbered, tugging at the sleeve of the soldiers nearest to her. The soldier's face twitched with impatience, and he backhanded her away. She fell in a heap in the corridor, her mouth splattered with blood, sobbing. The other men trampled past her, shouting.

Nico Smirnoff was asleep when they came into his room. They threw back the bedclothes and dragged him, shivering, out of his bed.

"What's wrong?" he mumbled. "What's happened? Is there a fire? Is—"

"There's a fire, all right, Smirnoff!" one of the guards shouted. "And your kind is going to roast in it! Where's Mikhailovich?"

"Here!" another voice interposed. "Let me through! Let me through!" Mikhailovich pushed his way through the crowd of men gathered around Nico Smirnoff and regarded the prisoner with pitiless eyes.

"Is this him?" he said, contemptuously. "Are you Nikolai Smirnoff?"

"Yes, yes," Nico said. He screwed up his eyes, trying to focus them properly. He felt fuzzy, disoriented. He was shaking with cold. Somehow it seemed important to convince them that it was not fear that was making him tremble. "I'm not afraid," he said. "You must understand. I'm not afraid."

"That's good," Mikhailovich said. "No need to be. You're among friends."

"We're no friends of his kind!" one of the Red Guards growled. "Look at this place!" His voice was threatening. At that moment they heard the unmistakable sound of champagne corks popping in the cellar. The big Red Guard grinned, his anger evaporating like a child's.

"Come on, comrades," he said to his fellows. "No use letting the boys drink down there on their own, is there?"

Cheering and laughing, they pushed out of the bedroom, clattering down the stairs to the cellar. Mikhailovich heard bottles smashing. They were breaking the necks off the bottles rather than wrestle with the corks. Drunken pigs, he thought.

"You don't remember me, do you?" he asked as he pulled up Nico

416

Smirnoff. He released his grip, and Nico slumped into a sitting position on the disordered bed. "You don't know who I am."

"No," Nico mumbled. "Don't know. Cold. Cold." He tried to crawl back into the bed, but Mikhailovich grabbed him and turned him around so that their faces were only inches apart.

"I'm your long-lost cousin," Mikhailovich said. "From Paris."

"Nikki?" Nico whispered. "Nikki Smirnoff?"

"Mikhail Mikhailovich," the man opposite him said.

"Please," Nico said. "I'm sick. Cold."

"You come with me," Mikhailovich said. "I'll fix you up." He put his shoulder under Nico's arm and hoisted him off the bed. Stickthin and light as a feather, he thought contemptuously. No meat and no guts. "Come on."

"Where?" Nico said. "Where are we going?"

"We're going to have a drink," Mikhailovich said. He helped Nico down the stairs into the cellar. Some of the men were already well on the way to being drunk. They set up a roar of mock welcome when they saw Nico Smirnoff.

"Here he is, comrades," Mikhailovich said. "Your host doesn't want you to drink his liquor without the pleasure of his company. You, give him a drink."

A glassful of wine was put into Nico's hand. He looked at it stupidly. "I'm not—I can't drink this," he said. "The doctor—"

"Drink it up, comrade," one of the men said, roughly. He took Nico's chin in his hand and forced open his mouth, pouring the wine into it. Nico coughed and spluttered and choked, and the soldiers roared with laughter, pounding him on the back. Someone filled another glass and they poured that into him, too, and another and more, drink after drink until he was drooling, stupid, lollingly drunk. The soldiers were all drunk, too, and one or two of them were turning ugly. Mikhailovich knew the signs.

"Well, comrades," he said, "there's probably a few rubles lying around upstairs. These capitalists always have money, and plenty of it."

"What about it, Smirnoff?" one of the Red Guards shouted. "Have you got any money?"

"Losha money," Nico said. "Loshnlosha money."

"Upstairs?"

"Upshers. Downshers. Loshamoney."

The soldiers grabbed him and yanked him to his feet. He looked at them, frowning with confusion. What had he done now?

"Come on, you!" the soldiers growled, and frog-marched him up the stairs. They weren't careful anymore. If furniture got in their way, they kicked it aside. Nico saw one of them take a picture off the wall and smash it to pieces.

"Here!" he began. "Stop that, this—" His words were cut off by a brutal blow in the face. He fell to the floor, mind reeling, blood pouring from his cut lips. It wasn't fair, he thought. Why were they doing this?

"The money, Smirnoff!" someone was shouting. "Where's the money?" Why were they shouting? he wondered. He could hear them perfectly well. He could hear glass breaking, too, and the splintering sound of furniture being broken. He saw a man kick in the door of a wardrobe, tearing the broken pieces of wood aside and ripping the clothes out of it, throwing them anywhere. The word kept hammering in his ears: money, money, money! They were still shouting at him, and he looked up at their faces. One of them kicked him and it broke something inside him. He felt it go as clearly as if he had seen it happen. A low moan of pain escaped his broken lips.

"No," he said. "No money."

"Talk, you miserable bastard!" someone shouted. They all started kicking him. The pain swept over him like dark red sea, and he screamed at them, begging them to stop, trying to tell them that he'd give them anything, anything, if they'd stop; but it was too late for that. They kicked him a few more times for good measure, and then four of them picked him up and threw him at the window. He smashed through the wood and glass and out into the street two stories below. He was unconscious, so he did not feel his spine breaking on the piled ice and slush at the side of the Nikitski Boulevard.

After a little while, Mikhail Mikhailovich came out of the house. The sounds of wrecking were loud and clear in the still winter air, but he knew no one would venture near. He looked at the body lying on the ice in its bloodstained nightshirt. If he wasn't dead already, Nico Smirnoff certainly would be by the time the Red Guards left. Buttoning his leather coat against the icy wind, he hurried back toward the center of the city.

Vladimir listened to what the nurse had to say. His face showed no emotion; he was past all that. There was nothing he could do for Nico; perhaps there never had been.

"They didn't tell you who they were?" he said.

"They just said—just said—that we had been plotting against the Bolsheviks."

"Were they wearing uniforms?"

"Not all of them. The old man had a leather overcoat on."

"Which old man?"

"The old man who gave them orders. They all did what he said."

"What did he look like?"

"Old. Thin, like a skeleton. His face looked like a skull. Dark shadows under his eyes, pouches. Gray hair, almost white."

"Did he give a name?"

"They don't use names, that kind," the nurse said. "The comrades." Her voice was bitter. Her mouth was puffed and swollen. She had run from the house as soon as the soldiers turned their backs, terrified. She told no one what had happened until Vladimir appeared at her door. Even now she was afraid. If they saw him here, they might come after her.

"Thank you, anyway," Vladimir said. "For what you did."

"Wait," the nurse said. She had been sprawled on the floor, senses reeling, she remembered that. All the men had gone into Monsieur Smirnoff's bedroom. She heard them pulling him out of bed and heard him mumbling something about a fire. Then someone shouted the old man's name.

"Mikhailovich!" she said to Vladimir. "His name was—"

"Mikhailovich!" The effect her words had upon him was electric. He turned deathly pale, and for a moment Nurse Brodny thought he might pass out. Then the fire came back into his eyes.

"Thank you, thank you, *Gospozha* Brodny," Vladimir said. He pressed a note into her hands. She looked and saw that it was a hundred rubles. She started to thank him, but he was already striding swiftly down the street.

He went to the Tverskoi and talked to the soldier standing lackadaisical guard outside the building which had once housed the City Governor of Moscow.

"Damned cold, eh, comrade?" he said. "It can't be much fun standing around outside this place all day."

"Too true, brother," the soldier said, feelingly. He was just a youngster, Vladimir thought, not more than twenty.

"Cigarette?"

"I'm not supposed to smoke on duty."

"It's a free country, isn't it?"

The boy smiled. "Just the same, I'll keep it till later."

"I'm looking for a friend of mine. They told me he works here, but I don't like to bother him."

"What's his name?" the soldier said.

"His name is Mikhail Mikhailovich," Vladimir said. "He's an old man. Tall, thin, gray-haired. You know him?'

"Everybody knows him," the soldier said, scornfully. "He's a Deputy Commissar."

"Is that so," Vladimir said, with a respectful whistle. "I didn't know he was such a high-up."

"He's an important man," the soldier said. "Next to Comrade Abrikosov, he's in charge of this whole place."

"What time do they finish work?"

"They're here all hours," the soldier said. "I thought you said Mikhailovich was a friend of yours? Hasn't he told you all this himself?"

"I haven't seen him for a while," Vladimir said, disarmingly. "Not since Paris."

"Paris, eh? Lucky devil," the soldier said, with a grin. "I wouldn't mind spending a week's leave there."

"Neither would I," Vladimir agreed. They shook hands, and he walked up the boulevard toward the Pushkin statue near the Tverskaya Gate. Then he walked back again on the other side, crossing the street opposite the square-shaped building that housed the *Cheka*. There were benches on the grass island which divided the twin carriageway, a path where pigeons foraged hopefully. A watery sun brightened the sky. Vladimir sat huddled in his overcoat, waiting, waiting.

It was nearly six when he saw Boris Abrikosov come out, get into a waiting car and drive off. Vladimir got up and went back across the street. There was no one about. The young soldier smiled as he drew closer.

"Come back, have you?" he said.

"I was wondering, could I go inside and wait till Mikhail Mikhailovich comes down?" Vladimir said. "It's damned cold out here. As you well know."

"Well," the soldier said, "I'm not supposed to."

"Ah, come on, comrade," Vladimir said. "You don't want me to freeze to death, do you? Here, have another cigarette."

"Well," the soldier said, taking the cigarette. He looked right and left. "Go on, then. But if anyone asks you what you're doing in there, it's nothing to do with me."

"Don't worry, comrade," Vladimir said. "I won't let you down."

Vladimir went inside the house. He found himself in the hallway of what had once been a beautiful mansion. It was now defaced by makeshift plywood paneling, decorated haphazardly with revolutionary posters and notices of Bolshevik committee meetings. He went along the corridor. Some of the doors were open, and he could hear voices, telephones ringing. The doors were as makeshift as the walls of plywood. Some of them had labels stuck on them which indicated the activities of the occupants. Not all the doors were labeled. A man came out of one of the offices and stared at him.

"I have an urgent message for Comrade Mikhailovich," Vladimir said, hoping his voice sounded more confident than he was. "Which is his office?"

"Twenty-eight," the man said, without interest. "On your right."

He went along the corridor. There were three steps up to a half-level, which led into what might once have been a kitchen. On the right was a door marked "28." He could hear voices inside the room. He put his hand in his pocket and grasped the pistol. His palms were slick with sweat, and he was trembilng as he opened the door with his left hand. There was a counter in front of him, behind which sat a swarthy man with a heavy moustache who looked up without interest as Vladimir came through the door.

"Yes?" he said.

There were six or seven men in the room. He saw his quarry, and in the same moment Mikhailovich turned toward him. Recognition dawned in the old man's eyes, and he smiled his sour, contemptuous smile.

"Well, well, well," Mikhailovich said. "Look who's here. How did you get in, Smirnoff?"

"Charm," Vladimir said. The man with the moustache looked at Mikhailovich for guidance.

"It's all right," Mikhailovich said. "I'll take care of this." He came across to the counter. "What do you want, Smirnoff?"

"You know why I'm here," Vladimir said.

"No," Mikhailovich said, his very voice a taunt. "Why?"

"The nurse heard them call you by name, Nikki."

"Don't call me that!" Mikhailovich hissed. "Don't use that name here!"

"Why not?" Vladimir said, raising his voice. "Don't they know that you're a Smirnoff, too?" He shook his head sadly. "Tut, tut, cousin! Lying to your comrades like that."

"Shut your damned mouth!" Mikhailovich snapped. "Do you hear me? Or you'll get what your halfwit brother got."

"It was you, then," Vladimir said, gently. "Was it?"

"Yes, it was me," Mikhailovich said. He drew himself up. "And I'm proud of it. Proud of exterminating your slave-driving capitalist brothers, all of them!"

"Sokolnika?" Vladimir said, suddenly sickened.

"Yes, and your precious horses at Telegin!" Mikhailovich shouted. "We said we would bury your kind in thousands one day, didn't we? Well, the day has co—"

The revolver made a shocking sound as Vladimir pulled the trigger. The bullet smashed through the flimsy plywood of the counter and into Mikhailovich's belly. He was still reeling backward when Vladimir tore the gun from the pocket in which he had concealed it and shot the staggering man in the head. Mikhailovich fell in a sprawling heap over one of the desks and slid off it onto the grubby floor. The other men in the room stared at Vladimir for what seemed like an eternity, and then the one at the counter gave an inarticulate shout and leaped to grapple with him. Vladimir lashed out with the barrel of the gun, and the man fell backward with a sound like a wet scream. The rest of them froze where they stood.

He groped behind him for the door handle and opened it, keeping the men in the room covered. He saw their expressions change too late and felt the prod of the rifle barrel in his back. He sighed, and let his shoulders slump. It had been too much to hope for, anyway, he thought. He turned around. It was the young soldier who had been guarding the doorway.

"Put the gun on the floor," the soldier said. He didn't look quite so young and inexperienced anymore. Vladimir bent down to lay the pistol on the floor, and the soldier hit him with the butt of the rifle. Vladimir fell senseless to the floor. When he awoke, he was lying on a stone floor in an empty room with barred windows. A man in a leather overcoat was standing by the heavy door, a riding crop in his hand. He flicked the crop impatiently, once, twice. Vladimir looked up and saw the cold eyes and thin face of Boris Abrikosov. Boris smiled his hateful smile and flicked the riding crop lightly across Vladimir's shoulders.

"Welcome to the Lubyanka," he said.

31

FROM THE HOUSE there was a path that led up the hill through pine and birch groves and past a field of growing corn. Another verst or so farther on there was a slope, and at the bottom of this long incline there was a small lake. Every day, rain or shine, Tatiana walked up the hill and sat beside the lake. It had become her special place. Here, she sat and tried to imagine where Vladimir was and what he was doing. There had been no letters from him after the brief note that gave them the barest details of his brother's death. Was he in Moscow? Was he already on his way back to Dmitrovsk? She did not know, and so she filled the empty place in her life with daydreams. He would be back soon. They would go away again, back to the Crimea, or somewhere else. It would be like it was then. They would be together; she no longer even cared about marriage. Vladimir had been right. Marriage was for better times than these.

Life at Dmitrovsk was dull and uneventful. If you closed your eyes, she thought, you could imagine there had been no changes. The old Empire-style house with its rambling extensions and battered conservatory was the same as it had always been, the old servants solicitous, the peasants friendly. They had known the Tretyakovs for generations, and there was not a family in the entire area which had not at some time benefited from the ministrations of *Byelaya*, the lady in white, Sergei Tretyakov's wife. At Katrina's suggestion, he had already apportioned the land. It belonged to the people anyway, she said. So while the hurricane of revolution carried everything before it in other villages, Dmitrovsk was a haven of calm. Katrina encouraged tradesmen to ply their crafts. Dmitrovsk boasted a shoemaker and a tailor as well as a miller and a wheelwright. There was a good stock of wheat, and smoked and salted meat and fish had been stored so that no one would go hungry when winter came. They even had arms. All the rifles and pistols and grenades the young men had brought back with them from the front were stored in the house in the center of the village which housed the council. There was no demarcation between the occupants of the big house and the peasants; everyone had his own work to do. Maryka Makcheyeva helped Katrina in the "clinic." Tatiana was in charge of feeding poultry, cows, horses, sheep. They all shared the bigger chores: milking, cleaning out stables and cow barns, planting, picking fruit.

Every day refugees passed through the village. The children usually found them wandering across the empty steppe and told them where the village was. They were part of an endless stream of dispossessd, on their way to nowhere, bundles on their backs, clothes gray with dust, fathers, mothers, children, old grandmothers hobbling on sticks, looking for somewhere to settle again, begin again, hope again. There were many deserters: young boys in the remnants of uniforms, older men with dark, cunning, treacherous eyes that roamed over the bodies of the young women in the village. They were all on their way home, to Perm, to Ufa, to Samara and Simbirsk. They were all hungry, and many of them had been wounded. They all told stories like the ones Tatiana had heard from the boys in the Catherine Hospital in Petrograd. Katrina saw to it that all were given food and drink, and somewhere to sleep for the night. If their wounds were bad, their dressings dirty, she washed them, and cleaned and rebandaged them, before sending them on their way.

Every morning, every afternoon, and every evening, Katrina went to the village church to pray. Sergei always went with her. The villagers called him *Tyenka*, the little shadow.

Nothing seemed to interest him. He talked only in monosyllables and looked old, much older than his years, gray and dispirited, as though life itself was a burden that was crushing him. He plodded through his work with lackluster eyes and slumped shoulders, and nothing seemed to make him smile. Tatiana had tried many times to talk to him, but he always rebuffed her. There was no anger in the rebuff. Once in a while, she even thought she saw regret in his eyes, as if he were thinking of different times and a different world to which he had once belonged.

Oh, Vladimir, she thought as she sat beside the still water of the little lake. Where are you? Don't you know I need you?

A wood pigeon burst out of a tree, its wings creaking like a badly oiled wheel, startling her from her reverie. It had grown cooler.

There were dark clouds on the southern horizon and the tops of the trees were swaying in a newly born breeze. Time to go back, she sighed. Back to the same old routine. Do the chores, milk the cows, eat supper, read. Repeat the same old clichés: Nice day, wasn't it? Did you go for your walk? Do you think it will rain tomorrow? Were there many people at the clinic today? Were there any messages from the village? Always the same . . .

As she came through the straggling stand of birch and pine that crowned the hill above the farm, she heard shouting. Frowning, she quickened her pace. Then she heard shots and yells and the sound of breaking glass carrying clearly on the soft new breeze. She left the path and ran through the woods, her feet soundless on the heavy layer of pine needles. A blackbird skittered through the undergrowth and she jumped. Ahead there was a thick clump of bushes and beyond them the bright open ground that overlooked the farm.

Down below in the cobbled farmyard there were a dozen men. Some were in uniform. All wore the red armband of the Bolsheviks. She could see Sergei, his arms held by two burly fellows. A man in a long leather coat was reading something from a paper. Sergei stood with his head down, as though shamed beyond redemption. Two other men were holding Katrina, who was struggling ineffectually. There was no sign of Maryka. A crowd of peasants was watching the proceedings. Not one of them moved to defend Katrina or Sergei, or to protest the actions of the men in uniform. Tatiana saw one of the men produce a noosed rope and put it around Sergei's neck. Katrina screamed; the sound was blood-curdling, but it had no effect on the men holding her. Her white clothes were soiled and torn, as if she had fallen on muddy ground. Tatiana saw now that Katrina's face was bruised, and realized with sick certainty that they had raped her.

She lay on the warm ground, cold as death, and watched them drag Sergei Tretyakov across the cobbled yard. One of the men tossed the end of the rope over the joist of the hayloft and another caught it as it came down. They pulled on it, and Sergei was hoisted off his feet. Tatiana could hear the men shouting and laughing. Sergei did not struggle; his hands were tied behind his back and his feet bound together. He was hoisted up like a sack and then let down to the ground again three or four times. They were torturing him, and in doing so driving Katrina to the very edge of insanity. Tatiana put her hands over her ears; she could no longer bear to hear the screams.

She did not want to watch the sickening spectacle below, and yet she could not tear her eyes from it. The men hoisted Sergei up again, and this time they kept him there. His body contorted like a fish on a hook as his lungs fought for air, while below the men shouted vile things at the dying man. Katrina was no longer screaming. One of the men clamped a grubby fist across her mouth, and every time she tried to turn her head away from the swinging thing on the hayloft joists, he forced it back so that she had to watch.

The old man shouted something and some of the men ran across and grabbed Sergei's feet, lifting themselves off the ground, adding their weight to his, to speed his final agony. They swung like some obscene pendulum, right, left, right, left. No one else in the farmyard moved. The peasants watched as impassively as if they were watching sheep being shorn.

After a while it was all over. They cut Sergei's body down. The man in the leather coat shouted something to the villagers, and they cheered and surged forward. They took Sergei's body by the legs, dragging it across the cobblestones, and threw it into the back of the truck in which the Bolsheviks had arrived. Then Katrina was hustled across and manhandled into the truck. The men who had been inside the house came out dragging a struggling figure. It was Tatiana's mother. Maryka's mouth was a red smear, and her dress was torn from shoulder to waist. She walked as if something inside her was broken. The men bundled her into the truck alongside Katrina and then piled aboard themselves. Tatiana saw Katrina take her mother into her arms. As the truck bounced out of the farmyard, she caught sight of them clutching each other, their eyes dark smudges, white faces frozen with fear.

Tatiana never knew how long she stayed on the hillside, stiff with fear, with disbelief, with horror. It was dark when she finally stumbled down into the empty yard and pushed open the door of the deserted house. She walked through it like a ghost, from room to ruined room. They had smashed things for no other reason than that they had stood in front of them: vases, windows, chairs, anything. She went into her mother's room. Somehow it did not seem possible that the blood on the bed could be hers, and yet as repellent as the realization was, Tatiana knew that it must be.

As she went back downstairs, she heard the sound of a man's voice in the yard outside. She froze, her heart bounding into her throat, almost choking with fear. She heard a match strike and saw the soft yellow glow of an oil lamp. Then she heard footsteps; someone was coming into the house. Desperately, Tatiana tried to muster her thoughts. She had to hide. But where? The only place was the kitchen, and she could not move without being seen. Her only hope was to remain as still as she could, to pray that whoever it was would not come into the room. Dread drenched her like water as she saw the knob turn and the door swing open. She nearly fainted with relief when she saw that it was Aleksi, the old manservant.

"Who's there?" he said, sharply. "Speak up! I've a pistol here!" He's as terrified as I was, Tatiana thought, almost giggling with sheer relief.

"It's I, Aleksi," she whispered. "Mademoiselle Makcheyeva."

"Oh, praise God!" the old man said. His voice was tremulous. He lifted the lamp high, and Tatiana saw that his eyes were full of tears.

"Oh, what is to become of us all, mademoiselle?" the old man said. "What is going to happen to us?"

"Who were they, those men?"

"The man in the leather coat said they were from the *Cheka*. What is the *Cheka*, mademoiselle?"

"I don't know," Tatiana said. "Where have they taken Madame Tretyakov and Madame Makcheyeva? Did they say?"

"I don't know, mademoiselle," the old man whimpered. "I was hiding in the barn. I was afraid. They started shouting, smashing things. I thought they were going to kill us all."

"Saddle a horse," Tatiana said to him. "Hurry, now. A good horse."

The old man got to his feet unsteadily. He nodded as though arriving at a difficult decision. "I don't saddle the horses," he muttered. "That's not my task. But I suppose—"

"Hurry!" Tatiana hissed. "If you value your mistress's life."

She ran to her room, tearing off her clothes and dressing in divided skirt, blouse, jacket, boots. She was panting with emotion, not really thinking, acting in the vacuum of shock. She ran along the landing, and as she did, she tumbled over a heavy book that lay outside Katrina's room. With an impatient exclamation, Tatiana was about to kick it to one side when she noticed that it was not a book but a scrapbook, full of yellowing cuttings from newspapers. The headline of one caught her eye: MASS MURDERER STRIKES AGAIN! ANOTHER VICTIM OF GOSPODIN PALATCH IN MOSCOW! She ran down the stairs and out into the yard. Old Aleksi came toward her, leading the roan with the white blaze that Tatiana had ridden many times. His name was Thunder.

"Where will you go, mademoiselle?" the old man asked, shakily. "What can you do on your own?"

"I don't know, Aleksi," she said. "But I must try to find my mother."

"What shall I do, mademoiselle?"

"Stay here," she said. "I'll be back as soon as I can."

She did not know whether what she said was true or not. She had no real idea where she was going to look for her mother and Katrina. All she knew was that she could not stay a moment longer in that house of atrocity. It reeked of blood and evil. She put the horse into a canter and did not look back. She knew that if she did, she would see the old man standing in the middle of the yard watching her. Uprooted, bewildered, he had nowhere else to go. The Tretyakov family had given him the only home he knew. There must be thousands like him all over Russia, Tatiana thought.

She did not go to the village. There was no way of knowing whether the *Cheka* detachment had left, nor the mood of the peasants. She swung around the huddle of huts and came down to a ford about two versts west of the village. She dismounted and walked to the edge of the trickling stream. The tracks of the truck were etched in the hardened mud at the bank of the ford, clearly visible in the bright moonlight. She tried to remember what lay on the road between Dmitrovsk and Malinka, the next village. Nothing, she thought; just the old quarry.

And then she knew, and it turned her blood to ice. She remounted slowly and gigged the horse into motion. No need to push him, she thought, no more need of haste. How her leaden heart knew that they were all dead she could not have said, but she knew it. The horse plodded on quietly, and ten minutes later Tatiana saw the quarry on her left.

It was about forty feet deep, with yellowish, muddy water lying at the bottom. There were tire marks from the edge of the road to where the ground fell away sharply, a steep slate cliff. The water shone dully golden in the moonlight, not a ripple on its surface. The only sound was that of the horse cropping the thin flattened grass.

Tatiana walked around the edge of the quarry, peering down. She searched for almost an hour before she saw anything. At first she thought that it was a dead branch, then realized with an awful chill of horror that what she was looking at was a woman's arm, clothed in what might once have been white.

"Katrina?" she whispered.

The bodies looked like lumps of rock, huddled in the shadow of gray stone at the foot of the cliff. Desperately, Tatiana ran along the edge looking for some way down to the foot of the quarry. Eventually she found a path, and scrambling, skittering, sliding, and falling, she made her way to where the three crumpled forms lay. It was ghastly, awful. They had just thrown them over and then riddled them with bullets. She knelt by her mother's body. In death, despite the cuts and abrasions, Maryka's face was peaceful and still beautiful. She was lying on her back, eyes open, staring sightlessly at the black sky. Tatiana closed her mother's eyes and kissed the dear dead lips. It was like kissing stone. She laid Maryka's hands across her breast and composed her clothing decently. Maryka had always been a modest woman, and Tatiana did not want to let death shame her.

Katrina lay half in and half out of the water, one arm flung across a jagged rock, as if her last gesture had been to reach upward toward Heaven. The once-white habit she had worn was bespattered with blood. Her body seemed heavy as lead. Tatiana waded into the shallow water, feeling her boots swallowed to the ankles in the miry guck under it. She heaved at Katrina's body, trying to pull her onto the sticky clay at the water's edge. It was like trying to move a rock. You never realized how heavy the dead were. Panting, fighting to keep the nausea back, Tatiana floundered and slid and pulled and cursed in the yellow muck until, every muscle in her body quivering like aspen leaves, she collapsed alongside Katrina's body on the wet clay. Her brain was empty, and her mouth hung open with exhaustion. She stared dully at Sergei's corpse, which lay face down in the water. I can't, Sergei, she said, not even able to speak. I'm sorry, but I can't.

After what seemed like a long, long time, she stood up. Her mother and Katrina lay side by side, their faces turned toward each other, as if they had fallen asleep talking. Tatiana kept half-expecting one of them to speak, to move, to spite all death. She looked up at the cliff top, where the horse stood. It seemed a thousand feet high. She looked down at her clothes, which were mud-caked and slimy. Her boots were thickly coated with the yellow clay. There was no more that she could do here. Tomorrow she could send Aleksi and some of the villagers to bring the bodies home. She nodded. She would face all this tomorrow, she told herself. She found her way back to the zigzag footpath that led to the top of the quarry and clambered, as slowly as an old, old woman, to the top.

Still she shed no tears; it was as if the very capacity to weep had left her. She stumbled across to the horse and climbed into the saddle. "Come on, boy," she said. "Take us home." It was not until she was halfway back to the farm that she realized that, like old Aleksi, she no longer had any home to go to. And then she cried.

Four days later, Tatiana arrived in Moscow. She was wearing the clothes of one of the servants' wives, her long blonde hair hidden beneath a cotton scarf. She looked like any one of the thousands of women on the city's streets: pinch-faced, undernourished, frightened. She still did not know how she had lived through the things that had happened to her. She retained her sanity by repeating, like a litany, the words "I won't think about it now. I'll find Vladimir first and tell him what happened, and he'll know what to do."

Old Aleksi told her the whole story after they buried Katrina and Maryka. The villagers would not bring Sergei's body back from the quarry, and Aleksi told her why. He told her about the *Cheka* official in his leather coat with the indictment and the order for the summary execution of Sergei Tretyakov. He was accused of having murdered a dozen children, in Moscow and in the town of Orsha.

"He denied it," Aleksi said. "He told them it was completely untrue."

"Of course he did!" Tatiana said.

"They said the proof was incontrovertible," Aleksi went on. "There were fingerprints. They said he could be identified."

"What did he say?"

"Nothing. Because Madame came into the room. She had a book. It was full of pieces cut from newspapers. Like a scrapbook." Tatiana remembered the book she had seen on the landing, full of headlines about the child murderer, the one they had called Citizen Butcher. An awful fear began to stir inside her.

"No," she whispered. "Oh, God, no."

"Madame told the official that it was true," Aleksi said. "She said that the master was the one, that she had found out about it, protected him, that he was ill."

"Oh, Aleksi," Tatiana whispered. "It can't be true."

"Madame said that the master would be placed in a hospital, as soon as times were more settled. In the meantime, she would stand surety for him. The man from the *Cheka* just laughed. 'We don't want surety from the likes of you,' he said. 'We're here to hang

Sergei Tretyakov, murderer of children and enemy of the people.'"

"No!" Katrina shouted. "No, you can't do that, you can't!" She flew at the *Cheka* officer, trying to push him away from Sergei. Through all this, Sergei stood like a statue, almost as if he was not aware of what was going on. The *Cheka* officer thrust Katrina away from him impatiently.

"Take her out of here!" he snapped to his men. "Keep her away from me."

"What shall we do with her, then?" one of the men asked. The *Cheka* officer just looked at him, and the men grinned like wolves. They dragged Katrina, screaming, out of the room. Sergei frowned, like a man reading a newspaper who is disturbed by noise.

"All right," the *Cheka* officer said. "Come on, you." Sergei followed him docilely out into the cobbled courtyard.

"No better than animals," the old servant said to Tatiana. "That's what they were: animals."

Some things were beyond boundaries Tatiana did not know existed. She could not encompass it now, and so she told herself that she would do so later, when she felt stronger, when there was more time. There was a fault in the skein of time, and she told herself that if she waited, it would correct itself.

She could not believe the changes she saw in the streets of Moscow. There was refuse everywhere, and the entire station was carpeted with the husks of sunflower seeds dropped by the soldiers and peasants waiting there in huddled, oxlike groups. Huge red banners flapped emptily on the front of office buildings. More than once she had to step off the sidewalk to avoid a band of drunken soldiers. She saw soldiers everywhere, even more slovenly than the ones with whom she had shared the packed train that shunted interminably toward Moscow from Orel. They said there were bandits on the track, but they never saw any.

There were lines everywhere. The faces of the people standing in line were expressionless, without hope, without fear, without life. They looked like some strange breed of cattle. There were crowds around a *kvass* cart, shouting, gesticulating.

"I've no more!" the owner of the cart was shouting. "I can't sell you what I haven't got!"

"Crook!" someone yelled. "Profiteer!"

"You have no right to call me that," the *kvass* vendor said, a hurt expression on his broad-cheekboned face. "No right at all."

Tatiana walked from the station through the narrow streets,

heading toward the center of the city. Sailors called after her. There were students, workers, Red Guards everywhere, lounging against the walls, smoking cigarettes. They were all dirty, unshaven, as if they had not washed for weeks. The sidewalks were littered with cigarette butts, torn bits of newspaper, old broad-sheets. The horses pulling the *droshke* looked starved, skeletal. Most of the bigger houses were occupied by soldiers or civilians wearing red armbands.

She came to the wide Christnoprudni Boulevard. There was an armored car on the opposite side at the corner of a narrow street. The building outside which it was parked was flying an American flag. All at once, as if it were only an hour ago, she heard David Castle's voice. *Our Moscow Consulate is in the Archangelski Pereulok. The Consul's name is Snodgrass.* They had all laughed, secure in the huge Rolls-Royce. She went to the door of the building. There was a brass plate that said "Consulate of the United States of America." A soldier stood by the door. He was only a boy, fair-haired, quite good-looking.

"You can't go in there, sweetheart." He grinned.

"I have an appointment," Tatiana said. "With the Consul."

"What's his name?"

"Snodgrass," Tatiana said.

"Well, in that case," the soldier said.

She went inside. There was a marble hallway with doors on both sides. The one to her left was open, and a woman sitting at a desk looked up.

"Can I help you?" she said.

"I'm looking for Mr. Snodgrass," Tatiana said.

"Have you an appointment?"

"No," Tatiana said.

"I'm sorry," the woman said firmly. "Mr. Snodgrass sees no one without an appointment." She went back to her work, head down, as if Tatiana had disappeared the moment she finished speaking.

"Can you tell me whether David Castle is still in Petrograd?"

The woman looked up again, her expression somewhere between annoyance and surprise.

"You know Mr. Castle?"

"We're old friends."

"He's working with the American Red Cross Mission," the woman said.

"I didn't know," Tatiana said.

"He only just joined them. Are you going to see him?"

432

"In Petrograd, you mean?"

"No, no," the woman said impatiently. "He's not in Petrograd. The Red Cross Mission is here in Moscow, at the Elite Hotel."

"The Elite Hotel," Tatiana repeated, as if the words themselves were a passport to Vladimir. She thanked the woman and left the Consulate. The soldier outside grinned at her as she passed.

"Everything all right?" he asked.

"Yes," she said. "Everything is perfect."

The Elite Hotel was not one of the best in Moscow, but it was spacious and bustling. From the moment she set foot inside it, Tatiana felt as if she was in a different world. All around her she heard foreign accents: English, American, French. It was a long time since she had heard French spoken. She went to the desk and asked for Castle. The concierge picked up his phone and dialed a number.

"Your name?" he said.

"Makcheyeva. Tatiana Makcheyeva."

The concierge repeated the name into the telephone. He nodded and hung up. "He says if you will wait?"

Tatiana went to a seat in the center of the foyer. The Elite was built in the old style, with lots of ornate carvings and gilt, mirrors everywhere, vast chandeliers overhead. She could hear music somewhere. Glasses clinked in the bar. Fashionably dressed women walked by on the arms of well-dressed men. It was as though everything outside was unreal, and this was the real world. A door swung open, and she caught the aroma of food from the restaurant. For the first time she realized how hungry she was. She had not eaten since leaving Orel the preceding afternoon.

"Hello."

She looked up. Castle stood before her, frowning slightly the way people do when they don't recognize someone. He is still good-looking, she thought, remembering the first day they had met. The light-brown hair was longer, and there was some gray in it. There were lines around the eyes and mouth and a deep sadness in the fine green eyes that had not been there that sunny day at the Khoduin-skoe Pole.

"You don't remember me?"

"I'm so sorry," he said. "I didn't recognize you at first. You've cha—you look different."

"The clothes?" she gestured at her dress. "It's best to look like this."

433

"But you must tell me all about yourself," he said. "How are your parents? Your brothers?"

"They're dead," Tatiana said, and all at once she began to cry. She made no sound, but the tears streamed from her eyes as if they would never stop.

"Here!" Castle said. "Come here, sit down. Forgive me, I really didn't know—"

"It's not that," Tatiana said. "It's not just that."

"What is it?"

"I need your help."

"You have it without asking," he said. "What can I do?"

"Vladimir," she sniffled, wiping her eyes with the soft white handkerchief he gave her.

"Vladimir Smirnoff?"

"I don't know where he is, or what's happened to him. I don't know what to do."

"Listen, this sounds like a long story," Castle said. "And you look all in."

"I'm all right," she said.

"You haven't eaten."

"No," she said.

"Then let's start there," Castle said. He took her arm and led her to the elevator. His suite was on the fourth floor. The corridors were bustling with people, American or English by the look of them.

"Now," he said. "Sit there. Would you like to wash?"

"I'd—do you think I could have a bath?"

"Sure," he said. "I'll see to the food while you're doing it. Just go ahead—no one will bother you."

He went out, closing the door behind him. She recalled another evening, Castle playing American ragtime on the piano, all the boys dancing. Vanya, Ilya, dear sweet Roma. All dead. Nicky Vasnetsov, Vasya, Andrei. I won't think about that now, she told herself. She went into the bathroom and turned on the taps. The water was not very hot, but it did not matter. It was a huge bathroom, with marble walls and floor and tall mirrors. The bath was vast, and Tatiana slid into it with a groan that was almost sexual. She felt utterly drained, soiled, grubby. She closed her eyes.

Later, wrapped in Castle's terrycloth dressing gown, warm and well fed, she told him of the events which had overtaken the Smirnoff family. He shook his head in disbelief.

"I didn't see any of them again after—after Senka died," he said.

434

"I had the feeling they didn't want to see me. Vladimir thought I was responsible for his brother's death, and in a way I was."

"He only talked about it a little," Tatiana said. "I think it was Irina, not Senka, that he blamed you for."

"Yes," Castle said, and she saw that sadness in his eyes again. "Irina."

"Did you love her very much?"

"Yes," Castle said. " 'But that was in another country—.' " Whatever he had been going to say, he did not finish.

He looked at his watch. "It's nearly four now," he said. "You stay here, get some rest. I'll go and talk to a few people. I'll be back at, say, seven. Maybe you'd like to have dinner with me?"

He was gone before she could answer, leaving Tatiana once more in the grip of the strange lethargy which had swamped her earlier. It was as though every ounce of energy had been drained from her. She could not hope, nor was she afraid. She was not tired, and yet she could not move. She was impatient with herself for being this way, and yet her brain simply refused to consider any more complicated train of thought than the dimensions of the room, the color of the carpets.

It was much later than seven when Castle came back, and the streets outside were dark. Tatiana sat by the window, watching the people outside without interest. She looked up as the American came in and switched on the lights. His face was grave, and her heart turned over.

"What is it?" she said, afraid to hear.

"He's under arrest, Tatiana," Castle said. "For murder."

"Murder? Vladimir?"

"He killed a *Chekist*."

"It's not—true. He wouldn't kill anyone."

"He walked into a government office and killed a man called Mikhail Mikhailovich. He's awaiting trial, they say."

"Where?"

"They won't tell me. I'll try to find out tomorrow."

"Tomorrow?"

"I can't get hold of the people I want," he said. "Not till tomorrow."

"Couldn't we go to see them—these *Cheka* people?"

"Tomorrow, yes." He regarded her sadly. "There's more, I'm afraid," he said. "Nico Smirnoff is dead. His house was looted and burned. Anarchists, probably—they're all over the city. There isn't a

435

house on the Povarskaya they haven't occupied. They stay in them until the cellars are emptied and then move on to another. Nobody tries to stop them. They're dangerous, heavily armed. They'd shoot their own mothers for a bottle of vodka. Half a bottle."

"Another one," Tatiana said. "Another one dead. It's like a curse."

"I think we need a drink," Castle said. He got up and went into the bedroom and came back with a bottle of champagne.

"I don't want any," Tatiana said. "I couldn't drink it."

"Doctor's orders," Castle said, filling a glass and handing it to her.

"I can't, I can't," Tatiana said. The tears came again, as unbidden as the first time. She sat soundlessly, staring at nothing, the glass of wine sparkling in her hand, her face wet with tears. "He's dead, I know he is. Everyone is dead."

"No," he said. "Don't think that."

"Oh, David," Tatiana said. She ran to him as unthinkingly as a child and huddled against him, her whole body racked by sobs she could no longer contain. He held her tight and stroked her hair, trying to find the right words to say. He had not held a woman in his arms since Irina, and as the thought occurred to him, he felt a huge, slow, deep throb of regret and sorrow for all the things that never would be.

"It's going to be all right, Tatiana," he said. "Don't cry. It's going to be all right."

She cried for a long time, while he held her and rocked her gently in his arms. When she stopped, he picked her up in his arms and took her into the bedroom. It was like a dream, like flying, she thought. He laid her down on the bed and pulled the coverlet over her.

"Sleep," he whispered. "Tomorrow is another day."

He went out and closed the door behind him, and Tatiana snuggled down on the soft pillows, falling asleep almost instantly. Outside the bedroom door, Castle caught sight of his own reflection in one of the mirrors.

"Well, Sir Galahad," he said. "Get on your horse."

Then he made a call to a man he knew who worked for the Foreign Office.

"Call me back," he said when he had finished talking. He sat in the half-darkened room, thinking of nothing. Two glasses of champagne later, the telephone jangled. He picked it up quickly; it was Petrov at the Foreign Office.

436

"What?" he said, when Petrov reported his findings.

"Vladimir Petrovich Smirnoff," Petrov repeated heavily, "is being held at the Lubyanka. The Commissar to whom you should speak is Boris Abrikosov."

"God Almighty," Castle said.

"Not quite," Petrov observed sourly. "But near enough. You know Comrade Abrikosov?"

"I know him," Castle said.

"Good luck," Petrov said. "You'll need it."

32

CASTLE went to see Robins early next morning, leaving Tatiana asleep in the hotel, ordering breakfast so that it would be ready for him when he got back. A small piece of salty fish on rubbery bread, some tea. It wasn't exactly luxury, but it was a lot better than most people in Russia were getting. The Commissars and the Party higher-ups were doing all right, though. They were saying now that Kerensky had escaped from the Winter Palace disguised as a nurse. People believed it; it was one of those stories that people like to believe.

Robins's offices were already a bustle of activity. In the months that followed the collapse of the Provisional Government, the Red Cross Mission had managed to get food and medical supplies to a quarter of a million children in Moscow and Petrograd. With the Germans getting perilously close to the capital, the government was moved to Moscow. Robins brought his people to the new capital shortly after Lenin made peace with the Germans at Brest-Litovsk. He told Castle that the Germans' treatment of the Russian delegation was so humiliating that one of the Russian generals went out after the formalities were concluded and shot himself.

He knew that Robins and Lenin were close. After Teddy Roosevelt, with whom Robins had campaigned during the "Bull Moose" election of 1912 as Vice-President, and his other hero, Cecil Rhodes, Robins thought Lenin a great man. He was like a kid about it, Castle thought. He told Robins he wanted to see the Bolshevik leader.

"What do you want? Can I help?"

Castle told him about Tatiana, about Vladimir Smirnoff and the rest of it. Robins listened with pursed lips and then shook his head.

"I don't think he'd go for it, son," he said. "If this Smirnoff killed

438

a *Chekist,* Lenin won't raise a finger to save him from the firing squad. And even if he did, I doubt Dzerzhinsky would sit still for it."

"Let me try," Castle said. "I have an ace in the hole."

"All right," Robins said. "I'll see what I can do."

When Castle got back to his suite, Tatiana was dressed and sitting at the small table drinking tea. She smiled as he came in.

"Good morning," she said.

"Hello," Castle said. "You look as if you slept well."

"Thank you, David," Tatiana said, softly. "For last night."

"Listen," he said, "I found out where Vladimir is."

"He's all right?" she said, jumping up from the chair. "Tell me where he is."

"He's all right," Castle said. "But you can't go to him. He is in the Lubyanka."

"The Lubyanka?"

"That's the special prison the *Cheka* use. It's their headquarters, that big Gothic place on the Lubyanskaya, the old offices of the All-Russia Insurance Company."

"Couldn't we go there?" Tatiana said. "Couldn't we talk to whoever is in charge?"

"That's the problem, Tatiana," Castle said. "The man in charge is Boris Abrikosov."

"Boris Ab?—" She was too stunned to say the rest of his name. Vladimir was in the hands of the one man in the world who most wished him harm.

"I must go to him," she said. "Perhaps he'll listen to me."

"You know better than that," Castle said.

"I can't just sit here and do nothing."

"Tatiana, listen to me," Castle said, making his voice sharp. "I'm going to see Lenin. I may be able to persuade him—"

"Lenin, Lenin," she said. "He won't help you; none of them will. All they know is lying and stealing and killing. They're all the same, all of them!"

"No matter what you think of them," Castle said, "they're the ones who hold the keys to Vladimir's cell, Tatiana. If you approach Abrikosov, you'll get nowhere. Let me try my way."

"All right," she said, thinking, thinking. "All right."

She knew what would happen if he asked Lenin to help. Lenin would say no. It was as simple as that. If Castle asked all of them— Lenin and Trotsky and Stalin and Dzerzhinsky and Zinoviev and everyone else in the Central Executive Committee—they'd all turn down their thumbs, like the Roman emperors of old. They would not so much as lift a telephone on behalf of someone like Vladimir Smirnoff, and if the American thought otherwise, he was a fool. She was not going to sit around in his hotel room hoping that his futile plan would work. There was only one way to get Vladimir out of the Lubyanka.

"I've got to go out for a while," Castle said. "You'll wait here?"

"Certainly," Tatiana lied. "Where are you going?"

"To the Kremlin," Castle said. "I'll be back as soon as I can."

She gave him twenty minutes. She did not tie up her hair or wear the hat. She looked in the mirror. The dress was frumpy, the shoes a mockery, but they would have to do. She went out of the hotel and hurried across town. Half an hour later, she was at the main entrance to the forbidding black building which housed the *Cheka*. A Red Guard barred her way, his rifle held horizontally.

"Your papers?" he snapped.

"Kindly send word to Comrade Commissar Abrikosov that I am here," Tatiana said.

"I don't run errands for women," the man sneered. His fellow guard sniggered. Tatiana managed to summon a withering glance which she directed at the man. He shifted uncomfortably.

"You had better inform Comrade Commissar Abrikosov that I am here," she said. "Otherwise you will bear the brunt of his displeasure when he hears that you have been offensive to me."

The guard stared at her and she stared back, hoping that the trembling of her legs would not give her away. Please, dear God, she thought, make him do it.

"Name?" the guard said, surly as a bear.

"Tatiana Makcheyeva."

"Business?"

Tatiana looked away regally, and the man stood irresolute for a moment. Then, with a curse, he turned and stamped into the guard office in the archway leading to the inner court. After a minute or two he came out. His face was changed, and his manner was humbly respectful.

"You're to go right up," he said. "Third floor. Someone will meet you."

Tatiana nodded and walked past the man, who trotted after her and laid a grimy hand on her arm. "Lady?" he said. "Don't tell him anything, will you? I'm only doing what they told me to do."

"I know you are," Tatiana said, and walked on. She did not feel sorry for the man. He was a brute who respected only someone stronger than himself. Let him worry, she thought. It will do him good. The arched doors of the building lay before her. She pushed through them into a stone-floored hall, at the far side of which were three elevators. She waited until the operator slid back the gates and got in.

"Third," she said. The man looked at her speculatively and said nothing. He stank of garlic, and the front of his jacket was stained with food. He opened the gates without a word. Tatiana stepped out and saw Boris Abrikosov waiting.

"Well, Tatiana," he said, his voice a satin whip. "This is an unexpected pleasure."

The Kremlin was in pretty poor shape, Castle thought as he walked through Cathedral Square. It was still the vast fortress of the Tsars, enormous, powerful, but wartime neglect and the Moscow street fighting had left the royal palaces and the offices surrounding them filthy and barely fit for human habitation. Lenin's room in the old Tsar's palace was untidy and bare but for a writing desk and a few plain chairs. He looked up impatiently as the Red Guard showed Castle in, a man with much on his mind and no time for pleasantries.

"Mr. Robins says you have asked to see me," he said.

"It's kind of you to spare me the time," Castle said.

It was the first time he had been as near to the Bolshevik leader as this, and he studied him closely. There was nothing about Lenin to suggest the dynamism of the man. He looked like a somewhat overweight shoe clerk, with his short, thick neck and plump red face. He had a high forehead and a slightly pug nose, a short, broad-shouldered body. Only in the eyes did Castle see Lenin's self-confidence and sense of conscious superiority. He reminded himself not to forget it was there.

"You will oblige me by being brief," Lenin said.

"I'll try," Castle said. "Your *Cheka* have a man in the Lubyanka. His name is Vladimir Smirnoff."

"I do not deal in *Cheka* affairs," Lenin said, dismissively. "You must discuss such matters with Felix Dzerzhinsky."

"I want to talk to the organ grinder," Castle said. "Not the monkey."

That made Lenin look up sharply, and for a moment Castle thought he had gone too far. Then Lenin smiled.

"You are bold, Mr. Castle. What is Smirnoff accused of?"

"Murder. He killed a *Chekist*."

"And you want what?"

"I want you to order his release."

Lenin's laugh was short and sharp, a bark of disbelief. "You can't be serious," he said.

"I most certainly am," Castle said. "You know who the Smirnoffs are, of course."

"I know who they were," Lenin corrected him.

"Have you any idea how much they contributed to Party funds in the old days?"

"Yes," Lenin said. "I have a very good idea."

"Yet you don't want to help them now?"

"Not particularly. They are no use to us in this new world we're building. They always were bloodsuckers, and they always will be."

"You wouldn't consider an exchange?"

"What sort of exchange, Mr. Castle? What have you to offer?"

"Three little words," Castle said. "The Petersburg Plan."

There was a profound silence. Lenin's steely eyes bored into his, weighing, watchful.

"You could be bluffing," Lenin said.

"All you have to do is call me."

"I could take . . . other steps."

"You'd be wasting your time."

"Ah," Lenin said. "You have put it in writing."

"Something like that."

"It would be . . . unfortunate," Lenin said slowly, "if details of the Petersburg Plan were to become public knowledge at this time. Our situation is somewhat precarious, and a spy scandal would not help at all. A month from now, two, and it will not matter."

"Which is why I'm here," Castle said. "Now."

"We weathered it before, you know. Last July. We could simply deny it. Sit you out. The public's memory is short."

"If you think that," Castle said, "we've got nothing more to talk about. What you have to do is ask yourself whether you need that kind of trouble just to keep one more enemy of the people in prison."

"You're persuasive," Lenin said. "Might I ask you for some earnest of your knowledge?"

"The name of the German *apparat* is AMSA—the special section of the Foreign Ministry known as *Sonderabteilung*. Your middleman is Ganetsky, who in turn works for the German High Command's Stockholm agent, 'Fatty' Parvus, alias Helphand. His man in Petrograd was Fritz Sukhotin, and Sukhotin's bagman was Frederick Streicher, the banker. There were others—" He stopped as Lenin held up a peremptory hand.

"Enough," Lenin said, and scribbled something on a piece of paper. "Take this to Dzerzhinsky. He'll do the rest." He paused for a moment, frowning. "Tell me, why is this Smirnoff fellow so important to you?" he asked.

"He's not," Castle said. "I'm doing this for . . . someone I used to know."

"Ah," Lenin said, softly. "*Cherchez la femme.*"

"She's dead," Castle said, harshly.

"About the Petersburg Plan," Lenin said. "Who else knew about it except you?"

"Only one man knew the whole story. He's dead."

"His name?"

"Michael Tereschenko. He was executed at the Peter and Paul two days after the storming of the Winter Palace."

"For what?"

"I never found out," Castle said.

Lenin rose from his chair and extended his hand. "Can I trust you, Castle?"

"Yes," Castle said. Again Lenin nodded, smiling this time. "I believe I can," he said.

Castle came down the stairs and out into the Sobornaya. The white tower of Ivan Veliki with its golden dome reared up into the sky on his right. He hurried through the Nikolskaya Gate into Red Square. There was a *droshky* at the curb, the decrepit nag twitching its tatty tail. For ten rubles the driver agreed to take him back to the Elite. Castle rushed into his suite waving the piece of paper authorizing Vladimir's release. There was no one there.

"Damn it all to Hell!" he shouted at the heedless walls. He knew where Tatiana had gone, and he knew what would happen to her when she got there. He ran down the stairs, hoping to God he was not too late.

"I should have killed you," Vladimir said.

"Yes, you should," Boris said, turning his back as though suddenly wearied of the whole charade. He ostentatiously lit a cigarette as Vladimir was taken to the execution post and tied to it. The sergeant barked out commands and the two soldiers moved into position, rifles at port. There was no last cigarette, no comfort at all. Just the dank prison walls, the bare yard, the glimpse of empty gray sky above, Boris Abrikosov smoking a cigarette. Not much for a man to take to Heaven, Vladimir thought. He closed his eyes as the sergeant shouted an order and the soldiers raised their rifles.

"Ready!" the sergeant shouted. His voice bounced off the bare walls, *deee-eee-eee-ee*. The rifle bolts made their metallic sound.

"Aim!" Tatiana, he thought. Tatiana.

"Fire!"

There was a thin clicking sound, nothing more. Then coarse, roaring laughter from the sergeant and the soldiers. There had been no bullets in the rifles. It had all been a sadistic charade. Vladimir tried to blink away the tears of fear and relief and could not. His legs and body trembled. He could not stop them, and he was ashamed.

"Well, well," he heard Boris Abrikosov say. "You live another day, cousin."

"What?" Vladimir said, weakly. "What do you mean?"

"Never fear," Boris said, blowing cigarette smoke through half-smiling lips. "We shall try again tomorrow."

Now finally Vladimir surrendered hope and knew that Boris knew it. It was not enough that he die. Abrikosov wanted him to die over and over, to march him out here day after day expecting to be killed, never knowing if he would be, until in the end he would embrace death, beg for it. No, Vladimir thought, I won't give him that. His head came up. He straightened his back as they unfastened the chains, and when they tried to take his arms, he shook them off with tatterdemalion dignity. If there was nothing left to do but to die, Vladimir thought, he could at least do it well.

Seven times he underwent the gut-wrenching ordeal, the whole ghastly ceremony. And seven times he was led back to his filthy corner in the fetid cell. On the eighth day they came for him in the afternoon, and this time he knew they were going to kill him.

"You always said you wanted me," Tatiana said.

"I did," Boris said. His tongue slid over his thin lips and she felt his eyes on her body. Her skin went cold, but she knew she must go on.

"If you will release Vladimir, I will stay with you," she said. "I will be your mistress, your wife, your woman, whatever you want."

"You mean it?" he said.

"I mean it."

"You must love him a very great deal."

"Will you release him?"

"If I thought you meant what you say . . ." he said, as though unsure of her. "If I thought for a moment that you were sincere . . ."

"If you have a Bible, I will swear upon it." Please, God, she prayed, don't let him see my fear. She unbuttoned the dress she was wearing and let it fall apart. She had nothing on underneath it. She saw the heat come into his eyes.

"Take it off," he whispered. His voice was heavy, thick in his throat. She could hear his breathing. He got up and crossed the room, turning the key in the door as she slipped out of the dress and stood naked. He was standing behind her and she was afraid to turn and face him. When he touched her, she flinched visibly. His hands roamed over her body, her buttocks, fondling her breasts. He turned her around and looked her over, like a farmer buying a horse.

She did not see him pick up the riding crop, but she heard its sudden whistle as he struck her across the back with all his strength. The pain was blinding. She felt as if he had laid a red-hot iron across her skin, and she shrieked with agony, lurching forward against the edge of the desk. Before her scream had properly left her throat, Boris hit her again, another wicked, terrible blow that flayed skin from her body and spattered the cream-painted wall with tiny pinpoints of blood. She sank gasping to her knees, blinded by tears of pain, her mind a blank of terror.

"Lesson one, bitch," he said, and tossed the crop contemptuously into the corner of the room. "You no longer have anything to offer that I want."

Tatiana looked up at him. He towered over her, the empty eyes burning with deep rage. She had never seen such hatred in any human's expression.

"Get up!" Boris snapped. She tried to obey, but her legs would not function. She was paralyzed by pain and fear, and she shook her head to let him know she could not move. He made an impatient sound and grabbed a handful of her hair, yanking her to her feet and thrusting her into the wooden chair. She sat with her head hanging, shivering with pain, her mind out of focus. All she could think was that he was going to kill her. She felt debased; she could not stop her hands and legs from trembling. When finally she made herself look at him, he was standing behind the desk again, looking as though nothing had happened.

"Lesson two," he said. "When I tell you to do something, do it. You understand?"

She managed to nod, and he seemed satisfied. He picked up the telephone and dialed a number. "We'll be down in a few minutes," he said into the receiver. "Get everything ready." Then he looked at Tatiana again with those merciless, empty eyes. She watched him without hope, without any feeling that she could identify, as he reached into his desk drawer and brought out some photographs. He laid them on the desk before her.

"Look at them, bitch," he said. It took a few moments for her eyes to focus. When they did, she found she was looking at photographs of dead children, terribly mutilated. The pictures were clinical and ghastly. Shuddering, Tatiana averted her head.

"I said look at them," he said, softly. He had the riding crop in his hand, and he flicked her very lightly across the shoulders with it. Tatiana gasped with fear, but she kept her head turned away from the awful images on the desk. Boris reached across the desk and grabbed her hair. He forced her head around and down, until she could not shut out the dreadful things he wanted her to see.

"You know what those are, eh?" Boris said, panting slightly from the effort of holding her. "You know who did all that?"

"Yes," she managed, as he twisted her bunched hair in his hands to make her speak. "Yes."

"Your darling Sergei," he said. "Did you know he butchered little girls for fun, eh? And that the nun he was married to knew about it?"

"No," she whispered.

"Yes!" he shouted. "You knew!"

"I . . . didn't," Tatiana whimpered. His grip on her hair was like a vise. She felt as if her head was bursting with the pain. "Until the *Cheka* came . . ."

"Ah, yes, the *Cheka* came," he said, releasing her. "And who do you think sent them, you empty-headed little trollop?"

She frowned; it took her a moment to realize what he was saying. Sergei had been hung by his orders, her mother and Katrina shot at the behest of this monster. She felt the heat of hatred burst inside her like a bomb and she came off the chair with her hands clawed, nothing in her mind except the desire to tear the sneering face into a bloody mask. She had no chance, of course; Boris simply slapped her back into the chair with a hand like a piece of wood. Her mouth numbed by the blow, a thin trickle of blood worming its way down her chin, Tatiana slumped sobbing in the chair, her humiliation total.

"You . . . you utter . . ."

"Don't bother to call me names, bitch," he said, eyes still alight with that angry fire. "You have not yet begun to experience the humiliation I have in store for you. Before I'm finished, you'll kiss my feet for a kind word."

"I'd rather die," Tatiana said, her voice little more than a whisper. "I'd rather die, you hateful monster!"

"Hateful, am I?" Boris shouted, making her jump with fright. "You don't even know what hate is, you stupid bitch. I've lived on hate for years, waiting for this day, waiting for the day I finished them off, every damned one of them! You want to know about hate, do you, bitch? Well, by God, I'm going to show you! Put your clothes on."

He threw her dress at her and watched her struggle into it, smiling without the slightest pity when she flinched as the material dragged across the torn skin of her back. Then he unlocked the door and grabbed her wrist, pulling her out into the corridor.

"You want to see Vladimir Smirnoff, eh?" he said. "Well, see him you shall, for one last time before we shoot him as an enemy of the people."

"No!" Tatiana said. "Oh, God, not that!" She tried to pull herself free of his grip, but his hands were like iron. After the first few attempts, Tatiana gave up. She was afraid he might break her arm, so fierce was his expression. He marched her down the gray-green corridors to the elevator. Once in a while a clerk would pass them, or an orderly carrying a sheaf of papers. Every one of them kept his head averted. No one even looked at Tatiana; it was as if she was invisible. They went down to the ground floor and then along corridors and through doors. Clerks looked up as they went past and then looked quickly down at their work again. Two soldiers stood guarding a heavy wooden door at the end of the stone corridor into which Boris dragged her.

"Everything ready?" he snapped.

"Yes, Comrade Commissar," one of the soldiers said. "They're just bringing him."

Almost as the guard stopped speaking, they heard the tramp of marching feet on the stone floor, and two Red Guards came along the corridor toward them. Between them walked Vladimir. His head was held high, but she could see he had been beaten. There was blood on his clothes, and his cheekbones were bruised badly. He did not see her at first because it was dark in the corridor.

"Tatiana!" he croaked. "Tatiana?"

"Keep moving, you!" the sergeant shouted. "Left, right, left, right!"

"Vladimir!" Tatiana screamed. "Oh, God, no, please, no!"

In the courtyard she saw the six-foot stake and the chains, the pitted stone wall behind it. The soldiers moved into position as the sergeant put the chains around Vladimir's body. Tatiana turned her head away, blinded by tears.

"Watch!" Boris Abrikosov hissed. He took hold of her chin in his iron grip and forced her head around so that she was looking into the courtyard. She saw through the blur of her tears that the firing squad was ready.

"Ready!" the sergeant shouted. The rifle bolts went *slokasloka* and the metallic sound bounced off the walls.

"Stop this execution immediately, Commissar Abrikosov! Stop it!" a voice said. Boris whirled around to see three men standing in the corridor. One of them was the American, Castle, the second a dark-haired man who looked like a red Indian. The third man, the one who had spoken, was Felix Dzerzhinsky.

"Aim!" the sergeant shouted.

"Stop!" Boris shouted hoarsely. "Stop the execution!" The sergeant looked around, astonishment on his face. Then he saw Boris come through the archway with the squat figure of Felix Dzerzhinsky behind him. The sergeant was afraid of Boris, but he was terrified of the chief architect of the *Cheka*. Dzerzhinsky was a man of mild voice and perfect manners, but his deeply sunken eyes held the fire of fanaticism and perhaps madness. They never twitched. He did not blink like other men, as if his eyelids were paralyzed. The unnerving stare and total lack of expression had a galvanic effect on the sergeant.

"Stop, stop!" he shouted. He was so anxious to please the *Cheka* chief that he ran in front of the rifles himself, his arms raised high.

"What is this?" Boris hissed to Dzerzhinsky. "Comrade Commissar, I demand to know by what authority you stop this execution."

"I need no authority but my own, comrade," Dzerzhinsky said, his voice level and unhurried. Boris paled slightly; the deadly reminder that he was at Dzerzhinsky's disposal did not escape him.

"This man is to be released into the custody of the United

States," Castle said. "This is Mr. Robins of the American Red Cross, who is here to witness that release. My name is—"

"I know who you are," Boris snarled.

"Raymond," Castle said softly. "I wonder if you could look after the young lady. Take her out to the car."

"Here—!" Boris began. He saw Dzerzhinsky's eyes on him and said no more. The soldiers brought Vladimir over to where the three men were standing, and Castle said, "I've come to take you out of here."

"Out?" Vladimir frowned.

"You're free," Castle said. "By special order of Lenin himself."

"This man is an enemy of the people!" Boris shouted. "A self-confessed murderer! He is a capitalist oppressor of the working classes. I protest his release most strongly."

"I note your protest, comrade," Dzerzhinsky said.

"I'm taking him to the Brest Station, Comrade Dzerzhinsky," Castle said. "There's a Red Cross train waiting. He'll be in Lvov by nightfall."

"Excellent." Dzerzhinsky's voice was as mild as milk, but there was no mistaking his meaning. "And you, sir?"

"You won't have to worry about me, either," Castle said.

"Even better." Dzerzhinsky smiled.

Robins was waiting in the big limousine, the engine already running as they came out of the Lubyanka into the daylight. Passersby gaped at Vladimir, but no one tried to stop them. They roared past the Kremlin and turned into the Tverskaya. No one spoke. Vladimir and Tatiana sat close together, their hands entwined. They saw the Brest Station come into sight, and Castle turned to grin at them.

"Your train is waiting," he said.

"I don't know what to say to you," Vladimir said. "I don't know how to thank you."

"Don't try," Castle said, hoping they would not notice how closely he was watching the street. They went into the station together, and Robins showed the guards the Red Cross papers he had prepared for Vladimir and Tatiana.

"I won't come to the train," Castle said. "I have to meet someone."

He watched them walk up the platform toward their carriage and then turned to face the entrance. Irina, he thought, I hope I'm doing the right thing. I owe the Smirnoffs three lives: yours, Sasha's and Senka's. The second bell rang. Five minutes, Castle thought. Maybe I was wrong.

Two minutes before the final bell, he saw the commotion at the entrance that he had been expecting. A uniformed man was shouting something to the Red Guards standing around the station, and a group of them ran with him toward the platform beside which the Red Cross train stood panting. Hello, Boris, Castle thought. He had been certain that Boris's fanaticism would overwhelm his fear of Dzerzhinsky, and he had been right. Boris rushed toward the gate on the platform, a pistol in his hand. He was shouting at the guards to stop the train when Castle stepped out from behind the ice-cream vendor's stand and shot him.

The bullet knocked Boris over sideways in a strange, slewing run. He crashed into a luggage trolley, scattering bags, his legs kicking high. The four soldiers who had been running behind him looked at Castle in paralyzed disbelief as he stepped forward and shot the squirming man on the ground again. Boris jerked convulsively and straightened out, dead. Castle turned toward the Red Guards as the sound of the whistle announced the train's departure. The soldiers all fired at once, and Castle was cut down as if someone had struck him with some mighty club. Irina, he thought as he died; we're even now.

The Red Cross train moved slowly out of the Brest Station, its occupants unaware of what had happened. Vladimir and Tatiana sat facing each other in the second carriage, empty of everything except relief. There were clean clothes in the bags Robins had given them, a little money. They were leaving everything else behind, all the years of their lives, everything they had ever owned.

"We'll start again, Vladimir," Tatiana whispered. "It will be like it was before."

"Yes," he said. He was watching the Russian countryside slip past. "One day."

They were silent for a while. There was no sound but the insistent *takatatak* of the wheels.

"He asked me to tell you something," Tatiana said, after what seemed like a long time. "David Castle asked me to tell you that he did it for Irina."

"Irina," Vladimir said. He shook his head. "I can't seem to remember clearly what she looked like . . . isn't that strange? It's as if I'm in a sort of dream, knowing I'm awake. I know I'm leaving Russia forever, but I can't believe it's actually happening."

"It isn't there anymore, Vladimir," she said, softly. "We're leaving their Russia, not ours."

"I wish I'd known him better," Vladimir said. "I wonder if we'll

450

ever see him again?" He fell silent again, staring out of the window. How thin he looks, Tatiana thought, how exhausted. The devil's smile she knew of old was wan now, and hesitant. She was going to have to be strong for both of them. Somehow the thought no longer oppressed her. All she had longed to do was to pass the burden on, to tell him and then forget the awful things she had seen, the humiliation she had suffered. But she knew now that she would never tell him any of it, not about Sergei, not about Katrina and Maryka, not about the awful photographs she had seen or the contemptuous humiliation she had suffered at the hands of Boris Abrikosov. She felt a surge of hatred for the man that brought a wave of pain into the raw cuts on her back. I hope someone kills him, she thought.

"We haven't got much, you know," Vladimir said. "A few thousand rubles. The vodka formula. It's not much."

"It will be enough," Tatiana said. "As long as we're together."

"You mean it, don't you?" he said, looking intently into her eyes.

"Of course I do."

"It's strange," he said, shaking his head. "All that time, even when we were . . . closest . . . I used to think it was Sergei you really wanted. Not me."

"I love you," she said. "Nobody else. Not now, not ever."

She kissed his broken lips and his poor bruised face, all her own pain forgotten. He took her two hands in his and held them very tightly.

"You're not afraid, are you?" he said, and there was wonder in his voice. "You're not afraid at all."

"No," Tatiana said. "Not anymore. I'll never be afraid again."

They held each other close, like two children lost in some vast forest. The train thundered on toward the sunset.